MESSAGES

MESSAGES

Building Interpersonal Communication Skills

FOURTH EDITION

Joseph A. DeVito

Hunter College
of the
City University of New York

An imprint of Addison Wesley Longman, Inc.

New York • Reading, Massachusetts • Menlo Park, California • Harlow, England
Don Mills, Ontario • Sydney • Mexico City • Madrid • Amsterdam

Editor-in-Chief: Priscilla McGeehon
Acquisitions Editor: Donna Erickson
Development Manager: Lisa Pinto
Marketing Manager: John Holdcroft
Supplements Editor: Mark Toews
Project Coordination and Text Design: Electronic Publishing Services Inc., NYC
Cover Designer: Kay Petronio
Cover Manager: Nancy Danahy
Cover Photos: PhotoDisk, Inc.
Full Service Production Manager: Valerie L. Zaborski
Photo Researcher: Photosearch, Inc.
Print Buyer: Denise Sandler
Electronic Page Makeup: Electronic Publishing Services Inc., NYC
Printer and Binder: World Color Book Services
Cover Printer: Phoenix Color Corps.

For permission to use copyrighted material, grateful acknowledgment is made to the copyright holders on p. 377, which are hereby made part of this copyright page.

Library of Congress Cataloging-in-Publication Data

DeVito, Joseph A.
    Messages : building interpersonal communication skills / Joseph A.
DeVito. —4th ed.
        p.   cm.
    Includes bibliographical references and index.
    ISBN 0-321-02509-1
    1. Interpersonal communication.   I. Title.
BF637.C45D5   1999   98-29692
158.2—dc21   CIP

Please visit our website at http://longman.awl.com

ISBN 0-321-02509-1 (paperbound)

ISBN 0-321-05562-4 (casebound)

2345678910–WCT–010099

Brief Contents

Detailed Contents vii
Specialized Contents xii
Preface xix

PART I. MESSAGES ABOUT THE SELF AND OTHERS 1

CHAPTER 1 INTERPERSONAL COMMUNICATION 1

CHAPTER 2 THE SELF 37

CHAPTER 3 PERCEPTION 65

CHAPTER 4 LISTENING 87

PART II. MESSAGES SPOKEN AND UNSPOKEN 110

CHAPTER 5 VERBAL MESSAGES 110

CHAPTER 6 NONVERBAL MESSAGES 138

CHAPTER 7 EMOTIONAL MESSAGES 169

CHAPTER 8 CONVERSATION MESSAGES 192

PART III. MESSAGES IN CONTEXT 229

CHAPTER 9 INTERPERSONAL COMMUNICATION AND CULTURE 229

CHAPTER 10 INTERPERSONAL COMMUNICATION
AND RELATIONSHIPS 256

CHAPTER 11 INTERPERSONAL COMMUNICATION
AND CONFLICT 290

CHAPTER 12 INTERPERSONAL COMMUNICATION
AND POWER 316

Appendix. Writing about Interpersonal Communication 343

Glossary of Interpersonal Communication Concepts
and Skills 348

Bibliography 363

Photo Credits 377

Index 378

Detailed Contents

Specialized Contents   xii

Preface xix

PART I. MESSAGES ABOUT THE SELF AND OTHERS 1

CHAPTER 1 **INTERPERSONAL COMMUNICATION 1**

Nature of Interpersonal Communication 3
*Source-Receiver 6 • Interpersonal Competence 8
Messages 14 • Channel 15
Noise 15 • Context 16 • Ethics 17*

Principles of Interpersonal Communication 20
*Interpersonal Communication Involves Both Content and
Relationship Messages 20 • Interpersonal
Communication is a Process of Adjustment 24
Interpersonal Communication is Inevitable, Irreversible,
and Unrepeatable 25 • Interpersonal Communication
Serves a Variety of Purposes 26*

Culture and Interpersonal Communication 27
*The Relevance of Culture 31 • The Aim of a Cultural
Perspective 33*

CHAPTER 2 **THE SELF 37**

Self-Concept and Self-Awareness 38
Self-Concept 38 • Self-Awareness 42
Self-Disclosure 45

Factors Influencing Self-Disclosure 47 • The Rewards of Self-Disclosure 51 • Dangers of Self-Disclosure 52 Guidelines for Making Self-Disclosures 53 • Guidelines for Responding to Self-Disclosures 54

Apprehension 58
Apprehensive Behaviors 58 • Culture and Speaker Apprehension 59 • Managing Communication Apprehension 60 • Empowering Apprehensives 62

CHAPTER 3 PERCEPTION 65

Interpersonal Perception 66
Sensing 67 • Organizing 67 • Interpreting-Evaluating 68

Interpersonal Perception Principles 71
First Impressions: Primacy and Recency 72 • Implicit Personality Theories 73 • Self-Fulfilling Prophecies 74 Stereotypes 76 • Attribution 76

Increasing Accuracy in Perception 80
Become Critically Aware of Your Perceptions 80 Check Your Perceptions 81 • Reduce Uncertainty 82 Be Culturally Sensitive 84

CHAPTER 4 LISTENING 87

The Listening Process 89
Receiving 90 • Understanding 91 • Remembering 91 Evaluating 92 • Responding 93

Listening, Culture, and Gender 96
Listening and Culture 96 • Listening and Gender 98

Increasing Listening Effectiveness 102
Participatory and Nonparticipatory Listening 102 Empathic and Objective Listening 103 Nonjudgmental and Critical Listening 104 • Surface and Depth Listening 106

PART II. MESSAGES SPOKEN AND UNSPOKEN 110

CHAPTER 5 VERBAL MESSAGES 110

The Nature of Language 111
Language Meanings Are in People 111 • Meanings Depend on Their Context 112 • Language Is Both Denotative and Connotative 112 • Language Varies in Directness 113 • Language Varies in Abstraction 116

Disconfirmation 120
Sexism 122 • Heterosexism 123 • Racism 124 Cultural Identifiers 125

Using Verbal Messages Effectively and
Critically 128

Language Symbolizes Reality (Partially) 129
Language Expresses Both Facts and Inferences 131
Language Is Relatively Static 132 • Language Can
Obscure Distinctions 133

CHAPTER 6 NONVERBAL MESSAGES 138

The Nature and Function of Nonverbal
Communication 139

Accenting 140 • Complementing 140
Contradicting 140 • Regulating 140 • Repeating 140
Substituting 141

The Channels of Nonverbal Communication 141

The Body 141 • Facial Communication 144 • Eye
Movements 145 • Space Communication 146
Artifactual Communication 149 • Touch
Communication 152 • Paralanguage 153
Silence 155 • Time Communication 156 • Smell
Communication 159

Culture and Nonverbal Communication 161

CHAPTER 7 EMOTIONAL MESSAGES 169

Emotions and Emotional Communication 171

The Body, Mind, and Culture in Emotions 171
Emotions, Arousal, and Expression 173 • Principles of
Emotional Communication 179

Obstacles in Communicating Emotions 180

Societal Rules and Customs 180 • Fear 182
Inadequate Interpersonal Skills 183

Guidelines for Communicating Emotions 184

Understand Your Emotions 184 • Decide If You Wish to
Express Your Feelings 184 • Assess Your
Communication Options (Effectiveness and Ethics) 186
Describe Your Feelings 186 • Identify the Reasons for
Your Feelings 186 • Anchor Your Feelings to the
Present 187 • Own Your Own Feelings 187

CHAPTER 8 CONVERSATION MESSAGES 192

The Conversation Process 195

Step One. The Opening 197 • Step Two.
Feedforward 198 • Step Three. Business 199 • Step
Four. Feedback 199 • Step Five. The Closing 201
Reflections on the Stages of Conversation 202

Conversation Management 205

Opening Conversations 206 • Maintaining
Conversations 207 • Repairing Conversations 213
Closing Conversations 214

Conversation Effectiveness 216

General Conversational Skills 216 • Specific Conversational Skills 220

PART III. MESSAGES IN CONTEXT 229

CHAPTER 9 INTERPERSONAL COMMUNICATION AND CULTURE 229

Culture and Intercultural Communication 231

How Cultures Differ 239

Individual and Collective Cultures 239 • High-and-Low Context Cultures 241 • Masculinity-Femininity 242

Improving Intercultural Communication 246

Recognize and Reduce Your Ethnocentrism 246 • Be Mindful 246 • Face Fears 248 • Recognize Differences 248 • Recognize Differences Among the Culturally Different Group 249 • Avoid Overattribution 249 • Recognize Meaning Differences in Verbal and Nonverbal Messages 249 • Avoid Violating Cultural Rules and Customs 250 • Avoid Evaluating Differences Negatively 250 • Recognize the Normalcy of Culture Shock 251

CHAPTER 10 INTERPERSONAL COMMUNICATION AND RELATIONSHIPS 256

Relationships and Relationship Stages 257

Contact 260 • Involvement 261 • Intimacy 264 Deterioration 266 • Repair 267 • Dissolution 268 Movement Among the Stages 270

Relationship Theories 272

Attraction Theory 272 • Relationship Rules Approach 275 • Social Penetration Theory 276 Social Exchange Theory 278 • Equity Theory 278

Improving Relationship Communication 281

Empathic Understanding 282 • Self-Disclosures 282 Openness to Change 282 • Fair Fighting 282 Reasonableness 283 • Cultural Differences 283 Gender Differences 285

CHAPTER 11 INTERPERSONAL COMMUNICATION AND CONFLICT 290

The Nature of Interpersonal Conflict 291

Culture and Conflict 292 • Gender and Conflict 293 Content and Relationship Conflicts 293 • Online Conflicts 295 • The Negatives and Positives of Conflict 296 • Before and After the Conflict 297

A Model of Conflict Resolution 299

Define the Conflict 299 • Examine Possible Solutions 300 • Test the Solution 301 • Evaluate the Solution 301 • Accept or Reject the Solution 301

Conflict Management Strategies 302

Avoidance and Fighting Actively 304 • Force and Talk 305 • Defensiveness and Supportiveness 306 Face-Detracting and Face-Enhancing Strategies 307 Blame and Empathy 308 • Silencers and Facilitating Open Expression 308 • Gunnysacking and Present Focus 309 • Fighting Below and Above the Belt 309 Verbal Aggressiveness and Argumentativeness 310

CHAPTER 12 INTERPERSONAL COMMUNICATION AND POWER 316

Self-Esteem 318

Substitute Self-Destructive Beliefs with Self-Affirming Beliefs 318 • Seek Out Nourishing People 318 • Work on Projects That Will Result in Success 319

Speaking with Power 319

Some People Are More Powerful than Others 320 • All Interpersonal Messages Have a Power Dimension 323 Some People Are More Machiavellian than Others 324 Power Follows the Principle of Less Interest 328 Power Has a Cultural Dimension 329 • Power Is Frequently Used Unfairly 331

Assertive Communication 335

Nonassertive, Aggressive, and Assertive Communication 336 • Principles for Increasing Assertive Communication 338

Appendix. Writing about Interpersonal Communication 343

Glossary of Interpersonal Communication Concepts and Skills 348

Bibliography 363

Photo Credits 377

Index 378

Specialized Contents

Listening
Listening Boxes

1. That Other Part of Communication (Chapter 1) 19
2. Listening to Yourself (Chapter 2) 44
3. Listening to Other Perspectives (Chapter 3) 71
4. Ethical Listening (Chapter 4) 93
5. Try Active Listening (Chapter 4) 100
6. Gender Differences in Verbal Messages (Chapter 5) 117
7. Gender Differences in Nonverbal Messages (Chapter 6) 150
8. Listening to the Emotions of Others (Chapter 7) 182
9. Listening to Gossip (Chapter 8) 215
10. Racist, Sexist, and Heterosexist Attitudes (Chapter 9) 239
11. Listening to Stage Talk (Chapter 10) 279
12. Messages in Conflict (Chapter 11) 303
13. Listening to Empower (Chapter 12) 335

Skill Development
How To... Boxes

1. Communicate in the Organization (Chapter 1) 29
2. Facilitate Self-Disclosure (Chapter 2) 56
3. Avoid Attribution Errors (Chapter 3) 77
4. Avoid Being a Difficult Listener (Chapter 4) 106
5. Be Polite on the Net (Chapter 5) 118

6. Communicate Power without Words (Chapter 6) 158

7. Communicate with the Grief Stricken (Chapter 7) 189

8. Avoid Becoming a Conversationally Difficult Person (Chapter 8) 204

9. Become Effective in Intercultural Communication (Chapter 9) 245

10. Deal with Relationship Breakup (Chapter 10) 269

11. Deal with Complaints (Chapter 11) 298

12. Be a Power Holder (Chapter 12) 327

Skill Building Exercises

1. Ethics in Interpersonal Communication (Chapter 1) 19

2. Explaining Interpersonal Difficulties (Chapter 1) 29

3. Cultural Beliefs (Chapter 1) 35

4. The Sources of Your Cultural Beliefs (Chapter 2) 46

5. To Disclose or Not to Disclose? (Chapter 2) 55

6. Using Performance Visualization to Reduce Apprehension (Chapter 2) 63

7. Perceiving My Selves (Chapter 3) 69

8. Perspective Taking (Chapter 3) 78

9. Barriers to Accurate Perception (Chapter 3) 85

10. Reducing Barriers to Listening (Chapter 4) 95

11. Typical Man, Typical Woman (Chapter 4) 99

12. Paraphrasing to Ensure Understanding (Chapter 4) 107

13. Climbing the Abstraction Ladder (Chapter 5) 118

14. Confirming, Rejecting, and Disconfirming (Chapter 5) 129

15. Thinking with E-Prime (Chapter 5) 135

16. Integrating Verbal and Nonverbal Messages (Chapter 6) 141

17. Communicating Nonverbally (Chapter 6) 160

18. Artifacts and Culture: The Case of Gifts (Chapter 6) 165

19. Communicating Your Emotions (Chapter 7) 181

20. Expressing Negative Feelings (Chapter 7) 183

21. Communicating Emotions Effectively (Chapter 7) 188

22. Gender and the Topics of Conversation (Chapter 8) 203

23. Formulating Excuses (Chapter 8) 215

24. Responding Effectively (Chapter 8) 227

25. How Do You Talk? As a Woman? As a Man? (Chapter 9) 239

26. Random Pairs (Chapter 9) 244

27. Confronting Intercultural Difficulties (Chapter 9) 253

28. Changing the Distance Between You (Chapter 10) 271
29. Applying Theories to Problems (Chapter 10) 280
30. From Culture to Gender (Chapter 10) 287
31. Dealing with Conflict Starters (Chapter 11) 299
32. Generating Win-Win Solutions (Chapter 11) 302
33. Increasing Productive Conflict Management (Chapter 11) 313
34. Rewriting Unrealistic Beliefs (Chapter 12) 320
35. Managing Power Plays (Chapter 12) 334
36. Analyzing and Practicing Assertiveness (Chapter 12) 340

Readings on Interpersonal Skills

1. How to Really Talk to Another Person (Chapter 1) 22
2. Self-Confidence: The Art of Being You (Chapter 2) 41
3. What Do You Do When You Meet a Blind Person... (Chapter 3) 79
4. Want to Do Better on the Job?—Listen Up! (Chapter 4) 101
5. Ten Things You Should Never Say to Anyone (Chapter 5) 127
6. Deconstructing Your Cubicle (Chapter 6) 150
7. Keeping Your Cool at Work (Chapter 7) 184
8. Attack by Question (Chapter 8) 205
9. Values Across Cultures (Chapter 9) 234
10. Tips for Happier Visits with Parents (Chapter 10) 281
11. How to Take the Bite out of Criticism (Chapter 11) 303
12. Direct Clear Language (Chapter 12) 338

Critical Thinking
Sidebars

1. Critical thinking comprises a variety of skills. (Chapter 1) 10
2. Critical thinking is always useful. (Chapter 1) 11
3. Critical thinking is especially useful in interpersonal communication. (Chapter 1) 21
4. Critical thinking is essential for mastering interpersonal skills. (Chapter 1) 27
5. Learn to transfer the skills of critical thinking. (Chapter 1) 33
6. Develop critical thinking attitudes. (Chapter 2) 38
7. Critical thinking can be aided by hidden knowledge. (Chapter 2) 43
8. Use different thinking styles to think critically. (Chapter 2) 50
9. Keep the brain in critical thinking condition. (Chapter 2) 60
10. Critical thinking sometimes needs to be suspended. (Chapter 2) 62
11. Recognize your role in perception. (Chapter 3) 66
12. Practice flexibility when examining information. (Chapter 3) 68

13. Examine your assumptions. (Chapter 3) 73

14. Beware of halos. (Chapter 3) 74

15. Look for a variety of cues. (Chapter 3) 76

16. Exercise your brain. (Chapter 3) 80

17. Look for contradictory cues. (Chapter 3) 81

18. Examine your assumptions (again). (Chapter 4) 90

19. Consider the source. (Chapter 4) 92

20. Read from a wide variety of sources to acquire information. (Chapter 4) 96

21. Interact with a wide variety of people to acquire information. (Chapter 4) 98

22. Distinguish between hypotheses and conclusions. (Chapter 4) 103

23. Listen for truth and accuracy. (Chapter 4) 105

24. Don't confuse snarl and purr words with objective descriptions. (Chapter 5) 113

25. Approach new ideas positively and critically. (Chapter 5) 114

26. Use the abstraction ladder as a critical thinking tool. (Chapter 5) 116

27. Don't be fooled by words that sound impressive but mean little. (Chapter 5) 130

28. Don't be influenced by weasel words. (Chapter 5) 133

29. Examine your self-interest assumptions about lying and ethics. (Chapter 6) 144

30. Examine your "altruistic" assumptions about lying and ethics. (Chapter 6) 146

31. Be careful of confusing relationship and causal assertions. (Chapter 6) 153

32. Evaluate causal assertions. (Chapter 6) 155

33. Carefully assess cues to lying before making judgments. (Chapter 6) 161

34. Consider recency. (Chapter 7) 177

35. Distinguish emotional from logical reasons. (Chapter 7) 180

36. Evaluate your assumptions for expressing emotions. (Chapter 7) 184

37. Evaluate your assumptions against expressing emotions. (Chapter 7) 187

38. Use comparison to highlight similarities and differences. (Chapter 8) 195

39. Altercast to gain other perspectives. (Chapter 8) 198

40. Apply concepts from one area to another. (Chapter 8) 201

41. Altercast with those different from yourself. (Chapter 8) 203

42. Altercast with role reversal. (Chapter 8) 210

43. Categorize to see relationships and connections. (Chapter 8) 219

44. Use analysis to understand individual elements. (Chapter 9) 230

45. Use synthesis to understand connections and relationships. (Chapter 9) 231

46. Bring your cultural assumptions to consciousness for careful analysis. (Chapter 9) 236

47. Examine the generality of generalizations with "Except-ional Analysis." (Chapter 9) 237

48. See the middle ground; don't be blinded by extremes. (Chapter 9) 243

49. Beware of your confirmation and disconfirmation biases. (Chapter 9) 246

50. Resist figurative analogies as evidence. (Chapter 10) 268

51. Assess different theories with Ockham's Razor. (Chapter 10) 273

52. Examine the reliability of research. (Chapter 10) 275

53. Examine the validity of research. (Chapter 10) 277

54. Be careful of generalizing from anecdotal evidence. (Chapter 10) 283

55. Examine your assumptions about conflict. (Chapter 11) 292

56. Critically evaluate your decision making processes. (Chapter 11) 299

57. Look at a problem with three critical thinking hats. (Chapter 11) 300

58. Look at a problem with three more critical thinking hats. (Chapter 11) 301

59. Critically evaluate your communication strategies before applying them. (Chapter 12) 322

60. Beware the ties that bind. (Chapter 12) 323

61. Use the simple checklist to assemble your information. (Chapter 12) 337

62. Be mindful and flexible about assertive communication. (Chapter 12) 340

Barriers to Critical Thinking

1. Maintaining unrealistic beliefs about interpersonal communication (Chapter 1) 4

2. Viewing communication as linear or interactional (Chapter 1) 5

3. Failing to see communication occurring within a context (Chapter 1) 17

4. Failing to decode relationship messages (Chapter 1) 22

5. Accepting cultural beliefs uncritically (Chapter 1) 34

6. Failing to understand cultural differences in self-disclosure (Chapter 2) 49

7. Failing to appreciate gender differences in self-disclosure (Chapter 2) 49

8. Failing to perceive the dyadic effect (Chapter 2) 50

9. Being unduly influenced by primacy or recency (Chapter 3) 73

10. Seeing others through implicit personality theories (Chapter 3) 74

11. Making and fulfilling prophecies (Chapter 3) 75

12. Stereotyping (Chapter 3) 76

13. Thinking through the self-serving bias (Chapter 3) 77

14. Thinking under the influence of the fundamental attribution error (Chapter 3) 77

15. Failing to check perceptions (Chapter 3) 82

16. Listening through preconceived attitudes (Chapter 4) 94

17. Hearing what you expect to hear (Chapter 4) 103

18. Listening offensively (Chapter 4) 104

19. Filtering out unpleasant or difficult messages (Chapter 4) 105

20. Assimilating messages into your own biases (Chapter 4) 105

21. Sharpening (Chapter 4) 105

22. Looking for meaning only in words (Chapter 5) 112

23. Thinking intensionally (Chapter 5) 131

24. Thinking in allness terms (Chapter 5) 131

25. Confusing fact and inferences (Chapter 5) 132

26. Thinking in static terms (Chapter 5) 132

27. Thinking indiscriminately (Chapter 5) 134

28. Polarizing (Chapter 5) 134

29. Failing to see the interconnection between verbal and nonverbal messages (Chapter 6) 140

30. Drawing conclusions (rather than hypotheses) about personality from people's nonverbal behaviors (Chapter 6) 155

31. "Reading" nonverbal messages through one's own cultural and gender rules (Chapter 6) 165

32. Failing to appreciate cultural and gender differences in emotional expression (Chapter 7) 179

33. Confusing emotional expression with feelings (Chapter 7) 179

34. Maintaining unexamined assumptions imposed by social rules and customs (Chapter 7) 181

35. Maintaining unrealistic and unexamined fears about emotional expression (Chapter 7) 183

36. Failing to see the influence of cultural maxims (Chapter 8) 209

37. Talking mindlessly (Chapter 8) 217

38. Being inflexible (Chapter 8) 219

39. Thinking with a closed mind (Chapter 9) 236

40. Thinking with ethnocentrism (Chapter 9) 247

41. Thinking mindlessly (Chapter 9) 248

42. Thinking by overattribution (Chapter 9) 249

43. Maintaining unrealistic beliefs about relationships (Chapter 10) 263

44. Failing to see cultural differences in relationships (Chapter 10) 284

45. Failing to appreciate gender and cultural variations in approaches to conflict (Chapter 11) 293

46. Failing to distinguish relational from content conflicts (Chapter 11) 294

47. Dealing with ill-defined conflicts (Chapter 11) 301

48. Maintaining unrealistic beliefs about the self (Chapter 12) 318

49. Maintaining unrealistic self-destructive beliefs (Chapter 12) 318

50. Failing to recognize that power is a part of all communication (Chapter 12) 334

Self Tests

1. What Do You Believe about Interpersonal Communication? (Chapter 1) 4

2. What's Your Cultural Awareness? (Chapter 1) 32

3. What Do You Have a Right to Know? (Chapter 2) 47

4. How Willing to Self-Disclose Are You? (Chapter 2) 51

5. How Apprehensive Are You? (Chapter 2) 59

6. How Accurate Are You at People Perception? (Chapter 3) 71

7. How Do You Listen? (Chapter 4) 95

8. Gender Differences (Chapter 5) 117

9. How Confirming Are You? (Chapter 5) 120

10. Can You Distinguish Facts from Inferences? (Chapter 5) 131

11. What Time Do You Have? (Chapter 6) 175

12. How Do You Feel about Communicating Feelings? (Chapter 7) 175

13. How Satisfying Is Your Conversation? (Chapter 8) 194

14. How Flexible Are You in Communication? (Chapter 8) 217

15. Are You a High Self-Monitor? (Chapter 8) 223

16. What Are Your Cultural Beliefs and Values? (Chapter 9) 232

17. How Open Are You Interculturally? (Chapter 9) 237

18. Individual and Collectivist Cultures (Chapter 9) 239

19. What Do You Believe about Relationships? (Chapter 10) 262

20. What Kind of Lover Are You? (Chapter 10) 265

21. How to Criticize (Chapter 11) 303

22. How Verbally Aggressive Are You? (Chapter 11) 310

23. How Argumentative Are You? (Chapter 11) 312

24. How Machiavellian Are You? (Chapter 12) 325

25. How Powerful Are You? (Chapter 12) 327

26. How Assertive Is Your Communication? (Chapter 12) 335

Preface

It's a pleasure and an honor to present this fourth edition of *Messages: Building Interpersonal Communication Skills.* This book was written (and revised for this edition) in response to the need for a text that emphasizes **critical thinking** by integrating it into all aspects of interpersonal communication, emphasizes the development of **interpersonal skills** (the practical skills for personal, social, and professional success), emphasizes the influence of **culture and gender** on just about every aspect of interpersonal communication, and emphasizes **listening** as an essential (but too often neglected) part of interpersonal communication.

Messages answers these needs by providing thorough coverage of each of these major elements. Chapter 1 discusses critical thinking, interpersonal skills, culture and gender, and listening as integral components of interpersonal competence. Material presented throughout the book reinforces this discussion and creates a foundation for students to understand these concepts and then apply what they have learned through real-life examples and exercises.

EXTENSIVE CRITICAL THINKING COVERAGE

Messages emphasizes the role of critical thinking as an essential part of effective and responsible interpersonal communication. The goals here are to explain the nature and principles of critical thinking and to provide opportunities for students to apply these principles to their own interpersonal communication. Critical thinking is integrated in this edition following a simple five-step process: (Step 1) understanding the nature and function of critical thinking, (Step 2) mastering the skills (techniques, strategies) of critical thinking, (Step 3) avoiding the barriers to critical thinking, (Step 4) engaging in careful and frequent self-appraisal, and (Step 5) applying critical thinking to a wide variety of situations. To enable students to effectively navigate through these five stages, the text contains several key features:

- **Critical thinking sidebars** explain the nature of critical thinking (Step 1 of the five-step process) and then move to Step 2 by providing a wide variety of specific skills for thinking critically about interpersonal communication or about anything else. Sidebars in the first two chapters explain what critical thinking is and lay the foundation for understanding its nature and goals. Those in the remaining chapters offer critical thinking principles, techniques, and applications that are more closely keyed to the text content, for example, examining assumptions about culture, relationships, and conflict; examining a problem from a variety of perspectives; and distinguishing between emotional and logical reasoning, relationship and causal assertions, and hypotheses and conclusions. This material appears in the margins of the text and helps to link the critical thinking concepts to specific text discussions, but also allows them to stand apart as ideas useful beyond the world of interpersonal communication.

- **Advice on avoiding barriers to critical thinking** (Step 3), such as uncritically accepting cultural beliefs and values, overattribution, offensive listening, and the failure to check perceptions, is integrated throughout the text. This advice is identified in the text with a critical thinking question in the margin prefaced with a Caution, Barrier to Critical Thinking icon.

- **Self-appraisal tests** (Step 4) are presented throughout the text to facilitate careful and frequent self-analysis, self-appraisal, and self-assessment. Some of these tests are standard research instruments used in studying interpersonal communication (for example, the tests of communication satisfaction, love style, verbal aggressiveness, argumentativeness, and communication flexibility). Others were developed to encourage students to interact more personally with the material covered in the text (for example, the tests of cultural awareness and beliefs, listening styles, individual and collective cultural orientations, and power).

- **Critical thinking questions** are presented in the margins and coordinated with the text material to provide frequent opportunities to evaluate (Step 5) and apply the principles and theories discussed in the text. In a similar way, marginal quotations—new to this edition—present different views on the text's topics and invite students to discuss and challenge them. Critical thinking questions are also integrated into many of the pedagogical features of the text, for example, skill building exercises, self-tests, and listening boxes.

SKILL DEVELOPMENT FOCUS

- *Messages* emphasizes the development of practical interpersonal communication skills such as increasing accuracy in interpersonal perception, expressing emotions effectively, and dealing constructively with interpersonal conflict. Interpersonal skills are presented throughout the text in the context of the concepts and principles of interpersonal communication.

- Interpersonal power and empowerment skills are emphasized throughout the text and show students how building these skills can be useful at home and at work. Chapter 12, "Interpersonal Communication and Power," discusses such issues as increasing power through self-esteem, managing power plays, speaking with power, and assertiveness. Empowering apprehensives and empowering through listening are also discussed in Chapters 2 and 12 respectively, further highlighting these important skills.

- Also, new to this edition, each chapter contains a **How to . . .** box that focuses on a specific skill and explains how it can be used to communicate more effectively. How To . . . boxes consider skills such as facilitating self-disclosure, communicating power nonverbally, communicating with the grief stricken, interacting effectively in intercultural situations, and dealing with relationship breakups.
- **Skill-building exercises** are also presented three times in each chapter. These exercises cover a wide variety of skills such as the appropriateness of self-disclosure, taking the perspective of another person, reducing barriers to listening, paraphrasing to ensure understanding, and applying theories to relationship problems.
- **Chapter opening grids** identify the skills covered within each chapter.
- **Skills checklists** in the chapter summary immediately reinforce the skills covered.
- The **glossary of concepts and skills** at the end of the book provides an easy way to find definitions of technical terms.
- Finally, each chapter contains a **skills-oriented reading** which provides an additional perspective on the skills covered in each of the chapters.

ATTENTION TO CULTURE AND GENDER

Comprehensive and fully integrated coverage of cultural diversity and gender in interpersonal communication is highlighted throughout the text.

Chapter 9, "Interpersonal Communication and Culture," covers cultural issues in interpersonal communication in depth, focusing on the nature of culture and of intercultural communication, cultural differences, such as individualism and collectivism, high and low context, and masculine and feminine, as well as ways to improve intercultural communication.

Integrated discussions of culture and gender are expanded from the previous edition throughout the text, including:

The role of culture in interpersonal communication—cultural awareness, the relevance of culture, and the aim of a cultural perspective—is presented in Chapter 1, "Interpersonal Communication," and establishes culture as a fundamental concept in all forms of interpersonal communication.

Cultural teachings as a source of self-concept, culture's influence on self-disclosure, and cultural influences on apprehension are integrated into Chapter 2, "The Self."

Chapter 3, "Perception," includes discussions of the role of stereotypes in perception and the importance of cultural sensitivity in perceptual accuracy.

Cultural and gender differences in listening are now discussed in a major section in Chapter 4, "Listening."

Gender and cultural differences in directness; language as a cultural institution and cultural maxims; sexism, heterosexism, and racism in language; and cultural identifiers (ways to talk to and about people from different cultures) are now included in Chapter 5, "Verbal Messages."

Chapter 6, "Nonverbal Messages," now includes a major section on culture and nonverbal communication, covering nonverbal taboos, cultural significance of color, monochronic and polychronic time orientations, the social clock, and nonverbal differences between men and women.

The role that culture and gender play in emotions and the varied societal rules and customs that influence emotional communication are covered in Chapter 7, "Emotional Messages."

Chapter 8, "Conversation Messages," covers the conversational taboos in different cultures, cultural sensitivity as a metaskill, suggestions for communicating with the deaf, and conversational maxims and their cultural and gender differences.

Chapter 9, "Interpersonal Communication and Culture," as noted above, is devoted entirely to interpersonal communication and culture.

The numerous culture and gender differences in friendship and love relationships are discussed in Chapter 10, "Interpersonal Communication and Relationships."

Chapter 11, "Interpersonal Communication and Conflict," discusses how different cultures view and deal with interpersonal conflict, the cultural aspects of face-enhancing and face-detracting strategies of conflict, and gender differences in conflict strategies.

The cultural dimension of power and especially the vast differences between high power and low power distance cultures are considered at length in Chapter 12, "Interpersonal Communication and Power."

EMPHASIS ON LISTENING

Listening—too often neglected or given only minor importance in most interpersonal communication texts—is emphasized in the fourth edition of *Messages* in two major ways. First, a separate chapter on listening (Chapter 4) covers the listening process from receiving to responding, the role of culture and gender in listening, and guidelines for increasing listening effectiveness. Second, and new to this edition, each of the chapters contains a **Listening** box. These boxes discuss specific listening skills as they relate to the other topics in the text, for example, listening to other perspectives is presented in "Perception" (Chapter 3), listening to the emotions of others in "Emotional Messages" (Chapter 7), the ways to listen in conflict situations in "Interpersonal Communications and Relationships" (Chapter 10), and listening to empower in "Interpersonal Communication and Power" (Chapter 12). With the separate chapter on listening that provides the fundamentals of effective listening and the Listening boxes in each chapter that relate to specific interpersonal contexts, *Messages* offers effective and comprehensive coverage of listening.

EXTENSIVE PEDAGOGICAL APPARATUS

Messages also contains a variety of interactive pedagogical features that help students better understand and more effectively master the skills of interpersonal communication by asking them to respond and relate their experiences to the material presented in the text.

Chapter opening grids present the major topics of the chapter with their corresponding goals and skills. The grids link the main concepts covered in each chapter with the corresponding goals (cognitive learning objectives) and skills (behavioral learning objectives) students should master after reading the chapter.

13 Listening boxes—new to this edition—highlight listening as an integral part of the interpersonal communication process. A complete listing of these boxes is presented in the Specialized Contents on page x.

12 How to . . . boxes—also new to this edition—focus on specific skills and present practical ways of mastering them in interpersonal situations. A complete listing of these boxes is presented in the Specialized Contents on page x.

26 Self-tests encourage students to assess themselves on such issues as self-disclosure, people perception, self-monitoring, relationship beliefs, and assertiveness. New to this edition are Self-tests dealing with cultural awareness in Chapter 1, rights to information about another person in Chapter 2, cultural beliefs and values in Chapter 9, individual and collectivist cultures in Chapter 9, personal power in Chapter 12, and Machiavellian tendencies in Chapter 12. A complete listing of Self-tests appears in the Specialized Contents on page xvi.

Critical Thinking Sidebars explain the nature and principles of critical thinking and are presented in the text's margins. A complete listing of the critical thinking sidebars—approximately half of which are new to this edition—appears in the Specialized Contents on page xii.

Critical Thinking Questions, also in the margins, ask students to apply what they have learned to specific situations.

Thinking Critically About . . . questions in the Self-tests, exercises, and featured boxes require critical analysis and application and ask for students' active involvement.

A variety of **quotations** appears in the margins and offers different perspectives on topics covered in the text inviting comment and discussion.

36 Skill building exercises are positioned after each major heading in the text. Many are new to this edition:

Cultural Beliefs (1.3)
Using Performance Visualization to Reduce Apprehension (2.3)
Perceiving My Selves (3.1)
Typical Man, Typical Woman (4.2)
Thinking in E-Prime (5.3)
Integrating Verbal and Nonverbal Messages (6.1)
Artifacts and Culture (6.3)
Gender and the Topics of Conversation (8.1)
How Do You Talk? As a Woman? As a Man? (9.1)
From Culture to Gender (10.3)
Generating Win-Win Solutions (11.2)
Rewriting Unrealistic Beliefs (12.1)

A listing of all Skill Building Exercises appears in the Specialized Contents on page xi.

Vocabulary quizzes at the end of each chapter highlight key terms and make learning them easier and more enjoyable.

Chapter summaries contain both content and skills summaries. The skills summaries are presented as checklists.

An appendix, **Writing About Interpersonal Communication,** is new to this edition and offers a variety of writing experiences that may be integrated into the course such as personal experience, explanation of a concept or principle, review, and research (pages 343-347). Suggestions for paper topics are provided in this appendix as well as in many of the critical thinking questions in the margins; the writing suggestions in the text's margins appear in italics.

A combined **glossary of concepts and skills,** also new to this edition, offers brief definitions of significant terms in interpersonal communication and identifies the related skills when appropriate (pages 348-362).

A complementary reading appears in each chapter, providing a different perspective from that given in the text. Five of these articles are new to this edition. A complete listing of these readings appears in the Specialized Contents on page xii.

Some Chapter-by-Chapter Changes

Numerous improvements were made in each of the chapters. Here is a brief summary of the major changes.

Chapter 1, "Interpersonal Communication." A graduated presentation of the communication model—from linear, through interactional, to transactional—has been added. A new table on the areas of interpersonal communication and relationships provides an overview of this rapidly growing area. The process of adjustment, including communication accommodation, has been added to the section on principles of interpersonal communication. A new diagram incorporating the purposes, motives, and results of interpersonal communication is included with the discussion of interpersonal purposes. A new section, Culture and Interpersonal Communication, establishes culture as a major focus of the text and explains the relevance and aim of a cultural perspective. This section includes a new self-test allowing for the exploration of cultural awareness.

Chapter 2, "The Self." New sections on cultural teachings as a source of self-concept, apprehension, and culture and ways to empower apprehensives have been added. A new self-test explores what people feel they have a right to know about friends or lovers.

Chapter 3, "Perception." The discussion of attribution errors has been expanded and now includes the fundamental attribution error (as well as self-serving biases and overattribution). The entire section on accuracy in perception has been expanded and revised and now includes becoming aware of perceptions, perception checking, reducing uncertainty (along with its cultural variations), and cultural sensitivity.

Chapter 4, "Listening." A major new section on the relevance of culture and gender to listening has been added. Also new is a discussion of difficult listeners and how to avoid becoming one of them.

Chapter 5, "Verbal Messages." This entire chapter has been completely revised to include a more general introduction to language and the principles for increasing verbal effectiveness. New and expanded topics include directness and its cultural and gender variations, politeness, language variations in abstraction, and the rules of netiquette. A new section on cultural identifiers offers useful advice on talking to and about members of different cultural groups.

Chapter 6, "Nonverbal Messages." The discussion of body communication has been expanded and now includes body appearance as well as body movements. Facial management techniques and the facial feedback hypothesis have been added to the discussion of facial communication. Smell as a form of nonverbal communication has also been integrated. A greatly expanded treatment of culture and nonverbal communication is now provided and includes such topics as nonverbal gestures that can create intercultural misunderstanding, cultural variations in the meanings of colors, monochronic and polychronic time orientations, and the social clock.

Chapter 7, "Emotional Messages." A table illustrating commonly used emoticons and a new section on the principles of emotional communication, such as emotional contagion and cultural variations on emotional expression, have been added as well as new sections on cultural and gender differences in emotional expression.

Chapter 8, "Conversation Messages." New sections include conversational taboos around the world, good and bad excuses, communicating with the deaf, cultural and gender differences in conversation, and a discussion of computer communication skills.

Chapter 9, "Interpersonal Communication and Culture." Two new self-tests—on cultural beliefs and individual/collectivist cultures—have been added as well as a discussion of cultural masculinity and femininity. A new section, Improving Intercultural Communication, streamlines and brings together the principles and the barriers to intercultural communication.

Chapter 10, "Interpersonal Communication and Relationships." New material on the advantages and disadvantages of interpersonal relationships, including online relationships, and the role of culture and gender on relationships has been added.

Chapter 11, "Interpersonal Communication Conflict." An expanded discussion of win-win conflict resolution and sections on face-enhancing and face-detracting conflict strategies, the role of listening in conflict, the nature of online conflicts, and gender differences in conflict are now included.

Chapter 12, "Interpersonal Communication and Power." A new discussion of Machiavellianism has been added to the section on principles of power. Two new Self-tests, on power and on Machiavellianism, have been included. The cultural dimension of power distance has been added. Sexual harassment and power plays are both presented as ways of exercising power unfairly.

SUPPLEMENTS

Messages comes with a variety of useful supplements.

The Exchange Web Site (http:/longman.awl.com/exchange/)

The Exchange is Longman's online guide to interpersonal communication providing additional resources to students and instructors including: online interpersonal communication scenarios asking students to choose responses, an Internet Relay Chat tutorial that guides students through the process of real-time discussions, an assignment bank for instructors wishing to incorporate the World Wide Web into their classes, and reference links for students and instructors for over 30 Web sites related to interpersonal communication.

Interpersonal Communication Video

Prepared by Jean Civikly and Tom Jewell of the University of New Mexico, the video covers concepts such as perception, ethics, self-disclosure, sexual harassment, and dysfunctional relationships. It includes segments written and performed by students from the University of New Mexico. An extensive 120-page Instructor's Guide accompanies the video and provides the complete script, a list of related concepts, questions for class discussion, exercises, and additional resources and references for each of the eight episodes.

Instructor's Manual and Test Bank with Transparency Masters

Prepared by Harriet B. Harral of Texas Christian University, the Instructor's Manual provides chapter overviews and learning and skill objectives for each chapter. The manual provides ideas to activate class discussions and contains exercises to illustrate the concepts, principles and skills of interpersonal communication. In addition, the test bank portion of the manual contains numerous multiple choice, true-false, short answer, and essay test questions. The Instructor's Manual includes more than 100 transparency masters that frame key concepts and skills.

PowerPoint CD-ROM

New to this edition, the transparency masters will now be available as PowerPoint presentation slides on CD-ROM. The Instructor's Manual includes handouts so students can follow along and take notes as the slides are being discussed.

Interpersonal Communication TestGen-EQ

The test bank portion of the Instructor's Manual is available on our computerized testing system, TestGen-EQ. This fully networkable testing software is available in Windows and Macintosh. TestGen-EQ's friendly graphical interface enables instructors to easily view, edit, and add questions, transfer questions to tests, and print tests in a variety of fonts and forms. Search and sort features let the instructor quickly locate questions and arrange them in preferred order.

The Interpersonal Challenge 3

This highly interactive game has been expanded and streamlined. The game now contains 200 questions covering such topics as perception, interpersonal relationships, ethical dilemmas, and intercultural communication. Instructions for playing the game have been completely revised; as a result the game will play faster and more smoothly with small groups in and out of the classroom.

Transparencies

In addition to the transparency masters included in the Instructor's Manual, Longman is pleased to offer a package of color transparencies. These transparencies reproduce many of the figures and tables from the text. Included in this transparency package is a convenient grid which offers suggestions for using the transparencies in the classroom and how to best integrate them with the text material.

The Longman Communication Video Library

Numerous videos are available for use with this text. Current videos cover such topics as effective listening, fear of communication, interpersonal relationships, interviewing, small group communication, and public speaking. Since new titles are being added regularly, consult your local Longman sales representative for the latest information.

Study Guide and Activity Manual

Prepared by Marylin Kelly of McLennan Community College, the Study Guide provides for a broad spectrum of abilities, from teaching basic level college skills to challenging the advanced student. The guide contains objectives, study methods, chapter outlines, expanded vocabulary tests, sample test items, and chapter summary charts. The guide also includes activities for reinforcing learning, demonstrating skills, and a selection of readings from popular magazines and books that address topics of interpersonal communication.

Brainstorms

This booklet, subtitled "How to Think More Creatively About Communication or Anything Else," integrates critical thinking into the interpersonal communication course. **Brainstorms** introduces the creative thinking process (its nature, values, characteristics, and stages) and its relationship to communication, and it provides 19 specific tools for thinking more creatively about communication (or anything else). The discussion of each tool includes its purposes, the specific techniques to follow in using the tool, and at least one exercise or application to get started using the tool. Creative thinking sidebars and relevant quotations add to the interactive pedagogy. Guides for coordinating the creative thinking tools with the topic of the textbook are provided as well.

ACKNOWLEDGMENTS

I want to thank the many people who contributed to this revision. As with all revisions, this one owes a great debt to those who reviewed earlier manuscripts and editions. I return their comments repeatedly. Thank you:

Phil Backlund, *Central Washington University;* Kimberly Batty-Herbert, *Clovis Community College;* Josie Cuerpo Buelow, *Skyline College;* D. Jean Christy, *Deleware Technical and Community College;* Mary Forestieri, *Lane Community College;* Roger Garrett, *Central Washington University;* Bruce Gutknecht, *University of North Florida;* Jeffrey C. Hahner, *Pace University;* Paul Harper, *Oklahoma State University;* Idahlynn Karre, *University of Northern Colorado;* Richard Katula, *Northeastern University;* Marilyn Kelly, *McLennan Community College;* Sandra M. Ketrow, *University of Rhode Island;* James P. Murtha, *Harford Community College;* Patricia D. Richardson, *Cecil Community College;* Anthony B. Schroeder, *Eastern New Mexico University;* Ann M. Scroggie, *Sante Fe Community College;* Margaret R. Ward, *Delta College;* Kent Zimmerman, *Sinclair Community College;* Elliott M. Zinner, *Cuyahoga Community College*

I am grateful to the following individuals who reviewed the manuscript and provided helpful suggestions: Leonard J. Barchak, *McNeese State University;* Doug Hoehn, *Community College of Philadelphia;* David Hudson, *Golden West College;* Thomas Huebner, *William Carey College;* Meg Kreiner, *Spokane Community College;* Polly Rogers, *Arapahoe Community College;* Nancy Willets, *Cape Cod Community College;* and Dianna Wynn, *Prince George's Community College.*

I also wish to thank the people at Longman who contributed so much energy, support, and helpful suggestions. Thank you Priscilla McGeehon, editor-in-chief; Donna Erickson, acquisitions editor; Lisa Pinto, development manager; John Holdcroft, marketing manager; and Lisa Ziccardi, supplements editor. The people at Electronic Publishing Services were equally helpful. I especially wish to thank Jodi Isman, production editor; Jo Anne Chernow, designer; and Teresa Barensfeld, copy editor.

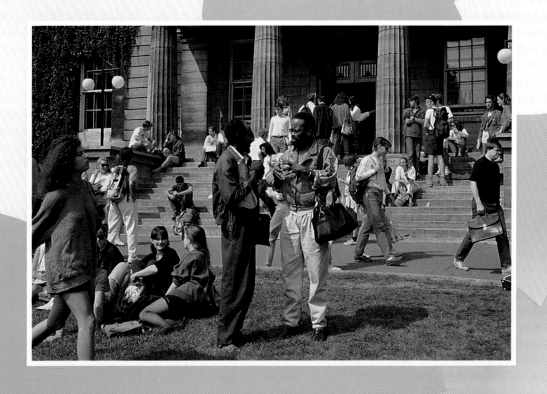

1

Interpersonal Communication

CHAPTER TOPICS	LEARNING OBJECTIVES	SKILL OBJECTIVES
	After completing this chapter, you should be able to	*After completing this chapter, you should be able to*
Nature of Interpersonal Communication	1. Define *interpersonal communication* and its major elements	Interact interpersonally with a recognition of all significant elements
Principles of Interpersonal Communication	2. Explain the principles of interpersonal communication	Engage in interpersonal communication with a clear recognition of its essential principles
Culture and Interpersonal Communication	3. Explain the role of culture in interpersonal communication	Interact interpersonally with an understanding of cultural differences

Grace and Mark have been dating for the last three years. Although they're deeply in love, there are lots of problems facing their relationship. Grace wants to continue her education and become an accountant; Mark wants to continue working at the local gas station. Grace wants to wait to have children; Mark wants lots of children as soon as possible. Grace wants to have her mother live with them; Mark is opposed. Whenever one of them brings up one of these problems, they get into an argument and often stay angry for days at a time. Both Grace and Mark feel that once they get married, they will work out these and any other problems that arise. Love, they feel, will conquer all.

Reno has five children, two preteens and three teenagers. For most of his life Reno has worked as a superintendent of a large condo complex in Boston. Although he's deeply interested in the lives of his wife and children, he feels he's often ignored. His children rarely confide in him and whenever there is important news they go to their mother. Reno feels left out of the family; he feels his only function is to earn money and has seriously considered leaving his family and starting another life in another city.

For the last 14 years, Karla has worked in a toy factory in Minnesota which was recently purchased by a Japanese investment firm. The production department, which Karla had headed for the last four years, has been reorganized and is now run by three people—two Japanese businessmen and Karla. Although production is up, morale is down. Karla used to handle most problems informally by talking with the crew over lunch or at company parties. Now, all problems are handled by this team at formal business meetings. Karla feels that the new owners have virtually eliminated her job and that she is being kept on just because the union contract protects her. She's thinking of asking for a transfer or seeking a position with another company.

These situations all revolve around problems in interpersonal communication. All these people would profit from learning the principles and skills of interpersonal communication. Whether in a romantic or friendship relationship, a long-established family, or a work environment, the principles of interpersonal communication are powerful tools for dealing with problems such as these. Mark and Grace, for example, don't seem to know how to resolve interpersonal differences. Their belief that love will conquer all prevents them from seeing the difficulties that confront their relationship now and that will not go away with marriage. Because they don't know how to resolve interpersonal conflicts, their disagreements and the ways in which they talk about them only aggravate the situation. Instead of improving their relationship, the conflicts and the attempts at resolution damage it further. The guidelines for conflict resolution discussed in Chapter 11 would help Mark and Grace considerably.

Reno feels left out and doesn't know how to facilitate the self-disclosures of his children or his wife. Nor does he know how to communicate his own feelings. So, it's not surprising that his children have learned that he's not the parent to go to with feelings. He wants involvement, but doesn't know how to get it. The suggestions for facilitating self-disclosure and for communicating empathy and support discussed in Chapters 2 and 8 would prove helpful to Reno.

Karla is having trouble communicating in this new intercultural setting. Although morale is down throughout the plant, the new owners are unaware of it largely because no one has voiced concern. Karla's self-esteem has been damaged; she feels she's lost her importance and doesn't know how to deal with it. Karla would profit from the discussion of self-esteem in Chapter 12 as well as the discussions of culture throughout this text and especially those dealing with improving intercultural communication given in Chapter 9.

> What other problems might Grace and Mark, Reno, and Karla be experiencing? What suggestions might you make to help them deal with their communication problems?

These situations and many like them can be understood and improved by mastering the skills of interpersonal communication. That's what this book is about. It's about problems like these and many others. So important have interpersonal skills become that the U.S. Department of Labor, in its report, "What Work Requires of Schools"—a report based on interviews with managers, employers, and workers who described the skills needed to function effectively at their jobs—identified interpersonal skills as one of five skills essential for a nation and an individual to be economically competitive in the world marketplace (*The New York Times*, July 3, 1991, p. A17). And, in a study conducted by the Collegiate Employment Research Institute of Michigan State University of over 500 employers, "good oral, written, and interpersonal communication skills were reported among the most notable deficiencies observed in new college graduates" (Scheetz, 1995).

This book, then, is about improving your interpersonal skills so that you'll be more effective in a wide variety of interpersonal communication situations: with your family; with supervisors, coworkers, and subordinates on the job; and with acquaintances, friends, and lovers.

Before you begin studying this exciting and practical area, examine your own beliefs about interpersonal communication by taking the self-test on page 4.

NATURE OF INTERPERSONAL COMMUNICATION

Interpersonal communication is communication that occurs between two persons who have a relationship between them. It occurs when you send or receive messages and when you assign meaning to such messages. Interpersonal communication is always distorted by noise, occurs within a context, and involves some opportunity for feedback.

Interpersonal communicators are conscious of one another and of their connection with one another. They're interdependent; what one person thinks and says impacts on what the other thinks and says. Interpersonal communication includes the conversations that take place between an interviewer and a potential employee, a son and his father, two sisters, a teacher and a student, two lovers, and two friends. Even the stranger asking for directions from a local resident has a relationship with that person.

> If your lips would keep from slips
> Five things observe with care;
> To who you speak, of whom you speak,
> And how, and when, and where.
>
> —*W. E. Norris*

SELF-TEST

What Do You Believe About Interpersonal Communication?

Instructions: Respond to each of the following statements with T if you believe the statement is usually true and F if you believe the statement is usually false.

_____ 1. Good interpersonal communicators are born, not made.

_____ 2. The more you communicate, the better your communication will be.

_____ 3. Unlike speaking or writing, effective listening really cannot be taught.

_____ 4. Opening lines such as "Hello, how are you?" or "Fine weather today" serve no useful interpersonal purpose.

_____ 5. The best way to communicate with someone from another culture is in the same way you communicate with someone from your own culture.

_____ 6. When verbal and nonverbal messages contradict each other, people believe the verbal message.

_____ 7. Complete openness should be the goal of any meaningful interpersonal relationship.

_____ 8. Interpersonal conflict is a good sign that your relationship is in trouble.

_____ 9. Effective interpersonal communicators do not rely on "power tactics"; power is irrelevant among close friends or romantic partners.

_____ 10. Fear of speaking is detrimental; the effective speaker has to learn to eliminate it.

Thinking Critically About Interpersonal Communication Beliefs All 10 statements have a bit of truth in them and because of this they're often believed as generalizations about communication. Actually, all 10 statements are a lot more false than they are true. As you read this book, you'll discover not only why these statements are basically false but some problems that can arise when you act as if these misconceptions are true.

CAUTION

How might **maintaining unrealistic beliefs about interpersonal communication** prevent you from acquiring needed communication skills? Might such beliefs prevent you from critically evaluating your own interpersonal communication?

In early theories, the communication process was viewed as linear. In this **linear** view of communication the speaker spoke and the listener listened; after the speaker finished speaking, the listener would speak. Communication was seen as proceeding in a relatively straight line. Speaking and listening were seen as taking place at different times; when you spoke, you didn't listen, and when you listened, you didn't speak (Figure 1.1).

This linear model was soon replaced with an **interactional** view in which the speaker and the listener were seen as exchanging turns at speaking and listening. For example, A spoke while B listened and then B (exchanging the listener's

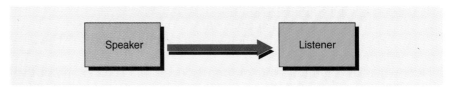

Figure 1.1

The Linear View of Human Communication

Communication researchers Judy Pearson and Paul Nelson (1994) suggest that you think of the speaker as passing a ball to the listener who either catches it or fumbles it. Can you think of another analogy or metaphor for this linear view of communication?

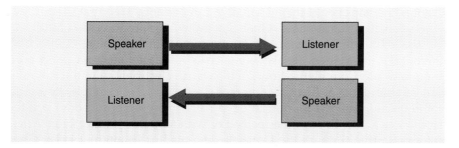

Figure 1.2

The Interactional View

In this view, continuing with the ball-throwing analogy, the speaker would pass the ball to the listener who would then pass the ball back or fumble (Pearson & Nelson, 1994). What other analogy would work here?

role for the speaker's role) spoke in response to what A said and A listened (Figure 1.2). Speaking and listening were still viewed as separate acts that did not overlap and that were not performed at the same time by the same person.

A more satisfying view and the one held currently sees communication as a **transactional** process where each person serves simultaneously as speaker and listener. At the same time that you send messages, you're also receiving messages from your own communications and from the reactions of the other person (Figure 1.3). At the same time that you're listening, you're also sending messages. In a transactional view, each person is seen as both speaker and listener, as simultaneously communicating and receiving messages (Watzlawick, Beavin, & Jackson, 1967; Watzlawick, 1977, 1978; Barnlund, 1970; Wilmot, 1987).

Also, in a transactional view the elements of communication are seen as *inter*dependent (never *in*dependent). Each exists in relation to the others. A change in any one element of the process produces changes in the other elements. For example, you're talking with a group of your friends and your mother enters the group. This change in "audience" will lead to other

CAUTION

How might **viewing communication as linear or interactional** lead you to incorrectly evaluate what goes on in interpersonal communication?

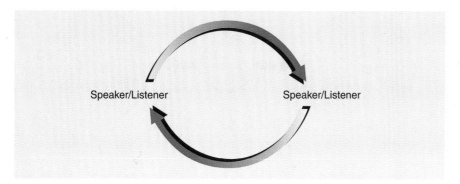

Figure 1.3

The Transactional View

In this view a complex ball game is underway where each player could send and receive any number of balls at any time. Players would be able to throw and catch balls at the very same time (Pearson & Nelson, 1994). Can you think of any other analogies for this transactional view of communication?

changes; perhaps you'll change what you say or how you say it. Regardless of what change is introduced, other changes will be produced as a result.

Throughout this explanation of interpersonal communication—and in fact, throughout this text—we make reference to both face-to-face and electronic communication. No matter how sophisticated, electronic communication is still very similar to ordinary face-to-face interactions. For example, electronic communication allows for the same types of communication as does face-to-face interaction with one other person or with a small or large group. When communicating through the Internet—in e-mail or in Internet Relay Chat groups, say—you encode your thoughts through your keyboard and send them via modem in a way that is very similar to how you encode your thoughts into words and send these through the air.

With this basic definition, the transactional perspective, and an understanding that interpersonal communication occurs in many different forms, we can expand our model as in Figure 1.4 and look at each of the essential elements in interpersonal communication: source-receiver, messages, feedback, feedforward, channel, noise, context, competence, and ethics.

Source-Receiver

Interpersonal communication involves at least two persons. Each formulates and sends messages (source functions) and each receives and understands messages (receiver functions). The hyphenated term **source-receiver** emphasizes that each person is both source and receiver.

> Visit the Website of a communication department (use a search engine such as Yahoo! or Infoseek and the key words *communication department*). What kinds of courses do they offer? How do these courses define communication? What types of interpersonal communication courses are offered?

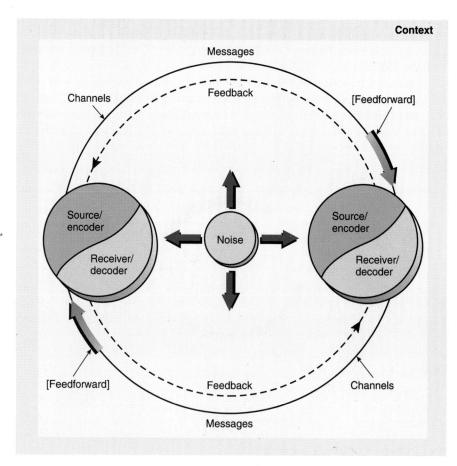

Figure 1.4
The Process of Interpersonal Communication

This model puts into visual form the various elements of the interpersonal communication process. How would you diagram the interpersonal communication process?

In what ways does speech differ from sign language as a form of interpersonal communication? Does the model of communication described earlier apply equally to both speech and sign language communication? Do the principles described in this chapter apply to both speech and to sign language communication?

By putting your meanings into sound waves (or gestures, facial expressions, or postural adjustments) you're putting your thoughts and feelings into a code, a process called *en*coding. By translating sound (and light) waves into ideas, you're taking them out of the code they're in, a process called *de*coding. So, we can call speakers (or more generally senders), *encoders* (those who put their meanings *into* a code). And we can call listeners (or more generally receivers) *decoders* (those who take meanings *out of* a code). Since encoding and decoding activities are combined in each person, the hyphenated term **encoding-decoding** is used to emphasize this inevitable dual function.

Usually you encode an idea into a code that the other person understands; for example, you would use words and gestures for which both you and the other person have similar meanings. At times, however, you may want to exclude others and so, for example, you might speak in a language that only one of your listeners knows or use jargon to prevent others from understanding. At other times, you may assume incorrectly that the other person knows your code and, for example, use words or gestures the other person simply doesn't understand.

Another obvious difference between face-to-face and computer communication is that in face-to-face interaction the individuals are usually clearly identified. In computer-mediated communication, however, you may remain anonymous. You may also pose as someone you're not—a person of another sex or race, for example, or even someone who is significantly older or younger than you really are, or someone of significantly different status (Saunders, Robey, & Vaverek, 1994). In face-to-face communication your physical self—the way you look, the way you're dressed—greatly influences the way your messages will be interpreted. In computer-mediated communication, you reveal your physical self through your own descriptions. Although you may send photos of yourself via computer, you can also send photos of others and claim they're of yourself. There is, in short, much greater opportunity for presenting yourself as you want when communicating via computer.

For interpersonal communication to occur, meanings must be encoded and decoded. If Jamie has his eyes closed and is wearing stereo headphones as his dad is speaking to him, interpersonal communication is not taking place simply because the messages—verbal and nonverbal—are not being received.

Interpersonal Competence

Your ability to communicate effectively is your **interpersonal competence.** It includes your understanding of interpersonal communication and your ability to communicate messages that reflect this understanding. For example, your competence includes the knowledge that in certain contexts and with certain listeners one topic is appropriate and another is not; and it includes the ability to adjust messages on the basis of this knowledge. Competence includes understanding the rules of nonverbal communication—for example, the appropriateness of touching, vocal volume, and physical closeness; and it includes the ability to use the wide variety of nonverbal messages to achieve specific goals. In short, interpersonal competence includes knowing how interpersonal communication works and the ability to adjust your messages according to the context of the interaction, the person with whom you're interacting, and a host of other factors discussed throughout this text.

The greater your competence, the greater your own power to accomplish successfully what you want to accomplish—asking for a raise or a date; establishing temporary work relationships, long-term friendships, or romantic relationships; communicating empathy and support; or gaining compliance or resisting the compliance tactics of others. Whatever your interpersonal goal, increased competence will help you accomplish it more effectively.

The goal of this text is not to tell you how to communicate in any given situation. That would be impossible, since each situation and each person is different. Rather, the goal of this text is to expand your interpersonal competence by providing you with

- a wide range of communication options, ways of communicating you may not have considered before, and opportunities to practice mastering these options
- the insight and understanding to evaluate situations and to make reasonable judgments about which ways of communicating will work best

Thus, the greater your competence, the more ways you'll have available for communicating your meanings and the greater the likelihood that you'll evaluate the situation intelligently and elect to use the most effective communication options. The greater your interpersonal competence, the more effective you're likely to be in communicating with friends, lovers, and family; with colleagues on the job; and in just about any situation where you'll interact with another person.

Interpersonal competence depends on **critical thinking,** an understanding of interpersonal communication and mastery of its **skills,** is specific to a given **culture,** and relies heavily on the often overlooked skills of **listening.** These four themes are not the only ones that could have been chosen for highlighting in a course in interpersonal communication. But, they seem the most crucial and the most practical for today's college student. Understanding the nature of these four dimensions of competence and how they are highlighted in this text will enable you to gain the most from your studying and working with this material.

Sooner or later, false thinking brings wrong conduct.
—Julian Huxley

Competence and Critical Thinking

Without critical thinking there can be no competent exchange of ideas, no competent communication. Because of the central importance of critical thinking, it's given prominence in this text in unique ways. The presentation can best be understood by explaining the steps you need to take to become a critical thinker (Figure 1.5) and the resources this text provides to help you make that climb.

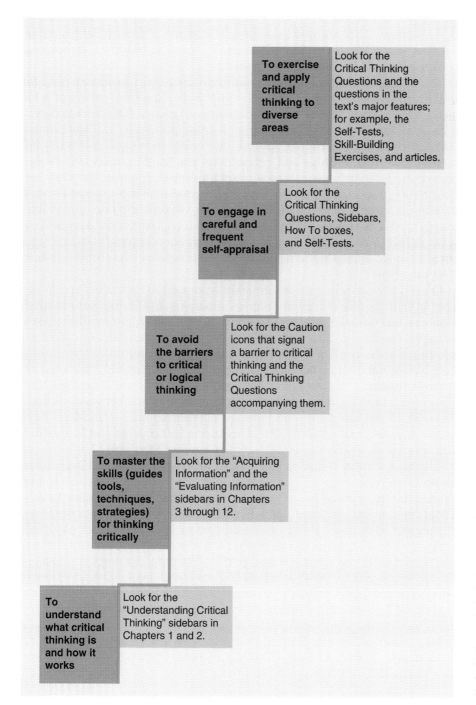

To exercise and apply critical thinking to diverse areas — Look for the Critical Thinking Questions and the questions in the text's major features; for example, the Self-Tests, Skill-Building Exercises, and articles.

To engage in careful and frequent self-appraisal — Look for the Critical Thinking Questions, Sidebars, How To boxes, and Self-Tests.

To avoid the barriers to critical or logical thinking — Look for the Caution icons that signal a barrier to critical thinking and the Critical Thinking Questions accompanying them.

To master the skills (guides tools, techniques, strategies) for thinking critically — Look for the "Acquiring Information" and the "Evaluating Information" sidebars in Chapters 3 through 12.

To understand what critical thinking is and how it works — Look for the "Understanding Critical Thinking" sidebars in Chapters 1 and 2.

Figure 1.5
The Steps of Critical Thinking

This five part characterization seeks to identify the major steps in mastering critical thinking. It's not intended to imply that in thinking critically you follow a neat linear route from Step 1 to Step 2 through to Step 5. Nor is it to claim that these are the only steps to competence in critical thinking. There are many routes to becoming a critical thinker; this is only one of them. Other approaches can be found in a variety of sources (for example, Sternberg, 1987; deBono, 1987; Potts, 1994; Savin, 1995) Can you think of other steps that could be included?

Understanding Critical Thinking

Critical thinking comprises a variety of skills.

1. To ask and answer questions of clarification or challenge
2. To draw and evaluate conclusions
3. To organize your thoughts and speak or write them coherently
4. To distinguish between logical and illogical inferences
5. To weigh the truth of arguments instead of just accepting them on faith
6. To make connections between new knowledge and what you already know
7. To obtain relevant and valid information
8. To evaluate the quality and reasonableness of ideas
9. To define a problem precisely
10. To explore and evaluate possible strategies for solving a problem

Numbers 1–2 are from Ennis (1987); 3–4 from Nickerson (1987); 5–6 from McCarthy (1991); 7–8 from Adams and Hamm (1991); and 9–10 from Bransford, Sherwood, and Sturdevant (1987).

First, to be a critical thinker, it's crucial **to understand what critical thinking is and how it works (Step 1).** To achieve this aim, **Understanding Critical Thinking sidebars** appearing in the first two chapters explain, for example, the values you'll derive from critical thinking, how critical thinking relates to interpersonal communication and particularly to interpersonal skills, how you can best transfer critical thinking skills learned here to other areas, and the kinds of attitudes that encourage critical thinking.

Second, it's necessary **to master the skills (guides, tools, techniques, strategies) for thinking critically (Step 2).** Although there are a wide variety of skills that could be included—every critical thinking theorist has her or his own list—most cluster under two general and broad headings: **Acquiring Information** and **Evaluating Information.**

The skills focusing primarily on acquiring information, provided in **Acquiring Information sidebars,** cover such topics as looking for a variety of cues before drawing conclusions, being especially alert to cues that contradict your own beliefs and values, approaching new ideas positively, acquiring information from a wide variety of sources, and categorizing and comparing to help you see relationships and connections you might not see otherwise. Some critical thinking theorists consider many of the techniques for acquiring information, especially those that help you get different perspectives on a problem, as *creative thinking.* In actual practice, it's difficult if not impossible to separate the two. A more complete explanation of creative thinking and its relationship to critical thinking and communication is presented in *Brainstorms: How to Think Creatively About Communication or About Anything Else* (DeVito, 1996).

Once you've acquired the information, you need to evaluate it and to assess its value and relevance to different situations. **Evaluating Information sidebars** deal with the skills for assessing and evaluating information (ideas, evidence, conclusions, theories) and include, for example, evaluating your assumptions about conflict, emotional expression, and culture; identifying your own biases in thinking about people and events; being mindful and flexible when evaluating your communication options and conclusions; recognizing your own role in interpersonal perception; distinguishing between relationship and causal assertions and between hypotheses and conclusions; and evaluating anecdotal evidence. These **Acquiring Information** and **Evaluating Information sidebars** appear throughout Chapters 3 through 12.

Third, as a critical thinker you'll want **to avoid uncritical, illogical, or sloppy thinking (Step 3).** These barriers to critical thinking are integrated throughout the text and include, for example, maintaining unrealistic beliefs about communication, about the self, and about relationships; uncritical acceptance of cultural beliefs; errors in interpersonal perception such as giving undue emphasis to what occurs first (or last), stereotyping, overattribution, and the failure to check perceptions; offensive listening; filtering out messages that contradict your cherished beliefs and values; giving greater attention to words than to things; failing to discriminate among people covered by the same label; giving undue emphasis to extremes while ignoring the large middle area; and ethnocentrism (seeing your own cultural values as superior and those of other cultures as inferior). These sections are signaled in the text by a **Caution Icon** and a **Critical Thinking question** that asks you to view this as a barrier to logical and sensible thinking.

Fourth, to be an effective critical thinker you need **to engage in careful and frequent self-appraisal (Step 4).** You can't think very critically about conflict, for example, if you maintain unexamined (and faulty) assumptions about the role of conflict in an interpersonal relationship. No one knows you better than you do, so analyze your own attitudes and beliefs and how they may influence your interpersonal interactions. The greater your self-understanding, the better you'll be able to think logically and rationally about the host of interpersonal communication issues raised throughout this text. *Messages* will help you in assessing yourself through a number of devices. Many of the **Critical Thinking questions** and **Critical Thinking sidebars** contained throughout the text ask you to reflect on your own attitudes and behaviors, to bring these to conscious awareness and make them available for critical analysis. Perhaps the most obvious and most enjoyable means for self-appraisal are the **26 self-tests** presented throughout the text. These self-tests ask you to pause, reflect, and assess your own communication thoughts and behaviors on, for example, your level of communication apprehension, your accuracy in perceiving other people, your flexibility and ability to adjust to new and different situations, your touching behavior, and the kind of lover you are.

Fifth, you need **to exercise and apply critical thinking to diverse areas—** in this case, areas of interpersonal communication **(Step 5).** To achieve this goal, questions are presented in the margins asking you to think critically about the issues raised in the text.

Critical thinking questions focusing on interpersonal communication are also presented in each of the self-tests, the **Skill Building Exercises,** readings, and even the photos. To achieve a similar purpose, a variety of quotations also appear in the margins; view these as implied questions. Ask yourself what the quotation means for interpersonal communication and whether or not you agree with it (and, of course, why).

Competence and Interpersonal Skills

This text explains the theory and research in interpersonal communication in order to provide you with a firm foundation in understanding how interpersonal communication works. With that understanding as a foundation, you'll be better able to develop and master the very practical skills of interpersonal communication. To enable you to achieve this goal, a variety of skills are presented to help you, for example, increase your accuracy in people perception, improve verbal and nonverbal messages, engage in conversations with greater satisfaction, manage conflict more effectively, and communicate with power. As already noted, these skills will prove useful for all forms of interaction, face-to-face interaction as well as online. Throughout the text a broad range of skills is discussed: empathy, openness, supportiveness, flexibility, active listening, and assertiveness, for example. These skills are highlighted in a variety of ways.

Skills are discussed **throughout the text** along with the relevant theory and research on which they're based. The discussions of conversation effectiveness in Chapter 8, improving intercultural communication in Chapter 9, improving relationship communication in Chapter 10, and managing conflict in Chapter 11 are examples of this integration of skills.

Skill Building Exercises appear at the end of each major section of the chapter, providing opportunities to practice some of the skills discussed in the text,

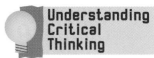

Understanding Critical Thinking

Critical thinking is always useful. Regardless of what you're working on, critical thinking will prove of value. It's relevant in your interpersonal relationships and in your professional life and will prove valuable in solving problems, improving relationships, and resolving interpersonal conflicts. Critical thinking is universal across all areas of knowledge and experience. Although this book focuses on interpersonal communication, probably your most important form of human behavior, critical thinking will prove of value in the arts and humanities, social sciences, sciences, and in just about any situation you can think of.

If people knew how hard I worked to get my mastery, it wouldn't seem so wonderful after all.

—*Michelangelo*

for example, reducing apprehension, communicating your emotions—even negative ones, formulating excuses, and confronting intercultural difficulties.

A special **How To box** appears in every chapter. Each box singles out one specific area of interpersonal communication and identifies its relevant skills, for example, encouraging someone to self-disclose, talking to the grief stricken, engaging in conversation, and dealing with complaints.

Each chapter also contains a **reprinted article**—usually from the popular press—focusing on the skills of interpersonal communication, for example, developing self-confidence, listening on the job, handling criticism, and talking with parents.

Competence and Culture

Culture refers to the lifestyle of a group of people. It's their values, beliefs, artifacts, ways of behaving, and ways of communicating. Culture includes all that members of a social group have produced and developed—their language, ways of thinking, art, laws, and religion.

Culture is transmitted from one generation to another not through genes but through communication and learning, especially from the teachings of parents, peer groups, schools, religious institutions, and government agencies. Because most cultures teach women and men different attitudes and ways of communicating, many of the gender differences we observe may be considered cultural. So, while not minimizing the biological differences between men and women, we consider gender differences as, in part, cultural.

Competence is culture specific; communications that are effective in one culture will not necessarily be effective in another. For example, giving a birthday gift to a close friend would be appreciated by members of many cultures and in some cases would be expected. But, among Jehovah Witnesses, it would be frowned upon since they don't celebrate birthdays (Dresser, 1995). Because of the vast cultural differences that impact on interpersonal communication, the role of culture is discussed in every chapter. To give you a glimpse of how culture is related to the topics of interpersonal communication, here are examples:

- Chapter 1, which introduces interpersonal communication, also introduces and defines culture, discusses its importance, and explains the aim of the cultural perspective taken in this text.
- The chapter on the self (Chapter 2) discusses culture and its role in self-concept and in self-disclosure, and the cultural influences on apprehension.
- Chapter 3, on interpersonal perception, covers the role of stereotypes in perception and the importance of cultural sensitivity in perceptual accuracy.
- The listening chapter (4) identifies the cultural and gender differences that influence listening effectiveness.
- Gender and cultural differences in directness; sexism, heterosexism, and racism in language; and cultural identifiers (ways to talk to and about people from different cultures) are discussed in Chapter 5, which deals with verbal messages.
- Chapter 6, which focuses on nonverbal communication, discusses topics such as nonverbal messages that can create problems with members of different cultures, the meanings that different cultures give to colors, and the ways different cultures view time.

- The chapter on emotions (7) considers the role that culture and gender play in emotions and the varied societal rules and customs that influence emotional expression.
- Chapter 8, which covers the entire process of conversation, covers the conversational taboos of different cultures, cultural sensitivity, suggestions for communicating with the deaf, and how the rules of conversation differ on the basis of culture and gender.
- Chapter 9 is devoted entirely to interpersonal communication and culture and discusses the nature of culture and of intercultural communication, how cultures differ, and ways to improve intercultural communication.
- The chapter on interpersonal relationships (10) discusses the influence of culture on the way we think about relationships—in the research conducted, in the theories developed, and even in the questions we ask—and the culture and gender differences and similarities in friendship and love relationships.
- Chapter 11, on interpersonal conflict, considers the cultural and gender differences in viewing and in managing conflict.
- The final chapter (12), on interpersonal power, discusses the cultural dimension of power, particularly the differences between high power and low power distance cultures—the degree to which power is unevenly distributed in a society.

Competence and Listening

Competence in interpersonal communication is often viewed as "speaking effectiveness," with little attention paid to listening. But, in actual practice, listening is an integral part of interpersonal communication; you cannot be a competent communicator if you're a poor listener. Both speaking and listening skills are crucial to the development of interpersonal competence. Listening, therefore, is given special prominence in this text.

There's no one so deaf as the one who will not listen.
—*Yiddish proverb*

First, **an entire chapter is devoted to listening (Chapter 4)** and covers the nature and importance of listening, the steps you go through in listening, the role of culture and gender in listening, and ways to increase your listening effectiveness.

Second, **13 "Listen To . . ." boxes are positioned throughout the text** to illustrate how listening relates to the topic of the chapter and to provide a variety of specific listening skills. Among the topics these boxes address are: the importance of listening to yourself; the role of gender differences; sexist, heterosexist, and racist listening; ways to listen during conflict; and how to listen to empower others.

As you read this text, you'll see that these four dimensions of competence are not separate and distinct from one another but rather interact and overlap. For example, as already noted, critical thinking pervades the entire interpersonal communication process, but it also serves as a foundation for your cultural awareness, listening effectiveness, and skill development. Similarly, an awareness of cultural differences will make you a more effective listener, a more discerning user of skills, and a more logical thinker. So, as you read the text and work actively with the concepts, remember that all parts—the regular text, the boxed features, the material in the margins, and the summaries and vocabulary tests at the end of the chapters—contribute to one overarching aim: to increase your interpersonal communication competence.

Visit Longman's website for interpersonal communication (it's called "The Exchange") at http://longman.awl.com/ exchange. How might the material on this website help you learn the skills of interpersonal communication?

Messages

For interpersonal communication to exist, messages that express your thoughts and feelings must be sent and received. Interpersonal communication may be verbal or nonverbal but it's usually a combination of both. You communicate interpersonally with words and with gestures and touch, for example. Even the clothes you wear communicate as does the way you walk and the way you shake hands, comb your hair, sit, smile, or frown. Everything about you has the potential to send interpersonal messages.

In face-to-face communication your messages are both verbal and nonverbal; you supplement your words with facial expressions, body movements, and variations in vocal volume and rate, for example. When you communicate through a keyboard your message is communicated basically with words. This does not mean, however, that you cannot communicate emotional meanings; in fact, some researchers have argued that using diagrams, pictures, and varied typefaces enable you to communicate messages that are rich in emotional meaning (Lea & Spears, 1995). Similarly, you can use **emoticons** (see the discussion in Chapter 7). But, basically, your message is communicated with words. Because of this, sarcasm, for example, is difficult to convey unambiguously with just words whereas in face-to-face communication you might wink or smile to indicate that your message should not be taken seriously or literally.

Feedback

Feedback is a special type of message. When you send a message in speaking to another person, you get **feedback** from your own messages. You hear what you say, you feel the way you move, you see what you write. On the basis of this information, you may correct yourself, rephrase something, or perhaps smile at a clever turn of phrase. This is self-feedback.

You also get feedback from others. The person with whom you're speaking is constantly sending you messages that comment on how he or she is receiving and responding to your messages. Nods of agreement, smiles, puzzled looks, and questions asking for clarification are all examples of feedback.

Notice that in face-to-face communication you can monitor the feedback of the other person as you're speaking. In computer-mediated communication that feedback will come much later and thus is likely to be more clearly thought out and perhaps more closely monitored.

Feedforward

Much as feedback contains information about messages already sent, **feedforward** is information about messages before you send them. Opening comments such as "Wait until you hear this" or "I'm not sure of this, but…" or "Don't get me wrong, but…." are examples of feedforward. These messages tell the listener something about the messages to come or about the way you'd like the listener to respond. Nonverbally, feedforward is given by your facial expression, eye contact, and physical posture, for example; with these nonverbal messages you tell the other person something about the messages you'll be sending. For example, a smile may signal a pleasant message while eye avoidance may signal that the message to come is difficult and perhaps uncomfortable to express. A book's table of contents, preface, and (usually) its first chapter are also examples of feedforward.

How does feedback work in conversation between persons with impaired hearing? Between a person with impaired hearing and one with normal hearing? Between persons who are blind? Between a person who is blind and one who is sighted?

I am not sure I have learned anything else as important. I have been able to realize what a prime role what I have come to call 'feedforward' has in all our doings.

—I. A. Richards

How does feedforward operate in your college class lectures? What kinds of feedforward can you find in this book? Are these feedforward messages helpful to you as you listen to the lecture or read the text?

Channel

The communication **channel** is the medium through which message signals pass. The channel works like a bridge connecting source and receiver. Normally two, three, or four channels are used simultaneously. Thus, for example, in face-to-face interactions, you speak and listen, using the vocal-auditory channel. You also, however, make gestures and receive these signals visually, using the visual channel. Similarly, you emit odors and smell those of others (chemical channel). Often you touch one another, and this too communicates (tactile channel).

Another way to classify channels is by the means of communication. Thus, face-to-face contact, telephones, e-mail, movies, television, smoke signals, and telegraph would be types of channels. Of most relevance today, of course, is the difference between face-to-face and computer-mediated interpersonal communication, interaction through e-mail, chat lines, and usenet groups.

Noise

Noise interferes with your receiving a message someone is sending or with their receiving your message. Noise may be physical (others talking loudly, cars honking, illegible handwriting, "garbage" on your computer screen), physiological (hearing or visual impairment, articulation disorders), psychological (preconceived ideas, wandering thoughts), or semantic (misunderstood meanings). Technically, noise is anything that distorts the message, anything that prevents the receiver from receiving the message.

A useful concept in understanding noise and its importance in communication is "signal-to-noise ratio." Signal refers to information that you'd find useful and noise refers to information that is useless (to you). So, for example, a mailing list or newsgroup that contains lots of useful information would be high on signal and low on noise; those that contained lots of useless information would be high on noise and low on signal.

"Do you mind? I happen to be on the phone!"

Since messages may be visual as well as spoken, noise too may be visual. Thus, the sunglasses that prevent someone from seeing the nonverbal messages from your eyes would be considered noise as would blurred type on a printed page. Table 1.1 identifies these four major types of noise in more detail.

All communications contain noise. Noise cannot be totally eliminated, but its effects can be reduced. Making your language more precise, sharpening your skills for sending and receiving nonverbal messages, and improving your listening and feedback skills are some ways to combat the influence of noise.

Context

How would you describe noise on the Internet? (Noise or any of the major concepts discussed in this section would make great topics for a concept paper.)

Communication always takes place within a context that influences the form and the content of communication. At times this context is so natural that you ignore it, like street noise. At other times the context stands out, and the ways in which it restricts or stimulates your communications are obvious. Think, for example, of the different ways you'd talk at a funeral, in a quiet restaurant, and at a rock concert.

The context of communication has at least four dimensions: physical, cultural, social-psychological, and temporal. The room, workplace, or park in which communication takes place—the tangible or concrete environment—is the *physical dimension.* When you communicate face-to-face you're both in essentially the same physical environment. In computer-mediated communication you may both be in drastically different environments; one of you may be on a beach in San Juan while another is in a Wall Street office.

The *cultural dimension* refers to the rules and norms, the beliefs and attitudes of the people communicating that are passed from one generation to another. For example, in some cultures it's considered polite to talk to strangers; in others it's something to be avoided. In some cultures direct eye contact between child and adult signifies directness and honesty; in others it signifies defiance and arrogance.

Table 1.1. Four Types of Noise

One of the most important skills in communication is to recognize the types of noise and to develop ways to combat them. Consider, for example, what kinds of noise occur in the classroom? What kinds of noise occur in your family communications? What kinds occur at work? What can you do to combat these kinds of noise?

Types of Noise	Definition	Example
Physical	Interference that is external to both speaker and listener, it interferes with the physical transmission of the signal or message	Screeching of passing cars, hum of computer, sunglasses
Physiological	Physical barriers within the speaker or listener	Visual impairments, hearing loss, articulation problems, memory loss
Psychological	Cognitive or mental interference	Biases and prejudices in senders and receivers, closed-mindedness, inaccurate expectations, extreme emotionalism (anger, hate, love, grief)
Semantic	Speaker and listener assigning different meanings	People speaking different languages, use of jargon or overly complex terms not understood by listener, dialectical differences in meaning

How many kinds of potential noise can you identify in this photo? How would you combat these noise sources to make sure your message got through?

The *social-psychological dimension* includes, for example, the status relationships among the participants such as who is the employer and who is the employee or who is the salesperson and who is the store owner. The formality or informality, friendliness or hostility, and cooperativeness or competitiveness of the interaction are also part of the social-psychological dimension.

The *temporal* or *time dimension* refers to where a particular message fits into the sequence of communication events. For example, if you tell a joke about sickness immediately after your friend tells you she is sick, the joke will be perceived differently than the same joke told as one of a series of similar jokes to your friends in the locker room of the gym.

In what way might your evaluation of a communication act—say, talking with work colleagues about your weekend—be distorted by **failing to see communication occurring within a context?**

Ethics

Interpersonal communication also involves questions of **ethics.** There is a moral dimension to any interpersonal communication act which is separate from its effectiveness dimension (Jaksa & Pritchard, 1994; Bok, 1978). For example, while it may be effective to lie in selling a product, it would not be ethical. The decisions you make concerning communication are guided by what you consider right and by what you consider effective.

A general principle that provides a foundation for viewing interpersonal communication ethics is the notion of choice, the assumption that people have a right to make their own choices. Communications are ethical when they facilitate an individual's freedom of choice by presenting that person with accurate information or bases for choice. Communications are unethical when they interfere with an individual's freedom of choice by preventing that person from securing information relevant to the choice.

He who accepts evil without protesting against it is really cooperating with it.
    —*Martin Luther King, Jr.*

Ethical dimensions of interpersonal communication are integrated throughout the text and include, for example: ethical listening (Chapter 4), ethics and lying (Chapter 6), ethics and emotional expression (Chapter 7), and the ethics of gossip (Chapter 8). In addition, a wide variety of ethical issues are raised in the critical thinking questions that appear in the margins. Skill Building Exercise 1.1 introduces a number of ethical dilemmas to get you started thinking about the moral dimension of interpersonal interaction.

You can gain an additional perspective on interpersonal communication by looking at the major divisions or areas of the field as identified in Table 1.2.

Visit http://owl.english.purdue. edu/, a Website devoted to useful information about writing. What additional suggestions can you find there that would be useful to add to those given in the appendix on Writing About Interpersonal Communication?

Table 1.2. The Areas of Interpersonal Communication and Relationships

This table is intended as a guide for identifying some of the important areas under the general topic of interpersonal communication and relationships rather than as a formal outline of the field. The six areas of interpersonal communication are not independent but interact and overlap. For example, interpersonal interaction is a part of all the other areas; similarly, intercultural communication can exist in any of the other areas. The related academic areas suggest the close ties among fields of study.

General Area	Selected Topics	Related Academic Areas
Interpersonal interaction: communication between two people	Characteristics of effectiveness Conversational processes Self-disclosure Active listening Nonverbal messages in conversation Online interaction	Psychology Education Linguistics Counseling
Health communication: communication between health professional and patient	Talking about AIDS Increasing doctor-patient effectiveness Communication and aging Therapeutic communication	Medicine Psychology Counseling Health care
Family communication: communication within the family system	Power in the family Dysfunctional families Family conflict Heterosexual and homosexual families Parent-child communication	Sociology Psychology Family Studies Social Work
Intercultural communication: communication among members of different races, nationalities, religions, genders, and generations	Cross-generational communication Male-female communication Black-Hispanic-Asian-Caucasian communication Prejudice and stereotypes in communication Barriers to intercultural communication The Internet and cultural diversity	Anthropology Sociology Cultural studies Business
Business and organizational communication: communication among workers in an organizational environment	Interviewing strategies Sexual harassment Upward and downward communication Increasing managerial effectiveness Leadership in business	Business Management Public relations Computer science
Social and personal relationships: communication in close relationships, such as friendship and love	Relationship development Face-to-face and online relationships Relationship breakdown Repairing relationships Gender differences in relationships Increasing intimacy Verbal abuse	Psychology Sociology Anthropology Family studies

SKILL BUILDING EXERCISE 1.1

Ethics in Interpersonal Communication

Here are a few communication situations that raise ethical issues. Consider each of these five questions that others might ask you. For each question there are extenuating circumstances that may militate against your responding fully or even truthfully. Consider each question and the mitigating circumstances (these are noted under the **Thoughts** you're thinking as you consider your possible answer). How do you respond?

Question [A friend asks your opinion] How do I look?
Thought *You look terrible but I don't want to hurt your feelings.*

Question [A romantic partner asks] Do you love me?
Thought *You don't want to commit yourself but you don't want to end the relationship either. You want to allow the relationship to progress further before making any commitment.*

Question [An interviewer asks] You seem a bit old for this type of job. How old are you?
Thought *I am old for this job but I need it anyway. I don't want to turn the interviewer off* because I really need this job. Yet, I don't want to reveal my age either.*

Question [A parent asks] Did my son (15 years old) tell you he was contemplating suicide? OR Is my daughter (22 years old) taking drugs?
Thought *Yes, but I promised I wouldn't tell anyone.*

Question [A potential romantic partner asks] What's your HIV status?
Thought *I've never been tested, but now is not the time to talk about this. I'll practice safe sex so as not to endanger my partner.*

Thinking Critically About Ethics   What ethical principles did you use in making your decisions? Assume that you asked the question, what response would you prefer? Would your questions and the expected answers differ if you were communicating by computer, say with e-mail or in a chat room? Are your preferred responses the same responses you would give? If there are discrepancies, how do you account for them?

LISTENING

That Other Part of Communication

In the popular mind, communication is often taken as synonymous with speaking. Listening is either neglected or regarded as something apart from "real communication." But, as emphasized in the model of communication presented earlier and as stressed throughout this book, listening is integral to all communication; it's a process that is coordinate with speaking.

If you measured importance by the time you spend on an activity, then listening would be your most important communication activity. In one study, con-ducted in 1926 (Rankin), listening occupied 45% of a person's communication time; speaking was second with 30%; reading (16%) and writing (9%) followed. In another study of college students, conducted in 1980 (Barker, Edwards, Gaines, Gladney, & Holley), listening also occupied the most time: 53% compared to reading (17%), speaking (16%), and writing (14%). What percentages would you assign for your own listening, speaking, reading, and writing time?

[The next Listening box appears on page 44.]

In face-to-face communication, both people interact in real time. In computer communication this real time interaction occurs only sometimes. In e-mail, snail mail, and newsgroup communication, for example, the sending and receiving may be separated by several days or much longer. In Internet Relay Chat groups or IRCs, on the other hand, communication takes place in real time; the sending and receiving take place (almost) simultaneously.

All generalizations are false, including this one.
—*Alexander Chase*

PRINCIPLES OF INTERPERSONAL COMMUNICATION

Another way to define interpersonal communication is to consider its major principles. These principles, although significant in terms of explaining theory, also have very practical applications. These principles will provide insight into such practical issues as:

- why disagreements so often center on trivial issues and yet seem so difficult to resolve
- why you'll never be able to mindread, to know just what another person is thinking
- how communication expresses power relationships
- why you and your partner often see the causes of arguments very differently

Interpersonal Communication Involves both Content and Relationship Messages

Interpersonal messages refer to the real world, to something external to both speaker and listener. At the same time, they also refer to the relationship between the parties. For example, a supervisor may say to a trainee, "See me after the meeting." This simple message has a content message that tells the trainee to see the supervisor after the meeting. It also contains a relationship message that says something about the connection between the supervisor and the trainee. Even the use of the simple command shows there is a status difference that allows the supervisor to command the trainee. You can appreciate this most clearly if you visualize this command being made by the trainee to the supervisor. It appears awkward and out of place because it violates the normal relationship between supervisor and trainee.

Many conflicts arise because people misunderstand relationship messages and cannot clarify them. Other problems arise when people fail to see the difference between content messages and relationship messages. A good example occurred when my mother came to stay for a week at a summer place I had. On the first day she swept the kitchen floor six times. I had repeatedly told her that it did not need sweeping, that I would be tracking in dirt and mud from the outside. She persisted in sweeping, however, saying that the floor was dirty. On the content level, we were talking about the value of sweeping the kitchen floor. On the relationship level, however, we were talking about something quite different. We were each saying, "This is my house." When I realized this, I stopped complaining about the relative usefulness of sweeping a floor that did not need sweeping. Not surprisingly, she stopped sweeping.

Ignoring Relationship Considerations

Examine the following interchange and note how relationship considerations are ignored:

Messages	*Comments*
PAUL: I'm going bowling tomorrow. The guys at the plant are starting a team.	He focuses on the content and and ignores any relationship implications of the message.
JUDY: Why can't we ever do anything together?	She responds primarily on a relationship level and ignores the content implications of the message, and expresses her displeasure at being ignored in his decision.
Paul: We can do something together any time; tomorrow's the day they're organizing the team.	Again, he focuses almost exclusively on the content.

This example reflects research findings that show that men focus more on content messages. Women focus more on relationship messages (Wood, 1994). Once you recognize this gender difference, you can increase your sensitivity to the opposite sex.

CATHY   **BY CATHY GUISEWITE**

Being Sensitive to Relationship Considerations

Here is essentially the same situation but with the added sensitivity to relationship messages and to gender differences.

Messages	*Comments*
PAUL: The guys at the plant are organizing a bowling team. I'd sure like to be on the team. I'd like to go to the organizational meeting tomorrow. Okay?	Although he focuses on content, he shows awareness of the relationship dimensions by asking if this would be okay and by expressing his desire rather than his decision to attend this meeting.
JUDY: That sounds great but I'd really like to do something together tomorrow.	She focuses on the relationship dimension but also acknowledges his content orientation. Note too that she does not respond defensively, as if she has to defend herself or her emphasis on relationship aspects.
PAUL: How about your meeting me at Luigi's and we can have dinner after the organizational meeting?	He responds to the relationship aspect—without abandoning his desire to join the bowling team—and seeks to incorporate it into his communications. He tries to negotiate a solution that will meet both Judy's and his needs.
JUDY: That sounds great. I'm dying for spaghetti and meatballs.	She responds to both messages, approving of both his joining the team and of their dinner date.

CAUTION

How might your evaluation of a message be distorted by **failing to appreciate relationship messages?**

Arguments over the content dimension—such as what happened in a movie—are relatively easy to resolve. You may, for example, simply ask a third person what took place or see the movie again. Arguments on the relationship level, however, are much more difficult to resolve, in part, because people seldom recognize that the argument is a relationship one.

This article, which discusses seven rules for talking effectively with another person, serves as a kind of preview of some of the practical applications to be drawn from this text. As you read the article try to imagine specific applications of Malcolm Boyd's principles to your own interpersonal communication, for example, those in your family or at work.

How to Really Talk to Another Person

Malcolm Boyd

One of my favorite news clippings of all time was written early in the century and concerns the first two automobiles ever to have appeared on the streets of a major American city. Its opening sentence went something like this:

"The only two automobiles in town collided today at the intersection of State and Main."

But we don't need to be in cars to collide. People bump into one another all the time—in their families, their jobs, their social

Source: From "How to Really Talk to Another Person," by Malcolm Boyd, *Parade,* February 19, 1989. Reprinted with permission from the author and *Parade,* copyright © 1989.

relationships and in the public arena. Somehow, we get our signals crossed because we just don't communicate clearly. This article will offer seven basic rules to help keep you collision-free when exchanging ideas.

Communication failures are stumbling blocks to good living. We hear examples of them every day: "I didn't mean to say that." "She misunderstood me." "He lied."

The resultant damage to human feelings, to business, to property and finances—even to international relations—is inestimable. We can avoid all this only by communicating clearly, honestly and effectively.

1. **Listen with an inner ear—to hear what actually is meant, rather than what is said with words.** War, peace, love, hate—at crucial times, everything may hang on this ability. Of course, people should say what they mean, but sometimes they just can't. Only by listening carefully and deeply to others—and observing their actions, as well as their words—can we truly communicate.

2. **Listen to the concerns of others. Don't concentrate solely on your own ideas.** You already *know* what *you* think. Find out what others think and address *their* ideas. You might learn something, and others, seeing that you take them seriously, may be moved to take you seriously in return. Nothing is more deadly than I-I/me-me. Make it *we* and *us*. You'll get a bigger audience than a sky-writer does—and people may even be willing to help you cross your Ts in the process.

3. **It is important to know when *just* to listen.** Sometimes, a barrier suddenly falls between two people with a very close relationship. When it happens to you, try not to panic. No matter how close two people may be with one another, there are times when one person withdraws. This may occur for any reason—from midlife crisis to job anxiety to personal pain to a deep sense of loss. Usually it has nothing to do with *you,* specifically. Yet it affects you acutely.

   If ever there was a time to listen, this is it. Be patient and supportive. Be quiet and wait. Be ready to respond to communications the other person initiates. Sometimes, by simply listening, you say more about how you feel than words could say. The other person will hear you and be grateful.

   Try always to listen with a clear head and an open mind, which leads to the next rule:

4. **Assume nothing.** Too often we assume something is one thing and later find that it is something else entirely.

   We all have found that appearances are deceptive. We assume: *This* person couldn't possibly cheat. (But he does!) *That* relationship is more solid than the Rock of Gibraltar. (But it isn't.) Pat, the well-groomed, smiling man, obviously is bright, and Mike, the thrown-together one, is a dolt. (The reverse is true.)

   Making assumptions in human relations—and letting them affect our point of view, untested—can be fatal. Did you ever have a feeling that someone was out to "get" you? It's too easy to persuade ourselves that someone is telling a lie, gossiping maliciously, being unfaithful or trying to get our job. However, if we act on an assumption as though it were a fact and make a false judgment, not only might we end up with egg on our faces, but we also could create very real losses for ourselves.

   Misreading signs of human behavior can have very serious repercussions. I learned long ago that a seemingly

unfriendly attitude might indicate nothing more than that someone is suffering—from a toothache or a troubled life at home. Look for the real (not the assumed) person behind the stranger you meet. It's important to remember always that we're communicating with another distinctively individual human being who lives and breathes and feels the need to like and be liked.

We've explored listening as a surefire way to be heard. Now let's address *how to talk to another person.* And the cardinal rule here is this:

5. **Say what you mean.** It never ceases to amaze me that some people offhandedly tell such outright lies as: "I like it." "Your job is safe." "I'll be back in five minutes." They say things they don't mean. Result: hurt, confusion, resentment. Once we stop telling the truth about small things, it's just a small step to spinning a veritable spiderweb of falsehoods. Then, finding we're caught in that web, we start to tell bigger lies. Saying what we mean keeps confusion to a minimum.

6. **Before speaking, always ask yourself: What is the message that's needed?** It wouldn't be quite so hard to communicate clearly if we first answered these questions: What do those I'm talking to need to know? What is the best way for me to say it and to get straight to the point? How do I get them to listen?

   The rules for talking and listening are very similar. The key to the deepest secret of communication lies in *truly understanding what must be communicated.* If, for example, you're trying to *give* information to others, you must first find out what they need to know. If you're trying to *get* information, ask clearly for what you need to know. If, after listening carefully, you don't get what you need—or you don't understand what you get—say so and ask questions to clarify matters. Too often, we short-circuit our messages by telling people what we think they ought to know, rather than finding out what it is they need to know.

7. **Remember that communication is in the present.** "I should've said" just doesn't cut it. This moment—now—might change your life forever. Be open to communicating with that person who comes your way today. Don't miss your chance! ⸗

Thinking Critically About "How to Really Talk to Another Person" Can you imagine instances in which Boyd's suggestion to "listen with an inner ear" might be carried to extremes and create rather than resolve communication difficulties? How can you blend Boyd's "It is important to know when *just* to listen" with the recommendation to listen critically? Are the two principles both useful but in different situations? Can you identify an example from a television drama or sitcom that illustrates the dangers of making assumptions about others? How might Boyd's suggestions be useful to an employee beginning work in a large office of more experienced colleagues? Would you modify any of these rules if you were communicating over the Internet, say with e-mail or in a chat room?

Interpersonal Communication Is a Process of Adjustment

Interpersonal communication can take place only to the extent that the people talking share the same communication system. We can easily understand this when dealing with speakers of two different languages; much miscommunication is likely to occur. The principle, however, takes on particular relevance when you realize that no two people share identical communication systems. Parents and children, for example, not only have very different vocabularies but also, even more important, have different meanings for some of the terms they have in common (consider, for example, the differences between parents and children for such terms as "music," "success," and "family"). Different cultures and social groups, even when they share a common language, also have different nonverbal communication systems. To the extent that these systems differ, communication will be hindered.

Part of the art of interpersonal communication is learning the other person's signals, how they're used, and what they mean. People in close relationships—either as intimate friends or as romantic partners—realize that learning the other person's signals takes a long time and, often, great patience. If you want to understand what another person means—by a smile, by saying "I love you," by arguing about trivial matters, or by self-deprecating comments—you have to learn his or her system of signals. Furthermore, you have to share your own system of signals with others so that they can better understand you. Although some people may know what you mean by your silence or by your avoidance of eye contact, others may not. You cannot expect others to decode your behaviors accurately without help.

This principle is especially important in intercultural communication, largely because people from different cultures use different signals and sometimes the same signals to signify quite different things. Focused eye contact means honesty and openness in much of the United States. But, that same behavior may signify arrogance or disrespect in Japan and in many Hispanic cultures if, say, engaged in by a youngster with someone significantly older.

How do you see the principle of adjustment working in everyday conversation? What happens when people do not adjust to each other?

Communication Accommodation

An interesting theory largely revolving around adjustment is **communication accommodation theory.** This theory holds that speakers will adjust to or accommodate to the speaking style of their listeners to gain, for example, social approval and greater communication efficiency (Giles, Mulac, Bradac, & Johnson, 1987). For example, when two people have a similar speech rate, they seem to be more attracted to each other than to those with dissimilar rates (Buller, LePoire, Aune, & Eloy, 1992). Speech rate similarity has also been associated with greater sociability and intimacy (Buller & Aune, 1992). Also, the speaker who uses language intensity similar to that of listeners is judged to have greater credibility than the speaker who uses intensity different from that of listeners (Aune & Kikuchi, 1993). Still another study found that roommates who had similar communication attitudes (both were high in communication competence and willingness to communicate and low in verbal aggressiveness) were highest in roommate liking and satisfaction (Martin & Anderson, 1995). Although this theory has not been tested on computer communication, it would make the prediction that styles of written communication in e-mail or chat rooms would also evidence accommodation.

Have you witnessed communication accommodation? What specific form did it take?

As illustrated throughout this text, communication characteristics are influenced greatly by culture (Albert & Nelson, 1993). Thus, the communication similarities that lead to attraction and more positive perceptions are more likely to be present in *intra*cultural communication than in *inter*cultural encounters. This may present an important (but not insurmountable) obstacle to intercultural communication.

Interpersonal Communication Is Inevitable, Irreversible, and Unrepeatable

Communication is **inevitable.** Often communication is intentional, purposeful, and consciously motivated. Sometimes, however, you communicate even though you might not think you are, or might not even want to. Take, for example, the student sitting in the back of the room with an "expressionless" face, perhaps staring out the window. The student might think that she or he is not communicating with the teacher or with the other students. On closer inspection, however, you can see that the student *is* communicating something—perhaps lack of interest or simply anxiety about a private problem. In any event, the student is communicating whether she or he wishes to or not. You cannot *not* communicate.

In addition, you cannot *not* influence the person you interact with (Watzlawick, 1978). Persuasion, like communication, is also inevitable. The issue, then, is not whether you will or will not persuade or influence another; rather, it's how you'll exert your influence.

Communication is **irreversible.** Notice that only some processes can be reversed. For example, you can turn water into ice and then reverse the process by turning the ice back into water. Other processes, however, are irreversible. You can, for example, turn grapes into wine, but you cannot reverse the process and turn wine into grapes. Interpersonal communication is an irreversible process. Although you may try to qualify, deny, or somehow reduce the effects of your message, you cannot withdraw what you have said. Similarly, once you press the send key, your e-mail is in cyberspace and impossible to reverse.

Because of irreversibility, be careful not to say things you may wish to withdraw later. Similarly, monitor carefully messages of commitment, messages sent in anger, or messages of insult or derision. Otherwise you run the risk of saying something you'll be uncomfortable with later.

Communication is **unrepeatable.** The reason is simple: Everyone and everything are constantly changing. As a result, you can never recapture the exact same situation, frame of mind, or relationship dynamics that defined a previous interpersonal act. For example, you can never repeat meeting someone for the first time, comforting a grieving friend, or resolving a specific conflict.

You can, of course, try again as you do when you say, "I'm sorry I came off so pushy, can we try again?" Notice, however, that even when you say this, you have not erased the initial impression. Instead you try to counteract this initial (and perhaps negative) impression by going through the motions again. In doing so, you try to create a more positive impression that you hope will lessen the original negative effect.

Face-to-face communication is evanescent; it fades after you have spoken. There is no trace of your communications outside of the memories of the

Speech is pulling a straw out of thatch; once out it cannot be replaced.
—Hausa proverb

Don't let your tongue say what your head may pay for.
—Italian proverb

Can you identify at least one way you can get yoursself into trouble by acting as if communication is always intentional (rather than inevitable), reversible (rather than irreversible), and repeatable (rather than unrepeatable)? *(If you've experienced these situations, they might prove interesting for a personal experience paper.)*

parties involved or of those who overheard your conversation. In computer-mediated communication, however, the messages are written and may be saved, stored, and printed. Both face-to-face and computer-mediated messages may be kept confidential or revealed publicly. But, computer messages may be made public more easily and spread more quickly than face-to-face messages. And, of course, in the case of written messages there is clear evidence of what you have said and when you said it.

Interpersonal Communication Serves a Variety of Purposes

Great minds have purposes, others have wishes.
—Washington Irving

Interpersonal communication can be used to accomplish a variety of purposes (see Figure 1.6). Understanding how interpersonal communication serves these varied purposes will help you more effectively achieve your own interpersonal purposes. Interpersonal communication enables you to **learn,** to better understand the external world—the world of objects, events, and other people. Although a great deal of information comes from the media, you probably discuss and ultimately "learn" or internalize information through interpersonal interactions. In fact, your beliefs, attitudes, and values are probably influenced more by interpersonal encounters than by the media or even formal education. Throughout interpersonal communication you also learn about yourself. By talking about yourself with others, you gain valuable feedback on your feelings, thoughts, and behaviors. Through these communications, you also learn how you appear to others—who likes you, who dislikes you, and why.

Interpersonal communication helps you **relate.** One of the greatest needs people have is to establish and maintain close relationships. You want to feel loved and liked, and in turn you want to love and like others. Such relationships help to alleviate loneliness and depression, enable you to share and heighten your pleasures, and generally make you feel more positive about yourself.

Very likely, you **influence** the attitudes and behaviors of others in your interpersonal encounters. You may wish them to vote a particular way, try a new diet, buy a new book, listen to a record, see a movie, take a specific course, think in a particular way, believe that something is true or false, or value some idea—the list is endless. A good deal of your time is probably spent in interpersonal persuasion.

How would you go about finding answers to the following questions *(any one of these would make an excellent research paper):* (1) Are interpersonal communication skills related to relationship success—to success as a friend, lover, parent? (2) How is effective teaching related to the use of feedback and feedforward? (3) What are the most important interpersonal skills for success in business? (4) Are women more sensitive to relationship messages than men? and (5) Does communication accommodation take place on the Internet as it does in face-to-face communication?

Talking with friends about your weekend activities, discussing sports or dates, telling stories and jokes, and, in general, just passing the time serve a **play** function. Far from frivolous, this purpose is an extremely important one. It gives your activities a necessary balance and your mind a needed break from all the seriousness around us. Everyone has an inner child, and that child needs time to play.

Therapists of various kinds serve a helping function professionally by offering guidance through interpersonal interaction. But everyone interacts to **help** in everyday interactions: you console a friend who has broken off a love affair, counsel another student about courses to take, or offer advice to a colleague about work. Success in accomplishing this helping function, professionally or otherwise, depends on your knowledge and skill in interpersonal communication.

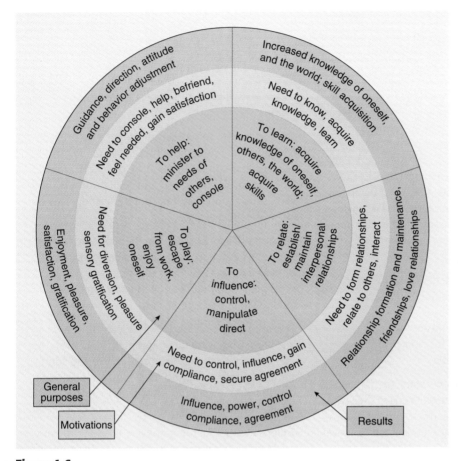

Figure 1.6

Why You Engage in Interpersonal Communication

This figure illustrates the five purposes of interpersonal communication discussed in the text and relates these purposes to the motives you have for engaging in interpersonal communication and the results you want to achieve. The innermost circle contains the general purposes, the middle circle the motivations, and the outer circle the results that you might hope to achieve by engaging in interpersonal communication. A similar typology of purposes comes from research on motives for communicating. In a series of studies, Rubin and her colleagues (Rubin, Fernandez-Collado, & Hernandez-Sampieri, 1992; Rubin & Martin, 1994; Rubin, Perse, & Barbato, 1988; Rubin & Rubin, 1992; Graham, 1994; and Graham, Barbato, & Perse, 1993) have identified six primary motives for communication: pleasure, affection, inclusion, escape, relaxation, and control. How do these compare to the five purposes discussed here?

CULTURE AND INTERPERSONAL COMMUNICATION

As noted earlier, culture refers to the beliefs, ways of behaving, and artifacts of a group that are transmitted through communication and learning rather than through genes. Gender is considered a cultural variable largely because cultures teach boys and girls different attitudes, beliefs, values, and ways of communicating and relating to one another. So, you act like a man or a

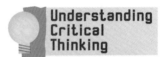

Understanding Critical Thinking

Critical thinking is essential for mastering interpersonal skills. Throughout this text, you'll find numerous recommendations for communicating more effectively. As you read them keep in mind that skills are almost always too general; they are rarely specific enough for automatic application to any given situation. So, ask yourself: What is there about your unique and specific situation that you need to take into account in deciding what to do? What are your communication options? Which seem the most promising? Can you play these through in your mind? Also, recognize that although great effort has been made to indicate cultural differences and variation, most of the research reported here is based on college students in the United States. So, before using your skills, it's always appropriate to ask if there are cultural differences that might bear on the skill and its successful application.

HOW TO...
Communicate in the Organization

You can gain an interesting perspective on interpersonal messages by looking at the way they're treated in the business world in an organizational context.

Upward communication refers to messages sent from the lower levels of the hierarchy to the upper levels, for example, line worker to manager, faculty member to dean. It gives subordinates a sense of belonging to and being a part of the organization. And it provides management with the opportunity to get new ideas from workers. Management can make upward communication more effective by

- Establishing some nonthreatening system for upward communication, for example, anonymous questionnaires, suggestion boxes
- Listening and responding to these messages
- Having convenient channels for worker-to-management communication available

Downward communication refers to messages sent from the higher levels of the hierarchy to the lower levels. Orders and explanations of new procedures are examples. Management can make downward communication more effective by

- Using a vocabulary understood by the workers, keeping technical jargon to a minimum
- Providing workers with sufficient information for them to function effectively
- Recognizing that too much information can overload the channels; this can often lead to the really important information being ignored because it's buried with lots of irrelevant notices and memos

Lateral communication refers to messages between equals—manager to manager or worker to worker. Lateral communication helps to disseminate organizational information and build morale and worker satisfaction. Lateral communication can be made more effective by

- A shared willingness to explain the specialized jargon that comes with each specialty in an organization
- Workers who are willing to see their own specialty in perspective rather than as the only important subdivision of the organization

Informal or grapevine communication follows no formal lines. Grapevine messages grow along with the formal communications; the more active the formal communication system, the more active the information system. Informal communication can be made more effective by

- Understanding that the grapevine is a vital means of information transmission; it's quick and generally quite accurate
- Realizing that although it's generally accurate, it's also generally incomplete and therefore it often needs to be followed up with more information
- Not communicating information you do not want sent through the grapevine

[The next How To box appears on page 56.]

woman in part because of what your culture has taught you about how men and women should act. This does not, of course, deny that biological differences also play a role in the differences between male and female behavior. In fact, recent research continues to uncover biological roots of behavior we once thought were entirely learned, like happiness and shyness, for example (McCroskey, 1997).

Because your interpersonal communications are heavily influenced by the culture in which you were raised, culture is given a prominent place in this text. In this section we explain the relevance of culture to interpersonal communication and the aims and benefits of a cultural perspective.

A walk through any large city, many small towns, and through just about any college campus will convince you that the United States is largely a

SKILL BUILDING EXERCISE 1.2

Explaining Interpersonal Difficulties

Using the principles of interpersonal communication just discussed, try *describing* what is going on in the following cases. These scenarios are extremely brief and are written only as aids to stimulate you to think more concretely about the axioms.

1. Grace feels that her fiancé Tom—in not defending her proposal at a company for which both work—created a negative attitude and encouraged others to reject her ideas. Tom says that he felt he could not defend her proposal because others in the room would have felt his defense was motivated by their relationship. So, he felt it was best to say nothing.

2. A couple together for 20 years argues about the seemingly most insignificant things—who takes out the garbage, who does the dishes, who decides where to eat, and on and on. The arguments are so frequent and so unsettling that they're seriously considering separating.

3. In the heat of a big argument, Harry said he didn't want to ever see Peggy's family again. "They don't like me and I don't like them," he said.

Peggy reciprocated and said she felt the same way about his family. Now, weeks later, there is still a great deal of tension between them especially when they're with one or both families.

4. Pat and Chris have been online friends for the last two years, communicating with each other at least once a day. Recently, Pat wrote a number of things that Chris interpreted as insulting and as ridiculing Chris's feelings and dreams. Chris wrote back that these last messages were greatly resented and then stopped writing. Pat has written every day for the last two weeks to try to patch things up; but Chris won't respond.

Thinking Critically About Interpersonal Difficulties   Although the instructions ask you to describe what is going on in these situations, did you also think of recommendations for reducing the communication problems? What advice would you give these people? What principle would you find especially useful in explaining what is going on to each of the people involved?

Can you identify one specific interpersonal encounter in which all five purposes were served?

collection of lots of different cultures (see Figure 1.7). These cultures coexist somewhat separately but also with each influencing the others. This co-existence has led some researchers to refer to these cultures as co-cultures (Shuter, 1990; Samovar & Porter, 1991; Jandt, 1995). Here are a few random facts to further support the importance of culture generally and of intercultural communication in particular (*Time*, December 2, 1993, p. 14):

- Over 30 million people in the United States speak languages other than English in their homes.
- In urban school systems, such as New York; Fairfax County, Virginia; Chicago; and Los Angeles, over 100 languages are spoken.

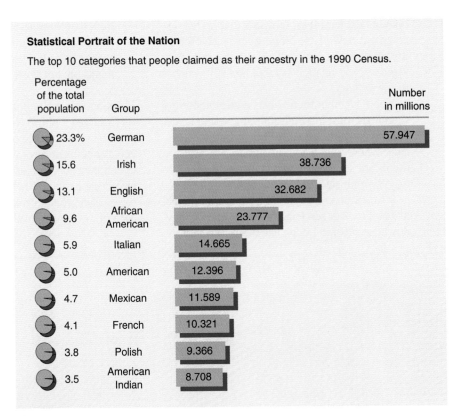

Statistical Portrait of the Nation

The top 10 categories that people claimed as their ancestry in the 1990 Census.

Percentage of the total population	Group	Number in millions
23.3%	German	57.947
15.6	Irish	38.736
13.1	English	32.682
9.6	African American	23.777
5.9	Italian	14.665
5.0	American	12.396
4.7	Mexican	11.589
4.1	French	10.321
3.8	Polish	9.366
3.5	American Indian	8.708

Figure 1.7

Ancestry of United States Residents

With immigration patterns changing so rapidly, the portrait illustrated here is likely to look very different in the coming years. For example, by 2030, it's predicted that the U.S. population will be 73.6% white, 12% African American, 10.2% Hispanic, and 3.3% Asian American. By 2050 it's predicted that the percentages will be: 52.8% white, 24.5% Hispanic, 13.6% African American, and 8.2% Asian American (figures projected by the Census Bureau and reported in *New York Times*, March 14, 1996, p. A16). To what factors might you attribute these projections? What will your own state, city, or town look like in 2030? In 2050? That is, in what ways will it resemble or differ from the predictions for the nation as a whole?

- Over 50% of the residents of Miami and Hialeah in Florida, Union City in New Jersey, and Huntington Park and Monterey Park in California are foreign-born.
- The foreign-born population of the United States in 1990 totaled almost 20 million, approximately 8% of the total U.S. population.
- 30% of the United States Nobel Prize-winners (since 1901) were foreign-born.

In addition, we're living in a time of great gender changes. Many men, for example, are doing a great deal more in caring for their children, and the term "house husband" is becoming increasingly common and perhaps a little less negative. More obvious perhaps is that many women are becoming much more visible in fields once occupied exclusively by men—politics, law enforcement, the military, and the clergy are just some examples. And, of course, women are increasingly entering corporate executive ranks; the glass ceiling may not have disappeared but it is cracked.

You may wish to continue this cultural awareness experience by taking the accompanying self-test on page 32, "What's Your Cultural Awareness?"

The Relevance of Culture

There are lots of reasons for the cultural emphasis you'll find in this book. Most obviously, perhaps, are the vast demographic changes taking place throughout the United States. While the United States was once a country largely populated by Europeans, it's now a country greatly influenced by the enormous number of new citizens from Latin and South America, Africa, and Asia. And the same is even more true on college and university campuses throughout the United States. With these changes have come different interpersonal customs and the need to understand and adapt to new ways of looking at communication.

As a people we've become increasingly sensitive to cultural differences. American society has moved from an assimilationist perspective (people should leave their native culture behind and adapt to their new culture) to one that values cultural diversity (people should retain their native cultural ways). And, with some notable exceptions—hate speech, racism, sexism, homophobia, and classism come quickly to mind—we're more concerned with saying the right thing and ultimately with developing a society where all cultures can coexist and enrich each other. At the same time, the ability to interact effectively with members of other cultures often translates into financial gain and increased employment opportunities and advancement prospects.

Today, most countries are economically dependent on each other. Our economic lives depend on our ability to communicate effectively across different cultures. Similarly, our political well-being depends in great part on that of other cultures. Political unrest in any part of the world—South Africa, Eastern Europe, and the Middle East, to take a few examples—affects our own security. Intercultural communication and understanding seem now more crucial than ever.

The rapid spread of communication technology has brought foreign and sometimes very different cultures right into our living rooms. News from foreign countries is commonplace. We see nightly—in vivid color—what is going on in remote countries. Technology has made intercultural communication easy, practical, and inevitable. The media bombard us daily with evidence of racial tensions, religious disagreements, sexual bias, and, in general,

How relevant do you think cultural differences are to your own current interpersonal interactions? How relevant will cultural differences be to you in the next 10 or 15 years? (A personal experience paper could easily be built around your intercultural experiences and what you've learned about communication from them.)

SELF-TEST
What's Your Cultural Awareness?

You may find it interesting to take the accompanying self-test as a way of beginning to think about your thinking about the world and culture generally.

1. The major language of education in India is
   (a) English   (b) Hindi   (c) Urdu
2. The major ancestral group in the United States (as of the 1990 census) was
   (a) German   (b) Irish   (c) Mexican
3. The largest number of Africans are
   (a) Christians   (b) Muslims   (c) Tribal religionists
4. The nation with the highest literacy rate (100%) is
   (a) Cuba   (b) Kyrgyzstan   (c) United States
5. The nation holding the most U.S. patents granted to residents of areas outside the United States and its territories is
   (a) France   (b) Germany   (c) Japan
6. It's predicted that in 2000 the country with the longest expectation of life at birth will be
   (a) Italy   (b) Japan   (c) Switzerland
7. Based on projected census figures for 2020, the country with the largest population will be (we're purposely omitting China—that would be too easy)
   (a) India   (b) Indonesia   (c) United States
8. The nation whose per capita annual income is less than $1,000 is
   (a) Nigeria   (b) Pakistan   (c) Philippines
9. The state with the largest number of Native Americans (defined by the U.S. Department of commerce, Bureau of the Census, as American Indian, Eskimo, and Aleut) is
   (a) Arizona   (b) California   (c) Oklahoma
10. The divorce rate is highest for which country?
    (a) Japan   (b) Sweden   (c) United States

Thinking Critically About Your Cultural Awareness This test was designed to get you thinking about what you think about the world and different cultures. The answers (all from current almanacs) are as follows: (1) English. (2) The answers are given in Figure 1.7. (3) The largest number of Africans are Christian (327,204,000 Africans are Christian) with Muslims (278,250,800), and tribal religionists (70,588,000) the next largest groups. (4) Of the nations listed in this question, only Kyrgyzstan has a literacy rate of 100% along with such other countries as Armenia, Australia, and Andorra. Cuba has a literacy rate of 99% (along with North Korea, Denmark, the Czech Republic, Ireland, and Barbados). The literacy rate for the United States is 97%. These figures contrast sharply with those nations which have literacy rates below 50%, for example, Iran, Bangladesh, Senegal, Uganda, Afghanistan. (5) Japan holds the largest number of patents, Germany is second, and France is third. (6) Japan will have the longest life span, Switzerland will be second, Italy will be third. (7) China is projected to have the greatest population with 1,424,725,000; India will rank a close second with a projected population of 1,320,746,000; the United States will be a distant third with 323,113,000; Indonesia will be fourth with 276,474,000; and Pakistan will be fifth with 275,100,000. By 2100, it's predicted, India will have the world's largest population. (8) All three nations listed have per capita annual incomes of less than $1,000. (9) The three states listed have the greatest Native American population. Oklahoma ranks first with 252,420; California second with 242,164; and Arizona third with 203,527. The three states with the fewest are Vermont (1,696), Delaware (2,019), and New Hampshire (2,134). (10) The divorce rate is highest in the United States (4.7 per 1,000 population); Sweden has a divorce rate of 2.22; and Japan has a divorce rate of 1.27.

Do these questions and their answers surprise you in any way? For example, are you surprised that the United States is not in the top three in terms of life span? Are you surprised at the religions of Africa? Are you surprised that the divorce rate in the United States is twice as high as it is in Sweden? Can you trace any of these surprises to stereotypes you might have of certain countries?

How important is intercultural communication to you? Will its importance change for you in the next 5 or 10 years?

Understanding Critical Thinking

Learn to transfer the skills of critical thinking. Here are three suggestions for transferring the skills of critical thinking covered here to a wide variety of situations (Sternberg, 1987):

• Think about the principles flexibly; recognize exceptions to the rule. Note especially that the principles discussed here come largely from research and theory conducted in the United States on college students. Ask yourself if they apply to other situations.

• Compare current situations with those you experienced earlier. What are the similarities and differences? For example, most people repeat relationship problems because they fail to see the similarities (or differences) between the old and the new relationship.

• Look for situations at home, work, and school where you could transfer the skills discussed here. For instance, you might consider how the irreversibility of communication relates to communication problems at home or at work.

the problems caused when intercultural communication fails. And, of course, the Internet has made intercultural communication as easy as writing a note on your computer. You can now just as easily communicate by e-mail with someone in Europe or Asia, for example, as you can with someone in another city or state.

Still another reason is that interpersonal competence is specific to a given culture; what proves effective in one culture may prove ineffective in another. For example, in the United States corporate executives get down to business during the first several minutes of a meeting. In Japan, business executives interact socially for an extended period and try to find out something about each other. Thus, the communication principle influenced by U.S. culture would advise participants to get down to the meeting's agenda during the first five minutes. The principle influenced by Japanese culture would advise participants to avoid dealing with business until everyone has socialized sufficiently and feels well enough acquainted to begin negotiations. Neither principle is right and neither is wrong. Each is effective within its own culture, and ineffective outside its own culture.

The Aim of a Cultural Perspective

Because culture permeates all forms of communication, it's necessary to understand its influences if you're to understand how communication works and master its skills. As illustrated throughout this text, culture influences

In a small group, with the class as a whole, or in a brief paper discuss how your beliefs, attitudes, and values were influenced by the culture in which you were raised. How were they taught? How was the importance of each communicated? What penalties are incurred for going against these beliefs, attitudes, and values? How did you learn about these penalties?

communications of all types (Moon, 1996). It influences what you say to yourself and how you talk with friends, lovers, and family in everyday conversation. It influences how you interact in groups and how much importance you place on the group versus the individual. It influences the topics you talk about and the strategies you use in communicating information or in persuading. And it influences how you use the media and the credibility you attribute to them.

A cultural emphasis helps distinguish what is universal (true for all people) from what is relative (true for people in one culture and not true for people in other cultures) (Matsumoto, 1994). The principles for communicating information and for changing listeners' attitudes, for example, will vary from one culture to another. If you're to understand communication, then you need to know how its principles vary and how the principles must be qualified and adjusted on the basis of cultural differences.

And of course this cultural understanding is needed to communicate effectively in a wide variety of intercultural situations. Success in interpersonal communication—on your job and in your social life—will depend on your ability to communicate effectively with persons who are culturally different from yourself.

This emphasis on culture does not imply that you should accept all cultural practices or that all cultural practices are equal (Hatfield & Rapson, 1996). For example, cockfighting, fox hunting, and bullfighting are parts of the culture of some Latin American countries, England, and Spain, but you need not find these activities acceptable or equal to a cultural practice in which animals are treated kindly. Further, a cultural emphasis does not imply that you have to accept or follow even the practices of your own culture. For example, even if the majority in your culture find cock fighting acceptable, you need not agree with or follow the practice. Similarly, you can reject your culture's values and beliefs, its religion or political system, or its attitudes toward the homeless, the handicapped, or the culturally different. Of course, going against your culture's traditions and values is often very difficult. But, it's important to realize that while culture *influences,* it does not *determine* your values or behavior. Often, for example, personality factors (your degree of assertiveness, extroversion, or optimism, for example) will prove more influential than culture (Hatfield & Rapson, 1996).

As demonstrated throughout this text, cultural differences exist throughout the interpersonal communication spectrum—from the way you use eye contact to the way you develop or dissolve a relationship (Chang & Holt, 1996). But, these should not blind you to the great number of similarities existing among even the most widely separated cultures. Close interpersonal relationships, for example, are common in all cultures, though they may be entered into for very different reasons by members of different cultures. Further, when reading about these differences, remember that these are usually matters of degree. Thus, for example, most cultures value honesty but not all value it to the same degree. The advances in media and technology and the widespread use of the Internet, for example, are influencing cultures and cultural change and are perhaps homogenizing different cultures, lessening the differences and increasing the similarities. They're also Americanizing different cultures because the dominant values and customs evidenced in the media and on the Internet are in large part American, a product of America's current dominance in both media and technology.

CAUTION

How might **accepting cultural beliefs uncritically** prevent you from achieving accurate self-awareness? Can you identify beliefs that you have that you've never examined critically?

Visit the National Communication Association's website at http://www.natcom.org. What kinds of information are available? How can this information help you in learning about communication?

SKILL BUILDING EXERCISE 1.3.

Cultural Beliefs

Review the following cultural maxims. Select any one that seems especially interesting and identify

A. The meaning of the maxim
B. The cultural value(s) it embodies and speaks to
C. The similarity or difference between it and what your own culture teaches

1. A penny saved is a penny earned.
2. All that glitters is not gold.
3. All will come to those who wait.
4. Blessed are the meek.
5. Blood is thicker than water.
6. Children should be seen and not heard.
7. Do unto others as you would have others do unto you.
8. Don't put off 'til tomorrow what you can do today.
9. God is just.
10. Honesty is the best policy.
11. If you've got it, flaunt it. Blow your own horn.
12. It's better to light a candle than to curse the darkness.
13. Love thy neighbor.
14. Never give a sucker an even break.
15. No one likes a sore loser.
16. Nothing succeeds like success.
17. Patience is a virtue.
18. Real men don't cry.
19. Respect your elders.
20. Self-praise smells bad.
21. Smile though your heart is breaking.
22. Stick with your own kind.
23. Tell it like it is.
24. The apple doesn't fall far from the tree.
25. There's no defense like a good offense.
26. Throw caution to the wind.
27. Time is money.
28. Time waits for no one.
29. Tomorrow will take care of itself.
30. What goes around comes around.

Thinking Critically About Cultural Maxims.   Try sharing your responses with others, especially with members of different cultures. Are your meanings similar? Do any of the maxims contradict any of your own values or beliefs? Do you see any problems with any of these maxims? For example, do any of them advocate values that would provide obstacles to your achiev-ing your goals?

SUMMARY OF CONCEPTS AND SKILLS

In this chapter we explored the nature of interpersonal communication. We then looked at several principles of interpersonal communication and last at the centrality of culture:

1. Interpersonal communication is a transactional process that takes place between two people who have a relationship.
2. Essential to an understanding of interpersonal communication are the following elements: source-receiver, encoding-decoding, messages (including feedback and feedforward), channel, noise (physical, physiological, psychological, and semantic), context (physical, cultural, social-psychological, and temporal), competence, and ethics.
3. Interpersonal communication is:

   • both content and relationship messages: we communicate about objects and events in the world but also simultaneously about the relationship between us
   • a process of adjustment by which we each adjust to the specialized communication system of the other
   • inevitable (communication will occur whether we want it to or not), irreversible (once something is received, it remains communicated and cannot be erased from a listener's memory), and

unrepeatable (no communication act can ever be repeated exactly)

- purposeful; throughout interpersonal communication we learn, relate, influence, play, and help

4. Interpersonal communication is heavily influenced by culture, that is, by the beliefs, attitudes, and values taught and practiced by cultural members.

Several interpersonal skills were also noted in this chapter. You'll gain most from this brief experience if you think carefully about each skill and try to identify instances from your recent communications in which you did or did not act on the basis of the specific skill. Evaluate your own mastery of these skills using the following rating scale: 1 = almost always, 2 = often, 3 = sometimes, 4 = rarely, and 5 = almost never.

_____ 1. Interact interpersonally with a recognition that all the elements of communication are in a constant state of transaction, with each influencing each other element.

_____ 2. Distinguish between content and relationship messages and respond to both.

_____ 3. Adjust your messages to the unique communication system of the other.

_____ 4. Communicate *after* thinking, especially in light of the inevitability, unrepeatability, and irreversibility characteristics of interpersonal communication.

_____ 5. Communicate with a recognition of the variety of purposes that interpersonal interaction may serve.

_____ 6. Use the principles of interpersonal communication with a recognition of its cultural context.

VOCABULARY QUIZ. THE LANGUAGE OF INTERPERSONAL COMMUNICATION

Match the terms of interpersonal communication with their definitions. Record the number of the definition next to the appropriate term.

7	interpersonal communication	_____	relationship message
10	encoding	**2**	source-receiver
1	feedback	**9**	social comparison process
4	semantic noise		
5	cultural context	_____	communication as a transactional process
3	feedforward		

1. Messages sent back to the source in response to the source's messages.
2. Each person in the interpersonal communication act.
3. Information about messages that are yet to be sent.
4. Interference that occurs when the receiver does not understand the meanings intended by the sender.
5. The rules and norms, the beliefs and attitudes of the people communicating.
6. Communication as an ongoing process in which each part depends on each other part.
7. Communication that takes place between two persons who have a relationship between them.
8. Messages referring to the connection between the two people in communication.
9. The process of comparing yourself to others.
10. The process of sending messages, for example, in speaking or writing.

The Self

CHAPTER TOPICS	LEARNING OBJECTIVES	SKILL OBJECTIVES
	After completing this chapter, you should be able to	*After completing this chapter, you should be able to*
Self-Concept and Self-Awareness	1. Define *self-concept* and *self-awareness* and the suggestions for increasing self-awareness	Analyze your self-concept and increase self-awareness
Self-Disclosure	2. Explain the nature of self-disclosure, its potential rewards and dangers, and the guidelines for making and responding to disclosures	Self-disclose and respond to the disclosures of others appropriately
Apprehension	3. Define *communication apprehension,* its causes, and ways for managing it	Manage your fear of communicating; communicate with confidence in a variety of contexts

Aesop, the great writer of fables, tells the story of Mercury, one of the gods of Ancient Rome. Although only a lesser god, Mercury aspired to be more. So, one day, disguised as an ordinary man, he entered a sculptor's studio where he saw statues of the gods and goddesses for sale. Eyeing a statue of Jupiter, one of the major gods, Mercury asked the price. "A crown," the sculptor said. Mercury laughed for he thought that such a low price; maybe Jupiter was not that important after all. Then he asked the price of a statue of Juno, another major god. "Half a crown," said the sculptor. This seemed to please Mercury who thought that surely his likeness would command a much higher price. So, pointing to a statue of himself, he proudly asked its price. "Oh, that; I'll give that one free if you buy the other two."

Understanding Critical Thinking

Develop critical thinking attitudes.

As a critical thinker, be willing to:

- Analyze yourself as a critically thinking communicator. Self-analysis is essential if you're to use this material in any meaningful sense. Be open-minded to new ideas, even those that contradict your existing beliefs.
- Observe the behaviors of those around you as well as your own. See in real life what you read about here; it will then have clearer application to your own day-to-day interactions.
- Delay conclusions until you've collected sufficient information. But do realize that at some point thinking needs to give way to action and you'll need to make a decision.
- Analyze and evaluate ideas instead of accepting them just because they appear in a textbook or are mentioned by an instructor.

Mercury was engaging in "social comparison"—a way of gaining insight into his own self-concept; he was comparing his reputation to the reputations of others. By doing so, Mercury got a good idea of his own relative importance. In this chapter we look at self-concept and self-awareness and particularly how you develop your image of yourself and how you can increase your own self-awareness. With this as a foundation we then look at self-disclosure, the process of revealing yourself to another person, and speaker apprehension and some ways to reduce your own fear of communication.

SELF-CONCEPT AND SELF-AWARENESS

Central to all forms of interpersonal communication is your self-concept—the image of you that others have, the comparisons you make between yourself and others, and the way you interpret and evaluate your own thoughts and behaviors. Equally significant is the degree to which you're self-aware, the degree to which you know yourself. Let's look first at self-concept.

Self-Concept

Your self-concept is your image of who you are. It's how you perceive yourself: your feelings and thoughts about your strengths and weaknesses and your abilities and limitations. Self-concept develops from the image that others have of you; the comparisons between yourself and others; your cultural experiences in the realms of race, ethnicity, gender, and gender roles; and your evaluation of your own thoughts and behaviors (Figure 2.1).

Other's Images of You

If you wished to see the way your hair looked, you'd probably look in a mirror. But, what would you do if you wanted to see how friendly or how assertive you are? According to the concept of the *looking-glass self* (Cooley, 1922), you would look at the image of yourself that others reveal to you through their behaviors and especially through the way they treat you and react to you.

Of course, you would not look to just anyone. Rather, you would look to those who are most significant in your life—to your *significant others*. As a child you would look to your parents and then to your elementary school teachers, for example. As an adult you might look to your friends and romantic partners. If these significant others think highly of you, you'll see a positive self-image reflected in their behaviors; if they think little of you, you'll see a more negative image.

Social Comparisons

Another way you develop self-concept is to compare yourself with others, to engage in what is called social comparisons (Festinger, 1954). Again, you don't choose just anyone. Rather, when you want to gain insight into who you are and how effective or competent you are, you look to your peers. For example, after an examination you probably want to know how you performed relative to the other students in your class. This gives you a clearer idea as to how effectively you performed. If you play on a baseball team, it's important to know your batting average in comparison with the batting average of others on the team. Absolute scores on the exam or of your batting average may

> However much we guard against it, we tend to shape ourselves in the image others have of us.
> —*Eric Hoffer*

> I am only one,
> But still I am one.
> I cannot do everything.
> But still I can do something;
> And because I cannot do everything
> I will not refuse to do the something that I can do.
> —*Edward Everett*

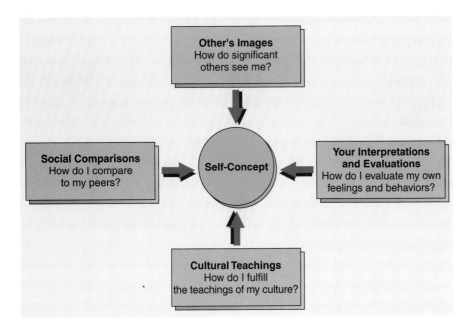

Figure 2.1
The Sources of Self-Concept

This diagram depicts the four sources of self-concept, the four contributors to how you see yourself. As you read about self-concept, consider the influence of each factor throughout your life. Which factor influenced you most as a preteen? Which influences you the most now? Which will influence you the most 25 or 30 years from now?

be helpful in telling you something about your performance, but you gain a different perspective when you see your score in comparison with those of your peers.

Cultural Teachings

Through your parents, teachers, and the media, your culture instills in you a variety of beliefs, values, and attitudes—about success (how you should define and achieve it); the relevance of a person's religion, race, or nationality; and the ethical principles you should follow in business and in your personal life. These teachings provide benchmarks against which you can measure yourself. Your success in, for example, achieving what your culture defines as success, will contribute to a positive self-concept. Your failure to achieve what your culture teaches (for example, not being married by the time you're thirty) may contribute to a negative self-concept.

When you demonstrate the qualities that your culture (or organization, because organizations are much like cultures) teaches, you'll see yourself as a cultural success and you'll be rewarded by other members of the culture (or organization). Seeing yourself as culturally successful and getting rewarded by others will contribute positively to your self-concept. When you fail to demonstrate such qualities, you're more likely to see yourself as a cultural failure and to be punished by other members of the culture, contributing to a more negative self-concept.

Your Own Observations, Interpretations, and Evaluations

Access one of the online entertainment industry Websites (for example, www.boxoff.com, http://us.imdb.com, or www.buzzmag.com) and research the question: What makes a hit movie (or music album or television series)? What does this say about "self-concept"?

You also observe, interpret, and evaluate your own behavior. For example, let's say you believe that lying is wrong. If you lie, you will probably evaluate this behavior in terms of your internalized beliefs about lying and will react negatively to your own behavior. You might, for example, experience guilt as a result of your behavior contradicting your beliefs. On the other hand, let's say that you pulled someone out of a burning building at great personal risk. You

What kinds of information about yourself do you seek from social comparisons? With whom do you compare yourself?

would probably evaluate this behavior positively; you would feel good about this behavior and, as a result, about yourself.

The more you understand why you view yourself as you do, the better you'll understand who you are. You can gain additional insight into yourself by looking more closely at self-awareness and especially at the Johari model of the self.

This article reinforces and applies much of the material in this chapter to some very common self-confidence problems. Self-esteem, also noted in this article, is discussed in Chapter 12. You may want to reread this article after reading the section on self-esteem.

Self-Confidence: The Art of Being You

Joshua Halberstam

Why do we come to see ourselves as inept or unworthy? If we were born with a confident sense of self more or less intact, how did we manage to lose it—and how do we get it back? These are urgent questions, because in our complicated world, the demand for self-confidence confronts us at every turn.

Confidence means trust. When we confide in someone, we entrust them with our secrets; we take them into our *confidence*. When we are *self*-confident, we trust ourselves. We believe that we have what it takes to accomplish what we need to accomplish; we also trust ourselves not to fall apart if we fail to accomplish it.

Self-confidence can be closely aligned with self-esteem, but confidence as a term is usually applied to performance and skill mastery ("I'm confident I can win the game." "I'm confident at cocktail parties." "I'm confident about my job qualifications."), whereas self-esteem reflects a value judgment about oneself, one's morals, principles, and spirituality. So it is possible to have self-esteem without being confident, or to be confident, say, as a computer whiz, without having an overall sense of self-esteem.

The concern with confidence is first and finally a very personal frustration. Male or female, it is the result of one's own individual history, one's own character. It is in our private psychological story that the problem takes hold. And here is where we can find its solution.

Self-confidence is so intimately tied to self-evaluation that in order to figure out why we do or don't have sufficient self-confidence, we first need to look at the ways in which we judge ourselves. How do we come to believe that we are charming, callous, talented, sexy, stupid, or kind?

It appears that we base our opinions of ourselves on two primary sources, the first being our own experience and the second being what *we think* people think of us.

Ask Donna why she considers herself clumsy, for instance, and she'll tell you about the two occasions, five years apart no less, when she spilled wine at a party. You've been at dozens of parties with her over the years and never seen her do anything the least ungraceful; why she is so wedded to this image of herself as a klutz is baffling to you. But many of us, like Donna, allow our failures and embarrassments to burn themselves into our memories while at the same time taking our accomplishments for granted. Empir-

ical research confirms that losing hurts more than winning feels good: In other words, like it or not, there's no contest as to which makes the bigger emotional impression. So big an impression that, as in Donna's case, a mere awkward incident, which somehow resonates with a trigger experience from childhood, can assume the status of a full-blown character flaw. Self-confidence suffers when we lose perspective about our imperfections as being just a part of the entire context of our lives—a mix of talents and limitations, successes and failures, and everything in between.

I THINK I CAN'T, I THINK I CAN'T

The great danger of all such behaviors is that they can so easily turn into defeatist self-fulfilling prophecies. Like long-term viruses, negative self-fulfilling prophecies invade the psyche and take up permanent residence there.

Michelle's antipathy for math is typical. After an unhappy encounter with an arithmetic exam back in the fifth grade, she proclaimed that she was "lousy at math." She then stayed away from the subject and, sure enough, eventually became *truly* lousy at math. Now, years later, in order to advance in her job Michelle finds herself obliged to become computer savvy—which, she hastens to add, requires "math-like thinking"—and worries that she has a built-in block against learning it. Until she jettisons this tired label, she's absolutely right.

The second way we self-evaluate is by attempting to see ourselves as others see us. Of course, the opinions we ascribe to others are often based on mere imaginings. The arrogant err on the positive side, thinking they are more respected than they in fact are; others err in the opposite direction.

It's not always easy to know or believe how you are perceived, particularly when it comes to nonquantifiable attributes. A recent study of eighth graders showed that their judgment about their popularity was far more askew than their judgment about their athletic prowess. That's probably true for grown-ups as well.

More to the point, it's even more difficult for others to size *you* up. No one reads another person like a book. No one can know you better than you know yourself.

Sometimes it *is* helpful to get feedback from others. You aren't funny, for example, if no one laughs at your jokes. If your friends constantly say you're cheap, maybe you are. It's worth looking into. In these matters, disregarding the opinion of others is not a show of confidence, but of conceit.

On the other hand, if you hitch your sense of self to the judgments of others, even those of your nearest and dearest, you are not *self*-confident. You let others dictate who you are. You'd do better ultimately to form your own opinion of yourself, about the things that go to the core of your character. You can consider and respect the views of others, but don't elevate these above your own.

When you don't have confidence, you also tend to ignore or reject compliments, while taking criticism, particularly self-criticism, more to heart. A great deal of research in personality assessment demonstrates that those of us who are not particularly good at evaluating the impressions we create tend to disregard compliments: "Sure, people say that I've got a wonderful sense of humor, but they're just being polite."

KNOW THYSELF

If you have a dependency on the perception of others, you need to break the habit. You need to repeat, as with a mantra, that you have the power to know yourself better than anyone else does, both your strengths and your weaknesses. You don't need to determine what they think. You need to take a good hard look at yourself and decide what *you* think. (Not easy, granted; this takes practice.) And if you're stacking the deck against yourself, toting up every failure, large or small, while forgetting or demeaning your accomplishments, it's time to start playing fair. Because just as defeatist thinking can lead to self-fulfilling prophecies, so can positive thinking reinforce itself over the long run and actually change the reality: Convince yourself that you'll blow everyone away at the interview and the likelihood becomes greater that you will. Talk yourself into things, not out of them. If those are your two choices, what do you have to lose?

Thinking Critically About "Self-Confidence"

1. What do you think of Halberstam's definition of self-confidence as trust in yourself? How would you define it?
2. Most people can easily accept intellectually the idea that it's rational and normal to lack confidence about some things. But many find it difficult to accept the idea emotionally. Can you accept this emotionally?
3. In the text four sources of self-concept are identified: others' images of you, social comparisons, your own evaluations and cultural teachings. Halberstam identifies two: your own experience and what you think people think of you. How would you explain the sources of your self-concept?

Source: "The Art of Being You" by Joshua Halberstam as appeared in *Self,* January 1994. Copyright ©1994 by Joshua Halberstam. reprinted by permission of the author.

Self-Awareness

Since you control your thoughts and behaviors largely to the extent that you understand who you are, it's crucial to develop heightened self-awareness. We can begin this discussion by looking at a model of the four selves.

Your Four Selves

Assume that the model of the four selves in Figure 2.2 represents you. The model is divided into quadrants, each of which contains a different self.

Your Open Self.   Your **open self** represents all the information, behaviors, attitudes, feelings, desires, motivations, and ideas that characterize you. The type of information included here might vary from your name and sex to your age, religious affiliation, and batting average. The size of your open self changes depending on the situation and the individuals you're interacting with. Some people probably make you feel comfortable and support you. To them, you would open yourself wide. To others you might prefer to leave most of yourself closed or unknown.

Visualize the entire model as of constant size but each section as variable, sometimes small, sometimes large. Note that a change in the open self area—or in any area—will cause a change in the other quadrants. For example, your disclosure enlarges your open self and shrinks your hidden self.

The Johari model emphasizes that the several aspects of the self are not separate and distinct pieces. Rather, they're parts of a whole that interact with each other. Like the model of interpersonal communication, this model of the self is a transactional one: each part is dependent on each other part.

Your Blind Self.   Your **blind self** represents all the things about yourself that others know but of which you're ignorant. These include, for example, your habit of rubbing your nose when you get angry, your defense mechanisms, and your repressed experiences.

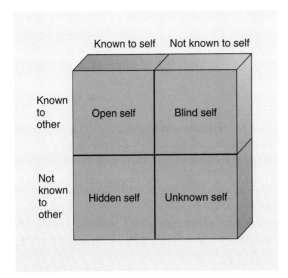

Figure 2.2
The Johari Window
This diagram is a commonly used tool for examining what you know and don't know about yourself. It will also prove an effective way of explaining the nature of self-disclosure, covered later in this chapter. The window gets its name from its inventors, *Jo*seph Luft and *Har*ry Ingham. When interacting with your peers, which self is your largest? Your smallest?

From *Group Processes: An Introduction to Group Dynamics,* 3rd ed., by Joseph Luft. Copyright © 1984 by Mayfield Publishing. Reprinted by permission.

Interpersonal communication depends on both parties sharing the same basic information about each other. Where blind areas exist, communication will be more difficult. Yet blind areas always exist. You can shrink your blind area, but you can never totally eliminate it.

Your Hidden Self.   Your **hidden self** contains all that you know of yourself but that you keep to yourself. This area includes all your successfully kept secrets. In any interaction, this area includes everything you have not revealed and perhaps seek actively to conceal. When you move information from this area to the open area—as in, say, telling someone a secret, you're self-disclosing, a process examined later in this chapter.

Your Unknown Self.   Your **unknown self** represents truths that exist but that neither you nor others know. We infer the existence of this unknown self from dreams, psychological tests, or therapy. For example, through therapy you might become aware of your high need for acceptance and how this influences the way you allow people to take advantage of you. With this insight, this information moves from the unknown self to the hidden self and perhaps to the open self.

Increasing Self-Awareness

The Johari window is particularly helpful in increasing your self-awareness. Self-awareness is crucial for several reasons. Perhaps most obviously, self-awareness will help you identify your strengths and weaknesses so that you can capitalize on your strengths. More important, you can also direct your energies to correcting your weaknesses.

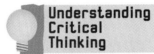
Understanding Critical Thinking

Critical thinking can be aided by hidden knowledge.   Much knowledge resides in the unconscious. Consider an example. Students were asked to press a button corresponding to where an X would appear on a computer screen (Goleman, 1992; Stine & Bewares, 1994). They were offered a reward of $100 if they could identify the system of rules governing where the X would appear on the screen. Now, the interesting thing about this was that the students could not state the system of rules governing the appearance of the X. But, they were able to predict where the X would appear next. The system of rules that they had to follow to predict where the X would appear was apparently in their unconscious, below the level of conscious awareness. The critical thinking techniques discussed throughout this text will help you to tap into this reservoir of knowledge.

Self-awareness will also help improve your interpersonal communication. For example, if you know you have difficulty telling jokes (the punch line never seems to come out right), then you can avoid this type of communication or elect to improve and perfect your joke-telling abilities. Still another benefit is that self-awareness will give you greater control over yourself. If you know, for example, that you upset people by talking about yourself too much, then you begin to change this behavior.

Embedded in the discussion of the Johari window were suggestions on how to increase your own self-awareness. We make these explicit here. In the final chapter we return to the self and consider the nature of self-esteem and how to increase it.

Listen to Others.   You can learn a great deal about yourself from seeing yourself as others do. Conveniently, others are constantly giving you the very feedback you need to increase self-awareness. In every interpersonal interaction,

LISTENING
Listening to Yourself

We all talk to ourselves; some just silently and some out loud. Self-talk is important because it influences your self-concept, the way you feel about yourself, the degree to which you like yourself, and the extent to which you consider yourself a valuable person. By listening carefully to what you tell yourself, you'll gain in self-awareness. Listen especially to two types of statements: self-destructive statements and self-affirming statements.

Self-destructive statements are those that damage the way you feel about yourself and prevent you from building meaningful and productive relationships. They may be about yourself ("I'm not creative," "I'm boring"), your world ("The world is an unhappy place," "People are out to get me"), or your relationships ("All the good people are already in relationships," "If I ever fall in love, I know I'll be hurt").

Recognizing that you may have internalized such beliefs is a first step to eliminating them. A second step involves recognizing that these beliefs are in fact unrealistic and self-defeating. Cognitive therapists (for example, Ellis, 1988; Ellis & Harper, 1975; Beck, 1988; Glaser, 1987; Murphy, 1997) argue that you can accomplish this by understanding why these beliefs are unrealistic and substituting more realistic ones. With training you can learn to rid yourself of ineffective self-evaluations and behaviors and to substitute more effective ones. For example, you might try substituting the unrealistic belief that you have to please others (always and in everything you do) with a more realistic

belief that it would be nice if others were pleased with you, but it certainly isn't essential (Ellis, 1988). You can choose, for example, to eliminate despair and to choose happiness (Howatt, 1997).

Self-affirming statements, on the other hand, are positive and self-supportive. Remind yourself of your successes from time to time. Focus on your good deeds, positive qualities, strengths, and virtues. Also, look carefully at the good relationships you have with friends, coworkers, and relatives. Concentrate on your potential, not your limitations (Brody, 1991). Throughout this process, be careful not to delude yourself into thinking you have no faults. Rather, be realistic; approach any real inadequacies with the belief that you can change them into strengths. Here is just a small sampling of self-affirmations that you may wish to say to yourself and, most important, listen to:

1. I'm a competent person.
2. I'm worth loving and having as a friend.
3. I'm growing and improving.
4. I'm empathic and supportive.
5. I facilitate open communication.
6. I can accept my past but can also let it go.
7. I can forgive myself and those who have hurt me.
8. I'm open minded and listen fairly to others.
9. I can apologize.
10. I'm flexible and can adjust to different situations.

[The next Listening box appears on page 71.]

people comment on you in some way—on what you do, what you say, how you look. Sometimes these comments are explicit: "loosen up," "don't take things so hard," "you seem angry." Often they're "hidden" in the way in which others look at you or in what they talk about. Pay close attention to this kind of information (both verbal and nonverbal) and use it to increase your own self-awareness. In the discussions of verbal and nonverbal communication (Chapters 5 and 6) we offer suggestions and insights for reading these hidden messages.

Increase Your Open Self.   Revealing yourself to others will help increase your self-awareness. At the very least, you'll bring into focus what you may have buried within. As you discuss yourself, you may see connections that you had previously missed. With feedback from others, you may gain still more insight. All this will help to increase your self-awareness. Also, by increasing your open self, you increase the chances that others will reveal what they know about you.

Seek Information About Yourself.   Seek out information to reduce your blind self. Encourage people to reveal what they know about you. You need not be so blatant as to say, "Tell me about myself" or "What do you think of me?" You can, however, use some situations that arise every day to gain self-information. "Do you think I came down too hard on the kids today?" "Do you think I was assertive enough when asking for the raise?" Seek this self-awareness in moderation. If you do it too often, your friends will soon look for someone else to talk with.

Another way to seek out information about yourself is to visualize how you're seen by your parents, teachers, friends, the stranger on the bus, your neighbor's child. Recognize that each of these people sees you differently; to each you're a different person. Yet, you're really *all* of them. The experience will surely give you new and valuable perspectives on yourself. It will convince you that you're actually a different person, depending on who you're interacting with. For example, my colleagues see me as serious and always doing a hundred things at the same time. My students, however, see me as humorous and laid back.

Still another way to seek information about yourself is to dialogue with yourself. No one knows you better than you know yourself. The problem is that we seldom, if ever, ask ourselves about ourselves. So, ask yourself who are you? What are your strengths? What are your weaknesses? What are your goals?

> The worst of all deceptions is self-deception.
> —*Plato*

SELF-DISCLOSURE

The Johari window leads naturally into an examination of self-disclosure, why and how you reveal your hidden self. More specifically, we here consider the nature of self-disclosure and the rewards and dangers of self-disclosing. Most important, we offer guidelines to help you make decisions about your own self-disclosures and your responses to the disclosures of others.

Self-disclosure is a type of communication in which you reveal information about yourself. Therefore, overt statements as well as slips of the tongue and unconscious nonverbal movements may be self-disclosing communications. Self-disclosure may also involve your reactions to the feelings of others, for example, when you tell your friend you're sorry she was fired.

Only new knowledge represents "disclosure." To tell someone something about yourself that he or she already knows would not be self-disclosure. Self-disclosure may involve information that you tell others freely or information

SKILL BUILDING EXERCISE 2.1

The Sources of Your Cultural Beliefs

This exercise is designed to increase your awareness of your cultural beliefs and how you got them. For any one of the beliefs noted below, try to answer these six questions:

What were you taught? Phrase it as specifically as possible, for example: I was taught to believe that . . . .

Who taught you? Parents? Teachers? Television? Peers? Coaches?

How were you taught? By example? Explicit teaching?

When were you taught this? As a child? As a high school student? As an adult?

Where were you taught this? In your home? Around the dinner table? At school? In the playground?

Why do you suppose you were taught this? What motives led your parents or teachers to teach you this belief?

Beliefs

1. The nature of God (for example, belief in the existence of God, organized religion, atheism, an afterlife)
2. The importance of family (respect for elders, interconnectedness, responsibilities to other family members)
3. The meaning of and means to success (the qualities that make for success, financial and relational "success")
4. The rules for sexual appropriateness (sex outside of committed relationships, same-sex and opposite sex relationships)
5. The role of education (the role of education in defining success, the obligation to become educated, education as a way of earning a living)
6. Male-female differences (recognizing differences, feminism)
7. Intercultural interactions (friendship and romance with those of other religions, races, nationalities; importance of ingroup versus outgroup)
8. The importance of money (amount that's realistic or desirable, and professional goals, relative importance compared to relationships, job satisfaction)
9. The meaning of life (major goal in life, this life versus an afterlife)
10. Time (the importance of being on time, the value of time, wasting time, adherence to the social time table of your peers—doing what they do at about the same age)

Thinking Critically About Beliefs and Interpersonal Communication

In what one way did each of these beliefs influence your interpersonal communication style? If you have the opportunity for interaction in small groups, a good way to gain added insight into cultural beliefs is for volunteers to talk about the belief they selected, how they answered each of the six questions, and how the belief influences their own way of communicating interpersonally. If the principles for effective interpersonal and intercultural communication (Chapters 8 and 9) are followed, this simple interchange should result in formidable interpersonal and intercultural insight.

that you normally keep hidden. It may supply information ("I earn $45,000") or reveal feelings ("I'm feeling really depressed"). Self-disclosure can vary from the insignificant ("I'm a Sagittarius") to the highly revealing ("I'm currently in an abusive relationship," "I'm always depressed").

Self-disclosure involves at least one other individual. It cannot be *intra*personal communication (communication with yourself). Nor may we "disclose" in a way that makes it impossible for another person to understand. To be self-disclosure, someone must receive and understand the information.

At this point you may want to explore your own feelings about self-disclosure, especially those feelings concerning what you feel you have a right to know about someone with whom you are a friend or lover.

SELF-TEST

What Do You Have a Right to Know?

At some point in a relationship, people may feel that the other person has an obligation to disclose and that they have a right to know certain information. At what point—if any—do you feel you have the right to know the types of information listed here? Record your feelings for romantic relationships in the first column and for friendship relationships in the second column. Use numbers from 1 to 10 to indicate at what point you would feel you have a right to know this information by visualizing a relationship as existing on a continuum from initial contact at 1 to extreme intimacy at 10. If you feel you would never have the right to know this information use an X.

Initial Contact   Extreme Intimacy
1   10

Romantic Relationships	Friendship Relationships	Information You Feel You Have the Right to Know
_____	_____	1. HIV status
_____	_____	2. History of family genetic disorders
_____	_____	3. The existence and number of children the person has
_____	_____	4. Past sexual experiences
_____	_____	5. Marital history
_____	_____	6. Annual salary, net financial worth
_____	_____	7. Affectional orientation
_____	_____	8. Race and nationality
_____	_____	9. Religion and religious beliefs
_____	_____	10. Social and political beliefs and attitudes

Thinking Critically About Your Right to Know In which type of relationship do you have the greater right to know? In which type of relationship is more information never another's right to know (the Xs in your responses)? In which relationship does the right to know come earlier? Try formulating in one sentence exactly what you feel gives one person the right to know information about another person.

Factors Influencing Self-Disclosure

A number of factors influence whether or not you disclose, and to whom you disclose. Among the most important factors are who you are, your culture, your gender, who your listeners are, and what your topic is.

Who You Are

Highly sociable and extroverted people self-disclose more than those who are less sociable and more introverted. People who are apprehensive about talking in general also self-disclose less than do those who are more comfortable in communicating.

Would this photo seem strange to you if instead of six women it featured six men? What has your culture taught you about self-disclosure? Did it provide different "rules" for men and for women?

   Competent people engage in self-disclosure more than less competent people. Perhaps competent people have greater self-confidence and more positive things to reveal. Similarly, their self-confidence may make them more willing to risk possible negative reactions (McCroskey & Wheeless, 1976).

Your Culture

Different cultures view self-disclosure differently. People in the United States, for example, disclose more than do those in Great Britain, Germany, Japan, or Puerto Rico (Gudykunst, 1983). American students also disclose more than do students from nine different Middle East countries (Jourard, 1971). Similarly, American students self-disclose more on a variety of controversial issues and also self disclose more to different types of people than do Chinese students (Chen, 1992). Singaporean-Chinese students consider more topics to be taboo and inappropriate for self-disclosure than their British colleagues (Goodwin & Lee, 1994). Among the Kabre of Togo, secrecy is a major part of their everyday interaction (Piot, 1993).

   Some cultures (especially those high in masculinity) view the disclosing of one's inner feelings as a weakness. Among some groups, for example, it would be considered "out of place" for a man to cry at a happy occasion like a wedding while that same display of emotion would go unnoticed in some Latin cultures. Similarly, in Japan it's considered undesirable for colleagues to reveal personal information whereas in much of the United States it's expected (Barnlund, 1989; Hall & Hall, 1987).

   In some cultures—for example, Mexican—there is a strong emphasis on discussing all matters in a positive mode, and this undoubtedly influences the way Mexicans approach self-disclosure as well. Negative self-disclosures, in contrast, are usually made to close intimates and then only after considerable time has elapsed in a relationship. This pattern is consistent with evidence showing that self-disclosure and trust are positively related (Wheeless &

Grotz, 1977). Additional research, for example, finds that the Hispanic reluctance to disclose negative issues (for example, one's positive HIV status) is creating serious problems in preventing and in treating HIV infection (Szapocznik, 1995).

These differences aside, there are also important similarities across cultures. For example, people from Great Britain, Germany, the United States, and Puerto Rico are all more apt to disclose personal information—hobbies, interests, attitudes, and opinions on politics and religion—than information on finances, sex, personality, and interpersonal relationships (Jourard, 1970). Similarly, one study showed self-disclosure patterns among American males to be virtually identical to those among Korean males (Won-Doornink, 1991).

Your Gender

The popular stereotype of gender differences in self-disclosure emphasizes the male reluctance to speak about himself. For the most part, research supports this view and shows that women disclose more than men. This is especially true in same-sex dyads; women disclose more intimately (and with more emotion) when talking with other women than with men (Shaffer, Pegalis, & Bazzini, 1996). Men and women, however, make negative disclosures about equally (Naifeh & Smith, 1984).

More specifically, women disclose more than men about their previous romantic relationships, their feelings about their closest same-sex friends, their greatest fears, and what they don't like about their partners (Sprecher, 1987). Women also seem to increase the depth of their self-disclosures as the relationship becomes more intimate, while men seem not to change their self-disclosure levels. Men, for example, have more taboo topics that they will not disclose to their friends than do women (Goodwin & Lee, 1994). Finally, women even self-disclose more to members of the extended family than do men (Komarovsky, 1964; Argyle & Henderson, 1985; Moghaddam, Taylor, & Wright, 1993). One notable exception occurs in initial encounters. Here men will disclose more intimately than women, perhaps "in order to control the relationship's development" (Derlega, Winstead, Wong, & Hunter, 1985).

Men and women give different reasons for avoiding self-disclosure (Rosenfeld, 1979), but both genders share this reason: "If I disclose, I might project an image I do not want to project." In a society in which image is so important—in which one's image is often the basis for success or failure—this reason is not surprising. Other reasons for avoiding self-disclosure, however, are unique to men or women. Lawrence Rosenfeld (1979) sums up males' reasons for self-disclosure avoidance: "If I disclose to you, I might project an image I do not want to project, which could make me look bad and cause me to lose control over you. This might go so far as to affect relationships I have with people other than you." Men's principal objective in avoiding self-disclosure is to maintain control. The general reason women avoid self-disclosure, says Rosenfeld, is that "if I disclose to you, I might project an image I do not want to project, such as my being emotionally ill, which you might use against me and which might hurt our relationship." Women's

How might **failing to understand cultural differences in self-disclosure** distort your evaluation of a person's disclosure messages?

One recent study suggests that gender differences in self-disclosure may be changing. In this study men and women discussed how their family relationships had changed since they entered college. Here men disclosed more than women (Leaper et al., 1995). What gender differences in self-disclosure do you observe? *(This could be the subject of an excellent review paper where you research and organize what is known about gender differences and self-disclosure. Search the databases for ERIC, Psychlit, and Sociofile using key words gender + self-disclosure.)*

How might **failing to appreciate gender differences in self-disclosure** lead to faulty conclusions about another person's self-disclosures?

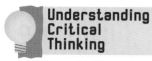

Understanding Critical Thinking

Use different thinking styles to think critically.

Here are five main types of thinking, all of which are useful to the critical thinker (Harrison & Bramson, 1984):

- The **synthesist** combines a variety of different things into something new; wants to integrate diverse elements into a new meaningful whole.
- The **idealist** looks for ideal solutions to problems and is greatly concerned with the impact of different solutions on people. The idealist asks, "What is good for the world?"
- The **pragmatist** is practical and looks for solutions that will get the job done. The important question is "What will work?"
- The **analyst** looks for the one best solution, which is almost invariably the scientific solution. The analyst asks, "What's the most logical solution?"
- The **realist** looks for concrete results and is concerned with identifying the relevant facts in any given decision process.

CAUTION

Has anyone ever misinterpreted your feelings because of **failing to perceive the dyadic effect?**

principal objective for avoiding self-disclosure is "to avoid personal hurt and problems with the relationship."

Your Listeners

Self-disclosure occurs more readily in small groups than in large groups. Dyads or groups of two people are the most hospitable setting for self-disclosure. With one listener, you can attend to the responses carefully. You can monitor the disclosures, continuing if there is support from your listener and stopping if there is not. With more than one listener, such monitoring becomes difficult since the listeners' responses are sure to vary.

Sometimes self-disclosure takes place in group and public speaking situations. In consciousness-raising groups and in meetings like those of Alcoholics Anonymous, members may disclose their most intimate problems to ten or perhaps hundreds of people at one time. In these situations, group members are pledged to be totally supportive. These and similar groups are devoted specifically to encouraging self-disclosure and to giving each other support for the disclosures.

Because you disclose, generally at least, on the basis of support you receive, you probably disclose to people you like (Derlega, Winstead, Wong, & Greenspan, 1987; Collins & Miller, 1994) and to people you trust (Wheeless & Grotz, 1977). You probably also come to like those to whom you disclose (Berg & Archer, 1983; Collins & Miller, 1994). And, not surprisingly, you're more likely to disclose to people who are close to you in age (Parker & Parrott, 1995).

At times self-disclosure occurs more in temporary than permanent relationships—for example, between strangers on a train or plane, a kind of "in-flight intimacy" (McGill, 1985). In this situation, two people set up an intimate self-disclosing relationship during a brief travel period, but they don't pursue it beyond that point. In a similar way, you might set up a relationship with one or several people on the Internet and engage in significant disclosure. Perhaps knowing you'll never see these other people and that they will never know where you live or work or what you look like makes it a bit easier.

You're more likely to disclose when the person you're with discloses. This **dyadic effect** (what one person does, the other person does likewise) probably leads you to feel more secure and reinforces your own self-disclosing behavior. Disclosures are also more intimate when they're made in response to the disclosures of others (Berg & Archer, 1983).

Your Topic

You're also more likely to disclose about some topics than others. For example, you're probably more likely to self-disclose information about your job or hobbies than about your sex life or financial situation (Jourard, 1968, 1971a). You're also more likely to disclose favorable information than unfavorable information. Generally, the more personal and negative the topic, the less likely you would be to self-disclose.

The self-test below, "How Willing to Self-Disclose Are You?", focuses on the influences of the five factors just discussed: you, your culture, your gender, your listeners, and your topic.

CHAPTER 2: The Self   **51**

Instructions: Respond to each statement below by indicating the likelihood that you would disclose such items of information to, say, other members of this class. Use the following scale:

1 = would definitely self-disclose
2 = would probably self-disclose
3 = don't know
4 = would probably not self-disclose
5 = would definitely not self-disclose

_____ 1. My attitudes toward different nationalities and races.
_____ 2. My feelings about my parents.
_____ 3. My sexual fantasies.
_____ 4. My past sexual experiences.
_____ 5. My ideal mate.
_____ 6. My drinking and/or drug-taking behavior.
_____ 7. My personal goals.
_____ 8. My unfulfilled desires.
_____ 9. My major weaknesses.
_____ 10. My feelings about the people in this group.

Thinking Critically About Self-Disclosure

This test, and ideally its discussion with others who also complete it, should get you started thinking about your own self-disclosing behavior and especially the factors that influence it. How does your own personality influence your self-disclosure behavior? How has your culture and your gender influenced what you feel is appropriate self-disclosure? Are you more likely to disclose interpersonally than in small group or public situations? Are there certain people to whom you feel relatively free to disclose to and others to whom you feel much less free? Are there certain topics you're less willing to disclose than others? Are you more likely to disclose positive secrets rather than negative ones? Are there topics about which you wish you had the opportunity to self-disclose but somehow can't find the right situation for such self-disclosing?

The Rewards of Self-Disclosure

Research shows that self-disclosure helps to increase self-knowledge, communication and relationship effectiveness, and physiological well-being.

Self-Disclosure Gives Self-Knowledge

One reward of self-disclosure is that you gain a new perspective on yourself, a deeper understanding of your own behavior. Through self-disclosure you may bring to consciousness a great deal that you might otherwise keep from conscious analysis. For example, as Tony talks about the difficulties he had living with an alcoholic father, he may remember details of his early life or entertain new feelings.

Even self-acceptance is difficult without self-disclosure. You accept yourself largely through the eyes of others. Through self-disclosure and subsequent support, you may be in a better position to see the positive responses to you. And you're more likely to respond by developing a more positive self-concept.

Self-Disclosure Increases Communication Effectiveness

You understand the messages of another person largely to the extent that you understand the person. For example, you can tell when a friend is serious and when joking, when someone is being sarcastic out of fear and when out of resentment. Self-disclosure is an essential condition for getting to know another individual.

Couples who engaged in significant self-disclosure are found to remain together longer than couples who do not (Sprecher, 1987). Self-disclosure helps us achieve a closer relationship with the person to whom we self-disclose (Schmidt & Cornelius, 1987). Without self-disclosure, meaningful relationships seem impossible to develop.

Interestingly enough we also come to increase our affection for our partner when we self-disclose. Think about your own self-disclosures. Have you come to increase your liking for someone after you disclosed to this person? Do others seem to like you more after they disclosed to you?

Self-Disclosure Promotes Physiological Health

People who self-disclose are less vulnerable to illnesses (Pennebaker, 1991). For example, bereavement over the death of someone very close is linked to physical illness for those who bear this alone and in silence. But it's unrelated to any physical problems for those who share their grief with others. Similarly, women who suffer sexual trauma normally experience a variety of illnesses (among them, headaches and stomach problems). Women who kept these experiences to themselves, however, suffered these illnesses to a much greater extent than did those who talked with others about these traumas. The physiological effort required to keep your burdens to yourself seems to interact with the effects of the trauma to create a combined stress that can lead to a variety of illnesses.

Dangers of Self-Disclosure: Risks Ahead

Confiding a secret to an unworthy person is like carrying grain in a bag with a hole.
—*Ethiopian proverb*

As is usually the case, when the potential rewards are great, so are the risks. Self-disclosure is no exception; the risks can be personal, relational, and professional and can be considerable.

Personal Risks

If you self-disclose certain aspects of your life, you may face rejection from even the closest friends and family members. Those who disclose they have AIDS, for example, may find that their friends and family no longer want to be quite as close as before.

Relationship Risks

Even in close and long-lasting relationships, self-disclosure can cause problems. Total self-disclosure may prove threatening to a relationship by decreasing trust. Self-disclosures concerning infidelity, romantic fantasies, past indiscretions or crimes, lies, or hidden weaknesses and fears could easily have such negative effects.

Professional Risks

The extensive media coverage of the gays and lesbians in the military who are coming out in protest of the "don't ask, don't tell" policy illustrate the professional dangers that self-disclosure may entail. Openly gay and lesbian military personnel, as well as those in law enforcement, health care agencies, education, and fire departments—to name just a few—may find themselves confined to desk jobs, prevented from further advancement, or even charged with criminal behavior and fired. Similarly, politicians who disclose they have been "in therapy" may lose party and voter support. Teachers who disclose former or current drug use or cohabitation with students may find themselves denied tenure and eventually falling victim to "budget cuts."

Guidelines for Making Self-Disclosures

In trying to answer your first question, "Should I disclose?" consider the following questions.

What Is Your Motivation for Self-Disclosing?

Self-disclose out of a concern for the relationship, for the others involved, and for yourself. Some people self-disclose out of a desire to hurt the listener rather than from a desire to improve the relationship (for example, children telling their parents that they never loved them or telling a relationship partner that he or she stifled emotional development). However, let's say that you feel ignored and unimportant because your partner devotes all available time to professional advancement. Instead of letting these feelings smolder and turn into resentment, it might be helpful to the relationship to disclose them.

Is This Self-Disclosure Appropriate?

Appropriate self-disclosures include honest expressions of feelings ("I feel uncomfortable when you criticize me in front of my friends"), past behaviors that another has a right to know ("I was married when I was 17; we divorced two years later"), or personal abilities or lack of them that impact on others ("I never hung wallpaper before but I'll do my best"). Self-disclose in an atmosphere where your listener can give open and honest responses. Don't wait until you're boarding the bus to say to your friend, "I got some really bad news today. I'll tell you about it later."

> Never reveal all of yourself to other people; hold back something in reserve so that people are never quite sure if they really know you.
>
> —*Michael Korda*

How would you describe the dangers of self-disclosing on the job to your subordinates? To your coworkers? To your superiors? What kinds of self-disclosure would be especially dangerous?

Is the Other Person also Disclosing?

During your disclosures, give the other person a chance to reciprocate with his or her own disclosures. If the other person does not do so, then reassess your own self-disclosures. The lack of reciprocity may signal that this person, at this time and in this context, does not welcome your disclosures. Therefore, disclose gradually and in small increments so that you can retreat if the responses are not positive enough. Lack of reciprocity may also be due to cultural differences; in some cultures, significant self-disclosure only takes place after an extremely long acquaintanceship or may be considered inappropriate among, say, opposite sex friends.

Will This Self-Disclosure Impose Burdens?

Carefully weigh the potential problems that the self-disclosure may cause. Can you, if you were to disclose your previous prison record, afford to lose your job? If you were to disclose your previous failed romantic relationships, would you be willing to risk discouraging your present relational partner?

Ask yourself whether you're making unreasonable demands on the listener. For example, consider the person who discloses an affair with a neighbor to his or her own mother-in-law. This type of situation places an unfair burden on the mother-in-law. She is now in a bind either to break her promise of secrecy or to allow her own child to believe a lie. Parents often place unreasonable burdens on their children by self-disclosing marital problems or infidelities or self-doubts. They fail to realize that the children may be too young or too emotionally involved to deal effectively with this information. Often such disclosures do not make the relationship a better one. Instead they may simply add tension and friction.

In making your choice between disclosing and not disclosing, keep in mind—besides the advantages and dangers already noted—the irreversible nature of communication discussed in Chapter 1. No matter how many times you may try to qualify something or "take it back," once you have said something, you cannot withdraw it. You cannot erase the conclusions and inferences listeners have made on the basis of your disclosures. This is not to suggest that you therefore refrain from self-disclosing, but only to suggest that it's especially important here to recognize the irreversible nature of communication.

Guidelines for Responding to Self-Disclosures

When someone discloses to you, it's usually a sign of trust and affection. In serving this most important receiver function, keep the following in mind.

Practice the Skills of Effective and Active Listening

The skills of effective listening are discussed in detail in Chapter 4. These are especially important when listening to self-disclosures. Listen with empathy. Listen with an open mind. Repeat in your own words what you think the speaker has said so you can be sure you understand both the thoughts and the feelings. Express an understanding of the speaker's feelings to allow the speaker the opportunity to see these through the eyes of another individual. Ask questions to ensure your own understanding and to signal your own interest and attention.

How important is self-disclosure in your relationship life? In your professional life? How would you describe yourself in terms of self-disclosure? Do you find your level of self-disclosure satisfactory? If not, what might you do to change this? How would you describe the self-disclosure that takes place on television talk shows? Could you see yourself being a guest on such a show? (Your experiences with self-disclosure and the insights you've gained from these experiences would make an interesting personal experience paper.)

One response that is seldom mentioned in discussions of disclosure is to say that you simply don't want to hear the disclosure. Have you ever said this? Has anyone ever responded to your attempted self-disclosure with a refusal to listen? Under what conditions would such refusals be appropriate? Under what conditions would they be inappropriate?

Support the Discloser

Express support for the person during and after the disclosures. Try to avoid making judgments. Concentrate on understanding and empathizing with the discloser. Make your supportiveness clear to the discloser through your verbal and nonverbal responses. Nod your head to show you understand and echo the feelings and thoughts of the person. Maintain eye contact and otherwise show your positive attitudes toward the discloser and the act of disclosing.

Keep the Disclosures Confidential

When a person discloses to you, it's because she or he wants you to know these feelings and thoughts. If the discloser wishes others to share these, then it's up to her or him to disclose them. If you reveal these disclosures to others, it probably will inhibit this person's future disclosures. As a result, your relationship will suffer. In addition to keeping the disclosures confidential, avoid using them against the person at some later time. Many self-disclosures expose a vulnerability, a weakness. If you later turn around and use these against the person, you betray the confidence and trust invested in you.

It's interesting to note that one of the netiquette rules of e-mail is that you shouldn't forward mail to third parties without the writer's permission. This rule is a useful one for self-disclosure generally: Maintain confidentiality; don't pass on disclosures made to you to others without the person's permission.

Access the *New York Times,* the *Washington Post,* the *Wall Street Journal,* or any online newspaper for an article on the self (self-concept self-awareness, self-disclosure) that discusses recent research. On the basis of this article, what can you add to this chapter?

SKILL BUILDING EXERCISE 2.2

To Disclose or Not to Disclose?

Whether you should self-disclose is one of the most difficult decisions you have to make in interpersonal communication. Here are several instances of impending self-disclosure. For each, indicate whether you think the self-disclosure would be appropriate and why.

1. A mother of two teenaged children (one boy, one girl) has been feeling guilty for the past year over a romantic affair she had with her brother-in-law while her husband was in prison. They have been divorced for the last few months. She wants to self-disclose this affair and her guilt to her children.
2. Tom wants to break up his engagement with Cathy. Tom has since fallen in love with another woman and wants to end his relationship with Cathy. Tom wants to call Cathy on the phone, break his engagement, and disclose his new relationship.
3. Sam has been living in a romantic relationship with another man for the past several years. Sam wants to tell his parents, with whom he has been

very close throughout his life, but can't get up the courage to do so. He decides to tell them in a long letter.
4. Mary and Jim have been married for 12 years. Mary has been honest about most things and has self-disclosed a great deal to Jim—about her past romantic encounters, her fears, her ambitions, and so on. Yet, Jim doesn't reciprocate. He almost never shares his feelings and has told Mary almost nothing about his life before they met. Mary wonders if she should continue her pattern of self-disclosure.

Thinking Critically About Self-Disclosure

What are your reasons for your judgments? Which self-disclosure do you think will prove most effective? Least effective? Which disclosures seem appropriate to the receiver? Are the intended methods (phone call, letter) likely to prove effective? Will the self-disclosure help accomplish what the person wishes to accomplish?

HOW TO ...
Facilitate Self-Disclosure

Learning to facilitate the disclosures of others is a delicate art and one that is best explained by example. Consider, therefore, the first act of "Tommy's Family," a dialogue written to illustrate the failure to facilitate another's disclosures. Note the specific ways in which Tommy's father, mother, and sister fail to help him share his feelings.

Family:

Tommy, 12 years old, and obviously troubled

Frank, Tommy's father

Millie, Tommy's mother

Sally, Tommy's teenage sister

"TOMMY'S FAMILY"

Act I. The Failure

[Tommy enters living room, throws books down on coffee table, and goes to the refrigerator.]

Frank (*to Millie*):

	What's wrong with him?
Millie:	I don't know. He's been acting strange the last few days.
Sally:	*Acting* strange? He *is* strange. Weird.

[Tommy comes back into the living room, sits down and stares into space]

Frank:	Well, when you're 12 years old that's the way it is. I remember when I was 12. When I was your age, the big thing was girls. You got a girl, Tommy?
Sally:	Hey Mom, how about driving me to the mall? I gotta get a new dress for next week.
Millie:	Okay. I need a few things at K-Mart. You need anything, Tommy? You don't want to come with us, do you?
Sally:	Please say no. If people see us together, they'll think we're related. God! My life would be ruined. People would ignore me. No one would talk to me.
Frank:	Okay. Okay. That's enough. You two go to the mall. I'm going bowling with Pete and Joe. Tommy will be okay home alone.

Tommy:	Yeah.
Sally:	Mom, let's go.
Millie:	All right. I just have to call Grandma and see if she's okay.
Sally:	Oh, that reminds me. I have to call Jack. Lori left him for a college guy and he's really down in the dumps. I thought I'd call to cheer him up.
Millie:	Can't you do that when we get back?
Sally:	Yeah, I guess.
Frank:	Well, you guys have fun. I'm off to bowl another 200 game. Joe is still bowling under 140 so Pete and I are going to try to give him a few tips.
Millie:	Hello, Mom? How are you doing? Is the arthritis acting up? I figure that with this weather it must be really bad.
Sally:	Come on, Mom.

[Frank exits; Tommy turns on TV]

In this dialogue Tommy's father, mother, and sister illustrate the typical failure to help another person share feelings. Although Tommy gave enough signals—throwing books down on the coffee table, saying nothing, staring into space—nobody showed any real concern and nobody encouraged him to talk about what was on his mind. Note too that even though the father was aware that Tommy was disturbed, he directed his question to Millie instead of Tommy. And in his comment he expressed negative evaluation ("What the hell is wrong with him?"). Even if Tommy wanted to talk about his feelings, his father effectively closed the door to any empathetic communication.

Note also that the few comments addressed to Tommy (for example, the father's "You got a girlfriend?" and the mother's "You don't want to come with us, do you?") fail to consider Tommy's *present* feelings. The father's comment is intimidating and seems more a reference to his own macho image than a question about Tommy. The mother's comment is negative and, in effect, asks Tommy not to join them.

But the most damaging part of this interaction occurs when father, mother, and sister not only ignore Tommy's feelings and problems, but each expresses concern for someone else—sister for Jack, father for Joe, and mother for Grandma. Their comments tell Tommy that he is not worth their time and energy but that others are. Even when both the father and mother ignore the put-downs of Tommy's sister (normal as they may be among young children), they reinforce the idea that Tommy is unworthy. In their silence, they communicate agreement.

Act II. The Success

[Tommy enters living room, throws books down on coffee table, and goes to the refrigerator.]

Father (*calling into the kitchen*):
Hey, Tommy, what's up? You look pretty angry.

Tommy: It's nothing. Just school.

Sister: He's just weird, Dad.

Father: You mean "weird" like the mad scientist in the old movies?

Sister: No. You know what I mean—he's different.

Father: Oh, well that's something else. That's great. I'm glad Tommy is different. The world doesn't need another clone and Tommy is certainly no clone. At 12 years old, it's not easy being unique. Right Tommy?

Tommy (*to sister*):
Yeah, unique.

Father (*to mother and daughter*):
Are you still planning to go to the mall?

Sister: Yeah, I have to get a new dress.

Mother: And I need some things at K-Mart. Are you going bowling?

Father: Well, I was planning on it but I thought I might cancel and stay home. Tommy, you got any plans? If not, how about doing something together?

Tommy: No. You want to go bowling.

Father: I can bowl anytime. After all, what's another 200 game? It's hardly a challenge. Come on. How about we take a drive to the lake and take a swim—just the two of us. And I'd like to hear about what's going on in school.

Tommy: Okay, let's go. I need to put on my trunks. You know I can swim four lengths without stopping.

Father: Four lengths? Well, I got to see that. Get those trunks on and we're out of here.

Sister: Mom, let's go-o-o-o.

Mother: Okay. Okay. Okay. But, I have to call Grandma first to see if she's all right.

Father: Let me say hello too.

Mother (*to Tommy and sister*):
You two want to talk to Grandma too?

Sister: Of course. I got to tell her about this great new guy at school.

Mother: Oh, I want to hear about this, too. Well, we'll have plenty of time to talk in the car.

Tommy: Hey Mom, I gotta tell Grandma about my new bike. So let me talk first so Dad and I can get to the lake.

[later, Tommy and Father in car]

Father (*puts arm on Tommy's shoulder*):
School got you down?

Tommy: It's this new teacher. What a pain. I can't understand what he's talking about. Maybe I'm just stupid.

Father: What don't you understand?

Tommy: I don't know. He calls it pregeometry. What's pregeometry?

This interaction is drastically different from the previous one and illustrates three ways you can use to facilitate self-disclosure.

1. Address feelings directly. Notice that Tommy's feelings are addressed immediately and directly by his father.
2. Show concern for the other person and the other person's feelings. The father shows concern for Tommy's feelings by asking him about his feelings and then about school. He shows that he cares for Tommy by defending him. For example, he turns Sally's negative comment into a positive one (from "weird" to "unique") and gives up bowling to be with Tommy. He continues to show caring and concern by putting Tommy first—ahead of his bowling and ahead of his friends, Pete and Joe.

(continued)

(continued)

3. Be supportive rather than evaluative. The father further helps Tommy to disclose by being supportive and nonevaluative. Instead of asking Tommy "What's wrong with you?" he reflects Tommy's feelings, using the information that Tommy has already revealed ("School got you down?"). This is a good example of active listening (see Skills boxes in Chapters 7 and 8).

This dialogue is just an introductory one and merely sets the stage for meaningful self-disclosure. Both Tommy and his father are comfortable and away from any distractions. Tommy knows that his father is interested in him and that he is not going to find fault with him or otherwise give him a hard time. The atmosphere is supportive and nonthreatening.

[The next How To box appears on page 77.]

APPREHENSION

You'll profit most from this discussion if you first take the brief test provided in the "Apprehension Questionnaire." This test measures your apprehension in interpersonal communication situations.

"Apprehension" in interpersonal communication refers to a feeling of fear or anxiety about a situation in which one must communicate. Some people develop negative feelings about communication and therefore expect the worst of themselves when they're called upon to speak. To those who feel high anxiety in such circumstances, it just doesn't seem worthwhile to try. This is not to say that apprehensives are ineffective or unhappy people. Most of them have learned or can learn to deal with their communication anxiety or fear.

"Communication apprehension," researchers note, "is probably the most common handicap . . . suffered by people in contemporary American society" (McCroskey & Wheeless, 1976). According to surveys of college students, between 10 and 20% suffer "severe, debilitating communication apprehension," while another 20% suffer from "communication apprehension to a degree substantial enough to interfere to some extent with their normal functioning."

Apprehensive Behaviors

We can also look at apprehension in more behavioral terms (Richmond & McCroskey, 1996). Generally, we see a decrease in the frequency, strength, and likelihood of engaging in communication transactions. High apprehensives avoid communication situations and, when forced to participate, do so as little as possible. This reluctance to communicate shows itself in a variety of forms. For example, in small group situations, apprehensives will not only talk less but will also avoid the seats of influence, for example, those in the direct line of sight of the group leader. High apprehensives are less likely to be seen as leaders in small group situations regardless of their actual behaviors. Even in classrooms, they avoid seats where they can be easily called on, and they maintain little direct eye contact with the instructor, especially when a question is likely to be asked. Closely related to this is the finding that apprehensives have more negative attitudes toward school, earn poorer grades, and are more likely to drop out of college (McCroskey, Booth-Butterfield, & Payne, 1989).

How would you describe your history of apprehension? That is, has your apprehension changed over your life time? Can you identify specific times when your apprehension seemed to change significantly? (Your experiences with apprehension—your own or someone close to you—would make an interesting personal experience paper.)

SELF-TEST
How Apprehensive Are You?

Instructions: This questionnaire is composed of six statements concerning your feelings about communication with other people. Please indicate in the space provided the degree to which each statement applies to you by marking whether you (1) strongly agree, (2) agree, (3) are undecided, (4) disagree, or (5) strongly disagree with each statement. There are no right or wrong answers. Some of the statements are similar to other statements; do not be concerned about this. Work quickly; record your first impression.

_____ 1. While participating in a conversation with a new acquaintance, I feel very nervous.

_____ 2. I have no fear of speaking up in conversations.

_____ 3. Ordinarily I am very tense and nervous in conversations.

_____ 4. Ordinarily I am very calm and relaxed in conversations.

_____ 5. While conversing with a new acquaintance, I feel very relaxed.

_____ 6. I'm afraid to speak up in conversations.

Scoring: Compute your score as follows:

1. Begin with the number 18; it's just used as a base so that you won't wind up with negative numbers.
2. To 18, add your scores for items 2, 4, and 5.
3. Subtract your scores for items 1, 3, and 6 from your Step 2 total.
4. The result (which should be somewhere between 6 and 30) is your apprehension score for interpersonal conversations. The higher the score, the greater your apprehension. A score above 18 indicates some degree of apprehension.

Source: From *Introduction to Rhetorical Communication,* 7th ed. by James C. McCroskey. Copyright ©1997 by James C. McCroskey. Reprinted by permission of the author.

Apprehensives disclose little and avoid occupations with heavy communication demands (for example, teaching or public relations). Within their occupation, they're less desirous of advancement, largely because with advancement comes an increased need to communicate. High apprehensives are also less satisfied with their jobs, probably because they're less successful in advancing and in developing interpersonal relationships. High apprehensives are even less likely to get job interviews.

Apprehensives also engage more in steady dating, a finding that is not unexpected. One of the most difficult communication situations is asking for a date, especially a first date, and developing a new relationship. Consequently, once a dating relationship has been established, the apprehensive is reluctant to give this up and go through the anxiety of another first date and another get-acquainted period.

Culture and Speaker Apprehension

Interacting with members of cultures different from your own can create uncertainty, fear, and anxiety, all of which contribute to speaker apprehension (Stephan & Stephan, 1985).

When you're speaking with people from cultures very different from your own, you're likely to be more uncertain about the situation and about their possible responses (Gudykunst & Nishida, 1984; Gudykunst, Yang, & Nishida, 1985). When you're sure of the situation and can predict what will

How has your own level of communication apprehension influenced your communications, relationships, and general interactions?

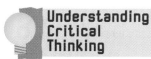

Understanding Critical Thinking

Keep the brain in critical thinking condition. According to Isaac Asimov in *The Brain* (1983; Stine & Benares, 1994), at about 21 years of age the brain begins to lose brain cells. In fact, the average brain loses approximately 10,000 brain cells every day. That comes to 3,650,000 cells per year. But, a normal brain with 200 billion cells will hardly notice the loss. Nevertheless, here are some suggestions for age-proofing yourself: "Keep your job. Don't retire. Ever. Stay physically healthy. Become an expert in something—anything. Take up the piano. Take a course in something. Learn to roll with the punches. Do cross-word puzzles. Go out with friends or find new playmates. Learn French in four years, not four weeks. Turn off the TV. Stock your life with rich experiences of all kinds. Play with toys. Lots of them. Different ones. Skip bingo. Play bridge instead" (White, 1993).

happen, you're more likely to feel comfortable and at ease. But when the situation is uncertain and you cannot predict what will happen, you're likely to become more apprehensive (Gudykunst & Kim, 1992).

Such situations can also engender fear. You might, for example, have a greater fear of saying something that will prove offensive or of revealing your own prejudices. The fear is easily transformed into apprehension.

These situations can also create anxiety. For example, if your prior relationships with members of a culturally different group were few or if they were unpleasant, then you're likely to experience greater anxiety when dealing with these members than if these prior experiences were numerous and positive (Stephan & Stephan, 1985).

Your thoughts and feelings about the other people will also influence your apprehension. For example, if you hold stereotypes and prejudices, or if you feel that you're very different from these other people, then you're likely to experience more apprehension than if you saw them as similar to you.

Managing Communication Apprehension

Although most of us suffer from some communication apprehension, we can successfully manage it and control it at least somewhat. Here are some suggestions (Beatty, 1988; McCroskey, 1982; Richmond & McCroskey, 1996).

Acquire Communication Skills and Experience

If you lack skills in typing, you can hardly expect to type very well. Yet we rarely assume that a lack of interpersonal skills and experience can cause difficulty with communication and create apprehension. It can. If you never asked for a date and had no idea how to do it, it would be natural to feel apprehension in doing so. And, research shows that all [qy] skills will help reduce interfo[qy] interaction and dating anxiety (Allen et al., 1998). In this course you're gaining the skills of effective interpersonal interaction. Engage

"How will you ever know whether you're a flying squirrel if you don't give it a shot?"

in experiences—even if these prove difficult at first—to help you acquire the skills you need most. The more preparation and practice you put into something, the more comfortable you'll feel with it.

Focus on Success

The more you perceive a situation as one in which others will evaluate you, the greater your apprehension will be (Beatty, 1988). Employment interviews and asking for a date, for example, are anxiety-provoking largely because they're highly evaluative. Similarly, your prior history in similar situations influences the way you respond to new ones. Prior success generally (though not always) reduces apprehension. Prior failure generally (though not always) increases apprehension. If you see yourself succeeding, you'll stand a good chance of doing just that. So, think positively. Visualize others giving you positive evaluations. Concentrate your energies on doing the best job you can in any situation you find yourself in. You now have new skills and new experiences, and these will increase your chances for success.

> If you can't get a compliment any other way, pay yourself one.
> —*Mark Twain*

Reduce Unpredictability

The more unpredictable the situation, the greater your apprehension is likely to be. Ambiguous situations and new situations are unpredictable. Therefore, you naturally become anxious. In managing apprehension, therefore, try to reduce any unpredictability. When you're familiar with the situation and with what is expected of you, you're better able to predict what will happen. This will reduce the ambiguity and perceived newness of the situation. So, if you're going to ask the boss for a raise, become familiar with as much of the situation as you can. If possible, sit in the chair you'll sit in; then rehearse your statement of the reasons you deserve the raise and the way in which you'll present them.

Put Apprehension in Perspective

Whenever you engage in a communication experience, remember that the world won't end if you don't succeed. Also, remember that other people are not able to perceive your apprehension as sharply as you do. You may feel a dryness in your throat and a rapid heartbeat; however, no one knows this but you.

How would you go about seeking answers to such questions as these? *(Any one of these would make excellent topics for a research paper.)*

- What is the relationship between self-disclosure and self-awareness? Do people with great self-awareness self-disclose more than do those with little self-awareness?
- Do men and women differ in the topics they self-disclose to their best friends? To their romantic partners?
- Do men and women experience apprehension differently?
- Are there cultural differences in apprehension? In the evaluation of apprehensive people?

Some research suggests that people respond more negatively to those they perceive as apprehensive than to those they perceive as more confident and less fearful (Richmond & McCroskey, 1996). Do you respond more negatively to those you see as apprehensive than to those you see as less fearful? Would you prefer to work with one type rather than the other? Would you prefer to date one type rather than the other?

Understanding Critical Thinking

Critical thinking sometimes needs to be suspended. Sometimes it's important to suspend critical thinking to allow ideas to flow freely, without any analysis and critical scrutiny. A useful way to learn to suspend critical thinking is to practice brainstorming, a technique for generating ideas. After selecting a problem, you storm your problem with as many ideas as you can think of following these four rules:
• Don't criticize; suspend evaluations until you're finished brainstorming.
• Strive for quantity; the more ideas the better.
• Combine and extend ideas.
• Develop the wildest ideas possible. It's easier to tone an idea down than to build it up.
   Try brainstorming—alone or in a group—with one of these topics or one of your own: *What makes a great life-partner? How can communication between healthcare workers and patients be improved? How can we promote greater intercultural understanding?* After you've generated as many ideas as you can—in, say, 5 or 10 minutes—then think about them critically.

Empowering Apprehensives

At the same time that you want to manage and perhaps lessen your own apprehension, consider the values and means of empowering others to manage and better control their apprehension. Here are some suggestions based largely on the insights of apprehension researchers (Carducci & Zimbardo, 1996; McCroskey, 1996).

• Don't overprotect the shy person, especially the shy child, but don't push her or him to communicate either. If you constantly rush to the child's aid every time he or she experiences social anxiety, the child will never learn how to cope with it. At the same time, if you push them to communicate, you may push them into situations that will only worsen their anxiety. Instead, be supportive (indirectly). Nudge, instead of push, the child (or the adult) to try out new communication situations. But, don't make decisions for them; apprehensives can communicate if they have to or if they have an extreme desire to do so.

• Demonstrate your understanding and empathy for the other person's fear of communicating but don't assume that the communication apprehensive wants to be like you. Most communication apprehensives are quite happy as they are and don't want to be different. At the same time, don't minimize their fear of communication situations, something those with little apprehension often do. Practice active listening, should you sense they wish to discuss their communication anxiety.

• Help the shy person develop self-confidence. Often apprehensives lack self-confidence and may feel inadequate in social situations. Expressing positiveness may help. But don't assume that you can "cure" their apprehension.

• In social gatherings with shy people make sure that you don't monopolize the conversation and that you give the shy people opportunities to speak; ask their opinions, for example. With a child, consider enrolling him or her in preschool to give the child opportunities to learn to communicate with peers before entering regular school. Consider making

SKILL BUILDING EXERCISE 2.3

Using Performance Visualization to Reduce Apprehension

Performance visualization is a technique designed specifically to reduce the outward manifestations of speaker apprehension and also to reduce negative thinking (Ayres & Hopf, 1993, 1995). Try reducing your own communication apprehension by following these two simple suggestions.

1. The first part of performance visualization is to develop a positive attitude and a positive self-perception. So, visualize yourself in the role of being an effective speaker. Visualize yourself communicating as a fully and totally confident individual. Look at your listeners and speak. Throughout your conversation see yourself as fully in control of the situation. See your listeners in rapt attention from the time you begin to the time you stop. Throughout this visualization, avoid all negative thoughts. As you visualize yourself an effective speaker, take special note of how you walk, look at your listeners, respond to questions, and especially how you feel about the whole experience.

2. The second part of performance visualization is designed to help you model your performance on that of an especially effective speaker. So, view a particularly competent speaker and make a mental movie of it. Try selecting one on video so you can replay it several times. As you review the actual and mental movie, begin to shift yourself into the role of speaker. Become this effective speaker.

Thinking Critically About Reducing Apprehension   If you went through these two steps, how did you feel? What other suggestions might you add to help reduce negative thinking? What other techniques might help reduce communication apprehension?

---

professional assistance available for helping those who want to reduce their apprehension.

- When appropriate, try to steer the conversation in the direction of the shy person's expertise and area of competence. Another useful aid is to provide alternatives for the communication apprehensive (other than talking) for them to demonstrate their competence.
- Avoid making a shy person the center of attention. That is exactly what they do not want. And never make their fear of communicating the topic of a group conversation. Saying, "Oh Jane; she's so bright but she never talks" only makes it more difficult for Jane to even open her mouth

SUMMARY OF CONCEPTS AND SKILLS

In this chapter we explored the self in interpersonal communication. We looked at the four selves and how to increase self-awareness. Next we looked at self-disclosure, the process of revealing ourselves to others, and some of its advantages and disadvantages. We then explored apprehension, what causes it and how it can be managed effectively.

1. The self-concept is the image that you have of yourself and is developed from the images of you that others have and that they reveal to you, the comparisons you make between yourself and others, and the way you interpret and evaluate your own thoughts and behaviors.

2. The four selves are the open self (what we and others know about us), the blind self (what others know but we do not know), the hidden self (what we know but keep hidden from others), and the unknown self (what neither we nor others know).

3. We may increase self-awareness by asking ourselves about ourselves, listening to others, actively seeking information about ourselves, seeing ourselves from different perspectives, and increasing our open selves.

4. Self-disclosure is a type of communication in which we reveal information about ourselves to others.
5. Self-disclosure is generally reciprocal; the self-disclosures of one person stimulate the self-disclosures of the other person.
6. Both men and women avoid self-disclosure for fearing to project a negative image. Men also avoid self-disclosure so they can maintain control. Women also avoid self-disclosure to avoid personal hurt and to create problems for the relationship.
7. Through self-disclosure you may gain self-knowledge, increase communication effectiveness, enhance the meaningfulness of your interpersonal relationships, and promote physical health.
8. There are also serious dangers in self-disclosing. Your interpersonal, social, and business relationships may be severely damaged if your self-disclosures are not positively received.
9. Communication apprehension refers to a feeling of fear or anxiety about communication situations.
10. Persons with high apprehension behave differently from persons with low apprehension. High apprehensives communicate less and avoid situations and occupations that demand lots of communication. High apprehensives are less likely to be seen as leaders, have more negative attitudes toward school, and are more likely to drop out of college. High apprehensives are also less satisfied with their jobs and engage more in steady dating.
11. Techniques for managing communication apprehension include acquiring communication skills and experience, focusing on success, reducing unpredictability, and being familiar with the situation.

Check your ability to apply these skills. You'll gain most from this brief experience if you think carefully about each skill and try to identify instances from your recent communications in which you did or did not act on the basis of the specific skill. Use a rating scale such as the following: 1 = almost always, 2 = often, 3 = sometimes, 4 = rarely, and 5 = almost never.

_____ 1. Analyze your own self-concept and seek to discover the sources that influenced it.
_____ 2. Become aware of your own communication patterns, especially as these relate to self-disclosing messages.
_____ 3. Engage in activities that increase self-awareness.
_____ 4. Regulate self-disclosures on the basis of the topic, listener, purposes, and so on.
_____ 5. Critically weigh the potential rewards and costs of self-disclosure before disclosing.
_____ 6. Self-disclose appropriately.
_____ 7. Respond to the self-disclosures of others as appropriate.
_____ 8. Manage the fear of communicating in interpersonal situations.
_____ 9. Communicate in interpersonal encounters with confidence.

VOCABULARY QUIZ. THE LANGUAGE OF THE SELF

Match the terms listed here with their definitions. Record the number of the definition next to the name of the concept.

_____ Johari model

_____ the open self

_____ the blind self

_____ the hidden self

_____ the unknown self

_____ self-awareness

_____ self-disclosure

_____ the dyadic effect

_____ communication apprehension

_____ gender and culture

1. Fear or anxiety over communicating.
2. The part of the self that contains information about the self that is known to others but unknown to oneself.
3. The tendency for the behaviors of one person to stimulate behaviors in the other person, usually used to refer to the tendency of one person's self-disclosures to stimulate the listener to self-disclose, also.
4. The part of the self that contains information about the self that is known to oneself and to others.
5. The part of the self that contains information about the self known to oneself but unknown to (hidden from) others.
6. A diagram of the four selves.
7. A knowledge of oneself.
8. The process of revealing something significant about ourselves to another individual or to a group, something that would not normally be known by them.
9. The part of the self that contains information about the self that is unknown to oneself and to others.
10. Two of the factors that influence self-disclosure.

Perception in Interpersonal Communication

CHAPTER TOPICS	LEARNING OBJECTIVES	SKILL OBJECTIVES
	After completing this chapter, you should be able to	*After completing this chapter, you should be able to*
Interpersonal Perception	1. Explain what perception is and how it works	Perceive others with the recognition that you're a major part of your own perceptions
Interpersonal Perception Principles	2. Define the processes that influence perception (*primacy and recency, the self-fulfilling prophecy, implicit personality theory, stereotyping,* and *attribution*) and the barriers to accurate perception that each of these can create	Perceive others while avoiding such common barriers as seeing what you want or expect to see, fulfilling your own predictions, and seeing an individual primarily as a member of a group, mindreading, and the self-serving bias
Increasing Accuracy in Perception	3. Identify the strategies for increasing accuracy in interpersonal perception	Use the strategies for increasing your accuracy in interpersonal perception

In a small compartment on a train, there were four people: an American grandmother with her attractive young granddaughter, a Mr. Wonderful, and an evil Martian officer. As the train passed through a dark tunnel, the lights went out and all that was heard was a loud kiss and an even louder slap. No one spoke. But as the train emerged from the tunnel and the lights went back on, the grandmother thought: Well, I'm glad that my granddaughter didn't allow anyone to kiss her without slapping his face. And the granddaughter thought: Isn't it peculiar that one of these men would kiss grandmother. It's even stranger that she would slap him so hard without saying anything." And the evil Martian officer thought: This Mr. Wonderful sure is clever. He kisses the girl and the other guy gets slapped. And Mr. Wonderful thought: What a clever fellow I am. I make a kissing noise and get a chance to slap the evil Martian.

Evaluating Information

Recognize your role in perception. Recognize that your own physiological and psychological states will influence what your senses pick up and the meaning you give to your perceptions. The sight of raw clams may be physically upsetting when you have a stomach ache but mouth-watering when you're hungry. Psychologically, your own biases and stereotypes will influence what you perceive, for example, seeing only the positive in people you like and only the negative in people you do not like.

This story, adapted from one told by Alfred Korzybski, the founder of the approach to language known as General Semantics, illustrates that each person perceives the world differently and often in very distorted ways. This chapter focuses on perception, its stages and principles, and the techniques for making it more accurate.

INTERPERSONAL PERCEPTION

Perception is the process by which you become aware of, organize, and interpret the many stimuli bombarding your senses. **Interpersonal** or **people perception** concerns your sensing, organizing, and interpreting-evaluating information about people and their messages.

Perception is complex. There is no one-to-one relationship between the messages that occur "out there" in the world and the messages that eventually get to your brain. Perception takes place in three stages that flow into one another and overlap: sensation, organization, and interpretation-evaluation. These stages are not separate; they're continuous and blend into and overlap one another (see Figure 3.1).

Sensing

At this first stage you sense the stimuli; one or more of your five senses responds to a stimulus. You **hear** a new Michael Jackson recording. You **see** an old buddy from your Army days. You **smell** perfume on the person sitting next to you on the bus. You **taste** chocolate ice cream. You **feel** a sweaty palm as you shake hands with a new employee. That is, you take in information through your five senses.

Naturally, you don't perceive everything; rather, you engage in *selective perception*. For example, when you're daydreaming in class, you don't hear what the instructor is saying until your own name is called. Then you wake up. You know the teacher called your name, but you don't know why. This is a clear example of the principle that you perceive what is meaningful to you and do not perceive what is not meaningful. From among all the stimuli bombarding our senses, we select and attend only to those that meet our immediate needs.

In addition to meaningfulness, you're more likely to perceive stimuli that are greater in *intensity* than surrounding stimuli and stimuli that have *novelty* value (Lahey, 1989). For example, television commercials normally play at a greater intensity than regular programming to ensure that you'll take special notice of them. You're also more likely to notice the student who dresses in a novel way rather than the one who dresses like everyone else. For example, you'll quickly perceive the student who shows up to class in a tuxedo or to a formal party in shorts.

An obvious implication here is that what you do perceive is only a very small portion of what you could perceive. Much as you have limits on how far you can see, you also have limits on the amount of stimulation that you can take in at any given time. A major goal of education and of critical thinking is to train us to perceive and make sense of what exists, whether it be art, politics, music, communication, social problems, or any other source of sensory stimulation.

Organizing

At the second stage, you organize the stimulations. One frequently used principle is *proximity* or physical closeness. You perceive things that are physically close together as a unit. For example, you would perceive people who are often together, or messages spoken one immediately after the other, as units. You also assume that the verbal and nonverbal signals sent at about the same time are related and constitute a unified whole (*temporal* principle).

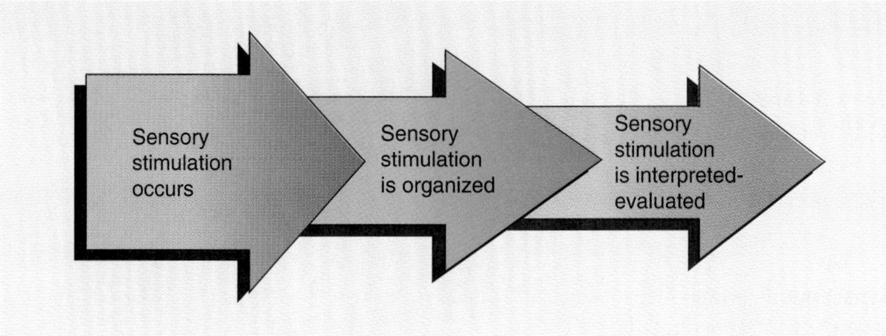

Has "selective perception" ever created problems for you? Do you engage in selective perception when listening to people talk about you? For example, are you more likely to attend to the positives than the negatives? Can you see this tendency in the behaviors of your friends? *(This would make an interesting personal experience paper.)*

Figure 3.1
The Perception Process.

This diagram identifies the three stages in the process of perception. It also illustrates that each stage overlaps with the next one and that the perception process moves from the general to the more specific. How would you illustrate the process of perception?

Sensory stimulation occurs

Sensory stimulation is organized

Sensory stimulation is interpreted-evaluated

Another principle is *similarity.* You perceive things that are physically similar, things that look alike, as belonging together. Thus, for example, you'd perceive as belonging together things that are similar in color, size, or shape. This principle of similarity would lead you to see people who dress alike as belonging together. You might assume that people who work at the same jobs, who attend the same church, or who live in the same building belong together.

You use the principle of *contrast* when you note that some items (people or messages, for example) don't belong together; they're too different from each other to be part of the same perceptual organization. So, for example, in a conversation or a public speech listeners will focus their attention on changes in intensity or rate since these contrast with the rest of the message.

Another principle is *closure:* You perceive a message that is actually incomplete as a complete whole. For example, you see someone gesturing angrily, but can't quite make out the words. So, you assume that the verbal message is an expression of anger. You may even fill in specific words on the basis of the words you do hear.

Be aware, of course, that these principles will not yield information that is *necessarily* true. The information provided by these principles should serve only as hypotheses or possibilities that need to be investigated further, not as conclusions that are necessarily true.

Interpreting-Evaluating

The third stage in the perceptual process is *interpretation-evaluation.* We hyphenate these terms to emphasize that they're interrelated. This third stage is a highly subjective process.

It is with our judgments as with our watches; no two go just alike, yet each believes his own.
—*Alexander Pope*

What cues do you look for when judging other people after first meeting them?

WHAT DO YOU LIKE IN A MAN?

©1991 Stivers

Mark Stivers

Try creating a cartoon comparable to this one but titled "What I like in a friend (or lover)?" or "What I dislike in a friend (or lover)?"

In interpersonal perception there is much room for disagreement. Although we may all sense the same external stimulus, we will each interpret-evaluate it differently. For example, two people may both hear the sound of a popular rock group. Your friend, Danny, who plays the violin, may judge it as terrible noise, while to Alex it may sound like great music. The sight of someone we have not seen for years (a former husband or wife, for example) may bring joy to one person and anxiety to another. A sweaty palm may be perceived by one person to mean nervousness and by another to mean excitement. The accompanying cartoon, "What do you like in a man?" provides a humorous slant on the inevitable differences in interpretation and evaluation.

How would you describe the stages you go through in making sense out of the stimuli "out there" in the world? Does the three-part model presented here (sensation, organization, evaluation) adequately describe the process? What else would you add?

SKILL BUILDING EXERCISE 3.1
Perceiving My Selves

The purpose of this exercise is to explore how you perceive yourself and how you think others perceive you and the reasons for any differences in the two perceptions. In some instances and for some people, these two perceptions will be the same; in most cases and for most people, however, they'll be different.

Following this brief introduction are nine lists of items (animals, birds, colors, communications media, dogs, drinks, music, transportation, and sports). Read over each list carefully, trying to look past the purely physical characteristics of the objects to their "personalities" or "psychological meanings."

1. For each of the nine lists, indicate the one item that best represents how you perceive yourself—not your physical self, but your psychological and philosophical self. Mark these items MM (Myself to Me).

2. In each of the nine lists, select the one item that best represents how you feel others perceive you. Think of "others" as acquaintances—neither passing strangers nor close friends, but people you meet and talk with for some time—for example, people in this class. Mark these items MO (Myself to Others).

(continued)

(continued)

Thinking Critically About Self-Perception.   After all nine lists are marked for both MMs and MOs, consider the differences either alone or with a group of five or six others. Your objective is to get a better perspective on how your self-perception compares with the perception of you by others. Consider why you selected the items you did and specifically what each selected item means to you at this time. If you are doing this in a group, ask others why they see you as they do. Also, welcome suggestions from group members as to why they think you selected the items you did. You might also wish to integrate consideration of some or all of the following questions into your thinking and discussion:

• How different are the items marked MM from those marked MO? Why do you suppose this is so? Which is the more positive? Why?
• If discussing this in a group, consider how accurate you were in the items you marked MO. Do members of the group see you as you think they do? If not, why not?
• Would you show these forms to your best same-sex friend? Your best opposite-sex friend? Your parents? Your children?

Animals

_____ bear
_____ deer
_____ dinosaur
_____ fox
_____ lion
_____ monkey
_____ rabbit
_____ turtle

Birds

_____ chicken
_____ eagle
_____ ostrich
_____ owl
_____ parrot
_____ swan
_____ turkey
_____ vulture

Colors

_____ black
_____ blue
_____ gray
_____ pink
_____ puce
_____ red
_____ white
_____ yellow

Communications Media

_____ book
_____ e-mail
_____ film
_____ fourth-class mail
_____ radio
_____ special delivery
_____ telephone
_____ television

Dogs

_____ boxer
_____ Doberman
_____ greyhound
_____ husky
_____ mutt
_____ pit bull
_____ poodle
_____ St. Bernard

Drinks

_____ beer
_____ champagne
_____ hot chocolate
_____ milk
_____ prune juice
_____ Scotch
_____ water
_____ wine

Sports

_____ auto racing
_____ baseball
_____ boxing
_____ bullfighting
_____ chess
_____ figure skating
_____ tennis
_____ wrestling

Transportation

_____ bicycle
_____ 18-wheeler
_____ horse and wagon
_____ jet plane
_____ motorcycle
_____ Rolls Royce
_____ trailer
_____ yacht

Music

_____ country-western
_____ folk
_____ jazz
_____ opera
_____ popular
_____ rap
_____ rock
_____ rhythm and blues

LISTENING
Listening to Other Perspectives

"Galileo and the Ghosts" is a technique for seeing a problem or person or situation through the eyes of a particular group of people (DeVito, 1996). It involves setting up a mental "ghost-thinking team," much like executives and politicians hire ghostwriters to write their speeches or corporations and research institutes maintain think tanks. In this ghost-thinking technique, you select a team of four to eight "people" you admire, for example, historical figures like Aristotle or Picasso, fictional figures like Wonder Woman or Captain Picard, or persons from other cultures or of a different sex or affectional orientation.

You pose a question or problem and then ask yourself how this team of ghosts would answer your question or solve your problem, allowing yourself to listen to what they have to say. Of course, you're really listening to yourself but yourself acting in the role of another person. The technique forces you to step outside your normal role and to consider the perspective of someone totally different from you. If you wish, visualize yourself and your ghost-thinking team seated around a conference table, in a restaurant having lunch, or even jogging in the park. Choose the team members and the settings in any way you would like. Use whatever works for you and change it any time you want.

Your ghost team analyzes your problem with perspectives different from your own. In the ghost-thinking technique each team member views your problem from his or her unique perspective. As a result, your perception of the problem will change. Your team members then view this new perception and perhaps analyze it again. As a result, your perception of the problem changes again. The process continues until you achieve a solution or decide that this technique has yielded all the insight its going to yield.

In interpersonal communication and relationships, this technique might be used to see an issue or problem from the point of view of your romantic partner, parent, or child. In a small group setting, it might help you to see an issue from management or the employees' points of view. And in public speaking, it could help you visualize your task from the perspective of different audiences.

Try creating your own think tank, your own ghost-thinking team. Share your selections with others and then, if you wish, trade team members with others from your class to revise your team. Limiting your team to four to eight people will keep it more manageable. Once you have your ghost team in place, try asking their advice on such questions as these: How can I become a more responsive relationship partner? How can I become less apprehensive in formal communication situations such as interviewing or public speaking? How can I increase my assertive communication?

[The next Listening box appears on page 93.]

INTERPERSONAL PERCEPTION PRINCIPLES

Before beginning this section, take the perception test presented below. This test asks you to assess your own tendencies in perceiving people.

SELF-TEST
How Accurate Are You at People Perception?

Instructions: Respond to each of the following statements with TRUE if the statement is usually or generally accurate in describing your behavior and FALSE if the statement is usually or generally inaccurate in describing your behavior. Try to avoid the tendency to give what you feel is the desirable answer; just be truthful.

_____ 1. I base most of my impressions of people on the first few minutes of our meeting.

_____ 2. When I know some things about another person I can fill in what I don't know.

_____ 3. I make predictions about people's behaviors which generally prove to be true.

(continued)

(continued)

_____ 4. I have clear ideas of what people of different national, racial, and religious groups are really like.

_____ 5. I generally attribute a person's attitudes and behaviors to their most obvious physical or psychological characteristic.

_____ 6. I avoid making assumptions about what is going on in someone else's head on the basis of his or her behavior.

_____ 7. I pay special attention to the behavior of people that might contradict my initial impressions.

_____ 8. On the basis of my observations of people, I formulate guesses (that I am willing to revise) about them rather than make firmly held conclusions.

_____ 9. I reserve making judgments about people until I learn a great deal about them and see them in a variety of situations.

_____ 10. After I formulate an initial impression I check my perceptions by, for example, asking questions or by gathering more evidence.

Thinking Critically About Interpersonal Perception This brief test was designed to raise issues about your perceptual tendencies. As you read the remainder of this self-test and chapter ask yourself how the concepts and principles discussed here relate to your own perceptual patterns and how you might make them more effective and accurate. The first five questions refer to your tendencies to make judgments of others on the basis of (1) first impressions, (2) implicit personality theories, (3) self-fulfilling prophecies, (4) stereotypes, and (5) attribution. Ideally you would have answered FALSE to these five questions. These processes are covered in the discussion of Interpersonal (People) Perception.

Questions 6 through 10 refer to specific guidelines for increasing accuracy in people perception: (6) avoiding mindreading, (7) being alert to contradictory cues, (8) formulating hypotheses rather than conclusions, (9) delaying conclusions until more evidence is in, and (10) checking your perceptions. Ideally you would have answered TRUE to these five questions. These suggestions for increasing accuracy in people perception are covered in the Critical Thinking sidebars and in the final section, Increasing Accuracy in Perception.

Five processes influence interpersonal perception (Cook, 1984; Fiske & Taylor, 1984; Kleinke, 1986). These processes influence the judgments you make about other people and they influence the accuracy of your judgments about them. The five processes are: first impressions, implicit personality theories, self-fulfilling prophecies, stereotypes, and attribution.

First Impressions: Primacy and Recency

Assume that you have watched a miniseries on television in which half the episodes were extremely dull and half were extremely exciting. At the end of the season you evaluate the series. Would your evaluation be more favorable if the dull episodes came first (and the exciting episodes came last) or if the exciting episodes came first (and the dull episodes came last)? If what comes first exerts more influence, we have a *primacy effect*. If what comes last (or is the most recent) exerts more influence, we have a *recency effect*.

CAUTION

Can you identify a specific instance where your thinking was distorted by your **being unduly influenced by primacy or recency?**

Beware of First Impressions: Barriers to Accurate Perception

First impressions are inevitable. People will always draw conclusions about a new acquaintance, for example, merely on the basis of what he or she looks like

How would you describe the first impression that people form of you? What specific cues do you communicate to give these impressions?

Evaluating Information

Examine your assumptions. This is a puzzle you've probably seen many times, but it helps illustrate an important principle. The objective is to connect all 9 dots with 4 straight continuous lines; there can be no breaks between your 4 lines. Try it for a few minutes before reading on.

If you had difficulty solving this "simple" problem, you probably added the restriction that the dots represented a square and that your lines could not extend beyond this square. With this assumption, the problem becomes impossible to solve. But, once you abandon this assumption, the problem becomes simple. This puzzle further illustrates the need to become aware of your assumptions and to discard those that get in the way of critical thinking.

or dresses like, or does in a single evening. Further, first impressions have a way of establishing a filter through which later information is sifted. For example, if the new teacher in your son's daycare center seems particularly nervous the first day on the job, you may always think of this teacher as a nervous person from that day on. At the same time, we prevent information that is inconsistent with our initial perception from getting through. After being on the job a week, the teacher may be much calmer, but you might not notice it because you're relying on this first impression of a nervous, ill-at-ease teacher.

Implicit Personality Theories

Each of us has a subconscious or implicit system of rules that tells us which characteristics of an individual go with other characteristics. Consider, for example, the following brief statements. Note the characteristic in parentheses that best seems to complete the sentence.

Pablo is energetic, eager, and (intelligent, stupid).
Leonid is bright, lively, and (thin, fat).
Jim is handsome, tall, and (flabby, muscular).
Elena is attractive, intelligent, and (likable, unlikable).
Jenny is bold, defiant, and (extroverted, introverted).
Midori is cheerful, positive, and (attractive, unattractive).

It's not important which words you selected. There are no right or wrong answers. However, certain words probably "seemed right" and others "seemed wrong." Why did some seem right? Why did others seem wrong? Probably, it was your implicit personality theory, the system of rules that tells you what characteristics go with other characteristics. Your theory may tell you, for instance, that a person who is energetic and eager is also intelligent rather than stupid. There is, of course, no logical reason why a stupid person could not be energetic and eager.

Visit a "lifestyle" Website, for example, www.afronet.com/ (people of color), http://www.asiaconnect.com.my/ (Asian community), http://www.planetout.com (gays and lesbians), http://www.latino.net (all-Spanish), http://www.bizwomen.com (executive women). What can you learn about perception from such Websites? *(An interesting review paper could center on the Websites for a particular group of people and their potential value in interpersonal communication.)*

Evaluating Information

Beware of halos. If you believe an individual has several positive qualities, you may see the person as having a "halo" and are more likely to conclude that she or he has other positive qualities (the "halo effect"). The "reverse halo effect" operates similarly; if you know a person has several negative qualities, you're more likely to conclude that the person also has other negative qualities. Both of these effects will distort your perceptions, will lead you to see what may not be there. So, beware of halos—whether positive or negative.

How might **seeing others through implicit personality theories** short circuit your thinking processes and force you to rely on (often) unexamined assumptions? Do you have implicit personality theories that you've never critically examined?

As you might expect, the implicit personality theories that people hold differ from culture to culture, group to group, and even person to person. For example, the Chinese have a concept called *shi gu* which refers to "someone who is worldly, devoted to his or her family, socially skillful, and somewhat reserved" (Aronson, Wilson, & Akert, 1994, p. 190). This concept is not easily encoded in English, as you can tell by trying to find a general concept that covers this type of person. In English, on the other hand, we have a concept of the "artistic type," a generalization which seems absent in Chinese. Thus, although it's easy for speakers of English or Chinese to refer to specific concepts—such as socially skilled or creative—each language creates its own generalized categories. Thus, in Chinese the qualities that make up *shi gu* are more easily seen as going together than they might be for an English speaker; they're part of the implicit personality theory of more Chinese speakers than English speakers.

Similarly, consider the different personality theories that "graduate students" and "blue collar high school dropouts" might have for "college students." Likewise, an individual may have had great experiences with doctors, and so may have a very positive personality theory of doctors, whereas another person may have had negative experiences with doctors, and might thus have developed a very negative personality theory.

Beware of Implicit Theories: Barriers to Accurate Perception

Theories about personality characteristics that go with other characteristics can lead you to draw inaccurate conclusions. For example, some energetic and eager people are stupid. Some bold and defiant people are shy. Become aware of your implicit theories of personality. You will then see each person as that person really is and not as your theory tells you that person should be. To internalize this notion, focus on yourself and identify the ways in which you would violate the implicit personality theories of others.

Self-Fulfilling Prophecies

Prophecies, predictions about what will or will not happen in the future, are all around us: Stocks will go up, bonds will go down. Job opportunities in technology and communication will grow. Women will break through the glass ceiling in the next several years. A special type of prophecy is the *self-fulfilling prophecy* (Rosenthal & Rubin, 1978; Dusek, Hall, & Neger, 1984). It occurs when you make a prediction that comes true *because* you made the prediction and *because* you acted as if it were true. People give subtle cues or hints about how they expect the other person to act, and the person begins to act accordingly. The four basic steps in the self-fulfilling prophecy should clarify this important concept and its implications for interpersonal perception.

1. You make a prediction or formulate a belief about a person or a situation. (For example, you predict that Anna is awkward in interpersonal situations.)
2. You act toward that person as if the prediction or belief is true. (For example, you act toward Anna as if Anna were awkward.)
3. Because you act as if the belief is true, it becomes true. (For example, because of the ways in which you act toward Anna, Anna becomes tense and acts awkwardly.)
4. You observe *your* effect on the person or the resulting situation and what you see strengthens your beliefs. (For example, you observe Anna's awkwardness and this reinforces your belief that Anna is in fact awkward.)

In one study, for example, high school teachers had made the prophecy that boys are more assertive and talked more in class than girls. The teachers then behaved as if this prophecy were true and actually encouraged boys to talk more than girls (Sadker & Sadker, 1985).

If you expect people to act a certain way, your predictions will frequently come true because of the self-fulfilling prophecy phenomenon. Consider, for example, what would happen if you were to go on a blind date predicting that your date will be boring. If the date does prove a disaster, you may have made it so. You may have acted in a way that encouraged your date to behave as a boring person by, say, doing all the talking yourself. You then perceive your date as boring because he or she doesn't talk. You thus fulfill your own prophecy.

Beware of Self-Fulfilling Prophecies: Barriers to Accurate Perception

Prophecies are inevitable. The problem occurs when you act as if the prediction is true and, by your behaviors, make the prediction come true. For example, a problem occurs when you act toward your new supervisor as if she is lacking in useful information. Therefore you don't try very hard to listen to what your supervisor says and you mentally argue with her. You don't maintain customary eye contact. You don't go to her for suggestions. As a result of your behavior, she doesn't communicate anything of value to you. Meanwhile, based on your behavior, your supervisor has been making prophecies about you.

Become aware of your predictions. Notice the ways in which your own behaviors may contribute to making predictions come true.

A widely known example of the self-fulfilling prophecy is the Pygmalion effect. In one study, for example, teachers were told that certain pupils—whose names were actually selected at random—were expected to do exceptionally well, that they were late bloomers. At the end of the term, these students actually performed at a higher level than the others (Rosenthal & Jacobson, 1968; Insel & Jacobson, 1975). The teachers' expectations probably generated extra attention to the students, thereby positively affecting their performance. Has someone's predictions about you ever influenced you? *(Your experience with the self-fulfilling prophecy would make an interesting personal experience paper.)*

CAUTION

How might **making and fulfilling prophecies** distort your thinking? How can it make you see what you expect to see instead of what really is? Have you ever had such an experience?

Of course, you also make predictions about yourself; you predict that you'll do poorly in an examination and so you don't read the questions carefully and don't make any great effort to organize your thoughts or support your statements. Or, you make the prediction that people don't like you and so you don't extend yourself to others. You can also make positive predictions about yourself and these too will influence your behavior. For example, you can assume that others will like you and so you approach them with a positive attitude and demeanor. Generally, how do your predictions influence your achieving your personal and professional goals?

Acquiring Information

Look for a variety of cues. In making a judgment about, say, a place to work, you'd use a variety of cues—salary, opportunity for advancement, benefits package, and the working environment, for example. After examining these cues, you'd make a judgment about the suitability of this job. In a similar way, it's useful to use a variety of cues when making a judgment about a person.

Stereotypes

Stereotyping is a commonly used shortcut in people perception. Originally, "stereotype" was a printing term that referred to the plate that printed the same image repeatedly. A sociological or psychological stereotype, then, is a fixed impression of a group of people. Most people have stereotypes based on race, nationality, religion, affectional orientation, socioeconomic class, age, or occupation.

Because of these stereotypes, you may perceive a person primarily as having the characteristics of a group rather than as a unique individual. If you meet a homeless person, for example, you might apply the stereotypical characteristics for homeless people (for example, uneducated, dirty, having no family or a family that doesn't care) to this homeless individual. And so, without other information, you assume that any homeless person you might meet would have these characteristics. You see these characteristics whether they're present or not. Further, you may not see characteristics that may be present (for example, the homeless person's political activism or deep religious beliefs) but contradict these stereotypes.

Stereotypes pose especially powerful barriers in intercultural communication. The reason is simple: Our stereotypes of groups to which we do not belong—for example, other racial, national, or religious groups—are likely to be more inaccurate and negative than the stereotypes of groups to which we ourselves belong (Gudykunst, 1991).

Stereotypes distort your ability to perceive people accurately. They prevent you from seeing an individual as an individual. Conversely, sometimes others see you only as a member of the group to which they assign you and they overlook your own individuality.

Beware of Stereotyping: Barriers to Accurate Perception

When you stereotype a person and put that person into a group, you no longer perceive that person as an individual. Instead, you see the person as one of "them." "Them" may be a national, racial, or religious group. "Them" may be a social class (the rich, the poor, the street people). "Them" may be an occupational group (college teachers, waiters, actors). When you stereotype an individual, you prevent yourself from seeing this person's uniqueness.

Don't allow stereotypes to prevent you from seeing the individual, the person who is unlike every other person in the world, just like you're unlike every other person. After all, you aren't like every other person of your religion or nationality or race. In the same way, neither are others.

CAUTION

Think critically about your own **stereotyping.** Do you maintain stereotypes? How much evidence do you have that this stereotype effectively covers individual members of the group you're likely to meet?

Attribution

Attribution is a process by which we try to explain the motivation for a person's behavior. Perhaps the major way we do this is to ask if the person is in control of the behavior. If people are in control of their own behaviors, then we feel justified in praising them for positive behaviors and blaming them for negative behaviors. You probably make similar judgments based on controllability in many situations. Consider, for example, how you would respond to such situations such as Doris failing her history exam or Sidney's car being repossessed because he failed to keep up the payments.

Very likely you would be sympathetic to Doris and Sidney if you felt that they were *not* in control of what happened, for example, if the examination was unfair or if Sidney couldn't make his car payments since he lost his job

What stereotypes, if any, would your family or friends have of the people depicted in this photograph? What stereotypes, if any, do you have?

because of discrimination. On the other hand, you would probably not be sympathetic or might blame these people for their problems if you felt that they were in control of what happened, for example, if Doris partied instead of studying and if Sidney gambled his payments away.

Generally, research shows that if we feel people are in control of negative behaviors, we will come to dislike them. If we feel people are not in control of negative behaviors, we will come to feel sorry for them and not blame them for their negative circumstances.

The major problems with attribution and how to avoid them are covered in the following skills box.

CAUTION

Have you ever misevaluated a situation because your were **thinking through the self-serving bias?**

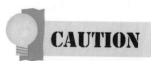

CAUTION

Has **thinking under the influence of the fundamental attribution error** ever led you to develop erroneous conclusions?

HOW TO ...
Avoid Attribution Errors

Three major attribution problems can interfere with accuracy in perception. The **self-serving bias** operates when you evaluate your own behaviors and take credit for the positive and deny responsibility for the negative. Thus, you're more likely to attribute your own negative behaviors to uncontrollable factors. For example, after getting a D on an exam, you're more likely to attribute it to the difficulty or unfairness of the text. However, you're likely to attribute your positive behaviors to controllable factors, to your own strength or intelligence or personality. For example, after getting an A on an exam, you're more likely to attribute it to your ability or hard

work (Bernstein, Stephan, & Avis, 1979). So, this self-serving bias may distort your attributions. To prevent this, consider the potential influences of both internal and external factors on both positive and negative behaviors. Ask yourself to what extent your negative behaviors may be due to internal (controllable) factors and your positive behaviors to external (uncontrollable) factors. Just asking the question will prevent you from mindlessly falling into the self-serving bias.

The second problem is **overattribution.** This is the tendency to single out one or two obvious characteristics of a person and attribute everything that person

(continued)

(continued)

does to these one or two characteristics. For example, if the person had alcoholic parents or is blind or was born into great wealth, there is often a tendency to attribute everything that person does to such factors. And so we say, Sally has difficulty forming meaningful relationships because she grew up in a home of alcoholics, Alex overeats because he's blind, and Lillian is irresponsible because she never had to work for her money. To prevent overattribution, recognize that most behaviors and personality characteristics result from a lot of factors. Realize that you almost always make a mistake when you select one factor and attribute everything to it. So, when you make a judgment, ask yourself if other factors might be operating here. Are there other factors that might be creating difficulties for Sally to form relationships, for Alex to control his eating habits, and for Lillian to behave responsibly?

A third problem is called the **fundamental attribution error,** the tendency to conclude that people do what they do because that's the kind of people they are, not because of the situation they are in. When Pat is late for an appointment, you're more likely to conclude that Pat is inconsiderate or irresponsible or a "scatterbrain" rather than attribute the lateness to the bus breaking down or to a traffic accident. When you commit the fundamental attribution error you overvalue the contribution of internal factors and undervalue the influence of external factors. To prevent making this error, ask yourself if you're giving undue emphasis to internal factors. Ask yourself what external factors might have accounted for another's behavior.

When you explain your own behavior you also favor internal explanations, although to a lesser extent than when explaining the behaviors of others. In one study, for example, managers who evaluated their own performance and that of their subordinates used more internal explanations when evaluating the behavior of their subordinates than they did in evaluating their own (Martin & Klimoski, 1990). One reason for giving greater weight to external factors in explaining your own behavior than you do in explaining the behavior of others is that you know the situation surrounding your own behavior. You know, for example, what's going on in your love life and you know your financial condition, so you naturally see the influence of these factors. But you rarely know as much about others, so you're likely to give less weight to external factors in their cases.

This fundamental attribution error is at least in part culturally influenced. For example, in the United States people are more likely to explain behavior by saying that people did what they did because of who they are. But when Hindus in India were asked to explain why their friends behaved as they did, they gave greater weight to external factors than did Americans in the United States (Miller, 1984; Aronson, 1994). Further, Americans have little hesitation in offering causal explanations of a person's behavior ("Pat did this because . . ."). Hindus, on the other hand, are generally reluctant to explain a person's behavior in causal terms (Matsumoto, 1994).

[The next How To box appears on page 106.]

SKILL BUILDING EXERCISE 3.2

Perspective Taking

Taking the perspective of the other person and looking at the world through this perspective, this point of view, rather than through your own is crucial in achieving mutual understanding. For each of the specific behaviors listed below, identify specific circumstances that would lead to a *positive perception* and specific circumstances that might lead to a *negative perception.* The first one is done for you.

1. Giving a beggar in the street a twenty-dollar bill.
   Positive perception: *Grace once had to beg to get money for food. She now shares all she has with those who are like she once was.*
   Negative perception: *Grace is a first class snob. She just wanted to impress her friends, to show them that she has so much money she can afford to give $20 to a total stranger.*

2. Ignoring a homeless person who asks for money.
3. A middle-aged man walking down the street with his arms around a teenage girl.
4. A mother refusing to admit her teenage son back into her house.

Thinking Critically About Perspective Taking. The following should have been clear from this experience. Often, in perceiving a person, you may assume a specific set of circumstances and on this basis evaluate specific behaviors as positive or negative. Also, you may evaluate the very same specific behavior positively or negatively depending on the circumstances that you infer to be related to the behavior. Clearly, if you're to understand the perspective of another person, you need to understand the reasons for their behaviors and need to resist defining circumstances from your own perspective.

This article, prepared as a pamphlet by The Lighthouse Inc., an agency that "helps people of all ages overcome vision impairment," addresses many questions that create interpersonal difficulties between blind and sighted persons.

What Do You Do When You Meet A Blind Person . . .

GIVE A BLIND PERSON THE SAME RESPECT AND CONSIDERATION YOU WOULD GIVE A SIGHTED PERSON

 On the Street

Ask if assistance would be helpful. Sometimes a blind person prefers to get along unaided. If the person wants your help, offer your elbow. You will then be walking a half-step ahead and the movements of your body will indicate when to change direction, when to stop and start, and when to step up or down at curbside as you cross a street.

 Giving Directions

Your verbal directions should be given with the blind person as the reference point, not yourself. Example: "You are facing Lexington Avenue and you will have to cross it as you continue east on 59th Street."

 Handling Money

When giving out bills, indicate the denomination of each one so the blind person can identify it and put it away. Coins are identified by touch.

 Safety

Half-open doors are a hazard to everyone, particularly to a person who is blind. Keep doors closed or wide open.

 Dining Out

Guide blind people to the table in the restaurant by offering your arm. Then place their hand on the back of the chair so they can seat themselves. Read the menu aloud and describe the table setting. Encourage the waiter to speak directly to the blind person rather than to you. Describe the placement of the food using an imaginary clock face as a reference (e.g., vegetables are at 2 o'clock, salad plate is at 11 o'clock).

 Traveling

Just as a sighted person enjoys hearing a description of unfamiliar scenery from a tour guide, a blind person likes to hear about the indoor and outdoor sights while traveling.

 Guide Dogs

Guide dogs are working animals, not pets. Do not distract a guide dog by petting it or by seeking its attention.

Remember

Talk with a blind person as you would with a person who can see. Speak in a normal tone. You can use common expressions such as "See you later" and "Did you see that?"

If you enter a room in which a blind person is alone, make your presence known by speaking or introducing yourself. In a group, address blind people by name if they are expected to reply. Excuse yourself when you are leaving.

Always ask before you try to help someone. Grabbing a person's arm or pushing them is dangerous and discourteous.

When you accompany blind people, offer to describe whatever is around you.

Thinking Critically About Communication Between Blind and Sighted Persons

1. What is the popular perception that sighted people have of blind people? That blind people have of sighted people? How do these popular perceptions interfere with meaningful interpersonal communication?

2. Can you identify communication problems that might occur between persons with and without significant physical disabilities that illustrate the barriers of first impressions, personality theories, self-fulfilling prophecies, stereotypes, and attribution?

3. What would you include in a pamphlet with the same general purpose but titled "What Do You Do When You Meet a Person in a Wheelchair"? "What Do You Do When You Meet a Person Who Is Hearing Impaired"?

Source: Reprinted by permission of The Lighthouse Inc.

INCREASING ACCURACY IN PERCEPTION

Successful interpersonal communication depends largely on the accuracy of your interpersonal perception. As a preface, realize that in addition to your perception of another's behaviors (verbal or nonverbal), you can also perceive what you think another person is feeling or thinking (Laing, Phillipson, & Lee, 1966; Littlejohn, 1996). You can, for example, perceive Pat kissing Chris. This is a simple, relatively direct perception of some behavior. But you can also sense (or perceive)—on the basis of the kiss—that Pat loves Chris. Notice the difference: you have observed the kiss but have not observed the love. (Of course, you could continue in this vein and, from your conclusion that Pat loves Chris, conclude that Pat no longer loves Terry. That is, you can always formulate a conclusion on the basis of a previous conclusion. The process is unending.)

The important point to see here is that when your perceptions are based on something observable (here, the kiss), you have a greater chance of being accurate when you describe this kiss or even when you interpret and evaluate it. As you move further away from your actual observation, however, your chances of being accurate decrease—when, for example, you try to describe or evaluate the love. Generally, when you draw conclusions on the basis of what you think someone is thinking as a result of the behavior, you have a greater chance of making errors than when you stick to conclusions about what you observe yourself.

We've already identified the potential barriers that can arise with each of the perceptual processes, for example, the self-serving bias, overattribution, and the fundamental error in attribution. There are, however, additional suggestions we want to offer.

Become Critically Aware of Your Perceptions

When you become aware of your perceptions, you'll be able to subject them to logical analysis and critical thinking. Here are a few suggestions:

- Avoid early conclusions. On the basis of your observations of behaviors, formulate hypotheses to test against additional information and evidence rather than drawing conclusions you then look to confirm. Delay formulating conclusions until you have had a chance to process a wide variety of cues.
- Avoid the one-cue conclusion. Look for a variety of cues pointing in the same direction. The more cues pointing to the same conclusion, the more likely your conclusion will be correct. Be especially alert to contradictory cues, ones that refute your initial hypotheses. It's relatively easy to perceive cues that confirm your hypotheses but more difficult to

We must always tell what we see. Above all, and this is more difficult, we must always see what we see.

—*Charles Peguy*

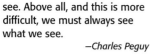

Acquiring Information

Exercise your brain. Exercise is not only useful for the body; it's also useful to the brain. Exercise increases the amount of oxygen that goes to the brain and that increases mental activity. Similarly, exercise releases endorphins which lessen many of the negative emotions like depression or anger. Thus, when you're having difficulty thinking clearly or when negative feelings get in the way of clear thinking, try exercising. The increase in the oxygen supply to the brain and the release of endorphins are likely to give you a thinking boost.

The sparrow flying in the rear of the hawk thinks the hawk is fleeing.

—*Japanese proverb*

acknowledge contradictory evidence. At the same time, seek validation from others. Do others see things in the same way you do? If not, ask yourself if your perceptions may be in some way distorted.

- Avoid mind reading; avoid trying to read the thoughts and feelings of another person just from observing their behaviors. Regardless of how many behaviors you observe and how carefully you examine them, you can only *guess* what is going on in someone's mind. A person's motives are not open to outside inspection; you can only make assumptions based on overt behaviors.
- Beware of your own biases. Know when your perceptual evaluations are unduly influenced by your own biases: for example, perceiving only the positive in people you like and only the negative in people you do not like.
- Be mindful of whether (or how much) your needs and wants are influencing what you see and what you don't see, a principle Curtis in the accompanying cartoon seems to ignore.

Check Your Perceptions

Perception checking is another way to reduce uncertainty and to make your perceptions more accurate. In its most basic form, perception checking consists of two steps:

1. Describe what you see or hear, recognizing that even descriptions are not really objective but are heavily influenced by who you are, your emotional state, and so on. At the same time, you may wish to describe what you think is happening. Again, try to do this as descriptively (not evaluatively) as you can. Sometimes you may wish to offer several possibilities.

   - You've called me from work a lot this week. You seem concerned that everything is all right at home.
   - You've not wanted to talk with me all week. You say that my work is fine but you don't seem to want to give me the same responsibilities that other editorial assistants have.

2. Ask the other person for confirmation. Do be careful that your request for confirmation does not sound as though you already know the answer. So avoid phrasing your questions defensively. Avoid saying, for

Visit the Website for the Institute for Propaganda Analysis (http://carmen.artsci.washington.edu/propaganda/home.html). What can you learn about critical thinking from this Website? Can you find a principle that could be used as a critical thinking sidebar? Try writing it up.

The sins of others are before our eyes; our own are behind our backs.

—*Seneca*

Acquiring Information

Look for contradictory cues. In searching for cues (or information or evidence) to help you make a judgment or reach a conclusion, be especially alert to contradictory cues, cues that refute your initial hypotheses. It's easy to perceive cues that confirm your hypotheses or conclusions but more difficult to acknowledge contradictory evidence.

CURTIS   **By RAY BILLINGSLEY**

example, "You really don't want to go out, do you? I knew you didn't when you turned on that lousy television." Instead, ask for confirmation in as supportive a way as possible: "Would you rather watch TV?"

- Are you worried about me or the kids?
- Are you pleased with my work? Is there anything I can do to improve my job performance?

As these examples illustrate, the goal of perception checking is not to prove that your initial perception is correct but to explore further the thoughts and feelings of the other person. With this simple technique, you lessen your chances of misinterpreting another's feelings. At the same time, you give the other person an opportunity to elaborate on his or her thoughts and feelings.

Reduce Uncertainty

We all have a tendency to reduce uncertainty, a process that enables us to achieve greater accuracy in perception. In large part we learned about uncertainty and how to deal with it from our culture.

Culture and Uncertainty

People from different cultures differ greatly in their attitudes toward uncertainty and how to deal with it, attitudes that impact on perceptual accuracy. People in some cultures do little to avoid uncertainty and have little anxiety about not knowing what will happen next. Uncertainty to them is a normal part of life and is accepted as it comes. Members of these cultures do not feel threatened by unknown situations. Other cultures do much to avoid uncertainty and have a great deal of anxiety about not knowing what will happen next; uncertainty is seen as threatening and something that must be counteracted. Table 3.1 presents the countries who have the greatest anxiety over or feel most threatened by uncertainty and those that have the lowest.

CAUTION

Has another person's **failing to check perceptions** about what you were feeling ever led to this person drawing inaccurate inferences about you?

Table 3.1. Uncertainly Avoidance and Culture.

There are wide differences within each culture as well as between cultures. These rankings are based on average scores obtained by members of these cultures (Hofstede, 1997). The countries are listed in order: Greece had the strongest uncertainty avoidance score, Portugal was second, Guatemala third, and so on. Singapore had the weakest uncertainty avoidance score, Jamaica was second, Denmark third, and so on. Countries listed together had the same score. How does your own culture treat uncertainty and its reduction?

Strong uncertainty avoidance	*Weak uncertainty avoidance*
Greece	Singapore
Portugal	Jamaica
Guatemala	Denmark
Uruguay	Sweden
Belgium, El Salvador	Hong Kong
Japan	Ireland
Yugoslavia	Great Britain
Peru	Malaysia
France, Chile, Spain, Costa Rica, Panama, Argentina	India
Turkey, South Korea	Philippines
Mexico	United States

The clear sighted do not rule the world, but they sustain and console it.

—*Agnes Repplier*

Greece ranks the highest in uncertainty avoidance; Greeks seem to have the strongest anxiety about the future and the uncertain. How anxious are you about uncertainty? Did you learn this attitude from your culture?

The potential for communication problems when people come from cultures with different attitudes toward uncertainty can be great. For example, managers from cultures with weak uncertainty avoidance will accept workers who work only when they have to and will not get too upset when workers are late. Managers from cultures with strong uncertainty avoidance will expect workers to be busy at all times and will have little tolerance for lateness.

Because weak uncertainty avoidance cultures have great tolerance for ambiguity and uncertainty, they minimize the rules governing communication and relationships (Hofstede, 1997; Lustig & Koester, 1996). People who do not follow the same rules as the cultural majority are readily tolerated. Different approaches and perspectives may even be encouraged in cultures with weak uncertainty avoidance. Strong uncertainty avoidance cultures create very clear-cut rules for communication. It's considered unacceptable for people to break these rules.

Students from weak uncertainty avoidance cultures appreciate freedom in education and prefer vague assignments without specific timetables. These students will want to be rewarded for creativity and will easily accept the teacher's (sometimes) lack of knowledge. Students from strong uncertainty avoidance cultures prefer highly structured experiences where there is very little ambiguity—specific objectives, detailed instructions, and definite timetables. These students expect to be judged on the basis of the right answers and expect the teacher to have all the answers all the time (Hofstede, 1997).

Geert Hofstede (1997, p. 119), who conducted much of the cultural research reported here, claims that those cultures which have strong uncertainty avoidance believe "What is different, is dangerous." Weak uncertainty avoidance cultures believe "What is different, is curious." Does your experience support this distinction?

Strategies for Reducing Uncertainty

Communication involves a gradual process of reducing uncertainty about each other (Berger & Bradac, 1982; Gudykunst, 1995). A variety of strategies can help reduce uncertainty. Observing another person while he or she is engaged in an active task, preferably interacting with others in more informal social situations, will often reveal a great deal about the person since people are less apt to monitor their behaviors and more likely to reveal their true selves in informal situations.

You can also manipulate the situation in such a way that you observe the person in more specific and more revealing contexts. Employment interviews, theatrical auditions, and student teaching are some of the ways situations can be created to observe how the person might act and react and hence to reduce uncertainty about the person.

New members of Internet chat groups usually lurk before joining the group discussion. Lurking, reading the exchanges between the other group members without saying anything yourself, will help you learn about the people in the group and about the group itself.

Another way to reduce uncertainty is to collect information about the person through asking others. You might inquire of a colleague if a third person finds you interesting and might like to have dinner with you.

And of course you can interact with the individual. For example, you can ask questions: "Do you enjoy sports?" "What did you think of that computer science course?" "What would you do if you got fired?" You also gain knowledge of another by disclosing information about yourself. Your self-disclosure can help to create an environment that encourages disclosures from the person about whom you wish to learn more.

You probably use these strategies all the time to learn about people. Unfortunately, many people feel that they know someone well enough after only observing the person from a distance or from rumors. A combination of information—including and especially your own interactions—is most successful at reducing uncertainty.

Be Culturally Sensitive

You can increase your accuracy in perception by recognizing and being sensitive to cultural differences, especially those concerning values, attitudes, and beliefs. You can easily see and accept different hairstyles, clothing, and foods. In basic values and beliefs, however, you may assume that down deep we're really all alike. We aren't. When you assume similarities and ignore differences, you may fail to perceive a situation accurately. Take a simple example. An American invites a Filipino coworker to dinner. The Filipino politely refuses. The American is hurt and feels that the Filipino does not want to be friendly. The Filipino is hurt and concludes that the invitation was not extended sincerely. Here, it seems, both the American and the Filipino assume that their customs for inviting people to dinner are the same when, in fact, they aren't. A Filipino expects to be invited several times before accepting a dinner invitation. When an invitation is given only once it's viewed as insincere.

Within every cultural group there are wide and important differences. As all Americans are not alike, neither are all Indonesians, Greeks, Mexicans, and so on. When you make assumptions that all people of a certain culture are alike, you're thinking in stereotypes. Recognizing differences between another culture and your own and recognizing differences among members of a particular culture will help you perceive the situation more accurately.

How would you go about finding answers to such questions as these *(any of which would make excellent topics for research papers):* Is the tendency to judge by first impressions universal? That is, do all cultures judge people very quickly? What other characteristics do people who have a lot of stereotypes possess? In what ways are people with a lot of stereotypes different from people with few stereotypes? Are people who attribute controllability to the homeless more negative in their evaluation of homelessness than those who attribute a lack of controllability? Do different cultures hold different implicit personality theories? Do men and women hold different theories?

SKILL BUILDING EXERCISE 3.3
Barriers to Accurate Perception

This exercise is designed to reinforce an understanding of the processes of perception. Read the following dialogue and identify the processes of perception that may be at work here.

PAT: All I had to do was to spend two seconds with him to know he's an idiot. I said I went to Graceland and he asked what that was. Can you believe it? Graceland! The more I got to know him, the more I realized how stupid he was. A real loser; I mean, really.

CHRIS: Yeah, I know what you mean. Well, he is a jock, you know.

PAT: Jocks! The worst. And I bet I can guess who he goes out with. I'll bet it's Lucy.

CHRIS: Why do you say that?

PAT: Well, I figure that the two people I dislike would like each other. And I figure you must dislike them, too.

CHRIS: Definitely.

PAT: By the way, have you ever met Marie? She's a computer science major, so you know she's bright. And attractive—really attractive.

CHRIS: Yes, I went out of my way to meet her, because she sounded like she'd be a nice person to know.

PAT: You're right. I knew she'd be nice as soon as I saw her.

CHRIS: We talked at yesterday's meeting. She's really complex, you know. I mean really complex. Really.

PAT: Whenever I think of Marie, I think of the time she helped that homeless man. There was this homeless guy—real dirty—and he fell, running across the street. Well, Marie ran right into the street and picked this guy up and practically carried him to the other side.

CHRIS: And you know what I think of when I think of Lucy? The time she refused to visit her grandmother in the hospital. Remember? She said she had too many other things to do.

PAT: I remember that—a real selfish egomaniac. I mean really.

Thinking Critically About the Barriers to Perception. Seeing the processes of perception and especially the barriers to accurate perception operate in ourselves and in others with whom we interact is a lot more difficult. For the next several days, record all personal examples of the five barriers to accurate perception. Record also the specific context in which they occurred. Consider such questions as: What barrier seems most frequent? What problems did the barrier cause? What advantages do you gain when you avoid making first impressions? When you avoid using implicit theories? When you avoid making prophecies? When you avoid stereotyping? What disadvantages are there in avoiding these shortcuts to people perception?

SUMMARY OF CONCEPTS AND SKILLS

In this chapter we surveyed the role of perception in interpersonal communication, examined how perception works, and identified its three main stages (sensation, organization, and interpretation-evaluation). Next we looked at the processes that influence people perception (first impressions, implicit personality theories, self-fulfilling prophecies, stereotypes, and attribution) and how these processes can create barriers to accurate interpersonal perception. We then considered ways of increasing our perceptual accuracy.

1. *Perception* is the process that enables you to become aware of the many stimuli impinging on your senses. *Interpersonal* or *people perception* is the process by which you become aware of and interpret-evaluate other people.

2. You can think about perception as occurring in three stages. Sensory stimulation occurs. Sensory stimulation is organized. Then sensory stimulation is interpreted and evaluated.

3. Perception is influenced by a number of processes: (1) first impressions, (2) self-fulfilling prophecies,

(3) implicit personality theories, (4) stereotyping, and (5) attribution.

4. *First impressions* refers to the tendency to form a general impression and then filter subsequent information through the image you derived from the initial encounter. If what occurs first exerts greatest influence, you have a primacy effect. If what occurs last exerts greatest influence, you have a recency effect.

5. The *self-fulfilling prophecy* occurs when you make a prediction that comes true *because* you made the prediction and *because* you acted as if it were true.

6. *Implicit personality theory* refers to the private personality theory that you hold and that influences how you perceive other people.

7. *Stereotyping* refers to developing and maintaining fixed, unchanging perceptions of groups of people and using these to evaluate individual members of these groups. You thus fail to see their individual, unique characteristics.

8. *Attribution* refers to the process by which you try to explain the motivation for a person's behavior. Your perception of whether or not the person was in control of the behavior will influence your evaluation of the behavior.

9. In achieving more accurate perception avoid the barriers that the various processes of perception may set up. Therefore, beware of your first impressions. Beware of your implicit personality theories. Beware of trusting your prophecies and acting as if these were true. Beware of forming stereotypes and relying on these to draw conclusions about other people. Beware of the self-serving bias, overattribution, and the fundamental attribution error.

10. Further increase your accuracy in interpersonal perception by becoming critically aware of your perceptions and the influences on them, checking your perceptions, reducing uncertainty, and being culturally aware and sensitive.

Check your ability to apply these skills. You'll gain most from this brief experience if you think carefully about each skill and try to identify instances from your recent communications in which you did or did not act on the basis of the specific skill. Use a rating scale such as the following: 1 = almost always, 2 = often, 3 = sometimes, 4 = rarely, and 5 = almost never.

_____ 1. Perceive others with the recognition that I am a major part of my own perceptions.

_____ 2. Perceive others with the recognition that my perceptions and evaluations of others are potentially influenced by the tendency to formulate impressions after the first meeting, implicit personality theories, self-fulfilling prophecies, stereotypes, and attribution processes.

_____ 3. Perceive others while avoiding such common barriers as giving undue emphasis to what occurs first or last, fulfilling my own prophecies, filtering what I perceive through my own implicit personality theories, seeing an individual primarily as a member of a group, and the self-serving bias, overattribution, and the fundamental attribution error.

_____ 4. Increase accuracy in perception by becoming critically aware of my perceptions, checking my perceptions, reducing uncertainty, and being culturally sensitive.

VOCABULARY QUIZ. THE LANGUAGE OF INTERPERSONAL PERCEPTION

Match the terms dealing with interpersonal perception listed here with their definitions. Record the number of the definition next to the name of the appropriate concept.

_____ perception

_____ implicit personality theory

_____ stereotype

_____ proximity

_____ the fundamental attribution error

_____ self-fulfilling prophecy

_____ mindreading

_____ perception checking

_____ self-serving bias

_____ primacy

1. A process involving overvaluing the contribution of internal factors and undervaluing the influence of external factors in explaining behavior.
2. A way of increasing accuracy in perception that focuses on describing what you think is going on and then asking for confirmation.
3. A theory of personality that each individual maintains, complete with rules or systems, through which others are perceived.
4. The tendency to see things that are physically close to each other as belonging together, as forming a unit.
5. The process of becoming aware of objects and events from the senses.
6. A fixed impression of a group of people.
7. The condition by which what comes first exerts greater influence than what comes last.
8. The situation in which we make a prediction and then act in a way to make that prediction come true.
9. A tendency that leads us to take credit for the positive things and to deny responsibility for the negative things.
10. Drawing conclusions about what is going on in the mind of another person, for example, motives or intentions.

Listening in Interpersonal Communication

CHAPTER TOPICS	LEARNING OBJECTIVES	SKILL OBJECTIVES
	After completing this chapter, you should be able to	*After completing this chapter, you should be able to*
The Listening Process	1. Define *listening*, its stages, purposes, and major obstacles	Listen more effectively at each of the five stages of listening
Listening, Culture, and Gender	2. Explain some of the cultural and gender differences in listening	Interact with a clear understanding of the cultural and gender listening differences
Increasing Listening Effectiveness	3. Define and explain the four principles for effective listening	Regulate your listening on the basis of participation, empathy, judgment, and depth

EXAMPLE NO. 1

Foreman: Hey, Al, I don't get this production order. We can't handle this run today. What do they think we are?

Supervisor: But that's the order. So get it out as soon as you can. We're under terrific pressure this week.

Foreman: Don't they know we're behind schedule already because of that press breakdown?

Supervisor: Look, Kelly, I don't decide what goes on upstairs. I just have to see that the work gets out and that's what I'm gonna do.

Foreman: The guys aren't gonna like this.

Supervisor: That's something you'll have to work out with them, not me.

EXAMPLE NO. 2

Foreman: Hey, Ross, I don't get this production order. We can't handle this run today. What do they think we are?

Supervisor: Sounds like you're pretty sore about it, Kelly.

Foreman: I sure am. We were just about getting back to schedule after that press breakdown. Now this comes along.

Supervisor: As if you didn't have enough work to do, huh?

Foreman: Yeah. I don't know how I'm gonna tell the guys about this.

Supervisor: Hate to face 'em with it now, is that it?

Foreman: I really do. They're under a real strain today. Seems like everything we do around here is rush, rush.

Supervisor: I guess you feel like it's unfair to load anything more on them.

Foreman: Well, yeah. I know there must be plenty of pressure on everybody up the line, but—well, if that's the way it is . . . guess I'd better get the word to 'em.

These examples, supplied by Carl Rogers and Richard Farson (1981), reflect an essential difference in listening techniques. As you read this chapter, think about what the supervisor does in Example 2 but not in Example 1. Why do the supervisor's responses in Example 1 create problems? Why do the supervisor's responses in Example 2 prove more effective?

In Example 1 the supervisor uses common but ineffective listening. In Example 2 the supervisor uses effective listening techniques.

Throughout this chapter we explain the differences between ineffective and effective listening. More specifically, this chapter examines the listening process and some of the reasons we listen. It focuses on some of the cultural and gender differences observed in listening and the implications of these differences for effective interpersonal listening. The chapter's major emphasis is on the obstacles to effective listening, how these can be eliminated, and how you can listen more effectively.

Listening serves a variety of purposes—to learn, relate, influence, play, and help. Table 4.1 identifies these purposes along with the potential benefits you might derive from accomplishing these purposes.

How effective a listener are you? Are you satisfied with this level of listening? How might you go about improving your listening behavior? Are you satisfied with the level of listening that others give you? How might you go about increasing this level?

THE LISTENING PROCESS

Listening can be described as a series of five steps: receiving, understanding, remembering, evaluating, and responding. The process is visualized in Figure 4.1. Note that the listening process is a circular one. The responses of Person

Access the ERIC database for an article on listening. What is the thesis or theme of the article? Does it offer any practical suggestions for improving listening? An interesting review paper could be written on such an article.

Table 4.1. The Purposes and Benefits of Effective Listening.

These purposes are, of course, the same as the purposes of interpersonal communications discussed in Chapter 1.

Effective listening will result in increasing your ability to	Because you will	For example,
learn: to acquire knowledge of others, the world, and yourself, so as to avoid problems, and make more reasonable decisions	profit from the insights of others and acquire more information relevant to decisions you'll be called upon to make in business or in personal life	listening to Peter about his travels to Cuba to learn more about Peter and about life in another country; listening to the difficulties your sales staff has may help you improve sales training
relate, to gain social acceptance and popularity	find that people come to like those who are attention and supportive	others will increase their liking for you once they feel you have genuine concern for them
influence the attitudes and behaviors of others	find that people are more likely to respect and follow those they feel have listened to them	workers are more likely to follow your advice once they feel you have listened to their insights and concerns
play	know when to suspend evaluative thinking and when to engage in supportive and accepting listening	listening to your coworkers' anecdotes will enable you appreciate the relationships between the worlds of work and of play
help others	hear more, empathize more, and come to understand others more deeply	listening to your child's complaints about her teacher will put you in a better position to help your child with school

Figure 4.1

The Five Stages of Listening.

This model depicts the various tags involved in listening. This model, and the suggestions for listening improvement throughout this chapter, draws on a variety of previous theories and models that listening researchers have developed (for example, Nichols & Stevens, 1957; Nichols, 1961; Barker, 1990; Steil, Barker, & Watson, 1983; Brownell, 1987; Alessandra, 1986; Nichols, 1995). Note that receiving or hearing is not the same thing as listening but is in fact only the first step in a five-step process. How would you further distinguish between hearing and listening? Can you identify people you know who "hear" but don't "listen"?

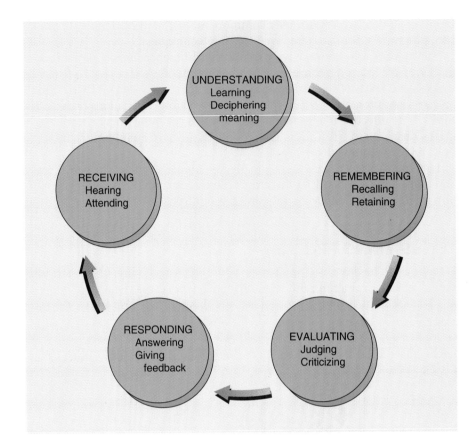

Evaluating Information

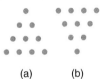

(a)   (b)

Examine your assumptions (again). Try to change Figure (a) into Figure (b) by moving only 3 circles. Try this for a few minutes before reading on.

If you had difficulty with this, it's likely that you focused your attention on moving the top 3 circles. Your unstated assumptions might be: (1) the rows with fewest circles should be moved or (2) entire rows must be moved. These are assumptions that many people make and that prevent solving the problem.

A serve as the stimuli for Person B whose responses, in turn, serve as the stimuli for Person A, and so on.

Each of these stages involves various dangers or barriers which need to be avoided as you make your way from receiving to responding.

Receiving

Listening is a much more extensive process than hearing. Hearing is essentially the first stage of listening, receiving. Listening begins (but does not end) with receiving messages the speaker sends which are both verbal and nonverbal; they consist of words as well as gestures, facial expressions, and the like. At this stage you note not only what is said (verbally and nonverbally) but also what is omitted. You not only receive, for example, your friend's request for a loan, but also the omission of any stated intention to pay you back in a reasonable time. The following suggestions should prove useful in making receiving more effective:

- focus your attention on the speaker's verbal and nonverbal messages, on what is said and not said
- avoid distractions in the environment; if necessary, shut off the stereo or tell your assistant to hold all calls
- focus your attention on the speaker, not on what you'll say next
- maintain your role as listener; avoid interrupting the speaker until he or she is finished

Understanding

Understanding occurs when you learn what the speaker means. Understanding includes both the thoughts that are expressed as well as the emotional tone that accompanies them, for example, the urgency or the joy or sorrow expressed in the message. In achieving understanding:

- relate the speaker's new information to what you already know (In what way will this new proposal change our present health care?)
- see the speaker's messages from the speaker's point of view; avoid judging the message until it's fully understood as the speaker intended it
- ask questions for clarification, if necessary; ask for additional details or examples if needed
- rephrase (paraphrase) the speaker's ideas to check on your understanding of the speaker's thoughts and feelings

The one who listens, understands.

—West African proverb

Remembering

Messages that you receive and understand need to be retained at least for some period of time. In some small group and public speaking situations you can augment your memory by taking notes or by taping the messages. In most interpersonal communication situations, however, such note taking would be considered inappropriate, although you often do write down a phone number, an appointment, or directions.

What you remember is not what was actually said, but what you think (or remember) was said. Memory for speech is not reproductive, it is reconstructive. You don't simply reproduce in your memory what the speaker said; rather, you reconstruct the messages you hear into a system that makes sense to you—a concept noted in the discussion of perception in Chapter 3. To illustrate this important concept, try to memorize the list of 12 words presented below (Glucksberg & Danks, 1975). Don't worry about the order; only the number remembered counts. Take about 20 seconds to memorize as many words as possible. Don't read any further until you have tried to memorize the list.

Memory's like an athlete; keep it in training; take it for cross-country runs.

—James Hilton

Word List

BED	AWAKE
DREAM	NIGHT
COMFORT	SLUMBER
REST	TIRED
WAKE	EAT
SOUND	SNORE

Now close the book and write down as many words from the list as you can remember. Don't read any further until you have tested your own memory. If you're like my students, you not only remembered most of the words, but also added at least one word: "sleep." Most people recall "sleep" being on the list, but, as you can see, it wasn't. What happened was that you didn't just reproduce the list; you reconstructed it. In this case you gave the list meaning by including the word "sleep." This happens with all types of messages; they are reconstructed into a meaningful whole and in the process, a distorted version is often remembered.

To insure more accurate remembering:

- identify the central ideas and the major support advanced.
- summarize the message in an easier to retain form but do not ignore crucial details or qualifications.
- repeat names and key concepts to yourself or, if appropriate, aloud.
- if this is a formal talk with a recognizable organizational structure, identify this pattern and use it (see it in your mind) to organize what the speaker is saying.

Evaluating

Evaluating consists of judging the messages. At times you may try to evaluate the speaker's underlying intent, often without much conscious awareness. For example, Elaine tells you she is up for a promotion and is really excited about it. You may then try to judge her intention. Does she want you to use your influence with the company president? Is she preoccupied with the possible promotion, thus telling everyone? Is she looking for a pat on the back? Generally, if you know the person well, you'll be able to identify the intention and respond appropriately.

In other situations, the evaluation is more in the nature of a critical analysis. For example, you would evaluate proposals advanced in a business meeting while listening to them. Are they practical? Will they increase productivity?

Evaluating Information

Consider the source. You acquire information from a wide variety of sources—newspapers, television, friends, family members, instructors, textbooks, and so on. But, not all sources are equally reliable or trustworthy. A report on the addictiveness of tobacco from a cigarette company and one from an independent research organization should obviously be viewed very differently. Similarly, don't attribute the same reliability to an article on the Web, which just about anyone can post, as you'd attribute to one in a professional research journal that requires its articles be reviewed by a group of impartial researchers before publication. So, always consider the source when evaluating information.

Some people, when they get older, lose some memory ability. But, it's far less than most people's stereotypes.

What is the evidence? Are there more practical alternative proposals? At this stage of listening try to

- resist evaluation until you fully understand the speaker's point of view.
- assume that the speaker is a person of goodwill and give the speaker the benefit of any doubt by asking for clarification on issues you object to (are there any other reasons for accepting this new proposal?).
- distinguish facts from inferences (see Chapter 5), opinions, and personal interpretations by the speaker.
- identify any biases, self-interests, or prejudices that may lead the speaker to unfairly slant information presented.

Responding

Responding occurs in two phases: (1) responses you make while the speaker is talking and (2) responses you make after the speaker has stopped talking. Responses made while the speaker is talking should be supportive and should acknowledge that you're listening. These include what nonverbal researchers call *backchanneling cues,* such as "I see," "yes," "uh-huh," that let the speaker know you're paying attention (more on this in Chapter 8).

Responses after the speaker has stopped talking are generally more elaborate and might include empathy ("I know how you must feel"); asking for clarification ("Do you mean this new health plan will replace the old one or will it be just a supplement?"); challenging ("I think your evidence is weak"); and agreeing ("You're absolutely right and I'll support your proposal when it comes up for a vote"). In responding:

- be supportive of the speaker throughout the talk by using varied backchanneling cues; using only one—for example, saying "uh-huh" throughout—will make it appear that you're not listening but are merely on automatic pilot
- express support for the speaker in your final responses
- own your own responses; state your thoughts and feelings as your own; use "I" messages (say "I think the new proposal will entail greater expense than you outlined" rather than "Everyone will object to the plan's cost")

> Silence gives consent, or a horrible feeling that nobody's listening.
> *—Franklin P. Jones*

Access the Websites of several major corporations and examine their job openings. Try www.name of corporation.com or one of the search engines or directories. Do they mention communication skills or listening in their descriptions of the kind of person they want to fill the position? *(This could make an interesting review paper: What communication skills do corporations want?)*

LISTENING
Ethical Listening

Most discussions of ethics focus exclusively on the speaker. But, interpersonal communication is a two-way process; both speaker *and* listener share in the success or failure of the interaction. So too, both share in the moral implications of the interpersonal communication exchange. Two principles govern ethical listening.

Give the speaker an honest hearing. First, as a listener, give the speaker an honest hearing. Listen fully and openly. Try to put aside prejudices and preconceptions so you can evaluate the speaker's message fairly. Then, accept or reject the speaker's ideas on the basis of the information offered, and not on the basis of some bias. Of course, you will see any given topic from your own point of view. As a listener, however, try to see the topic, and particularly the specific purpose, from the speaker's point of view as well. Try to empathize with the speaker. You don't have to agree with the speaker. Try, however, to understand emotionally as well as intellectually what the speaker means. Only after you have achieved empathic understanding should you evaluate the speaker, the speech, or the purpose.

Respond honestly. As the speaker should be honest with the listener, the listener should be honest with
(continued)

LISTENING
Ethical Listening [continued]

the speaker. This means giving open and honest feedback to the speaker. It means reflecting honestly on the questions that the speaker raises. It means providing an appropriate evaluation and critique. Much as the listener has a right to expect an active speaker, the speaker has the right to expect an active listener. The speaker has a right to expect a listener who will actively deal with, rather than just passively hear, the message.

As illustrated throughout this text, culture influences all aspects of communication; listening is no exception. Consider these questions involving ethical listening and cultural differences. To what extent are your answers a statement of culture-specific ethical principles?

- Do you listen differently (for example, less or more openly) to a speech by a person from a different

culture as opposed to someone from your own? Do you hear yourself saying, "Oh, the speaker's just saying that because he or she is Asian or gay or Jewish?"

- Would you listen honestly to a speaker explaining religious beliefs and practices that are very different from your own? On a 10-point scale, with 10 being the highest, how open are you to listening to opposing religious perspectives?
- Would you attribute similar credibility (all other things being equal) to a speaker from a different culture than you would one from your own culture? Do you feel that people from your own culture are generally more competent or more trustworthy that those from other cultures?

[The next Listening box appears on page 100]

CAUTION

How might **listening through preconceived attitudes** prevent you from acquiring the information you need to render logical judgments? Have you ever listened through preconceived attitudes only to discover later that your attitudes distorted the messages you received?

Are you a supportive listener? An expressive listener? Do you own your own responses?

Before reading about the principles of effective listening, examine your own listening habits and tendencies by taking the accompanying self-test. The "desirable" answers are obvious, of course; but, try to give responses that are true for you in most of your listening experiences.

SELF-TEST
How Do You Listen?

Instructions: Respond to each question with the following scale:

1 = always
2 = frequently
3 = sometimes
4 = seldom
5 = never

_____ 1. I listen by participating; I interject comments throughout the conversation.

_____ 2. I listen to what the speaker is saying and feeling; I try to feel what the speaker feels.

_____ 3. I listen without judging the speaker.

_____ 4. I listen to the literal meanings that a speaker communicates; I don't look too deeply into hidden meanings.

_____ 5. I listen with minimal participation; I generally remain silent and take in what the other person is saying.

_____ 6. I listen objectively; I focus on the logic of the ideas rather than on the emotional meaning of the message.

_____ 7. I listen critically, evaluating the speaker and what the speaker is saying.

_____ 8. I look for the hidden meanings; the meanings that are revealed by subtle verbal or nonverbal cues.

Thinking Critically About Listening These statements focus on the ways of listening discussed in this chapter. All ways are appropriate at times and all ways are inappropriate at times. It depends. So, the only responses that are really inappropriate are "always" and "never" responses. Effective listening is listening that is appropriate to the specific communication situation. Review these statements and try to identify situations in which each statement would be appropriate and situations in which each statement would be inappropriate.

SKILL BUILDING EXERCISE 4.1
Reducing Barriers to Listening

Visualize yourself ready to talk with the following people on the topics noted. What barriers to listening (from any stage: receiving, understanding, remembering, evaluating, and responding) might arise in each encounter? What would you do to prevent these barriers from interfering with effective listening?

1. A friend tells you he's HIV positive.

2. A male instructor argues that the feminist movement is dead.

3. A lesbian mother argues that current adoption laws are discriminatory.

4. A coalition of homeless people claims the right to use public spaces.

5. A politician says that relationships between different races will never be better.

(continued)

(continued)

6. A Catholic priest argues that people need to remain virgins until marriage.
7. An 80-year-old relative argues that abortion, regardless of the circumstances, is murder.
8. A telephone company representative asks that you switch to their new long distance system.

Thinking Critically About Barriers to Listening.   In thinking about these situations, consider, for example: How would your initial expectations influence your listening? How would you assess the person's credibility (even before you begin to talk)? How will this influence your listening? Will you begin listening with a positive, negative, or neutral attitude? How might these attitudes influence your listening?

LISTENING, CULTURE, AND GENDER

Listening is difficult, in part, because of the inevitable differences in the communication systems between speaker and listener. Because each person has had a unique set of experiences, each person's communication and meaning system is going to be different from every other persons'. When speaker and listener come from different cultures or are of different genders, the differences and their effects are naturally so much greater. Let's look first at culture.

Listening and Culture

The culture in which you were raised will influence your listening in a variety of ways. Here we look at some of these: language and speech, nonverbal differences, direct and indirect styles, balance of story versus evidence, credibility, and feedback.

Language and Speech

Even when speaker and listener speak the same language, they speak it with different meanings and different accents. No two speakers speak exactly the same language. Every speaker speaks an idiolect; a unique variation of the language (King & DiMichael, 1992). Speakers of the same language will, at the very least, have different meanings for the same terms because they have had different experiences.

Speakers and listeners who have different native languages and who may have learned English as a second language will have even greater differences in meaning. Translations are never precise and never fully capture the meaning in the other language. If your meaning for "house" was learned in a culture in which everyone lived in their own house with lots of land around it, then communicating with someone whose meaning was learned in a neighborhood of high-rise tenements is going to be difficult. Although you'll each hear the same word, the meanings you'll each develop will be drastically different. In adjusting your listening—especially when in an intercultural setting—understand that the speaker's meanings may be very different from yours even though you each know the same language.

Acquiring Information

Read from a wide variety of sources to acquire information.   Read a variety of different types of material, for example, plays, newspapers, novels, how-to books, poetry, and even comic books and children's books. Visit relevant and diverse Websites. Also, try to expose yourself to different points of view; avoid falling into the trap of reading only that which supports your current positions. The more diverse your reading—in type and point of view—the more likely you'll be able to see issues and problems from different perspectives. Similarly, expose yourself to the best that television has to offer—especially programs that can provide you with new and different perspectives.

Still another part of speech is that of accents. In many classrooms throughout the country, there are a wide range of accents. Those whose native language is a tonal one such as Chinese (where differences in pitch signal important meaning differences) may speak English with variations in pitch that may seem puzzling to others. Those whose native language is Japanese may have trouble distinguishing "l" from "r" since Japanese does not include this distinction. The native language acts as a filter and influences the accent given to the second language.

Nonverbal Behavioral Differences

Speakers from different cultures have different display rules, cultural rules which govern what nonverbal behaviors are appropriate and which are inappropriate in a public setting. As you listen to another person, you also "listen" to their nonverbals. If these are drastically different from what you expect on the basis of the verbal message, they may be seen as a kind of noise or interference or they may be seen as contradictory messages. Also, different cultures may give very different meanings to the same nonverbal gesture.

Direct and Indirect Styles

Some cultures—Western Europe and the United States, for example—favor a direct style in communication; they advise us to "say what you mean and mean what you say." Many Asian cultures, on the other hand, favor an indirect style; they emphasize politeness and maintaining a positive public image rather than absolute truth. Listen carefully to persons with different styles of directness. Consider the possibility that the meanings the speaker wishes to communicate with, say, indirectness, may be very different from the meanings you would communicate with indirectness.

Credibility

What makes a speaker credible or believable will vary from one culture to another. In some cultures, people would claim that competence is the most important factor in, say, choosing a teacher for their preschool children. In other cultures, the most important factor might be the goodness or morality of the teacher. Similarly, members of different cultures may perceive the credibility of the various media very differently. For example, members of a repressive society in which the government controls television news may come to attribute little credibility to such broadcasts. After all, this person might reason, television news is simply what the government wants you to know. This may be hard to understand or even recognize by someone raised in the United States, for example, where the media are free of such political control.

Feedback

Members of some cultures give very direct and very honest feedback. Speakers from these cultures—the United States is a good example—expect the feedback to be an honest reflection of what their listeners are feeling. In other cultures—Japan and Korea are good examples—it's more important to be positive than to be truthful, and so people of these cultures may respond with positive feedback (say, in commenting on a business colleague's proposal) even though they don't feel it. Listen to feedback, as you would all messages, with a full recognition that various cultures view feedback very differently.

If people around you will not hear you, fall down before them and beg their forgiveness, for in truth you are to blame.
—*Fyodor Dostoyevsky*

Try describing your own culture's teachings and rules as they might influence listening in the classroom or at your place of work. *(This would make an interesting concept paper; you might try organizing your paper around the concepts covered in this chapter: language and speech differences, nonverbal behavior differences, direct and indirect styles, credibility, and feedback. Or, try describing the gender differences you've observed.)*

Have you witnessed any of the cultural differences discussed in this chapter in your recent interactions? What can you add to what is said here?

Listening and Gender

Deborah Tannen opens her chapter on listening in her best selling *You Just Don't Understand: Women and Men in Conversation* (1990) with several anecdotes illustrating that when men and women talk, men lecture and women listen. The lecturer is positioned as the superior, as the teacher, the expert. The listener is positioned as the inferior, the student, the nonexpert.

Women, according to Tannen, seek to build rapport and establish a closer relationship and so use listening to achieve these ends. For example, women use more listening cues that let the other person know they are paying attention and are interested. Men not only use fewer listening cues but interrupt more and will often change the topic to one they know more about or one that is less relational or people-oriented, or to one that is more factual, for example, sports statistics, economic developments, or political problems. Men, research shows, play up their expertise, emphasize it, and use it in dominating the conversation. Women play down their expertise.

Now, you might be tempted to conclude from this that women play fair in conversation and that men don't; for example, men consistently seek to put themselves in a position superior to women. But, that may be too simple an explanation. Research shows, however, that men communicate this way not only with women but with other men as well. Men are not showing disrespect for their female conversational partners but are simply communicating as they normally do. Women, too, communicate as they do not only with men but also with other women.

Tannen argues that the goal of a man in conversation is to be accorded respect and so he seeks to display his knowledge and expertise even if he has to change the topic to one he knows a great deal about. Women, on the other hand, seek to be liked and so they express agreement, rarely interrupt men to take a turn as speaker, and give lots of cues (verbally and nonverbally) to indicate that they are listening.

Acquiring Information

Interact with a wide variety of people to acquire information. Interact with different people and participate in different experiences—especially people and experiences of different cultures. Avail yourself of the great number of mailing lists and newsgroups. Seeing an issue from the viewpoint of someone of the opposite sex; a different affectional orientation; or a different age, religion, or culture can give you insights you might not have considered before. Pride yourself for diversity of thought rather than single mindedness.

Do you notice differences in the way in which men and women listen? Can you offer specific examples to bolster your conclusions?

Men and women also show that they are listening in different ways. A woman is more apt to give lots of listening cues such as interjecting *yeah, uh-uh,* nodding in agreement, and smiling. A man is more likely to listen quietly, without giving lots of listening cues as feedback. Tannen also argues, however, that men do listen less to women than women listen to men. The reason, says Tannen, is that listening places the person in an inferior position whereas speaking places the person in a superior position.

There is no evidence to show that these differences represent any negative motives on the part of men to prove themselves superior or of women to ingratiate themselves. Rather, these differences in listening are largely the result of the way in which men and women have been socialized. Can men and women change these habitual ways of listening (and speaking)?

Do you engage in much active listening? Do your close friends practice active listening when they listen to you? Can you give a specific example of active listening that you were recently involved in? *(Your experience with active listening would make an interesting personal experience paper.)*

SKILL BUILDING EXERCISE 4.2.

Typical Man. Typical Woman.

How would you describe the listening behavior of a typical (even stereotypical) man and a typical woman in each of the following situations?

1. Your steady dating partner wants to talk about the state of the relationship; things have not been going well.
2. Your supervisor has criticized your work just about every day this week. You've been under a lot of pressure lately and you now have to go for your quarterly evaluation interview.
3. A close friend has a drug problem, mainly tranquilizers. During a chance meeting your friend complains about losing another job and not being able to meet this month's rent payments.

Thinking Critically About Gender Differences in Listening. Now that the stereotypes are out in the open, consider their accuracy. How accurate are these stereotypes in describing the listening behavior of the men and women you've interacted with? Can you think of more examples supporting the stereotype or contradicting it?

LISTENING TO . . .

Try Active Listening

Active listening, an approach to listening developed by Thomas Gordon (1975), is especially important in relationship communication. It's a method for encouraging the other person to explore his or her thoughts and talk about them.

Active listening serves several important functions. For one thing, it enables you to check on your understanding of what the speaker meant. When you reflect back to the speaker what you perceived to be the speaker's meanings (one of the techniques to be discussed in the next box), he or she can then confirm or deny your perceptions. Future messages will have a better chance of being meaningful.

Active listening also enables you to express acceptance of the speaker's feelings. Remember that a person's feelings—whether you see these as logical or illogical, reasonable or unreasonable—are extremely important to that person. Acceptance of these feelings is to the speaker a prerequisite for talking about them.

And perhaps most important, active listening stimulates the speaker to explore feelings and thoughts. Active listening helps encourage the speaker to explore and express thoughts and feelings. When you use active listening you provide Angela, who has expressed worry about getting fired, with the opportunity to explore these feelings in greater detail. You give Charlie, who hasn't had a date in four months, the opportunity to reflect openly on his feelings about dating and about his own loneliness. Active listening sets the stage for a dialogue of mutual understanding rather than one of attack and defense. In providing the speaker with the opportunity to talk feelings through, the active listener helps the speaker deal with them.

Here are three techniques for effective active listening.

1. Paraphrase the speaker's thoughts. State in your own words what you think the speaker meant. This will help ensure understanding, since the speaker will be able to correct your restatement. It will show the speaker that you're interested in what is being said. Everyone wants to feel attended to, especially when angry or depressed. The paraphrase also gives the speaker a chance to elaborate on or extend what was originally said. When you echo the speaker's thought, the speaker may then elaborate on his or her feelings. In your paraphrase, be especially careful that you do not lead the speaker in the direction you think he or she should go. Make your paraphrases as close to objective descriptions as you can. Practice in paraphrasing is provided in Skill Building Exercise 4.3, page 107.

2. Express understanding of the speaker's feelings. In addition to paraphrasing the content, echo the feelings you felt the speaker expressed or implied. ("I can imagine how you must have felt. You must have felt really horrible.") Just as the paraphrase enables you to check on your perception of the content, the expression of feelings enables you to check on your perception of the speaker's feelings. This expression of feelings will also provide the speaker with the opportunity to see his or her feelings more objectively. It's helpful especially when the speaker feels angry, hurt, or depressed. We all need that objectivity; we need to see our feelings from a somewhat less impassioned perspective if we are to deal with them effectively. When you echo the speaker's feelings, you also give the speaker permission to elaborate on these feelings. In echoing these feelings, be careful that you do not over- or understate the speaker's feelings. Just try to restate the feelings as accurately as you can.

3. Ask questions. Ask questions to ensure your own understanding of the speaker's thoughts and feelings and to secure additional information ("How did you feel when you saw that grade?"). The questions should be designed to provide just enough stimulation and support for the speaker to express the thoughts and feelings he or she wants to express. Questions should not pry into unrelated areas or challenge the speaker in any way. These questions will further confirm your interest and concern for the speaker.

[The next Listening To box appears on page 117.]

Here in a brief article are useful suggestions for listening more effectively in business settings. The suggestions, however, can easily be applied to the classroom or the home, for example.

Want To Do Better On the Job?—Listen Up!

Diane Cole

When Linda S., an Ohio banking executive, learned she would not be promoted she asked her boss why. He had barely begun to speak when she blurted out, "I know that whatever the reason I can do better!"

Exasperated, he replied, "You always interrupt before you even know what I'm going to say! How can you do better if you never listen?"

"Most people value speaking—which is seen as active—over listening, which is seen as passive," explains Nancy Wyatt, professor of speech communication at Penn State University and co-author with Carol Ashburn of *Successful Listening* (Harper and Row, 1988).

And there are other reasons we might fail to tune in.

We may become so fixed on what WE think that we tune out important information. Or we may react emotionally to a phrase or style the speaker uses and miss the main point. Or we're just too busy to pay attention to what is being said.

Sound familiar? If so, listen up, for changing your ways will pay big dividends.

You'll stop wasting time on misunderstood assignments at work. People will start to see you as a perceptive, smart and sensitive person who understands their needs. And that will open new opportunities on the job, suggests Lyman K. Steil, Ph.D., president of Communication Development Inc., a consulting firm based in St. Paul, Minn.

You can also develop an ear for the crucial but unspoken words in conversation that signal problems in your business relationships.

Here are some suggestions for learning to listen to what is said—and not said—more effectively.

- Control distractions: Give a speaker your full attention or you're likely to miss the main point.

   Many interruptions cannot be avoided, but you can limit their effect.

   If you must take a call while a co-worker is explaining something important, make a choice and devote yourself to one conversation at a time.
- Identify the speaker's purpose: Tune into the speaker's agenda. Is he or she there to let off steam, solve a problem, share information or just schmooze?

   Once you know, you can respond in the way he or she wants and expects.

   Learning to listen may also keep you from inadvertently getting caught in the cross fire of office politics.
- Don't finish other people's sentences: Many people have this bad habit. Just observe yourself: Do you cut people off before they finish a thought? Are you so busy thinking about what you want to say that you can't resist breaking in?

   "That often happens because the interrupter is bright, thinks she has grasped the point and wants to show off how much she knows," says Dee Soder, Ph.D., president of Endymion, a New York City-based executive-consulting firm. "What happens instead is that interrupters are perceived as being arrogant and interested only in themselves."

   To break the habit of interrupting, bite your tongue and follow up with your comments only after the other person has had his or her say.

Soder suggests you might even have to literally sit on your hands to keep your gestures from speaking for you.

Finally, if you're not certain that the speaker has finished, ask!
- Don't let the speaker's style turn you off: It's easy to tune out when less-than-favorite speakers clear their throats.

   One high school teacher confesses that for a long time she found a colleague's slow, deliberate drawl so grating that she simply could not listen to him.

   "It was only when I was forced to work with him and had to concentrate on WHAT he was saying rather than HOW that I realized how smart and helpful he was and now we're best friends at work."
- Don't be distracted by buzzwords: What springs to mind when you hear the label "feminist" or "right-to-lifer"? If you're like most people emotions take over and you stop paying careful attention to the point a speaker is trying to make.
- Listen for what is not being said: Sometimes it's important to "hear between the lines."

   "Many people like to avoid conflict and so the person speaking is very reluctant to say anything negative," says Soder.

   When you suspect that a delicate or negative subject is being studiously avoided, you have to be prepared to delve deeper and ask the speaker, "Tell me more about that. Could you please explain?"
- Show you are listening: Think about what your body language is revealing.

   Are you making good eye contact and leaning slightly forward in a way that indicates "I'm open to what you're saying"? Or are you tapping your foot and looking out of the window as if to say, "I have more important things to do than listen to you"?
- Make a note of it: Jotting down a word or two can remind you later of the main purpose behind the assignment your boss is giving you.

   A brief note can also help you remember the point you would like to raise after the speaker finishes.
- Make sure you heard it right: Many misunderstandings could be prevented if we'd just make sure we heard what we thought we heard.

   So when in doubt don't be afraid to ask, "Let me make sure I understand what you're saying." It's a hearing test well worth taking.

Thinking Critically About "Listen Up!"   How would you characterize the listening that goes on at your job? What is the greatest listening problem? Which of the suggestions are you most apt to violate? Can you identify reasons why you don't follow the suggestion? How might you apply these suggestions to communication in your own family?

Source: "Want to do better on the job?—Listen up!" by Diane Cole as appeared in *Working Mother,* March 1991. Copyright © 1991 by Diane Cole. Reprinted by permission of the author.

INCREASING LISTENING EFFECTIVENESS

Because you listen for a variety of purposes, the principles of effective listening should vary from one situation to another. The following four dimensions of listening illustrate the appropriateness of different listening modes for different communication situations.

Participatory and Nonparticipatory Listening

The key to effective listening in most situations is to participate actively. Perhaps the best preparation for participatory listening is to *act* like you're participating (physically and mentally) in the communication exchange. For many people, this may be the most abused rule of effective listening. Recall, for example, how your body almost automatically reacts to important news: Almost immediately you assume an upright posture, cock your head to the speaker, and remain relatively still and quiet. You do this almost reflexively because this is how you listen most effectively. Even more important than this physical alertness is mental alertness. As a listener, participate in the communication interaction as a partner with the speaker, as one who is emotionally and intellectually ready to engage in the sharing of meaning.

In much of the United States, effective participatory listening is expressive. Let the listener know that you're participating in the communication interaction. Nonverbally, maintain eye contact, focus your concentration on the speaker rather than on others present, and express your feelings facially. Verbally, ask appropriate questions, signal understanding with "I see" or "yes," and express agreement or disagreement as appropriate.

Nonparticipatory listening, however, is not without merit. Nonparticipatory listening—listening without talking or directing the speaker in any obvious way, listening by giving only minimal responses—is a powerful means of communicating acceptance. This is the kind of listening that people ask for when they say, "just listen to me." They are essentially asking you to suspend your judgment and "just listen." This form of listening allows the speaker to develop his or her thoughts and ideas in the presence of another person who accepts but does not evaluate, who supports but does not intrude. By listening with only minimal participation, you provide a supportive and receptive environment. Once that has been established, you may wish to participate in a more active way, verbally and nonverbally.

Another form of nonparticipatory listening is just to sit back, relax, and let the auditory stimulation wash over you without exerting any significant energy and especially without your directing the stimuli in any way, as in listening to music for pure enjoyment rather than to make critical evaluations.

In regulating participatory and nonparticipatory listening, keep the following guidelines in mind:

- Avoid preoccupation with yourself or with external issues. Avoid focusing on your own performance in the interaction or on rehearsing your responses. Avoid, too, focusing on matters that are irrelevant to the interaction, on what you did Saturday night or your plans for this evening. Even in nonparticipatory listening, devote full attention to the speaker.

Listening, not imitation, may be the sincerest form of flattery.
—Joyce Brothers

Visit the International Listening Association's website at http://www.listen.org. What resources are available to someone learning about listening

- Because you can process information faster than the average rate of speech, there is often a time lag. Use this time to summarize the speaker's thoughts, formulate questions, draw connections between what the speaker says and what you already know. Avoid the tendency to let your mind wander to perhaps more pleasant thoughts.
- Be careful lest you fail to hear what the speaker is really saying and instead hear what you expect. You know that Lin frequently complains about grades, so when Lin tells you about problems with a teacher, you automatically "hear" Lin complaining (again) about grades.
- When listening with only minimal participation attend carefully to what the person is saying; make sure that you don't minimize your participation to the point where it looks like you stopped listening.

Empathic and Objective Listening

If you're to understand what a person means and what a person is feeling, listen empathically. To empathize with others is to feel with them, to see the world as they see it, to feel what they feel. Empathy will enable you to understand another's meaning more fully.

There is no easy method of achieving empathy. But it's something you should work toward. Popular students might intellectually understand why an unpopular student feels depressed, but that will not enable them to understand emotionally the feelings of depression. To accomplish that, they must put themselves in the position of the unpopular student, role-play a bit, and begin to feel that student's feelings and think his or her thoughts. Then the popular students will be in a better position to understand, to genuinely empathize. (See Chapter 7 for specific suggestions for developing and communicating empathy.)

Although empathic listening is the preferred response for most communication situations, there are times when you need to go beyond empathy and

CAUTION

How can **hearing what you expect to hear** (a rather natural tendency) prevent you from listening openly about what is being said? Have you ever "heard" what you expected to hear, only to find out later that what you heard was different from what was said?

Evaluating Information

Distinguish between hypotheses and conclusions. On the basis of your observations of behaviors, formulate hypotheses to test against additional information and evidence rather than draw conclusions you then look to confirm. Delay formulating conclusions until you have had a chance to process a variety of cues. At the same time, seek additional evidence. For example, compare your perceptions with those of others. Do others see things in the same way you do? If not, ask yourself if your perceptions may be in some way distorted.

"I can't get off the phone, he won't stop listening!"

Courtesy Jerry Marcus

Would it be more difficult to empathize with someone who is overjoyed because of winning the lottery for $7 million or with someone who is overcome with sadness because of a death of a loved one? How easy or difficult would it be for you to empathize with someone who was depressed because the expected raise of $40,000 turned out to be only $25,000? In what situations is it easiest for you to experience empathy? In what situations is it difficult?

measure the meanings and feelings against some objective reality. It's important to listen to a friend tell you how the entire world hates him or her and to understand how your friend feels and why. But then you need to look a bit more objectively at your friend and at the world and perhaps see the paranoia or self-hatred at work. Sometimes you have to put your empathic responses aside and listen with objectivity and detachment.

In adjusting your empathic and objective listening focus, keep the following recommendations in mind:

- Seek to understand both thoughts and feelings. Don't consider your listening task finished until you've understood what the speaker is feeling as well as thinking.
- Avoid "offensive listening," the tendency to listen to bits and pieces of information that will enable you to attack the speaker or find fault with something the speaker has said.
- Beware of the "friend-or-foe" factors that may lead you to distort messages because of your attitudes toward another person. For example, if you think Freddy is stupid, then it will take added effort to listen objectively to Freddy's messages and to hear anything that is clear or insightful.

CAUTION

How might **listening offensively** distort your ability to acquire the information you need? Can you identify two or three people to whom you listen offensively? Do some people listen offensively to you? Has this type of listening ever created problems for you?

Nonjudgmental and Critical Listening

Effective listening is both nonjudgmental and critical. It involves listening with an open mind with a view toward understanding. But, it also involves listening critically with a view toward making some kind of evaluation or judgment. Clearly, listening for understanding (nonjudgmentally) should come first. Only after you have fully understood the message should you evaluate or judge. Listening with an open mind is often difficult. It's not easy, for example, to listen to arguments against some cherished belief or to criticisms of something you value highly. Listening often stops when a hostile or critical remark is made. Admittedly, to continue listening with an open mind is difficult, yet it is in precisely these situations that it's especially important to listen fairly.

Supplement open-minded listening with critical listening. Listening with an open mind will help you understand the messages; listening with a critical mind will help you analyze and evaluate the messages. This is especially true in the college environment. It's easy simply to listen to a teacher and take down what is said. Yet, it's important that you also evaluate and critically analyze what is said. Teachers have biases, too; at times consciously and at times unconsciously, these biases creep into scholarly discussions. Identify and bring these to the surface. The vast majority of teachers will appreciate critical responses. Such responses show that someone is listening and will help to stimulate further examination of ideas.

In adjusting your nonjudgmental and critical listening, focus on the following guidelines:

- Keep an open mind. Avoid prejudging. Delay evaluation until you have fully understood the intent and the content of the message being communicated.

- Avoid filtering out difficult messages. Avoid distorting messages through oversimplification or leveling—the tendency to eliminate details and to simplify complex messages so that they're easier to remember.
- Avoid filtering out unpleasant or undesirable messages, messages that may run counter to your fundamental beliefs, for example; you may miss the very information you need to change your assumptions or your behaviors.
- Recognize your own biases; we all have them. These may interfere with accurate listening and cause you to distort message reception through the process of *assimilation*—the tendency to interpret what you hear or think you hear according to your own biases, prejudices, and expectations. For example, are your ethnic, national, or religious biases preventing you from appreciating the speaker's point of view? Biases may also lead to *sharpening*—the tendency for a particular item of information to take on increased importance because it seems to confirm the listener's stereotypes or prejudices.
- Use critical listening when evaluations and judgments are called for. Use nonjudgmental listening when support is needed.

CAUTION

Is your classroom listening ever characterized by your **filtering out unpleasant or difficult messages?** What effects might this have?

CAUTION

In what ways can **assimilating messages into your own biases** distort the meanings you create? How might it distort your evaluations of people?

CAUTION

How does **sharpening** work in gossip? If you've ever witnessed sharpening, what effect did it have on people's perceptions?

Which of the suggestions for adjusting your listening between nonjudgmental and critical listening do you regularly follow? What one suggestion do you follow least often?

Evaluating Information

Listen for truth and accuracy. Listening critically also depends on assessing the truth and accuracy of the message. Thus, in addition to keeping an open mind and delaying judgments, it's necessary to focus on other issues as well:

- Is the message logical and accurate as far as you understand it? Is this car really that great? Are there any disadvantages to this particular car?
- Is the message relatively complete? Is the relevant information presented in sufficient detail? Have crucial parts been left out? Have all the costs been identified?

HOW TO ...
Avoid Being a Difficult Listener

Poet Walt Whitman once said, "To have great poets, there must be great audiences, too." The same is true of interpersonal interaction; to have great interpersonal communication, there must be great listeners as well as great talkers. There must be great speakers-listeners. Here, in brief, are a few types of listeners that make conversation difficult. It's easy to see others in these roles. It's harder but more important to see ourselves as listeners who make conversation difficult.

- The **static listener** gives no feedback, remains relatively motionless, reveals no expression. You wonder, Why isn't she reacting? Am I not producing sound?
- The **monotonous feedback** giver seems responsive but the responses never vary; regardless of what you say, the response is the same. Am I making sense? Why is he still smiling? I'm being dead serious.
- The **overly expressive listener** reacts to just about everything with extreme responses. Why is she so expressive? I didn't say anything that provocative. She'll have a heart attack when I get to the punchline.
- The **reader/writer** reads or writes, while "listening" and only occasionally glances up. Am I that boring? Is last week's student newspaper more interesting than I am?

- The **eye avoider** looks all around the room and at others but never at you. Why isn't he looking at me? Do I have spinach on my teeth?
- The **preoccupied listener** listens to other things at the same time, often with headphones with the sound so loud that it interferes with your own thinking. When is she going to shut that music off and really listen? Am I so boring that my talk needs background music?
- The **waiting listener** listens for a cue to take over the speaking turn. Is he listening to me or rehearsing his next interruption?
- The **thought-completing** listener listens a little and then finishes your thought. Am I that predictable? Why do I bother saying anything? He already knows what I'm going to say.

Is there any way that you (as a speaker) can help your listeners become less difficult? That is, how can you prevent your listeners from giving monotonous feedback? From avoiding eye contact? As a listener what can you do to prevent yourself from falling into one of these difficult modes?

[The next How To box appears on page 118.]

Surface and Depth Listening

In Shakespeare's *Julius Caesar*, Marc Antony, delivering Caesar's funeral oration, says: "I come to bury Caesar, not to praise him. . . . The evil that men do lives after them. . . . The good is oft interred with their bones." And later: "For Brutus is an honourable man. . . . So are they all, all honourable men." But Antony, as we know, did come to praise Caesar and to convince the crowd that Brutus was not an honorable man. He came to incite the crowd to avenge the death of Caesar, his friend.

In most messages there is an obvious meaning that a literal reading of the words and sentences reveals. But there is most often another level of meaning. Most messages exist on two or three levels at the same time. For example, on one level, the friend who asks you how you like his or her new haircut is asking for your opinion. On another level, perhaps a more important level, your friend may be asking you to say something positive about him or her. Your friend may be asking for positive stroking, asking you to say something pleasant and supportive.

Become sensitive to different levels of meaning. If you respond only to the surface-level communication (the literal meaning), you'll miss the opportunity

Watch a movie and try to identify as many types of listening as you can. Were the different types of listening used appropriately? *(An interesting review paper could be built around the role of listening in a particular film—how listening helped to define the characters or advance the plot, helped or hindered relationship development.)*

to make meaningful contact with the other person's feelings and real needs. If you say to your parent who complains about work, "You're always complaining. I bet you really love working so hard," you may be failing to answer this very real call for understanding and appreciation.

In regulating your surface and depth listening, consider the following guidelines:

- Focus on both verbal and nonverbal messages. Recognize both consistent and inconsistent "packages" of messages and take these cues as guides for inferring the meaning the speaker is trying to communicate. Ask questions when in doubt. Listen also to what is omitted. Remember that you communicate by what you leave out as well as by what you include.

- Listen for both content and relational messages (Chapter 1). The student who constantly challenges the teacher is on one level communicating disagreement over content; the student is debating the issues. However, on the relationship level, the student may be objecting to the instructor's authority or authoritarianism. If the instructor is to deal effectively with the student, both types of messages must be addressed.

- Do not disregard the literal (surface) meaning of interpersonal messages in your attempt to uncover the more hidden (deep) meanings. Balance your attention between the surface and the underlying meanings. Respond to the various levels of meaning in the messages of others as you would like others to respond to yours—sensitively but not obsessively, readily but not over ambitiously.

Can you identify an example from your own experience in which messages were communicated on two different levels but either you or the other person listened to and responded to only one level? *(This could be the start of an interesting personal experience paper.)*

How would you go about seeking answers to such questions as these *(any of which would make suitable research paper topics):* Is listening efficiency influenced by the sex of the speaker and listener? For example, is listening more efficient when speaker and listener are the same sex or opposite sex? Does it make a difference? Of what value is listening competency in business and industry? Are men or women better at demonstrating empathy? Would some cultures respond negatively to active listening?

SKILL BUILDING EXERCISE 4.3.

Paraphrasing to Ensure Understanding

One of the most important skills that helps ensure effective listening is paraphrasing. For each of the messages presented below, write a paraphrase that you think would be appropriate. After you complete the paraphrases, ask another person if he or she would accept them as objective restatements of thoughts and feelings. Rework the paraphrases until the other person agrees that they are accurate. A sample paraphrase is provided in the first example.

1. I can't deal with my parents' constant fighting. I've seen it for the last 10 years and I really can't stand it anymore.
Paraphrase: *You have trouble dealing with their fighting. You seem really upset by this last fight.*
2. Did you hear I got engaged to Jerry? Our racial and religious differences are really going to cause

difficulties for both of us. But, we love each other. We'll work it through.
3. I got a C on that paper. That's the worst grade I've ever received. I just can't believe that I got a C. This is my major. What am I going to do?
4. I can't understand why I didn't get that promotion. I was here longer and did better work than Thompson. Even my two supervisors said I was the next in line for the promotion. And now it looks like another one won't come along for at least a year.
5. That rotten, inconsiderate pig just up and left. He never even said goodbye. We were together for six months and after one small argument he leaves without a word. And he even took my bathrobe—that expensive one he bought for my last birthday.

(continued)

(continued)

6. I'm just not sure what to do. I really love Chris. She's the sweetest kid I've ever known. I mean she'd do anything for me. But, she really wants to get married. I do too and yet I don't want to make such a commitment. I mean that's a long term thing. And, much as I hate to admit it, I don't want the responsibility of a wife, a family, a house. I really don't need that kind of pressure.

Thinking Critically About Paraphrasing.
How might paraphrasing be of value in interpersonal conflict situations? In intercultural communication situations? Can you identify situations where paraphrasing would be inappropriate?

SUMMARY OF CONCEPTS AND SKILLS

In this chapter we defined listening, explored its five stages, and identified some of the reasons we listen. We then looked at the wide cultural and gender differences in listening. Last, we looked at the types of listening and how best to adjust your listening to achieve maximum effectiveness.

1. *Listening* may be viewed as a five-step process: receiving, understanding, remembering, evaluating, and responding. Listening difficulties and obstacles exist at each of these stages.
2. We listen for a variety of reasons: to learn, to relate, to influence, to play, and to help.
3. Cultural differences in accents, in nonverbal behaviors, in the directness of the style of communicating, in the way they see credibility, and in the feedback they give and expect may create listening difficulties.
4. Men and women seem to listen with different purposes in mind and with different behaviors.
5. Effective listening depends on varying your listening behavior appropriately between participatory and nonparticipatory, empathic and objective, nonjudgmental and critical, and surface and depth listening.

Check your ability to apply these skills. You'll gain most from this brief experience if you think carefully about each skill and try to identify instances from your recent communications in which you did or did not act on the basis of the specific skill. Use a rating scale such as the

following: 1 = almost always, 2 = often, 3 = sometimes, 4 = rarely, and 5 = almost never.

_____ 1. In receiving messages, focus attention on the speaker's verbal and nonverbal messages, avoid interrupting

_____ 2. In understanding messages, relate the new information to what you already know; ask questions and paraphrase to ensure understanding

_____ 3. In remembering messages, identify the central ideas, summarize the message in an easier to retain form, and use repetition (aloud or to yourself) to help with key terms and names

_____ 4. In evaluating messages, try first to understand fully what the speaker means and try to identify any biases and self-interests that may lead to an unfair presentation of material

_____ 5. In responding to messages, express support and own your own responses

_____ 6. In listening and in speaking, recognize the cultural differences that can create barriers to mutual understanding.

_____ 7. In listening, be careful to recognize that women and men may listen with different purposes in mind and that they may act differently, but mean the same thing, or act similarly, but mean different things.

_____ 8. Regulate and adjust your listening between participatory and nonparticipatory, empathic and objective, nonjudgmental and critical, and surface and depth listening.

VOCABULARY QUIZ. THE LANGUAGE OF LISTENING

Match these terms about listening with their definitions. Record the number of the definition next to the term.

__7__ listening

__6__ leveling

__5__ sharpening

__8__ assimilation

__9__ empathic listening

__10__ supportive listening

__2__ nonparticipatory listening

__1__ memory

__4__ paraphrase

__3__ evaluating

1. A reconstructive, not a reproductive, process.
2. Listening while giving only minimal responses and not directing the speaker in any way.
3. An essential stage in the listening process where we make judgments about a message.
4. A restatement of something said in your own words.
5. The procedure where details of what we have heard become heightened and emphasized.
6. The reduction of the number of details that we remember of something we have heard.
7. A process of receiving, understanding, remembering, evaluating, and responding to messages.
8. The tendency to reconstruct messages so they reflect our own attitudes, prejudices, needs, and values.
9. Placing ourselves into the position of the speaker so that we feel as the speaker feels.
10. Listening without judgment or evaluation; listening for understanding.

Verbal Messages

CHAPTER CONCEPTS	CHAPTER OBJECTIVES	CHAPTER SKILLS
	After completing this chapter, you should be able to	*After completing this chapter, you should be able to*
The Nature of Language	1. Identify the characteristics of language and their implications for human communication	Communicate with a recognition that meanings are in people, are context based, have both denotative and connotative meanings, vary in directness, are culturally based institutions, and vary in abstraction
Disconfirmation	2. Explain disconfirmation, distinguish it from confirmation and rejection, and explain the nature of sexist, hetereosexist, and racist language	Regulate your confirmations as appropriate, especially avoiding sexist, heterosexist, and racist language and, in general, language that puts down other groups
Using Verbal Messages Effectively and Critically	3. Explain the suggestions for using verbal messages effectively	Identify conceptual distortions in your own and in the language of others and avoid them in your own messages

A couple on the second night of their honeymoon are sitting at a hotel bar. The woman strikes up a conversation with the couple next to her. The husband refuses to communicate with the couple and becomes antagonistic toward his wife and the couple. The wife then grows angry because he has created such an awkward and unpleasant situation. Each becomes increasingly disturbed, and the evening ends in a bitter conflict with each convinced of the other's lack of consideration. Eight years later, they analyze this argument. Apparently "honeymoon" had meant different things to each. To the husband it was a "golden opportunity to ignore the rest of the world and simply explore each other." He felt his wife's interaction with the other couple implied there was something lacking in him. To the wife "honeymoon" meant an opportunity to try out her new role as wife. "I had never had a conversation with another couple as a wife before," she said. "Previous to this I had always been a 'girl friend' or 'fiancee' or 'daughter' or 'sister.'"

This example—taken from Ronald D. Laing, H. Phillipson, and A. Russell Lee in *Interpersonal Perception* (1966; also Watzlawick, 1977)—illustrates the confusion that can result when you look for meaning in the words and not in the person. It's just one of the ways you can fail to communicate your meaning, one of the topics of this chapter.

THE NATURE OF LANGUAGE

In communication you use two major signal systems—the verbal and the nonverbal. This chapter focuses on the verbal system: language as a system for communicating meaning, how it can be used effectively and how it creates problems when it isn't.

Language Meanings Are in People

If you wanted to know the meaning of the word "love," you'd probably turn to a dictionary. There you'd find, according to Webster's: "the attraction, desire, or affection felt for a person who arouses delight or admiration

Think about the implication of the principle that meanings are in people for intercultural communication. Consider, for example, the differences in meaning for such words as *woman* to an American and an Iranian, *religion* to a born-again Christian and an atheist, and *lunch* to a Chinese rice farmer and a Wall Street executive. What communication principles might help you more effectively communicate your meaning in these situations?

CAUTION

How might **looking for meaning only in words** limit your ability to acquire information and accurately evaluate a situation? Have others ever misinterpreted the meaning you wanted to communicate because they failed to look for meaning in you?

Visit http://www.ccil.org/jargon/, http://www.onelook.com/, http://c.gp.cs.cmu.edu:5103/prog/webster/ or any electronic dictionary and browse through the terms and definitions. How is an online dictionary different from a print one? *(An interesting review paper could be written on online dictionaries or, in fact, on any online database that would be of value to the student of interpersonal communication.)*

or elicits tenderness, sympathetic interest, or benevolence." This is the denotative meaning.

But where would you turn if you wanted to know what Pedro means when he says "I'm in love"? Of course, you'd turn to Pedro to discover his meaning. It's in this sense that meanings are not in words but in people. Consequently, to uncover meaning, you need to look into people and not merely into words.

Also recognize that as you change, you also change the meanings you created out of past messages. Thus, although the message sent may not have changed, the meanings you created from it yesterday and the meanings you create today may be quite different. Yesterday, when a special someone said, "I love you," you created certain meanings. But today, when you learn that the same "I love you" was said to three other people or when you fall in love with someone else, you drastically change the meanings you perceive from those three words.

Meanings Depend on Their Context

Verbal and nonverbal communications exist in a context, and that context to a large extent determines the meaning of any verbal or nonverbal behavior. The same words or behaviors may have totally different meanings when they occur in different contexts. For example, the greeting, "How are you?" means "Hello" to someone you pass regularly on the street but means "Is your health improving?" when said to a friend in the hospital. A wink to an attractive person on a bus means something completely different from a wink that signifies a put-on or a lie. Similarly, the meaning of a given signal depends on the other behavior it accompanies or is close to in time. Pounding a fist on the table during a speech in support of a politician means something quite different from that same gesture in response to news of a friend's death. Divorced from the context, it's impossible to tell what meaning was intended from just examining the signals. Of course, even if you know the context in detail, you still might not be able to decipher the meaning of the message.

Especially important is the cultural context, a context emphasized throughout this text. The cultural context will influence not only the meaning assigned to speech and gesture but whether your meaning is friendly, offensive, lacking in respect, condescending, sensitive, and so on.

Language is Both Denotative and Connotative

Two general types of meaning are essential to identify: denotation and connotation. **Denotation** refers to the meaning you'd find in a dictionary; it's the meaning that members of the culture assign to a word. **Connotation** refers to the emotional meaning that specific speakers-listeners give to a word. Take as an example the word *death*. To a doctor this word might mean (or denote) the time when the heart stops. This is an objective description of a particular event. On the other hand, to the dead person's mother (upon being informed of her son's death), the word means (or connotes) much more. It recalls her son's youth, ambition, family, illness, and so on. To her it's a highly emotional, subjective, and personal word. These emotional, subjective, or personal reactions are the word's connotative meaning. The denotation of a word is its objective definition. The connotation of a word is its subjective or emotional meaning.

How would you describe this dinner scene in denotative terms? In connotative terms? Which of these two descriptions is more likely to be accurate? Why?

Evaluating Information

Don't confuse snarl and purr words with objective descriptions. Semanticist S. I. Hayakawa (Hayakawa & Hayakawa, 1990) coined the terms "snarl words" and "purr words" to further clarify the distinction between denotative and connotative meaning. Snarl words are highly negative ("She's an idiot." "He's a pig." "They're a bunch of losers."). Sexist, racist, and heterosexist language and hate speech provide lots of other examples. Purr words are highly positive ("She's a real sweetheart." "He's a dream." "They're the greatest.").

Although they may sometimes seem to have denotative meaning and refer to the "real world," snarl and purr words are actually connotative in meaning. They don't describe people or events but rather, they reveal the speaker's feelings about these people or events.

Language Varies in Directness

Think about how you'd respond to someone saying the following sentences.

1A. I'm so bored; I have nothing to do tonight.
2A. I'd like to go to the movies. Would you like to come?
1B. Do you feel like hamburgers tonight?
2B. I'd like hamburgers tonight. How about you?

Statements 1A and 1B are relatively indirect; they're attempts to get the listener to say or do something without committing the speaker. Statements numbered 2A and 2B are more direct—they state more clearly the speaker's preferences and then ask the listeners if they agree. A more obvious example of an indirect message occurs when you glance at your watch to communicate that it's late and that you had better be going. Indirect messages have both advantages and disadvantages.

Advantages of Indirect Messages

Indirect messages allow you to express a desire without insulting or offending anyone; they allow you to observe the rules of polite interaction. So instead of saying, "I'm bored with this group," you say, "It's getting late and I have to get up early tomorrow," or you look at your watch and pretend to be surprised by the time. Instead of saying, "This food tastes like cardboard," you say, "I just started my diet" or "I just ate." In each instance you're stating a preference but are saying it indirectly so as to avoid offending someone. Not all direct requests, however, should be considered impolite. In one study of Spanish and English speakers, for example, no evidence was found to support the assumption that politeness and directness were incompatible (Mir, 1993).

Sometimes indirect messages allow you to ask for compliments in a socially acceptable manner, such as saying, "I was thinking of getting a nose job." You hope to get the desired compliment: "A nose job? You? Your nose is perfect."

Disadvantages of Indirect Messages

Indirect messages, however, can also create problems. Consider the following dialogue in which an indirect request is made:

PAT: You wouldn't like to have my parents over for dinner this weekend, would you?

CHRIS: I really wanted to go to the shore and just relax.

PAT: Well, if you feel you have to go to the shore, I'll make the dinner myself. You go to the shore. I really hate having them over and doing all the work myself. It's such a drag shopping, cooking, and cleaning all by myself.

Given this situation, Chris has two basic alternatives. One is to stick with the plans to go to the shore and relax. In this case Pat is going to be upset and Chris is going to be made to feel guilty for not helping with the dinner. A second alternative is to give in to Pat, help with the dinner, and not go to the shore. In this case Chris is going to have to give up a much-desired plan and is likely to resent Pat's "manipulative" tactics. Regardless of which decision is made, one person wins and one person loses. This win–lose situation creates resentment, competition, and often an "I'll get even" attitude. With direct requests, this type of situation is much less likely to develop. Consider:

PAT: I'd like to have my parents over for dinner this weekend. What do you think?

CHRIS: Well, I really wanted to go to the shore and just relax.

Regardless of what develops next, both individuals are starting out on relatively equal footing. Each has clearly and directly stated a preference. Although at first these preferences seem mutually exclusive, it might be possible to meet both persons' needs. For example, Chris might say, "How about going to the shore this weekend and having your parents over next weekend? I'm really exhausted; I could use the rest." Here is a direct response to a direct request. Unless there is some pressing need to have Pat's parents over for dinner this weekend, this response may enable each to meet the other's needs.

Gender and Cultural Differences in Directness

The popular stereotype in much of the United States holds that women are indirect in making requests and in giving orders. This indirectness communicates powerlessness, discomfort with their own authority. Men, the stereotype continues, are direct, sometimes to the point of being blunt or rude. This directness communicates power and comfort with one's own authority.

Deborah Tannen (1994) provides an interesting perspective on these stereotypes. Women are, it seems, more indirect in giving orders and are more likely to say, for example, "It would be great if these letters could go out today" rather than "Have these letters out by 3." But, Tannen (1994b, p. 84) argues that "issuing orders indirectly can be the prerogative of those in power" and does in no way show powerlessness. Power, to Tannen, is the ability to chose your own style of communication.

Acquiring Information

Approach new ideas positively and critically.   A useful critical thinking tool for all kinds of verbal communication is responding to new ideas with the four-step technique called PIP'N (DeVito, 1996): **P**araphrase, state in your own words what you think the other person is saying to ensure that you're both talking about the same thing; **I**nteresting, say why you think this idea might be interesting to you, to others, to the organization; **P**ositive, say something positive. What's good about it? How might it solve a problem?; and **N**egative, state any negatives that you think the idea might entail. Might it prove expensive? Difficult to implement? Is it directed at insignificant issues?

Because the emphasis in Internet communication—in e-mail, Internet relay chat (IRC) groups, or in newsgroups—is on speed (in sending, reading, and responding), directness (and the brevity it entails) is preferred. This cultural preference is seen in the emphasis on practically eliminating introductory and concluding comments in messages, in using abbreviations to express commonly used phrases (BTW for "by the way"), in having "signatures" that automatically "sign" your e-mails, and in enabling you to quote relevant sections of an e-mail you're answering. What role does directness play in other forms of computer communication, for example, IRC groups or newsgroups?

Men, however, are also indirect but in different situations (Rundquist, 1992; Tannen, 1994a, b). According to Tannen, men are more likely to use indirectness when they express weakness, reveal a problem, or admit an error. Men are more likely to speak indirectly in expressing emotions other than anger. Men are also more indirect when they refuse expressions of increased romantic intimacy. Men are thus indirect, the theory goes, when they're saying something that goes against the masculine stereotype.

Many Asian and Latin American cultures stress the value of indirectness largely because it enables a person to avoid appearing criticized or contradicted and thereby losing face. A somewhat different kind of indirectness is seen in the greater use of intermediaries to resolve conflict among the Chinese than among North Americans, for example (Ma, 1992). In most of the United States, however, you're taught that directness is the preferred style. "Be up front" and "tell it like it is" are commonly heard communication guidelines. Contrast these with the following two principles of indirectness found in the Japanese language (Tannen, 1994b):

omoiyari, close to empathy, says that listeners need to understand the speaker without the speaker being specific or direct. This style obviously places a much greater demand on the listener than would a direct speaking style.

sassuru advises listeners to anticipate a speaker's meanings and use subtle cues from the speaker to infer his or her total meaning.

It's interesting to note that almost all the etiquette books are written by women. If you doubt this, look through the etiquette section in any large bookstore. Why do you think this is so? *(A useful review paper could be written on one of the popular etiquette books and its relationship to interpersonal communication.)*

Are you generally more direct when talking with members of the same sex? Members of the opposite sex? Are you generally more direct with members of your own culture? Members of other cultures?

Acquiring Information

Use the abstraction ladder as a critical thinking tool.
To gain a different perspective on a question, vary its level of abstraction. For example, if your problem is "How can I write better progress reports?" you might gain a different perspective by asking questions at higher and lower levels of abstraction:
   Higher level of abstraction: How can I become a more effective writer?
   Original question: How can I write better progress reports?
   Lower level of abstraction: How can I write better openings for these reports?
   Notice that the level of abstraction on which you phrase your question influences the answers you generate. The higher level question focuses attention on improving writing in general; sentence length, organizational strategies, writing dialogue, and the like are possible directions this question suggests. The lower level question focuses attention on a more specific area and might suggest previewing summary recommendations, opening with questions, or identifying the objectives of the report. Try generating different perspectives by phrasing higher and lower level abstractions for each of these questions: *How can I become a better relationship partner? How can I become a better listener? How can I become more popular with my peers?*

In thinking about direct and indirect messages, it's important to realize the ease with which misunderstandings can occur. For example, a person who uses an indirect style of speech may be doing so to be polite and may have been taught this style by his or her culture. If you assume, instead, that the person is using indirectness to be manipulative, because your culture regards it so, then miscommunication is inevitable.

Language Varies in Abstraction

Consider the following list of terms:

- entertainment
- film
- American film
- recent American film
- *Titanic*

At the top is the general or abstract entertainment. Note that "entertainment" includes all the other items on the list plus various other items—television, novels, drama, comics, and so on. "Film" is more specific and concrete. It includes all of the items below it as well as various other items such as Indian film or Russian film. It excludes, however, all entertainment that is not film. "American film" is again more specific than film and excludes all films that are not American. "Recent American film" further limits American film to a time period. *Titanic* specifies concretely the one item to which reference is made.

The more general term—in this case, "entertainment"—conjures up a number of different images. One person in the audience may focus on television, another on music, another on comic books, and still another on radio. To some, "film" may bring to mind the early silent films. To others, it brings to mind high-tech special effects. To still others, it recalls Disney's animated cartoons. *Titanic* guides the listener still further—in this case to

LISTENING
Gender Differences in Verbal Messages

The best way to start thinking about gender differences in language is to think about your own beliefs. These beliefs influence what you hear (or think you hear) and the interpretations you give to what you hear. The following self-test will help.

SELF-TEST: GENDER DIFFERENCES

Instructions: Here are 10 statements about the "differences" between the speech of women and men. For each of the following statements, indicate whether you think the statement describes Women's Speech (W), Men's Speech (M), or Women's and Men's Speech Equally (WM).

_____ 1. This speech is logical rather than emotional.

_____ 2. This speech is vague.

_____ 3. This speech is endless, less concise, and jumps from one idea to another.

_____ 4. This speech is highly businesslike.

_____ 5. This speech is more polite.

_____ 6. This speech uses weaker forms (for example, the weak intensifiers like *so* and *such*) and fewer exclamations.

_____ 7. This speech contains more tag questions (for example, questions appended to statements that ask for agreement, such as "Let's meet at 10 o'clock, *OK?*").

_____ 8. This speech is more euphemistic (contains more polite words as substitutes for some taboo or potentially offensive terms) and uses fewer swear words.

_____ 9. This speech is generally more effective.

_____ 10. This speech is less forceful and less in control.

Thinking Critically About Gender Differences.

After responding to all 10 statements, consider the following: (1) On what evidence did you base your answers? (2) How strongly do you believe that your answers are correct? (3) What do you think might account for sex differences in verbal behavior? That is, how did the language differences that might distinguish the sexes come into existence? (4) What effect might these language differences (individually or as a group) have on communication (and relationships generally) between the sexes? *Don't read any further* until you have responded to the above statements and questions.

The 10 statements were drawn from the research of Cheris Kramarae (1974a, 1974b, 1977, 1981; see also Coates and Cameron, 1989), who argues that these "differences"—with the exception of statements 5 and 8 (women's speech is often more "polite")—are actually stereotypes of women's and men's speech, which are not in fact confirmed in analyses of actual speech. According to Kramarae, then, you should have answered Women's and Men's Speech Equally for statements 1, 2, 3, 4, 6, 7, 9, and 10 and Women's Speech for statements 5 and 8. Perhaps you see these "differences" in cartoons or on television, and this teaches you that they actually characterize real speech.

Reexamine your answers to the above 10 statements. Were your answers based on your actual listening to the speech of women and men or might they have been based on what you think you heard based on your beliefs about women's and men's speech?

[The next Listening To box appears on page 150.]

---

one film. But, note that even though *Titanic* identifies one film, different listeners are likely to focus on different aspects of the film, perhaps its special effects, perhaps its love story, perhaps its historical accuracy, perhaps its financial success.

Effective verbal messages include words from a wide range of abstractions. At times a general term may suit your needs best; at other times a more specific term may serve better. Generally, however, the specific term will prove the better choice. As you get more specific—less abstract—you more effectively guide the images that come to your listeners' minds.

If women speak and hear a language of connection and intimacy, while men speak and hear a language of status and independence, then communication between men and women can be like cross-cultural communication, prey to a clash of conversational styles. Instead of different dialects, it has been said they speak different genderlects.
—*Deborah Tannen*

SKILL BUILDING EXERCISE 5.1.
Climbing the Abstraction Ladder

The **abstraction ladder** is a device to illustrate the different levels of abstraction on which different terms exist (Figure 5.1). Notice that as you go from "animal" to "pampered white toy poodle" you're going down in terms of abstraction, you're getting more and more specific. As you get more specific, you more clearly communicate your own meanings and more easily direct the listener's attention to what you wish. For each of the terms listed below, indicate at least four possible terms that indicate increasing specificity. The first example is done for you.

Thinking Critically About Abstractions.
The general suggestion for effective communication is to use abstractions sparingly and to express your meanings specifically with words that are low in abstraction. However, are there situations when terms high in abstraction would be more effective than specific terms? How would you describe advertisements for cosmetics in terms of high and low abstraction? Advertisements for cereals? Advertisements for cat and dog food? How would you describe political campaign speaking in terms of abstraction?

Level 1	Level 2 ore specific than 1	Level 3 more specific than 2	Level 4 more specific than 3	Level 5 more specific than 4
house	mansion	large brick house	brick mansion	Governor's mansion
desire				
car				
toy				
magazine				
sports				

HOW TO . . .
Be Polite on the Net

The rules of **netiquette** are the rules for communicating politely over the Internet. Much as the rules of etiquette provide guidance in communicating in social situations, the rules of netiquette provide guidance for communicating over the net. These rules, as you'll see, are helpful in making Internet communication more pleasant and easier, achieving greater personal efficiency, and putting less strain on the system and other users. Here are several guidelines suggested by computer researchers (Shea, 1994; James & Weingarten, 1995; Barron, 1995).

• *Read the FAQs.* Before asking questions about the system, read the frequently asked questions; your question has probably been asked before and you'll put less strain on the system.

• *Don't shout.* WRITING IN CAPS IS PERCEIVED AS SHOUTING. It's okay to use caps occasionally to achieve emphasis. If you wish to give emphasis, underline, _like this_, or *like this*.

• *Lurk before speaking.* Lurking refers to reading the posted notices and reading the conversations without contributing anything; in computer communication, lurking is good, not bad. Lurking will help you learn the rules of the particular group and will help you avoid saying things you'd like to take back.

- *Don't contribute to traffic jams.* Try connecting during off hours, whenever possible. If you're unable to connect, try later, not immediately. It only puts added strain on the system and you're likely to still be unable to connect. In securing information try local information sources before trying more distant sources; it requires fewer connections and less time. And be economical in using files (for example, photographs) that may tie up lines for long periods of time.

- *Be brief.* Follow the maxim of quantity by communicating only the information that is needed; follow the maxim of manner by communicating clearly, briefly, and in an organized way.
- *Treat newbies kindly;* you were one once yourself.

[The next How To box appears on page 158.]

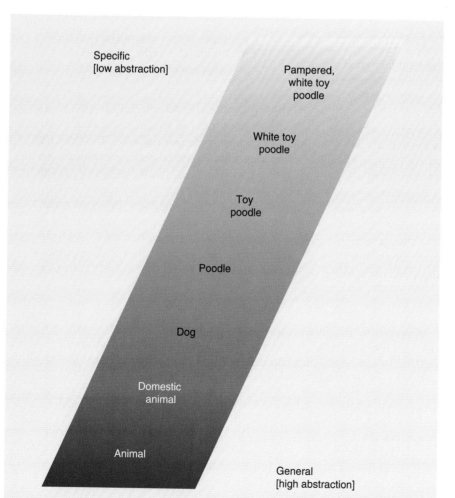

Figure 5.1
The abstraction ladder.

As you go up in abstraction, you get more general; as you go down in abstraction, you get more specific. How would you arrange the following terms in order of abstraction, from most specific to most general: vegetation, tree, elm tree, thing, organic thing, blooming elm tree?

DISCONFIRMATION

Before reading about disconfirmation, take the self-test to examine your own behavior.

SELF-TEST

How Confirming Are You?

Instructions: In your typical communications, how likely are you to display the following behaviors? Use the following scale in responding to each statement:

5 = always
4 = often
3 = sometimes
2 = rarely
1 = never

_____ 1. I acknowledge the presence of another person both verbally and nonverbally.

_____ 2. I acknowledge the contributions of the other person by, for example, supporting or taking issue with what the person says.

_____ 3. During the conversation, I make nonverbal contact by maintaining direct eye contact, touching, hugging, kissing, and otherwise demonstrating acknowledgment of the other person.

_____ 4. I communicate as both speaker and listener, with involvement, concern, and respect for the other person.

_____ 5. I signal my understanding of the other person both verbally and nonverbally.

_____ 6. I reflect back the other person's feelings as a way of showing that I understand these feelings.

_____ 7. I ask questions as appropriate concerning the other person's thoughts and feelings.

_____ 8. I respond to the other person's requests by, for example, returning phone calls and answering letters within a reasonable time.

_____ 9. I encourage the other person to express his or her thoughts and feelings.

_____ 10. I respond directly and exclusively to what the other person says.

Thinking Critically About Confirmation and Disconfirmation. All 10 statements are phrased so that they express confirming behaviors. Therefore, high scores (say, above 35) reflect a strong tendency to engage in confirmation. Low scores (say, below 25) reflect a strong tendency to engage in disconfirmation. Don't assume, however, that all situations call for confirmation and that only insensitive people are disconfirming. You may wish to consider the situations in which disconfirmation would be—if not an effective response—at least a legitimate one.

Visit http://www.albion.com/netiquette/index/html, a home page for Websites devoted to netiquette. Visit one or more of the recommended Websites. What other rules of netiquette can you find that have special relevance to interpersonal communication?

A useful way to introduce disconfirmation and its alternatives, confirmation and rejection, is to consider a specific situation: Pat arrives home late one night. Chris is angry and complains about Pat's coming home so late. Consider some responses Pat might make:

1. Stop screaming. I'm not interested in what you're babbling about. I'll do what I want, when I want. I'm going to bed.

2. What are you so angry about? Didn't you get in three hours late last Thursday? When you went to that office party? So, knock it off.

3. You have a right to be angry. I should have called when I was going to be late but I got involved in an argument at work and I couldn't leave until it was resolved.

In (1) Pat dismisses Chris's anger and even indicates a dismissal of Chris as a person. In (2) Pat rejects the validity of Chris's reasons for being angry but does not dismiss Chris's feelings of anger or Chris as a person. In (3) Pat acknowledges Chris's anger and the reasons for being angry. In addition, Pat provides some kind of explanation and in doing so shows that Chris's feelings and Chris as a person are important and deserve to know what happened. The first response is an example of disconfirmation, the second of rejection, and the third of confirmation.

The psychologist William James once observed that "No more fiendish punishment could be devised, even were such a thing physically possible, than that one should be turned loose in society and remain absolutely unnoticed by all the members thereof." In this often-quoted observation, James identifies the essence of disconfirmation (Watzlawick, Beavin, & Jackson, 1967; Veenendall & Feinstein, 1995).

Disconfirmation is a communication pattern in which you ignore someone's presence as well as that person's communications. You say, in effect, that this person and what he or she has to say are not worth serious attention or effort, that this person and his or her contributions are so unimportant or insignificant that there is no reason to concern ourselves with them.

Note that disconfirmation is not the same as *rejection*. In rejection you disagree with the person; you indicate your unwillingness to accept something the other person says or does. In disconfirming someone, however, you deny that person's significance; you claim that what this person says or does simply does not count.

Confirmation is the opposite communication pattern. In confirmation you not only acknowledge the presence of the other person but you also indicate your acceptance of this person, of this person's definition of self, and of your relationship as defined or viewed by this other person.

Disconfirmation and confirmation may be communicated in a wide variety of ways. Table 5.1 shows just a few and parallels the self-test presented earlier so that you can see clearly not only the confirming but also the opposite

How confirming are the majority of your interpersonal messages? (Confirmation, disconfirmation, and rejection [and sexism, racism, and heterosexism] would all make suitable topics for a concept paper.)

Table 5.1. Confirmation and Disconfirmation.

This table parallels the self-test presented earlier in this unit so that you can see clearly not only the confirming but also the opposite, disconfirming behaviors. As you review this table, try to imagine a specific illustration for each of the ways of communicating disconfirmation and confirmation (Pearson, 1993; Galvin & Brommel, 1996).

Confirmation	Disconfirmation
1. Acknowledge the presence and the contributions of the other by either supporting or taking issue with what the other says (self-test items 1 and 2).	1. Ignore the presence and the messages of the other person; express (nonverbally and verbally) indifference to anything the other says.
2. Make nonverbal contact by maintaining direct eye contact, touching, hugging, kissing, and otherwise demonstrating acknowledgment of the other; engage in dialogue—communication in which both persons are speakers and listeners, both are involved, and both are concerned with each other (items 3 and 4).	2. Make no nonverbal contact; avoid direct eye contact; avoid touching the other person; engage in monologue—communication in which one person speaks and one person listens, there is no interaction, and there is no real concern or respect for each other.
3. Demonstrate understanding of what the other says and means and reflect these feelings to demonstrate your understanding (items 5 and 6).	3. Jump to interpretation or evaluation rather than working at understanding what the other means; express your own feelings, ignore feelings of the other, or give abstract intellectualized responses.
4. Ask questions of the other concerning both thoughts and feelings and acknowledge the questions of the other, return phone calls, answer letters (items 7 and 8).	4. Make statements about yourself, ignore any lack of clarity in the other's remarks; ignore the other's requests; fail to answer questions, return phone calls, answer letters.
5. Encourage the other to express thoughts and feelings and respond directly and exclusively to what the other says (items 9 and 10).	5. Interrupt or otherwise make it difficult for the other to express himself or herself; respond only tangentially or by shifting the focus in another direction.

disconfirming behaviors. As you review this table, try to imagine a specific illustration for each of the ways of communicating disconfirmation and confirmation (Pearson, 1993; Galvin & Brommel, 1996).

You can gain insight into a wide variety of offensive language practices by viewing them as types of disconfirmation, as language that alienates and separates. The three obvious practices are sexism, heterosexism, and racism.

Sexism

The National Council of Teachers of English has proposed guidelines for nonsexist (gender-free, gender-neutral, or sex-fair) language. These concern the use of generic "man," the use of generic "he" and "his," and sex role stereotyping (Penfield, 1987).

Generic Man. The word *man* refers most clearly to an adult male. To use the term to refer to both men and women emphasizes "maleness" at the expense of "femaleness." Similarly, the terms *mankind* or *the common man* or even *cavemen* imply a primary focus on adult males. Gender-neutral terms can easily be substituted. Instead of *mankind,* you can say *humanity, people,* or *human beings.* Instead of *the common man,* you can say *the average person* or *ordinary people.* Instead of *cavemen,* you can say *prehistoric people* or *cave dwellers.*

Similarly, the use of such terms as *policeman* or *fireman* and other terms that presume maleness as the norm and femaleness as a deviation from this norm are clear and common examples of sexist language. Consider using nonsexist alternatives for these and similar terms; make these alternatives (for example, *police officer* and *firefighter*) a part of your active vocabulary. What alternatives can you offer for each of such terms as these: man, mankind, countryman, manmade, the common man, manpower, repairman, doorman, fireman, stewardess, waitress, salesman, mailman, and actress.

Generic He and His. The use of the masculine pronoun to refer to any individual regardless of sex is certainly declining. But, it was only as recently as 1975 that all college textbooks, for example, used the masculine pronoun as generic. There seems to be no legitimate reason why the feminine pronoun could not alternate with the masculine pronoun in referring to hypothetical individuals, or why such terms as *he or she* or *her or him* could not be used instead of just *he* or *him.* Alternatively, you can restructure your sentences to eliminate any reference to gender. For example, the NCTE Guidelines (Penfield, 1987) suggest that instead of saying, "The average student is worried about his grades" say "The average student is worried about grades." Instead of saying, "Ask the student to hand in his work as soon as he is finished," say, "Ask students to hand in their work as soon as they're finished."

Sex Role Stereotyping. The words you use often reflect a sex role bias, the assumption that certain roles or professions belong to men and others belong to women. In eliminating sex role stereotyping, avoid, for example, making the hypothetical elementary school teacher female and the college professor male. Avoid referring to doctors as male and nurses as female. Avoid noting the sex of a professional with terms such as "female doctor" or "male nurse." When you're referring to a specific doctor or nurse, the person's sex will become clear when you use the appropriate pronoun: "Dr. Smith wrote the prescription for her new patient" or "The nurse

Julia Stanley, for example, researched terms indicating sexual promiscuity and found 220 terms referring to a sexually promiscuous woman but only 22 terms for a sexually promiscuous man (Thorne, Kramarae, & Henley, 1983). Assuming the widely held assumption that the importance of a concept to a culture is reflected in the number of terms for the concept that the language has, how would you explain this difference in terms for promiscuity for men and for women?

recorded the patient's temperature himself." Here are a few additional examples. How would you rephrase these?

1. You really should get a second doctor's opinion. Just see what he says.
2. Johnny went to school today and met his kindergarten teacher. I wonder who she is.
3. Everyone needs to examine his own conscience.
4. The effective communicator is a selective self-discloser; he discloses to some people about some things some of the time.
5. The effective waitress knows when her customers need her.
6. The history of man is largely one of technology replacing his manual labor.

Heterosexism

A close relative of sexism is heterosexism. The term is a relatively new addition to the list of linguistic prejudices. As the term implies, heterosexism refers to language used to disparage gay men and lesbians. As with racist language, you see heterosexism in the derogatory terms used for lesbians and gay men as well as in more subtle forms of language usage. For example, when you qualify a profession—as in "gay athlete" or "lesbian doctor" you're in effect stating that athletes and doctors are not normally gay or lesbian. Further, you're highlighting the affectional orientation of the athlete and the doctor in a context where it may have no relevance. This practice, of course, is the same as qualifying by race or gender already noted.

Still another instance of heterosexism—and perhaps the most difficult to deal with—is the presumption of heterosexuality. Usually, people assume the person they're talking to or about is heterosexual. Usually, they're correct since the majority of the population is heterosexual. At the same time, however, note that it denies the lesbian and gay identity a certain legitimacy. The practice is very similar to the presumption of whiteness and maleness that we

In what ways does this photo comment on sex role stereotyping? If you were one of these construction engineers, what interpersonal communication problems (if any) would you anticipate?

have made significant inroads in eliminating. Here are a few additional suggestions for avoiding heterosexist, or what some call "homophobic," language.

- Avoid offensive nonverbal mannerisms that parody stereotypes when talking about gay men and lesbians.
- Avoid "complimenting" gay men and lesbians because "they don't look it." To gay men and lesbians, it's not a compliment. Similarly, expressing disappointment that a person is gay—often thought to be a compliment when said in such comments as "What a waste!"—is not really a compliment.
- Avoid the assumption that every gay or lesbian knows what every other gay or lesbian is thinking. It's very similar to asking a Japanese why Sony is investing heavily in the United States or, as one comic put it, asking an African-American "What do you think Jesse Jackson meant by that last speech?"
- Avoid denying individual differences. Saying things like *lesbians are so loyal* or *gay men are so open with their feelings,* which ignore the reality of wide differences within any group, are potentially insulting to all groups.
- Avoid "overattribution," the tendency to attribute just about everything a person does, says, and believes to being gay or lesbian. This tendency helps to recall and perpetuate stereotypes (see Chapter 3).
- Remember that relationship milestones are important to all people. Ignoring anniversaries or birthdays of, say, a relative's partner is resented by everyone.

Racism

According to Andrea Rich (1974), "any language that, through a conscious or unconscious attempt by the user, places a particular racial or ethnic group in an inferior position is racist." Racist language expresses racist attitudes. It also, however, contributes to the development of racist attitudes in those who use or hear the language.

Racist terms are used by members of one culture to disparage members of other cultures—their customs or their accomplishments. Racist language emphasizes differences rather than similarities and separates rather than unites members of different cultures. Generally, racist language is used by the dominant group to establish and maintain power over other groups. The social consequences of racist language in terms of employment, education, housing opportunities, and general community acceptance are well known.

Many people feel that it's permissible for members of a culture to refer to themselves with racist terms. That is, Asians may use the negative terms referring to Asians, Italians may use the negative terms referring to Italians, and so on. This issue is seen clearly in rap music where performers use such racial terms (*The New York Times,* 24 January 1993, 1, 31). The reasoning seems to be that groups should be able to laugh at themselves.

It's interesting to note that the terms denoting some of the major movements in art—for example, "impressionism" and "cubism"—were originally applied negatively. The terms were adopted by the artists themselves and eventually became positive. A parallel can be seen in the use of the word "queer" by some lesbian and gay organizations. Their purpose in using the term is to cause it to lose its negative connotation.

Many interviewers when they come to talk to me, think they're being progressive by not mentioning in their stories any longer that I'm black. I tell them, "Don't stop now. If I shot somebody you'd mention it."
—*Colin Powell*

One possible problem, though, is that such terms may not lose their negative connotations and may simply reinforce the negative stereotypes that society has already assigned to certain groups. By using these terms, members may come to accept the labels with their negative connotations and thus contribute to their own stereotyping.

It has often been pointed out (M. Davis, 1973; Bosmajian, 1969) that there are aspects of language that may be inherently racist. For example, in one examination of English there were found 134 synonyms for *white*. Of these 44 have positive connotations (for example, "clean," "chaste," and "unblemished") and only 10 have negative connotations (for example, "whitewash" and "pale"). The remaining were relatively neutral. Of the 120 synonyms for *black,* 60 have unfavorable connotations ("unclean," "foreboding," and "deadly") and none have positive connotations.

Cultural Identifiers

Perhaps the best way to avoid sexism, heterosexism, and racism is to examine the preferred cultural identifiers to use (and not to use) in talking about members of different cultures. As always, when in doubt, find out. The preferences and many of the specific examples identified here are drawn largely from the findings of the Task Force on Bias-Free Language of the Association of American University Presses (Schwartz, 1995). Realize that not everyone would agree with these recommendations; they're presented here—in the words of the Task Force—"to encourage sensitivity to usages that may be imprecise, misleading, and needlessly offensive" (Schwartz, 1995 p. ix). They're not presented so that you can "catch" someone being "politically incorrect" or label someone "culturally insensitive."

Generally: The term *girl* should only be used to refer to very young females and is equivalent to *boy.* Neither term should be used for people older than, say, 13 or 14. *Girl* is never used to refer to a grown woman, nor is *boy*

Consider this situation: An instructor at your school persists in calling the female students girls, refers to gay men and lesbians as "queers," and refers to various racial groups with terms that most people would consider inappropriate. To the objection that these terms are offensive, the instructor claims the right to free speech and argues that to prevent instructors from using such terms would be a restriction on free speech, which would be a far greater wrong than being culturally or politically incorrect or insensitive. How would you comment on this argument?

"It doesn't have a damn thing to do with political correctness, pal.
I'm a sausage, and that guy's a wienie."

used to refer to persons in blue collar positions, as it once was. *Lady* is negatively evaluated by many because it connotes the stereotype of the prim and proper woman. *Woman* or *young woman* is preferred. *Older person* is preferred to *elder, elderly, senior,* or *senior citizen* (which technically refers to someone older than 65).

Generally: *Gay* is the preferred term to refer to a man who has an affectional orientation for other men and *lesbian* is the preferred term for a woman who has an affectional orientation for other women. (*Lesbian* means "homosexual woman" so the phrase *lesbian woman* is redundant.) This preference for the term *lesbian* is not universal among homosexual women; in one survey, for example, 58% preferred "lesbian"; 34% preferred "gay" (Lever, 1995). *Homosexual* refers to both gay men and lesbians but more often to a sexual orientation to members of one's own sex. *Gay* and *lesbian* refer to a life style and not just to sexual orientation. *Gay* as a noun, although widely used, may prove offensive in some contexts, for example, "We have two gays on the team." Although used within the gay community in an effort to remove the negative stigma through frequent usage, the term *queer*—as in "queer power"—is often resented when used by outsiders. Because most scientific thinking holds that one's sexuality is genetically determined rather than being a matter of choice, the term *sexual orientation* rather than *sexual preference* or *sexual status* (which is also vague) is preferred.

Generally: Most African Americans prefer *African American* to *black* (Hecht, Ribeau, and Collier, 1993) though *black* is often used with *white* and is used in a variety of other contexts (for example, Department of Black and Puerto Rican Studies, the *Journal of Black History,* and Black History Month). The American Psychological Association recommends that both terms be capitalized but the *Chicago Manual of Style* (the manual used by most newspapers and publishing houses) recommends using lower case. The terms *negro* and *colored* are used in the names of some organizations (for example, the United Negro College Fund and the National Association for the Advancement of Colored People), but not outside of these contexts.

White is generally used to refer to those whose roots are in European cultures and is usually used to not include Hispanics. On the analogy of *African American* comes the phrase *European American.* Few *European Americans,* however, would want to be called that; most would prefer their national origins emphasized, for example, *German American* or *Greek American.* This preference may well change as Europe moves into a more cohesive and united entity. *People of color*—a more literary-sounding term appropriate perhaps to public speaking but sounding awkward in most conversations—is preferred to *nonwhite,* which implies that whiteness is the norm and nonwhiteness is a deviation from that norm. The same is true of the term *non-Christian.*

Generally: *Hispanic* is used to refer to anyone who identifies himself or herself as belonging to a Spanish-speaking culture. *Latina* (female) and *Latino* (male) refer to those whose roots are in one of the Latin American countries—for example, Dominican Republic, Nicaragua, or Guatemala. *Hispanic American* refers to those U.S. residents whose ancestry is a Spanish culture and includes Mexican, Caribbean, and Central and South Americans. In emphasizing a Spanish heritage, the term is really inadequate in referring to those large numbers in the Caribbean and South America whose origins are French or Portuguese. *Chicana* (female) and *Chicano* (male) refer to those with roots in Mexico, though it often connotes a nationalist attitude

(Jandt, 1995) and is considered offensive by many Mexican Americans. *Mexican American* is preferred.

Inuk (pl. *Inuit*) was officially adopted at the Inuit Circumpolar Conference to refer to the group of indigenous people of Alaska, Northern Canada, Greenland, and Eastern Siberia. This term is preferred to *Eskimo* (a term the U.S. Census Bureau uses), which was applied to the indigenous peoples of Alaska by Europeans and derives from a term that means "raw meat eaters" (Maggio, 1997).

Indian refers only to someone from India and is incorrectly used when applied to members of other Asian countries or to the indigenous peoples of North America. *American Indian* or *Native American* are preferred, even though many Native Americans refer to themselves as *Indians* and *Indian people.* The term *native American* (with a lower case *n*) is most often used to refer to persons born in the United States. Although the term technically could refer to anyone born in North or South America, people outside the United States generally prefer more specific designations such as *Argentinean, Cuban,* or *Canadian.* The term *native* means an indigenous inhabitant; it's not correctly used to mean "someone having a less developed culture."

Muslim is the preferred form (rather than the older *Moslem*) to refer to a person who adheres to the religious teachings of Islam. *Quran* (rather than *Koran*) is the preferred term for the scriptures of Islam. The terms "Mohammedan" or "Mohammedanism" are not considered appropriate since they imply worship of Muhammad, the prophet, "considered by Muslims to be a blasphemy against the absolute oneness of God" (Maggio, 1997, p. 277).

Although there is no universal agreement, generally *Jewish people* is preferred to *Jews;* and *Jewess* (a Jewish female) is considered derogatory. *Jew* should only be used as a noun and is never correctly used as a verb or an adjective (Maggio, 1997).

When history was being written with a European perspective, it was taken as the focal point and the rest of the world was defined in terms of its location from Europe. Thus, Asia became the East or the orient and Asians became *Orientals*—a term that is today considered inappropriate or "Eurocentric." Thus, people from Asia are *Asians* just as people from Africa are *Africans* and people from Europe are *Europeans.*

> What cultural identifiers do you prefer? Have these preferences changed over time? How can you let other people know the designations that you want and those that you don't want to be used to refer to you? An interesting exercise—especially in a large and multicultural class—is for each student to write anonymously his or her preferred cultural identification on an index card and have them all read aloud.

This very clever article illustrates some of the most important principles of effective interpersonal communication in the form of ten statements that are likely to create problems.

10 Things You Should Never Say to Anyone

George J. Thompson, Ph.D., with Jerry B. Jenkins

There are some things you should never say to another human being. I'm not talking about calling people names or hurling insults at them—you already know better than to do that! I'm referring to the things we tend to blurt out when we're upset, when we often say things we regret later. The statements that follow are the ten most common troublemakers. Here's why you should never say these things to anyone and what to do if someone says them to you.

1. **"You wouldn't understand."** No matter who this is said to, it is taken as a putdown. Even if you're sure the person won't understand what you're feeling or what you're about to say, remember that she wouldn't be talking to you if she didn't care. She *wants* to understand, and you can probably help her. Better to say, "This might be difficult to understand, but . . ." or "Let me try to explain this . . . ."

2. **"Because those are the rules."** We've all heard this statement or some variation of it ("Because I said so," "Because I'm the boss," "Sorry, I don't make the rules"). Is it ever a satisfactory explanation? No. Any time you fall back on this nonexplanation, it means you don't have a legitimate answer. Rather than reinforcing your position, a statement like this makes you appear more concerned with your own authority than with the other person's welfare. And you may be challenged by someone with the guts to say, "So what? The rules are wrong."

3. **"It's none of your business."** Here is the slam dunk of verbal abuse. The phrase angers people because it brusquely cuts them off and brands them as outsiders. It also exposes you as someone who doesn't have a good answer to the question.

   Instead of saying, "It's none of your business," explain why you aren't at liberty to answer. If it's a confidential matter, say so—and explain why. For instance, "There are other people involved who wouldn't want me to say anything without their knowledge or permission, and I want to honor that."

4. **"What do you want *me* to do about it?"** What a cop-out! This rhetorical question, almost always accompanied by sarcasm, is nothing but an evasion of responsibility. It's often said by untrained salesclerks in response to complaints, but it's also heard among friends, spouses, and co-workers at the end of their rope.

   When you say, "What do you want *me* to do about it?" you can count on two problems: the one the person came to you with and the one you just created by trying to duck responsibility. A better alternative is to offer to help sort out the problem and find a solution.

5. **"Calm down!"** No matter what tone you use, this command just doesn't work. In fact, it almost always makes people more upset. If you've ever tried this on your friends or family, you know. Ordering someone to "Calm down" negates that person's feelings and implies that she has no right to be upset. Rather than reassuring her that things will improve—which should be your goal—you make her feel that she needs to defend her reaction to you.

6. **"What's the problem?"** This snotty, useless phrase signals the beginning of a you-versus-me battle, rather than a what-can-*we*-do discussion. The typical response is to get defensive: It's not *my* problem; *you're* the problem!"

   Asking someone, "What's your problem?" is not going to get you anywhere near a solution. Rather, say, "What's the matter? How can I help?" Then you can start a real discussion of the issue.

7. **"You never . . ." or "You always . . ."** These absolute generalizations are usually untrue. Is it true that a child *never* cleans up her room? (Okay, bad example. That may be true!) Is it true that your spouse is *always* late? Accusatory generalizations are not only false, they also indicate that you

have both lost perspective *and* will soon lose the attention of your listener.

8. **"I'm not going to say this again."** This is almost always an empty promise. If you're trying so hard to emphasize a point, chances are you won't be able to let it go with only one final reminder. After all, what are you going to do if you still don't get satisfaction? This threat traps you, because if you're really not going to repeat yourself, you're left with one option, action. If you're not prepared to act, you lose credibility.

9. **"I'm doing this for your own good."** This statement is guaranteed to turn any listener into an instant cynic. No one believes it. It begs the sarcastic comeback, "Sure, I'll bet you are."

10. **"Why don't you be reasonable?"** Not once in my life has anyone come up to me and said, "You know what? I'm way out in left field today, totally irrational." People may know they're a little forgetful or out of it, but they're not going to admit to being unreasonable. So you're only inviting conflict by asking someone a question like this.

    A better plan of action is to allow the person to become more reasonable by being reasonable with her. Use a language of reassurance, saying things like, "Let me see if I understand your position" and then paraphrasing her own words. That not only assures you that you're hearing the person correctly, but it also enables her to see her position through your eyes. That approach starts to absorb a person's tension and makes her feel your support. Then you can help her think more logically and less destructively, without making the insulting charge implied in the question.

Thinking Critically About "10 Things You Should Never Say."   Can you identify a specific instance in which one of these 10 things were said and caused interpersonal difficulties? Which of these 10 things irritates you the most? Do you disagree with any of the suggestions offered in this article? When might one or more of these statements be appropriate? As you can see this article was addressed to an audience of women. The assumption in including it here is that it's equally relevant to men. Is it? Would the article have differed if it appeared in a "men's magazine" (which, by the way, hardly ever contain "relationship-type" articles)?

Source: From *Verbal Judo,* by George Thompson, Ph. D., and Jerry B. Jenkins. Copyright © 1993 by George Thompson and Jerry B. Jenkins. Reprinted by permission of William Morrow & Company.

USING VERBAL MESSAGES EFFECTIVELY AND CRITICALLY

> It is not only true that the language we use puts words in our mouths; it also puts notions in our heads.
>
> *–Wendell Johnson*

A chief concern in using verbal messages is to recognize what critical thinking theorists call "conceptual distortions," mental mistakes, misinterpretations, or reasoning fallacies. Avoiding these distortions and substituting a more critical, more realistic analysis is probably the best way to improve your own use of verbal messages.

SKILL BUILDING EXERCISE 5.2.
Confirming, Rejecting, and Disconfirming

Classify the following responses as confirmation, rejection, or disconfirmation.

Enrique receives this semester's grades in the mail; they're a lot better than previous semesters' grades but are still not great. After opening the letter, Enrique says: "I really tried hard to get my grades up this semester." Enrique's parents respond:

_____ 1. Going out every night hardly seems like trying very hard.

_____ 2. What should we have for dinner?

_____ 3. Keep up the good work.

_____ 4. I can't believe you've really tried your best; how can you study with the stereo blasting in your ears?

_____ 5. I'm sure you've tried real hard.

_____ 6. That's great.

_____ 7. What a rotten day I had at the office.

_____ 8. I can remember when I was in school; got all B's without ever opening a book.

Pat, who has been out of work for the past several weeks, says: "I feel like such a failure; I just can't seem to find a job. I've been pounding the pavement for the last five weeks and still nothing." Pat's friend responds:

_____ 1. I know you've been trying real hard.

_____ 2. You really should get more training so you'd be able to sell yourself more effectively.

_____ 3. I told you a hundred times; you need that college degree.

_____ 4. I've got to go to the dentist on Friday. Boy, do I hate that.

_____ 5. The employment picture is real bleak this time of the year but your qualifications are really impressive. Something will come up soon.

_____ 6. You're not a failure. You just can't find a job.

_____ 7. What do you need a job for? Stay home and keep house. After all, Chris makes more than enough money to live in style.

_____ 8. What's five weeks?

_____ 9. Well, you'll just have to try harder.

Thinking Critically About Confirmation, Rejection, and Disconfirmation.

Generally, communication experts would advise you to be more confirming than disconfirming. Can you identify situations where disconfirmation would be a more effective response than confirmation? Are there situations when confirmation would be inappropriate?

Can you provide examples of a confirmatory, rejecting, and disconfirmatory response to your friend's: "I haven't had a date in the last four months. I'm getting really depressed over this"? Another example: Your friend tells you of relationship problems: "Pat and I just can't seem to get along anymore. Every day is a hassle. Every day, there's another conflict, another battle. I feel like walking away from the whole mess."

Language Symbolizes Reality (Partially)

Language symbolizes reality; it's not the reality itself. Of course, this is obvious. But consider: Have you ever reacted to the way something was labeled or described rather than to the actual item? Have you ever bought something because of its name rather than because of the actual object? If so, you were probably responding as if language were the reality, a distortion called _intensional orientation_.

You cannot fill your belly by painting pictures of bread.
—*Chinese proverb*

Intensional Orientation

Intensional orientation (the *s* in *intensional* is intentional) refers to the tendency to view people, objects, and events in the way they're talked about—

the way they're labeled. For example, if Sally is labeled "uninteresting," you would, responding intensionally, evaluate her as uninteresting even before listening to what she had to say. You'd see Sally through a filter imposed by the label "uninteresting." **Extensional orientation,** on the other hand, is the tendency to look first at the actual people, objects, and events and only afterwards at their labels. In this case, it would mean looking at Sally without any preconceived labels, guided by what she says and does, not by the words used to label her. If the people in the accompanying cartoon see themselves as "upper-middle class" because they've been labeled as such, they'd be responding intensionally. If, on the other hand, they realize that their lives won't change just because their label changed, they'd be responding extensionally.

The way to avoid intensional orientation is to extensionalize. Recognize that language provides labels for things and should never be given greater attention than the actual thing. Give your main attention to the people, things, and events in the world as you see them and not as they're presented in words, something the king in the accompanying cartoon seems not to recognize. For example, when you meet Jack and Jill, observe and interact with them. Then form your impressions. Don't respond to them as "greedy, money-grubbing landlords" because Harry labeled them this way. Don't respond to Carmen as "lazy and inconsiderate" because Elaine told you she was.

Allness

A related distortion is to forget that language only symbolizes a portion of reality, never the whole. When you assume that you can know all or say all about anything you're into a pattern of behavior called **allness.** You never see all of anything. You never experience anything fully. You see a part, then conclude what the whole is like. You have to draw conclusions on the basis of insufficient evidence (you always have insufficient evidence). A useful device to

Evaluating Information

Don't be fooled by words that sound impressive but mean little. Doublespeak is language that fails to communicate; it comes in four basic forms (Lutz, 1996). **Euphemisms** make the negative and unpleasant appear positive and appealing, for example, calling the firing of 200 workers "downsizing" or "reallocation of resources." **Jargon** is the specialized language of a professional class (for example, the computer language of the hacker); it becomes doublespeak when used to communicate with people who aren't members of the group and who don't know this specialized language. **Gobbledygook** is overly complex language that overwhelms the listener instead of communicating meaning. **Inflated language** makes the mundane seem extraordinary, the common exotic ("take the vacation of a lifetime; explore unsurpassed vistas"). All four forms can be useful in some situations, but, when spoken or listened to mindlessly, they may obscure meaning and distort perceptions.

"I now decree you all upper-middle-class."

help combat the tendency to think that all can or has been said about anything is to end mentally each statement with etc.—a reminder that there is more to learn, more to know, and more to say—that every statement is inevitably incomplete. Some people overuse the *etc.* They use it not as a mental reminder, but as a substitute for being specific. This obviously is to be avoided and merely adds to the conversational confusion.

To avoid allness, recognize that language symbolizes only a part of reality, never the whole. Whatever someone says—regardless of what it is or how extensive it is—is only part of the story.

Language Expresses Both Facts and Inferences

Language enables you to form statements of both facts and inferences without making any linguistic distinction between the two. Similarly, when you speak or listen to such statements you often don't make a clear distinction between statements of facts and statements of inference. Yet, there are great differences between the two. Barriers to clear thinking can be created when inferences are treated as facts, a tendency called **fact–inference confusion.**

For example, you can say, "She's wearing a blue jacket," as well as "He's harboring an illogical hatred." Although the sentences have similar structures, they're different. You can observe the jacket and the blue color, but how do you observe "illogical hatred"? Obviously, this is not a descriptive but an inferential statement. It's one you make on the basis not only of what you observe, but on what you infer. For a statement to be considered factual it must be made by the observer after observation and must be limited to what is observed (Weinberg, 1958).

There is nothing wrong with making inferential statements. You must make them to talk about much that is meaningful to you. The problem arises when you act as if those inferential statements are factual. You may test your ability to distinguish facts from inferences by taking the accompanying fact-inference test (based on the tests constructed by Haney, 1973).

CAUTION

Thinking intensionally, by focusing attention on the way something is talked about instead of the way it exists in the physical world, prevents you from seeing things objectively. Are there some topics about which you generally think intensionally?

CAUTION

Thinking in allness terms shuts down your critical thinking facilities; after all, if you already know everything about something, there's no point in learning further—a sure critical thinking killer. Are there some topics that you think about in allness terms?

SELF-TEST
Can You Distinguish Facts from Inferences?

Carefully read the following report and the observations based on it. Indicate whether you think the observations are true, false, or doubtful on the basis of the information presented in the report. Write T if the observation is definitely true, F if the observation is definitely false, and ? if the observation may be either true or false. Judge each observation in order. Do not reread the observations after you have indicated your judgment, and do not change any of your answers.

A well-liked college teacher had just completed making up the final examinations and had turned off the lights in the office. Just then a tall, broad figure with dark glasses appeared and demanded the examination. The professor opened the drawer. Everything in the drawer was picked up and the individual ran down the corridor. The dean was notified immediately.

_____ 1. The thief was tall, broad, and wore dark glasses.

_____ 2. The professor turned off the lights.

_____ 3. A tall figure demanded the examination.

_____ 4. The examination was picked up by someone.

(continued)

(continued)

———— 5. The examination was picked up by the professor.

———— 6. A tall, broad figure appeared after the professor turned off the lights in the office.

———— 7. The man who opened the drawer was the professor.

———— 8. The professor ran down the corridor.

———— 9. The drawer was never actually opened.

———— 10. Three persons are referred to in this report.

Thinking Critically About Facts and Inferences After you answer all 10 questions, form small groups of five or six and discuss the answers. Look at each statement from each member's point of view. For each statement, ask yourself "How can you be absolutely certain that the statement is true or false?" You should find that only one statement can be clearly identified as True and only one as False; eight should be marked "?".

CAUTION

Confusing facts and inferences distorts the important distinction between statements that are verifiably true and statements that are assumptions. Can you identify an episode of a situation comedy that revolved around fact-inference confusion?

To avoid fact-inference confusion, phrase inferential statements not as factual but as tentative. Recognize that they may prove to be wrong. Inferential statements should leave open the possibility of alternatives. If, for example, you treat the statement "Our biology teacher was fired for poor teaching" as factual, you eliminate any alternatives. When making inferential statements, be psychologically prepared to be proved wrong. If you're prepared to be wrong, you will be less hurt if you're shown to be wrong. Be especially sensitive to this distinction when you're listening. Most talk is inferential. Beware of the speaker who presents everything as fact. Analyze closely and you'll uncover a world of inferences.

Language Is Relatively Static

Language changes only very slowly, especially when compared to the rapid change in people and things. **Static evaluation** is the tendency to retain evaluations without change while the reality to which they refer is changing. Often a verbal statement you make about an event or person remains static—"That's the way he is; he's always been that way"—while the event or person may change enormously. Alfred Korzybski (1933) used an interesting illustration. In a tank you have a large fish and many small fish, the natural food for the large fish. Given freedom in the tank, the large fish will eat the small fish. If you partition the tank, separating the large fish from the small fish by a clear piece of glass, the large fish will continue to attempt to eat the small fish but will fail, knocking instead into the glass partition.

CAUTION

How might **thinking in static terms** hinder your ability to see changes and so distort critical thinking? Can you name things (people, institutions, countries, religions) that never change? Can you name things that you treat *as if* they never change? How does this influence the way you think about them?

Eventually, the large fish will "learn" the futility of attempting to eat the small fish. If you now remove the partition, the small fish will swim all around the big fish, but the big fish will not eat them. In fact, the large fish will die of starvation while its natural food swims all around. The large fish has learned a pattern of behavior, and even though the actual territory has changed, the map remains static.

While you'd probably all agree that everything is in a constant state of flux, do you act as if you know this? Do you act in accordance with the notion of change or just accept it intellectually? Do you realize, for example, that because you've failed at something once, you need not fail again? Your evaluations of yourself and of others must keep pace with the rapidly changing real world; otherwise your attitudes and beliefs will be about a world that no longer exists.

The "date" is a device that helps to keep language (and thinking) up-to-date and helps guard against static evaluation. The procedure is simple: date your statements and especially your evaluations. Remember that Pat Smith$_{1996}$ is not Pat Smith$_{1999}$; academic abilities$_{1996}$ are not academic abilities$_{1999}$. T. S. Eliot, in *The Cocktail Party,* said, "What we know of other people is only our memory of the moments during which we knew them. And they have changed since then . . . at every meeting we are meeting a stranger." In listening, look carefully at messages that claim that what was true still is. It may or may not be. Look for change.

Language Can Obscure Distinctions

Language can obscure distinctions among people or events that are covered by the same label but are really quite different (indiscrimination) and by making it easy to focus on extremes rather than on the vast middle ground between opposites (polarization).

Indiscrimination

Each word in the language can refer to lots of things; most terms are general ones that refer to a wide variety of individuals. The words "teacher" or "textbook" or "computer program" refer to lots of specific people and things. When you allow the general term to obscure the specific differences (say, among teachers or textbooks), you're into a pattern called **indiscrimination.**

Indiscrimination refers to the failure to distinguish between similar but different people, objects or events. It occurs when you focus on classes and fail to see that each is unique and needs to be looked at individually. Everything is unique. Everything is unlike everything else.

Our language, however, provides you with common nouns, such as teacher, student, friend, enemy, war, politician, and liberal. These lead you to focus on similarities—to group together all teachers, all students, and all politicians. At the same time, the terms divert attention away from the uniqueness of each person, each object, and each event.

This misevaluation is at the heart of stereotyping on the basis of nationality, race, religion, sex, and affectional orientation. A stereotype, you'll remember from Chapter 3, is a fixed mental picture of a group that is applied to each individual in the group without regard to his or her unique qualities.

Most stereotypes are negative and denigrate the group to which they refer. Some, however, are positive. A particularly glaring example is the popular stereotype of Asian American students as successful, intelligent, and hardworking.

Whether the stereotypes are positive or negative, they create the same problem. They provide you with shortcuts that are often inappropriate. For instance, when you meet a particular person, your first reaction may be to pigeonhole him or her into some category—perhaps religious, national, or academic ("She's a typical academic—never thinks of the real world."). Then you assign to this person all the qualities that are part of your stereotype.

Evaluating Information

Don't be influenced by weasel words. A weasel is a slippery rodent; just when you're going to catch it, it slips away. Weasel words are words whose meanings are difficult to pin down. For example, the medicine that claims to work better than Brand X doesn't specify how much better or in what respect it performs better. Is it possible that it performs better in one respect and less effective on the other nine measures? "Better" is a weasel word. "Like" is another word often used for weaseling, as when a claim is made that "Brand X will make you feel like a new man." Exactly what such a claim means is impossible to pin down. Other weasel words are "helped," "virtually," "as much as," and "more economical." Try looking for weasel words; you'll often find them lurking in the promises of advertisers and politicians.

Regardless of the category you use or the specific qualities you're ready to assign, you fail to give sufficient attention to the individual's unique characteristics. Two people may both be Christian, Asian, and lesbian, for example, but each will be different from the other. Indiscrimination is a denial of another's uniqueness.

A useful antidote to indiscrimination (and stereotyping) is the index. This mental subscript identifies each individual as an individual even though both may be covered by the same label. Thus, politician$_1$ is not politician$_2$, teacher$_1$ is not teacher$_2$. The index helps you to discriminate among without discriminating against. Although the label "politician," for example, covers all politicians, the index makes sure that each is thought about as an individual.

Polarization

Another way in which language can obscure differences is in its predominance of extreme terms and its relative lack of middle terms, a system that often leads to **polarization.** You can appreciate the role language plays in fostering polarization by trying to identify the opposites of the following terms: *happy, long, wealth, life, healthy, up, left, legal, heavy, strong.* This should have been relatively easy and you probably identified the opposites very quickly. Now, however, identify the middle term, the term referring to the middle ground between the italicized terms and the opposites you supplied. These terms should have been more difficult to come up with and should have taken you more time and effort. Further, if you compared your responses with others, you'd find that most people agreed on the opposites; most people would have said *unhappy, short, poverty,* and so on. But, when it comes to the middle terms, the degree of agreement would be much less. Language, thus, makes it easy to focus on opposites and relatively difficult to talk about the middle areas.

How does indiscrimination operate in intercultural communication? Can you recall specific examples you've witnessed?

Polarization is the tendency to look at the world in terms of opposites and to describe it in extremes—good or bad, positive or negative, healthy or sick, intelligent or stupid. It's often referred to as the fallacy of "either-or" or "black and white." Most people exist somewhere between the extremes. Yet there's a strong tendency to view only the extremes and to categorize people, objects, and events in terms of these polar opposites.

Problems are created when opposites are used in inappropriate situations. For example, "The politician is either for us or against us." These options do not include all possibilities. The politician may be for us in some things and against us in other things, or may be neutral. During the Vietnam War, people were categorized as either hawks or doves. But clearly many people were neither and many were hawks on certain issues and doves on others.

In correcting this tendency to polarize, beware of implying (and believing) that two extreme classes include all possible classes—that an individual must be one or the other, with no alternatives ("Are you pro-abortion or pro-life?"). Most people, most events, most qualities exist between polar extremes. When others imply that there are only two sides or alternatives, look for the middle ground.

How would you go about finding answers to questions such as these *(any of which would make suitable research paper topics)?*
- Does the use of derogatory language about your own groups influence your self-concept?
- What are the effects of using racist, sexist, and heterosexism language on your campus? At home? With your close friends?
- Do the definitions of what constitutes confirmation, rejection, and disconfirmation vary from one culture to another?

SKILL BUILDING EXERCISE 5.3.

Thinking with E-Prime

The expression *E-prime* (*E'*) refers here to the mathematical equation E − e = E' where E = the English language and e = the verb *to be*. E', therefore, stands for normal English without the verb *to be*. D. David Bourland, Jr. (1965–1966; Wilson, 1989), argued that if you wrote and spoke without the verb *to be*, you'd describe events more accurately. (A symposium of 18 articles on E-prime appears in the Summer 1992 issue of *ETC.: A Review of General Semantics.*) The verb *to be* often suggests that qualities are in the person or thing rather than in the observer making the statement. It's easy to forget that these statements are evaluative rather than purely descriptive. For example, when you say, "Johnny is a failure," you imply that failure is somehow within Johnny instead of a part of someone's evaluation of Johnny. This type of thinking is especially important in making statements about yourself. When you say, for example, "I'm not good at mathematics" or "I'm unpopular" or "I'm lazy," you imply that these qualities are *in* you. But these are simply evaluations that may be incorrect or, if at least partly accurate, may change. The verb *to be* implies a permanence that is simply not true of the world in which you live.

To appreciate further the difference between statements that use the verb *to be* and those that do not, try to rewrite the following sentences without using the verb *to be* in any of its forms—*is, are, am, was,* etc.

1. I'm a poor student.
2. They're inconsiderate.
3. What is meaningful communication?
4. Is this valuable?
5. Happiness is a dry nose.
6. Love is a useless abstraction.
7. This Web site is meaningless.
8. Was the movie any good?
9. Dick and Jane are no longer children.
10. This class is great.

Thinking Critically About E-Prime.   Did you ever describe yourself with the verb "to be" and thereby imply that these qualities were *in* you or that the quality was now and would always be an integral part of you? Might thinking in E-prime have proven more productive?

SUMMARY OF CONCEPTS AND SKILLS

In this chapter we considered verbal messages. We discussed the nature of language and the ways in which language works; the concept of disconfirmation and how it relates to sexism, heterosexism, and racist language; and the ways in which language can be used more effectively.

1. Language meanings are in people, not in things.
2. Meanings are context-based; the same message in different context will likely mean something different.
3. Language is both denotative (objective and generally easily agreed upon) and connotative (subjective and generally highly individual in meaning).
4. Language varies in directness; language can state exactly what you mean or it can hedge and state your meaning very indirectly.
5. Language is a cultural institution; each culture has its own rules identifying the ways in which language should be used.
6. Language varies in abstraction; language can vary from extremely general to extremely specific.
7. Disconfirmation refers to the process of ignoring the presence and the communications of others. Confirmation refers to accepting, supporting, and acknowledging the importance of the other person.
8. Sexist, heterosexist, and racist language puts down and negatively evaluates various cultural groups.
9. Using language effectively involves eliminating conceptual distortions and substituting more accurate assumptions about language, the most important of which are:

   - Language symbolizes reality; it's not the reality itself.
   - Language can express both facts and inferences and distinctions need to be made between them.
   - Language is relatively static; because reality changes so rapidly, you need to constantly revise the way you talk about people and things.
   - Language can obscure distinctions in its use of general terms and in its emphasis on extreme rather than middle terms.

The study of language, disconfirmation, and popular conceptual distortions has important implications for developing the skills of effective communication. Check your ability to apply these skills. Use a rating scale such as: (1) = almost always, (2) = often, (3) = sometimes, (4) = rarely, (5) = hardly ever.

_____ 1. I recognize that meaning is in people and not in things and therefore focus on what the person means as well as what the words mean.
_____ 2. I look for both the connotative and the denotative meanings when listening.
_____ 3. I recognize the cultural and gender differences in the rules for using language; each culture has its own rules that must be recognized and taken into consideration if communication is to be effective.
_____ 4. I am generally confirming in my communications and acknowledge others and their contributions.
_____ 5. I avoid disconfirmation through sexist, heterosexist, and racist language.
_____ 6. I avoid responding (intensionally) to labels as if they're objects; instead, I respond extensionally and look first at the reality and only then at the words.
_____ 7. I distinguish facts from inferences and respond to inferences with tentativeness.
_____ 8. I mentally date my statements and thus avoid static evaluation.
_____ 9. I avoid indiscrimination by treating each person and situation as unique.
_____10. I avoid using negative allness statements (particularly those using always and never) in conflict situations.
_____11. I avoid polarization by using "middle ground" terms and qualifiers in describing the world and especially people.

VOCABULARY QUIZ. THE LANGUAGE OF LANGUAGE

Match these terms about language with their definitions. Record the number of the definition next to the term.

10	polarization	2	static evaluation
9	intensional orientation	8	indiscrimination
3	connotative meaning	7	language sexism
1	fact-inference confusion	6	level of abstraction
4	confirmation	5	netiquette

1. Treating inferences as if they were facts.
2. The denial of change in language and in thinking.
3. The emotional, subjective aspect of meaning.
4. A communication pattern in which we acknowledge the presence of and signal the acceptance of another person.
5. The rules for polite communication on the Internet.
6. The degree of generality or specificity of a term.
7. Language derogatory to one sex, generally women.
8. The failure to see the differences among people or things covered by the same label.
9. A focus on the way things are talked about rather than on the way they exist in the world.
10. An almost exclusive focus on extremes, often to the neglect or omission of the vast middle ground.

Nonverbal
Messages

CHAPTER CONCEPTS	LEARNING GOALS	SKILLS GOALS
	After completing this chapter, you should be able to	*After completing this chapter, you should be able to*
Nonverbal Communication	1. Define nonverbal communication and identify its major functions	Use nonverbal messages in conjunction with verbal messages to express a variety of functions
The Channels of Nonverbal Communication	2. Define the nonverbal channels and provide examples of the messages that can be communicated through each	Use a wide variety of nonverbal communication forms to encode and decode meanings
Culture and Nonverbal Communication	3. Explain why the interpretation of nonverbal messages is influenced by culture	Use nonverbal behaviors with an awareness of cultural differences and influences

Bob leaves his apartment at 8:15 A.M. and stops at the corner drugstore for breakfast. Before he can speak, the counterman says, "The usual?" Bob nods yes. While he savors his danish, a fat man pushes onto the adjoining stool and overflows into his space. Bob scowls and the man pulls himself in as much as he can. Bob has sent two messages without speaking a syllable.

George is talking to Charley's wife at a party. Their conversation is entirely trivial, yet Charley glares at them suspiciously. Their physical proximity and the movements of their eyes reveal that they are powerfully attracted to each other.

José Ybarra and Sir Edmund Jones are at the same party and it is important for them to establish a cordial relationship for business reasons. Each is trying to be warm and friendly, yet they will part with mutual distrust and their business transaction will probably fall through.

José, in Latin fashion, moved closer and closer to Sir Edmund as they spoke, and this movement was miscommunicated as pushiness to Sir Edmund, who kept backing away from this intimacy, which was miscommunicated to José as coldness. The silent languages of Latin and English cultures are more difficult to learn than their spoken languages.

In these three examples, supplied by nonverbal researchers Edward and Mildred Hall (1971), you see the powerful messages communicated without words—the subject of this chapter.

NONVERBAL COMMUNICATION

Nonverbal communication is communication without words. You communicate nonverbally when you gesture, smile or frown, widen your eyes, move your chair closer to someone, wear jewelry, touch someone, raise your vocal volume, or even when you say nothing. In this chapter we look at these nonverbal messages—how they interact with verbal messages, the types of nonverbal messages, and the cultural variations in nonverbal communication.

Begin your reading of nonverbal communication with the following suggestions in mind:

- *Analyze your own nonverbal communication patterns.* If you're to use this material in any meaningful way, for example, to change some of your behaviors, then self-analysis is essential.
- *Observe. Observe. Observe.* Observe the behaviors of those around you and your own. See in everyday behavior what you read about here and discuss in class.
- *Resist the temptation to draw conclusions from nonverbal behaviors.* Instead, develop hypotheses (educated guesses) about what is going on and test the likelihood of their being correct on the basis of other evidence.
- *Connect and relate.* Although the areas of nonverbal communication are presented separately in textbooks, in actual communication situations, they all work together.

In face-to-face communication you blend verbal and nonverbal messages to best convey your meanings. Here are six ways in which nonverbal messages are used with verbal messages; these will help to highlight this important verbal–nonverbal interaction (Knapp & Hall, 1992).

Accenting

Nonverbal communication is often used to emphasize some part of the verbal message. You might, for example, raise your voice to underscore a particular word or phrase, bang your fist on the desk to stress your commitment, or look longingly into someone's eyes when saying "I love you."

Complementing

Nonverbal communication may add nuances of meaning not communicated by your verbal message. Thus, you might smile when telling a story (to suggest that you find it humorous) or frown and shake your head when recounting someone's deceit (to suggest your disapproval).

Contradicting

You may deliberately contradict your verbal messages with nonverbal movements—for example, by crossing your fingers or winking to indicate that you're lying.

Regulating

Movements may be used to control, or to indicate your desire to control, the flow of verbal messages, as when you purse your lips, lean forward, or make hand gestures to indicate that you want to speak. You might also put up your hand or vocalize your pauses (for example, with "um" or "ah") to indicate that you have not finished and are not ready to relinquish the floor to the next speaker.

Repeating

You can repeat or restate the verbal message nonverbally. You can, for example, follow your verbal "Is that all right?" with raised eyebrows and a questioning look, or motion with your head or hand to repeat your verbal "Let's go."

CAUTION

How can **failing to see the interconnection between verbal and nonverbal messages** prevent you from seeing the broad picture, from appreciating the nuances that, say, nonverbal messages give to verbal messages? Can you think of a specific instance where you or others failed to see a message as a package of verbal and nonverbal signals? How did this distort your analysis of the situation?

SKILL BUILDING EXERCISE 6.1.

Integrating Verbal and Nonverbal Messages

Think about how you integrate verbal and nonverbal messages in your own everyday communications. Try reading each of the following statements and describing (rather than acting out) the nonverbal messages that you would use in making these statements in normal conversation.

1. I couldn't agree with you more.
2. Absolutely not, I don't agree.
3. Hurry up; we're an hour late already.
4. You look really depressed. What happened?
5. I'm so depressed I can't stand it.
6. Life is great, isn't it? I just got the job of a lifetime.
7. I feel so relaxed and satisfied.
8. I'm feeling sick; I feel I have to throw up.
9. You look fantastic; what did you do to yourself?
10. Did you see that accident yesterday?

Thinking Critically About Verbal and Nonverbal Messages. This experience was probably a lot more difficult than it seemed at first. The reason is that we're generally unaware of the nonverbal movements we make; often they function below the level of conscious awareness. What values might there be to bringing these processes to consciousness? Can you identify any problems with this?

Substituting

You may also use nonverbal communication to take the place of verbal messages. For instance, you can signal "OK" with a hand gesture. You can nod your head to indicate yes or shake your head to indicate no.

THE CHANNELS OF NONVERBAL COMMUNICATION

Nonverbal communication is probably most easily explained by identifying the various channels through which messages pass. Here we cover 10 channels: body, face, eye, space, artifactual, touch, paralanguage, silence, time, and smell.

The Body

Two areas of the body are especially important in communicating messages. First, the movements you make with your body communicate and second, the general appearance of your body communicates.

Body Movements

Nonverbal researchers identify five major types of body movements: emblems, illustrators, affect displays, regulators, and adaptors (Ekman & Friesen, 1969; Knapp & Hall, 1996).

Emblems are body gestures that directly translate into words or phrases, for example, the OK sign, the thumb's up for "good job," and the V for victory. You use these consciously and purposely to communicate the same meaning as the words. Emblems are culture-specific; so be careful when using your culture's emblems in other cultures. For example, when President Nixon visited Latin America and gestured with the OK sign he thought communicated something positive, he was quickly informed that this gesture was not universal. In Latin America the gesture has a far more negative

The body says what words cannot.

—*Martha Graham*

meaning. Here are a few differences in meaning across cultures of the emblems you may commonly use (Axtell, 1991):

- In the United States, to say "hello" you wave with your whole hand moving from side to side but in a large part of Europe that same signal means "no." In Greece, however, this would be considered insulting to the person to whom you're waving.
- The V for victory common throughout much of the world, if used in England with the palm facing your face, it's insulting as the raised middle finger is in the United States.
- In Texas the raised fist with little finger and index finger raised is a positive expression of support because it represents the Texas longhorn steer. But, in Italy it's an insult that means that "your spouse is having an affair with someone else." In parts of South America it's a gesture to ward off evil, and in parts of Africa it's a curse: "may you experience bad times."
- In the United States and in much of Asia hugging is rarely exchanged among acquaintances but among Latins and Southern Europeans hugging is a common greeting gesture, which if withheld may communicate unfriendliness.

Illustrators enhance (literally "illustrate") the verbal messages they accompany. For example, when referring to something to the left, you might gesture toward the left. Most often you illustrate with your hands, but you can also illustrate with head and general body movements. You might, for example, turn your head or your entire body toward the left. You might also use illustrators to communicate the shape or size of objects you're talking about.

Affect displays are not only movements of the face (smiling or frowning, for example) but also of the hands and general body (body tenseness or relaxing posture, for example) that communicate emotional meaning. You use affect displays to accompany and reinforce your verbal messages and also as substitutes for words—for example, you might just smile while saying how happy you are to see your friend or you might just smile. Or, you might rush to greet someone with open arms. Because affect displays are primarily centered in the facial area, we consider these in more detail in the next section. Affect displays are often unconscious; you smile or frown, for example, without awareness. At other times, however, you may smile with awareness, consciously trying to convey your pleasure or satisfaction.

Regulators are behaviors that monitor, control, coordinate, or maintain the speaking of another individual. When you nod your head, for example, you tell the speaker to keep on speaking; when you lean forward and open your mouth, you tell the speaker that you would like to say something.

Adaptors are gestures that satisfy some personal need, for example, scratching to relieve an itch or moving your hair out of your eyes. *Self-adaptors* are self-touching movements (for example, rubbing your nose). *Alter-adaptors* are movements directed at the person with whom you're speaking, for example, removing lint from a person's jacket or straightening their tie or folding your arms in front of you to keep others at a comfortable distance from you. *Object-adaptors* are those gestures focused on objects, for example,

Visit the Macmillan library (http://www.mcp.com/). How might this Website help you in mastering the skills of interpersonal and especially nonverbal communication?

NAME AND FUNCTION	EXAMPLES
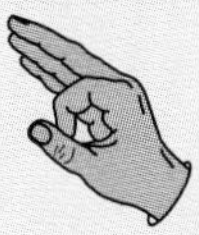 EMBLEMS directly translate words or phrases	"Okay" sign, "come here" wave, hitchhiker's sign
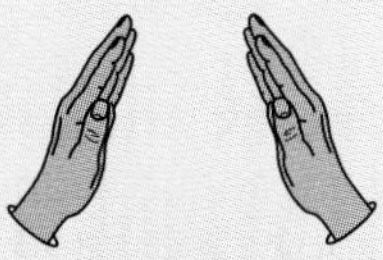 ILLUSTRATORS accompany and literally "illustrate" verbal messages	Circular hand movements when talking of a circle; hands far apart when talking of something large
 AFFECT DISPLAYS communicate emotional meaning	Expressions of happiness, surprise, fear, anger, sadness, disgust/contempt
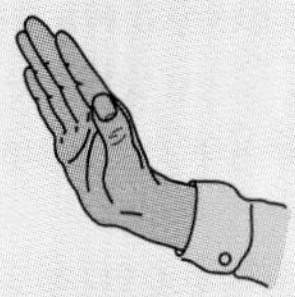 REGULATORS monitor, maintain, or control the speaking of another	Facial expressions and hand gestures indicating "keep going," "slow down," or "what else happened?"
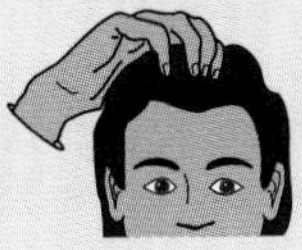 ADAPTORS satisfy some need	Scratching one's head

Figure 6.1

Five Body Movements.

Can you give at least one additional example of each of these five body movements?

doodling on or shredding a styrofoam coffee cup. Figure 6.1 summarizes these five movements.

Body Appearance

Your general body appearance also communicates. Height, for example, has been shown to be significant in a wide variety of situations. Tall presidential candidates have a much better record of winning the election than do their shorter opponents. Tall people seem to be paid more and are favored by interviewers over shorter applicants (Keyes, 1980; DeVito & Hecht, 1990; Knapp & Hall, 1992; Jackson & Ervin, 1992).

Your body also reveals your race through skin color and tone and may also give clues as to your more specific nationality. Your weight in proportion to your height will also communicate messages to others as will the length, color, and style of your hair.

Your general attractiveness is also a part of body communication. Attractive people have the advantage in just about every activity you can name. They get better grades in school, are more valued as friends and lovers, and are preferred as coworkers (Burgoon, Buller, & Woodall, 1995). Although we normally think that attractiveness is culturally determined—and to some degree it is—recent research seems to be showing that definitions of attractiveness are becoming universal (Brody, 1994). A person rated as attractive in one culture is likely to be rated as attractive in other cultures—even cultures that are widely different in appearance.

It is only the shallow people who do not judge by appearances.
—*Oscar Wilde*

Facial Communication

Throughout your interpersonal interactions, your face communicates, especially your emotions. Facial movements alone seem to communicate the degree of pleasantness, agreement, and sympathy felt; the rest of the body doesn't provide any additional information. But, for other aspects, for example, the intensity with which an emotion is felt, both facial and bodily cues are used (Graham, Bitti, & Argyle, 1975; Graham & Argyle, 1975).

Some nonverbal researchers claim that facial movements may express at least the following eight emotions: happiness, surprise, fear, anger, sadness, disgust, contempt, and interest (Ekman, Friesen, & Ellsworth, 1972). Others propose that in addition, facial movements may also communicate bewilderment and determination (Leathers, 1997).

Try to express surprise using only facial movements. Do this in front of a mirror and try to describe in as much detail as possible the specific movements of the face that make up surprise. If you signal surprise like most people, you probably use raised and curved eyebrows, long horizontal forehead wrinkles, wide-open eyes, a dropped-open mouth, and lips parted with no tension. Even if there were differences—and clearly there would be from one person to another—you could probably recognize the movements listed here as indicative of surprise.

Of course, some emotions are easier to communicate and to decode than others. For example, in one study, happiness was judged with an accuracy ranging from 55 to 100%, surprise from 38 to 86%, and sadness from 19 to 88% (Ekman, Friesen, & Ellsworth, 1972). Research finds that women and girls are more accurate judges of facial emotional expression than men and boys (Hall, 1984; Argyle, 1988).

Facial Management Techniques

As you learned the nonverbal system of communication, you also learned certain facial management techniques; for example, to hide certain emotions and to emphasize others. Table 6.1 identifies four types of facial management techniques that you will quickly recognize (Malandro, Barker, & Barker, 1989).

These facial management techniques are learned along with display rules which tell you what emotions to express when; they're the rules of appropriateness. For example, when someone gets bad news in which you may secretly take pleasure, the display rule dictates that you frown and otherwise nonverbally signal your displeasure. If you violate these display rules, you will be judged insensitive.

Facial Feedback Hypothesis

The facial feedback hypothesis holds that your facial expressions influence physiological arousal (Lanzetta, Cartwright-Smith, & Kleck, 1976; Zuckerman, Klorman, Larrance, & Spiegel, 1981). In one study, for example, participants held a pen in their teeth to simulate a sad expression and then rated a series of photographs. Results showed that mimicking sad expressions actually increased the degree of sadness the subjects reported feeling when viewing the photographs (Larsen, Kasimatis, & Frey, 1992).

Further support for this hypothesis comes from a study which compared participants who (1) felt emotions such as happiness and anger with those who (2) both felt and expressed these emotions. In support of the facial feedback hypothesis, subjects who felt and expressed the emotions became

Evaluating Information

Examine your self-interest assumptions about lying and ethics.   What assumptions do you hold about the ethics of lying? Each of the situations below presents an occasion for a lie which basically benefits the liar. Is it ethical to lie to:

1. get what you deserve but can't get any other way, for example, a well-earned promotion or raise or another chance with your relationship partner?
2. keep hidden information about yourself that you simply don't want to reveal to anyone, for example, your affectional orientation, your financial situation, or your religious beliefs?
3. get yourself out of an unpleasant situation, for example, to get out of an extra office chore, a boring conversation, or a conflict with your partner?

Table 6.1. Facial Management Techniques.

Can you identify a specific situation in which you or someone with whom you interacted used one of these techniques?

Technique	Function	Example
Intensifying	To exaggerate a feeling	Exaggerating surprise when friends throw you a party, to make your friends feel better
Deintensifying	To underplay a feeling	To cover up your own joy in the presence of a friend who didn't receive such good news
Neutralizing	To hide a feeling	To cover up your sadness so as not to depress others
Masking	To replace or substitute the expression of one emotion for another	To express happiness in order to cover up your disappointment at not receiving the gift you had expected

emotionally aroused faster than did those who only felt the emotion (Hess, Kappas, McHugo, & Lanzetta, 1992).

Generally, research finds that facial expressions can produce or heighten feelings of sadness, fear, disgust, and anger. But, this effect does not occur with all emotions; smiling, for example, doesn't seem to make us feel happier (Burgoon, Buller, & Woodall, 1996). Further, it has not been demonstrated that facial expressions can eliminate one feeling and replace it with another. So, if you're feeling sad, smiling will not eliminate the sadness and replace it with gladness. A reasonable conclusion seems to be that your facial expressions can influence some feelings but not all (Burgoon, Buller, & Woodall 1996; Cappella, 1993).

Eye Movements

From Ben Jonson's poetic observation "Drink to me only with thine eyes, and I will pledge with mine" to the scientific observations of contemporary researchers (Hess, 1975; Marshall, 1983), the eyes are regarded as the most important nonverbal message system.

The messages communicated by the eyes (a study known technically as **oculesis**) vary depending on the duration, direction, and quality of the eye behavior. For example, in every culture there are strict, though unstated, rules for the proper duration for eye contact. In our culture, the average length of gaze is 2.95 seconds. The average length of mutual gaze (two persons gazing at each other) is 1.18 seconds (Argyle & Ingham, 1972; Argyle, 1988). When eye contact falls short of this amount, you may think the person is uninterested, shy, or preoccupied. When the appropriate amount of time is exceeded, you might perceive the person as showing unusually high interest.

The direction of the eye also communicates. In much of the United States, you're expected to glance alternatively at the other person's face, then away, then again at the face, and so on. The rule for the public speaker is to scan the entire audience, not focusing for too long or ignoring any one area of the audience. When you break these directional rules, you communicate different meanings—abnormally high or low interest, self-consciousness, nervousness over the interaction, and so on. The quality—how wide or how narrow your eyes get during interaction—also communicates meaning, especially interest level and such emotions as surprise, fear, and disgust.

From a man's face, I can read his character; if I can see him walk, I know his thoughts.
—*Petronius*

Take a close look at popular plush toy animals and Beanie Babies. Are their pupils larger than normal? What do these pupils communicate? *(An interesting research paper could be written on the nonverbal messages in children's toy animals.)*

Evaluating Information

Examine your "altruistic" assumptions about lying and ethics. Each of these situations presents an occasion for a lie that basically benefits another person. Is it ethical to lie to:

1. achieve some greater good, for example, to lie to someone to prevent her or him from committing suicide or getting depressed, or to lie to prevent a burglary or theft?

2. enable the other person to save face, for example, to agree with an idea you find foolish or to compliment someone when it is undeserved?

3. get someone to do something in his or her own best interests, for example, to diet, to stop smoking, or to study harder?

The Functions of Eye Movements

With eye movements you can serve a variety of functions. One such function is to seek feedback. In talking with someone, we look at her or him intently, as if to say, "Well, what do you think?" As you might predict, listeners gaze at speakers more than speakers gaze at listeners. In public speaking, you might scan hundreds of people to secure this feedback.

A second function is to inform the other person that the channel of communication is open and that he or she should now speak. You see this regularly in conversation when one person asks a question or finishes a thought and then looks to you for a response.

Eye movements may also signal the nature of a relationship, whether positive (an attentive glance) or negative (eye avoidance). You can also signal your power through "visual dominance behavior" (Exline, Ellyson, & Long, 1975). The average speaker, for example, maintains a high level of eye contact while listening and a lower level while speaking. When people want to signal dominance, they may reverse this pattern—maintaining a high level of eye contact while talking but a much lower level while listening.

By making eye contact you psychologically lessen the physical distance between yourself and another person. When you catch someone's eye at a party, for example, you become psychologically close, though physically far apart.

Eye Avoidance Functions

The eyes are "great intruders," observed sociologist Erving Goffman (1967). When you avoid eye contact or avert your glance, you help others to maintain their privacy. You might do this when you see a couple arguing in public. You turn your eyes away (though your eyes may be wide open) as if to say, "I don't mean to intrude; I respect your privacy." Goffman refers to this behavior as **civil inattention.**

Eye avoidance can also signal lack of interest—in a person, a conversation, or some visual stimulus. At times, you might hide your eyes to block off unpleasant stimuli (a particularly gory or violent scene in a movie, for example) or close your eyes to block out visual stimuli and thus heighten other senses. For example, you might listen to music with your eyes closed. Lovers often close their eyes while kissing, and many prefer to make love in a dark or dimly lit room.

What messages do you communicate with your facial expression and eye movements? Have others ever misinterpreted the meaning of your meanings? (This could be the start of an interesting personal experience paper.)

Space Communication

Your use of space to communicate (an area of study known technically as **proxemics**) speaks as surely and loudly as words and sentences. Speakers who stand close to their listener, with their hands on the listener's shoulders and their eyes focused directly on those of the listener, communicate something very different from speakers who stand in a corner with arms folded and eyes downcast. Similarly, for example, the territory you occupy or own and the way you protect this territory also communicates (an area of study known as **territoriality**). The executive office suite on the top floor with huge windows, private bar, and plush carpeting communicates something totally different from the six-by-six-foot cubicle occupied by the rest of the workers.

In the fifteenth and sixteenth centuries in Italy, women put drops of belladonna (which literally means "beautiful woman") into their eyes to dilate the pupils so they would look more attractive. Contemporary research supports the logic of these women; people judge dilated pupils as more attractive (Hess, 1975). Your pupils also enlarge when you're interested in something or emotionally aroused. Perhaps you judge dilated pupils as more attractive because you judge an individual's dilated pupils as showing interest in you. More generally it's claimed that pupils dilate in response to positively evaluated attitudes and objects and constrict in response to negatively evaluated attitudes and objects (Hess, 1985). Do you find this generally true? In what other contexts would pupils dilate? Constrict?

Spatial Distances

Edward Hall (1959, 1966) distinguishes four distances that define the type of relationship between people and the type of communication in which they're likely to engage (see Table 6.2). In **intimate distance,** ranging from actual touching to 18 inches, the presence of the other individual is unmistakable. Each person experiences the sound, smell, and feel of the other's breath. You use intimate distance for lovemaking, comforting, and protecting. This distance is so short that most people do not consider it proper in public.

Personal distance refers to the protective "bubble" that defines your personal distance, ranging from 18 inches to 4 feet. This imaginary bubble keeps you protected and untouched by others. You can still hold or grasp another person at this distance but only by extending your arms; allowing you to take certain individuals such as loved ones into your protective bubble. At the outer limit of personal distance, you can touch another person only if both of you extend your arms. At this distance you conduct much of your interpersonal interactions, for example, talking with friends and family.

Social distance, ranging from 4 to 12 feet, you lose the visual detail you have at personal distance. You conduct impersonal business and interact at a social gathering at this social distance. The more distance you maintain in your interactions, the more formal they appear. In offices of high officials, the desks are positioned so the official is assured of at least this distance from clients.

Table 6.2. Relationships and Proxemic Distances.

Note that these four distances can be further divided into close and far phases and that the far phase of one level (say, personal) blends into the close phase of the next level (social). Do your relationships also blend into one another or are, say, your personal relationships totally separated from your social relationships?

Relationship	Distance
Intimate Relationship	**Intimate Distance** 0 _____ 18 inches close phase · · · far phase
Personal Relationship	**Personal Distance** 1½ _____ 4 feet close phase · · · far phase
Social Relationship	**Social Distance** 4 _____ 12 feet close phase · · · far phase
Public Relationship	**Public Distance** 12 _____ 25+ feet close phase · · · far phase

Why would it be difficult to engage in intimate communication in public distance? Why would it be difficult to conduct impersonal business (say, banking) at intimate distance?

Public distance, from 12 to more than 25 feet, protects you. At this distance you could take defensive action if threatened. On a public bus or train, for example, you might keep at least this distance from a drunkard. Although at this distance you lose fine details of the face and eyes, you're still close enough to see what is happening.

Influences on Space Communication

Several factors influence the way you relate to and use space in communicating. Here are a few examples of how status, culture, subject matter, gender, and age influence space communication (Burgoon, Buller, & Woodall, 1995).

People of equal **status** maintain shorter distances between themselves than do people of unequal status. When status is unequal, the higher-status person may approach the lower-status person more closely than the lower-status person would approach the higher-status person.

Members of different **cultures** treat space differently. For example, those from northern European cultures and many Americans stand fairly far apart when conversing, compared with those from southern European and Middle Eastern cultures who stand much closer. It's easy to see how those who normally stand far apart may interpret the close distances of others as pushy and overly intimate. It's equally easy to appreciate how those who normally stand close may interpret the far distances of others as cold and unfriendly.

When discussing personal **subjects** you maintain shorter distances than with impersonal subjects. Also, you stand closer to someone praising you than to someone criticizing you.

Your **gender** also influences your spatial relationships. Women generally stand closer to each other than men. Similarly, when someone approaches another person, he or she will come closer to a woman than to a man. As people **age** there is a tendency for the spaces to become larger. Children stand much closer than do adults. These findings provide some evidence that these distances are learned behaviors.

Territoriality

Territoriality, a term from ethology (the study of animals in their natural habitat), refers to the ownership-like reaction toward a particular space or object. The size and location of human territory also say something about status. An apartment or office in midtown Manhattan or downtown Tokyo is extremely high-status territory since the cost restricts it to the wealthy.

Status is also indicated by the unwritten law granting the right of invasion. In some cultures and in some organizations, for example, higher-status individuals have more of a right to invade the territory of others than vice versa. The president of a large company can invade the territory of a junior executive by barging into her or his office, but the reverse would be unthinkable.

Like animals, humans also mark their territory (Hickson & Stacks, 1988). For example, you might place an item of clothing or a book at a table in the cafeteria to claim this seat as your territory. Or, you might have initials on your brief case. Other types of markers are used to separate one territory from another, for example, the bar used at the supermarket checkout to separate your groceries from the person behind you or the arm rest used in a theater to separate your seat from those next to you.

Artifactual Communication

Artifactual messages are those made by human hands. Thus, color, clothing, jewelry, and the decoration of space would be considered artifactual. Let's look at each of these briefly.

Do you sit in the same seat in class? Do you get disturbed when someone else sits in that seat? How would you explain "seat claiming behavior" in terms of territoriality?

How would you describe your own territorial behavior? How do you respond to territorial encroachment? What types of markers do you use? *(Any of the technical terms used in this chapter, for example, territoriality, proxemics, and markers, would make interesting topics for a concept paper.)*

"Never let her catch you in her garden … Humans are very territorial."

© 1994. Reprinted courtesy of Bunny Hoest and Parade Magazine.

LISTENING

Gender Differences in Nonverbal Messages

Men and women communicate differently in their nonverbal messages as well as in their verbal messages. Here are a few findings from research on nonverbal sex differences (Burgoon, Buller, & Woodall, 1989; Eakins & Eakins, 1978; Pearson, West, & Turner, 1995; Arliss, 1991). What reasons can you think of that might account for these differences? Would these reasons differ from one culture to another? What problems might these differences create when men and women try to listen to each other?

1. Women smile more than men.
2. Women stand closer to each other than men do and are generally approached more closely than men.
3. Both men and women, when speaking, look at men more than at women.
4. Women both touch and are touched more than men.
5. Men extend their bodies, taking up greater areas of space, than women.

[The next Listening box appears on page 182.]

Visit one of the Websites of a large multinational corporation. What can you learn about nonverbal communication from such elements as the general design, colors, movement, fonts, or spacing used? Can you point out any way that the Website can be visually improved?

Color Communication

There is some evidence that colors affect us physiologically. For example, respiratory movements increase with red light and decrease with blue light. Similarly, eye blinks increase in frequency when eyes are exposed to red light and decrease when exposed to blue. This seems consistent with our intuitive feelings about blue being more soothing and red more arousing. After changing a school's walls from orange and white to blue, the blood pressure of the students decreased while their academic performance increased.

Color also influences perceptions and behaviors (Kanner, 1989). People's acceptance of a product, for example, is largely determined by its packaging, especially its color. The very same coffee taken from a yellow can was described as weak; from a dark brown can, too strong; from a red can, rich; and from a blue can, mild. Even your acceptance of a person may depend on the colors worn. Consider, for example, the comments of one color expert (Kanner, 1989): "If you have to pick the wardrobe for your defense lawyer heading into court and choose anything but blue, you deserve to lose the case . . . ." Black is so powerful it could work against the lawyer with the jury. Brown lacks sufficient authority. Green would probably elicit a negative response.

This brief article pokes fun at some of the ways people decorate their offices but makes the serious point that our nonverbal signals may not communicate what we want them to. Although written for a men's magazine, the insights apply to women as well.

Deconstructing Your Cubicle
Think Before You Tack Up That NRA Banner

Yutaka Kawachi

You'd like to think the trinkets you keep in your office express something unique about your personality. Whatever novelty you use to dress up your office, be aware that some of these doodads send subtle messages that would be better left suppressed.

We inspected our own cubicles and came up with a list of some of the more annoying junk that should remain at home:

A Trophy You've Won

What you think it says about you: You're a winner.
What it really says: Your house doesn't have a garage.

A Coffee Mug with A Cute Saying ("Damn, I'm Good!)

What you think it says about you: You're quite the irreverent guy.

What it really says: Your coffee mug is wittier than you are.

Fishing/Hunting Gear

What you think it says about you: You have outside interests.

What it really says: Yes, and they should remain outside the office.

Jefferson Airplane Poster

What you think it says about you: You wear a business suit, but at heart you're a rebel.

What it really says: You wear a business suit, but your life stopped in 1968.

Gym Stuff

What you think it says about you: You're an active guy.

What it really says: You're an active guy whose office smells like a locker room.

Anything from The Franklin Mint

What you think it says about you: You have a vintage Corvette at home just like the scale model on your desk.

What it really says: You couldn't afford a real vintage Corvette, so you bought the $79.95 model instead.

A Babe Calendar

What you think it says about you: You're one hot dude.

What it really says: You're one big sexual-harassment settlement waiting to happen.

A Framed Diploma

What you think it says about you: You're an accomplished fellow.

What it really says: Secretly, you always wanted to be a doctor.

A Half-Eaten Cheeseburger

What you think it says about you: You're such a go-getter, you barely have time to eat lunch.

What it really says: You're a slob.

Thinking Critically About "Deconstructing Your Cubicle."   Do you agree with the suggestions made in the article? What reasons might you offer to support or refute the suggestions in the article? Try writing a similar article but address it to the woman executive about to enter a new position. What items would you suggest she avoid displaying? What items would you suggest she should display? What reasons can you advance for each of your suggestions?

Source: From "Deconstructing Your Cubicle" by Yutaka Kawachi, *Men's Health*, December 1996. Reprinted by permission of *Men's Health* Magazine. Copyright © 1996 Rodale Press, Inc. All rights reserved.

Clothing and Body Adornment

People make inferences about who you are—in part—by the way you dress. Whether these inferences are accurate or not, they will influence what people think of you and how they react to you. Your socioeconomic class, your seriousness, your attitudes (for example, whether you're conservative or liberal), your concern for convention, your sense of style and perhaps even your creativity will all be judged—in part at least—by the way you dress (Molloy, 1977; Burgoon, Buller, & Woodall, 1996; Knapp & Hall, 1992). Similarly, college students will perceive an instructor dressed informally as friendly, fair, enthusiastic, and flexible and the same instructor dressed formally as prepared, knowledgeable, and organized (Malandro, Barker, & Barker, 1989).

The way you wear your hair communicates about who you are—from caring about being up-to-date to a desire to shock, to perhaps a lack of concern for appearances. Men with long hair will generally be judged as less conservative than those with shorter hair. Your jewelry also communicates messages about you. Wedding and engagement rings are obvious examples that communicate specific messages. College rings and political buttons likewise communicate specific messages. If you wear a Rolex watch or large precious stones, for example, others are likely to infer that you're rich. Men who wear earrings will be judged differently from men who don't. What judgments are

A popular defense tactic in sex crimes against women, gay men, and lesbians is to blame the victim by referring to the way the victim was dressed and to imply that the victim, by virtue of the clothing worn, provoked the attack. Currently, New York and Florida are the only states that prohibit defense attorneys from referring to the way a sex-crime victim was dressed at the time of the attack (*The New York Times* July 30, 1994, p. 22). What do you think of this? If you do not live in New York or Florida, have there been proposals in your state to similarly limit this popular defense tactic?

made will depend on who the receiver is, the communication context, and all the factors identified throughout this text.

Space Decoration

The way you decorate your private spaces also communicates about you. The office with mahogany desk and bookcases and oriental rugs communicates your importance and status within the organization just as the metal desk and bare floors indicate a worker much further down in the hierarchy.

Similarly, people will make inferences about you based on the way you decorate your home. The expensiveness of the furnishings may communicate your status and wealth; their coordination, your sense of style. The magazines may reflect your interests while the arrangement of chairs around a television set may reveal how important watching television is to you. And, bookcases lining the walls reveal the importance of reading. In fact, there is probably little in your home that would not send messages that others would not use in making inferences about you. Computers, widescreen televisions, well-equipped kitchens, and oil paintings of great grandparents, for example, all say something about the people who live in the home.

Similarly, the lack of certain items will communicate something about you. Consider what messages you would get from a home where there is no television, phone, or books.

Touch Communication

Touch communication (known technically as **haptics**) is perhaps the most primitive form of communication (Montague, 1971). Touch develops before the other senses; even in the womb the child is stimulated by touch. Soon after birth the child is fondled, caressed, patted, and stroked. In turn, the child explores its world through touch and quickly learns to communicate a variety of meanings through touch.

What inferences would you make about the owner of this home solely on the basis of what appears in this photo?

The Meanings of Touch

Nonverbal researchers have identified the major meanings of touch (Jones & Yarbrough, 1985):

- Positive emotion. Touch may communicate such positive feelings as support, appreciation, inclusion, sexual interest or intent, and affection.
- Playfulness. Touch often communicates our intention to play, either affectionately or aggressively.
- Control. Touch may also direct the behaviors, attitudes, or feelings of the other person. In attention-getting, for example, you touch the person to gain his or her attention, as if to say "look at me" or "look over here."
- Ritual. Ritualistic touching centers on greetings and departures, for example, shaking hands to say "hello" or "goodbye" or hugging, kissing, or putting your arm around another's shoulder when greeting or saying farewell.
- Task-relatedness. Task-related touching occurs while you're performing some function, for example, removing a speck of dust from another person's face or helping someone out of a car.

Recognize that different cultures will view these types of touching differently. For example, some task-related touching, viewed as acceptable in much of the United States, would be viewed negatively in some cultures. Among Koreans, for example, it's considered disrespectful for a store owner to touch a customer in, say, handing back change; it's considered too intimate a gesture. Members of other cultures, expecting some touching, may consider the Korean's behavior cold and insulting.

Touch Avoidance

Much as we touch and are touched, we also avoid touch from certain people and in certain circumstances. Researchers in nonverbal communication have found some interesting relationships between touch avoidance and other significant communication variables (Andersen & Leibowitz, 1978; Hall, 1996). For example, touch avoidance is positively related to communication apprehension; those who fear oral communication also score high on touch avoidance. Touch avoidance is also high with those who self-disclose little. Both touch and self-disclosure are intimate forms of communication; thus people who are reluctant to get close to another person by self-disclosing also seem reluctant to get close by touching.

Older people have higher touch-avoidance scores for opposite-sex persons than do younger people. As we get older we're touched less by members of the opposite sex. This decreased frequency may lead us to avoid touching.

Males score higher on same-sex touch avoidance than do females, which matches our stereotypes. Men avoid touching other men, but women may and do touch other women. On the other hand, women have higher touch-avoidance scores for opposite-sex touching than do men.

Paralanguage

Paralanguage refers to the vocal (but nonverbal) dimension of speech. It refers to how you say something, not what you say. A traditional exercise to increase a student's ability to express different emotions, feelings, and attitudes is to

Evaluating Information

Be careful of confusing relationship and causal assertions. The statement "touch avoidance is positively related to communication apprehension" indicates a relationship between "touch avoidance" and "communication apprehension." It states that these two things are found together often enough to be significant beyond chance. It does *not* claim that "apprehension" *causes* people to avoid touch. Some third factor—say, low self-esteem, for example—may cause both touch avoidance and apprehension. When you encounter relationship assertions, ask, for example:

- Does the relationship hold for all people? For young and older couples? Heterosexual and homosexual couples? Does it hold in all cultures?
- How are the terms defined? For example, what is "significant" self-disclosure? How much longer does "remain together longer" mean?

How would you describe the rules of touch avoidance for passengers on a commuter train? For students at a football stadium? For members of your family at dinner?

repeat a sentence while accenting or stressing different words. One popular sentence was, "Is this the face that launched a thousand ships?" Significant differences in meaning are easily communicated depending on where the stress is placed. Consider the following variations:

1. *Is* this the face that launched a thousand ships?
2. Is *this* the face that launched a thousand ships?
3. Is this *the face* that launched a thousand ships?
4. Is this the face *that launched* a thousand ships?
5. Is this the face that launched *a thousand ships?*

Each sentence communicates something different; in fact, each asks a different question although the words are the same. All that distinguishes the sentences is stress, one aspect of paralanguage.

In addition to stress or pitch, paralanguage includes such vocal characteristics as rate, volume, and rhythm as well as the vocalizations you make in crying, whispering, moaning, belching, yawning, and yelling (Trager, 1958, 1961; Argyle, 1988). A variation in any of these features communicates. When you speak quickly, for example, you communicate something different from when you speak slowly. Even though the words might be the same, if the speed (or volume, rhythm, or pitch) differs, the meanings people receive will also differ.

What nonverbal cues should you look for in judging whether someone likes you? List them in the order of their importance, using 1 for the cue that is of most value in making your judgment, 2 for the cue that is next most valuable, and so on down to perhaps 10 or 12. Do you really need two lists? One for judging a woman's liking and one for a man's?

Judgments About People

Paralanguage cues are often used as a basis for making judgments about people, for example, their emotional state or even their personality. Listeners can accurately judge the emotional states of speakers from vocal expression alone if both speaker and listener speak the same language. Paralanguage cues are not so accurate when used to communicate emotions to those who speak a different language (Albas, McCluskey, & Albas, 1976). In these studies, speakers recite the alphabet or numbers while expressing emotions. Some emotions are easier to identify than others; it's easy to distinguish between hate and sympathy but more difficult to distinguish between fear and anxiety. And, of course, listeners vary in their ability to decode, and speakers in their ability to encode, emotions (Scherer, 1986).

Less reliable are judgments made about personality. Some, for example, may conclude that those who speak softly feel inferior, believing that no one wants to listen and nothing they say is significant, or that people who speak loudly have overinflated egos and think everyone in the world wants to hear them.

Judgments About Communication Effectiveness

The rate or speed at which people speak is the aspect of paralanguage that has received the most attention (MacLachlan, 1979). It's of interest to the advertiser, the politician, and, in fact, anyone who tries to convey information or influence others. It's especially important when time is limited or expensive.

In one-way communication (when one person is doing all or most of the speaking and the other person is doing all or most of the listening), those who talk fast (about 50% faster than normal) are more persuasive. People agree more with a fast speaker than with a slow speaker and find the fast speaker more intelligent and objective.

When we look at comprehension, rapid speech shows an interesting effect. When the speaking rate is increased by 50%, the comprehension level drops only by 5%. When the rate is doubled, the comprehension level drops only 10%. These 5 and 10% losses are more than offset by the increased speed; thus the faster rates are much more efficient in communicating information. If the speeds are more than twice normal speech, however, comprehension begins to fall dramatically.

Exercise caution in applying this research to all forms of communication (MacLachlan, 1979). For example, if you increase your rate to increase efficiency, you may create so unnatural an impression that others will focus on your speed instead of your meaning.

Silence

Like words and gestures, silence too communicates important meanings and serves important functions (Johannesen, 1974; Jaworski, 1993). Silence allows the speaker *time to think,* time to formulate and organize his or her verbal communications. Before messages of intense conflict, as well as those confessing undying love, there is often silence. Again, silence seems to prepare the receiver for the importance of these future messages.

Some people use silence as a weapon *to hurt* others. We often speak of giving someone "the silent treatment." After a conflict, for example, one or both individuals might remain silent as a kind of punishment. Silence used to hurt others may also take the form of refusing to acknowledge the presence of another person, as in disconfirmation (see Chapter 5); here silence is a dramatic demonstration of the total indifference one person feels toward the other.

Sometimes silence is used as a *response to personal anxiety,* shyness, or threats. You may feel anxious or shy among new people and prefer to remain

CAUTION

Might **drawing conclusions (rather than hypotheses) about personality from people's nonverbal behaviors** prevent you from seeking further information and hinder you from seeing evidence contrary to your conclusion? Have you ever drawn conclusions about another person and then acted as if these conclusions were accurate when they weren't? Has anyone ever drawn conclusions in this way about you?

Evaluating Information

Evaluate causal assertions. The statement "In one-way communication . . . those who talk fast . . . are more persuasive" not only states a relationship between "talking speed" and "persuasiveness" but also states that the type of relationship is a *causal* one: talking faster than normal causes (leads to, contributes to, influences) persuasion. In thinking critically about causal assertions, try to ask:

- How strong is the causal connection? Is this true of all types of self-disclosure? How significant is the persuasive effect?
- Might factors intervene to prevent the cause from producing the effect? For example, what would happen in a situation in which there was a great deal of noise? Might the noise prevent this causal relationship from holding?
- Does this causal connection operate in all cultures? For example, are there cultures where fast-talking might have negative effects?

Drawing on my fine command
of language, I said nothing.
                —*Robert Benchley*

silent. By remaining silent you preclude the chance of rejection. Only when the silence is broken and an attempt to communicate with another person is made do you risk rejection.

Silence may be used *to prevent communication* of certain messages. In conflict situations silence is sometimes used to prevent certain topics from surfacing and to prevent one or both parties from saying things they may later regret. In such situations silence often allows us time to cool off before expressing hatred, severe criticism, or personal attacks, which, we know, are irreversible.

Like the eyes, face, or hands, silence can also be used *to communicate emotional responses* (Ehrenhaus, 1988). Sometimes silence communicates a determination to be uncooperative or defiant; by refusing to engage in verbal communication, you defy the authority or the legitimacy of the other person's position. Silence is often used to communicate annoyance, usually accompanied by a pouting expression, arms crossed in front of the chest, and nostrils flared. Silence may express affection or love, especially when coupled with long and longing stares into each other's eyes.

How do you respond to silence? For example, when you're with friends, does silence make you uncomfortable? Are there some people with whom you're comfortable in silence?

Of course, you may also use silence when you simply have *nothing to say,* when nothing occurs to you, or when you do not want to say anything. James Russell Lowell expressed this best: "Blessed are they who have nothing to say, and who cannot be persuaded to say it." Silence may also be used to say nothing and thus avoid responsibility for any wrongdoing (Beach, 1990–1991).

Time Communication

Temporal communication (known technically as **chronemics**) concerns the use of time—how you organize it, react to it, and the messages it communicates (Bruneau, 1985, 1990). Consider, for example, the emphasis you place on the past, present, and future. In a past orientation, you have special reverence for the past. You relive old times and regard the old methods as the best. You see events as circular and recurring, so the wisdom of yesterday is applicable also to today and tomorrow. In a present orientation, however, you live in the present; for now, not tomorrow. In a future orientation, you look toward and live for the future. You save today, work hard in college, and deny yourself luxuries because you're preparing for the future. Before reading more about time, take the accompanying time test yourself.

Whether it's the best of times
or the worst of times, it's the
only time we've got.
                —*Art Buchwald*

SELF-TEST

What Time Do You Have?

Instructions: For each statement, indicate whether the statement is true (T) or untrue (F) of your general attitude and behavior.

_____   1. Meeting tomorrow's deadlines and do-
              ing other necessary work comes be-
              fore tonight's partying.
_____   2. I meet my obligations to friends and
              authorities on time.

_____   3. I complete projects on time by making
              steady progress.
_____   4. I am able to resist temptations when I
              know there is work to be done.

Source: From "Time in Perspective: What Time Do You Have?," by Alexander Gonzalez and Philip G. Zimbardo, *Psychology Today,* March 1980. Reprinted with permission from *Psychology Today* magazine, copyright © 1980 Sussex Publishers, Inc.

_____ 5. I keep working at a difficult, uninteresting task if it will help me get ahead.

_____ 6. If things don't get done on time, I don't worry about it.

_____ 7. I think that it's useless to plan too far ahead because things hardly ever come out the way you planned anyway.

_____ 8. I try to live one day at a time.

_____ 9. I live to make better what is, rather than to be concerned about what will be.

_____ 10. It seems to me that it doesn't make sense to worry about the future, since fate determines that whatever will be, will be.

_____ 11. I believe that getting together with friends to party is one of life's important pleasures.

_____ 12. I do things impulsively, making decisions on the spur of the moment.

_____ 13. I take risks to put excitement in my life.

_____ 14. I get drunk at parties.

_____ 15. It's fun to gamble.

_____ 16. Thinking about the future is pleasant to me.

_____ 17. When I want to achieve something, I set subgoals and consider specific means for reaching those goals.

_____ 18. It seems to me that my career path is pretty well laid out.

_____ 19. It upsets me to be late for appointments.

_____ 20. I meet my obligations to friends and authorities on time.

_____ 21. I get irritated at people who keep me waiting when we've agreed to meet at a given time.

_____ 22. It makes sense to invest a substantial part of my income in insurance premiums.

_____ 23. I believe that "A stitch in time saves nine."

_____ 24. I believe that "A bird in the hand is worth two in the bush."

_____ 25. I believe it is important to save for a rainy day.

_____ 26. I believe a person's day should be planned each morning.

_____ 27. I make lists of things I must do.

_____ 28. When I want to achieve something, I set subgoals and consider specific means for reaching those goals.

Thinking Critically About Your Time Perspective This time test measures seven different factors. If you selected true (T) for all or most of the questions within any given factor, you're probably high on that factor. If you selected untrue (F) for all or most of the questions within any given factor, you're probably low on that factor. As you read down the list of factors, consider how you measure up on each factor and especially about how your time attitude impacts on your life—as a student, as a friend, as a family member.

The first factor, measured by questions 1–5, is a future, work motivation, perseverance orientation. These people have a strong work ethic and are committed to completing a task despite difficulties and temptations. The second factor (questions 6–10) is a present, fatalistic, worry-free orientation. High scorers on this factor live one day at a time, not necessarily to enjoy the day but to avoid planning for the next day or anxiety about the future.

The third factor (questions 11–15) is a present, pleasure-seeking, partying orientation. These people enjoy the present, take risks, and engage in a variety of impulsive actions. The fourth factor (questions 16–18) is a future, goal-seeking and planning orientation. These people derive special pleasure from planning and achieving a variety of goals.

The fifth factor (questions 19–21) is a time-sensitivity orientation. People who score high are especially sensitive to time and its role in social obligations. The sixth factor (questions 22–25) is a future, practical action orientation. These people do what they have to do—take practical actions—to achieve the future they want.

The seventh factor (questions 26–29) is a future, somewhat obsessive daily planning orientation. High scorers on this factor make daily "to do" lists and devote great attention to specific details.

The time orientation you develop depends on your socioeconomic class and your personal experiences. Gonzalez and Zimbardo (1985), who developed this scale and upon whose research these findings are based, observe: "A child with parents in unskilled and semiskilled occupations is usually socialized in a way that promotes a present-oriented fatalism and hedonism. A child of parents who are managers, teachers, or other professionals learns future-oriented values and strategies designed to promote achievement." Not surprisingly, in the United States future income is positively related to future orientation; the more future-oriented you are, the greater your income is likely to be.

Different time perspectives also account for much intercultural misunderstanding, since different cultures often teach their members drastically different time orientations. For example, members from some Latin cultures would rather be late for an appointment than end a conversation abruptly or before it has come to a natural end. So, the Latin sees this behavior as politeness. But, others may see this as impolite to the person with whom he or she had the appointment (Hall & Hall, 1987).

HOW TO . . .
Communicate Power without Words

Your nonverbal communication will greatly influence the interpersonal power you're seen to possess. Just as you make judgments of the power of someone based on his or her nonverbals, so others are making judgments of you. Here are some suggestions for communicating power without words (Lewis, 1989; Burgoon, Buller, & Woodall, 1995).

• Other things being equal, dress relatively conservatively if you want to influence others; conservative clothing is associated with power and status.

• Respond visibly but in moderation; an occasional nod of agreement or a facial expression that says "that's interesting" are usually sufficient. Responding with too little or too much reaction is likely to be perceived as powerless. Too little response says you aren't listening and too much response says you aren't listening critically. Use backchanneling cues—head nods and brief oral responses that say you're listening.

• Use facial expressions and gestures as appropriate; these help you express your concern for the other person and for the interaction and help you establish your charisma, an essential component of credibility.

• Avoid adaptors—playing with your hair or a pencil or drawing pictures on a styrofoam cup; they signal that you're uncomfortable and hence that you lack power. These body movements show you to be more concerned with yourself than with the speaker. The lack of adaptors, on the other hand, make you appear in control of the situation and comfortable in the role of listener.

• When you break eye contact, direct your gaze downward; otherwise, you will communicate a lack of interest in the other person.

• Use consistent packaging; be especially careful that your verbal and nonverbal messages do not contradict each other.

• To communicate dominance with your handshake, exert more pressure than usual and hold the grip a bit longer than normal.

• Walk slowly and deliberately. To appear hurried is to appear as without power, as if you were rushing to meet the expectations of another person who had power over you.

• Maintain an open posture. When around a table or in an audience resist covering your face, chest, or stomach with your hands. This type of posture is often interpreted as indicating defensiveness and may therefore communicate a feeling of vulnerability and hence powerlessness.

• Avoid interrupting the speaker. The reason is simple: not interrupting is one of the rules of business communication that powerful people follow and powerless people don't. Completing the speaker's thoughts (or what you think is the speaker's thought) has a similar powerless effect.

[The next How To box appears on page 189.]

Similarly, the future-oriented person who works for tomorrow's goals will frequently look down on the present-oriented person as lazy and poorly motivated for enjoying today and not planning for tomorrow. In turn, the present-oriented person may see those with strong future orientations as obsessed with amassing wealth or rising in status.

Smell Communication

Smell communication, or **olfactics,** is extremely important in a wide variety of situations and is now "big business" (Kleinfield, 1992). There is some evidence (though clearly not very conclusive evidence), for example, that the smell of lemon contributes to a perception of health, the smell of lavender and eucalyptus seems to increase alertness, and the smell of rose oil seems to reduce blood pressure. Findings such as these have contributed to the growth of aromatherapy and to a new profession of aromatherapists (Furlow, 1996). Because humans possess "denser skin concentrations of scent glands than almost any other mammal" it has been argued that it only remains for us to discover how we use scent to communicate a wide variety of messages (Furlow, 1996, p. 41). Here are some of the most important messages scent seems to communicate.

- *Attraction messages.* Humans use perfumes, colognes, after-shave lotions, powders, and the like to enhance their attractiveness to others and to themselves. After all, you also smell yourself. When the smells are pleasant, you feel better about yourself.
- *Taste messages.* Without smell, taste would be severely impaired. For example, it would be extremely difficult to taste the difference between a raw potato and an apple without smell. Street vendors selling hot dogs, sausages, and similar foods are aided greatly by the smells that stimulate the appetites of passersby.
- *Memory messages.* Smell is a powerful memory aid; you can often recall situations from months and even years ago when you happen upon a similar smell.

What do you see as the ideal time orientation to have a happy life in this culture? To become wealthy in this culture? Can you identify other cultures where the ideal time orientation would be different? *(Your experience with people from different cultures who have different time orientations could make an interesting personal experience paper.)*

You can also signal power through "visual dominance behavior" (Exline, Ellyson, & Long, 1975). For example, the average speaker maintains a high level of eye contact while listening and a lower level while speaking. When you want to signal dominance, you might reverse this pattern, maintaining a high level of eye contact while talking but a much lower level while listening. Have you ever witnessed visual dominance behavior?

SKILL BUILDING EXERCISE 6.2.

Communicating Nonverbally

This exercise has several parts and asks you to explore the various channels of nonverbal communication discussed here in different ways.

1. The objective of this first exercise is to gain a greater understanding of the role of nonverbal channels in communicating emotions. Using any nonverbal channels you wish, communicate these primary emotions: happiness, surprise, fear, anger, sadness, disgust, contempt, and interest. In a small group discussion, brief talk, e-mail, or brief paper, describe the nonverbals you would use in communicating any one of these emotions. Consider as many of the 10 channels discussed here as possible.

2. Where would you sit in each of the four situations identified above? What would be your first choice? Your second choice?

   A. You want to polish the apple and ingratiate yourself with your boss.
   B. You aren't prepared and want to be ignored.
   C. You want to challenge your boss on a certain policy that will come up for a vote.
   D. You want to be accepted as a new (but important) member of the company.

   Why did you make the choices you made? Do you normally make choices based on such factors as these? What interpersonal factors—for example, the desire to talk to or the desire to get a closer look at someone—influence your day-to-day seating behavior?

3. Consider the meanings colors communicate. The color spectrum is presented in the accompanying photo with numbers from 1 to 25 to facilitate identifying the colors that you select for the objects noted below. Assume that you're working for an advertising agency and that your task is to select colors for these products: an herbal tea made from basil, a children's candy-flavored toothpaste, and a low-calorie ice cream. What major colors would you use? What colors would serve as accents?

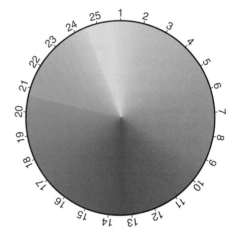

4. Consider how paralanguage variations can communicate praise and criticism by reading each of the following 10 statements, first to communicate praise and second, criticism. Then consider which paralanguage cues you used to communicate the praise and criticism. Although this exercise focused on paralanguage, did you also read the statements with different facial expressions, eye movements, and body postures?

   A. Now that looks good on you.
   B. You lost weight.
   C. You look younger than that.
   D. You're gonna make it.

E. That was some meal.

F. You really know yourself.

G. You're an expert.

H. You're so sensitive. I'm amazed.

I. Your parents are really something.

J. Are you ready? Already?

Thinking Critically About Communicating Nonverbally. How effective would you consider yourself as a nonverbal message sender? A nonverbal message receiver? With which channels are you most effective? Least effective?

- *Identification messages.* Smell is often used to create an image or an identity for a product. Advertisers and manufacturers spend millions of dollars each year creating scents for cleaning products and toothpastes, for example, which have nothing to do with their cleaning power. Instead, they function solely to help create an image for the product. There is also evidence that we can identify specific significant others by smell. For example, young children were able to identify the t-shirts of their brothers and sisters solely on the basis of smell (Porter & Moore, 1981). And one researcher goes so far as to advise: "If your man's odor reminds you of Dad or your brother, you may want genetic tests before trying to conceive a child" (Furlow, 1996, p. 41).

CULTURE AND NONVERBAL COMMUNICATION

Not surprisingly, nonverbal communication is heavily influenced by culture. Consider a variety of differences. At the sight of unpleasant pictures, members of some cultures (American and European, for example) will facially express disgust. Members of other cultures (Japanese, for example) will avoid facially expressing disgust (Ekman, 1985a; Matsumoto, 1991).

Although Americans consider direct eye contact an expression of honesty and forthrightness, the Japanese often view this as a lack of respect. The Japanese will glance at the other person's face rarely and then only for very short periods (Axtell, 1990a). Among some Latin Americans and Native Americans, direct eye contact between, say, a teacher and a student is considered inappropriate, perhaps aggressive; appropriate student behavior is to avoid eye contact with the teacher. Table 6.3 presents a variety of other nonverbal signals, identified by Axtell (1993), that can get you into trouble if used in certain cultures.

In the United States, living next door to someone means that you're expected to be friendly and to interact with that person. It seems so natural that Americans and members of many other cultures probably don't even consider that this cultural expectation is not shared by all cultures. In Japan, the fact that your house is next to another's does not imply that you should become close or visit each other. Consider, therefore, the situation in which a Japanese buys a house next to an American. The Japanese may see the American as overly familiar and as taking friendship for granted. The American may see

Evaluating Information

Carefully assess cues to lying before making judgments. Here are some communication behaviors that are frequently used to detect lying (Knapp & Hall, 1992; Miller & Burgoon, 1990; O'Hair, Cody, Goss, & Krayer, 1988; and Leathers, 1997). As you review these behaviors, try to imagine a situation in which these behaviors would signal not lying but some other intention. Generally, research finds that liars: smile less; respond with shorter answers, often simple "yes" or "no" responses; use fewer specifics and more generalities, for example, "we hung out;" shift their posture more; use more self-touching movements; blink more; use more and longer pauses; avoid direct eye contact with listener; appear less friendly and attentive; and make more speech errors.

Table 6.3. A Few Nonverbals That Can Get You into Trouble.

Can you identify other behaviors that can create cultural problems?

Communication Behavior	May be Considered
Blinking your eyes	Impolite in Taiwan
Folding your arms over your chest	Disrespectful in Fiji
Waving your hand	Insulting in Nigeria and Greece
Gesturing with the thumb up	Rude in Australia
Tapping your two index fingers together	A request that we sleep together in Egypt
Pointing with the index finger	Impolite in many Middle-Eastern countries
Bowing to a lesser degree than your host	A statement of superiority in Japan
With a clenched fist, inserting your thumb between your index and middle finger	Obscene in some southern European countries
Pointing at someone with your index and third fingers	A wish that evil fall on the person in some African countries
Resting your feet on a table or chair	Insulting in some Middle-Eastern countries

the Japanese as distant, unfriendly, and unneighborly. Yet, each person is merely fulfilling the expectations of his or her own culture (Hall & Hall, 1987).

Different cultures also assign different meanings to colors. Some of these cultural differences are illustrated in Table 6.4, but before looking at the table think about the meanings your own culture(s) gives to such colors as red, green, black, white, blue, yellow, and purple.

Touching, too, varies greatly from one culture to another. For example, African Americans touch each other more than do whites. Similarly, touching declines from kindergarten to the sixth grade for white but not for African

How many of the nonverbal cultural differences discussed here have you witnessed? Have you seen cultural differences in nonverbal communication not discussed here?

Table 6.4. Some Cultural Meanings of Color.

This table, constructed from the research reported by Henry Dreyfuss (1971), Nancy Hoft (1995), and Norine Dresser (1996), illustrates only some of the different meanings that colors may communicate and especially how they're viewed in different cultures. As you read this table, consider the meanings you give to these colors and where your meanings came from.

Color	Cultural Meanings and Comments
Red	In China, red signifies prosperity and rebirth and is used for festive and joyous occasions; in France and the United Kingdom, masculinity; in many African countries, blasphemy or death; and in Japan, anger and danger. Red ink, especially among Korean Buddhists, is used only to write a person's name at the time of death or on the anniversary of the person's death and creates lots of problems when American teachers use red ink to mark homework.
Green	In the United States, green signifies capitalism, go ahead, and envy; in Ireland, patriotism; among some Native Americans, femininity; to the Egyptians, fertility and strength; and to the Japanese, youth and energy.
Black	In Thailand, black signifies old age; in parts of Malaysia, courage; and in much of Europe, death.
White	In Thailand, white signifies purity; in many Muslim and Hindu cultures, purity and peace; and in Japan and other Asian countries, death and mourning.
Blue	In Iran, blue signifies something negative; in Ghana, joy; among the Cherokee, defeat; and for the Egyptian, virtue and truth.
Yellow	In China, yellow signifies wealth and authority; in the United States, caution and cowardice; in Egypt, happiness and prosperity; and in many countries throughout the world, femininity.
Purple	In Latin America, purple signifies death; in Europe, royalty; in Egypt, virtue and faith; in Japan, grace and nobility; and in China, barbarism.

Colors speak all languages
—*Joseph Addison*

American children (Burgoon, Buller, & Woodall, 1996). Similarly, Japanese touch each other much less than do Anglo-Saxons, who in turn touch each other much less than do southern Europeans (Morris, 1977; Burgoon, Buller, & Woodall, 1996).

Not surprisingly, the role of silence is seen differently in different cultures (Basso, 1972). Among the Apache, for example, mutual friends do not feel the need to introduce strangers who may be working in the same area or on the same project. The strangers may remain silent for several days. During this time they're looking each other over, trying to determine if the other person is all right. Only after this period do the individuals talk. When courting, especially during the initial stages, the Apache remain silent for hours; if they do talk, they generally talk very little. Only after a couple has been dating for several months will they have lengthy conversations. These periods of silence are generally attributed to shyness or self-consciousness. The use of silence is explicitly taught to Apache women, who are especially discouraged from engaging in long discussions with their dates. Silence during courtship is a sign of modesty to many Apache.

In Iranian culture there's an expression, *qahr,* which means to not be on speaking terms with someone, to give someone the "silent treatment." For example, when children disobey their parents or are disrespectful, or fail to do their chores as they should, they are given this silent treatment. With adults *qahr* may be instituted when one person insults or injures another. After a cooling off period, *ashti* (making up after *qahr*) may be initiated. *Qahr* lasts for

Speaking comes by nature, silence by understanding.
—*German Proverb*

How would you go about seeking answers to questions such as these *(Any of which would make suitable research paper topics):*

- Do high status people touch each other with the same frequency as lower status people?
- Do children who were born blind express emotions with the same facial expressions that sighted children use?
- Do men and women differ in the way they view time?
- What is the ideal outfit for a college instructor to wear on the first day of class?
- Do family photos on an executive's desk contribute to the executive's credibility? Is the relationship between photos and credibility the same for men and women?

a relatively short time between parents and children but longer between adults. *Qahr* is more frequently initiated between two women than between two men, but when men experience *qahr,* it lasts much longer and often requires the intercession of a mediator to establish *ashti* (Behzadi, 1994).

Time is another communication channel with great cultural differences. Two types of cultural time are especially important in nonverbal communication: formal and informal. In American culture, **formal time** is divided into seconds, minutes, hours, days, weeks, months, and years. Other cultures may use phases of the moon or the seasons to delineate time periods. In some colleges courses are divided into 50- or 75-minute periods that meet two or three times a week for 14-week periods called semesters. Eight semesters of fifteen or sixteen 50-minute periods per week equal a college education. Other colleges use quarters or trimesters. As these examples illustrate, formal time units are arbitrary. The culture establishes them for convenience.

Informal time refers to the use of general time terms—for example, "forever," "immediately," "soon," "right away," "as soon as possible." This area of time creates the most communication problems because the terms have different meanings for different people.

Another interesting distinction is that between **monochronic** and **polychronic time** orientations (Hall, 1959, 1976, 1987). Monochronic people or cultures (the United States, Germany, Scandinavia, and Switzerland are good examples) schedule one thing at a time. Time is compartmentalized; there is a time for everything, and everything has its own time. Polychronic people or cultures (Latin Americans, Mediterranean people, and Arabs are good examples), on the other hand, schedule a number of things at the same time. Eating, conducting business with several different people, and taking care of family matters may all be conducted at the same time. No culture is entirely monochronic or polychronic; rather these are general tendencies that are found across a large part of the culture. Some cultures combine both time orientations; Japanese and parts of American culture are examples where both orientations are found. Table 6.5, based on Hall (1987) identifies some of the distinctions between these two time orientations.

Attitudes toward time vary from one culture to another. In one study, for example, the accuracy of clocks was measured in six cultures—Japan, Indonesia, Italy, England, Taiwan, and the United States. Japan had the most accurate and Indonesia had the least accurate clocks. A measure of the speed at

Table 6.5. Monochronic and polychronic time.

Can you identify specific potentials for miscommunication that these differences might create when M-time and P-time people interact?

The Monochronic Person	The Polychronic Person
Does one thing at a time	Does several things at one time
Treats time schedules and plans very seriously; they may only be broken for the most serious of reasons	Treats time schedules and plans as useful (not sacred); they may be broken for a variety of causes
Considers the job the most important part of one's life, ahead of even family	Considers the family and interpersonal relationships more important than the job
Considers privacy extremely important, seldom borrows or lends to others, works independently	Is actively involved with others, works in the presence of and with lots of people at the same time

"Hello, I'm Nesbit. I'm three, and I'm right on track."

which people in these six cultures walked found that the Japanese walked the fastest, the Indonesians the slowest (LeVine & Bartlett, 1984).

Another interesting aspect of cultural time is your "social clock" (Neugarten, 1979). Your culture and your more specific society maintains a time schedule for the right time to do a variety of important things—for example, the right time to start dating, to finish college, to buy your own home, to have a child. And you no doubt learned about this clock as you were growing up, as has Nesbit in the accompanying cartoon. On the basis of this social clock, you then evaluate your own social and professional development. If you're on time with the rest of your peers—for example, you all started dating at around the same age or you're all finishing college at around the same age—then you will feel well adjusted, competent, and a part of the group. If you're late, you will probably experience feelings of dissatisfaction. Recent research, however, shows that this social clock is becoming more flexible; people are becoming more willing to tolerate deviations from the established, socially acceptable time-table for accomplishing many of life's transitional events (Peterson, 1996).

Seize the day, and put the least possible trust in tomorrow.
—Horace

CAUTION

Can you think of an instance where **"reading" nonverbal messages through your own cultural and gender rules** prevented you from accurately assessing another person or another's meaning?

SKILL BUILDING EXERCISE 6.3.

Artifacts and Culture: The Case of Gifts

An aspect of artifactual communication that's frequently overlooked is the giving of gifts, a practice in which rules and customs vary according to each culture. Here are a few situations where gift giving backfired and created barriers rather than bonds. These examples are designed to heighten your awareness of both the importance of gift giving and of recognizing intercultural differences. What might have gone wrong in each of these situations? These few examples should serve to illustrate the wide variations that exist among cultures in the meaning given to artifacts and in the seemingly simple process of giving gifts (Axtell, 1990a; Dresser, 1996).

(continued)

(continued)

1. You bring chrysanthemums to a Belgian colleague and a clock to a Chinese colleague. Both react negatively.
2. Upon meeting an Arab businessman for the first time—someone with whom you wish to do considerable business—you present him with a gift. He seems to become disturbed. To smooth things over, when you go to visit him and his family in Oman, you bring a bottle of your favorite brandy for after dinner. Your host seems even more disturbed now.
3. Arriving for dinner at the home of a Kenya colleague, you present flowers as a dinner gift. Your host accepts them politely but looks puzzled. The next evening you visit your Swiss colleague and bring 14 red roses. Your host accepts them politely but looks strangely at you. Figuring that the red got you in trouble, on your third evening out you bring yellow roses to your Iranian friend. Again, there was a similar reaction.
4. You give your Chinese friend a set of dinner knives as a gift but she doesn't open it in front of you; you get offended. After she opens it, she gets offended.
5. You bring your Mexican friend a statue of an elephant drinking water from a lake. Your friend says he cannot accept it; his expressions tell you he really doesn't want it.

Thinking Critically About Culture and Gifts. Here are some possible reasons: (1) Chrysanthemums in Belgium and clocks in China are both reminders of death and that time is running out. (2) Gifts given at the first meeting may be interpreted as a bribe and thus should be avoided. Further, since alcohol is prohibited by Islamic law, it should be avoided when selecting gifts for most Arabs. (3) In Kenya, flowers are only brought to express condolence. In Switzerland red roses are a sign of romantic interest. Also, an even number of flowers (or 13) is generally considered bad luck and should be avoided. Yellow flowers to Iranians signify the enemy and means that you dislike them. (4) The custom in China is simply not to open gifts in front of the donor. Knives (and scissors) symbolize the severing of a relationship. (5) Among many Latin Americans the elephant's upward trunk symbolizes the holding of good luck; an elephant's downward trunk symbolizes luck slipping away.

Are there gifts that you would consider culturally inappropriate for others to give you? What are your reasons? How did you learn about the cultural appropriateness of gifts? Have you ever given a culturally inappropriate gift? What happened?

A particularly interesting type of gift is the "Pygmalion gift," a gift designed to change the person into what the donor wants that person to become. The parent who gives the child books or science equipment may be asking the child to become a scholar. What messages have you recently communicated in your gift-giving behavior? What messages do you think others communicate to you by the gifts they give you?

SUMMARY OF CONCEPTS AND SKILLS

In this chapter we explored nonverbal communication—communication without words—and considered such areas as body movements, facial and eye movements, spatial and territorial communication, artifactual communication, touch communication, paralanguage, silence, and time communication.

1. The five body movements are emblems (nonverbal behaviors that rather directly translate words or phrases), illustrators (nonverbal behaviors that accompany and literally "illustrate" the verbal messages), affect displays (nonverbal movements that communicate emotional meaning), regulators (nonverbal movements that coordinate, monitor, maintain, or control the speaking of another individual), and adaptors (nonverbal behaviors

emitted without conscious awareness and that usually serve some kind of need, as in scratching an itch).

2. Facial movements may communicate a variety of emotions. The most frequently studied are happiness, surprise, fear, anger, sadness, and disgust/contempt. Facial Management Techniques enable you to control revealing the emotions you feel.

3. The Facial Feedback Hypothesis claims that facial display of an emotion can lead to physiological and psychological changes.

4. Eye movements may seek feedback, inform others to speak, signal the nature of a relationship, and compensate for increased physical distance.

5. Pupil size shows one's interest and level of emotional arousal. Pupils enlarge when one is interested in something or is emotionally aroused in a positive way.

6. Proxemics refers to the communicative function of space and spatial relationships. Four major proxemic distances are: (1) intimate distance ranging from actual touching to 18 inches; (2) personal distance, ranging from 18 inches to 4 feet; (3) social distance, ranging from 4 to 12 feet; and (4) public distance, ranging from 12 to more than 25 feet.

7. Your treatment of space is influenced by such factors as status, culture, context, subject matter, sex, age, and positive or negative evaluation of the other person.

8. Territoriality refers to your possessive reaction to an area of space or to particular objects.

9. Artifactual communication refers to messages that are human-made, for example, the use of color, clothing and body adornment, and space decoration.

10. Touch communication (or haptics) may communicate a variety of meanings, the most important being positive affect, playfulness, control, ritual, and task-relatedness. Touch avoidance refers to our desire to avoid touching and being touched by others.

11. Paralanguage refers to the vocal but nonverbal dimension of speech. It includes rate, pitch, volume, resonance, and vocal quality as well as pauses and hesitations. Based on paralanguage we make judgments about people, conversational turns, and believability.

12. Silence communicates a variety of meanings, from hurting another with the "silent treatment" to communicating deep emotional responses.

13. Time communication (chronemics) refers to the messages communicated by our treatment of time.

14. Smell can communicate messages of attraction, taste, memory, and identification.

15. Cultural variations in nonverbal communication are great. Different cultures, for example, assign different meanings to facial expressions and to colors, have different spatial rules, and treat time very differently.

Throughout our discussion we covered a variety of communication skills. Check your ability to apply these skills. Use the following rating scale: (1) = almost always, (2) = often, (3) = sometimes, (4) = rarely, (5) = almost never.

_____ 1. Recognize messages communicated by body gestures and facial and eye movements.

_____ 2. Take into consideration the interaction of emotional feelings and nonverbal expressions of the emotion; each influences the other.

_____ 3. Recognize that what you perceive is only a part of the total nonverbal expression.

_____ 4. Use eye movements to seek feedback, to inform others to speak, to signal the nature of your relationship with others, and to compensate for increased physical distance.

_____ 5. Give others the space they need, for example, giving more space to those who are angry or disturbed.

_____ 6. Use artifacts to communicate the desired messages.

_____ 7. Become sensitive to the touching behaviors of others and distinguish among those touches that communicate positive emotion, playfulness, control, ritual, and task-relatedness.

_____ 8. Recognize and respect each person's touch-avoidance tendency. Become especially sensitive to cultural and gender differences in touching preferences and in touch-avoidance tendencies.

_____ 9. Vary paralinguistic features (rate, pausing, quality, tempo, and volume) to communicate intended meanings.

_____10. Use silence to communicate intended meanings and become sensitive to the meanings communicated by the silence of others.

_____11. Be specific when using normally informal time terms.

_____12. Interpret time cues from the cultural perspective of the person with whom you're interacting.

VOCABULARY QUIZ. THE LANGUAGE OF NONVERBAL COMMUNICATION

Match the language of nonverbal communication with their definitions. Record the number of the definition next to the name of the effectiveness quality.

____4____ emblems

____1____ affect displays

____8____ proxemics

____9____ territoriality

____5____ haptics

____10____ paralanguage

____2____ chronemics

____7____ artifactual communication

____3____ social clock

____6____ psychological time

1. Movements of the facial area that convey emotional meaning—for example, anger, fear, and surprise.
2. The study of the communicative nature of time—how we treat time and how we use it to communicate.
3. The time which a culture establishes for appropriately achieving certain milestones.
4. Nonverbal behaviors that directly translate words or phrases—for example, the signs for OK and peace.
5. Touch or tactile communication.
6. One's orientation to the past, present, or future.
7. Communication that takes place through the wearing and arrangement of various artifacts—for example, clothing, jewelry, buttons, or the furniture in your house and its arrangement.
8. The study of the communicative function of space; the study of how people unconsciously structure their space—the distance between people in their interactions, the organization of space in homes and offices, and even the design of cities.
9. A possessive or ownership reaction to an area of space or to particular objects.
10. The vocal but nonverbal aspect of speech, for example, the rate, volume, pitch, and stress variations that communicate different meanings.

Emotional
Messages

CHAPTER TOPICS	LEARNING GOALS	SKILLS GOALS
	After completing this chapter, you should be able to	*After completing this chapter, you should be able to*
Emotions and Emotional Communication	1. Explain the nature of emotions, emotional expression, and emotional behavior; the role of the body, mind, and culture in emotions; and the principles of emotion	Communicate your positive and negative emotions more appropriately
Obstacles in Communicating Emotions	2. Identify and give examples of the major obstacles to effectively communicating emotions	Combat the common obstacles for communicating emotions
Guidelines for Communicating Emotions	3. Describe the guidelines for communicating more effectively and for responding to emotions	Communicate emotions and respond to the emotions of others more effectively

A young wife leaves her house one morning to draw water from the local well as her husband watches from the porch. On her way back from the well, a stranger stops her and asks for some water. She gives him a cupful, and then invites him home to dinner. He accepts. The husband, wife, and guest have a pleasant meal together. The husband, in a gesture of hospitality, invites the guest to spend the night—with his wife. He accepts. In the morning, the husband leaves early to bring home breakfast. When he returns, he finds his wife again in bed with the visitor.

The question is: At what point in this story does the husband feel angry?

The answer is: It depends on the culture to which you belong (Hupka, 1981). An American husband would feel rather angry at a wife who had an extramarital affair; and a wife would feel rather angry at being offered to a guest as if she were a lamb chop. But these reactions are not universal.

- A Pawnee Indian husband of the nineteenth century would be enraged at any man who dared ask his wife for water.
- An Ammassalik Eskimo husband finds it perfectly honorable to offer his wife to a stranger, but only once. He would be angry to find his wife and the guest having a second encounter.
- A Toda husband at the turn of the century in India would not be angry at all. The Todas allowed both husband and wife to take lovers, and women were even allowed to have several husbands. Both spouses might feel angry, though, if one of them had a *sneaky* affair; without announcing it publicly.

This report by Carole Wade and Carol Tavris (1998) illustrates that the emotions you feel depend, in part at least, on your culture. In this chapter we look at emotions and especially at the communication of emotions. What are emotions? What makes you experience emotion? Why do you find it difficult to express emotions? How can you learn to better communicate your emotions? How can you better deal with the emotions of others? These are some of the questions we examine in this chapter.

EMOTIONS AND EMOTIONAL COMMUNICATION

Communicating emotions is both difficult and important. It's difficult because our thinking often gets confused when we are intensely emotional. It's also difficult because we were not taught how to communicate emotions and we see few effective models whom we might imitate. Communicating emotions is also most important. Feelings represent a great part of your meanings. If you leave your feelings out or if you communicate these feelings inadequately, you will fail to communicate a great part of your meaning. Consider what your communications would be like if you left out your feelings when talking about failing a recent test, winning the lottery, becoming a parent, getting engaged, driving a car for the first time, becoming a citizen, or being promoted to supervisor. Emotional expression is so much a part of communication that even in the cryptic e-mail message style, emoticons are becoming more popular (Table 7.1).

> When dealing with people, remember you are not dealing with creatures of logic, but with creatures of emotion, creatures bristling with prejudice, and motivated by pride and vanity.
> —Dale Carnegie

The Body, Mind, and Culture in Emotions

Emotion involves at least three parts: bodily reactions (such as blushing when you're embarrassed); mental evaluations and interpretations (as in calculating the odds of drawing an inside straight at poker); and cultural rules and beliefs (for example, in the pride parents feel when their child graduates from college).

Table 7.1 Some Popular Emoticons

These are some of the popular emoticons (loosely, icons communicating emotions) used in e-mail. The first seven are popular in the United States, the last three are popular in Japan and illustrate how culture influences such symbols. In Japan it's considered impolite for a Japanese woman to show her teeth when she smiles and so the emoticon for a woman's smile shows a dot signifying a closed mouth.

Emoticon	Meaning
:-)	Smile; I'm kidding
:-(	Frown; I'm feeling down
*	Kiss
{}	Hug
{*****}	Hugs and kisses
This is important	Gives emphasis, calls special attention to
This is important	Substitutes for underlining or italics
⟨G⟩ ⟨grin⟩	Grin, I'm kidding
^.^	Woman's smile
^_^	Man's smile
^o^	Happy

Bodily reactions are the most obvious aspect of your emotional experience, since we can observe them easily. Such reactions span a wide range. They include, for example, the blush of embarrassment, the sweating palms that accompany nervousness, and the self-touching that goes with discomfort. When you judge people's emotions, you probably look to these nonverbal behaviors. You conclude that Ramon is happy to see you because of his smile and his open body posture. You conclude that Nobuko is nervous from her sweating hands, vocal hesitations, and awkward movements.

The mental part of emotional experience involves the evaluations and interpretations you make on the basis of your behaviors. For example, leading psychotherapist Albert Ellis (1988; Ellis & Harper, 1975), whose insights are used throughout this chapter, claims that your evaluations of what happens has a greater influence on your feelings than what actually happens. Let us say, for example, that your best friend, Sally, ignores you in the college cafeteria. The emotions you feel will depend on what you think this behavior means. You may feel pity if you figure that Sally is depressed because her father died. You may feel anger if you believe that Sally is simply rude and insensitive and snubbed you on purpose. Or, you may feel sadness if you believe that Sally is no longer interested in being friends with you.

In an interesting study that illustrates the influence that our interpretations have on the emotions we experience, students were asked how they felt when they failed or did well on a college examination (Weiner, Russell, & Lerman, 1979). Students who did poorly felt **angry** or **hostile** if they believed that others were responsible for their failure, for example, if they felt the instructor gave an unfair examination. Those who believed that they themselves were responsible for the failure felt **guilt** or **regret.** Students who did very well felt **proud** and **satisfied** if they believed their success was due to their own efforts. They felt **gratitude** and **surprise** (some even felt **guilt**) if they believed that their success was due to luck or chance. Have your own interpretations ever influenced the emotions you experienced? Have they ever not influenced the emotions you felt?

The culture you were raised in and live in gives you a framework for both interpreting the emotions in others and, as we'll see below in the section on Emotional Expression and Culture, for expressing emotions. A colleague of

> People *can* change their feelings. No matter what happens to them, they *can* creatively decide to feel one way or another about it. And they have quite a range of possible feelings to choose from!
> —*Albert Ellis*

Do you agree with Albert Ellis (1988) who argues that your actions and their consequences are not as important in influencing your feelings as are your beliefs about these actions and consequences? Can you give examples that support or refute Ellis's claim? *(This topic would make an interesting personal experience paper.)*

Generally speaking, how accurate do you think you are in judging the emotions of others from only their facial expressions? What specific facial cues do you use most in making your judgments?

mine gave a lecture in Beijing, China, to a group of Chinese college students. The students listened politely but made no comments and asked no questions after her lecture. At first, she concluded that the students were bored and uninterested. Later, she learned that Chinese students show respect by being quiet and seemingly passive. They think that asking questions would imply that she was not clear in her lecture. In other words, the culture—whether American or Chinese—influenced the interpretation of the feelings attributed to the students.

Emotions, Arousal, and Expression

How would you feel in each of the following situations?

1. You have just heard that you won the lottery.
2. Your best friend just died.
3. You were just told you got the job you applied for.
4. Your parents just told you they are getting divorced.

You would obviously feel very differently in each of these situations. In fact, each feeling is unique and unrepeatable. Yet, amid all these differences there is some similarity. For example, most people would claim that the feelings in 1 and 3 are more similar to each other than are 1 and 2. Similarly, 2 and 4 are more similar to each other than are 3 and 4.

There is some evidence that it's actually more difficult to judge when an intimate is lying than when a stranger is lying (Metts, 1989). Do you find this generally true? *(An interesting review paper could summarize what is known about nonverbal cues to lying. Still another paper could review one of the articles or books on nonverbal communication cited in this chapter.)*

"I've been thinking—it might be good for Andrew if he could see you cry once in a while."

Drawing by Weber; © 1993 The New Yorker Magazine, Inc.

Your Basic Emotions

To capture the similarities among emotions, many researchers have tried to identify basic or primary emotions. Robert Plutchik (1980; Havlena, Holbrook, & Lehmann, 1989) developed a most helpful model. In this model there are eight basic emotions (Figure 7.1).

The eight pieces of the pie represent the eight basic emotions: joy, acceptance, fear, surprise, sadness, disgust, anger, and anticipation. Emotions that are close to each other on this wheel are also close to each other in meaning. For example, joy and anticipation are more closely related than are joy and sadness or acceptance and disgust. Emotions that are opposite each other on the wheel are also opposite each other in their meaning. For example, joy is the opposite of sadness, anger is the opposite of fear.

In this model there are also blends. These are emotions that are combinations of the primary emotions. These are noted outside the emotion wheel. For example, according to this model, love is a blend of joy and acceptance. Remorse is a blend of disgust and sadness.

Emotional Arousal

If you were to describe the events leading up to emotional arousal, you would probably describe three stages: (1) an event occurs; (2) you experience an emotion: you feel surprise, joy, anger; (3) you respond physiologically: your heart beats faster, face flushes, and so on. Figure 7.2a depicts this common-sense view of emotions.

Psychologist William James and physiologist Carl Lange offered a different explanation. Their theory places the physiological arousal before the experience of the emotion. The James–Lange sequence is: (1) an event occurs; (2) you respond physiologically; and (3) you experience an emotion, for example, you feel joy or sadness. Figure 7.2b depicts the James–Lange view of emotions.

A third explanation is called the **cognitive labeling theory** (Schachter, 1964). According to this explanation, you interpret the physiological arousal

---

How accurately does Plutchik's model capture the nature of emotions? Would you make any changes in this model? For example, are there other emotions you feel are just as important as the ones included here?

Think critically about a recent situation in which you were emotionally aroused. What precipitated the emotional arousal? What did you do? For example, did you talk about your emotional state with others? If so, how did you describe it? Did you follow the suggestions made here? *(This would make an excellent personal experience paper topic.)*

Figure 7.1

A Model of the Emotions

Do you agree with the basic assumptions of this model? For example, do you see love as a combination of joy and acceptance and optimism as a combination of joy and anticipation? (Source: From *Emotion: A Psychoevolutionary Synthesis* by Robert Plutchik. Copyright © 1980 by Robert Plutchik. Reprinted by permission of HarperCollins Publishers, Inc.)

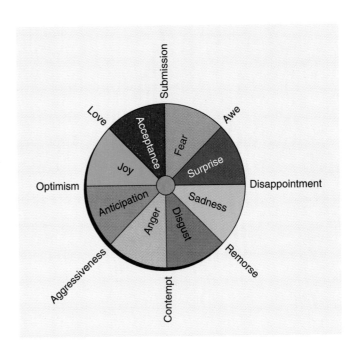

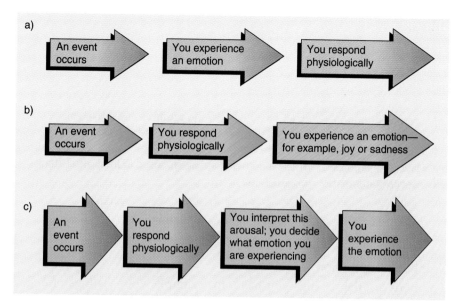

Figure 7.2
Three Views of Emotion
How would you describe emotional arousal?

and, on the basis of this, experience the emotions of joy, sadness, or whatever. The sequence of events goes like this: (1) an event occurs; (2) you respond physiologically; (3) **you interpret this arousal—that is, you decide what emotion you're experiencing;** and (4) you experience the emotion. Your interpretation of this arousal will depend on the situation you're in. For example, if you experience an increased pulse rate after someone you've been admiring smiles at you, you might interpret this as joy. You might, however, interpret that same increased heart beat as fear when three suspicious-looking strangers approach you on a dark street. It's only after you make this interpretation that you experience the emotion, for example, the joy or the fear. This sequence of events is pictured in Figure 7.2c.

Not one of these three explanations seems universally accepted. Each sheds some light on emotions but not enough to explain the entire process of emotional arousal. What would you want a theory of emotional arousal to explain?

SELF-TEST
How Do You Feel About Communicating Feelings?

Instructions: Respond to each of the following statements with T if you feel the statement is a generally true description of your attitudes about expressing emotions and with F if you feel the statement is generally a false description of your attitudes.

_____ 1. Expressing feelings is healthy; it reduces stress and prevents wasting energy on concealment.

_____ 2. Expressing feelings can lead to interpersonal relationship problems.

_____ 3. Expressing feelings can assist others in understanding you.

_____ 4. Emotional expression is often an effective means of persuading others to do as you wish.

_____ 5. Expressing emotions may lead others to perceive you negatively.

_____ 6. Emotional expression can lead to greater and not less stress; expressing anger, for example, may actually increase your feelings of anger.

Thinking Critically About Communicating Feelings
These statements are arguments that are often made for and against expressing emotions. Statements 1, 3,
(continued)

(continued)

and 4 are arguments made in favor of expressing emotions and 2, 5, and 6 are arguments made against expressing emotions. You can look at your responses as revealing (in part) your attitude favoring or opposing the expression of feelings. TRUE responses to statements 1, 3, and 4 and FALSE responses to statements 2, 5, and 6 would indicate a favorable attitude to expressing feelings; FALSE responses to statements 1, 3, and 4 and TRUE responses to statements 2, 5, and 6 indicate a negative attitude. Actually, there is evidence suggesting that expressing emotions can lead to all six outcomes—the positives and the negatives. These statements underscore the importance of critically assessing your options for emotional expression. These arguments are again raised in the Critical Thinking sidebars.

> Emotion is not something shameful, subordinate, second-rate; it is a supremely valid phase of humanity at its noblest and most mature.
>
> —*Joshua Loth Liebman*

Emotional Expression

Emotions are the feelings you have, for example, your feelings of anger, sorrow, guilt, depression, happiness, and so on. Emotional expression, on the other hand, is the way you communicate these feelings. Theorists do not agree over whether you can *choose* the emotions you feel. Some argue that you can, others argue that you cannot. You are, however, clearly in control of the ways in which you *express* your emotions. You do not have to express what you feel.

For example, if you feel anger, you may choose to express or not to express it. You do not have to express anger just because you feel angry. In fact, you may feel angry but outwardly act calmly, dispassionately, and lovingly. For example, if there are several promotions to be made in your office and you do not get the first one, you may feel anger. But, you may decide that to show your anger may hurt your chances for getting one of the other promotions. You may, therefore, decide to respond calmly on the assumption that this will help your advancement more than will an expression of anger.

Should you decide to communicate it, you need to make several decisions. For example, you would have to choose how to do so—face-to-face, letter, phone, e-mail, office memo. And you'd have to choose the specific emotions you will and those you will not reveal. And third, you'd have to choose the language in which you'd express your emotions.

Here is a list of terms for describing your emotions. It's based on the eight primary emotions identified by Plutchik. Notice that the terms included for each basic emotion provide you with lots of choices for expressing the intensity level you're feeling. For example, if you're extremely happy, then *bliss, ecstasy,* or *enchantment* may be appropriate descriptions. If you're mildly happy, then perhaps *contentment, satisfaction,* or *well-being* would be more descriptive. Look over the list and try grouping them into three levels of intensity: high, middle, and low. Before doing that, however, do look up the meanings of any words that are unfamiliar to you.

> **Happiness:** bliss, cheer, contentment, delight, ecstasy, enchantment, enjoyment, felicity, joy, rapture, gratification, pleasure, satisfaction, well-being

Surprise: amazement, astonishment, awe, eye-opener, incredulity, jolt, revelation, shock, unexpectedness, wonder, startle, catch-off-guard, unforeseen

Fear: anxiety, apprehension, awe, concern, consternation, dread, fright, misgiving, phobia, terror, trepidation, worry, qualm, terror

Anger: acrimony, annoyance, bitterness, displeasure, exasperation, fury, ire, irritation, outrage, rage, resentment, tantrum, umbrage, wrath, hostility

Sadness: dejection, depression, dismal, distress, grief, loneliness, melancholy, misery, sorrowful, unhappiness

Disgust: abhorrence, aversion, loathing, repugnance, repulsion, revulsion, sickness, nausea, offensiveness

Contempt: abhorrence, aversion, derision, disdain, disgust, distaste, indignity, insolence, ridicule, scorn, snobbery, revulsion, disrespect

Interest: attention, appeal, concern, curiosity, fascination, notice, spice, zest, absorb, engage, engross

> Visit one of the quotation sites (for example, http://www.cc.columbia.edu/acis/bartleby/bartlett/ or http://www.starlingtech.com/quotes/quotations). Locate a suitable quotation that might be used to highlight some aspect of emotional communication.

Emotional Expression and Culture

The chapter opening vignette provided an excellent example of the influence of culture on emotional expression and illustrates the role of **cultural display rules.** These are cultural teachings that advise members which emotions are permissible to express as well as the circumstances or contexts in which emotional expression is considered appropriate. For example, what is and what is not considered appropriate emotional expression in a romantic relationship will depend on the stage your relationship is at. You're more likely to inhibit any expression of your negative emotions in early stages of a relationship rather than after you've achieved some level of involvement or intimacy (Aune, Buller, & Aune, 1996). In one study, for example, Japanese and American students watched a particularly unpleasant film of an operation (Ekman, 1985a). The students were videotaped in both an interview situation about the film and alone while watching the film. When alone, both American and Japanese students showed very similar reactions. But in the interview, the American students displayed facial expressions indicating displeasure, whereas the Japanese students did not show any great emotion.

Similarly, cultural differences exist in decoding the meaning of a facial expression. For example, American and Japanese students judged the meaning of a smiling and a neutral facial expression. The Americans rated the smiling face as more attractive, more intelligent, and displaying greater sociability than the neutral face. The Japanese, however, rated the smiling face as more sociable but not as more attractive. The Japanese, in fact, rated the neutral face as the more intelligent (Matsumoto & Kudoh, 1993).

Similarly, Japanese women are not supposed to reveal broad smiles and so will hide their smile, sometimes with their hands (Ma, 1996). Recall from Table 7.1 that even the emoticon for a smiling woman in Japan is a closed mouth (^.^). Women in the United States, on the other hand, have no such restrictions and so are more likely to smile openly.

Americans are more apt, for example, to express negative emotions to their friends and positive emotions to relative strangers. In contrast, Poles and

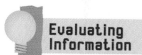

Evaluating Information

Consider recency. Recency is one criterion often used for evaluating research findings and information generally. For example, conclusions about power in the heterosexual relationship based on a study done 20 years ago would have to be examined in light of the tremendous changes that have taken place in our attitudes toward men and women and in sexual equality generally. Similarly, our research methods have improved greatly over the years; today's research is much more rigorous and generally more reliable than it was 20 years ago. But, this doesn't mean that the time the research was conducted is sufficient reason to consider one worthless and one worthwhile. There were a lot of worthwhile research studies done 20 years ago (and much earlier, of course) and a lot of worthless studies done yesterday. This is to say, however, that other things being equal (though of course other things are never really equal), findings from the more recent study will generally prove the more useful.

Hungarians are more likely to express negative emotions to strangers and positive emotions to friends (Matsumoto & Hearn, 1991).

And of course within American culture there are differences in display rules. For example, in one study Americans classified themselves into one of four categories: Caucasian, African American, Asian, and Hispanic/Latino. Here are a few findings just to make the point that different cultures teach different rules for the display of emotions (Matsumoto, 1994):

- Caucasians rated the expression of contempt as more appropriate than did Asians.
- African Americans and Hispanics felt disgust was less appropriate than did Caucasians.
- Hispanics rated public displays of emotion as less appropriate than did Caucasians.
- Caucasians rated the expression of fear as more appropriate than Hispanics.

Emotional Expression and Gender

Researchers agree that men and women experience emotions similarly (Oatley & Duncan, 1994; Cherulnik, 1979; Wade & Tavris, 1998). The differences that are observed are differences in emotional expression. Men and women seem to have different **gender display rules,** much as different cultures have different cultural display rules.

Women talk more about feelings and emotions and use communication for emotional expression more than men (Barbato & Perse, 1992). Even elementary and high schoolers show this gender difference. For example, a study of physical and sexual abuse among children in grades 5 to 12 found that girls were much more likely to turn to a friend in the face of abuse to talk about their feelings. Boy were more apt to spend time with a computer or exercising. Twenty-nine percent of the girls had not talked to anyone about the abuse in contrast to over 50 percent of the boys. Among those abused children who also

Some societies permit and even expect men to show strong emotions. They expect men to cry, to show fear, to express anger openly. Other societies—and many groups within general American culture—criticize men for experiencing and expressing such emotions. What did your culture teach you about gender and the expression of emotions, particularly strongly felt emotions and emotions that show weakness (for example, fear, discomfort, uncertainty)?

In 1972, Senator Edmund Muskie lost the Democratic presidential nomination—in the view of some political analysts—because he cried in public. Has the situation changed significantly? Would you vote for a candidate who cried in public? Would it matter if the candidate was a man or a woman?

What did you learn from your culture about the ways men and women should express emotions? How were these rules taught?

experienced depression, 40 percent of the boys said they had no one to talk to; less than 20 percent of the girls said they had no one to talk to (Lewin, 1998).

Women are also more likely to express socially acceptable emotions than are men (Brody, 1985). For example, women smile significantly more than men. In fact, women smile even when smiling is not appropriate—for example, when reprimanding a subordinate. Men, on the other hand, are more likely than women to express anger and aggression (Fischer, 1993; DePaulo, 1992; Wade & Tavris, 1998). Similarly, women are more effective at communicating happiness and men are more effective at communicating anger (Coats & Feldman, 1996).

Some research has also looked at reactions to emotional expression of men and women. In one case, participants watching a video of a courtroom trial rated women most guilty when they displayed extremely high or extremely little emotion. Women were rated least guilty when they expressed moderate levels of emotion. Men, on the other hand, were rated similarly regardless of the level of emotions they displayed (Salekin, Ogloff, McGarland, & Rogers, 1995).

Women also seem to respond well to men who express emotions (Werrbach, Grotevant, & Cooper, 1990). While watching a movie, a confederate of the experimenter displays a variety of emotions; participants were then asked what they thought of this person. Results showed that men were liked best when they cried and women were liked best when they did not cry (Labott, Martin, Eason, & Berkey, 1991).

Principles of Emotional Communication

Identifying several major principles of emotional communication should further explain how emotions work in communication.

Emotions Are Always Important

Although emotions are especially salient in conflict situations and in relationship development and dissolution, they are actually a part of all messages. Emotions are always present; sometimes to a very strong extent and sometimes only mildly. And they must be recognized as a part of the communication experience. This is not to say that emotions should always be talked about or that all emotions you feel should be expressed. In some instances, as we reiterate below, you might want to avoid revealing your emotions; for example, you might not want to reveal your frustration over a customer's indecision or your doubts about finding a job to your children.

Emotional Expression and Emotional Feeling Are Not the Same

Recall from our earlier discussion of facial management techniques that emotions are frequently disguised (Chapter 6). Remember that you can intensify, deintensify, neutralize, and mask your emotions so that others will think you're feeling something different from what you really are feeling. From this simple principle two useful corollaries can be derived:

- You cannot tell what other people are feeling simply from observing them. So, don't assume you can. It's far better to ask the person to clarify what he or she is feeling.
- Others cannot always tell what you're feeling from the way you act. So, if you want others to know how you feel, it's probably a good idea to tell them.

CAUTION

Can you think of a specific instance where **failing to appreciate the cultural and gender differences in emotional expression** lead you to miss another's meaning?

By starving emotions we become humorless, rigid and stereotyped; by repressing them we become literal, reformatory and holier-than-thou; encouraged, they perform life; discouraged, they poison it.
—Joseph Collins

CAUTION

How might **confusing emotional expression with feelings** lead you to make inferential leaps from, say, a person's facial expression to his or her feelings of depression? Can you recall an instance where someone confused your emotional expression with your feelings?

Emotions Are Communicated Both Verbally and Nonverbally

As with most meanings, emotions are encoded both verbally and nonverbally. Your words, the emphasis you give them, the gestures and facial expressions that accompany them all help to communicate your feelings. And conversely, emotions are decoded on the basis of both verbal and nonverbal cues. And of course emotions, like all messages, are most effectively communicated when verbal and nonverbal messages reinforce and complement each other.

Emotional Expression Can Be Both Good and Bad

Expressing emotions can be cathartic to oneself and can benefit the relationship. Expressing emotions can help you air dissatisfactions and perhaps reduce or even eliminate them. Through emotional expression you can come to understand each other better which may lead to a closer and more meaningful relationship.

On the other hand, expressing emotions may cause relationship difficulties. Expressing your anger with a worker's customary way of answering the phone, for example, may generate hostility; expressing jealousy when your partner spends time with friends may lead to a fear of being controlled and of losing autonomy.

Emotions Are Contagious

If you've ever watched an infant and mother interacting, you can readily see how quickly the infant mimics the emotional expressions of the mother. If the mother smiles, the infant smiles; if the mother frowns, the infant frowns. As the child gets older he or she begins to pick up more subtle expressions of emotions. A parent's anxiety or fear or anger, for example, is quickly identified and often mimicked by the child. In a study of college roommates, the depression of one roommate spread to the other over a period of just three weeks (Joiner, 1994). In short, emotions are contagious and are easily passed from one person to another. In conversation and in small groups, the strong emotions of one person can easily prove contagious to others present, which can be productive when the emotions are productive or unproductive when the emotions are unproductive.

OBSTACLES IN COMMUNICATING EMOTIONS

The expression of feelings is a part of most meaningful relationships. Yet, it's often very difficult. For that reason we need to consider the obstacles to effective emotional expression and to suggest some guidelines. Three major obstacles stand in the way of effective emotional communication: (1) society's rules and customs, (2) fear, and (3) inadequate interpersonal skills.

Societal Rules and Customs

If you grew up in the United States, you probably learned that many people frown on emotional expression. This is especially true for men and has been aptly called "the cowboy syndrome," a pattern of behavior seen in the old cowboy movies from which it gets its name (Balswick & Peck, 1971). The cowboy syndrome describes the closed and unexpressive male. This man is strong but silent. He never feels any of the softer emotions (for example, compassion, love, and contentment). He would never ever cry, experience fear, or

---

One of the greatest gifts you can give the people you love is to hear their anger and frustration without judging or contradicting them.
—Harold H. Bloomfield

Evaluating Information

Distinguish emotional from logical reasons. Part of thinking critically about messages involves identifying and analyzing emotional appeals and realizing that these do not constitute "logical proof." One popular emotional appeal is to pity. Advertisers use this appeal in commercials for children's orphanages; you're shown the hungry children and you feel pity. The objective, of course, is to get you to feel so much pity that you'll send in a contribution. People who beg for money often emphasize their difficulties in an effort to evoke pity and donations.

Another appeal is to guilt. If people do something for you, they may make you feel guilty unless you do something for them. Or they may present themselves in desperate need of money and make you feel guilty for having what you have and not sharing it.

Although you may wish to respond to these emotional expressions (that's up to you), try to separate emotional from logical reasons.

SKILL BUILDING EXERCISE 7.1.
Communicating Your Emotions

Communicating emotions is one of the most difficult of all communication tasks. Here are some situations to practice on. Visualize yourself in each of the following situations and respond as you think an effective communicator would respond.

1. A colleague at work has revealed some of the things you did while you were in college—many of which you would rather not have others on the job know about. You told your colleague these things in confidence and now just about everyone on the job knows. You're angry and decide to confront your colleague.

2. A close friend comes to your apartment in a deep depression, and tells you that her husband (his wife) of 22 years has fallen in love with another person and wants a divorce. Your friend is at a total loss as to what to do and comes to you for comfort and guidance.

3. A neighbor who has lived next door to you for the last 10 years and who has had many difficult financial times has just won the lottery worth several million dollars. You meet in the hallway of your apartment house.

4. Your grandmother is dying and calls you to spend some time with her. She says she knows she is dying and wants you to know how much she has always loved you and that her only regret in dying is not being able to see you anymore.

Thinking Critically About Communicating Your Emotions. If you have the opportunity, compare your responses with those of others. Can you derive two or three general principles for effectively communicating emotions from this experience?

---

feel sorry for himself. And he would never ask—as does our hero in the accompanying cartoon—for "a bigger emotional share." Unfortunately, many men grow up trying to live up to this unrealistic image. It's a syndrome that prevents open and honest expression. Researcher Ronald Levant (*Time*, January 20, 1992, p. 44) has argued that men's inability to deal with emotions as effectively as women is a "trained incompetence." Such training begins early in life when boys are taught to not cry and to ignore pain. This is not to suggest that men should, therefore, communicate their emotions more openly. Unfortunately, there are many who will negatively evaluate men who express emotions openly and often; such men may be judged ineffective, insecure, or unmanly.

Nor are women exempt from the difficulties of emotional expression. At one time, our society permitted and encouraged women to express emotions openly. The tide now is turning, especially for women in executive and managerial positions. Today, the executive woman is being forced into this same cowboy syndrome. She is not allowed to cry or to show any of the once acceptable "soft" emotions. She is especially denied these feelings while she is on the job.

For both men and women, the best advice (as with self-disclosure or any of the characteristics of effectiveness discussed earlier) is to selectively express your emotions. Carefully weigh the arguments for and against expressing your emotions. Consider the situation, the people you're with, the emotions themselves, and all the elements that make up the communication act. And, most important, consider your options for communicating—not only what you'll say but also how you'll say it.

CAUTION

How might **maintaining unexamined assumptions imposed by social rules and customs** prevent you from seeing other perspectives and trying out other behaviors?

LISTENING.

Listening to the Emotions of Others

Communicating your feelings is only half the process; the other half is listening (and recall that responding is one of the steps in interpersonal listening) to the feelings of others. You may feel awkward listening to the feelings of others. Sometimes you may feel like you're eavesdropping and overhearing matters that are really too personal. At other times you may feel awkward because you don't quite know what to say. Or, you may fear saying the wrong thing. Here are a few guidelines for making an often difficult process a little easier.

- Don't equate (as many men apparently do) "responding to another's feelings" with "solving the person's problems" (Tannen, 1990). It's usually more productive to view your task in more limited terms: to encourage the person to express and perhaps to clarify his or her feelings and to provide a supportive atmosphere.
- Empathize with the person. See the situation from the point of view of the speaker. Try to put yourself into the position of the other person. Be especially careful to avoid evaluating the other person's feel-

ings. To say, for example, "don't cry; (s)he wasn't worth it" or "you'll get promoted next year," can easily be interpreted to mean "your feelings are wrong or inappropriate" and this does nothing to help the person feel better or to clarify his or her own feelings.

- Focus on the other person. Avoid responding with your own problems. It's very easy, in hearing a friend talk of a broken love affair, to interject with your own similar past situations. And although this is often a useful technique for showing your understanding, it creates problems if it refocuses the conversation on you and away from the person who needs to talk.
- Show your interest in the other person and in this person's feelings by encouraging the person to explore his or her feelings. You might, for example, use simple encouragers like "I see" or "I understand." Or, ask questions that let the speaker know that you're listening and that you're interested in hearing more.

[The next Listening box appears on page 215.]

Fear

A variety of fears stand in the way of emotional expression. Emotional expression exposes a part of you that makes you vulnerable to attack. For example, if you express your love for another person, you risk being rejected. That is, by exposing a "weakness," you can now be easily hurt by the

"Rebecca, I'm looking for a bigger emotional share here."

uncaring and the insensitive. Of course, you might also fear hurting someone else by, say, voicing your feelings about past loves. Or, you may be angry and want to say something but fear risking the consequences of hurting the person and then feeling guilty yourself.

In addition, you might not reveal your emotions for fear of causing a conflict. Expressing how much you dislike Pat's friends, for example, may just create difficulties for the two of you and you may not be willing to risk the argument and its aftermath.

Because of these fears, you may deny to others and perhaps to yourself that you even have emotions. At least that's the way many people were taught to deal with them.

CAUTION

In what ways can **maintaining unrealistic and unexamined fears about emotional expression** needlessly narrow your options for communicating? Do you have fears that you've never really examined? How realistic are these fears?

Inadequate Interpersonal Skills

Perhaps the most important obstacle to effectively communicating emotions is the lack of interpersonal skills. Many people simply don't know how to express their feelings. Some people, for example, can only express anger through violence or avoidance. Others can deal with anger only by blaming and accusing others. Many cannot express love. They literally cannot say "I love you."

Expressing negative feelings is doubly difficult. Many suppress or fail to communicate negative feelings for fear of offending the other person or making matters worse. But, failing to express negative feelings will probably not help the relationship, especially if this is done frequently and over a long time. Learning to express negative feelings positively and constructively seems the better alternative and is addressed in "Skill Building Exercise 7.2. Expressing Negative Feelings."

SKILL BUILDING EXERCISE 7.2.

Expressing Negative Feelings

Here are three situations that would normally engender negative feelings. For each, indicate how you would express your negative feelings and also preserve and even improve the relationship you have with this other person.

1. You've called your friend, Jane, the last four times but she never seems to call you. You feel hurt and annoyed that Jane doesn't take the initiative and call you. You decide you have to tell her how you feel.

2. You and Ted have made an appointment to go to breakfast at 9 o'clock but Ted shows up at 10:30 with only a general and seemingly flimsy excuse. You've been waiting since 9 and are angry that he doesn't seem to care about the time you wasted. Since you don't want this to happen again, you decide to tell him how you feel.

3. You've been dating Chris for about six weeks. Everything seemed to be going fine until your birthday when Chris simply sent you a card. You expected something more. After all, you've been dating each other exclusively for six weeks. You feel that this shows that Chris doesn't really place much importance on the relationship and you want to get this feeling into the open.

Thinking Critically About Expressing Negative Feelings. Why is it more difficult for most people to express negative rather than positive feelings? Does your culture influence your willingness to express negative feelings? Are men and women expected to communicate negative feelings in different ways?

Evaluate your assumptions for expressing emotions. What assumptions do you hold about the values of expressing emotions? Do you think that:

1. emotional expression is healthy (that keeping emotions bottled up may lead to increased stress and a waste of energy)?
2. emotional expression makes you feel better (as, for example, when you get things off your chest)?
3. emotional expression helps you to get others to change or to do as you wish (it's often an effective way to gain compliance)?
4. emotional expression helps others to understand you better and may help to build more meaningful relationships?

GUIDELINES FOR COMMUNICATING EMOTIONS

Communicating your emotions and responding appropriately to the emotional expressions of others are as important as they are difficult. There are, however, a variety of suggestions that will make these tasks easier and more effective. Expressing emotions effectively begins with understanding your emotions and then deciding if and how you wish to express them.

Understand Your Emotions

Your first task is to understand the emotions you're feeling. For example, consider how you would feel if your best friend just got the promotion that you wanted or if your brother, a police officer, was shot while breaking up a street riot. Think about your emotions as objectively as possible. Think about both the bodily reactions you'd be experiencing as well as the interpretations and evaluations you'd be giving to these reactions. Further, identify the antecedent conditions (in as specific terms as possible) that may be influencing your feelings. Try to answer the question, "Why am I feeling this way?" or "What happened to lead me to feel as I do?"

Decide If You Wish to Express Your Feelings

Your second task is to decide if, in fact, you want to express your emotions. It will not always be possible to stop to think about whether you wish to express your emotions—at times you may respond almost automatically. More often than not, however, you will have the time and the chance to ask yourself whether you wish to express your emotions. When you do have this chance, remember that it isn't always necessary or wise to express every feeling you have. Remember, too, the irreversibility of communication discussed in Chapter 1; once you communicate something, you cannot take it back. Therefore, consider carefully the arguments for and against expressing your emotions for each decision you have to make.

This article applies many ideas discussed in this chapter to the business world and offers sound practical advice for dealing with emotions in a business context.

Keeping Your Cool at Work

We all know it's healthier to express our feelings than to keep them bottled up inside. But is a temper tantrum at the office good for your career? Probably not. So where do you find the happy medium between voicing your feelings and safeguarding your job?

Certainly, there's a fine line to be drawn. If you don't verbally air your feelings—or resolve them in some way—you're bound to act them out. That can mean sloppy work, irritability, sarcasm, or procrastination. Your body suffers, too: you may develop tension headaches, neck and back pain, fatigue, even ulcers.

"The truth is you *can* express emotions at work," says Venda Raye-Johnson, a Kansas City, Missouri, career counselor and coauthor of *Staying Up When Your Job Pulls You Down*, "as long as you do it in an acceptable way. But first you've got to get those emotions under control."

1. TAKE A TIME-OUT

Your boss unfairly criticizes a project you've slaved over—in front of others, no less. Your first reaction is to fight back: yell at her during the meeting and defend your work.

Don't do it! Instead, step back and buy yourself some time—from five minutes to five days, says Duffy Spencer, Ph.D., a management consultant in Long Island, New York, "Take as long as you need to analyze your feelings and switch from a reactive, blinded-by-emotion mind-set to a rational, thinking mode." What if you're being asked to respond? "You can say, 'I'm not sure about that; let me get back to you,'" Spencer notes.

2. ANALYZE YOUR FEELINGS

Once away from the situation, try doing a perception check, says Raye-Johnson. Stand back and ask yourself: What am I really upset about? Is there something about this situation that is "pushing my buttons"?

Sometimes we react strongly, not to the situation at hand but because it revives many old and painful feelings from our childhood. If that is the case, just realizing the parallel can help to calm you down.

Another way to gain some perspective is to ask yourself, Can I see why the other person behaved the way she did? Viewing a situation from another person's perspective allows you to understand that her or his intent may not have been vindictive.

3. EXPRESS YOURSELF

Even though you may now understand why you're feeling the way you do, you still need a positive outlet for your emotions. Tom Miller, Ph.D., a psychologist who lectures nationwide on self-discipline and emotional control, suggests, "Let out your feelings on paper. Unedited. Uncensored. Then review what you've written and destroy the evidence. Whatever you do, don't let your emotions churn around in your head. You need the cathartic release to get back in control and to see if you're overreacting."

Sometimes just being heard and having your emotions validated can restore your sense of balance. Try talking with friends, family, and *trusted* co-workers. Besides being a sounding board, they can also offer an objective assessment of the situation and your reaction to it.

If you *are* overreacting, it may stem from flagging self-esteem. "We're typically much harder on ourselves than we are on others and more likely to call ourselves 'zeros' in the face of a problem," says Miller. If you've been chewed out by your boss or passed over for a promotion, try boosting your self-worth with the "best friend test." "Put your best friend in your situation, and ask yourself if you would think she was a zero. Not likely," contends Miller. This test can help you see the error of your interpretations—and help you keep the calamity of the situation in perspective.

Deciding the Best Course of Action

Once you understand what's at the root of your feelings, the next step is to decide what you want to do about them. Surprisingly, one option is to do nothing.

The decision to confront a co-worker should be based on these two key issues:

- What you hope to gain by speaking out (respect, responsibility, and recognition are key goals).
- How likely you are to achieve your goals with the individual involved. If an idea of yours is stolen by an egotistic and credit-needy boss, even if you do speak out it's not likely you'll get far. And it may hurt you in the long run if you antagonize her.

When there is a concrete benefit to speaking up—you'll receive credit for your idea or will correct a damaging work situation—it's probably worth it to confront a colleague. However, plan your discussion carefully. Experts say the following techniques work best:

Be Assertive About Your Beliefs and Responsive to the Other Person's Perspective

"You want to get your needs across without alienating your co-worker," stresses Spencer. The best way to do this, explains Raye-Johnson, is to empathize with that person. "Let her know you understand her viewpoint. But also tell her how you see the situation, and make a statement about how you'd like to proceed."

Start Slow and Small

Even when your emotions are under control it's still possible to be overly confrontational, loud, or forceful. That's likely to make a co-worker feel as if she's being attacked—and it's likely to turn her off. "The goal of speaking out is to create a willingness in the other person to do what you want," says Miller. So start by calmly explaining your position and feelings. Then, as the conversation progresses and you get a sense of the other person's reactions, you can choose to strengthen your stance and push harder.

Stick to the Issue at Hand

Don't make the mistake of trying to bring up every sore issue from the past in one conversation. If you're telling your boss that you're disappointed you didn't get a recent plum assignment, don't throw in that you're also peeved about not being invited to certain meetings. Stick to one issue. And once you've made your point, stop, and wait for a response. Then go for an agreement or negotiation, advises Spencer.

Use the D.E.S.C. Script

Describe the situation; **E**xpress your feelings; **S**pecify what you want; and talk about the **C**onsequences. If you're upset because you're not receiving memos, tell your boss that you're feeling out of the loop and that if you were privy to memos you would be able to do a better job. Don't point the finger or talk about others. You'll get much further by using "I" statements and by emphasizing how co-workers can help you improve your performance, says Spencer.

Keeping Cool Under Pressure

It's an undeniable fact that we bring emotions to work. The key to managing these feelings is to know what drives them and *how* to express them. "You want people to know that you're concerned, annoyed, or upset," Miller explains, "but you don't want them to think you've handled the situation badly."

Politically, it's often probably best *not* to speak up—and certainly you should never confront someone when you're on "react." But keeping silent isn't the same as suppressing feelings, experts say. If it's not in your best interest to let emotions out at work, be sure to vent them at home, with friends, or on paper. At least one person will notice the effort—you—and your mind and body will thank you for it.

Thinking Critically About "Keeping Your Cool at Work." Do you believe it is "healthier to express our feelings than to keep them bottled up inside?" Can you imagine situations where this would not be true? With which of the three steps identified by Monson do you have the most difficulty? This article appeared in *New Woman* magazine. How would this article differ (if at all) if it appeared in *New Man* magazine? Can you detect a difference in the way emotions are handled as you go up the organizational hierarchy? Do people at the top of the hierarchy deal with their emotions in the same way as people at the bottom?

Source: "Keeping Your Cool At Work" by Nancy Monson as appeared in *New Woman*, October 1993, pp. 70, 72. Copyright © 1993 by Nancy Monson. Reprinted by permission of the author.

Assess Your Communication Options (Effectiveness and Ethics)

If you decide to express your emotions, your third task is to evaluate your communication options. Evaluate your options in terms of both effectiveness (what will work best and help you achieve your goal) and ethics (what is right or morally justified).

When thinking in terms of effectiveness, consider, for example, the time and setting, the persons you want to reveal these feelings to, and the available methods of communication. For example, should you arrange a special meeting with your supervisor to discuss your being passed up for promotion? Or, do you simply let your anger out immediately after you hear about it? What are the benefits or disadvantages of communicating your feelings of inadequacy to your spouse, your parents, your children, or your best friend? Is it better to ask for a date, confess your love, or ask for a divorce on the telephone, by letter, or face-to-face?

When thinking in terms of ethics, consider the legitimacy of appeals based on emotions. As a parent, for example, is it ethical to use appeals to fear to dissuade your teenage children from engaging in sexual relationships? From smoking? From taking drugs? From associating with people of another race or affectional orientation? Is your motive relevant in deciding whether such appeals are ethical or unethical? Is it ethical to use emotional appeals (say to guilt or to fear or to sympathy) to get a friend to loan you money? To take a vacation with you? To have sex with you?

Describe Your Feelings

General and abstract statements of emotional expression are usually ineffective. Consider, for example, the frequently-heard "I feel bad." Does it mean "I feel guilty" (because I lied to my best friend)? Does it mean "I feel lonely" (because I haven't had a date in the last two months)? Does it mean "I feel depressed" (because I failed that last exam)? Clearly, specificity helps. Describe also the intensity with which you feel the emotion. *I feel so angry I think I could have quit that job. I feel so hurt I want to cry.* Although you experience many emotions and feelings, you probably use few terms to describe them. Learn to describe these emotions and feelings in specific and concrete terms.

Identify the Reasons for Your Feelings

We can use the above examples to illustrate this principle. "I'm feeling guilty because I lied to my best friend." "I feel lonely; I haven't had a date for the last two months." "I'm really depressed from failing that last exam." If your feelings were influenced by something the person you're talking to did or said, describe this also. For example, *I felt so angry when you said you wouldn't help me. I felt hurt when you didn't invite me to the party.*

Identifying the reasons for your emotions will enable you to accomplish two important goals. First, it will help you to understand *how* you feel and *why* you feel as you do. Second, it will help you tell what you must do to reduce or get rid of these negative feelings. In the examples used, these

Emotion turning back on itself, and not leading on to thought or action, is the element of madness.

—*John Sterling*

might include avoiding lying, being more assertive about dating, and studying harder.

Anchor Your Feelings to the Present

Be especially careful not to fall into the trap of believing the negative statements you may say about yourself. Statements such as "I'm a failure" or "I'm foolish" or "I'm stupid" are especially destructive. These statements imply that failure, foolishness, and stupidity are *in* you and will *always* be in you. Instead, include references to the here-and-now. Coupled with specific description and the identification of the reasons for your feeling, such statements might look like this:

> "I feel like a failure right now; I've erased this computer file three times today."
>
> "I felt foolish when I couldn't think of that formula."
>
> "I feel stupid when you point out my grammatical errors."

Own Your Own Feelings

Perhaps the most important guideline for effective emotional communication is: own your feelings, take personal responsibility for your feelings (Proctor, 1991). Consider the following statements:

> "You make me angry."
>
> "You make me feel like a loser."
>
> "You make me feel stupid."
>
> "You make me feel like I don't belong here."

Note that in these statements the speaker is blaming the other person for the way he or she is feeling. Of course, you know—on more sober reflection—that

Evaluating Information

Evaluate your assumptions against expressing emotions. What assumptions do you hold about the dangers or problems of expressing emotions? Do you think that:

- emotional expression may create a snowball effect (expressing anger, for example, may make you more angry)?
- emotional expression may offend others and may damage your interpersonal relationships?
- emotional expression may expose your vulnerabilities, which others may take advantage of?
- emotional expression of doubt, confusion, or inferiority may lead others to evaluate you negatively?

Most examples of statements that show failure to own one's own feelings express negative judgments. But, you can also fail to own your own feelings when expressing positive evaluation as well, as in "The class seemed to enjoy the presentation" (instead of "I gave a really good speech") or "Everyone seems to think I know what I'm doing" (instead of "I finally mastered this business"). Do you own both positive and negative statements equally?

What would you say to Vinny or Doris? Vinny's dog—and lifelong companion—was run over by a bus. Vinny truly thought of the dog as a best friend. You see Vinny alone leaning against a car in the street. Doris's fiancé was in a car accident and will have to lose both his legs. You see her walking to the hospital.

no one can make anyone feel anything. Others may do things or say things to us, but it is we who interpret them. It is we who develop feelings as a result of the interaction between what these people say, for example, and our own interpretations. When we own our feelings, we take responsibility for them. We acknowledge that our feelings are *our* feelings. The best way to own our statements is to use *I-messages,* rather than the you-messages that were used above. With this acknowledgment of responsibility, the above statements would look like these:

"I get angry when you come home late without calling."
"I begin to think of myself as a loser when you criticize me in front of my friends."
"I feel so stupid when you use medical terms that I don't understand."
"When you ignore me in public, I feel like I don't belong here."

Note that these rephrased statements do not attack the other person and demand that he or she change certain behaviors. They merely identify

SKILL BUILDING EXERCISE 7.3.
Communicating Emotions Effectively

The 10 statements below are all ineffective expressions of feelings. For each statement (1) identify why the statement is ineffective (for example, what problem or distortion does the statement create) and (2) rephrase each of these into more effective statements in which you

• describe your feelings and their intensity as accurately as possible
• identify the reasons for your feelings and what influenced or stimulated you to feel as you do
• anchor your feelings to the present
• use I-messages to own your own feelings, to claim responsibility for these feelings, and to
• describe what (if anything) you want the other person to do because of your feelings

1. Your lack of consideration makes me so angry I can't stand it anymore.
2. You hurt me when you ignore me. Don't ever do that again.
3. I'll never forgive that louse. The hatred and resentment will never leave me.
4. I hate you. I'll always hate you. I never want to see you again. Never.

5. Look. I really can't bear to hear about your problems of deciding who to date tomorrow and who to date the next day and the next. Give me a break. It's boring. Boring.
6. You did that just to upset me. You enjoy seeing me get upset, don't you?
7. Don't talk to me in that tone of voice. Don't you dare insult me with that attitude of yours.
8. You make me look like an idiot just so you can act the role of the know-it-all. You always have to be superior, always the damn teacher.
9. I just can't think straight. That assignment frightens me to death. I know I'll fail.
10. When I left the interview, I let the door slam behind me. I made a fool of myself, a real fool. I'll never get that job. Why can't I ever do anything right? Why must I always make a fool of myself?

Thinking Critically About Communicating Emotions Effectively. Which of the five steps listed above, for rephrasing the statements, do you see violated most often in the expression of feelings? With which step do you have the most difficulty? In one sentence, how would you describe the difference between the ineffective and effective communication of feelings?

HOW TO . . .
Communicate with the Grief Stricken

Consider the wrong way:

I just heard that Harry died—I mean—passed away. I'm so sorry. I know exactly how you feel. But, you know, it's for the best. I mean the man was suffering. I remember seeing him last month; he could hardly stand up, he was so weak. And he looked so sad. He must have been in constant pain. It's better this way. He's at peace. You'll get over it. You'll see. Time heals all wounds. It was the same way with me and you know how close we were. I mean we were devoted to each other. Everyone said we were the closest pair they ever saw. And I got over it. So, how about we'll go to dinner tonight? We'll talk about old times. Come on, come on. Don't be a spoil sport. I really need to get out. I've been in the house all week. Come on, do it for me. After all, you have to forget; you have to get on with your own life. I won't take no for an answer. I'll pick you up at seven.

Obviously, this is not the way to talk to the grief-stricken (Miller, 1987; Zunin & Zunin, 1991). In fact, it was written to illustrate several popular mistakes. After you read the suggestions for communicating with the grief-stricken, you may wish to return to this "expression of sympathy" and analyze it again.

Grief is something everyone experiences at some time. Grief may be experienced because of illness or death, the loss of a highly valued relationship (for example, a romantic breakup or a divorce), the loss of certain physical or mental abilities, or the loss of material possessions (your house burning down or stock losses). Here are a few suggestions for easing this very difficult form of communication.

1. Confirm the other person and the person's feelings. For example, saying "You must miss him a great deal" confirms the person's feelings. This type of expressive support has been shown to lessen feelings of grief (Reed, 1993). Avoid disconfirming expressions: "You can't cry now; you have to set an example."

2. Give the grieving person permission to grieve. Let the person know that it's acceptable and okay with you if he or she grieves in the ways that feel most comfortable—for example, crying or talking about old times. This will be especially difficult with grieving men who have been raised to inhibit such emotional expression (Lister, 1991). Similarly, keep in mind that older people are often more reluctant to express their emotions than younger people are (McConatha & Lightner, 1994).

3. Avoid trying to force the grief-stricken to focus on the bright side; he or she may not be ready for this. Avoid expressions such as "You're so lucky you still have some vision left" or "It was better this way; Pat was suffering so much."

4. Encourage the grieving person to express feelings and talk about the loss. Most people who experience grief welcome the opportunity to talk about it. On the other hand, don't try to force the person to talk about experiences or feelings he or she may not be ready to share. Be especially sensitive to leave-taking cues. Don't try to force your presence on the grief-stricken or press the person to stay with you. When in doubt, ask.

5. Empathize with the grief-stricken person and communicate this empathic understanding. Let the grief-stricken know that you can feel (to even a small extent) what he or she is going through. Don't assume that your feelings (however empathic you are) are the same in depth or in kind.

[The next How To box appears on page 204.]

and describe your feelings about those behaviors. The rephrased statements do not encourage defensiveness. With I-message statements, it's easier for the other person to acknowledge these behaviors and to offer to change them.

Also use I-messages to describe what, if anything, you want the listener to do: *I'm feeling sorry for myself right now; just give me some space. I'll give you a call in a few days.* Or, more directly: *I'd prefer to be alone right now.*

Visit one of the Internet sites devoted to grief; lurk a while. What kinds of information do these sites provide? *(An interesting paper could review a Website on grief.)* Here are two general ones: http://www.yahoo.com/Society_and_Culture/death and http://www.katsden.com/death/index.html.

As noted in the text, men have an especially hard time expressing grief. Why do you think this is so?

SUMMARY OF CONCEPTS AND SKILLS

In this chapter we explored the nature and role of emotions in interpersonal communication. We examined the role of the body, mind, and culture in defining emotions and looked at some basic or primary emotions. More important, we looked at the obstacles to meaningful emotional communication and some guidelines that might help us communicate our feelings more effectively and also respond to the feelings of others.

1. Emotions consist of a physical part (our physiological reactions), a cognitive part (our interpretations of our feelings), and a cultural part (our cultural traditions influence our emotional evaluations and expressions).

2. Our primary emotions, according to Robert Plutchik, are: joy, acceptance, fear, surprise, sadness, disgust, anger, and anticipation.

3. Different views were presented to explain how emotions are aroused. One reasonable sequence is this: an event occurs, we respond physiologically, we interpret this arousal, we experience the emotion.

4. Emotional expression is largely a matter of choice, though it is heavily influenced by your culture and gender.

5. Useful principles of emotional communication include: Emotions are always important, emotional expression and emotional feeling are not the same thing, emotions are communicated both verbally and nonverbally, emotional expression can be both good and bad, and emotions are contagious.

6. Among the obstacles to effective communication of feelings are these: societal rules and customs, fear of making oneself vulnerable, denial, and inadequate communication skills.

7. The following guidelines should help make your emotional expression more meaningful. Understand your feelings, decide if you wish to express your feelings (not all feelings need be or should be expressed), assess your communication options, describe your feelings as accurately as possible, identify the reasons for your feelings, anchor your feelings and their expression to the present time, and own your own feelings.

8. In responding to the emotions of others try to see the situation from the perspective of the other person. Avoid refocusing the conversation on yourself. Show interest and provide the speaker with the opportunity to talk and explore his or her feelings. Avoid evaluating the feelings of the other person.

Check your ability to apply these skills. You will gain most from this brief experience if you think carefully about each skill and try to identify instances from your recent communications in which you did or did not act on the basis of the specific skill. Use a rating scale such as the following: 1 = almost always, 2 = often, 3 = sometimes, 4 = rarely, and 5 = almost never.

_____ 1. Identify destructive and constructive beliefs about emotions.
_____ 2. Identify and be able to describe emotions (both positive and negative) more clearly.
_____ 3. Use I-messages in communicating your feelings.
_____ 4. Communicate more effectively with the grief stricken.
_____ 5. Communicate emotions more effectively.
_____ 6. Respond to the emotions of others more appropriately by using, for example, active listening skills.
_____ 7. Evaluate the arguments for and against expressing emotions for each specific situation.

VOCABULARY QUIZ. THE LANGUAGE OF EMOTIONS

Match the terms concerning the communication of emotions with their definitions. Record the number of the definition next to the appropriate term.

__6__ emotion
__5__ James–Lange theory
__9__ cognitive labeling theory
__10__ emotional expression
__1__ cowboy syndrome

__2__ owning feelings
__3__ I-messages
__8__ emotional appeals
__7__ gender display rules
__4__ cultural display rules

1. The male's lack of ability to reveal the emotions he is feeling because of the belief that men should be strong and silent.
2. The process by which we take responsibility for our own feelings instead of attributing them to others.
3. Messages that explicitly claim responsibility for one's own feelings.
4. Rules for expressing and not expressing various emotions that different cultures teach its members.
5. Defines the sequence of events in feeling an emotion as follows: an event occurs, we respond physiologically, and we experience the emotion.
6. The feelings we have, for example, our feelings of guilt, anger, or sorrow.
7. Emotional expressions considered appropriate for one gender rather than another.
8. A nonlogical means of persuasion.
9. Defines the sequence of events in feeling an emotion as follows: an event occurs, we respond physiologically, we interpret this arousal (that is, we decide what emotion we are experiencing), and we experience the emotion.
10. The way one chooses to communicate one's feelings.

Conversation Messages

CHAPTER TOPICS	LEARNING GOALS	SKILLS GOALS
	After completing this chapter, you should be able to	*After completing this chapter, you should be able to*
The Conversation Process	1. Explain the five-step model of conversation	Follow the basic structure for conversation
Conversation Management	2. Explain the processes involved in opening, maintaining, and closing conversations	Initiate, maintain, and close conversations more effectively
Conversation Effectiveness	3. Explain the skills for conversational effectiveness	Use the principles of conversational effectiveness (openness, empathy, positiveness, immediacy, interaction management, expressiveness, and other orientation) with mindfulness, flexibility, cultural sensitivity, and metacommunication

Dear Ann:

Can you stand one more letter about parents who are "boring and repetitious"? I found solutions. May I share them?

Show interest. My father-in-law (74) brings up his World War II service every time we see him. So I ask questions. What part of the South Pacific? What were your duties? Do you still hear from people you served with? I ask him to pull out his maps and show me exactly where he was. It turns into a fascinating story and, of course, he loves it.

Your first Plymouth only cost $800? What color was it? Was it automatic? How many miles did you get on a gallon of gas? Do you have pictures of it? Where were you living then? I mention the car I am driving and laugh about the contrasts and comparison.

When Mom wants to talk about the past, I encourage her to tell us again about how she met Dad. She loves that story. Another favorite topic is the day I was born. Her eyes shine with delight every time she tells us how "babies come when they are ready—doctor or no doctor."

Our parents made room for us in their lives, whether they wanted to or not. So now it's our turn to make room for them.

/signed/ Seeing Myself in 40 Years*

In this letter to Ann Landers "Seeing Myself in 40 Years" shows unusual insight into conversational effectiveness, the topic of this chapter. Interpersonal researcher Margaret McLaughlin (1984) defines conversation as "relatively informal social interaction in which the roles of speaker and hearer are exchanged in a nonautomatic fashion under the collaborative management of all parties."

In this chapter we look at the conversation process—what it is, the principles you follow in conversing, how you manage a conversation (for example, opening, maintaining, and closing), and how you try to prevent and repair conversational problems.

Before reading about the process of conversation, think of your own conversations, the ones that were satisfactory and the ones that were unsatisfactory.

*Source: Courtesy of Ann Landers. Reprinted by permission of Creators Syndicate and Los Angeles Times Syndicate.

"The time has come,"
   the Walrus said,
"To talk of many things:
Of shoes—and ships—and
   sealing wax—
Of cabbages—and kings—
And why the sea is boiling hot—
And whether pigs have wings."
   —*Lewis Carroll*

You may find it helpful to think of a specific recent conversation as you respond to the accompanying self-test. This test will also make a great discussion stimulus if you and your conversational partner each complete the test with the same conversation in mind. Taking this test now will help highlight the characteristics of conversational behavior and what makes some conversations satisfying and others unsatisfying.

SELF-TEST
How Satisfying Is Your Conversation?

Instructions: Respond to each of the following statements by recording the number best representing your feelings, using this scale:

1 = strongly agree
2 = moderately agree
3 = slightly agree
4 = neutral
5 = slightly disagree
6 = moderately disagree
7 = strongly disagree

_____ 1. The other person let me know that I was communicating effectively.

_____ 2. Nothing was accomplished.

_____ 3. I would like to have another conversation like this one.

_____ 4. The other person genuinely wanted to get to know me.

_____ 5. I was very *dis*satisfied with the conversation.

_____ 6. I felt that during the conversation I was able to present myself as I wanted the other person to view me.

_____ 7. I was very satisfied with the conversation.

_____ 8. The other person expressed a lot of interest in what I had to say.

_____ 9. I did NOT enjoy the conversation.

_____ 10. The other person did NOT provide support for what he or she was saying.

_____ 11. I felt I could talk about anything with the other person.

_____ 12. We each got to say what we wanted.

_____ 13. I felt that we could laugh easily together.

_____ 14. The conversation flowed smoothly.

_____ 15. The other person frequently said things that added little to the conversation.

_____ 16. We talked about something I was NOT interested in.

Thinking Critically About Satisfying Conversations

To score your test, follow these steps:

1. Add the scores for items 1, 3, 4, 6, 7, 8, 11, 12, 13, and 14. This is your Step 1 total.

2. Reverse the scores for items 2, 5, 9, 10, 15, and 16. For example, if you responded to Question 2 with a 7, reverse this to 1; reverse 6 to 2; reverse 5 to 3; keep 4 as 4; reverse 3 to 5; reverse 2 to 6; and reverse 1 to 7. Add these reversed scores. This is your Step 2 total.

3. Add the totals from Steps 1 and 2 to get your communication satisfaction score. You may interpret your score along the following scale:

16	32	48	64	80	96	112
Extremely Satisfying	Quite Satisfying	Fairly Satisfying	Average	Fairly Unsatisfying	Quite Unsatisfying	Extremely Unsatisfying

More important than locating your score on this continuum is to identify the qualities that make a conversation satisfying for you. How will these qualities vary depending on the type of conversation, say, a business meeting with your supervisor and an intimate talk with a close friend?

Source: From "The Conceptualization and Measure of Interpersonal Communication Satisfaction" by Michael Hecht, *Human Communication Research* 4, 1978:253–264. Copyright © 1978 by Michael Hecht. Reprinted by permission of Sage Publications, Inc.

THE CONVERSATION PROCESS

Most often, of course, conversation takes place face-to-face. And this is the type of interaction that probably comes to mind when you think of conversation. But, especially today, much conversation takes place online. Online communication is becoming a part of people's experience throughout the world. Such communications are important personally, socially, and professionally. Three major online types of conversation and the ways in which they differ from each other and from face-to-face interaction may be noted here as a preface to the stages of the conversation process: e-mail, the mailing list group, and the Internet relay chat (IRC) group.

In **e-mail,** you usually type your letter in an e-mail program and send it (along with other documents you may wish to attach) from your computer via modem to your server (the computer at your school or at some commercial organization like America Online) which relays your message through a series of computer hook-ups and eventually to the server of the person to whom you're writing. Unlike face-to-face communication, e-mail does not take place in real time. You may send your message today but the receiver may not read it for a week and may take another week to respond. Much of the spontaneity created by real-time communication is lost here. You may, for example, be very enthusiastic about a topic when you send your e-mail but practically forget it by the time someone responds.

E-mail is more like a postcard than a letter and so can be read by others along the route. It is also virtually unerasable. Especially in large organizations, employees' e-mails are stored on hard disk or on backup tapes and may be retrieved for a variety of reasons. Currently, for example, large corporations are being sued because of sexist and racist e-mail that their employees wrote and that plaintiffs' lawyers have retrieved from archives long thought destroyed. Also, your e-mail can be easily forwarded to other people by anyone who has access to your files. And although this practice is considered unethical, it's relatively common. So, the principle that communication is irreversible (Chapter 1) and the disadvantages of self-disclosure (Chapter 2) are especially important with e-mail. Don't e-mail any message that you wouldn't want made public.

The **mailing list group** consists of a group of people interested in a particular topic who communicate with each other through e-mail. Generally, you subscribe to a list and communicate with all other members by addressing your mail to the group e-mail address. Any message you send to this address will be sent to each member who subscribes to the list. Your message is sent to all members at the same time; there are no asides to the person sitting next to you (as in face-to-face groups). The screen noted in the photo on the left on page 196 (top) will provide you with a list of 1500 mailing lists categorized by topic. The screen on the bottom shows one of the mailing lists that turned up in a request to search for mailing lists in "communication."

Internet relay chat (IRC) groups have proliferated across the Internet. These groups enable members to converse in real time in discussion groups called channels. At any one time, there may be perhaps 4000 channels and 20,000 users, so your chances of finding a topic you're interested in is high.

Unlike mailing lists, IRC communication takes place in real time; you see a member's message as it's being sent, there is virtually no delay. Like mailing

> Conversation is the socializing instrument par excellence, and in its style one can see reflected the capacities of a race.
>
> —*José Ortega y Gasset*

Acquiring Information

Use comparison to highlight similarities and differences. Here are several examples of face-to-face and computer communication. How does each form of communication differ from its counterpart?

1. Sending e-mail and snail mail
2. Talking face-to-face in a small group and in a chat room
3. Reading a commercial web site and a print catalogue or brochure
4. Using a search engine such as Yahoo! or Excite and a print reference work such as *Reader's Guide to Periodical Literature* or *Psychological Abstracts* to search for information on a specific topic
5. Reading a BBS and a cork-and-paper bulletin board

Another useful site for mailing lists is http://www.liszt.com, which contains over 60,000 lists. A list of frequently asked questions (FAQs) and mailing list addresses can be found at http://www.cis.ohio-state.edu/hypertext/faq/usenet/mail/mailing-lists/top.html. Of course, you could also go to one of the search engines and search for mailing lists you might find interesting. To locate a mailing list on a specific topic, you might e-mail your request to listserv@listserv.net. Send the message: list topic-of-interest, for example, list interpersonal communication. How many mailing lists can you find that might be appropriate to interpersonal communication?

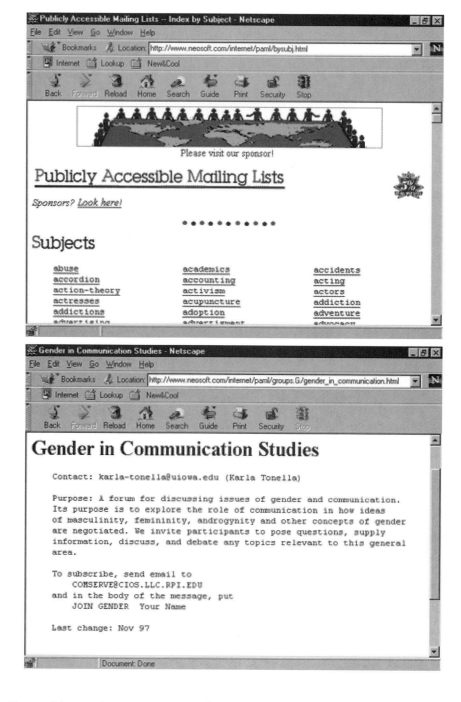

Visit one of the IRCs and lurk for 5 to 10 minutes. What characterizes the conversation on the channel you observed? What is the topic of conversation? What is the most obvious purpose of the group? If possible, try comparing your reactions with others who visited other channels.

lists and face-to-face conversation, the purposes of IRCs vary from communication that simply maintains connection with others (what many would call "idle chatter" or "phatic communion") to extremely significant. For example, IRCs were used to gather information on military activities during the Persian Gulf war and to provide an information database during the California earthquake in 1994 (Estabrook, 1997).

Communication on an IRC resembles the conversation you would observe at a large party. The total number of guests divide up into small groups varying from two on up and each discuss their own topic or version of a general topic. For example, in an IRC about travel, five people may be discussing the difficulties of traveling to communist countries, three people may be discussing airport security systems, and two people may be discussing bargain rates for cruises to Mexico all on this one channel dealing with travel. IRCs also allow you to "whisper," to communicate with just one other person without giving access to your message to other participants. So, although you may be communicating in one primary group (say, dealing with airport security), you also have your eye trained to pick up something particularly interesting in another group (much as you do at a party). IRCs also notify you when someone new comes into the group and when someone leaves. IRCs, like mailing lists, have the great advantage that they enable you to communicate with people you would never meet and interact with otherwise. Because IRCs are international, they provide excellent exposure to other cultures, other ideas, and other ways of communicating.

In face-to-face conversation you're expected to contribute to the ongoing discussion. In IRCs you can simply observe; in fact, you're encouraged to lurk—to observe the participants' interaction before you say anything yourself. In this way, you'll be able to learn the cultural rules and norms of the group.

With this basic understanding that conversation can take place in a wide variety of channels, we can look at the way in which conversation works. Conversation takes place in five steps: opening, feedforward, business, feedback, and closing (Figure 8.1).

Step One. The Opening

The first step is to open the conversation, usually with some verbal or nonverbal greeting: "Hi," "How are you?" "Hello, this is Joe," a smile, or a wave. You can accomplish a great deal in your opening (Krivonos & Knapp, 1975). First, your greeting can tell others that you're accessible, that you're available to them for conversation.

You can also reveal important information about the relationship between yourself and this other person. For example, a big smile and a warm "Hi, it's been a long time" signals that your relationship is still a friendly one, that you aren't angry any longer, or any of a number of other messages.

Your greeting also helps maintain the relationship. You see this function served between workers who pass each other frequently. This greeting-in-passing assures you that even though you do not stop and talk for an extended period that you still have access to each other.

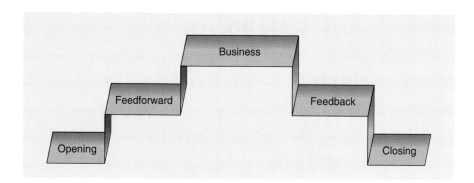

Figure 8.1
The Conversation Process

The process is viewed as occurring in five basic steps: opening, feedforward, business, feedback, and closing. Can you break down the conversation process into steps or stages that are significantly different from those identified here?

In normal conversation, your greeting is returned with a greeting from the other person that is similar in its formality and intensity. When it isn't—when the other person turns away or responds coldly to your friendly "good morning"—you know that something is wrong. Similarly, openings are generally consistent in tone with the main part of the conversation; a cheery "How ya doing today, big guy?" is not normally followed by news of a family death.

Step Two. Feedforward

At the second step, there is usually some kind of feedforward (see Chapter 1). Here you give the other person a general idea of what the conversation will focus on: "I got to tell you about Jack," "Did you hear what happened in class yesterday?" or "We need to talk about our vacation plans." When feedforwards are misused, for example, when they are overly long or insensitive, they can create conversational problems, as in the Hagar the Horrible cartoon.

As with the greeting, you can accomplish a great deal with feedforward, for example: (1) to open the channels of communication, (2) to preview the message, (3) to altercast, and (4) to disclaim. Let's look at each in more detail.

Phatic communion, messages that **open the channels of communication,** is a perfect example of feedforward. It's information that tells us that the normal, expected, and accepted rules of interaction will be in effect. It tells us another person is willing to communicate.

Feedforward messages frequently **preview other messages.** Feedforward may, for example, preview the content ("I'm afraid I have bad news for you"), the importance ("Listen to this before you make a move"), the form or style ("I'll tell you all the gory details"), and the positive or negative quality of subsequent messages ("You're not going to like this, but here's what I heard.").

Feedforward is often used to place the receiver in a specific role and to request that the receiver respond to you in terms of this assumed role. This process, known as **altercasting,** asks the receiver to approach your message from a particular role or even as someone else (Weinstein & Deutschberger, 1963; McLaughlin, 1984). For example, you might ask a friend, "As an advertising executive, what do you think of corrective advertising?" This question

Acquiring Information

Altercast to gain other perspectives. Altercasting is a powerful critical thinking tool. Putting yourself into the frame of mind of someone else can often bring considerable insights. Georges Simenon's detective, Inspector Maigret, used this technique in solving crimes. "I shall know the murderer," noted Maigret, "when I know the victim well." To help you better understand another person, consider using altercasting and casting yourself in the role of the other person. So, if you're a real estate sales representative, place yourself in the role of the home buyer and perhaps even go through the process of looking for a home as would a perspective buyer.

casts your friend into the role of advertising executive (rather than parent, Democrat, or Baptist, for example). It asks your friend to answer from a particular perspective.

When you use feedforward to **disclaim,** you try to ensure that your meaning will be understood and will not reflect negatively on you (Hewitt & Stokes, 1975; McLaughlin, 1984). Let us say, for example, that you fear your listeners will think your comment is inappropriate, or that they may rush to judge you without hearing your full account, or that you're not in full possession of your faculties. In these cases, you may use some form of disclaimer and say, for example, "This may not be the place to say this, but . . ." or "Just hear me out before you hang up." Here are five popular disclaimers, along with their definitions and examples.

- In **hedging** you disclaim the importance of the message to your own identity; you make it clear that listeners may reject the message without rejecting you: *I didn't read the entire report, but . . . .*
- In **credentialing** you try to avoid listeners' drawing undesirable inferences and so you seek to establish special qualifications: *Don't get the wrong idea; I'm not sexist, but . . . .*
- With **sin licenses** you announce that you will violate some social or cultural rule but should be "forgiven" in advance (a "license to sin"): *I realize that this may not be the time to talk about money, but . . . .*
- With **cognitive disclaimers** you seek to reaffirm your cognitive abilities in anticipation of any listener doubts: *I know you think I'm drunk, but I'm as sober and as lucid as . . . .*
- **Appeals for the suspension of judgment** ask listeners to delay making judgments until you have the chance to present a more complete account: *Don't say anything until I explain the real story.*

Step Three. Business

The third step is the "business," the substance or focus of the conversation. The business is conducted through an exchange of speaker and listener roles. Usually, brief (rather than long) speaking turns characterize most satisfying conversations.

"Business" is a good term to use for this stage because it emphasizes that most conversations are goal-directed. You converse to fulfill one or several purposes of interpersonal communication: to learn, relate, influence, play, or help (Chapter 1). The term is also general enough to include all kinds of interactions. Here you talk about Jack, what happened in class, or your vacation plans. This is obviously the longest part of the conversation and the reason for both the opening and the feedforward. Not surprisingly, each culture has its own conversational taboos, topics that should be avoided, especially by visitors from other cultures (Table 8.1).

Step Four. Feedback

The fourth step is the reverse of the second. Here you reflect back on the conversation to signal that the business is completed: "So, you may want to send Jack a get well card," "Wasn't that the craziest class you ever heard of?" or "I'll call for reservations while you shop for what we need." Throughout the interpersonal communication process, you exchange feedback—messages sent

Table 8.1 Conversational Taboos Around the World

This table identifies several examples that Roger Axtell in *Do's and Taboos Around the World* (1993) recommends that visitors from the United States avoid. These examples are not intended to be exhaustive, but rather should serve as a reminder that each culture defines what is and what is not an appropriate topic of conversation. Can you think of other examples?

Culture	Conversational Taboos
Belgium	Politics, language differences between French and Flemish, religion
Norway	Salaries, social status
Spain	Family, religion, jobs, negative comments on bullfighting
Egypt	Middle-Eastern politics
Nigeria	Religion
Libya	Politics, religion
Iraq	Religion, Middle-Eastern politics
Japan	World War II
Pakistan	Politics
Philippines	Politics, religion, corruption, foreign aid
South Korea	Internal politics, criticism of the government, socialism or communism
Bolivia	Politics, religion
Columbia	Politics, criticism of bullfighting
Mexico	Mexican-American war, illegal aliens
Caribbean	Race, local politics, religion

back to the speaker concerning reactions to what is said (Clement & Frandsen, 1976). Feedback tells the speaker what effect he or she is having on listeners. On the basis of this feedback, the speaker may adjust, modify, strengthen, de-emphasize, or change the content or form of the messages.

Feedback can take many forms. A frown or a smile, a yea or a nay, a pat on the back or a punch in the mouth are all types of feedback. Feedback can be looked upon in terms of five important dimensions: positive–negative, person focused–message focused, immediate–delayed; low monitoring–high monitoring, and critical–supportive. To use feedback effectively, then, you need to make educated choices along these dimensions (Figure 8.2).

Positive feedback (applause, smiles, head nods signifying approval) tells the speaker that his or her message is being well-received and that essentially the speaker should continue speaking in the same general mode. **Negative feedback** (boos, frowns and puzzled looks, and gestures signifying disapproval) tells the speaker that something is wrong and that some adjustment needs to be made. The art of feedback involves giving positive feedback without strings and giving negative feedback positively.

```
     Positive ____:____:____:____:____:____:____ Negative

Person-focused ____:____:____:____:____:____:____ Message-focused

   Immediate ____:____:____:____:____:____:____ Non-immediate

Low monitoring ____:____:____:____:____:____:____ High monitoring

   Supportive ____:____:____:____:____:____:____ Critical
```

Figure 8.2

Five Dimensions of Feedback.

Try classifying the last few examples of conversational feedback you encountered along these five dimensions. Can you identify other dimensions of feedback?

Feedback may be **person focused** ("You're sweet," "You have a great smile") or **message focused** ("Can you repeat that phone number?" "Your argument is a good one"). Especially in giving criticism it's important to make clear that your feedback relates to, say, the organization of the budget report and not to the person himself or herself.

Feedback can be **immediate** or **delayed.** Generally, the most effective feedback is that which is most immediate. In interpersonal situations, feedback is most often sent immediately after the message is received. Feedback, like reinforcement, loses its effectiveness with time. The longer you wait to praise or punish, for example, the less effect it will have. In other communication situations, however, the feedback may be delayed. Instructor evaluation questionnaires completed at the end of the course provide feedback long after the class began. In interview situations, the feedback may come weeks afterwards.

Feedback varies from the spontaneous and totally honest reaction (**low-monitored** feedback) to the carefully constructed response designed to serve a specific purpose (**high-monitored** feedback). In most interpersonal situations you probably give feedback spontaneously; you allow your responses to show without any monitoring. At other times, however, you may be more guarded as when your boss asks you how you like your job or when your grandfather asks what you think of his new motorcycle outfit.

Feedback is **supportive** when you console another or when you simply encourage the other to talk or when you affirm another's self-definition. **Critical** feedback, on the other hand, is evaluative. When you give critical feedback, you judge another's performance as in, for example, evaluating a speech or coaching someone learning a new skill.

Step Five. The Closing

The fifth and last step, the opposite of the first step, is the closing, the goodbye (Knapp, Hart, Friedrich, & Shulman, 1973; Knapp & Vangelisti, 1992). Most obviously, it signals the end of accessibility. Just as the opening signaled access, the closing signals the end of access. The closing may also signal some degree of supportiveness, for example, you might express your pleasure in interacting: "Well, it was good talking with you." In some conversations, the closing summarizes the interaction. Like the opening, the closing may be verbal or nonverbal but is usually a combination of both. Examples of verbal closings include expressing appreciation ("Well, I appreciate the time you've given me"), concern for the other's welfare ("Do take care of yourself"), reinforcement ("It was great seeing you again"), and leave-taking phrases ("goodbye," "so long"). Nonverbal closings include the breaking of eye contact, positioning your legs or feet toward the door and away from the person you're talking with, leaning forward, and placing your hands on your knees or legs (often accompanied by forward leaning) to signal the intention to stand up. As with openings, usually the verbal and the nonverbal

Acquiring Information

Apply concepts from one area to another. One way to gain additional information is to apply concepts from one area to another area. The more effectively you can do this, the greater your chances of seeing an idea from different perspectives. Try, for example, to apply the feedback model (Figure 8.2) to describe interpersonal relationships. Might it be argued, generally at least, that close personal relationships involve feedback that is strongly positive, person-focused, immediate, low in monitoring, and supportive? As relationships become less intimate, feedback generally moves toward the left ends of the scales and become negative, message-focused, delayed, high in monitoring, and critical. How would you go about testing this theory? To what other areas might this concept of feedback be applied?

are combined, for example, you might say "It was good seeing you again" while leaning forward with hands on your knees.

Reflections on the Stages of Conversation

Not all conversations will be easily divided into these five steps. Often the opening and the feedforward are combined as when you see someone on campus, for example, and say "Hey, listen to this" or when in a work situation, someone might say, "Well, folks, let's get the meeting going." In a similar way, the feedback and the closing might be combined: "Look, I've got to think more about this commitment, okay?"

As already noted, the business is the longest part of the conversation. The opening and the closing are usually about the same length and the feedforward and feedback are usually about equal in length. When these relative lengths are severely distorted, you may feel that something is wrong. For example, when someone uses a long feedforward or a too-short opening, you might suspect that what is to follow is extremely serious.

This model may also help identify conversational skill deficits and may help distinguish effective and satisfying from ineffective and unsatisfying conversations. Consider, for example, the following violations and how they can damage an entire conversation.

- Using openings that are insensitive, for example, "Wow, you've gained a few pounds."
- Using openers that fail to acknowledge the listener, for example, never asking "How are you?"
- Using overly long feedforwards that make you wonder if the speaker will ever get to the business

With what types of people do you find it easiest to communicate? Most difficult?

- Omitting feedforward before a truly shocking message (for example, the death or illness of a friend or relative) that leads you to see the other person as insensitive or uncaring
- Doing business without the normally expected greeting as when, for example, your doctor begins the conversation with, "Well, what's wrong?"
- Omitting feedback which leads you to wonder if the listener heard what you said or cared
- Omitting an appropriate closing that makes you wonder if the other person is disturbed or angry with you
- Not giving clear closure, say, on the phone, so it's not clear if the person wants to hang up or continue talking

Of course, each culture will alter these basic steps in different ways. In some cultures, the openings are especially short whereas in others the openings are elaborate, lengthy, and, sometimes, highly ritualized. It's easy in intercultural communication situations to violate another culture's conversational rules. Being overly friendly, too formal, or too forward may easily hinder the remainder of the conversation.

The reason why such violations may have significant consequences is that people are not aware of these rules and therefore do not see violations as simply cultural differences. Rather, we see the rule violator as too aggressive, too stuffy, or too pushy—almost immediately we dislike the person and put a negative cast on the future conversation.

Acquiring Information

Altercast with those different from yourself. Robert Olson (1980) recommends a type of altercasting in which you place yourself in the position of people very different from yourself and unconnected to your problem. Olson, for example, asked a child: How can I use my time more effectively? The child responded: "Eat less." This prompted Olson to think of using lunch time for important business conferences and discussions. A more dramatic example concerns Edwin Land who had just taken a picture of his small daughter. When she asked why she couldn't see the picture right away, Land began thinking of the developments that eventually led him to create the Polaroid camera (Rice, 1984).

SKILL BUILDING EXERCISE 8.1.

Gender and the Topics of Conversation

Below is a chart for recording the topics of conversation that you think would be extremely comfortable (and therefore highly likely to occur) and extremely uncomfortable (and therefore highly unlikely to occur) for men talking to men, for women talking to women, and for men and women talking to each other. Fill in each box with at least three topics. After you have completed the chart, the responses can be compared with those of others in a small group or with the entire class. One interesting way to do this is for one person to read out a topic (without revealing the particular box he or she put it in) and see if others can identify the "appropriate" box. This experience will give you a general idea of how widely held are one's beliefs about the topics that men and women talk about.

	Man to Man	Woman to Woman	Man to Woman	Woman to Man
Comfortable/ highly likely to occur	1. ____ 2. ____ 3. ____	1. ____ 2. ____ 3. ____	1. ____ 2. ____ 3. ____	1. ____ 2. ____ 3. ____
Uncomfortable/ highly unlikely to occur	1. ____ 2. ____ 3. ____	1. ____ 2. ____ 3. ____	1. ____ 2. ____ 3. ____	1. ____ 2. ____ 3. ____

Thinking Critically About Gender and Conversation   Why did certain topics seem more appropriately positioned in one box rather than another? What evidence did you use for classifying some topics as comfortable for men or for women, for example? Can you identify potential communication problems that might arise because of these differences in the likelihood of certain topics being discussed? How would you go about testing the accuracy of your predictions for which topics go in which boxes?

HOW TO . . .
Avoid Becoming a Conversationally Difficult Person

We all have our own gallery of what constitutes a conversationally difficult person. What would your list of *conversationally comfortable people* look like?

The Detour Taker begins to talk about the topic and then a key word or idea suggests another topic and off this person goes pursuing this other topic. The real problem arises when this person takes a detour off a detour and you forget what the original conversation was about. *Follow a logical pattern in conversation and avoid frequent and long detours.*

The Complainer complains—about everything and everyone. Life is difficult and others are only contributing to make things even worse. Family, friends, job, and school all create problems and this person never tires of listing each of them. *Again, be positive; emphasize what's good before what's bad.*

The Moralist seems to have an inside track on what is right and what is wrong. Often they appear as guests or as audience members on talk shows and you wonder where the producers found these people. The moralist's business is judgment and frequently interjects moral judgments into even the most mundane conversations: "You really shouldn't have said that," "You know, you should . . . ," and "Do you think that was right to do?" *Avoid evaluation and judgment; see the world through the eyes of the other person and (perhaps) the other culture.*

The Inactive Responder may hear you but you'd never know it from this person's reactions. Actually, there are no reactions—whether you talk of winning the lottery or the death of a loved one—this person remains expressionless. Sometimes you try especially hard to make your point in an interesting and dynamic way, but there are still no reactions and you may get the feeling that you're really talking to yourself. *Respond overtly with both verbal and nonverbal messages.*

The Story Teller has difficulty talking about the here-and-now and so tells stories. Mention a topic and the story teller has a ready tale that makes you sorry you ever mentioned the topic in the first place. Often the stories are interesting and are told with real enthusiasm, but they get in the way of two-way conversation. *Talk about yourself in moderation; be other-oriented.*

The Interrogator is a mixture of a police officer, lawyer, and teacher and seems to do nothing but ask questions. No sooner have you answered one question than you are shot with another and another and another. Generally you walk away from this person tired and annoyed that you have been grilled without saying anything in protest. *Ask questions in moderation—to secure needed information and not to get every detail imaginable.*

The Egotist is only interested in himself or herself and shows this by talking only about topics that are self-related. This person can connect even the most unusual topics to self-related concerns. Often this person has to leave just when the conversation changes to someone else. *Be other-oriented; focus on the other person as an individual; listen as much as you speak and speak about the listener at least as much as you speak about yourself.*

The Doomsayer is the ultimate negative thinker. No matter what you say, the doomsayer will read something negative into it. To the doomsayer, the past was a problem, the present is unsatisfying, and the future is bleak. Whatever you plan to do will result in some negative consequence. And even if you do nothing there will be negative consequences. The world conspires against us. *Be positive.*

The Arguer listens only to find something to take issue with. Only a few minutes go by before this person jumps on something you say to argue it isn't so. This person is the ultimate devil's advocate, not to fully test the validity of an argument but simply to argue—rather like some people play cards or watch television. *Be supportive but argue when it's appropriate; focus arguments on issues and behaviors rather than on personalities.*

The Thought Completer knows exactly what you're going to say and so says it for you. Often this person not only completes your sentence but goes on to complete your whole train of thought. Soon you get the idea that there is little reason for even opening your mouth. *Don't interrupt; assume that the speaker wants to finish her or his own thoughts.*

The Self-Discloser talks and talks and talks about himself or herself. Often the disclosures are too personal, sometimes to the point where we feel uncomfortable, almost as eavesdroppers in on someone else's life. Disclose selectively, in ways appropriate to your relationship with the listener.

The Advisor assumes that whenever you express a doubt or talk of a decision that you want his or her advice, proceeds to analyze in great depth the pros and cons of each alternative, and then provides the solution. The idea that you simply wanted to express a doubt never occurs to the conversational advisor. *Avoid giving unsolicited advice and don't assume that the ex-*

pression of a problem is asking you to come up with a solution.

The Psychiatrist analyzes everything you say, offers psychological reasons for why you do what you do, and frequently talks in psychobabble. Although untrained, the conversational psychiatrist traces the origin of your behaviors, mind-reads your motives, and tells you what you're going to do, when, and why. *Avoid playing the therapist; be a friend, lover, or parent, for example, rather than psychological counselor.*

[The next How To box appears on page 245.]

CONVERSATION MANAGEMENT

Speakers and listeners have to work together to make conversation an effective and satisfying experience. We can look at the management of conversations in terms of opening, maintaining, repairing, and closing conversations.

This article highlights the role of questions in conversation and raises a variety of issues about the appropriateness and effectiveness of questions.

Attack by Question

Jacques Lalanne

Questions have their place. Anyone who has seen a skillful lawyer break down a carefully constructed lie knows the value of effective questions, or cross-questions, as weapons.

But in everyday conversation, questions are usually a poor substitute for more direct communication. Questions are incomplete, indirect, veiled, impersonal and consequently ineffective messages that often breed defensive reactions and resistance. They are rarely simple requests for information, but an indirect means of attaining an end, a way of manipulating the person being questioned.

Where did you go?
Out.
What did you do?
Nothing.

This classic parent/child exchange illustrates in 10 words how ineffective questions may be. The parent isn't really asking for information, but making a charge. What comes across is: "You know you're not supposed to cross the street," or, "I told you not to go anywhere after eight o'clock," or, "You got your dress dirty again."

The child's answers, brief as they are, are just as devious. He's learned the hard way that a straightforward answer is likely to lead to trouble. So he uses evasion—"Out" or a half truth—"Nothing."

"When Did You Get Home?"
It's no surprise that questions make most of us feel uneasy. They remind us of times we'd rather forget. As children, before we learned the small skills of excuse and evasion, questions were often a prelude to accusations, advice, blame, orders, etc. At home we'd be asked what we did, or what we didn't do, and one seemed as bad as the other. At school, most questions seemed designed to ferret out what we didn't know rather than what we did.

When we become adults, the questions keep coming. As spouses, salespeople, bosses, even friends, we all use questions to manipulate in some way, convince of some truth, or convict of some error . . . .

A person asking questions may feel in control of a conversation, but that type of conversation isn't very nourishing for the questioner, either, because he's not really involved. Instead of examining our own feelings, as questioners we focus attention on the other person. We replace what is going on inside us with what is happening outside; facts take on more importance than feelings. For example, instead of saying, "I'm disappointed," we often ask, "When did you decide?" Joy and gratitude remain veiled behind "How did you prepare all that?" and instead of showing that we are worried, we ask, "Where were you, for heaven's sake?"

"I Was Afraid . . ."

It's easy to fall into the question-answer conversational trap, and we'd be better off consciously avoiding it. When we feel a question coming on, we could start listening to ourselves, identify our real feelings and express them, rather than hiding them in a question.

Instead of asking coolly, "Are you going out tomorrow afternoon?," we can become involved by revealing, "I'd appreciate it if you took me downtown tomorrow." The question, "What were you doing there so late?," does not express our real feelings as much as: "I was afraid you'd been in an accident!"

Personal disclosures of this kind involve risk. By showing our real feelings, we chance direct refusal or rejection. But we also create a warm climate for direct, fruitful contact with the other person—something the tepid questioning approach rarely accomplishes.

When a questioner has us in his clutches, we can break the spell by paying careful attention to the speaker's tone of voice, gestures, and other hints to see what the real message is, and then respond to that deeper meaning. Feedback establishes communication and lets it circulate.

It could work like this. "Where were you so late last night?" might be answered, "You seem quite worried about it," a response which opens the door to a discussion of what is really bothering the questioner. In answer to "Are you going out Friday night?," words such as "Maybe we can make plans for that night" get at the real message in considerably less time.

Beyond the Question Mark

Here are some everyday questions that work better as honest statements:

What time is it?
I'm tired. I'd like to go home now.
Is it far?
I don't feel up to a long trip this weekend.
Do you love me?
I wish you'd spend more time with me. You work every day and read in the evenings.
How much did you pay?
I hope we have some money left for the rest of the week.
Is it good?
I need to know if you like my soup. I made it the way you prefer.

Thinking Critically About "Attack by Question."   Can you recall recent questions that were addressed to you that would fall into the category Lalanne talks about here? Have you used such questions? Can you identify any advantages of using such questions?

Source: "Attack by Question" by Jacques Lalanne, *Psychology Today*, November 1975. Reprinted with permission from Psychology Today Magazine, copyright © 1975 Sussex Publishers, Inc.

Opening Conversations

Opening a conversation is especially difficult. At times you may not be sure of what to say or how to say it. You may fear being rejected or having someone not understand your meaning. One way to develop opening approaches is to focus on the elements of the interpersonal communication process we discussed in Chapter 1. From these we can derive several avenues for opening a conversation:

- *Self-references*. Say something about yourself. Such references may be of the name, rank, and serial number type of statement, for example: "My name is Joe, I'm from Omaha." On the first day of class students might say "I'm worried about this class" or "I took this instructor last semester; she was excellent."
- *Other references*. Say something about the other person or ask a question: "I like that sweater," "Didn't we meet at Charlie's?"
- *Relational references*. Say something about the two of you, for example, "May I buy you a drink?" "Would you like to dance?" or simply "May I join you?"
- *Context references*. Say something about the physical, cultural, social-psychological, or temporal context. The familiar "Do you have the time?" is of this type. But, you can be more creative, for example, "This place seems real friendly" or "That painting is just great."

Keep in mind two general rules. First, be positive. Lead off with something positive rather than something negative. Say, for example, "I really enjoy coming here" instead of "Don't you just hate this place?" Second, do not be too revealing; don't self-disclose too early in an interaction. If you do, people will think it strange.

The Opening Line

Another way of looking at the process of initiating conversations is to examine the infamous "opening line." Interpersonal researcher Chris Kleinke (1986) suggests that opening lines are of three basic types and provides some excellent examples.

Cute-flippant openers are humorous, indirect, and ambiguous about whether the one opening the conversation really wants an extended encounter. Examples include: "Is that really your hair?" "Bet I can outdrink you." "I bet the cherry jubilee isn't as sweet as you are."

Innocuous openers are highly ambiguous as to whether they are simple comments that might be made to just anyone or whether they are openers designed to initiate an extended encounter. Examples include: "What do you think of the band?" "I haven't been here before. What's good on the menu?" "Could you show me how to work this machine?"

Direct openers clearly show the speaker's interest in meeting the other person. Examples include: "I feel a little embarrassed about this, but I'd like to meet you." "Would you like to have a drink after dinner?" "Since we're both eating alone, would you like to join me?"

The most preferred opening lines by both men and women are generally those that are direct or innocuous (Kleinke, 1988). The least preferred lines by both men and women are those that are cute-flippant; women dislike these openers even more than men. Men generally underestimate how much women dislike the cute-flippant openers but probably continue to use them because they are indirect enough to cushion any rejection. Men also underestimate how much women actually like innocuous openers.

Women prefer men to use openers that are modest and to avoid coming on too strong. Women generally underestimate how much men like direct openers. Most men prefer openers that are very clear in meaning which may be because men are not used to having a woman initiate a meeting. Women also overestimate how much men like innocuous lines.

Maintaining Conversations

In maintaining conversations you follow a variety of principles and rules. Here we give an example of a general principle you follow and its several maxims and the ways in which the speaker and listener turns are exchanged in conversation.

The Principle of Cooperation

During conversation you probably follow the principle of cooperation, agreeing with the other person to cooperate in trying to understand what each is saying (Grice, 1975). If you didn't agree to cooperate, then communication would be extremely difficult, if not impossible. You cooperate largely by using four conversational maxims—principles that speakers and listeners in

What other methods seem to work for opening a conversation? Do you use similar or different methods when opening a conversation with a man as you do with a woman? Would you use similar or different methods depending on whether you wanted to establish a romantic-type or a business-type relationship?

Does your experience agree with or disagree with Chris Kleinke's conclusions about how men and women use and respond to opening lines? What evidence can you point to that supports or contradicts Kleinke's findings?

What types of conversation do you find stressful? Can you identify how you might reduce such stress?

the United States and in many other cultures follow in conversation. Although the names for these maxims may be new, the principles themselves will be easily recognized from your own experiences.

You follow the maxim of **quantity** when you're only as informative as necessary to communicate the intended meaning. Thus, you include information that makes the meaning clear but omit what does not. In following this principle, you give neither too little nor too much information. You see people violate this maxim when they try to relate an incident and digress to give unnecessary information. You find yourself thinking or saying, "Get to the point; so what happened?" This maxim is also violated when necessary information is omitted. In this situation, you find yourself constantly interrupting to ask questions: "Where were they?" "When did this happen?" "Who else was there?"

You follow the maxim of **quality** by saying what you know or assume to be true and by not saying what you know to be false. When you're in conversation, you assume that the other person's information is true—at least as far as he or she knows. When you speak with people who frequently violate this principle by lying, exaggerating, or minimizing major problems, you come to distrust what the person is saying and wonder what is true and what is fabricated.

You follow the maxim of **relation** when you talk about what is relevant to the conversation. Thus, if you're talking about Pat and Chris and say, for example, "Money causes all sorts of relationship problems," it is assumed by others that your comment is somehow related to Pat and Chris. This principle is frequently violated by speakers who digress widely and frequently interject irrelevant comments.

You follow the maxim of **manner** by being clear, by avoiding ambiguities, by being relatively brief, and by organizing you thoughts into a meaningful sequence. Thus, you use terms that the listener understands and omit or clarify terms that you suspect the listener will not understand. You see this maxim when you adjust your speech on the basis of your listener. For example, when talking to a close friend you can refer to mutual acquaintances and to experiences you've shared. When talking to a stranger, however, you either omit such references or explain them. Similarly, when talking with a child, you would simplify your vocabulary so that the child would understand your meaning.

Conversational Maxims, Culture, and Gender

The four maxims just discussed aptly describe most conversations as they take place in much of the United States. Recognize, however, that these maxims may not apply in all cultures; also, other cultures may have other maxims. Some of these maxims may contradict the advice generally given to persons communicating in the United States or in other cultures (Keenan, 1976). Here are a few maxims appropriate in cultures other than the culture of the United States, but also appropriate to some degree throughout the United States.

In research on Japanese conversations and group discussions, a maxim of preserving peaceful relationships with others may be noted (Midooka, 1990). The ways in which such peaceful relationships may be maintained will vary with the person with whom you're interacting. For example, in Japan, your status or position in the hierarchy will influence the amount of self-expression you're expected to engage in. Similarly, there is a great distinction made between public and private conversations. This maxim is much more important in public than it is in private conversations, in which the maxim may be and often is violated.

The maxim of self-denigration, observed in the conversations of Chinese speakers, may require that you avoid taking credit for some accomplishment or make less of some ability or talent you have (Gu, 1990). To put yourself down in this way is a form of politeness that seeks to elevate the person to whom you're speaking.

The maxim of politeness is probably universal across all cultures (Brown & Levinson, 1987). Cultures differ, however, in how they define politeness and in how important politeness is compared with, say, openness or honesty. Cultures also differ in the rules for expressing politeness or impoliteness and in the punishments for violating the accepted rules of politeness (Mao, 1994; Strecker, 1993).

In New York City, to take one example, politeness between cab drivers and riders has never been especially high and has promoted a great deal of criticism. In an attempt to combat this negative attitude, cab drivers have been given 50 polite phrases and are instructed to use these frequently: "May I open (close) the window for you?" "Madam (Sir), is the temperature O.K. for you?" "I'm sorry, I made a wrong turn. I'll take care of it, and we can deduct it from the fare" (*The New York Times* [May 6, 1996], p. B1).

Asian cultures, especially Chinese and Japanese, are often singled out because they emphasize politeness more and mete out harsher social punishments for violations than would most people in, say, the United States or Western Europe. This has led some to propose that a maxim of politeness operates in Asian cultures (Fraser, 1990). When this maxim operates, it may actually violate other maxims. For example, the maxim of politeness may require that you not tell the truth, a situation that would violate the maxim of quality.

CAUTION

How might **failing to see the influence of cultural maxims** distort your judgments about what another person in conversation means? Has this ever happened to you?

Log onto an international IRC channel (for example, #brazil, #finland, #italia, #polska). What can you learn about intercultural communication from just lurking on this channel? Do you feel that intercultural communication differences are more or less pronounced on the Internet than in face-to-face situations? *(An interesting paper could review one of these channels.)*

Acquiring Information

Altercast with role reversal. Altercasting is also useful when two people want to understand the perspective of the other; each might altercast and play the role of the other. In this **role reversal** you and your romantic partner might each play the part of the other in a mock argument. The reverse role playing allows you to see how your partner sees you and allows your partner to see how you see him or her.

In Internet communication, politeness is covered very specifically in its rules of netiquette, rules that are very clearly stated in most computer books (see discussion in Chapter 5). For example: find out what a group is talking about before breaking in with your own comment, be tolerant of newbies (those who are new to newsgroups or IRCs), don't send duplicate messages, don't attack other people (Barron, 1995).

There are also large gender differences (and some similarities) in the expression of politeness (Holmes, 1995). Generally, studies from a number of different cultures show that women use more polite forms than men (Brown, 1980; Wetzel, 1988; Holmes, 1995). For example, in informal conversation and in conflict situations women tend to seek areas of agreement more than do men. Young girls are more apt to try to modify disagreements while young boys are more apt to express more "bald disagreements" (Holmes, 1995). There are also similarities. For example, both men and women in both the United States and New Zealand seem to pay compliments in similar ways (Manes & Wolfson, 1981; Holmes, 1986, 1995) and both men and women use politeness strategies when communicating bad news in an organization (Lee, 1993).

Politeness also varies with the type of relationship. One researcher, for example, has proposed that politeness is greatest with friends and considerably less with strangers and intimates, and depicts this relationship as in Figure 8.3 (Wolfson, 1988; Holmes, 1995).

Conversational Turns

The defining feature of conversation is that the roles of speaker and listener are exchanged throughout the interaction. We accomplish this by using a wide variety of verbal and nonverbal cues to signal conversational turns—the changing (or maintaining) of the speaker or listener role during the conversation. Combining the insights of a variety of communication researchers (Duncan, 1972; Burgoon, Buller, & Woodall, 1995; Pearson & Spitzberg, 1990) we can look at conversational turns in terms of speaker cues and listener cues.

Speaker Cues. As a speaker you regulate the conversation through two major types of cues. *Turn-maintaining cues* enable you to maintain the role of speaker

Figure 8.3

Wolfson's Bulge Model of Politeness

Do you find this model a generally accurate representation of your own level of politeness in different types of relationships? Can you build a case for an inverted U theory (where politeness would be high for both strangers and intimates and low for friends)?

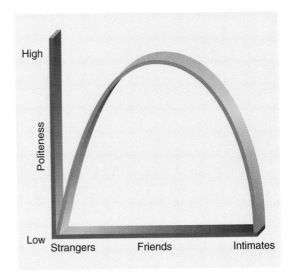

and may be communicated by, for example, audibly inhaling breath to show that you have more to say, continuing a gesture to show that your thought is not yet complete, avoiding eye contact with the listener so there is no indication that you're passing the speaking turn on to the listener, or vocalizing pauses (*er*, *umm*) to prevent the listener from speaking and to show that you're still talking

Turn-yielding cues tell the listener that you're finished and wish to exchange the role of speaker for the role of listener, and may be communicated by dropping your intonation, by a prolonged silence, by making direct eye contact with a listener, by asking a question, or by nodding in the direction of a particular listener.

Listener Cues. As a listener you can regulate the conversation by using three types of cues. *Turn-requesting cues* tell the speaker that you would like to take a turn as speaker, and may be communicated by using some vocalized *er* or *um* that tells the speaker that you would now like to speak as well as by opening your eyes and mouth as if to say something, by beginning to gesture with a hand, or by leaning forward.

Turn-denying cues indicate your reluctance to assume the role of speaker by, for example, intoning a slurred "I don't know," giving the speaker some brief grunt that signals you have nothing to say, avoiding eye contact with the speaker who wishes you to now take on the role of speaker, or engaging in some behavior that is incompatible with speaking—for example, coughing or blowing your nose.

Backchanneling cues communicate various meanings back to the speaker (without assuming the role of the speaker). For example, you can indicate your *agreement* or *disagreement* with the speaker through smiles or frowns, nods of approval or disapproval, brief comments such as "right," "exactly," "never" and such vocalizations as *hu-hah* or your *involvement* or boredom with the speaker through attentive posture, forward leaning, and focused eye contact that tell the speaker that you're involved in the conversation just as an inattentive posture, backward leaning, and avoidance of eye contact will communicate your lack of involvement. You can also request that the speaker pace the conversation differently (for example, asking the speaker to slow down by raising your hand near your ear and leaning forward and to speed

> Their remarks and responses were like a ping-pong game with each volley clearing the net and flying back to the opposition.
>
> —*Maya Angelou*

Although the general rule of conversation is to pass the role of speaker and listener back and forth often, there are times when this general principle should be broken. What are some of these situations?

up by continued nodding of your head or to give your *clarification;* a puzzled facial expression, perhaps coupled with a forward lean, will probably tell most speakers that you want some clarification.

Some of these backchanneling cues are actually interruptions. These interruptions, however, are generally confirming rather than disconfirming. They tell the speaker that we are listening and are involved (Kennedy & Camden, 1988).

One of the most often studied aspects of interruptions is gender differences. Do men or do women interrupt more? Research here is conflicting. These few research findings will give you an idea of some differing results (Pearson, West, & Turner, 1995).

- The more male-like the person's gender identity—regardless of the person's biological sex—the more likely that person is to interrupt (Drass, 1986).
- Men interrupt more than women (Zimmerman & West, 1975).
- There are no significant differences between boys and girls (ages 2–5) in interrupting behavior (Greif, 1980).
- Fathers interrupt their children more than mothers (Greif, 1980).
- Men and women do not differ in their interrupting (Roger & Nesshoever, 1987).

The various turn-taking cues and how they correspond to the conversational wants of speaker and listener are summarized in Figure 8.4.

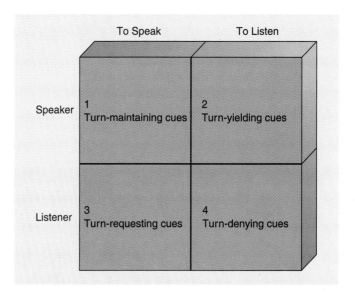

Figure 8.4

Turn-Taking and Conversational Wants

Quadrant 1 represents the speaker who wishes to speak (continue to speak) and uses turn-maintaining cues; Quadrant 2 the speaker who wishes to listen and uses turn-yielding cues; Quadrant 3 the listener who wishes to speak and uses turn-requesting cues; and Quadrant 4 the listener who wishes to listen (continue listening) uses turn-denying cues. Backchanneling cues would appear in Quadrant 4, since they are cues that listeners use while they continue to listen. Interruptions would appear in Quadrant 3, though they are not so much cues that request a turn but are actual take-overs of the speaker's position.

National Enquier.

Repairing Conversations

At times you may say the wrong thing, but because you can't erase the message (communication really is irreversible) you may try to account for it. Perhaps the most common way of doing this is with the excuse (Snyder, 1984; Snyder, Higgins, & Stucky, 1983).

You learn early in life that when you do something that others will view negatively, an excuse is in order to justify your performance. You're especially likely to offer an excuse when you say or are accused of saying something that runs counter to what is expected, sanctioned, or considered "right" by your listeners. Ideally, the excuse lessens the negative impact of the message.

Motives for Excuse Making

The major motive for excuse making seems to be to maintain self-esteem, to project a positive image to yourself and to others. You may also offer an excuse to reduce the stress that may be created by a bad performance. You may feel that if you can offer an excuse—especially a good one that is accepted by those around us—it will reduce the negative reaction and the subsequent stress that might accompany your (possible) poor performance.

Excuses enable you to take risks and engage in behavior that may be unsuccessful; you may offer an anticipatory excuse: "My throat's a bit sore, but I'll give the speech a try." The excuse is designed to lessen the criticism should you fail to deliver an acceptable speech.

Excuses also enable you to maintain effective interpersonal relationships even after some negative behavior. For example, after criticizing a friend's behavior and observing the negative reaction to your criticism, we might offer an excuse such as, "Please forgive me; I'm really exhausted. I'm just not thinking straight." Excuses place your messages—even your failures—in a more favorable light.

> To make excuses before they are needed is to blame one's self.
>
> —*Spanish proverb*

> Excuses are always mixed with lies.
>
> —*Arab proverb*

Have you heard (or used) any excuses lately? What functions did these excuses serve? Were they effective? How might they have been made more effective? In what types of situations do you find that excuses only aggravate the problems they were meant to solve?

Good and Bad Excuses

The most important question to most people is what makes a good excuse and what makes a bad excuse (Snyder, 1984; Slade, 1995). How can you make good excuses and thus get out of problems, and how can you avoid bad excuses and thus only make matters worse? Table 8.2 tries to answer this question.

Closing Conversations

Closing a conversation is almost as difficult as opening a conversation. It's frequently an awkward and uncomfortable part of interpersonal interaction. Here are a few ways you might consider for closing a conversation.

- Reflect back on the conversation and briefly summarize it to bring it to a close. For example, "I'm glad I ran into you and found out what happened at that union meeting. I'll probably be seeing you at the meetings."
- State the desire to end the conversation directly and to get on with other things. For example, "I'd like to continue talking but I really have to run. I'll see you around."
- Refer to future interaction. For example, "Why don't we get together next week sometime and continue this discussion."
- Ask for closure. For example, "Have I explained what you wanted to know?"
- Say that you enjoyed the interaction. For example, "I really enjoyed talking with you."

With any of these closings, it should be clear to the other person that you're attempting to end the conversation. Obviously, you'll have to use more direct methods with those who don't take these subtle hints, with those who don't realize that *both* persons are responsible for the interpersonal interaction and for bringing it to a satisfying closing.

To confess a fault freely is the next thing to being innocent of it.
—Publilius Syrus

If you were compiling a book on The World's Worst Excuses which one(s) would you include? Which would you include in The World's Best Excuses? (Your experiences with excuses (as sender or receiver) would make an interesting personal experience paper.)

What ways, in addition to those noted in this chapter, have you found for closing conversations?

Table 8.2 Good and Bad Excuses

The worst excuses are the "I didn't do it" type because they violate two of the essential characteristics of a good excuse; they fail to acknowledge responsibility and to correct the problem in the future. Can you identify other qualities of good and bad excuses?

Good Excuses	Bad Excuses
Are used in moderation	Are used too often
Avoid blaming others, especially those you work with	Blame others for your failures
Incorporate an acknowledgment of responsibility for doing something wrong (not for a lack of competence)	Avoid acknowledging responsibility or admitting to a lack of competence
Ask forgiveness	Avoid asking forgiveness (because the error is seldom admitted)
Promise that things will be better in the future, that this failure will never happen again	Fail to mention any ways in which this problem will not happen again

SKILL BUILDING EXERCISE 8.2.
Formulating Excuses

Although excuses are not always appropriate, they are often helpful in lessening possible negative effects of your mishap. Try formulating an appropriate excuse for each of the five situations listed below and develop a justification as to why you assume that this excuse will lessen any negative consequences. Three types of excuses that you might use as starting points are

- I didn't do it or I did do what I'm accused of not doing ("I didn't say that." "I wasn't even near the place." "I did try to get in touch with you to tell you I'd be late.")
- It wasn't so bad ("Sure I pushed him, but I didn't kill him.")
- Yes, but ("It was just my jealousy making those accusations.")

1. Because of some e-mail glitch, colleagues all receive a recent personal letter you sent to a friend in which you admit to having racist feelings. You even gave several examples. As you enter work, you see a group of colleagues discussing your letter. They aren't pleased.
2. Your boss accuses you of making lots of personal long distance phone calls from work, a practice explicitly forbidden.

3. In a discussion with your supervisor, you tell a joke that puts down lesbians and gay men. She tells you she finds the joke homophobic and offensive to everyone and, she adds, she has a gay son and is proud of it. Since you just started the job, you're still on probation and this supervisor's recommendation will count heavily.
4. Your friend tells you that he thinks you hurt Joe's feelings when you criticized his presentation.
5. Your history instructor is walking behind you and hears you and another student discussing your class. Your instructor clearly hears you say, "That last lecture was a total waste of time" but says nothing.

Thinking Critically About Excuses. Can you identify specific situations in which excuses would be inappropriate? What effects does repeated excuse-making have on a romantic relationship? Do you have stereotypes of people who consistently make excuses for just about everything they do?

LISTENING.
Listening to Gossip

There can be no doubt that everyone spends a great deal of time gossiping. In fact, gossip seems a universal among all cultures (Laing, 1993) and among some it's a commonly accepted ritual (Hall, 1993). Gossip is third-party talk about another person; the word "now embraces both the talker and the talk, the tattler and the tattle, the newsmonger and the newsmongering" (Bremner, 1980, p. 178). Gossip is an inevitable part of daily interactions; to advise anyone not to gossip would be absurd. Not gossiping would eliminate one of the most frequent and enjoyable forms of communication.

In some instances gossip is unethical (Bok, 1983). For example, it would generally be considered unethical to reveal information that you have promised to keep secret. Although this principle may seem too obvious to even mention, it seems violated in many cases. For example, in a study of 133 school executives, board presidents, and superintendents, the majority received communications that violated an employee's right to confidentiality (Wilson & Bishard, 1994). And in a study of elevator rides of medical personnel, 14 percent of these rides included gossip

(continued)

(continued)

about patients (Ubel, 1995). When there are significant reasons for not keeping such information confidential (Bok offers the example of the teenager who confides a suicide plan), the information should be revealed only to those who must know it, not to the world at large.

Gossip would also be considered unethical when it invades the privacy that everyone has a right to, for example, when it concerns matters that are properly considered private and when the gossip can hurt the individuals involved. Last, gossip would be considered unethical when it is known to be false and is nevertheless passed on to others. These conditions are not easy to identify in any given instance, but they do provide excellent starting points for asking whether or not discussing another person is ethical.

Under what conditions would revealing another person's secrets be ethical? Are there times when the failure to reveal such secrets would be unethical? Is it ethical to observe someone (without his or her knowledge) and report your observations to others? For example, would it be ethical to observe your communication professor on a date with a student or smoking marijuana and then report these observations back to your communication classmates? What ethical guidelines would you propose for talking about another person?

[The next Listening box appears on page 239.]

CONVERSATION EFFECTIVENESS

Because each conversation is unique, the qualities of interpersonal effectiveness cannot be applied indiscriminately. So, for example, although openness is a generally positive quality in, say romantic relationships, it may be quite inappropriate with your supervisor or postal worker. Obviously, you'll need to apply the specific skills selectively. Fortunately, there are general skills to help you regulate your more specific skills.

General Conversational Skills

Four general skills will prove especially valuable in helping you regulate your more specific skills; these are: mindfulness, flexibility, cultural sensitivity, and metacommunicational abilities.

Mindfulness

After you have learned a skill or rule you may have a tendency to apply it without thinking or "mindlessly," without, for example, considering the novel aspects of a situation. For instance, after learning the skills of active listening, many will use them in response to all situations. Some of these responses will be appropriate but others will prove inappropriate and ineffective. In interpersonal and even in small group situations (Elmes & Gemmill, 1990) apply the skills **mindfully** (Langer, 1989).

Langer (1989) offers several suggestions for increasing mindfulness:

- Create and recreate categories. See an object, event, or person as belonging to a variety of categories. Avoid storing in memory an image of a person, for example, with only one specific label; it will be difficult to recategorize it later.
- Be open to new information even if it contradicts your most firmly held stereotypes.
- Be willing to see your own and others' behaviors from a variety of perspectives.

CAUTION

Can you think of a specific conversation where either you or the other person were **talking mindlessly?** Did this mindlessness prevent critical analysis?

- Be careful of relying too heavily on first impressions; treat first impressions as tentative, as hypotheses.

Flexibility

Before reading about flexibility, take the following self-test (Martin & Rubin, 1994, 1995; Martin & Anderson, 1998):

SELF-TEST

How Flexible Are You in Communication?

Instructions: Here are some situations that illustrate how people sometimes act when communicating with others. The first part of each situation asks you to imagine that you are in the situation. Then, a course of action is identified and you are asked to determine how much your own behavior would be like the action described in the scenario. If it is *exactly* like you, mark a 5; if it is *a lot* like you, mark a 4; if it is *somewhat* like you, mark a 3; if it is *not much* like you, mark a 2; and if it is *not at all* like you, mark a 1.

Imagine

_____ 1. Last week, as you were discussing your strained finances with your family, family members came up with several possible solutions. Even though you already decided on one solution, you decided to spend more time considering all the possibilities before making a final decision.

_____ 2. You were invited to a Halloween party and assuming it was a costume party, you dressed as a pumpkin. When you arrived at the party and found everyone else dressed in formal attire, you laughed and joked about the misunderstanding, and decided to stay and enjoy the party.

_____ 3. You have always enjoyed being with your friend Chris, but do not enjoy Chris's habit of always interrupting you. The last time you met, every time Chris interrupted you, you then interrupted Chris to teach Chris a lesson.

_____ 4. Your daily schedule is very structured and your calendar is full of appointments and commitments. When asked to make a change in your schedule, you replied that changes are impossible before even considering the change.

_____ 5. You went to a party where over 50 people attended. You had a good time, but spent most of the evening talking to one close friend rather than meeting new people.

_____ 6. When discussing a personal problem with a group of friends, you noticed that many different solutions were offered. Although several of the solutions seemed feasible, you already had your opinion and did not listen to any of the alternative solutions.

_____ 7. You and a friend are planning a fun evening and you're dressed and ready ahead of time. You find that you are unable to do anything else until your friend arrives.

_____ 8. When you found your seat at the ball game, you realized you did not know anyone sitting nearby. However, you introduced yourself to the people sitting next to you and attempted to strike up a conversation.

_____ 9. You had lunch with your friend Chris, and Chris told you about a too-personal family problem. You quickly finished your lunch and stated that you had to leave because you had a lot to do that afternoon.

_____ 10. You were involved in a discussion about international politics with a group of acquaintances and you assumed that the members of the group were as knowledgeable as you on the

(continued)

(continued)

topic; but, as the discussion progressed, you learned that most of the group knew little about the subject. Instead of explaining your point of view, you decided to withdraw from the discussion.

_____ 11. You and a group of friends got into a discussion about gun control and, after a while, it became obvious that your opinions differed greatly from the rest of the group. You explained your position once again, but you agreed to respect the group's opinion, also.

_____ 12. You were asked to speak to a group you belong to, so you worked hard preparing a 30-minute presentation; but at the meeting, the organizer asked you to lead a question-and-answer session instead of giving your presentation. You agreed, and answered the group's questions as candidly and fully as possible.

_____ 13. You were offered a managerial position where every day you would face new tasks and challenges and a changing day-to-day routine. You decided to accept this position instead of one that has a stable daily routine.

_____ 14. You were asked to give a speech at a Chamber of Commerce breakfast. Because you did not know anyone at the breakfast and would feel uncomfortable not knowing anyone in the audience, you declined the invitation.

Thinking Critically About Flexibility

To compute your score:

1. Reverse the scoring for items 4, 5, 6, 7, 9, 10, and 14. That is, for each of these questions, substitute as follows:

   A. If you answered 5, reverse it to 1
   B. If you answered 4, reverse it to 2
   C. If you answered 3, keep it as 3
   D. If you answered 2, reverse it to 4
   E. If you answered 1, reverse it to 5

2. Add the scores for all 14 items. Be sure that you use the reversed scores for items 4, 5, 6, 7, 9, 10, and 14 instead of your original responses. Use your original scores for items 1, 2, 3, 8, 11, 12, and 13.

In general, you can interpret your score as follows:

- 65–70 = much more flexible than average
- 57–64 = more flexible than average
- 44–56 = about average
- 37–43 = less flexible than average
- 14–36 = much less flexible than average

Are you satisfied with your level of flexibility? What might you do to cultivate flexibility in general and communication flexibility in particular?

Source: From "Development of a Communication Flexibility Measure," by Matthew M. Martin and Rebecca B. Rubin, *The Southern Communication Journal* 59 (Winter 1994) pp. 171–178. Reprinted by permission of the Southern States Communication Association.

Although we provide general principles for effective interpersonal communication, be flexible when applying them and be sensitive to the unique factors in each situation. Thus, you may need to be frank and spontaneous when talking with a close friend about your feelings, but you may not want to be so open when talking with your grandmother about the dinner she prepared that you disliked.

Self-disclosure, for example, is beneficial sometimes and with some people but dangerous in other situations and with other people (Chapter 2). The same is true with the characteristics to be discussed here. Effective interpersonal communication depends on understanding the principles and applying them flexibly—with a consideration for all the elements in the communication act. Here are a few suggestions for cultivating flexibility:

- Recall the principle of indiscrimination (Chapter 5)—no two things or situations are exactly alike. Ask yourself what is different about this situation.
- Realize that communication always takes place in a context (Chapter 1); ask yourself what is unique about this specific context that might alter your communications. Will cultural differences play a role in this communication? Will gender differences come into play?
- Remember that everything is in a constant state of change (Chapter 5) and therefore responses that were appropriate yesterday may not be appropriate today. Responding protectively when your child is five might be appropriate; at 18 that same response may be inappropriate. Also, recognize that sudden changes may also exert great influence on communication: the death of a lover, the knowledge of a fatal illness, the birth of a child, a promotion are just a few examples.
- Recall that everyone is different. Thus, you may need to be frank and spontaneous when talking with a close friend about your feelings, but you may not want to be so open when talking with your grandmother about the dinner she prepared that you disliked.

Cultural Sensitivity

In applying the skills for interpersonal effectiveness be sensitive to the cultural differences among people (Kim, 1991). What may prove effective for upper income people working in the IBM subculture of Boston or New York, may prove ineffective for lower income people working as fruit pickers in Florida or California. What works in Japan may not work in Mexico. The direct eye contact that signals immediacy in most of the United States may be considered rude or too intrusive in Hispanic and other cultures. The empathy that most Americans will welcome may be uncomfortable for the average Korean (Yun, 1976). The specific conversational skills discussed below are considered generally effective in the United States and among most people living in the United States. But, note that these skills and the ways in which we communicate them verbally or nonverbally are specific to general United States culture.

Metacommunicational Ability

Much talk concerns people, objects, and events in the world. But you also talk about your talk. You **metacommunicate,** that is, you communicate about your communication. Your interpersonal effectiveness often hinges on this ability to metacommunicate. Let's say that someone says something positive but in a negative way; for example, the person says, "Yes, I think you did . . . a good job," but with no enthusiasm and an avoidance of eye contact. You are faced with several alternatives. You may, for example, respond to the message as positive or as negative. Another alternative, however, is to talk about the message and say something like, "I'm not sure I understand if you're pleased or displeased with what I did. You said you were pleased but I detect dissatisfaction in your voice. Am I wrong?" In this way, you may avoid lots of misunderstandings.

Acquiring Information

Categorize to See Relationships and Connections

Grouping things into categories helps you to see relationships that you may not see otherwise. Try to create as many categories (with at least three items each) as you can from the list of 30 items presented below. For example, one category might be "things that fly," which would include the airplane, bee, helicopter, mosquito, and parakeet. A less obvious category might be "things you moisten." Sharing these categories with others will give you an appreciation for the added perspectives that can be brought to bear on a concept by seeing it categorized in different ways.

$10 bill, airplane, bee, bologna, camera, dictionary, envelope, eye glasses, fax machine, hearing aid, helicopter, ice cream, microphone, milk, mosquito, paper clip, parakeet, pen, pocket knife, postage stamp, razor, ruler, scissors, screwdriver, telephone, television set, transparent tape, wall calendar, wallpaper, window

This experience should also demonstrate that a single item can be a member of lots of categories. For example, it allows you to see a screwdriver, not only in the category of tools, but also in the category of door stops, can openers, paperweights, nail cleaners, garden implements, and electrical current testers.

CAUTION

How might **being inflexible** prevent you from accurately perceiving people? Are you inflexible about any particular conversational practices?

Here are a few suggestions for using metacommunication:

- Give clear feedforward. This will help the other person get a general picture of the message that will follow and make understanding easier.
- Confront contradictory or inconsistent messages. At the same time, explain your own messages that may appear inconsistent to your listener.
- Explain the feelings that go with your thoughts. Often people communicate only the thinking part of their message with the result that listeners are not able to appreciate the other parts of your meaning.
- Paraphrase your own complex messages. Similarly, to check on your own understanding of another's message, paraphrase what you think the other person means and ask if you are accurate.
- Ask questions. If you have doubts about another's meaning, don't assume; instead, ask.
- When you do talk about your talk, do so only to gain an understanding of the other person's thoughts and feelings. Avoid substituting talk about talk for talk about a specific problem.

Specific Conversational Skills

The skills of conversational effectiveness we discuss here are (1) openness, (2) empathy, (3) positiveness, (4) immediacy, (5) interaction management, (6) expressiveness, and (7) other-orientation. These qualities are derived from a wide spectrum of ongoing research (Bochner & Kelly, 1974; Wiemann, 1977; Spitzberg & Hecht, 1984; Spitzberg & Cupach, 1984, 1989; Rubin, 1985, 1986; Rubin & Graham, 1988). As you read about these concepts, keep the general skills in mind.

Openness

Openness refers to three aspects of interpersonal communication. First, you should be willing to "self-disclose," to reveal information about yourself. Of course, these disclosures need to be appropriate to the entire communication act (see Chapter 2). There must also be an openness in regard to listening to the other person; you should be open to the thoughts and feelings of the person with whom you're communicating.

A second aspect of openness refers to your willingness to react honestly to the situations that confront you. We want people to react openly to what we say, and we have a right to expect this. We show openness by responding spontaneously and honestly to the communications and the feedback of others.

Third, openness calls for the "owning" of feelings and thoughts. To be open in this sense is to acknowledge that the feelings and thoughts you express are yours and that you bear the responsibility for them.

When you own your own messages, you use I-messages instead of you-messages. Instead of saying, "You make me feel so stupid when you ask what everyone else thinks but don't ask my opinion," the person who owns his or her feelings says "I feel stupid when you ask everyone else what they think but don't ask me." When you own your feelings and thoughts, when you use "I-messages," you say in effect, "This is how *I* feel," "This is how *I* see the situation," "This is what *I* think," with the *I* always paramount. Instead of saying, "This discussion is useless," you would say, "*I'm* bored by this discussion," or "*I* want to talk more about myself," or any other such statement that includes a reference to the fact that you're making an evaluation and not describing objective reality.

Why is it so important to be mindful, flexible, and culturally sensitive and to use metacommunication in your conversations? Can you give examples to illustrate the importance of these general skills from your own conversational experiences? *(Your experiences with these concepts in conversations would make an interesting personal experience paper.)*

There is no wisdom like frankness.

—*Benjamin Disraeli*

After reviewing the research on the empathic and listening abilities of men and women, Pearson, West, and Turner (1995) conclude: "Men and women do not differ as much as conventional wisdom would have us believe. In many instances, she thinks like a man, and he thinks like a woman because they both think alike." What kinds of experiences have you had that bear on this issue?

Empathy

To *empathize* with someone is to feel as that person feels. When you feel empathy for another, you're able to experience what the other is experiencing from that person's point of view. Empathy does *not* mean that you agree with what the other person says or does. You never lose your own identity or your own attitudes and beliefs. To *sympathize*, on the other hand, is to feel *for* the individual—to feel sorry for the person, for example. To empathize is to feel the same feelings in the same way as the other person does. Empathy, then, enables you to understand, emotionally and intellectually, what another person is experiencing. Here are a few suggestions for communicating empathy both verbally and nonverbally:

- Self-disclose. Express both the similarities between your experiences and the experiences of the other person. At the same time, however, acknowledge that you're aware of the differences. For example, *I never failed a course but I got enough D's to understand why you feel so down. I felt it was a kind of rejection from someone I really wanted to impress.*
- Avoid judgmental and evaluative (nonempathic) responses. Avoid *should* and *ought* statements that try to tell the other person how he or she *should* feel. For example, avoid expressions such as *don't feel so bad, don't cry, cheer up, in time you'll forget all about this,* and *you should start dating others; by next month you won't even remember her name.*
- Use reinforcing comments. Let the speaker know that you understand what the speaker is saying and encourage him or her to continue talking about this issue. For example, use comments such as *I see, I get it, I understand, yes,* and *right.*

- Demonstrate interest by maintaining eye contact (avoid scanning the room or focusing on objects or persons other than the person with whom you're interacting); maintaining physical closeness (avoid large spaces between yourself and the other person); leaning toward (not away from) the other person; and showing your interest and agreement with your facial expressions, nods, and eye movements.

Positiveness

You can communicate positiveness in interpersonal communication in at least two ways: (1) stating positive attitudes and (2) complimenting the person with whom you interact.

Attitudinal positiveness in interpersonal communication refers to a positive regard for oneself, for the other person, and for the general communication situation. Your feelings (whether positive or negative) become clear during conversation and greatly influence the satisfaction (or dissatisfaction) you derive from the interaction. Negative feelings usually make communication more difficult and can contribute to its eventual breakdown.

Positiveness is seen most clearly in the way you phrase statements. Consider these two sets of sentences:

1A. I wish you wouldn't handle me so roughly.
1B. I really enjoy it when you're especially gentle.

2A. You look horrible in stripes.
2B. You look your best, I think, in solid colors.

The A sentences are negative; they are critical and will almost surely encourage an argument. The B sentences, in contrast, express the speaker's thought clearly but are phrased positively and should encourage cooperative responses.

Another aspect of positiveness is **complimenting,** behavior that acknowledges the existence of some positive quality in another person or some action that you evaluate positively. Many people, in fact, structure interpersonal encounters almost solely for the purpose of getting complimented. People may buy new clothes to get complimented, compliment associates so that the associates compliment back, do favors for people to receive thanks, associate with certain people because they are generous with their compliments, and so on. Some people even enter relationships because they hold the promise of frequent compliments.

What constitutes an appropriate compliment will naturally vary with the culture (Dresser, 1996). For example, in the United States it would be considered appropriate for a teacher to publicly compliment a student on getting the highest grade in an examination or for a supervisor to compliment a worker for doing an exceptional job on some project. But, in other cultures (collectivist cultures, for example) this would be considered inappropriate because it singles out the individual and separates that person from the group. Similarly, the responses to compliments will vary from one culture to another (Chen, 1993). In the United States, a compliment is generally supposed to be accepted graciously; you did a good job and have a right to have that acknowledged. In more collectivist cultures, however, you're expected to deny your right to the compliment and to instead credit the group or the situation—"It was a very easy thing to do," "I didn't do it by myself," "Others deserve the credit," and so on.

There is nothing you can say in answer to a compliment. I have been complimented myself a great many times, and they always embarrass me—I always feel that they have not said enough.

—*Mark Twain*

Immediacy

Immediacy refers to the joining of the speaker and listener, the creation of a sense of togetherness. The communicator who demonstrates immediacy conveys a sense of interest and attention, a liking for and an attraction to the other person. People respond favorably to immediacy. Immediacy joins speaker and listener.

You can communicate immediacy in several ways:

- maintain appropriate eye contact and limit looking around at others; smile and otherwise express your interest
- maintain a physical closeness which suggests a psychological closeness; maintain a direct and open body posture
- Focus on the other person's remarks. Make the speaker know that you heard and understood what was said and will base your feedback on it.
- Reinforce, reward, or compliment the other person. Use such expressions as "I like your new outfit" or "Your comments were really to the point."

Interaction Management

The effective communicator controls the interaction to the satisfaction of both parties. In effective *interaction management,* neither person feels ignored or on stage. Each contributes to the total communication interchange. Maintaining your role as speaker or listener and passing back and forth the opportunity to speak are interaction management skills. If one person speaks all the time and the other listens all the time, effective conversation becomes difficult if not impossible. Depending on the situation, one person may speak more than the other person. This, however, should depend on the situation and not on one person being a "talker" and another a "listener."

Effective interaction managers avoid interrupting the other person. Interruption signals that what you have to say is more important than what the other person is saying and puts the other person in an inferior position. The result is dissatisfaction with the conversation. Similarly, keeping the conversation flowing and fluent without long and awkward pauses that make everyone uncomfortable are signs of effective interaction management.

One of the best ways to look at interaction management is to take the self-test, "Are You a High Self-Monitor?" This test will help you to identify the qualities that make for the effective management of interpersonal communication situations.

> Say nothing good of yourself, you will be distrusted; say nothing bad of yourself, you will be taken at your word.
> —*Joseph Roux*

SELF-TEST
Are You a High Self-Monitor?

Instructions: These statements concern personal reactions to a number of different situations. No two statements are exactly alike, so consider each statement carefully before answering. If a statement is true or mostly true, as applied to you, write T. If a statement is false or not usually true, as applied to you, write F.

_____ 1. I find it hard to imitate the behavior of other people.

_____ 2. I guess I do put on a show to impress or entertain people.

_____ 3. I would probably make a good actor.

_____ 4. I sometimes appear to others to be experiencing deeper emotions than I actually have.

_____ 5. In a group of people, I am rarely the center of attention.

(continued)

(continued)

_____   6. In different situations and with different people, I often act like very different persons.

_____   7. I can only argue for ideas I already
believe.

_____   8. In order to get along and be liked, I
tend to be what people expect me to
be rather than who I really am.

_____   9. I may deceive people by being friendly
when I really dislike them.

_____   10. I am always the person I appear to be.

Thinking Critically About Self-Monitoring.
To score your test, give yourself one point for each of
questions 1, 5, and 7 that you answered F. Give yourself one point for each of the remaining questions
that you answered T. Add up your points. If you're a
good judge of yourself and scored 7 or above, you're
probably a high self-monitoring individual; 3 or below,
you're probably a low self-monitoring individual.

Does your score correspond to the way in which
you view yourself? Does self-monitoring have an ethical dimension to it? That is, are there circumstances
when self-monitoring would be unethical? In what
situations are you likely to self-monitor?

Source: From "The Many Me's of the Self-Monitor," by Mark Snyder, as appeared in *Psychology Today,*
March 13, 1980. Reprinted by permission of the author.

Self-monitoring, the manipulation of the image that you present to others
in your interpersonal interactions, is integrally related to interpersonal interaction management. High self-monitors carefully adjust their behaviors on the
basis of feedback from others so that they produce the most desirable effect.
Low self-monitors communicate their thoughts and feelings with no attempt
to manipulate the impressions they create. Most of us lie somewhere between
the two extremes.

> Admonish your friends pri-
> vately, but praise them openly.
> —*Syrus*

Expressiveness

The *expressive* speaker communicates genuine involvement in the interpersonal interaction. He or she plays the game instead of just watching it
as a spectator. *Expressiveness* is similar to openness in its emphasis on involvement. It includes taking responsibility for your thoughts and feelings, encouraging expressiveness or openness in others, and providing
appropriate feedback.

This quality also includes taking responsibility for both talking and listening and for your own thoughts and feelings. In conflict situations, expressiveness involves fighting actively and stating disagreement directly. More
specifically, expressiveness may be communicated in a variety of ways. Here
are a few guidelines:

- Practice active listening by paraphrasing, expressing understanding of
the thoughts and feelings of the other person, and asking relevant
questions (as explained in Chapter 4).
- Avoid clichés and trite expressions that signal a lack of personal involvement and originality; they make it appear that there is nothing special in this specific conversation.
- Address messages (verbal or nonverbal) that contradict each other. Also
address messages that somehow seem unrealistic to you (for example,

> When we talk in company we
> lose our unique tone of voice,
> and this leads us to make state-
> ments which in no way corre-
> spond to our real thoughts.
> —*Friedrich Nietzsche*

statements claiming that the breakup of a long-term relationship is completely forgotten or that failing a course doesn't mean anything).

- Use I-messages to signal personal involvement and a willingness to share your feelings. Instead of saying "You never give me a chance to make any decisions," say "I'd like to contribute to the decisions that affect both of us."

Nonverbally you can communicate expressiveness by using appropriate variations in vocal rate, pitch, volume, and rhythm to convey involvement and interest and by allowing our facial muscles to reflect and echo this inner involvement. Similarly, the appropriate use of gestures communicates involvement. Too few gestures signal disinterest, while too many may signal discomfort, uneasiness, and awkwardness. The monotone and motionless speaker who talks about sex, winning the lottery, and fatal illness all in the same tone of voice, with a static posture and an expressionless face, is the stereotype of the ineffective interaction manager.

Other-Orientation

Other-orientation shows consideration and respect—for example, asking if it's all right to dump your troubles on someone before doing so or asking if your phone call comes at an inopportune time before launching into your conversation. Other-orientation involves acknowledging others' feelings as legitimate: "I can understand why you're so angry; I would be, too." *Other-orientation* is the opposite of self-orientation and is illustrated in the letter to Ann Landers that opened this chapter. It involves the ability to communicate attentiveness and interest in the other person and in what is being said.

You communicate other-orientation in a variety of ways:

- Use focused eye contact, smiles, head nods, leaning toward the other person, and displaying feelings and emotions through appropriate facial expression.
- Ask the other person for suggestions, opinions, and clarification as appropriate. Statements such as "How do you feel about it?" or "What do you think?" will go a long way toward focusing the communication on the other person.
- Express agreement when appropriate. Comments such as "you're right" or "that's interesting" help to focus the interaction on the other person, which encourages greater openness.
- Use backchanneling cues to encourage the other person to express himself or herself, for example, *yes, I see,* or even *aha* or *hmm* will tell the other person that you're interested in his or her continued comments.
- Use positive affect statements to refer to the other person and to his or her contributions to the interaction; for example, *I really enjoy talking with you* or *That was a clever way of looking at things* are positive affect statements that are often felt but rarely expressed.

Not surprisingly, other-orientation is especially important in communicating with a person who has a handicap such as deafness. Table 8.3 offers some useful suggestions for communicating with a deaf person.

How would you go about seeking answers to the following questions *(any one of which would make an interesting research paper topic)*: Are people who demonstrate the qualities of effective conversational management better liked than those who do not? Which quality of effectiveness is the most important in communication between healthcare provider and patient? What role does other-orientation play in first dates?

Table 8.3 Talking with a Deaf Person*

- Get the deaf person's attention before speaking.

- Key the deaf person into the topic of discussion.

- Speak slowly and clearly, but do not yell, exaggerate, or overpronounce.

- Look directly at the deaf person when speaking.

- Do not place anything in your mouth when speaking.

- Maintain eye contact with the deaf person.

- Use the words "I" and "you."

- Avoid standing in front of a light source, such as a window or bright light. The glare and shadows created on the face make it almost impossible for the deaf person to speechread.

- First repeat, then try to rephrase a thought if you have problems being understood, rather than repeating the same words again.

- Use pantomime, body language, and facial expression to help supplement your communication.

- Be courteous to the deaf person during conversation. If the telephone rings or someone knocks at the door, excuse yourself and tell the deaf person that you are answering the phone or responding to the knock.

- Use open-ended questions that must be answered by more than "yes" or "no." Do not assume that deaf persons have understood your message if they nod their heads in acknowledgment. A response to an open-ended question ensures that your information has been communicated.

*From "Tips for Communicating with Deaf People" Rochester Institute of Technology, National Technical Institute for the Deaf, 52 Lomb Memorial Drive, Rochester, NY 14623-5804; (716) 475-6906 (v/TTY), NTIDMC@rit.edu. Reprinted by permission.

A Note on Computer Communication Skills

Research has just begun to focus on the skills of computer communication. There is some evidence, for example, that small computer-communicating groups function in some ways better than face-to-face groups (Olaniran, 1994; Kiesler & Sproull, 1992; Harris, 1995). Compared with face-to-face groups, computer groups generated a greater number of unique ideas, proposed more unconventional or risky decisions, took longer to reach agreement, engaged in more explicit and outspoken advocacy, and had more equal participation among members.

In many cases, students preferred computer-mediated communication over face-to-face communication. The reason, it seems, was that in mediated communication the students didn't have to worry about the rules for interpersonal communication such as those for eye contact and body communication; it also lessened their concerns about shyness (Mendoza, 1995). The insights from students such as these are just beginning to be incorporated into interpersonal communication courses and textbooks (Harris, 1995).

Here are some guidelines for making your own online communication more effective:

- Watch your spelling. If you have a spell check, use it.

SKILL BUILDING EXERCISE 8.3.
Responding Effectively

This experience is designed to illustrate the characteristics of interpersonal effectiveness more concretely. For each of the situations presented below, develop responses that demonstrate one or more of the seven characteristics of conversational effectiveness: openness, empathy, positiveness, immediacy, interaction management, expressiveness, and other orientation. For purposes of this experience, try to formulate responses that focus as exclusively as possible on each one of these characteristics.

1. Katrina tells you of her upcoming marriage, the new house they plan to buy, and how much she is looking forward to moving to San Diego.
2. Kevin tells you about his fear of intimacy and how he feels this comes from being rejected by his parents when he was a young boy.
3. A friend you've known for years e-mails you and tells you he just found out he's HIV positive.
4. A neighbor tells you that she just won the lottery for $2 million.
5. Your relationship partner of 30 years tells you that he feels like a failure, never having accomplished what he set out to do or what others thought he would accomplish.

Thinking Critically About Responding Effectively.   Which of the characteristics of conversational effectiveness is easiest to demonstrate? Hardest? How does your relationship with the person influence your demonstrating these characteristics?

- Remember that what you write can easily be made public. So—to quote Sidney Biddle Barrows—"Never say anything on the [Internet] that you wouldn't want your mother to hear at your trial."
- Follow the rules of netiquette (Chapter 5) and avoid the potential sources of conflict such as spamming and flaming (Chapter 11).
- Clean up your writing—consider your choices for communicating mindfully.
- Be explicit of your good intentions; avoid the possibility of being misunderstood. If, for example, you think your sarcasm may not be interpreted as humor, then use an emoticon that shows you smiling :-).
- Follow the suggestions and guidelines for interpersonal communication generally; after all, they aren't that different.

Access ERIC, *Medline*, Psychlit, or Sociofile (databases of citations and abstracts of thousands of articles on communication and education, medicine, psychology, and sociology) and locate an article dealing with some aspect of conversation. What can you learn about conversation and interpersonal communication from this article? *(This would make an interesting review paper.)*

SUMMARY OF CONCEPTS AND SKILLS

In this chapter we looked at conversation and identified five stages that are especially important. We looked at the process of initiating, maintaining, repairing, and closing a conversation and at the skills of conversational effectiveness.

1. Conversation consists of five general stages: opening, feedforward, business, feedback, and closing.
2. The disclaimer (a statement that helps to ensure that your message will be understood as you wish and will not reflect negatively on you) is often used to prevent conversational problems. Hedges, credentialing, sin licenses, cognitive disclaimers, and appeals for the suspension of judgment are the major types of disclaimers.
3. Initiating conversations can be accomplished in various ways, for example, with self, other, relational, and context references.
4. Conversations are maintained by taking turns at speaking and listening; turn-maintaining and turn-yielding cues are used by the speaker and turn-requesting, turn-denying, and backchanneling cues are used by the listener.

5. Conversational closure may be achieved through a variety of methods; for example: Reflect back on conversation as in summarizing, directly state your desire to end the conversation, refer to future interaction, ask for closure, and state your pleasure with interaction.

6. Conversational repair is frequently undertaken through the excuse (a statement of explanation designed to lessen the negative impact of a speaker's messages). "I didn't do it," "It wasn't so bad," and "Yes, but" are the major types of excuses.

7. The skills of conversational effectiveness need to be applied with mindfulness, flexibility, cultural sensitivity, and metacommunication (as appropriate). Among the skills of conversational effectiveness are openness, empathy, positiveness, immediacy, interaction management, expressiveness, and other-orientation.

Check your ability to apply these skills. You will gain most from this brief experience if you think carefully about each skill and try to identify instances from your recent communications in which you did or did not act on the basis of the specific skill. Use a rating scale such as the following: 1 = almost always, 2 = often, 3 = sometimes, 4 = rarely, and 5 = almost never.

_____ 1. Follow the basic structure of conversations but deviate with good reason.

_____ 2. Regulate feedback in terms of positiveness, person and message focus, immediacy, monitoring, and supportiveness as appropriate to the situation.

_____ 3. Initiate conversations with a variety of people with comfort and relative ease.

_____ 4. Maintain conversations by smoothly passing the speaker turn back and forth.

_____ 5. Recognize when conversational repair is necessary and make the appropriate repairs in a timely fashion.

_____ 6. Close conversations with comfort and relative ease.

_____ 7. Apply the specific skills of interpersonal communication mindfully, flexibly, with cul-

tural sensitivity, and metacommunicate as appropriate.

_____ 8. Use the skills of conversational effectiveness (openness, empathy, positiveness, immediacy, interaction management, expressiveness, and other-orientation).

VOCABULARY QUIZ. THE LANGUAGE OF CONVERSATION

Match the terms listed here with their definitions. Record the number of the definition next to the term.

__2__ excuse

__4__ disclaimer

__10__ business

__1__ turn-yielding cues

__3__ feedforward

__8__ backchanneling cues

__7__ altercasting

__5__ conversation

__6__ immediacy

__9__ phatic communion

1. An interaction in which speaker and listener exchange their roles nonautomatically
2. A form of conversation repair
3. Information that tells the listener about the messages that will follow
4. A statement that aims to ensure that your message will be understood and will not reflect negatively on you
5. A conversation stage during which the major purpose of the interaction is accomplished
6. Cues that tell the listener that the speaker is finished and wishes to exchange the role of speaker for the role of listener
7. A kind of feedforward in which you place the listener in a specific role
8. Communicate information back to the speaker without assuming the role of speaker
9. Messages that open the channels of communication
10. The joining of speaker and listener

Interpersonal
Communication
and Culture

CHAPTER TOPICS	LEARNING GOALS	SKILLS GOALS
	After completing this chapter, you should be able to	*After completing this chapter, you should be able to*
Culture and Intercultural Communication	1. Define *intercultural communication* and explain why intercultural communication is so important today	Send and receive messages with a recognition of the influence of cultural factors
How Cultures Differ	2. Explain the ways in which cultures differ in terms of individualism and collectivism, high and low context, and masculinity and femininity	Communicate with the recognition that cultures differ in important ways that impact on interpersonal communication
Improving Intercultural Communication	3. Explain the guidelines for communicating effectively in intercultural situations	Follow the guidelines for intercultural communication

Evaluating Information

Use analysis to understand individual elements.   Analysis helps you appreciate the unique elements that make up a concept or person or event. For example, you might analyze a communication event into sources/receivers, messages, contexts, and feedback, for example—much as we described communication in the section, "The Concepts of Interpersonal Communication," in Chapter 1—and then analyze each of these concepts in detail. However, regardless of how thorough your examination of these parts might be, a full understanding requires seeing these pieces as they interact with each other. For example, to understand the appropriateness of self-disclosure in an intercultural situation, you would have to know the relationship between the speaker and listener, the context in which they interacted, the cultural backgrounds of the individuals, and how all these factors interacted with each other. For that, you need synthesis, the subject of the next critical thinking sidebar.

Nacirema culture is characterized by a highly developed market economy which has evolved in a rich natural habitat. While much of the people's time is devoted to economic pursuits, a large part of the fruits of these labors and a considerable portion of the day are spent in ritual activity. The focus of this activity is the human body, the appearance and health of which loom as a dominant concern in the ethos of the people. While such a concern is certainly not unusual, its ceremonial aspects and associated philosophy are unique.

The fundamental belief underlying the whole system appears to be that the human body is ugly and that its natural tendency is to debility and disease. Incarcerated in such a body, man's only hope is to avert these characteristics through the use of the powerful influences of ritual and ceremony. Every household has one or more shrines devoted to this purpose. The more powerful individuals in the society have several shrines in their houses and, in fact, the opulence of a house is often referred to in terms of the number of such ritual centers it possesses. Most houses are of wattle and daub construction, but the shrine rooms of the more wealthy are walled with stone. Poorer families imitate the rich by applying pottery plaques to their shrine walls.

While each family has at least one such shrine, the rituals associated with it are not family ceremonies but are private and secret. The rites are normally only discussed with children, and then only during the period when they are being initiated into these mysteries. I was able, however, to establish sufficient rapport with the natives to examine these shrines and to have the rituals described to me.

The focal point of the shrine is a box or chest which is built into the wall. In this chest are kept the many charms and magical potions without which no native believes he could live. These preparations are secured from a variety of specialized practitioners. The most powerful of these are the medicine men, whose assistance must be rewarded with substantial gifts. However, the medicine men do not provide the curative potions for their clients, but decide what the ingredients should be and then write them down in an ancient and secret language. This writing is understood only by the medicine men and by the herbalists who, for another gift, provide the required charm.

There remains one other kind of practitioner, known as a "listener." This witch-doctor has the power to exorcise the devils that lodge in the heads of people who have been bewitched. The Nacirema believe that parents bewitch their own children. Mothers are particularly suspected of putting a curse on children while teaching them the secret body rituals. The counter-magic of the witch-doctor is unusual in its lack of ritual. The patient simply tells the "listener" all his troubles and fears, beginning with the earliest difficulties he can remember. The memory displayed by the Nacirema in these exorcism sessions is truly remarkable. It is not uncommon for the patient to bemoan the rejection he felt upon being weaned as a babe, and a few individuals even see their troubles going back to the traumatic effects of their own birth.*

From these observations of anthropologist Horace Miner (1956) you might conclude that the Nacirema are a truly strange people. Look more carefully and you will see that we are the Nacirema and the rituals are our own (Nacirema is American spelled backwards). In the excerpt quoted, Miner describes the bathroom, the doctor writing prescriptions for the druggist, and the psychiatrist. This excerpt brings into focus the fact that cultural customs (our own and those of others) are not logical or natural. Rather, they are better viewed as useful or not useful to the members of that particular culture. The excerpt is an appropriate reminder against **ethnocentric** thinking (thinking your customs are right and others are wrong). It also awakens our consciousness, our mindful state, to our own customs and values.

CULTURE AND INTERCULTURAL COMMUNICATION

Culture, you'll recall from Chapter 1, refers to the lifestyle of a group of people, their values, beliefs, artifacts, ways of behaving, and ways of communicating. Culture includes all that members of a social group have produced and developed—their language, ways of thinking, art, laws, and religion—and that is transmitted from one generation to another through a process known as *enculturation.* You learn the values of your culture (that is, you become enculturated) through the teachings of your parents, peer groups, schools, religious institutions, and government agencies. You may wish to explore some of these cultural beliefs and values by taking the self-test, "What Are Your Cultural Beliefs and Values?" on the next page.

Acculturation refers to the processes by which a person's culture is modified through direct contact with or exposure to (say, through the mass media) another culture (Kim, 1988). For example, when immigrants settle in the United States (the host culture), their own culture becomes influenced by the host culture. Gradually, the values, ways of behaving, and beliefs of the host culture become more and more a part of the immigrants' culture. At the same time, of course, the host culture changes, too. Generally, however, the culture of the immigrant changes more. As Young Yun Kim (1988) puts it, "a reason for the essentially unidirectional change in the immigrant is the difference between the number of individuals in the new environment sharing the immigrant's original culture and the size of the host society."

The acceptance of the new culture depends on several factors (Kim, 1988). Immigrants who come from cultures similar to the host culture will become acculturated more easily. Similarly, those who are younger and

In this age of multiculturalism, how do you feel about Article II, Section 1, of the United States Constitution? The relevant section reads: "No person except a natural born citizen, or a citizen of the United States, at the time of the adoption of this Constitution, shall be eligible to the office of President."

Evaluating Information

Use synthesis to understand connections and relationships. In **synthesis** you combine elements into more meaningful wholes; you arrange and rearrange the elements into different patterns so you can see the problem from different perspectives. A synthesized explanation of communication would describe it as a set of interacting, interdependent elements—much as we described interpersonal communication in the transactional model and in the section on "Principles of Interpersonal Communication" in Chapter 1.

Both analysis and synthesis are helpful in achieving understanding of a complex process such as communication or intercultural interaction: analysis to understand the individual parts in detail and synthesis to understand how these parts interact and work together.

Source: From "Body Ritual Among the Nacirema" by Horace Miner. Reproduced by permission of the American Anthropological Association from *American Anthropologist,* 58:3, June 1958. Not for further reproduction.

SELF-TEST
What Are Your Cultural Beliefs and Values?

Here the extremes of 10 cultural differences are identified. For each characteristic indicate your own values:

A. if you feel your values are very similar to the extremes, select 1 or 7
B. if you feel your values are quite similar to the extremes, select 2 or 6
C. if you feel your values are fairly similar to the extremes, select 3 or 5
D. if you feel you're in the middle, select 4

Men and women are equal and are entitled to equality in all areas	Gender equality 1 2 3 4 5 6 7	Men and women are very different and should stick to the specific roles assigned to them by their culture
"Success" is measured by your contribution to the group	Group and individual orientation 1 2 3 4 5 6 7	"Success" is measured by how far you outperform others
Enjoy yourself as much as possible	Hedonism 1 2 3 4 5 6 7	Work as much as possible
Religion is the final arbiter of what is right and wrong; your first obligation is to abide by the rules of your religion	Religion 1 2 3 4 5 6 7	Religion is like any other social institution; it's not inherently moral or right just because it's a religion
Your first obligation is to your family; each person is responsible for the welfare of his or her family	Family 1 2 3 4 5 6 7	Your first obligation is to yourself; each person is responsible for himself or herself
Work hard now for a better future	Time orientation 1 2 3 4 5 6 7	Live in the present; the future may never come
Romantic relationships, once made, are forever	Relationship permanency 1 2 3 4 5 6 7	Romantic relationships should be maintained as long as they are more rewarding than punishing and dissolved when they are more punishing than rewarding
People should express their emotions openly and freely	Emotional expression 1 2 3 4 5 6 7	People should not reveal their emotions, especially those that may reflect negatively on them or others or make others feel uncomfortable
Money is extremely important and should be a major consideration in just about any decision you make	Money 1 2 3 4 5 6 7	Money is relatively unimportant and should not enter into life's really important decisions such as what relationship to enter or what career to pursue
The world is a just place; bad things happen to bad people and good things happen to good people; what goes around comes around	Belief in a just world 1 2 3 4 5 6 7	The world is random; bad and good things happen to people without any relationship to whether they are good or bad people

Thinking Critically About Cultural Beliefs, Values, and Communication This test was designed to help you explore the possible influence of your cultural beliefs and values on communication. If you visualize communication as involving choices, as already noted in Unit 1, then these beliefs will influence the choices you make and thus how you communicate and how you listen and respond to the communications of others. For example, your beliefs and values about gender equality will influence the way in which you communicate with and about the opposite sex. Your group and individual orientation will influence how you perform in work teams and how you deal with your peers at school and at work. Your degree of hedonism will influence the kinds of communications you engage in, the books you read, the television programs you watch. Your religious beliefs will influence the ethical system you follow in communicating. Review the entire list of 10 characteristics and try to identify one *specific* way in which each characteristic influences your communication.

better educated become acculturated more quickly than do older and less educated persons. Personality factors are also relevant. Persons who are risk takers and open-minded, for example, have a greater acculturation potential. Also, persons who are familiar with the host culture before immigration—whether through interpersonal contact or mass media exposure—will be acculturated more readily.

Intercultural communication, then, refers to communication that takes place between persons of different cultures and will be greatly influenced by both enculturation and acculturation processes. Intercultural communication occurs between persons who have different cultural beliefs, values, or ways of behaving. Figure 9.1 illustrates the ever-present influence of culture in communication.

This model illustrates that each communicator is a member of a different culture. Sometimes the cultural differences are slight—say, between persons from Canada and the United States. In other instances the differences are great—say, between persons from rural China and industrialized England.

What part does intercultural communication play in your personal, social, and professional life? Has this changed in the last five years? Is it likely to change in the next five years?

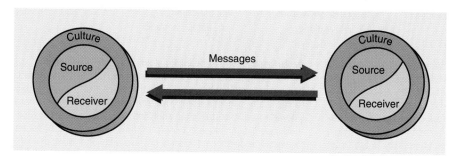

Figure 9.1

The Process of Intercultural Communication. The larger circles represent the culture of the individual communicator. The smaller circles represent the source/receiver. How would you represent the intercultural communication process?

This article contrasts the values of Americans, Japanese, and Arabs and explains how underlying values that we normally take for granted and rarely think about can exert powerful influences on how we communicate.

Values Across Cultures

To explain the cultural value contrast more clearly, we developed the accompanying table, which compares specific contrasting values of American, Japanese, and Arab cultures. Reading across the table from left to right provides perspective on the values of each culture.

In examining the table, we note that one of the top American values listed is freedom—freedom to choose your own destiny—whether it leads to success or failure. Japanese culture, on the other hand, finds a higher value in belonging. In this culture, you must belong to and support a group(s) to survive. Belonging to a group is more important to Japanese culture than individualism. Arab culture is less concerned with individualism or belonging to a group, concentrating instead on maintaining their own family security and relying on God for destiny. Individual identity is usually based on the background and position of each person's family.

The value American culture places on independence and individual freedom of choice naturally leads to the idea that everyone is equal regardless of age, social status, or authority. Japanese and Arab cultures, however, place more value on age and seniority. The Japanese individual will always give way to the feelings of the group, while Arabs respect authority and admire seniority and status.

In most business situations, Americans would come with a competitive attitude. The Japanese, conversely, value group cooperation in the pursuit of success. An Arab will make compromises in order to achieve a shared goal between two parties.

Cultural Contrasts in Value

Americans	Japanese	Arabs
1. Freedom	1. Belonging	1. Family security
2. Independence	2. Group harmony	2. Family harmony
3. Self-reliance	3. Collectiveness	3. Parental guidance
4. Equality	4. Age/Seniority	4. Age
5. Individualism	5. Group consensus	5. Authority
6. Competition	6. Cooperation	6. Compromise
7. Efficiency	7. Quality	7. Devotion
8. Time	8. Patience	8. Very patient
9. Directness	9. Indirectness	9. Indirectness
10. Openness	10. Go-between	10. Hospitality
11. Aggressiveness	11. Interpersonal	11. Friendship
12. Informality	12. Hierarchy	12. Formal/Admiration
13. Future-orientation	13. Continuation	13. Past and present
14. Risk-taking	14. Conservative	14. Religious belief
15. Creativity	15. Information	15. Tradition
16. Self-accomplishment	16. Group achievement	16. Social recognition
17. Winning	17. Success	17. Reputation
18. Money	18. Relationship	18. Friendship
19. Material possessions	19. Harmony with nature	19. Belonging
20. Privacy	20. Networking	20. Family network

In American culture, the phrase "time is money" is commonly accepted as a framework for the desire to finish a task in the shortest amount of time with the greatest profit. If a process is considered inefficient, it "wastes" time and money, and possibly will be abandoned. The Japanese, however, value high quality over immediate gain, and they patiently wait for the best possible result. Arab culture also values quality more than immediacy, but the trust in the business relationship is the most important value.

Americans emphasize individual achievement and are results-oriented; therefore, they value directness and openness when dealing with others, enabling individuals to finish tasks more quickly. Because of these values of directness and equal-ity, Americans tend to be informal when speaking and writing, often using first names. The Japanese prefer to follow an indirect, harmonious style when dealing with others. Go-betweens help to move the process along, and interpersonal harmony is considered more important than confrontation. The Arab culture, like the Japanese, avoids direct confrontation. However, Arabs prefer to negotiate directly in the spirit of hospitality and friendship until a compromise is reached.

Americans tend to be oriented toward the present and immediate gains, which explains why Americans value taking risks. To an American, accomplishing a task as quickly as possible brings the future closer. The Japanese, however, view time as a continuum, and are long-term oriented. As a result of their value of a long-term, quality-based relationship, the Japanese tend to be conservative and patient. The Arab culture believes that the present is a continuation of the past and that whatever happens in the future is due to fate and the will of God.

A principal value of American culture is individual achievement. When someone accomplishes something by him or herself, he or she expects and receives recognition for being a creative person, or the one who developed the best idea. The Japanese, because of their value of group achievement, seek information in order to help the entire group succeed. In Arab culture, the individual is not as important as preserving tradition. An Arab measures success by social recognition, status, honor, and reputation.

Thinking Critically About "Values Across Cultures." Are the observations of the authors consistent with what you know of these three cultures? What advice would you give an Arab or a Japanese who had just taken a position with an organization in the United States? What advice would you give an American who had just taken a position in an Arab country or in Japan? How might these differences in values influence American, Japanese, and Arab students studying, say, at your particular college?

Source: From *Multicultural Management*, pp. 62–64, by Farid Elashmawi and Philip R. Harris. Copyright © 1993 by Gulf Publishing Company. Used with permission. All rights reserved.

Note, too, that you send messages from your specific and unique cultural context. That context influences what you say and how you say it. Culture influences every aspect of your communication experience. And, of course, you receive messages through the filters imposed by a unique culture. Cultural filters, like filters on a camera, color the messages you receive. They influence what you receive and how you receive it. For example, some cultures rely heavily on television or newspapers for their news and trust them implicitly. Others rely on face-to-face interpersonal interactions, distrusting any of the mass communication systems. Some look to religious leaders for guides to behavior while others ignore them.

Communication between different cultures as well as communication between a smaller culture and the dominant or majority culture would be considered "intercultural communication." The model of intercultural communication presented in Figure 9.1 may just as logically be a model of communication between different smaller cultures or between a variety of other groups. The following types of communication may all be considered "intercultural" and, more important, subject to the same principles of effective communication identified in this chapter. The term *intercultural* is used broadly to refer to all forms of communication among persons from different groups as well as to the more narrowly defined area of communication between different cultures.

Visit one of the Websites for U.S. census data (for example, http://tiger.census.gov/cgi-bin/gazetteer). What interesting cultural information can you find that would be of value to someone learning the skills of interpersonal communication?

- Communication between cultures—for example, between Chinese and Portuguese, or between French and Norwegian.
- Communication between races (sometimes called *interracial communication*)—for example, between African Americans and Asian Americans.
- Communication between ethnic groups (sometimes called *interethnic communication*)—for example, between Italian-Americans and German-Americans.
- Communication between religions—for example, between Roman Catholics and Episcopalians, or between Muslims and Jews.
- Communication between nations (sometimes called *international communication*)—for example, between the United States and Argentina, or between China and Italy.

When you have to ask directions, you're confessing, in some way, your ignorance and your inability to control the situation by yourself. Men, according to Deborah Tannen (1990, 1994b), are especially reluctant to ask for directions because they want to maintain control; by asking for directions, they lose it. Do you find that men are more reluctant to ask for directions? Do you agree with Tannen's explanation?

Evaluating Information

Bring your cultural assumptions to consciousness for careful analysis. In thinking critically about communication or about any significant topic, it's crucial to identify your cultural assumptions and how they influence the way you view a topic. How do your cultural attitudes, beliefs, and values influence your responses to questions such as these?

1. Should Christian Science parents be prosecuted for preventing their children from receiving life saving treatment such as blood transfusions?
2. Should same sex marriages be legalized?
3. Should safe sex practices be taught in the schools?
4. Should assisted suicides be legalized?
5. What should be the fate of affirmative action?

CAUTION

Have you ever been guilty of **thinking with a closed mind** about gender differences? About racial differences? About religious differences? About affectional orientation?

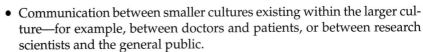

- Communication between smaller cultures existing within the larger culture—for example, between doctors and patients, or between research scientists and the general public.
- Communication between a smaller culture and the dominant culture—for example, between homosexuals and heterosexuals, or between senior citizens and the not-yet seniors.
- Communication between the sexes—between men and women. Some researchers would consider intergender communication as a separate area and only a part of intercultural communication when the two people are also from different races or nationalities. But, because gender roles are largely learned through culture, it seems useful to consider male-female communication as intercultural (Tannen, 1994b).

Regardless of your own cultural background, you will surely come into close contact with people from a variety of other cultures—people who speak different languages, eat different foods, practice different religions, and approach work and relationships in very different ways. It doesn't matter whether you're a longtime resident or a newly arrived immigrant. You are or soon will be living, going to school, working with, and forming relationships with people who are from very different cultures. Your day-to-day experiences are sure to become increasingly intercultural.

Consider your own willingness to engage in intercultural communication by taking the following self-test. It's designed to help you explore your openness to communicate with members of other cultures.

"Because my genetic programming prevents me from stopping to ask directions—that's why!"

Recently, the Emma Lazarus poem on the Statue of Liberty was changed. The words "the wretched refuse of your teeming shore" were deleted and the poem now reads:

> Give me your tired, your poor,
> Your huddled masses yearning to breathe free, . . .
> Send these, the homeless, tempest-tost to me
> I lift my lamp besides the golden door.

Harvard zoologist Stephen Jay Gould, commenting on this change, notes that with the words omitted, the poem no longer has balance or rhyme and, more important, no longer represents what Lazarus wrote (Gould, 1995). "The language police triumph," notes Gould, "and integrity bleeds." On the other hand, it can be argued that calling immigrants "wretched refuse" is insulting and degrading and that if Lazarus were writing today, she would not have used that phrase. How do you feel about this? Would you have supported the deletion of this line?

Acquiring Information

Examine the generality of generalizations with "except-ional analysis." *Except-ional analysis* is a useful technique when you want to see how general a generalization really is (Koberg & Bagnall, 1976a, b; Michalko, 1991). Applying except-ional analysis to the statement "No one likes a smart aleck," you might add "unless the smart aleck is a stand-up comic." To the statement "Money has nothing to do with happiness" you might add "unless you're comparing those above and those below the poverty line; in these cases money does make a difference." Here, for example, are generalizations that we seldom examine for exceptions. Ask yourself what are some actual or easily imagined exceptions to these generalizations: *Absence makes the heart grow fonder. Admit your mistakes. Be positive in conversation. Empathize with your relationship partner. Honesty is the best policy. Never betray a confidence. Work hard.*

I was raised to believe that excellence is the best deterrent to racism or sexism. And that's how I operate my life.
—Oprah Winfrey

SELF-TEST

How Open Are You Interculturally?

Instructions: Select a specific culture (national, racial, or religious) different from your own, and substitute this culture for the phrase *interculturally different person* in each question below. Indicate how open you would be to communicate in each of these situations, using the following scale:

5 = very open and willing
4 = open and willing
3 = neutral
2 = closed and unwilling
1 = very closed and unwilling

_____ 1. Talk with an interculturally different person while alone waiting for a bus.

_____ 2. Talk with an interculturally different person in the presence of those who are interculturally similar to you.

_____ 3. Have a close friendship with an interculturally different person.

(continued)

(continued)

_____ 4. Have a long-term romantic relationship with an interculturally different person.

_____ 5. Participate in a problem-solving group that is composed predominantly of interculturally different people.

_____ 6. Openly and fairly observe an information-sharing group consisting predominantly of interculturally different people.

_____ 7. Lead a group of interculturally different people through a problem-solving or information-sharing group.

_____ 8. Participate in a consciousness-raising group that is composed of one-half interculturally different people.

_____ 9. Listen openly and fairly to a conversation by an interculturally different person.

_____ 10. Ascribe a level of credibility for an interculturally different person identical to that ascribed to an interculturally similar person—all other things being equal.

Thinking Critically About Intercultural Openness This test was designed to raise questions rather than to provide answers. To calculate your scores, simply add your scores for all 10 questions. High scores (say, above 35) indicate considerable openness; low scores for any subset (say, below 20) indicate a lack of openness. Use these numbers for purposes of responding to the following questions rather than to indicate any absolute level of openness or closedness.

- Did you select the group on the basis of whether your attitudes were positive or negative? Why? What group would you be most open to interacting with? Least open?
- In which form of communication are you most open? Least open? Why?
- How open are you to learning about the importance of greater intercultural understanding and communication?
- How open are you to learning what members of other groups think of your cultural groups?

SKILL BUILDING EXERCISE 9.1.

How Do You Talk? As a Woman? As a Man?

Consider how you would respond in each of these situations if you were a typical woman and if you were a typical man.

1. A supervisor criticizes your poorly written report and says that it must be redone.
2. An associate at work tells you she may be HIV positive and is awaiting results of her blood tests.
3. You see two preteenaged neighborhood children fighting in the street; no other adults are around and you worry that they may hurt themselves.
4. An elderly member of your family tells you that he has to go into an old age home.
5. A colleague confides that she was sexually harassed and doesn't know what to do.
6. You're fed up with neighbors who act decidedly unneighborly—playing the television at extremely high volume, asking you to watch their two

young children while they go shopping, and borrowing things they rarely remember returning.

Thinking Critically About Women and Men Talking. Compare your responses with others and try to draw a profile of the following:
A. the typical woman as seen by women
B. the typical woman as seen by men
C. the typical man as seen by men
D. the typical man as seen by women

Consider the reasons for the profiles. For example, were the profiles drawn on the basis of actual experience? Popular stereotypes in the media? Evidence from research studies? How do these perceptions of the way women and men talk influence actual communication between women and men?

LISTENING.
Racist, Sexist, and Heterosexist Attitudes

Just as racist, sexist, and heterosexist attitudes will influence your language (as we note in the discussion of verbal messages in Unit 8), they also influence your listening.

In this type of listening, you only hear what the speaker is saying through your stereotypes. You assume that what the speaker is saying is unfairly influenced by the speaker's sex, race, or affectional orientation.

Sexist, racist, and heterosexist listening occur in a wide variety of situations. For example, when you dismiss a valid argument or attribute validity to an invalid argument, when you refuse to give someone a fair hearing, or when you give less credibility (or more credibility) to a speaker because the speaker is of a particular sex, race, or affectional orientation, you're practicing sexist, racist, or heterosexist listening. Put differently, sexist, racist, or heterosexist listening occurs when you listen differently to a person because of his or her sex, race, or affectional orientation when these characteristics are irrelevant to the communication.

But, there are many instances where these characteristics are relevant and pertinent to your evaluation of the message. For example, the sex of the speaker talking on pregnancy, fathering a child, birth control, or surrogate fatherhood is, most would agree, probably relevant to the message. And so it's not sexist listening to hear the topic through the sex of the speaker. It is sexist listening to assume that only one sex has anything to say that's worth hearing or that what one sex says can be discounted without a fair hearing. The same is true when listening through a person's race or affectional orientation.

Do you find this position a reasonable one to take? If not, how would you define sexist, racist, and heterosexist listening? Do you find this a useful concept in understanding effective communication? Do you find these types of listening operating in your classes? In your family? In your community? If you wanted to reduce this type of listening, how would you do it?

[The next Listening box appears on page 272.]

HOW CULTURES DIFFER

The ways in which cultures differ in terms of their (1) orientation (whether individual or collective), (2) context (whether high and low), and (3) masculinity-femininity impact significantly on interpersonal communication (Hofstede, 1997; Hall & Hall, 1987; Gudykunst, 1991). Another characteristic on which cultures differ is that of uncertainty, a topic discussed in Chapter 3.

Individual and Collective Cultures

Before reading about this concept, take the accompanying self-test to see where you and your own culture stand on this concept.

Visit one of the numerous travel Websites (for example, http://www.globalpassage.com/netstop, http://travel.epicurious.com/travel/g_cnt/home.html, http://www.travelchannel.com/, http://www.lonelyplanet.com/). What can you learn about intercultural communication from such sources? *(An interesting paper could be written reviewing one of these websites (or any of the websites noted in the chapter) and its usefulness for intercultural communication.)*

SELF-TEST
Individual and Collectivist Cultures

1 = almost always true
2 = more often true than false
3 = true about half the time and false about half the time
4 = more often false than true
5 = almost always false

_____ 1. My own goals rather than the goals of my group (for example, my extended family, my organization) are the more important.

_____ 2. I feel responsible for myself and to my own conscience rather than for the entire group and to the group's values and rules.

(continued)

(continued)

_____ 3. Success to me depends on my contribution to the group effort and the group's success rather than to my own individual success or to surpassing others.

_____ 4. I make a clear distinction between who is the leader and who are the followers and similarly make a clear distinction between members of my own cultural group and outsiders.

_____ 5. In business transactions, personal relationships are extremely important and so I would spend considerable time getting to know people with whom I do business.

_____ 6. In my communications I prefer a direct and explicit communication style; I believe in "telling it like it is," even if it hurts.

To compute your individualist–collectivist score, follow these steps:

1. Reverse the scores for items 3 and 5 such that

if your response was 1, reverse it to a 5
if your response was 2, reverse it to a 4
if your response was 3, keep it as 3
if your response was 4, reverse it to a 2
if your response was 5, reverse it to a 1

2. Add your scores for all six items, being sure to use the reverse scores for items 3 and 5 in your calculations. Your score should be between 6 (indicating a highly individualist orientation) to 30 (indicating a highly collectivist orientation).

3. Position your score on the following scale:

6	15	30
highly individualist	about equally individualist and collectivist	highly collectivist

Thinking Critically About Individual and Collective Orientation Does this scale and score accurately measure the way in which you see yourself on this dimension? Is this orientation going to help you achieve your personal and professional goals? Might it hinder you?

The distinction between individual and collective cultures revolves around the extent to which the individual's goals or the group's goals are given greater importance. Individual and collective tendencies are not mutually exclusive; this is not an all-or-none orientation but rather one of emphasis. Thus, you may, for example, compete with other members of your basketball team for most baskets or most valuable player award. At the same time, however, you will—in a game—act in a way that will benefit the group. In actual practice both individual and collective tendencies will help you and your team each achieve your goals.

At times, however, these tendencies may conflict; for example, do you shoot for the basket and try to raise your own individual score or do you pass the ball to another player who is better positioned to score the basket and thus benefit your team?

In an individualist culture, you're responsible for yourself and perhaps your immediate family; in a collectivist culture you're responsible for the entire group. Success, in an individualist culture, is measured by the extent to which you surpass other members of your group; you would take pride in standing out from the crowd. And your heroes—in the media, for example—are likely to be those who are unique and who stand apart. In a collectivist culture, success is measured by your contribution to the achievements of the group as a whole; you would take pride in your similarity to other members of your group. Your heroes, in contrast, are more likely to be team-players who do not stand out from the rest of the group's members.

In an individualist culture, you're responsible to your own conscience and responsibility is largely an individual matter. In a collectivist culture, you're responsible to the rules of the social group and responsibility for an accomplishment or a failure is shared by all members. Competition is promoted in individualist cultures while cooperation is promoted in collectivist cultures.

Distinctions between in-group members and out-group members are extremely important in collectivist cultures. In individualist cultures, where a person's individuality is prized, the distinction is likely to be less important.

Does the individualistic or collectivist nature of one's culture influence success in college? How would you go about researching this question?

High- and Low-Context Cultures

A high-context culture is one in which much of the information in communication is in the context or in the person—for example, information shared through previous communications, through assumptions about each other, and through shared experiences. The information is not explicitly stated in the verbal message. In a low-context culture most information is explicitly stated in the verbal message, and in formal transactions in written (contract) form.

To appreciate the distinction between high and low context, consider giving directions ("Where's the voter registration center?") to someone who knows the neighborhood and to a newcomer to your city. To someone who knows the neighborhood (a high-context situation) you can assume the person knows the local landmarks. So, you can give directions such as "next to the laundromat on Main Street" or "the corner of Albany and Elm." To the newcomer (a low-context situation), you cannot assume the person shares any information with you. So, you would have to use only those directions that even a stranger would understand, for example, "make a left at the next stop sign" or "go two blocks and then turn right."

High-context cultures are also collectivist cultures (Gudykunst & Ting-Toomey, 1991). These cultures (Japanese, Arabic, Latin American, Thai, Korean, Apache, and Mexican are examples) place great emphasis on personal relationships and oral agreements (Victor, 1992). Low-context cultures, on the other hand, are individualist cultures. These cultures (German, Swedish, Norwegian, and American are examples) place less emphasis on personal relationships and

How does your culture view interracial friendships? Interracial romantic relationships? Are there certain interracial relationships that are "approved" and others that are "disapproved?"

more emphasis on the written, explicit explanation, and, for example, on the written contracts in business transactions.

Members of high-context cultures spend lots of time getting to know each other before any important transactions take place. Because of this prior personal knowledge, a great deal of information is shared and therefore does not have to be explicitly stated. Members of low-context cultures spend less time getting to know each other and therefore do not have that shared knowledge. As a result everything has to be stated explicitly. High-context members, for example, rely more on nonverbal cues in reducing uncertainty (Sanders, Wiseman, & Matz, 1991).

When this simple difference is not understood, misunderstandings can easily result. For example, the directness characteristic of the low-context culture may prove insulting, insensitive, or unnecessary to the high-context cultural member. Conversely, to the low-context member, the high-context cultural member may appear vague, underhanded, or dishonest in his or her reluctance to be explicit or engage in communication that a low-context member would consider open and direct.

Another frequent source of misunderstanding related to high- and low-context cultures is face-saving (Hall & Hall, 1987). High-context cultures place a great deal more emphasis on face-saving. For example, they are more likely to avoid argument for fear of causing others to lose face whereas low-context members (with their individualist orientation) will use argument to win a point. Similarly, in high-context cultures criticism should only take place in private to enable the person to save face. Low-context cultures may not make this public-private distinction.

High-context cultures are reluctant to say "no" for fear of offending and causing the person to lose face. And so, for example, it's necessary to distinguish between the Japanese executive's "yes" when it means "yes" and when it means "no." The difference is not in the words used but in the way in which they are used. It's easy to see how the low-context individual may interpret this reluctance to be direct—to say "no" when you mean "no"—as a weakness or as an unwillingness to confront reality.

High-context cultures are reluctant to question the judgments of their superiors. And so, for example, if a product was being manufactured with a defect, workers might be reluctant to communicate this back to management (Gross, Turner, & Cederholm, 1987). Similarly, problems in procedures proposed by management might be detected by workers, but never communicated back to management. A knowledge of this tendency would alert a low-context management to look more deeply into the absence of communication. A summary of these differences as they relate to interpersonal communication is presented in Table 9.1.

Masculinity-Femininity

Cultures differ in the extent to which gender roles are distinct or overlap (Hofstede, 1997). In a highly "masculine" culture men are viewed as assertive, oriented to material success, and strong; women, on the other hand, are viewed as modest, focused on the quality of life, and tender. In a highly "feminine" culture, both men and women are supposed to be modest, oriented to maintaining the quality of life, and tender. On the basis of Hofstede's research, the 10 countries with the highest masculinity score (from the highest) are: Japan, Austria, Venezuela, Italy, Switzerland, Mexico, Ireland, Jamaica, Great Britain, and Germany. The 10 countries with the highest femininity score (from the highest) are: Sweden, Norway, Netherlands, Denmark, Costa

We hold these truths to be self-evident, that all men and women are created equal.
—*Elizabeth Cady Stanton*

Table 9.1 Some Individual and Collective Culture Differences

This table parallels the self-test presented earlier. As you read through this table, consider which statements you agree with and which you disagree with and how these beliefs influence your communications. This table is based on the work of Hofstede (1997), Hall and Hall (1987; Hall, 1983) and the interpretations by Gudykunst (1991) and Victor (1992). Can you identify additional differences between individual and collective cultures?

Individual (low-context) Cultures	Collective (high-context) Cultures
Your goals are most important	The group's goals are most important
You're responsible for yourself and to your own conscience	You're responsible for the entire group and to the group's values and rules
Success depends on your surpassing others; competition is emphasized	Success depends on your contribution to the group; cooperation is emphasized
Clear distinction is made between leaders and members	Little distinction is made between leaders and members; leadership is normally shared
Personal relationships are less important; hence, little time is spent getting to know each other in meetings	Personal relationships are extremely important; hence, much time is spent getting to know each other in meetings
Directness is valued; face-saving is seldom considered	Indirectness is valued; face-saving is a major consideration

Rica, Yugoslavia, Finland, Chile, Portugal, and Thailand. Out of 53 countries ranked, the United States ranked 15th most masculine.

A study of babies raised in Japan and the United States illustrates the ways in which cultures teach boys and girls differently (Otaki, Durrett, Richards, Nyquist, & Pennebaker, 1986). Boys raised in Japan are significantly noisier than girls; girls raised in the United States are significantly noisier than boys. This difference is most likely due to the ways in which mothers and, to a somewhat less extent, fathers, react to the babies. Both of these cultures are relatively high on masculinity and so not surprisingly teach girls and boys differently. In the United States, Japan, and Germany, for example, the emphasis on material success is seen in the importance that students place on grades. Students in such cultures are conditioned to strive to be the best and school failure is shameful and extremely significant. Students from more feminine cultures place greater emphasis on the quality of life and give much less importance to such issues as grades. Students here are content to be average and failing in school is unpleasant but nothing serious (Hofstede, 1997).

The masculine culture socializes its children to be assertive, ambitious, and competitive. And masculine organizations emphasize the bottom line and reward their workers on the basis of their contribution to the organization. The feminine culture socializes its children to be modest and to emphasize close interpersonal relationships. Feminine organizations are more likely to emphasize worker satisfaction and reward their workers on the basis of need; those who have large families, for example, may get raises that the single person would not get even if the single person contributed more to the organization.

Masculine cultures are more likely to confront conflicts directly and to competitively fight out any differences; they are more likely to emphasize win-lose conflict strategies. Feminine cultures are more likely to emphasize compromise and negotiation in resolving conflicts; they are more likely to emphasize win-win solutions.

Acquiring Information

See the middle ground; don't be blinded by extremes. In reading these sections on individualist and collective and high- and low-context cultures, be sure to see these concepts as identifying the opposites of a continuum but where individual cultures occupy positions somewhere between these opposites. Some cultures, of course, are more individual or more collective than others and so it's possible to arrange cultures in terms of their degree of individuality and to say that one culture is more individually oriented than another. Do be careful, however, that you don't use these terms to stereotype cultures and to obscure the great differences within any cultural group.

SKILL BUILDING EXERCISE 9.2.

Random Pairs

This exercise is designed to provide an opportunity for you to analyze communication and particularly intercultural communication *before* you get into the specifics of how cultures differ or how intercultural communication can be made more effective.

Refer to the table below and build an interpersonal communication act consisting of a source (plus identifiers), a message, and a receiver (plus identifiers) that would seem to involve some interesting cultural differ-ence. Once you've created your basic interpersonal act, explain the cultural factors (for example, individual and collective, high and low context, masculine and femi-nine, formal and informal) at work. Consider, too, the concepts discussed in earlier chapters. For example, are there likely to be significant self-concept differ-ences? Is apprehension likely to be a factor? Is self-dis-closure relevant here? Are certain perceptual or listening barriers especially likely to create problems?

Source–Sender	Further Identifiers	Message Situation	Receiver–Audience	Further Identifiers
1. Australian	1. Male MBA	1. Applying for an entry level office job	1. Australian	1. Male MBA
2. African American	2. Female, sightless and uneducated	2. Giving a speech to support a politician	2. African American	2. Female, sightless and uneducated
3. Latino	3. Male nursery school teacher	3. Asking for a date	3. Latino	3. Male nursery school teacher
4. Native American	4. Female PhD in physics	4. Giving a compliment	4. Native American	4. Female PhD in physics
5. Mexican	5. Male lawyer earning $400,000	5. Asking directions on a subway late at night	5. Mexican	5. Male lawyer earning $400,000
6. Jewish American	6. Father who owes three years child support	6. Asking for a sizable favor	6. Jewish American	6. "Deadbeat Dad" who owes child support
7. Asian	7. Gay male, uneducated	7. Working together on a project	7. Asian	7. Gay male, uneducated
8. European white	8. Lesbian, MD, mother of 4	8. Planning to marry	8. European white	8. Lesbian, MD, mother of 4
9. South African	9. Male welfare recipient for the last 7 years	9. Competing for leadership in an organization	9. South African	9. Male welfare recipient for the last 7 years
10. Japanese	10. Hearing impaired male, recent college graduate	10. Firing someone for incompetence	10. Japanese	10. Hearing impaired male, recent college graduate
11. Chinese	11. Female exconvict (armed robber)	11. Asking for a handout	11. Chinese	11. Female exconvict (armed robber)
12. Iranian	12. Homeless male, 25 years old	12. Complaining about poor service	12. Iranian	12. Homeless male, 25 years old
13. Ugandan	13. Male model	13. Buying an expensive sweater	13. Ugandan	13. Male model
14. German	14. Rap singer	14. Self-disclosing past indiscretions	14. German	14. Rap singer
15. Northern Irelander	15. Female HIV+ drug user	15. Opening a conversation	15. Northern Irelander	15. Female HIV+ drug user

Thinking Critically About Intercultural Communi-cation Between Random Pairs. If you were asked to give the two people involved in your interpersonal act advice to make their interaction more effective— even before they begin to speak—what would it be? What one rule would you ask them to follow? How likely is this communication dyad to succeed? To fail? What reasons can you offer for your prediction?

HOW TO . . .
Become Effective in Intercultural Communication

The characteristics of conversational effectiveness (discussed in detail in Chapter 8) are especially useful in intercultural communication, though caution needs to be exercised since there are likely to be important cultural differences in the way these characteristics are expected to be used. So, generally:

- Be **open** to differences among people. Be especially open to the different values, beliefs, and attitudes, as well as ways of behaving. Recognize, too, that a person's willingness to self-disclose or to respond to the openness of others is culturally influenced. Cultural differences may help to explain differences in openness and in responsiveness to openness.

- **Empathize** with the other person; put yourself into the position of the person from another culture. Try to see the world from this different perspective. Let the person know that you feel as he or she is feeling. Use facial expressions, an attentive and interested body posture, and understanding and agreement responses to communicate your empathy.

- Communicate **positiveness** to others; it helps put the other person at ease. It tells the other person that you're feeling good about interacting and are enjoying communicating. The appropriateness of positive statements about the self will vary greatly with the culture. For example, some cultures expect speakers to use self-denigrating comments and to minimize their own successes and abilities. Other cultures expect success and ability to be acknowledged openly and without embarrassment.

- Use **immediacy** to unite yourself with others and to surmount the differences. In intercultural communication this quality takes on special importance because of the great differences between you and the culturally different. Communicate a sense of togetherness to counteract the obvious intercultural differences, but realize that members of some cultures may prefer to maintain greater interpersonal and psychological distance from others.

- Engage in effective **interaction management,** for example, be especially sensitive to the differences in turn-taking. Many Americans, especially those from large urban centers, have the habit of interrupting or of completing the other person's sentences. Some cultures consider this especially rude.

- Communicate **expressiveness.** When differences among people are great, some feel uneasy and unsure of themselves. Counteract this by communicating genuine involvement in the interaction. Let the other person know that you're enjoying the interaction. Smile. Allow your facial muscles to express your interest and concern. Recognize, however, that some cultures may frown on too much expressiveness. So don't assume (necessarily) that the absence of expressiveness shows an unwillingness to participate in conversation; it may indicate just a difference in the way in which members of different cultures reveal their feelings.

- Be **other-oriented,** by, for example, focusing your attention and the conversation on the other person. See both the content and the relationship issues from the other person's point of view. Use the techniques already considered to show other-orientation, for example, active listening, asking questions, and maintaining eye contact (see Chapter 8). Some cultures, however, may find these techniques too intrusive, too direct. So, look carefully for feedback that comments on your own degree of other-orientation. Ask, for example, if your focus on the other person makes that person feel uncomfortable.

[The next How To box appears on page 269.]

How would you explain your cultural teachings in terms of masculine and feminine?

Evaluating Information

Beware of your confirmation and disconfirmation biases. Guard against the common tendency to seek out and evaluate information that supports or confirms your own position, your own bias (a confirmation bias). Similarly, guard against avoiding or finding fault with information that would contradict or disconfirm your position (disconfirmation bias). When acquiring and evaluating information ask yourself if you're being influenced by either of these biases. Bringing this possibility to consciousness will help you think more critically and more fairly about information.

How would you explain ethnocentrism? Can you give an example of your own ethnocentrism? Are your friends and relatives ethnocentric? How does this manifest itself in everyday interpersonal communications? *(Ethnocentrism or any of the important concepts covered in this chapter would make suitable concept paper topics.)*

IMPROVING INTERCULTURAL COMMUNICATION

Here are a variety of principles for increasing intercultural communication effectiveness—in conversation, on the job, in friendship and romantic relationships. These guidelines are based on the intercultural research of a wide variety of researchers (Barna, 1985; Ruben, 1985; Gudykunst, 1991; Hofstede, 1997).

Recognize and Reduce Your Ethnocentrism

Ethnocentrism, one of the biggest obstacles to intercultural communication, is the tendency to see others and their behaviors through your own cultural filters, often as distortions of your own behaviors. It's the tendency to evaluate the values, beliefs, and behaviors of your own culture as more positive, superior, logical, and natural than those of other cultures. To achieve effective interpersonal communication, you need to see both yourself and others as different but with neither being inferior or superior—not a very easily accomplished task.

Ethnocentrism exists on a continuum. People are not either ethnocentric or not ethnocentric; rather, most are somewhere between these polar opposites (see Table 9.2). Note also that your degree of ethnocentrism will depend on the group on which you're focusing. For example, if you're Greek-American, you may have a low degree of ethnocentrism when dealing with Italian-Americans but a high degree when dealing with Turkish-Americans or Japanese-Americans. Most important for our purposes is that your degree of ethnocentrism (and we are all ethnocentric to at least some degree) will influence your interpersonal (intercultural) communications.

Be Mindful

Being mindful rather than mindless (a distinction considered in Chapter 8), is generally helpful in intercultural communication situations. When you're in a mindless state, you behave with assumptions that would not normally pass

Table 9.2 The Ethnocentrism Continuum

Drawing from several researchers (Lukens, 1978; Gudykunst & Kim, 1984; Gudykunst, 1991), this table summarizes some interconnections between ethnocentrism and communication. In this table, five degrees of ethnocentrism are identified; in reality, of course, there are as many degrees as there are people. The "communication distances" are simply general terms that highlight the major communication attitude that dominates that level of ethnocentrism. Under "communications" are some ways people might interact given their particular degree of ethnocentrism. How would you have rated yourself on this scale five years ago? How would you rate yourself today?

CAUTION

How might **thinking with ethnocentrism,** by imposing assumptions (for example, other cultures are inferior) on your thinking, prevent objective and logical evaluation? Can you identify—if only to yourself—the areas in which you're ethnocentric?

Degrees of Ethnocentrism	Communication Distance	Communications
Low	Equality	Treats others as equals; evaluates other ways of doing things as equal to one's own
	Sensitivity	Wants to decrease distance between self and others
	Indifference	Lacks concern for others but is not hostile
	Avoidance	Avoids and limits interpersonal interactions with others; prefers to be with one's own kind
High	Disparagement	Engages in hostile behavior; belittles others; views one's own culture as superior to other cultures

intellectual scrutiny. For example, you know that cancer is not contagious and yet many people will avoid touching cancer patients. You know that people who cannot see do not have hearing problems and yet many people use a louder voice when talking to persons without sight. Approximately one-third of the participating college students said that they would not go swimming in a pool used by mental patients and that they would wash their hands after touching a mental patient (Wheeler, Farina, & Stern, 1984). When the discrepancies between available evidence and behaviors are pointed out and

Do you agree with the assumption that everyone is ethnocentric to some degree? If so, where would you place yourself on the ethnocentric continuum when the "other" is a person of the opposite sex? A member of a different affectional orientation? A member of a different race? A member of a different religion?

How might **thinking mindlessly** create intercultural difficulties? In what ways are you culturally mindless? In what ways are you culturally mindful?

your mindful state is awakened, you quickly realize that these behaviors are not logical or realistic.

When you deal with people from other cultures you're often in a mindless state and therefore function "nonrationally" in many ways. When your mindful state is awakened, as it is in textbook discussions such as this one, you may then resort to a more critical thinking mode, and recognize, for example, that other people and other cultural systems are different but not inferior or superior. Thus, these suggestions for increasing intercultural communication effectiveness may appear logical (even obvious) to your mindful state but are probably frequently ignored in your mindless state.

Face Fears

Another factor that stands in the way of effective intercultural communication is fear (Stephan & Stephan, 1985; Gudykunst, 1991). You may wish to think of your responses to the self test "How Open Are You Interculturally?" as you consider these specific types of fear. You may fear for your self-esteem. You may become anxious about your ability to control the intercultural situation or you may worry about your own level of discomfort.

You may fear that you will be taken advantage of by the member of this other culture. Depending upon your own stereotypes you may fear being lied to, financially duped, or made fun of. You may fear that members of this other group will react to you negatively. They may not like you or may disapprove of your attitudes or beliefs or they may even reject you as a person. Conversely, you may fear negative reactions from members of your own group. They might, for example, disapprove of your socializing with the interculturally different.

These fears—coupled with the greater effort that intercultural communication takes and the ease with which you communicate with those who are culturally similar—can easily create sufficient anxiety to make some people give up.

Recognize Differences

When you assume that all people are similar and ignore the differences between yourself and the culturally different, your intercultural efforts are likely to fail. This is especially true in the area of values, attitudes, and beliefs. It's easy to see and accept different hairstyles, clothing, and foods. But, when it comes to values and beliefs, it's easier to assume (mindlessly) that deep down we're all similar. We aren't. Henry may be a devout Baptist, while Carol may be an atheist, and Jan may be a Muslim. Each, consequently, sees his or her own life as having very different meanings because of the differences in their religious views. When you assume similarities and ignore differences, you may implicitly communicate to others that you feel your ways are the right ways and their ways are the wrong ways. The result is confusion and misunderstanding on both sides.

Has anyone ever assumed something about you (because you were a member of a particular culture) that was not true? Did you find this disturbing? *(Your experiences in these types of situations would make an interesting personal experience paper topic.)*

Recall from Chapter 8 the various maxims that different cultures use in communicating, for example, the principles of cooperation, peaceful relations, politeness, and self-denigration. Misunderstandings are easy when two people follow different maxims but assume there is sameness.

NON SEQUITUR

© 1993 Washington Post Writers Group. Reprinted with permission.

This cartoon can be appreciated on a number of different levels. On one level it depicts our tendency to be unconcerned with the possible pain of animals and people not like ourselves. On another level it depicts our inability to decipher what someone from another culture means by their nonverbal communication. On still another level it depicts our inability to empathize with those who are different from ourselves. What does it mean to you?

Recognize Differences Among the Culturally Different Group

Within every cultural group there are wide and important differences. Just as we know that all Americans are not alike (think of the various groups found in your city or just your own school), so neither are all Jamaicans, Koreans, Mexicans, and so on.

Within each culture there are many smaller cultures. These smaller cultures differ from each other and from the majority culture. Further, members of one smaller culture may share a great deal with members of that same smaller culture in another part of the world. For example, farmers in Indiana may have more in common with farmers in Borneo than with bankers in Indianapolis. For example, all will be concerned with and knowledgeable about weather conditions and their effects on crop growth, crop rotation techniques, and soil composition. Of course, in many other things these farmers, so similar when it comes to farming, may be drastically different on such issues as government subsidies, trade regulations, and sales techniques.

Avoid Overattribution

You'll recall from Chapter 3 that overattribution is the tendency to attribute too much of a person's behavior or attitudes to one of that person's characteristics (She thinks that way because she's a woman; he believes that because he was raised a Catholic). In intercultural communication situations, you see overattribution in two ways. First, it's the tendency to see too much of what a person believes or does as caused by the person's cultural identification. Second, it's the tendency to see a person as a spokesperson for that particular culture just because she or he is a member. As demonstrated in the discussion of perception in Chapter 3, people's ways of thinking and ways of behaving are influenced by a wide variety of factors; culture is just one of them.

Recognize Meaning Differences in Verbal and Nonverbal Messages

Earlier, we noted that meaning does not exist in the words we use (Chapter 5). Rather, it exists in the person using the words. This principle is especially important in intercultural communication. Consider the differences in meaning that might exist for the word *woman* to an American and an Iranian. What about *religion* to a Christian Fundamentalist and to an atheist or *lunch* to a Chinese rice farmer and a Wall Street executive?

CAUTION

In what ways can **thinking by overattribution,** because it prevents you from seeking and evaluating information other than the one or two factors that you assume are causing everything else (a kind of "allness"), hinder critical thinking? Have others ever committed overattribution when evaluating you? What problems did it create?

Are such statements as "Columbus discovered America in 1492" and "Ponce de Leon discovered Florida and claimed it for the King of Spain in 1513" ethnocentric? If so, how would you rephrase them so that they represent a more multicultural perspective?

Even when we use the same words—as would be the case between a New England prep school student and a homeless teenager in Los Angeles—the meanings of many terms (consider *security*, *future*, and *family*) would be drastically different.

When it comes to nonverbal messages, the potential differences are even greater. Thus, the over-the-head clasped hands that signify victory to an American may signify friendship to a Russian. To an American, holding up two fingers to make a V signifies victory. To certain South Americans, however, it's an obscene gesture that corresponds to our extended middle finger. Tapping the side of your nose will signify that you and the other person are in on a secret—if in England or Scotland—but that the other person is nosy—if in Wales. A friendly wave of the hand will prove insulting in Greece, where the wave of friendship must show the back rather than the front of the hand.

Avoid Violating Cultural Rules and Customs

Each culture has its own rules and customs for communicating. These rules identify what is appropriate and what is inappropriate. Thus, for example, if you lived in a middle-class community in Connecticut you would follow the rules of the culture and call the person you wish to date three or four days in advance. If you lived in a different culture, you might be expected to call the parents of your future date weeks or even months in advance. In this same Connecticut community, you might say, as a friendly gesture to people you don't ever want to see again, "come on over and pay us a visit." To members of other cultures, this comment is sufficient for them to visit at their convenience.

In some cultures, members show respect by avoiding direct eye contact with the person to whom they are speaking. In other cultures this same eye avoidance would signal lack of interest. In some Mediterranean cultures men walk arm-in-arm. Other cultures consider this inappropriate.

A good example of a series of rules for an extremely large and important culture that many people do not know appears in Table 9.3, "The Ten Commandments for Communicating with People with Disabilities." In looking over the list of suggestions, consider if you have seen any violations. Were you explicitly taught any of these principles?

Avoid Evaluating Differences Negatively

Be careful not to evaluate negatively the cultural differences that you do perceive. Be careful that you don't fall into the trap of ethnocentric thinking, evaluating your culture positively and other cultures negatively. For example, many Americans of Northern European descent evaluate negatively the tendency of many Hispanics and Southern Europeans to use the street for a gathering place, for playing Dominos, and for just sitting on a cool evening. Whether you like or dislike using the street in this way, recognize that neither is logically correct and neither is incorrect. This street behavior is simply adequate or inadequate for *members of the culture.*

Remember that you learned your behaviors from your culture. The behaviors are not natural or innate. Therefore, try viewing these variations nonevaluatively. See these as different but equal.

Table 9.3 Ten Commandments for Communicating with People with Disabilities

1. Speak directly rather than through a companion or sign language interpreter who may be present.
2. Offer to shake hands when introduced. People with limited hand use or an artificial limb can usually shake hands and offering the left hand is an acceptable greeting.
3. Always identify yourself and others who may be with you when meeting someone with a visual impairment. When conversing in a group, remember to identify the person to whom you're speaking.
4. If you offer assistance, wait until the offer is accepted. Then listen or ask for instructions.
5. Treat adults as adults. Address people who have disabilities by their first names only when extending that same familiarity to all others. Never patronize people in wheelchairs by patting them on the head or shoulder.
6. Do not lean against or hang on someone's wheelchair. Bear in mind that disabled people treat their chairs as extensions of their bodies.
7. Listen attentively when talking with people who have difficulty speaking and wait for them to finish. If necessary, ask short questions that require short answers, a nod, or shake of the head. Never pretend to understand if you're having difficulty doing so. Instead repeat what you have understood and allow the person to respond.
8. Place yourself at eye level when speaking with someone in a wheelchair or on crutches.
9. Tap a hearing-impaired person on the shoulder or wave your hand to get his or her attention. Look directly at the person and speak clearly, slowly, and expressively to establish if the person can read your lips. If so, try to face the light source and keep hands, cigarettes, and food away from your mouth when speaking.
10. Relax. Don't be embarrassed if you happen to use common expressions such as "See you later," or "Did you hear about this?" that seem to relate to a person's disability.

Source: From *The New York Times*, June 7, 1993. Courtesy of NYT Permissions.

Recognize the Normalcy of Culture Shock

Culture shock refers to the psychological reaction you experience at being in a culture very different from your own (Furnham & Bochner, 1986). Culture shock is normal; most people experience it when entering a new and different culture. Nevertheless, it can be unpleasant and frustrating and can sometimes lead to a permanently negative attitude toward this new culture. Understanding the normalcy of culture shock will help lessen any potential negative implications.

Part of culture shock results from your feelings of alienation, conspicuousness, and difference from everyone else. When you lack knowledge of the rules and customs of the new society, you cannot communicate effectively. You're apt to blunder frequently and seriously. The person experiencing culture shock may not know some very basic things:

- how to ask someone for a favor or pay someone a compliment
- how to extend or accept an invitation for dinner
- how early or how late to arrive for an appointment or how long to stay
- how to distinguish seriousness from playfulness and politeness from indifference
- how to dress for an informal, formal, or business function
- how to order a meal in a restaurant or how to summon a waiter

Anthropologist Kalervo Oberg (1960), who first used the term *culture shock,* notes that it occurs in stages. These stages are useful for examining many

Visit one of the online news organizations (for example, www.pbs.org/, www.npr.org, www.c/net.com, www.reutershealth.com, www.cnnfn.com) for a recent item on culture. Of what value might such information be to someone engaging in intercultural communication?

A commonly encountered case of culture shock occurs with international students. For example, for the 1993–94 academic year, there were 449,749 international students in the United States (*New York Times,* January 4, 1995, A17). The 10 countries sending the most students to the United States are China (44,381 students), Japan (43,770), Taiwan (37,581), India (34,796), South Korea (31,076), Canada (22,655), Hong Kong (13,752), Malaysia (13,718), Indonesia (11,744), and Thailand (9,537). If you're an international student, can you describe your culture shock experiences? If you're not an international student, can you visualize the culture shock you might experience if you were to study in another culture?

encounters with the new and the different. Going away to college, getting married, or joining the military, for example, can all result in culture shock.

At the first stage, the **honeymoon,** there is fascination, even enchantment, with the new culture and its people. You finally have your own apartment. You're your own boss. Finally, on your own! When in groups of people who are culturally different, this stage is characterized by cordiality and friendship among these early and superficial relationships. Many tourists remain at this stage because their stay in foreign countries is so brief.

At stage two, the **crisis stage,** the differences between your own culture and the new one create problems. No longer do you find dinner ready for you *unless* you do it yourself. Your clothes are not washed or ironed unless you do them yourself. Feelings of frustration and inadequacy come to the fore. This is the stage at which you experience the actual shock of the new culture. In one study of foreign students coming from over 100 different countries and studying in 11 different countries, it was found that 25% of the students experienced depression (Klineberg & Hull, 1979).

During the third period, the **recovery,** you gain the skills necessary to function effectively. You learn how to shop, cook, and plan a meal. You find a local laundry and figure you'll learn how to iron later. You learn the language and ways of the new culture. Your feelings of inadequacy subside.

At the final stage, the **adjustment,** you adjust to and come to enjoy the new culture and the new experiences. You may still experience periodic difficulties and strains, but on a whole, the experience is pleasant. Actually, you're now a pretty decent cook. You're even coming to enjoy it. You're making a good salary, so why learn to iron?

Time spent in a foreign country is not sufficient for the development of positive attitudes; in fact, the development of negative attitudes is often found. Rather, friendships with nationals is what is crucial for satisfaction with the new culture. Contacts only with other expatriates or sojourners is not sufficient (Torbiorn, 1982).

People may also experience culture shock when they return to their original culture after living in a foreign culture, a kind of reverse culture shock (Jandt, 1995). Consider, for example, the Peace Corps volunteers who work in a rural and economically deprived area. Upon returning to Las Vegas or Beverly Hills they, too, may experience culture shock. Sailors who served long periods aboard ship and then return to an isolated farming community might also experience culture shock. In these cases, however, the recovery period is shorter and the sense of inadequacy and frustration is less.

> I am not an Athenian or a Greek, but a citizen of the world.
>
> —Socrates

SKILL BUILDING EXERCISE 9.3.

Confronting Intercultural Difficulties

How might you deal with each of the following obstacles to intercultural understanding and communication?

1. Your friend makes fun of Radha who comes to class in her native African dress. You feel you want to object to this.
2. Craig and Louise are an interracial couple. Craig's family treats him fairly but virtually ignore Louise. They never invite Craig and Louise as a couple to dinner or to partake in any of the family affairs. The couple decide that they should confront Craig's family.
3. Malcolm is a close friend and is really an open-minded person. But, he has the habit of referring to members of other racial and ethnic groups with the most derogatory language. You decide to tell him that you object to this way of talking.
4. Tom, a good friend of yours, wants to ask Pat out for a date. Both you and Tom know that Pat is a lesbian and will refuse the date and yet Tom says he's going to have some fun and ask her anyway—just to give her a hard time. You think this is wrong and want to tell Tom you think so.
5. Your parents persist in holding stereotypes about other religious, racial, and ethnic groups. These stereotypes come up in all sorts of conversations. You're really embarrassed by these attitudes and feel you must tell your parents how incorrect you think these stereotypes are.
6. Lenny, a colleague at work, recently underwent a religious conversion. He now persists in trying to get everyone else—yourself included—to undergo this same religious conversion. Every day he tells you why you should convert, gives you literature to read, and otherwise persists in trying to convert you. You decide to tell him that you find this behavior offensive.

Thinking Critically About Intercultural Difficulties.   Why is it so difficult to call to the attention of friends or family their intercultural communication shortcomings? Of all the intercultural problems discussed in this chapter, with which do you have the greatest difficulty? Are these difficulties the result of attitudes and beliefs you hold? Habit and custom?

SUMMARY OF CONCEPTS AND SKILLS

In this chapter we explored culture and intercultural communication, the ways in which cultures differ, and suggestions for improving intercultural communication.

1. *Culture* refers to the specialized lifestyle of a group of people. It consists of their values, beliefs, artifacts, ways of behaving, and ways of communicating. Each generation teaches its culture to the next generation. It's transmitted through a process of *enculturation. Acculturation* refers to the processes by which your culture is modified through direct contact with or exposure to another culture.

2. Intercultural communication encompasses a broad range of communication. It includes at least the following: communication between cultures, between races, between ethnic groups, between religions, and between nations.

3. Cultures differ in the degree to which they teach individualist or collectivist orientations.

4. High-context cultures are those in which much of the information is in the context or in the person's nonverbals; low-context cultures are those in which most of the information is explicitly stated in the message.

5. Cultures differ in the degree to which gender roles are distinct or overlap. In a highly "masculine" culture men are viewed as assertive, oriented to material success, and strong; women are viewed as modest, focused on the quality of life, and tender.

6. Intercultural communication can be made more effective by, for example, reducing ethnocentrism, communicating mindfully, facing fears, recognizing cultural differences between yourself and others, recognizing cultural differences within any group, recognizing meaning differences, not violating cultural rules and customs, and not evaluating differences negatively.

Throughout this chapter, a variety of specific skills were considered. Check your ability to apply these skills. Use a rating scale such as the following: 1 = almost always, 2 = often, 3 = sometimes, 4 = rarely, and 5 = almost never.

_____ 1. Communicate with an understanding of the role of culture and how it influences the messages sent and the messages received.

_____ 2. Appreciate the communication differences in individual and collective cultures and adjust communications accordingly.

_____ 3. Respond to intercultural communications in light of high and low context differences.

_____ 4. Respond to intercultural communication in light of differences in masculinity and femininity.

_____ 5. Recognize and try to combat ethnocentric thinking.

_____ 6. Be mindful of the intercultural communication process.

_____ 7. Communicate in intercultural situations with a recognition of potential differences between yourself and the culturally different.

_____ 8. Communicate in intercultural situations with a recognition of the differences within any cultural group.

_____ 9. Communicate in intercultural situations with a recognition of the possible differences in meanings for both verbal and nonverbal signals.

_____10. Communicate in intercultural situations with a recognition of the possible differences in cultural rules and customs.

_____11. Communicate in intercultural situations without evaluating differences negatively.

_____12. Communicate interculturally with appropriate degrees of openness, empathy, positiveness, immediacy, interaction management, expressiveness, and other-orientation.

VOCABULARY QUIZ. THE LANGUAGE OF INTERCULTURAL COMMUNICATION

Match the terms of intercultural communication with their definitions. Record the number of the definition next to the appropriate term.

_____ high-context cultures

_____ acculturation

_____ intercultural communication

_____ low-context cultures

_____ ethnocentrism

_____ culture

_____ mindfulness

_____ enculturation

_____ individual cultures

_____ collective cultures

1. A culture in which most information is explicitly stated in the verbal message.

2. The specialized lifestyle of a group of people—consisting of their values, beliefs, artifacts, ways

of behaving, and ways of communicating—passed on from one generation to the next.

3. The process by which culture is transmitted from one generation to another by, for example, parents, peer groups, and schools.

4. Communication that takes place between persons of different cultures or who have different cultural beliefs, values, or ways of behaving.

5. The process through which a person's culture is modified through contact with another culture.

6. The tendency to evaluate other cultures negatively and our own culture positively.

7. That mental state in which we are aware of the logic that governs behaviors.

8. Cultures that emphasize competition, individual success, and where your responsibility is largely to yourself.

9. A culture in which much of the information in communication is in the context or the person and is not made explicit in the verbal message.

10. Cultures that emphasize the member's responsibility to the entire group rather than just to himself or herself.

Interpersonal Communication and Relationships

CHAPTER TOPICS	LEARNING GOALS	SKILLS GOALS
	After completing this chapter, you should be able to	*After completing this chapter, you should be able to*
Relationships and Relationship Stages	1. Explain the advantages and disadvantages of interpersonal relationships and the six-stage model of interpersonal relationships	Formulate both verbal and nonverbal messages appropriate to the relationship stage
Relationship Theories	2. Explain attraction, rules, social penetration, social exchange, and equity theories	Assess your own relationships in terms of attraction, rules, social penetration, social exchange, and equity theories
Improving Relationship Communication	3. Explain the suggestions for improving communication in relationships	Use empathy and self-disclosures, be open to change, fight fair, and be reasonable in relationship communication

The story is told that in ancient Greece, a young man, Pythias, was condemned to death by the tyrant Dionysius for speaking out against the government. Pythias begged Dionysius to delay his execution until he was able to put his family affairs in order. Dionysius agreed but insisted that someone remain in Pythias's place just in case he didn't come back. Damon, Pythias's friend, volunteered and agreed to be executed if Pythias did not return. Damon was then placed in prison while Pythias traveled home. On the day of the scheduled execution, Pythias was nowhere to be found. Without any anger or animosity toward his friend, Damon prepared for his death. But, just before the execution could be carried out, Pythias arrived and begged the court's forgiveness for his unavoidable delay; he was ready to be executed and asked that his friend be set free. Dionysius was so impressed by this friendship that he not only freed Damon but pardoned Pythias and asked if he could join the two of them in this extraordinary friendship.

O f course this is an exceptional story and an exceptional relationship. In a way, however, all relationships are exceptional and all tell exceptional stories.

RELATIONSHIPS AND RELATIONSHIP STAGES

Although we think of relationships as largely face-to-face interactions, the huge number of Internet relationships cannot be ignored. As the number of Internet users increases, commercial services are adding, expanding, and improving their services for computer relationships. Books such as Phyllis Phlegar's (1995) *Love Online: A Practical Guide to Digital Dating* and Linda K. Fuller's (1995) *Media-Mediated Relationships: Straight and Gay, Mainstream and Alternative Perspectives* attest to the growing importance of online relationships. Even the afternoon television talk shows have been focusing on computer relationships, especially getting people together who have established a relationship online but who have never met. Clearly, many are turning to the Internet to find a friend or, more often, a romantic partner. Some are using the Internet as their only means of interaction; others are using it as a way of beginning a relationship and intend to later supplement computer talk with photographs, phone calls, and face-to-face meetings.

Visit one of the online bookstores (for example, www.amazon.com, www.bookserve.com) for popular books on improving interpersonal relationships. What relationship themes dominate the popular market and, by implication, the popular mind?

Whether face-to-face or online, each person develops interpersonal relationships for different reasons, with the idea that relationships will provide several important advantages over a life without such relationships. For example, interacting with another person helps you lessen loneliness. People who have experienced long periods of isolation seem unanimous in claiming that the major difficulty was the lack of human contact, of someone to talk with. Also, we all need the stimulation of the ideas and personalities others provide.

Largely through contact with others, you learn about yourself. You see yourself in part through the eyes of others. If your friends see you as warm and generous, for example, you will also see yourself as warm and generous.

Relationships help you enhance your self-esteem, your sense of self-worth. Having a relational partner makes you feel worthy and desirable. When you're fortunate enough to have a supportive partner, your relationship enhances your self-esteem even more. The most general reason for establishing relationships is to maximize your physical, mental, and social pleasures and minimize your pains. You want to share with others both your good fortune and your pain.

Online relationships have a few additional advantages. For example, it's safe in terms of avoiding the potential for physical violence as well as sexually transmitted diseases from someone you really don't know. Unlike relationships established in face-to-face encounters where physical appearance tends to outweigh personality, on the Internet the person's inner qualities are communicated first. Friendship and romantic interaction on the Internet is a natural boon to shut-ins and the extremely shy that make traditional ways of meeting someone difficult. Another obvious advantage is that the number of people you can reach is so vast that it's relatively easy to find someone who matches what you're looking for. The situation is analogous to finding a book that covers just what you need from a library of millions of volumes rather than from a local library of several thousands. Still another advantage for many is that the socioeconomic and educational status of people on the Net is significantly higher than you're likely to find in bar or singles group.

Some researchers have argued that computer talk is more empowering for those with "physical disabilities or disfigurements" where face-to-face interactions are often superficial and often end with withdrawal (Lea & Spears, 1995; Bull & Rumsey, 1988). By eliminating the physical cues, computer talk equalizes the interaction and does not put the disfigured person, for example, at an immediate disadvantage in a society where physical attractiveness is so highly valued. You're more in control of what you want to reveal of your physical self and of course you may do it gradually.

There are also, however, disadvantages that need to be weighed. For example, close relationships put pressure on you to reveal yourself and to expose your vulnerabilities. While this is generally worthwhile in the context of a supporting and caring relationship, it may backfire if the relationship deteriorates and these weaknesses are used against you. Furthermore, many find no satisfaction in revealing themselves and no advantage in exposing weaknesses.

In close relationships one person's behavior influences the other person's, sometimes to great extents. Your time is no longer entirely your own. And although you enter a relationship to spend more time with this special person, you also incur time obligations with which you may not be happy. Similarly, if your money is pooled (as it is in many close relationships), then your financial successes have to be shared as do your partner's loses. On the positive side, of course, your partner shares your loses and you share in your partner's gains. Perhaps the obligation that creates the most difficulty is the emotional obligations you incur. To be emotionally responsive and sensitive is not always easy. When one person becomes ill, the pressures of care-taking increase sometimes to the point of breakdown.

Close relationships can result in abandoning other relationships. Sometimes, it involves someone you like but your partner can't stand. And so, you may give up this person or see him or her less often. More often, however, it's simply a matter of time and energy; relationships take a lot of both. You consequently have less to give to these other and less intimate relationships.

Once entered into, a relationship may prove difficult to get out of. In some cultures, for example, religious pressures may prevent married couples from separating. If children are part of the relationship, it may be emotionally difficult to exit. And, if lots of money is involved, dissolving a relationship can often mean giving up the fortune you have spent your life accumulating.

And, of course, your partner may break your heart. Your partner may leave you—against all your pleading and promises. Your hurt will be in proportion to how much you care and need your partner. The person who cares a lot is hurt a lot, the person who cares little is hurt little; it's one of life's little ironies.

There are also disadvantages that are perhaps unique to online relationships. For one thing, you can't see what the other person looks like. Unless you exchange photos or meet face-to-face you won't know what the person looks like. And even if photos are exchanged, how certain can you be that the

Are there other advantages and disadvantages of relationships that should be added to those identified here?

photos are of the person or that they were taken recently? In addition, you cannot hear their voices—which, as demonstrated in Unit 13, communicates a great deal of information. Of course, you can always add an occasional phone call to give you this added information.

People can present a false self with little chance of detection. For example, minors may present themselves as adults and adults may present themselves as children for illicit and illegal sexual communications and, perhaps, meetings. Similarly, you can present yourself as rich when you're poor, as mature when you're immature, as serious and committed when you're just enjoying the experience.

Another potential disadvantage—though some might argue is actually an advantage—is that computer interactions may become all-consuming and may substitute for face-to-face interpersonal relationships.

All relationships have the potential for bringing rewards and punishments, advantages and disadvantages; in an imperfect world, that's to be expected. The insights and skills of interpersonal communication and relationships, however, should stack the odds in favor of greater and longer lived advantages and fewer and shorter lived disadvantages.

The six-stage model shown in Figure 10.1 describes the significant stages you might go through in developing (and perhaps even dissolving) your relationships as you try to achieve your relationship goals. The stages describe the development of relationships, whether friendship or love. As a general description of relationships, the stages seem standard. The six stages are *contact, involvement, intimacy, deterioration, repair,* and *dissolution.* Each stage can be divided into an initial and a final phase.

> Communication is to a relationship what breathing is to maintaining life.
>
> —*Virginia Satir*

Contact

At the contact stage there is first *perceptual contact*—you see what the person looks like, you hear what the person sounds like, you might even smell the person. From this you get a physical picture: sex, approximate age, height, and so on. After this perception, there is usually *interactional contact.* Here the contact is superficial and impersonal. This is the stage of "Hello, my name is Joe"—the stage at which you exchange basic information that needs to come before any more intense involvement. This interactional contact may also be nonverbal as, for example, in the exchange of smiles (Table 10.1).

This is the stage at which you initiate interaction ("May I join you?") and engage in invitational communication ("May I buy you a drink?"). According to some researchers, it's at this stage—within the first four minutes of initial interaction—that you decide if you want to pursue the relationship or not (Zunin & Zunin, 1972).

At the contact stage, physical appearance is especially important because it's the most readily available to sensory inspection. Yet through both verbal and nonverbal behaviors, qualities such as friendliness, warmth, openness, and dynamism are also revealed at this stage.

If you like the individual and want to pursue the relationship, you go to the second stage, involvement. Here are the five most often used strategies that people use to move to greater involvement (Tolhuizen, 1989):

- Increase contact
- Give tokens of affection such as gifts, cards, or flowers
- Increase your own attractiveness, to make yourself more desirable

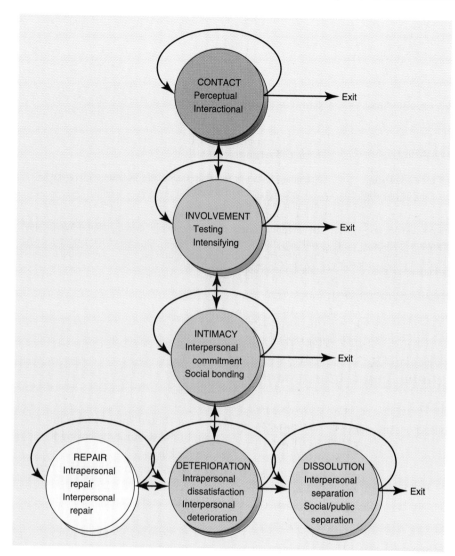

Figure 10.1
The Six Stages of Relationships.

Because relationships differ so widely, it's best to think of any relationship model as a tool for talking about relationships rather than as a specific map that indicates how you move from one relationship position to another. Are there other stages that you can identify that would further explain what goes on in relationships? Can you provide a specific example, from literature or from your own experience, that would illustrate some or all of these stages?

- Do things that suggest intensifying the relationships, for example, make your partner jealous
- Become more sexually intimate

Involvement

At this stage a sense of mutuality, of being connected, develops. During this stage you experiment and try to learn more about the other person. At the initial phase of involvement, there is a kind of *testing* that goes on. You want to see if your initial judgment—made perhaps at the contact stage—proves reasonable. And so you may ask questions—"Where do you work?" "What are you majoring in?"

If you're committed to getting to know the person even better, you continue your involvement by *intensifying* your interaction. Here you not only try to get to know the other person better but you also begin to reveal yourself. It's at this stage that you begin to share your feelings and your emotions. If this is to be a romantic relationship, you might date. If it's to be a friendship, you might share your mutual interests—go to the movies or to some sports event together.

I feel that the moment a date happens that it is a social encounter. And the question of sex needs to be negotiated from the first moment on.
—Camille Paglia

Table 10.1 The First Encounter

Here are just a few suggestions for opening an initial encounter. Can you offer additional suggestions?

Nonverbal Messages	*Verbal Messages*
Establish eye contact. The eyes reveal an interest in the other person. While maintaining eye contact, smile and further signal your positive attitude.	Introduce yourself. Try to avoid trite opening lines. It's probably best simply to say, "Hi, my name is Pat."
Concentrate your focus. Be careful, however, not to focus so directly that you make the person uncomfortable.	Focus the conversation on the other person; few people enjoy talking about anything more.
Decrease the physical distance between the two of you. Approach (though not to the point of discomfort) so that you make your interest clear.	Exchange favors or rewards. Be sincere but complimentary and positive. We like and are attracted more to positive than to negative people.
Maintain an open posture that communicates an openness, a willingness to interact with the other person. Hands crossed over the chest or clutched around your stomach are often taken to signal an unwillingness to let others enter your space.	Be energetic. Show your high energy level by responding facially with appropriate affect, smiling, talking in a varied manner, being flexible with your body posture and gestures, and asking questions as appropriate.

SELF-TEST
What Do You Believe About Relationships?

Instructions: For each of the following statements, select the number (1 to 7) of the category that best fits how much you agree or disagree. Enter that number on the line next to each statement.

7 = agree completely
6 = agree a good deal
5 = agree somewhat
4 = neither agree nor disagree
3 = disagree somewhat
2 = disagree a good deal
1 = disagree completely

_____ 1. If a person has any questions about the relationship, then it means there is something wrong with it.

_____ 2. If my partner truly loved me, we would not have any quarrels.

_____ 3. If my partner really cared, he or she would always feel affection for me.

_____ 4. If my partner gets angry at me or is critical in public, this indicates he or she doesn't really love me.

_____ 5. My partner should know what is important to me without my having to tell him or her.

_____ 6. If I have to ask for something that I really want, it spoils it.

_____ 7. If my partner really cared, he or she would do what I ask.

_____ 8. A good relationship should not have any problems.

_____ 9. If people really love each other, they should not have to work on their relationship.

_____ 10. If my partner does something that upsets me, I think it is because he or she deliberately wants to hurt me.

_____ 11. When my partner disagrees with me in public, I think it is a sign that he or she doesn't care for me very much.

_____ 12. If my partner contradicts me, I think that he or she doesn't have much respect for me.

_____ 13. If my partner hurts my feelings, I think that it is because he or she is mean.

_____ 14. My partner always tries to get his or her own way.

_____ 15. My partner doesn't listen to what I have to say.

Thinking Critically About Relationship Beliefs

Aaron Beck, one of the leading theorists in cognitive therapy and the author of the popular _Love Is Never Enough_, claims that all of these beliefs are unrealistic and may well create problems in your interpersonal relationships. The test was developed to help people identify potential sources of difficulty for relationship development and maintenance. The more statements that you indicated you believe in, the more unrealistic your expectations are.

Do you agree with Beck that these beliefs are unrealistic and that they will cause problems? Which belief is the most dangerous to the development and maintenance of an interpersonal relationship? Review the list and identify hypothetical or real examples why each belief is unrealistic (or realistic).

Source: From _Love Is Never Enough_ by Aaron T. Beck. Copyright © 1988 by Aaron T. Beck, M.D. Reprinted by permission of HarperCollins Publishers, Inc. Beck notes that this test was adapted in part from the Relationship Belief Inventory of N. Epstein, J. L. Pretzer, and B. Fleming, "The Role of Cognitive Appraisal in Self-Reports of Marital Communication," _Behavior Therapy_ 18 (1987):51–69.

Throughout the relationship process, but especially during the involvement and early stages of intimacy, partners test each other. Each person tests the other; each tries to find out how the other feels about the relationship. Among the strategies often used are these (Bell & Buerkel-Rothfuss, 1990; Baxter & Wilmot, 1984):

CAUTION

What effects might **maintaining unrealistic beliefs about relationships** have on the way people think about their friendship and love relationships?

- **Directness:** You might ask your partner directly how he or she feels or you might self-disclose your own feelings on the assumption that your partner will also self-disclose.
- **Endurance:** You subject your partner to various negative behaviors on the assumption that if your partner endures them, he or she is really serious about the relationship; for example, you can behave badly toward the partner, you can make requests that are inconvenient, and you can criticize yourself to an irritating degree.
- **Indirect suggestion:** For example, you might joke about a shared future together, touch more intimately, or hint that you're serious about the relationship on the assumption that similar responses from your partner will mean that the partner wishes to increase the intimacy of the relationship.
- **Public presentation:** For example, you might introduce your partner as your "boyfriend" or "girlfriend" and see how your partner responds.
- **Separation:** Separating yourself physically to see how the other person responds; if your partner calls, then you know that he or she is interested in the relationship.
- **Third party:** You might question mutual friends as to your partner's feelings and intentions.
- **Triangle:** You might set up a triangle and tell your partner that, for example, another person is interested in him or her and see how your partner reacts. If the news is met with interest, then this shows a lack of commitment to your relationship. If, on the other hand, your partner assures you of interest in you, it shows a stronger commitment.

How would you explain the cartoon to the right in terms of social exchange theory?

Intimacy

At the intimacy stage you commit yourself still further to the other person and, in fact, establish a kind of relationship in which this individual becomes your best or closest friend, lover, or companion. Usually the intimacy stage divides itself quite neatly into two phases: an *interpersonal commitment* phase in which you commit yourselves to each other in a kind of private way and a *social bonding* phase in which the commitment is made public—perhaps to family and friends, perhaps to the public at large through formal marriage. Here the two of you become a unit, a pair.

Commitment may take many forms; it may be an engagement or a marriage; it may be a commitment to help the person or to be with the person, or a commitment to reveal your deepest secrets. It may consist of living together or an agreement to become lovers. The type of commitment varies with the relationship and with the individuals. The important characteristic is that the commitment made is a special one; it's a commitment that you do not make lightly or to everyone. This intimacy stage is reserved for very few people at any given time—sometimes just one, sometimes two, three, or perhaps four. Rarely do people have more than four intimates, except in a family situation.

To many people, the intimacy stage is the stage of falling in love. This is the time you "become lovers" and commit yourselves to being romantic partners. It's interesting and important to note, however, that *love* means very different things to different people. To illustrate this important concept, take the following love test, "What Kind of Lover Are You?"

True love comes quietly, without banners or flashing lights. If you hear bells, get your ears checked.

—*Erich Segal*

Immature love says: "I love you because I need you."
Mature love says: "I need you because I love you."

—*Erich Fromm*

Truly loving means I put no strings on you, nor accept them from you. Each person's integrity is respected.

—*Virginia Satir*

What do you see as the major differences in the development of friendship and love relationships? Is it easier to turn a friendship into a love relationship or a love relationship into a friendship? Do you think gay men, lesbians, and heterosexuals differ in their ability to make the transition between love and friendship?

SELF-TEST

What Kind of Lover Are You?

Instructions: Respond to each of the following statements with T (if you believe the statement to be a generally accurate representation of your attitudes about love) or F (if you believe the statement does not adequately represent your attitudes about love).

_____ 1. My lover and I have the right physical "chemistry" between us.

_____ 2. I feel that my lover and I were meant for each other.

_____ 3. My lover and I really understand each other.

_____ 4. I believe that what my lover doesn't know about me won't hurt him/her.

_____ 5. My lover would get upset if he/she knew of some of the things I've done with other people.

_____ 6. When my lover gets too dependent on me, I want to back off a little.

_____ 7. I expect to always be friends with my lover.

_____ 8. Our love is really a deep friendship, not a mysterious, mystical emotion.

_____ 9. Our love relationship is the most satisfying because it developed from a good friendship.

_____ 10. In choosing my lover, I believed it was best to love someone with a similar background.

_____ 11. An important factor in choosing a partner is whether or not he/she would be a good parent.

_____ 12. One consideration in choosing my lover was how he/she would reflect on my career.

_____ 13. Sometimes I get so excited about being in love with my lover that I can't sleep.

_____ 14. When my lover doesn't pay attention to me, I feel sick all over.

_____ 15. I cannot relax if I suspect that my lover is with someone else.

_____ 16. I would rather suffer myself than let my lover suffer.

_____ 17. When my lover gets angry with me, I still love him/her fully and unconditionally.

_____ 18. I would endure all things for the sake of my lover.

Thinking Critically About Your Love Style This scale is designed to enable you to identify those styles that best reflect your own beliefs about love. "True" answers represent your agreement and "false" answers represent your disagreement with the type of love to which the statements refer.

Statements 1–3 are characteristic of the **eros lover.** If you answered "true" to these statements, you have a strong eros component to your love style. If you answered "false," you have a weak eros component. The eros lover seeks beauty and sensuality and focuses on physical attractiveness, sometimes to the exclusion of qualities we might consider more important and more lasting. The erotic lover has an idealized image of beauty that is unattainable in reality. Consequently, the erotic lover often feels unfulfilled.

Statements 4–6 refer to **ludus love,** a love that seeks entertainment and excitement and sees love as fun, a game. To the ludic lover, love is not to be taken too seriously; emotions are to be held in check lest they get out of hand and make trouble. The ludic lover retains a partner only so long as the partner is interesting and amusing. When the partner is no longer interesting enough, it's time to change.

Statements 7–9 refer to **storge love,** a love that is peaceful and tranquil. Like ludus, storge lacks passion and intensity. Storgic lovers do not set out to find lovers but to establish a companionlike relationship with someone they know and can share interests and activities. Storgic love is a gradual process of unfolding thoughts and feelings and is sometimes difficult to separate from friendship.

Statements 10–12 refer to **pragma love,** a love that seeks the practical and traditional and wants compatibility and a relationship in which important needs and desires will be satisfied. The pragma lover is concerned with the social qualifications of a potential mate even

(continued)

(continued)

more than personal qualities; family and background are extremely important to the pragma lover, who relies not so much on feelings as on logic.

Statements 13–15 refer to **manic love,** an obsessive love that needs to give and to receive constant attention and affection. When this is not given or when an expression of increased commitment is not returned, such reactions as depression, jealousy, and self-doubt are often experienced and can lead to the extreme lows characteristic of the manic lover.

Statements 16–18 refer to **agapic love,** a compassionate and selfless love. The agapic lover loves the stranger on the road and the annoying neighbor. Jesus, Buddha, and Gandhi practiced and preached this unqualified, spiritual love, a love that is offered without concern for personal reward or gain, without any expectation that the love will be returned or reciprocated.

Do your scores seem accurate reflections of what you think about love?

Source: From "A Relationship: Specific Version of the Love Attitudes Scale" by C. Hendrick and S. Hendrick, *Journal of Social Behavior and Personality* 5, 1990. Reprinted by permission of Select Press.

Deterioration

Although many relationships remain at the intimacy stage, some enter the stage of deterioration, the stage that focuses on the weakening of bonds between the parties and that represents the downside of the relationship progression. Relationships deteriorate for many reasons. When the reasons for coming together are no longer present or when they change drastically, relationships may deteriorate. Thus, for example, when your relationship no longer lessens your loneliness or provides stimulation or self-knowledge, or when it fails to increase your self-esteem or maximize pleasures and minimize pains, it may be in the process of deteriorating. Among the other reasons for deterioration are these (Blumstein & Schwartz, 1983):

- **Third party relationships** may appear to offer greater rewards than the present relationship.
- **Sexual satisfaction** decreases, which often encourages partners to look elsewhere (approximately 15% of a national survey of married or previously married Americans indicate they have cheated on a spouse, *New York Times,* October 19, 1993, p. A20).
- **Dissatisfaction with work** often spills over into relationships; most people are not able to separate work problems from their relationship lives.
- **Financial difficulties** create stress and general dissatisfaction, which often extends into relationships.
- **Unrealistic expectations** create resentment when they are not fulfilled.

What other problems can create relationship deterioration? What other communication patterns seem to characterize relationship deterioration?

The first phase of deterioration is usually *intrapersonal dissatisfaction.* You begin to feel that this relationship may not be as important as you had previously thought. You may experience personal dissatisfaction with everyday interactions and begin to view the future together negatively. If this dissatisfaction continues or grows, you will pass to the second phase, *interpersonal deterioration,* where you discuss these dissatisfactions with your partner.

During the process of deterioration, communication patterns change drastically. These patterns are in part a response to the deterioration (you communicate as you do because of the way you feel your relationship is deteriorating). However, the way you communicate also influences the fate of your relationships. The following patterns seem to characterize communication during relational deterioration:

- Withdrawal increases. Nonverbally, withdrawal is seen in the failure to look at each other or to touch each other. Verbally, there is less talking and less listening.
- Self-disclosing communications decline. When trust and closeness lessen, so does disclosure.
- Deception increases.
- Negative evaluations increase and positive evaluations decrease. Instead of praising, we criticize; instead of complimenting, we complain. Nonverbally, we smile, caress, and hold each other less.

Repair

The first phase of repair is *intrapersonal repair.* Here you would analyze what went wrong and consider ways of solving your relational difficulties. You might at this stage consider changing your behaviors or perhaps changing your expectations of your partner. You might also evaluate the rewards of your relationship as it is now and the rewards that would prevail if your relationship ended.

Should you decide that you want to repair your relationship, you might discuss this with your partner at the *interpersonal repair* level. (See Figure 10.2.) Here you might discuss the problems in the relationship, the corrections you would want to see, and perhaps what you would be willing to do and what you would want the other person to do. This is the stage of negotiating new agreements, new behaviors. You and your partner might try to solve your problems yourselves, seek the advice of friends or family, or perhaps enter professional counseling.

How would you distinguish between repair designed to maintain a relationship ("preventive maintenance," to keep the relationship satisfying and functioning smoothly) and repair designed to reverse deterioration ("corrective maintenance," to fix something that is broken or not functioning properly) (M. Davis, 1973)? Do these two kinds of repair rely on different strategies? *(Your experiences with relationship repair [preventive or corrective] would make an interesting personal experience paper.)*

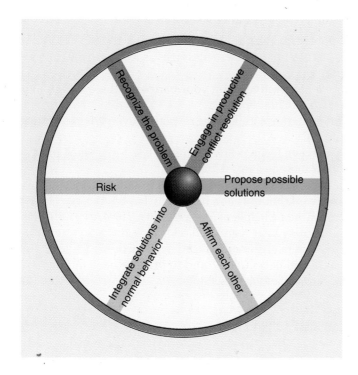

Figure 10.2
The Relationship Repair Wheel.

The wheel seems an apt metaphor for the repair process; the specific repair strategies—the spokes—all work together in constant process. The wheel is difficult to get started, but once in motion it becomes easier and, of course, it's easier to start when two people are pushing. How would you describe the repair process?

One way to improve communication during difficult times is to ask your partner for positive behaviors rather than to stop negative behaviors. How might you use this suggestion to replace such statements as: (1) I hate it when you ignore me at business functions. (2) I can't stand going to these cheap restaurants; when are you going to start spending a few bucks? (3) Stop being so negative; you criticize everything and everyone.

Research shows that when relationships break up, it's the more attractive person who leaves first (Blumstein & Schwartz, 1983). What other factors might account for who leaves first?

You can look at the strategies for repairing a relationship in terms of the following six suggestions, which conveniently spell out the word REPAIR, a useful reminder that repair is not a one-step but a multistep process: *Recognize* the problem, *Engage* in productive conflict resolution, *Pose* possible solutions, *Affirm* each other, *Integrate* solutions into normal behavior, and *Risk*.

- *Recognize the problem.* What is wrong with your present relationship (in concrete terms)? What changes would be needed to make it better (again, in specific terms)? Create a picture of your relationship as you would want it to be and compare that picture to the way the relationship looks now.
- *Engage in productive conflict resolution.* Interpersonal conflict is an inevitable part of relationship life. It's not so much the conflict that causes relationship difficulties but rather the way in which the conflict is approached (Chapter 11). If it's confronted with productive strategies, the conflict may be resolved and the relationship may actually emerge stronger and healthier. If, however, unproductive and destructive strategies are used, the relationship may well deteriorate further.
- *Pose possible solutions.* Ideally, you would ask, "What can we do to resolve the difficulty that will allow both of us to get what we want?"
- *Affirm each other.* For example, happily married couples engage in greater positive behavior exchange; they communicate more agreement, approval, and positive affect than do unhappily married couples (Dindia & Fitzpatrick, 1985).
- *Integrate solutions into normal behavior.* Make the solutions a part of your normal behavior.
- *Risk.* Risk giving favors without any certainty of reciprocity. Risk rejection by making the first move to make up or say you're sorry. Be willing to change, to adapt, to take on new tasks and responsibilities.

Throughout this process of repair, apply your interpersonal communication skills. Make them a normal part of your interactions. Here is just a handful of suggestions designed to refresh your memory.

- Look closely for relational messages that will help clarify motivations and needs. Respond to these messages as well as to the content messages (Chapter 1).
- Exchange perspectives with your partner and see the situation as your partner does (Chapter 3).
- Practice empathic and positive responses even when emotionally upset (Chapter 7).
- Own your own feelings and thoughts. Use I-messages and take responsibility for these feelings (Chapter 7).
- Use active listening techniques to help your partner explore and express relevant thoughts and feelings (Chapter 4).
- Remember the principle of irreversibility. Think carefully before saying things you may later regret (Chapter 1).
- Keep the channels of communication open. Be available to discuss problems, to negotiate solutions, and to practice new and more productive communication patterns (Chapter 8).

Dissolution

The dissolution stage, in both friendship and romance, is the cutting of the bonds tying you together. At first it usually takes the form of *interpersonal separation*, where you might not see each other any more. If you lived together, you would at this stage move into separate apartments and begin to lead lives apart from each other. If this relationship is a marriage, you might seek a legal separation. If this separation period proves workable and if the original relationship is not repaired, you may enter the phase of *social or public separation*. If this is a marriage, this phase would correspond to divorce. Avoidance of each other and a return to being "single" are among the primary identifiable features of dissolution. In some cases, however, the former partners change the definition of their relationship, and, for example, the ex-lovers become friends or the ex-friends become "just" business partners.

This final, "goodbye," phase of dissolution is the point at which you become an ex-lover or ex-friend. At times this is a stage of relief and relaxation; finally it's over. At other times this is the stage of anxiety and frustration, of guilt and regret, of resentment over the time ill-spent and now lost. In more materialistic terms, it's the stage where property is divided, where legal battles ensue over who should get what.

> After all, my estwhile dear,
> My no longer cherished,
> Need we say it was not love,
> Just because it perished?
> —*Edna St. Vincent Millay*

HOW TO . . .
Deal with Relationship Breakup

No matter how friendly the breakup, there is likely to be some emotional difficulty. Here are some suggestions for dealing with this.

1. Break the loneliness-depression cycle. Realize, first, that your feelings of loneliness and depression are not insignificant (Rubenstein & Shaver, 1982). Avoid *sad passivity*, a stage where you feel sorry for yourself, sit alone, and perhaps cry. This may actually make you feel worse. Temporary measures are *active solitude* (exercise, write, study, play computer games) and *distraction* (do things to put loneliness out of your mind, for example, take a long drive or shop). The most effective way to deal with loneliness is through *social action,* especially through helping those in need of assistance.

2. Take time out. Take some time for yourself. Renew your relationship with yourself. If you were in a long-term relationship, you probably saw yourself as part of a team, as one of a pair. Get to know yourself as a unique individual, standing alone now but fully capable of entering a meaningful relationship in the future.

3. Bolster self-esteem. If your relationship failed, you may experience a lowering of self-esteem. Take positive action to raise your self-esteem. As in dealing with loneliness, helping others is one of the best ways to raise your own self-esteem. Positive and successful experiences are most helpful in building self-esteem. So, engage in activities that you enjoy, that you do well, and that are likely to result in success. For more suggestions on self-esteem see the Listening box in Chapter 2 and the discussion in Chapter 12.

4. Seek support. Seek the support of others. It's an effective antidote to the discomfort and unhappiness that occurs when a relationship ends. Avail yourself of your friends and family for support. Tell your friends of your situation—in only general terms, if you prefer. Make it clear that you need support now. Seek out people who are positive and nurturing. Avoid negative individuals who will paint the world in even darker tones. Make the distinction between seeking support and seeking advice. If you feel you need advice, seek out a professional.

5. Avoid repeating negative patterns. Many enter second and third relationships with the same blinders and unrealistic expectations with which they entered earlier relationships. Ask, at the start of a new relationship, if you're entering a relationship modeled on the previous one. If the answer is yes, be especially careful that you don't repeat the problems. At the same time, avoid becoming a prophet of doom. Don't see in every new relationship vestiges of the old. Don't jump at the first conflict and say, "Here it goes again." Treat the new relationship as the unique relationship it is. Use past relationships and experiences as guides, not filters.

[The next How To box appears on page 298.]

Movement Among the Stages

Within each relationship and within each relationship stage, there are dynamic tensions between several opposites. The assumption made by this theory—called **relational dialectics theory**—is that all relationships can be defined by a series of opposites. For example, some research has found three such opposites (Baxter 1988, 1990; Baxter & Simon, 1993). The tension between **autonomy** and **connection** expresses your desire to remain an individual but also to be intimately connected to another person and to a relationship. The tension between **novelty** and **predictability** focuses on your two desires—for newness and adventure on the one hand and sameness and comfortableness on the other. The tension between **closedness** and **openness** relates to your desires to be in an exclusive relationship and, at the other extreme, one that is open to different people. The closedness-openness tension is more in evidence during the early stages of development. Autonomy-connection and novelty-predictability are more frequent as the relationship progresses.

A more obvious type of movement is depicted in Figure 10.1 by the different types of arrows. The **exit** arrows show that each stage offers the opportunity to exit the relationship. After saying "hello," you can say "goodbye" and exit. The vertical or **movement** arrows going to the next stage and back again represent the fact that you can move to another stage, either one that is more intense (say, from involvement to intimacy) or one that is less intense (say, from intimacy to deterioration). The **self-reflexive** arrows—the arrows that return to the beginning of the same level or stage—signify that any relationship may become stabilized at any point. You may, for example, continue to maintain a relationship at the intimate level without its deteriorating or going back to a less intense stage of involvement. Or we might remain at the "Hello, how are you?" stage—the contact stage—without getting any further involved. Numerous strategies designed to maintain a relationship have been identified. Table 10.2 gives examples.

> Do any of your relationships involve tension between such opposites as those described here? How do you deal with them?

> Can you think of examples where maintenance behaviors, affinity-seeking strategies or disengagement strategies (see box on 271) would be unethical? For example, would you consider it unethical for someone to engage in maintenance behaviors to achieve a selfish end (for example, to maintain a relationship because it's financially rewarding)? Would it be unethical for someone to use affinity-seeking strategies to get you to go on a date with her or him? To get you to vote for her or him? Would it be unethical to fabricate some justification for the desired breakup in order to avoid arguments and not hurt the other person? Would it be unethical to break up solely by behavioral deescalation—without ever saying anything directly about the desired breakup?

Table 10.2 Maintenance Behaviors

These strategies come from research by Dindia and Baxter, 1987; Canary, Stafford, Hause, and Wallace, 1993; and Dainton and Stafford, 1993. What additional strategies have you witnessed?

Maintenance Behaviors	Examples
Openness	You engage in direct discussion and listen to the other person, express empathy, self-disclose.
Togetherness	You spend time together, visit mutual friends, do things as a couple.
Positivity	You make your interactions positive, pleasant, and upbeat; do favors for the other person.
Ceremonial	You celebrate birthdays and anniversaries, discuss enjoyable past times.
Assurance	You express your love or tell your partner how important the relationship is and that your partner comes first.
Prosocial	You act especially polite, cheerful, and friendly, avoid criticism, and talk about a shared future.

SKILL BUILDING EXERCISE 10.1.
Changing the Distance Between You

Research in interpersonal communication has identified a wide variety of strategies that people use to change the interpersonal distance between them—to begin a relationship, to maintain it, to repair it, to dissolve it, and so on—topics we consider throughout this chapter. Here are two sets of strategies: (1) affinity-seeking strategies, strategies that people use to make others like them, to draw people closer to them—from the research of Bell & Daly (1984) and (2) disengagement strategies, strategies people use in trying to distance themselves from a close relationship partner—the research of Cody (1982). As you read down these two lists, try to recall situations in which you have used these strategies or had them used on you. What occasioned the use of the strategy? What specific form did it take? What effect(s) did it have?

AFFINITY-SEEKING STRATEGIES

Altruism: being of help to the other person

Assuming equality: presenting yourself as socially equal to the other

Comfortable self: presenting yourself as comfortable and relaxed when with the other

Conversational rule-keeping: following the cultural rules for polite, cooperative conversation with the other person

Dynamism: appearing active, enthusiastic, and dynamic

Inclusion of other: including the other person in your social activities and groupings

Listening: Listening to the other attentively and actively

Optimism: appearing optimistic and positive rather than pessimistic and negative

Self-concept confirmation: showing respect for the other person and helping him or her to feel positively

Self-inclusion: arranging circumstances so that you and the other person come into frequent contact

Sensitivity: communicating warmth and empathy

Similarity: demonstrating that you share significant attitudes and values

DISENGAGEMENT STRATEGIES

Positive tone is designed to maintain a positive relationship and to express positive feelings: *I really care for you a lot but I'm not ready for such a relationship.*

Negative identity management blames the other person and absolves yourself of blame: *I can't stand your jealousy, your checking up on me. I need my freedom.*

Justification gives reasons for the breakup: *I'm going away to college; there's no point in not dating others.*

Behavioral deescalation reduces the intensity of the relationship: avoid the other person, cut down on phone calls, reduce time spent together.

Deescalation reduces the exclusivity and hence the intensity of the relationship: *I'm not ready for so exclusive a relationship. We should see other people.*

Thinking Critical About Affinity-Seeking and Disengagement Strategies.   What other affinity-seeking strategies do you see used in interpersonal communication? Other disengagement strategies? Which affinity-seeking strategies do you use most often? Least often? What disengagement strategies do you use most often? Least often?

LISTENING.
Listening to Stage Talk

Learning to hear stage-talk messages—messages that express a desire to move the relationship in a particular way or to maintain it at a particular stage—will help you understand and manage your own interpersonal relationships, whether business or personal. Over the next few days listen carefully to all stage-talk messages. Listen to those messages referring to your own relationships as well as those messages that friends or coworkers disclose to you about their relationships. Collect these messages and classify them into the following categories.

1. **Contact messages** express a desire for contact: *Hi, my name is Joe.*
2. **Closeness messages** express a desire to increase closeness, involvement, or intimacy: *I'd like to see you more often.*
3. **Maintenance messages** express a desire to stabilize the relationship at one stage: *Let's keep it like this for a while. I'm afraid to get more involved at this point in my life.*
4. **Distancing messages** express a desire to distance oneself from a relationship. *I think we should spend a few weeks apart.*
5. **Repair messages** express a desire to repair the relationship: *Couldn't we discuss this and work it out? I didn't mean to be so dogmatic.*
6. **Dissolution messages** express a desire to break up or dissolve the existing relationship: *Look, it's just not working out as we planned; let's each go our own way.*

Share these collected messages with others in small groups or with the class as a whole. Consider, for example: (1) What types of messages are used to indicate the six different desires noted above? (2) Do people give reasons for their desire to move from one stage to another or to stabilize their relationship? If so, what types of reasons do they give? (3) Do men and women talk about relationship stages in the same way? (4) Do members of different cultures talk about relationships in the same way?

[The next Listening box appears on page 303.]

Movement through the various stages is usually a gradual process; you don't jump from contact to involvement to intimacy. Rather, you progress gradually, a few degrees at a time. Yet there are leaps that must and do take place. For example, during the involvement stage of a romantic relationship, the first kiss or the first sexual encounter requires a leap; it requires a change in the kind of communication and in the kind of intimacy to be experienced by the two people. Before you take these leaps, you probably first test the waters. Before the first kiss, for example, you may hold each other, look longingly into each other's eyes, and perhaps caress each other's face. You might do this (in part) to discover if the leap—the kiss, for example—will be met with a favorable response. No one wants rejection—especially of our romantic advances. Some of the major leaps or turning points identified by college students are identified in Table 10.3.

What disengagement strategies would you be most likely to use if you wanted to break up with someone you had been dating steadily for the last six months? Why?

RELATIONSHIP THEORIES

Several theories offer insight into why and how we develop and dissolve our relationships. Here we single out five such theories: attraction, relationship rules, social penetration, social exchange, and equity theories.

Attraction Theory

You're no doubt attracted to some people and not attracted to others. In a similar way, some people are attracted to you and some people are not. If you're like most people, then you're attracted to others on the basis of four

Table 10.3 Turning Points in Romantic Relationships

These major jumps or turning points provide an interesting perspective on how relationships develop. This table presents the five most frequently reported turning points in romantic relationships among college students and is based on the research of Baxter and Bullis (1986). Are these turning points similar to those that would occur in friendships?

Turning Point	Examples
Getting-to-know time	The first meeting, the time spent together studying, the first date
Quality time that enables the couple to appreciate each other and the relationship	Meeting the family or getting away together
Physical separation	Separations due to vacations or trips (not to breakups)
External competition	The presence of a new or old rival and demands that compete for relationship time
Reunion	Getting back together after physical separation.

major factors: attractiveness (physical appearance and personality), similarity, proximity, and reinforcement.

Attractiveness: Physical and Personality

When you say, "I find that person attractive," you probably mean either that (1) you find that person physically attractive or (2) you find that person's personality or behavior attractive. For the most part, you probably like physically attractive people rather than physically unattractive people, and you like people who have a pleasant rather than an unpleasant personality. Of course, we each would define "attractive" somewhat differently. However, recent research seems to be finding universals of attraction. For example, in one study both Japanese and Britons ranked faces as attractive when they had large eyes, looked youthful, had high cheekbones, and a narrow jaw (Brody, 1994).

Generally, people attribute positive characteristics to people they find attractive and negative characteristics to people they find unattractive. Those who are perceived as attractive are also perceived as more competent generally. Interestingly enough, those who are perceived as more competent in communication are also perceived as more attractive—in terms of working on a task, socially, and physically (Duran & Kelly, 1988).

Similarity

If you could construct your mate, it's likely that your mate would look, act, and think very much like you do. By being attracted to people like us, we validate ourselves; we tell ourselves that we are worthy of being liked, that we are attractive. Although there are exceptions, we generally like people who are similar to ourselves in nationality, race, ability, physical characteristics, intelligence, attitudes, and so on.

Evaluating Information

Assess different theories with Ockham's razor. Ockham's razor holds that the best explanation is the simplest; it's the one that requires the fewest assumptions. So, when evaluating several potential solutions, Ockham's razor tells you to select the one that is simplest. Consider, for example, the astrologers and psychics who claim to be able to tell you what will happen in the future. Now, you can conclude that the position of the stars, the way cards fall on a table, or vibrations in your voice contain cues to your future and that these people have special abilities to read these cues and so can tell you what will happen—financially, relationally, or occupationally. Or, you can conclude that these people are guessing or are just saying what most people want to hear. Ockham's razor would suggest that the second conclusion is the simpler and hence the more reasonable (Wade & Tarvis, 1998).

Another way to use Ockham's razor is to look at a problem and shave off all the incidentals that get in the way of a clear view of the problem. Or you can shave away the parts over which you have no control and focus your energies on what you can do to make your situation better. In this way the problem may be reduced to one that you can manage more easily.

It's been argued that you don't actually develop an attraction for those who are similar to you but rather develop a repulsion for those who are dissimilar (Rosenbaum, 1986). For example, you may be repulsed by those who disagree with you and therefore exclude them from those with whom you might develop a relationship. You're therefore left with a pool of possible partners who are similar to you. What do you think of this repulsion hypothesis? How would you go about testing it?

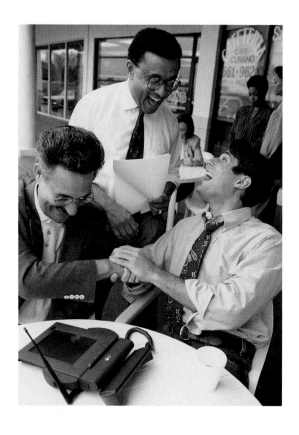

The "matching hypothesis" claims that people date and mate people who are very similar to themselves in physical attractiveness (Walster & Walster, 1978). When this does not happen—when a very attractive person dates someone of average attractiveness—you may begin to look for "compensating factors," factors that the less attractive person possesses that compensate or make up for being less physically attractive. What evidence can you find to support or contradict this theory? How would you go about testing this theory? *(Testing this theory would make an excellent research paper.)*

Sometimes people are attracted to their opposites, for example, a dominant person might be attracted to someone who is more submissive. Generally, however, people much prefer relationships with people who are similar. And, not surprisingly, relationships between persons who are similar last longer than relationships between dissimilar people (Blumstein & Schwartz, 1983).

Proximity

If you look around at people you find attractive, you would probably find that they are the people who live or work close to you. People who become friends are the people who have the greatest opportunity to interact with each other. Physical closeness is most important in the early stages of interaction, for example, during the first days of school (in class or in dormitories). It decreases (but always remains significant) as the opportunity to interact with more distant others increases.

Reinforcement

Not surprisingly, we are attracted to people who give us rewards or reinforcements. These may be social, as in the case of compliments or praise, or material, as in the case of the suitor whose gifts eventually win the hand of the beloved. When overdone, of course, reward can lose its effectiveness and may even lead to negative responses. The people who reward you constantly soon become too sweet to take, and in a short period you probably learn to discount whatever they say. Also, if the reward is to work, it must be perceived as genuine and not motivated by selfish concerns.

You're also attracted to people *you* reward (Jecker & Landy, 1969; Aronson, 1980). You come to like people for whom you do favors. For example, you

"I myself don't see much hope for an inter-utensil relationship."

have probably increased your liking for persons after buying them an expensive present or going out of your way to do them a special favor. In these situations, you justify your behavior by believing that the person was worth your efforts; otherwise, you would have to admit to spending your money and effort on people who do not deserve it.

Relationship Rules Approach

You can gain an interesting perspective on interpersonal relationships by looking at them in terms of the rules that govern them. The general assumption of this view is that relationships—friendship and love in particular—are held together by adherence to certain rules. When those rules are broken, the relationship may deteriorate and even dissolve.

Discovering relationship rules serves several functions. Ideally, these rules help identify successful versus destructive relationship behavior. In addition, these rules help pinpoint more specifically why relationships break up and how they may be repaired. Further, if we know what the rules are we will be better able to teach the social skills involved in relationship development and maintenance. Since these rules vary from one culture to another, it will be necessary to identify those unique to each culture so that intercultural relationships may be more effectively developed and maintained.

Friendship Rules

Column 1 in Table 10.4 presents some important rules of friendship (Argyle & Henderson, 1984). When these rules are followed, the friendship is strong and mutually satisfying. When these rules are broken, the friendship suffers and may die. Column 2 presents the abuses that are most significant in breaking up a friendship (Argyle & Henderson, 1984). Note that some rules for

---

What relationship rules do you demand be followed in a friendship relationship? In a romantic relationship? Can you identify specific rules that, if broken, would lead you to dissolve the relationship?

Evaluating Information

Examine the reliability of research. **Reliability** is a measure of consistency. When research is referred to as having "high reliability," it means that findings similar to those of this study are highly likely to be found in other studies, conducted at other times, and with other (but similar) participants. For example, a test to measure love style such as that presented here must be reliable; it must yield similar scores from one time to another. Intelligence tests are extremely reliable; your score on an intelligence test is likely to remain relatively consistent from one time to another. So, when you read research studies, look at their reliability. Ask yourself if these findings are likely to be found at other times.

Table 10.4 Keeping and Breaking Up a Friendship

Do these rules adequately describe the ways in which your friendships have been maintained or broken up? Can you think of additional rules that are important in friendships?

To Keep a Friendship	To Break Up a Friendship
Stand up for a friend in his or her absence.	Be intolerant of a friend's friends.
Share information and feelings about successes.	Discuss confidences between yourself and a friend with others.
Demonstrate emotional support.	Don't display any positive regard for a friend.
Trust each other; confide in each other.	Don't demonstrate any positive support for a friend.
Offer to help a friend when in need.	Nag a friend.
Try to make a friend happy when you're together.	Don't trust or confide in a friend.

maintaining a friendship directly correspond to the abuses that break up friendships. For example, it's important to "demonstrate emotional support" to maintain a friendship, but when emotional support is not shown, the friendship will prove less satisfying and may well break up. The strategy for maintaining a friendship would then depend on your knowing the rules and having the ability to apply the appropriate interpersonal skills (Trower, 1981; Blieszner & Adams, 1992).

> You can hardly make a friend in a year, but you can easily offend one in an hour.
> —*Chinese proverb*

Romantic Rules

Other research has identified the rules that romantic relationships establish and follow. Leslie Baxter (1986), for example, has identified eight major rules. Baxter argues that these rules both keep the relationship together and when broken lead to deterioration and eventually dissolution. The general form for each rule, as Baxter phrases it, is "If parties are in a close relationship they should . . . ."

1. "acknowledge one another's individual identities and lives beyond the relationship"
2. "express similar attitudes, beliefs, values, and interests"
3. "enhance one another's self-worth and self-esteem"
4. "be open, genuine and authentic with one another"
5. "remain loyal and faithful to one another"
6. "have substantial shared time together"
7. "reap rewards commensurate with their investments relative to the other party"
8. "experience a mysterious and inexplicable 'magic' in one another's presence"

Social Penetration Theory

Social penetration theory is not so much a theory of why relationships develop as what happens when they do develop; it describes relationships in terms of the number of topics that people talk about and their degree of "personalness" (Altman & Taylor, 1973). The *breadth* of a relationship refers to the number of topics you and your partner talk about. The *depth* of a relationship refers to the degree to which you penetrate the inner personality—the core of your individual.

We can represent an individual as a circle and divide that circle into various parts. These parts represent the topics or areas of interpersonal communication, or breadth. Further, visualize the circle and its parts as consisting of concentric inner circles, rather like an onion. These represent the different levels of communication, or the depth (see Figure 10.3). The circles contain eight topic areas (A through H) and five levels of intimacy (represented by the concentric circles).

When a relationship begins to deteriorate, the breadth and depth will, in many ways, reverse themselves, a process called *depenetration.* For example, while ending a relationship, you might cut out certain topics from your interpersonal communications. At the same time you might discuss the remaining topics in less depth. In some instances of relational deterioration, however, both the breadth and the depth of interaction increase. For example, when a couple breaks up and each is finally free from an oppressive relationship, they may—after some time—begin to discuss problems and feelings they would never have discussed when they were together. In fact, they may become extremely close friends and come to like each other more than when they were together. In these cases the breadth and depth of their relationship may increase rather than decrease (Baxter, 1983).

Evaluating Information

Examine the validity of research. **Validity** is a measure of the extent to which a test, say, measures what it claims to measure. Although intelligence tests are extremely reliable, there's considerable debate about their validity. To be valid, the test must measure what we normally think of as intelligence and not, say, knowledge of vocabulary or mathematical formulas. In reading research studies, ask yourself if the test or study actually measured what it claimed to measure. For example, did the test of love style used in this study really measure "love"? Look through the self-tests in this text; how would you judge their validity?

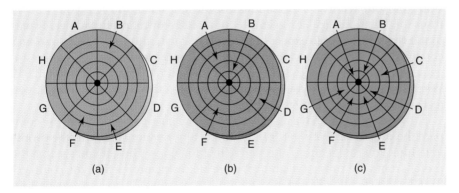

Figure 10.3
Social Penetration with (a) An Acquaintance, (b) A Friend, and (c) An Intimate.

Note that in circle (a) you discuss only three topic areas. You penetrate two only to the first level and one to the second level. In this type of interaction, you talk about three topic areas and discuss these at fairly superficial levels. This is the type of relationship you might have with an acquaintance. Circle (b) represents a more intense relationship. It's both broader and deeper. This is the type of relationship you might have with a friend. Circle (c) is a still more intense relationship, one with considerable breadth and depth. This is the type of relationship you might have with a lover, a parent, or a sibling. Does this theory adequately describe the types of communication you have with acquaintances, friends, and intimates? Does it adequately describe both face-to-face and online relationships?

Social Exchange Theory

Social exchange theory claims that you develop relationships that will enable you to maximize your profits (Chadwick-Jones, 1976; Gergen, Greenberg, & Willis, 1980; Thibaut & Kelley, 1959), a theory based on an economic model of profits and losses. The theory begins with the following equation:

$$Profits = Rewards - Costs$$

Rewards are anything that you would incur costs to obtain. Research has identified six types of rewards in a love relationship: money, status, love, information, goods, and services (Baron & Byrne, 1984). For example, to get the reward of money, you might have to work rather than play. To earn the grade of A in an interpersonal communication course, you might have to write a term paper or study more than you want to.

Costs are those things that you normally try to avoid. These are the things you consider unpleasant or difficult. Working over time, washing dishes and ironing clothes, watching your partner's favorite television show which you find boring, and doing favors for those you dislike might all be considered costs.

Using this basic economic model, social exchange theory claims that you seek to develop friendship and romantic relationships which will give you the greatest profits; that is, relationships in which the rewards are greater than the costs. The most preferred relationships, according to this theory, are those that give you the greatest rewards with the least costs.

You enter a relationship with a *comparison level*—a general idea of the kinds of rewards and profits that you feel you ought to get out of such a relationship. It's your realistic expectations concerning what you feel you deserve from this relationship. For example, in a study of married couples, it was found that most people expect high levels of trust, mutual respect, love, and commitment. Their expectations are significantly lower for time spent together, privacy, sexual activity, and communication (Sabatelli & Pearce, 1986). When the rewards that you get equal or surpass this comparison level, you feel satisfied with your relationship.

However, you also have a *comparison level for alternatives*. That is, you compare the profits that you get from your current relationship with the profits you think you can get from alternative relationships. Thus, if you see that the profits from your present relationship are below the profits that you could get from an alternative relationship, you might decide to leave your current relationship and enter this new, more profitable relationship.

Equity Theory

Equity theory uses the ideas of social exchange but goes a step further and claims that you develop and maintain relationships in which the *ratio* of your rewards compared to costs is approximately equal to your partner's (Walster, Walster, & Berscheid, 1978; Messick & Cook, 1983). For example, if you and a friend start a business and you put up two-thirds of the money and your friend puts up one-third, equity would demand that you get two-thirds of the profits and your friend get one-third. An equitable relationship, then, is simply one in which each party derives rewards that are

---

How important is money to your relationship decisions and relationship happiness? To what extent—if any—does your relationship happiness depend on money? *(The role of money in relationship satisfaction or in happiness generally would make an interesting research paper.)*

Test out the predictions of social exchange theory in your own relationships. Did the relationships that you pursued and maintained give you profits (rewards were greater than costs)? Equally important, were the relationships that you did not pursue or that you ended unprofitable (costs were greater than rewards)? How useful a theory is social exchange? *(Your own experiences with relationships analyzed in terms of costs and rewards would make an interpersonal personal experience paper.)*

proportional to their costs. If you contribute more toward the relationship than your partner, then equity requires that you should get greater rewards. If you each work equally hard then equity demands that you should each get approximately equal rewards. Conversely, inequity would exist in a relationship if you pay more of the costs (for example, you do more of the unpleasant tasks) but your partner enjoys more of the rewards. Inequity would also exist if you and your partner work equally hard, but one of you gets more of the rewards.

Much research supports this idea that people want equity in their interpersonal relationships (Ueleke et al., 1983). The general idea behind this is that if you are underbenefited (you get less than you put in), you'll be angry and dissatisfied. If, on the other hand, you are overbenefited (you get more than you put in), you'll feel guilty. Some research, however, has questioned this rather neat but intuitively unsatisfying assumption and found that the overbenefited person is often quite happy and contented; guilt from getting more than you deserve seems easily forgotten (Noller & Fitzpatrick, 1993).

Equity theory puts into clear focus the sources of relational dissatisfaction seen every day. For example, in a relationship both partners may have full-time jobs but one may also be expected to do the major share of the household chores. Thus, although both may be deriving equal rewards—they have equally good cars, they live in the same three-bedroom house, and so on—one partner is paying more of the costs. According to equity theory, this partner will be dissatisfied because of this lack of equity.

Equity theory claims that you will develop and maintain relationships and will be satisfied with relationships that are equitable. You will not develop, will terminate, and will be dissatisfied with, relationships that are inequitable. The greater the inequity, the greater the dissatisfaction, and the greater likelihood that the relationship will end.

A summary of these basic theories is presented in Table 10.5.

How equitable are your friendships? How equitable are your romantic relationships? If any are not equitable, are you the overbenefitted or the underbenefitted partner? How do you feel about this?

Table 10.5 Relationship Theories and Relationship Movement

This table summarizes the theories just considered and their basic assumptions on relationship development, maintenance, and deterioration. Can you think of specific examples in which the theories effectively explained what happened in a relationship? Can you think of examples where the relationship contradicted the theory's predictions?

Relationship Movement / Relationship Theories	Attraction	Relationship Rules	Social Penetration	Social Exchange	Equity
Development and increases toward intimacy	When attraction is great	When the relationship partners follow the rules	Depth and breadth increase	When the rewards are greater than the costs and especially when these rewards are more than you could get elsewhere	When the rewards and costs are distributed between the partners equitably
Maintenance, keep the relationship much as it is	When attraction is satisfactory	When the relationship rules are maintained or are broken with acceptable frequency	Depth and breadth remain at acceptable levels	When the rewards are greater and the costs are less than you expected or that you could get elsewhere	When the rewards and costs are distributed equitably or within acceptable limits of inequity
Deterioration and moves away from intimacy	When attraction is less than desired	When relationship rules are broken	Depth and breadth decrease	When the costs exceed the rewards or when you could get greater profit in another relationship	When the rewards and costs are distributed to an unacceptable inequitable degree

SKILL BUILDING EXERCISE 10.2.

Applying Theories to Problems

Read each of the following letters and *describe* each of the problems in terms of (1) attraction, (2) relationship rules, (3) reinforcement, (4) social exchange, and (5) equity theories.

LOVE AND AGE DIFFERENCE

I'm in love with an older woman. She's 51 and I'm 22 but very mature; in fact, I'm a lot more mature than she is. I want to get married but she doesn't; she says she doesn't love me but I know she does. She wants to break up our romance and "become friends." How can I win her over?

Signed, 22 and Determined

LOVE AND THE BEST FRIEND

Chris and I have been best friends for the last 10 years. Now, Chris fell in love and is moving to California. I became angry and hurt at the idea of losing my best friend and I said things I shouldn't have. Although we still talk, things aren't the same ever since I opened my big mouth. What should I do?

Signed, Big Mouth

LOVE AND SPORTS

My relationship of the last 20 years has been great—except for one thing: I can't watch sports on television. If I turn on the game, Pat moans and groans until I turn it off. Pat wants to talk; I want to watch the game. I work hard during the week and on the weekend I want to watch sports, drink beer, and fall asleep on the couch. This problem has gotten so bad that I'm seriously considering separating. What should I do?

Signed, Sports Lover

LOVE AND THE DILEMMA

I'm 29 and have been dating two really great people fairly steadily. Each knows about my relationship with the other and for a while they went along with it and tolerated what they felt was an unpleasant situation. They now threaten to break up if I don't make a decision. To be perfectly honest, I like both of them a great deal and simply need more time before I can make the decision and ask one to be my life mate. How can I get them to stay with the status quo for maybe another year or so?

Signed, Simply Undecided

Thinking Critically About Relationship Theories. Do the theories make any predictions about how these situations are likely to be resolved? Do they offer any suggestions as to what the individuals should do? Which theory offers the greatest insights into problems such as these?

IMPROVING RELATIONSHIP COMMUNICATION

You can improve communication in primary interpersonal relationships by applying the same principles that would improve communication in any other context. But to be most effective, these principles need to be adapted to the unique context of the primary relationship. The purpose of this section is to suggest how the general principles of effective communication may be best applied to primary relationships. Additional suggestions for improving communication within relationships are presented in Chapter 8, Conversation Messages.

Here are a variety of useful suggestions for reducing stress and increasing satisfaction when visiting parents.

Tips for Happier Visits with Parents

Visiting with parents can be stressful under the best circumstances. Start with a positive attitude by saying, "I'm here to have fun and visit with the people I love. I've been looking forward to this visit for quite a while and I know we are going to have a great time!" *Be aware that emotions are highest at the beginning and end of visits, so avoid overreaction to comments or questions that may seem confrontational. Accept your folks for their good points and keep in mind that they are people too and not just your parents.*

1. Establish a set of behavior ground rules to avoid old arguments. For example, you can say, *"I don't want to argue over little things, so I promise to be home early most nights (not be late for dinner, help around the house, etc.) if you promise not to bug me too much about what I wear (who I see, how I fix my hair, etc.)."*
2. Desensitize yourself to old disputes that set off arguments, and make an extra effort to show your parents that you are a mature and responsible adult. Nip tensions in the bud by saying, *"Let's get along and enjoy the short time we have to spend together."*
3. If your past visits have started off peacefully but after a time end up in old arguments, then plan for a shorter stay. If your parents protest, say, *"The quality of our visit is more important than how long we visit, especially if we end up arguing."*
4. Avoid criticizing your parents, even if they criticize you. Chances are, their opinions and values are not going to change. Your best response to parental criticism is, *"I understand you do not approve of my lifestyle, but I'm the one who must decide what is best for me."*

5. Spend plenty of time talking with your parents about the important, rewarding, and exciting things happening in their life as well as yours. You can say, *"So enough about me. How are your plans coming along for your dream vacation?"*
6. Limit your discussion of personal problems or complaints. You are visiting to share time with your parents. Don't expect them to solve your problems. Say, *"Don't worry, I can handle these problems on my own."*
7. Let your parents know that you are planning to spend time with friends as well. Set aside some free time to visit friends or go away for a day or two. Say, *"I'm also planning on spending some time with my friend Jody. We haven't seen each other for years and want to catch up on old times."*
8. Always be a gracious guest and offer assistance with the dishes or dinner, help around the house, or find other ways to show your appreciation. Always send a short note soon after your visit is over, saying, *"Thanks, I had a wonderful time!"*

Thinking Critically About "Tips for Happier Visits with Parents." What other suggestions might you offer for visiting parents? What suggestions would you offer parents visiting their children? Can you think of situations where one or more of these suggestions should *not* be followed?

Source: From *How to Talk to the People You Love,* by Dan Gabor. Reprinted by permission of the author.

Empathic Understanding

If meaningful communication is to be established, we must learn to see the world from the other person's point of view, to feel that person's pain and insecurity, to experience the other person's love and fear. Empathy is an essential ingredient if a primary relationship or a family is to survive as a meaningful and productive union. It's essential, for example, that the individuals be allowed—and in fact encouraged—to explain how and why they see the world, their relationship, and their problems as they do.

Self-Disclosures

The importance of self-disclosure in the development and maintenance of a meaningful interpersonal relationship has been noted repeatedly. Recall that total self-disclosure may not always be effective (Noller & Fitzpatrick, 1993). At times it may be expedient to omit, for example, past indiscretions, certain fears, and perceived personal inadequacies if these disclosures may lead to negative perceptions or damage the relationship in some way. In any decision to self-disclose, the possible effects on the relationship should be considered. But it's also necessary to consider the ethical issues involved, specifically the other person's right to know about behaviors and thoughts that may influence the choices he or she will make. Most relationships would profit from greater self-disclosure of present feelings rather than details of past sexual experiences or past psychological problems. The sharing of present feelings also helps a great deal in enabling each person to empathize with the other; each comes to better understand the other's point of view when these self-disclosures are made.

Openness to Change

Throughout any significant relationship, there will be many significant changes in each individual and in the relationship. Because persons in relationships are interconnected with each impacting on the other, changes in one person may demand changes in the other person. Thus, when one person goes back to college, for example, it will require changes in the other person as well. The willingness to be responsive to such changes, to be adaptable and flexible, will likely enhance relationship satisfaction and is included as an essential skill in the major theories of family functioning (Noller & Fitzpatrick, 1993).

Fair Fighting

Because conflict is inevitable, an essential relationship skill involves fair fighting. Winning at all costs, beating down the other person, getting one's own way, and the like have little use in a primary relationship or family. Instead, cooperation, compromise, and mutual understanding must be substituted. If we enter conflict with a person we love with the idea that we must win and the other must lose, the conflict has to hurt at least one partner, very often both. In these situations the loser gets hurt and frequently retaliates so that no one really wins in any meaningful sense. On the other hand, if we enter a conflict to achieve some kind of mutual understanding, neither party need be hurt. Both parties, in fact, may benefit from the clash of ideas or desires and from the airing of differences.

Having two bathrooms ruined the capacity to cooperate.
—Margaret Mead

Reasonableness

Some people expect their relationship to be perfect. Whether from the media, from the self-commitment to have a relationship better than one's parents, or from the mistaken belief that other relationships are a lot better than one's own, many people expect and look for perfection. But, of course, this is likely to result in disappointment and dissatisfaction with any existing relationships. Psychologist John DeCecco (1988) argues that relationships should be characterized by reasonableness: "*reasonableness* of need and expectation, avoiding the wasteful pursuit of the extravagant fantasy that *every* desire will be fulfilled, so that the relationship does not consume its partners or leave them chronically dissatisfied."

Cultural Differences

The research and theory discussed throughout this chapter derive in great part from research conducted in the United States and on heterosexual couples. This research and the corresponding theory reflect the way most heterosexual relationships are viewed in the United States. And although we paused periodically to note specific cultural differences, it's helpful to bring the influence of culture together now that we've covered a major part of our relationship discussion and to look at some of the more general issues.

For example, we assume in the model and in the discussion of relationship development that we voluntarily choose our relationship partners. We choose to pursue certain relationships and not others. In some cultures, however, your romantic partner is chosen for you by your parents. In some cases, your husband or wife is chosen to solidify two families or to bring some financial advantage to your family or village. Such an arrangement may have been entered into by your parents when you were an infant.

In the United States, researchers study and textbook authors write about dissolving relationships and how to manage after a relationship breaks up. It's assumed that you have the right to exit an undesirable relationship. But, that is not always true. In some cultures, you simply cannot dissolve a relationship once it's formed or once there are children. In the practice of Roman Catholicism, once people are validly married, they are always married and cannot dissolve that relationship.

As you may have noticed, equity is consistent with the capitalistic orientation of Western culture, where each person is paid, for example, according to his or her contributions. The more you contribute to the organization or the relationship, the more rewards you should get out of it. In other cultures, a principle of equality or need might operate. Under equality, each person would get equal rewards, regardless of their own individual contribution. Under need, each person would get rewards according to his or her individual need (Moghaddam, Taylor, & Wright, 1993). Thus, in the United States equity is highly correlated with relationship satisfaction and with relationship endurance (Schafer & Keith, 1980); but, in Europe, equity seems to be unrelated to satisfaction or endurance (Lujansky & Mikula, 1983).

In one study, for example, subjects in the United States and India were asked to read situations in which a bonus was to be distributed between a worker who contributed a great deal but who was economically well-off and a worker who contributed much less but who was economically needy. Their choices

Evaluating Information

Be careful of generalizing from anecdotal evidence. Often you'll hear people use anecdotes to prove a point: "Women are like that, I have three sisters." "That's the way Japanese managers are; I've seen plenty of them." These observations are often useful starting points for collecting evidence and systematically studying some aspect of communication. But, they are not evidence in any meaningful sense. One reason this type of "evidence" is inadequate is that it relies on usually just one or a few observations; it's usually a clear case of overgeneralizing on the basis of too little evidence. A second reason is that one person's observations may be unduly clouded by his or her own attitudes and beliefs; your attitudes toward women or the Japanese, for example, may influence your perception of their behaviors. A third reason is that there is no way to test the reliability and validity of these observations.

were to distribute the bonus equitably (on the basis of contribution), equally, or in terms of need (Berman, Murphy-Berman, & Singh, 1985; Moghaddam, Taylor, & Wright, 1993). Subjects from the United States distributed the bonus based on equity (49%) while only 16% of the subjects from India did this. Only 16% of the subjects from the United States said they would distribute the bonus based on need compared to 51% of the subjects from India.

A similar assumption of choice is seen in the research and theory on friendships. In most of the United States, interpersonal friendships are drawn from a relatively large pool. Out of all the people you come into regular contact with, you choose relatively few of these as friends. And now with computer discussion groups, the number of friends you can have has increased enormously, as has the range from which these friends can be chosen. In rural areas and in small villages throughout the world, however, you would have very few choices. The two or three other children your age become your friends; there is no real choice because these are the only possible friends you could make.

Some cultures consider sexual relationships to be undesirable outside of a formally sanctioned marriage whereas others consider it a normal part of relationships and view chastity as undesirable. Intercultural researchers Elaine Hatfield and Richard Rapson (1996, p. 36) recall a meeting of the International Academy of Sex Research where colleagues from Sweden and the United States were discussing ways of preventing AIDS. When members from the United States suggested teaching abstinence as a way of preventing AIDS, Swedish members asked, "How will teenagers ever learn to become loving, considerate sexual partners if they don't practice?" "The silence that greeted the question," note Hatfield and Rapson, "was the sound of two cultures clashing."

A cultural bias is also seen in the research on maintenance. It's assumed that relationships should be permanent or at least long-lasting. Consequently, it's assumed that people want to keep relationships together and will exert considerable energy to maintain them. Because of this bias, there is little research that has studied how to move effortlessly from one intimate relationship to another or that advises you how to do this more effectively and efficiently.

Culture influences heterosexual relationships by assigning different roles to men and to women. In the United States men and women are supposed to be equal, at least that is the stated ideal. As a result, both men and women can initiate relationships and both men and women can dissolve them. Both men and women are expected to derive satisfaction from their interpersonal relationships and when that satisfaction is not present, either may seek to exit the relationship. In Iran, on the other hand, only the man has the right to dissolve a marriage without giving reasons.

In some cultures, gay and lesbian relationships are accepted and in others are condemned. In some areas of the United States and in many other countries, "domestic partnerships" may be registered and these grant gay men, lesbians, and, in some cases, unmarried heterosexuals rights that were formerly only reserved for married couples, for example, health insurance benefits and the right to make decisions when one member is incapacitated. In Norway, Iceland, Sweden, and Denmark same sex relationships are legally sanctioned in much the same way as are heterosexual marriages.

How have your own cultural beliefs and values influenced your interpersonal relationships? *(This would make an excellent topic for a personal experience paper.)*

CAUTION

How can **failing to see cultural differences in relationships** create interpersonal misunderstandings?

In an interesting study on love, men and women from different cultures were asked the following question: "If a man (woman) has all the other qualities you desired, would you marry this person if you were not in love with him (her)? How would you answer this question? Results varied greatly from one culture to another (Levine, Sato, Hashimoto, & Verma, 1994). For example, 50.4% of the respondents from Pakistan said yes, 49% of those from India said yes, and 18.8% from Thailand said yes. At the other extreme were those from Japan (only 2.3% said yes), the United States (only 3.5% said yes), and Brazil (only 4.3% said yes).

Gender Differences

Gender differences are, like cultural ones, often considerable. Consider, first the case of friendship. Perhaps the best-documented finding—already noted in our discussion of self-disclosure—is that women self-disclose more than men do (for example, Dolgin, Meyer, & Schwartz, 1991). This difference holds throughout male and female friendships. Male friends self-disclose less often and with less intimate details than female friends do. Men generally do not view intimacy as a necessary quality of their friendships (Hart, 1990).

Women engage in significantly more affectional behaviors with their friends than do males (Hays, 1989). This difference, Hays notes, may account for the greater difficulty men experience in beginning and maintaining close friendships. Women engage in more casual communication; they also share greater intimacy and more confidences with their friends than do men. Communication, in all its forms and functions, seems a much more important dimension of women's friendships.

When women and men were asked to evaluate their friendships, women rated their same-sex friendships higher in general quality, intimacy, enjoyment, and nurturance than did men (Sapadin, 1988). Men, in contrast, rated their opposite-sex friendships higher in quality, enjoyment, and nurturance than did women. Both men and women rated their opposite-sex friendships similarly in intimacy. These differences may be due, in part, to our society's suspicion of male friendships; as a result, a man may be reluctant to admit to having close relationship bonds with another man.

Men's friendships are often built around shared activities—attending a ball game, playing cards, working on a project at the office. Women's friendships,

Visit one of the online newsgroups dealing with some aspect of this chapter. What are the goals of the group? What topics are discussed? Is there anything you can learn from these groups?

on the other hand, are built more around a sharing of feelings, support, and "personalism." Similarity in status, in willingness to protect one's friend in uncomfortable situations, in academic major, and even in proficiency in playing Password were significantly related to the relationship closeness of male-male friends but not of female-female or female-male friends (Griffin & Sparks, 1990). Perhaps similarity is a more important criterion for male friendships than it is for female or mixed-sex friendships.

The ways in which men and women develop and maintain their friendships will undoubtedly change considerably—as will all sex-related variables—in the next several years. Perhaps there will be a further differentiation or perhaps an increase in similarities. In the meantime, given the present state of research in gender differences, we need to be careful not to exaggerate and to treat small differences as if they were highly significant. "Let us," warns one friendship researcher, "avoid stereotypes or, worse yet, caricatures" (Wright, 1988).

Further, friendship researchers warn that even when we find differences, the reasons for them are not always clear (Blieszner & Adams, 1992). An interesting example is the finding that middle-aged men have more friends than middle-aged women and that women have more intimate friendships (Fischer & Oliker, 1983). But why is this so? Do men have more friends because they are friendlier than women or because they have more opportunities to develop such friendships? Do women have more intimate friends because they have more opportunities to pursue such friendships or because they have a greater psychological capacity for intimacy?

Gender differences in love also exist. In the United States, the differences between men and women in love are considered great. In poetry, novels, and the mass media, women and men are depicted as acting very differently when falling in love, being in love, and ending a love relationship. As Lord Byron put it in *Don Juan,* "Man's love is of man's life a thing apart,/'Tis woman's whole existence." Women are portrayed as emotional, men as logical. Women are supposed to love intensely; men are supposed to love with detachment. Women are supposed to be more relationship-oriented than men.

Women and men seem to experience love to a similar degree (Rubin, 1973). However, women indicate greater love than men do for their same-sex friends. This may reflect a real difference between the sexes, or it may be a function of the greater social restrictions on men. A man is not supposed to admit his love for another man. Women are permitted greater freedom to communicate their love for other women.

Men and women also differ in the types of love they prefer (Hendrick et al., 1984). For example, on one version of the love self-test presented earlier ("What Kind of Lover Are You? on page 265), men have been found to score higher on erotic and ludic love, whereas women score higher on manic, pragmatic, and storgic love. No difference has been found for agapic love. Men also demonstrate a greater tendency to incorporate erotic materials (as well as alcohol and drugs) into sexual relationships than women do (Purnine, Carey, & Jorgensen, 1994).

Another gender difference frequently noted is that of romanticism. Women have their first romantic experiences earlier than men. The median age of first infatuation for women was 13 and for men, 13.6; the median age for first time in love for women was 17.1 and for men, 17.6 (Kirkpatrick & Caplow, 1945; Hendrick et al., 1984).

We love because it's the only true adventure.
—*Nikki Giovanni*

Men were found to place more emphasis on romance than women (Kirk-patrick & Caplow, 1945; Knapp & Vangelisti, 1992). For example, when college students were asked the question posed in the photo caption on page 285 (*"If a man [woman] has all the other qualities you desired, would you marry this person if you were not in love with him [her]?"*), approximately two-thirds of the men responded no, which seems to indicate that a high percentage were concerned with love and romance. However, less than one-third of the women responded no. Further, when men and women were surveyed concerning their view on love—whether it's basically realistic or basically romantic—it was found that married women had a more realistic (less romantic) conception of love than did married men.

> The magic of first love is our ignorance that it can never end.
> —*Benjamin Disraeli*

SKILL BUILDING EXERCISE 10.3.
From Culture to Gender

This exercise is designed to help you explore how cultures teach men and women different values and beliefs and how these might in turn influence the ways in which men and women communicate in relationships.

Select one of the beliefs listed below and indicate how you think the "typical man" and the "typical woman" would view this belief, for example: *Men are more likely to believe that women make more effective parents than men or Women believe that men have a higher commitment to career and desire for success than women do.*

Try to identify one way you think these beliefs influence the typical man's, the typical woman's, and the typical male–female interpersonal interaction, for example: *As a result of a man's belief that women make better parents, men have a tendency to leave parenting behaviors up to the woman or Men's belief that women make better parents leads men to avoid making parenting decisions.*

Think critically about your beliefs. What evidence can you offer for your beliefs about gender differences and about how these cultural beliefs influence interpersonal communication?

You may wish to extend this journey by actually locating the evidence bearing on your hypotheses. One way to do this is to access the CD-ROM databases which your school library is likely to have, for example, ERIC, psychlit, or sociofile. Do a find search for "gender" and the key word of the proposition, for example, gender + friendship or gender + money. Try several variations for each combination, for example, gender + finances, men + money, gender differences + finance.

Some abstracts you'll find will give you the results of the study but others will just identify the hypotheses studied—to discover what was found, you'd have to consult the original research study.

BELIEFS

1. The three most important qualities necessary for developing a romantic relationship
2. The importance of money in a relationship and in defining one's success or achievement
3. The role of politeness in interpersonal relationships
4. The tendency to nurture others
5. Effectiveness in parenting
6. The tendency to think emotionally rather than logically
7. The likelihood of becoming hysterical in, say, an argument or when placed in a dangerous situation
8. High commitment to career and desire for success
9. The likelihood of becoming depressed because of real or imagined problems
10. The importance placed on winning—with friends, loved ones, and business associates

Thinking Critically About Culture and Gender.
On the basis of your analysis and research, would you revise your beliefs? State them with even stronger conviction? Urge caution in accepting such beliefs?

More recent research (based on the romanticism questionnaire presented here) confirms this view that men are more romantic. For example, "Men are more likely than women to believe in love at first sight, in love as the basis for marriage and for overcoming obstacles, and to believe that their partner and relationship will be perfect" (Sprecher & Metts, 1989). This difference seems to increase as the romantic relationship develops: men become more romantic and women less romantic (Fengler, 1974).

Men and women differ also in breaking up a relationship (Blumstein & Schwartz, 1983; Janus & Janus, 1993). Popular myth would have us believe that love affairs break up as a result of the man's outside affair. But the research does not support this. When surveyed as to the reason for breaking up, only 15% of the men indicated that it was their interest in another partner, whereas 32% of the women noted this as a cause of the breakup. These findings are consistent with their partners' perceptions as well: 30% of the men (but only 15% of the women) noted that their partner's interest in another person was the reason for the breakup.

In their reactions to broken romantic affairs, women and men exhibit both similarities and differences. For example, the tendency for women and men to recall only pleasant memories and to revisit places with past associations was about equal. However, men engaged in more dreaming about the lost partner and in more daydreaming generally as a reaction to the breakup than did women.

What gender differences in relationship attitudes and behaviors do you think cause most heterosexual couples the most difficulty?

SUMMARY OF CONCEPTS AND SKILLS

In this chapter we explored why we form interpersonal relationships and the pattern that most relationships seem to follow. We examined five major explanations for why we develop, maintain, and dissolve relationships: attraction, relationship rules, social penetration, social exchange, and equity.

1. We develop relationships to alleviate loneliness, to gain stimulation, to gain self-knowledge, to increase self-esteem, and to maximize pleasure and minimize pain.
2. We establish relationships in stages. Recognize at least these: contact, involvement, intimacy, deterioration, repair, and dissolution.
3. Attraction, relationship rules, social penetration, social exchange, and equity theories are five explanations of what happens when we develop, maintain, and dissolve interpersonal relationships.
4. Attraction depends on five factors: attractiveness (physical and personality), proximity (physical closeness), reinforcement, and similarity (especially attitudinal).
5. The matching hypothesis holds that we mate with and date those who are about equivalent to ourselves in physical attractiveness.

6. The relationship rules approach looks at relationships as held together by agreement and adherence to an agreed upon set of rules.
7. Social penetration describes relationships in terms of breadth and depth. Breadth refers to the number of topics we talk about. Depth refers to the degree of personalness with which we pursue topics.
8. Social exchange theory holds that we develop relationships which yield the greatest profits. We seek relationships in which the rewards exceed the costs and are more likely to dissolve relationships when the costs exceed the rewards.
9. Each person has a comparison level—a level of expectations for what he or she feels should be derived from the relationship. When this level is reached or exceeded, you feel satisfied. When it's not reached, you feel dissatisfied.
10. Equity theory claims that we develop and maintain relationships in which rewards are distributed in proportion to costs. When our share of the rewards is less than would be demanded by equity, we are likely to experience dissatisfaction and exit the relationship.
11. Suggestions for improving relationship communication include empathic understanding, self-disclosures, openness to change, fair fighting, reasonableness, and a recognition of cultural and gender differences.

Check your ability to apply these skills. Use a rating scale such as the following: 1 = almost always, 2 = often, 3 = sometimes, 4 = rarely, and 5 = almost never.

_____ 1. See relationships as serving a variety of functions but not necessarily all at the same time.

_____ 2. Formulate both verbal and nonverbal messages that are appropriate to the stage of the relationship.

_____ 3. End relationships with a measure of comfort and control.

_____ 4. Use affinity seeking strategies as appropriate.

_____ 5. Examine your own relationships in terms of the insights of attraction, rules, social penetration, social exchange, and equity theories.

_____ 6. Use empathy and self-disclose as appropriate.

_____ 7. Be open to change and see relationships and people as ever changing.

_____ 8. Engage in conflict fairly.

_____ 9. Be reasonable in relationship expectations.

_____ 10. Take into consideration cultural and gender differences.

VOCABULARY QUIZ. THE LANGUAGE OF INTERPERSONAL RELATIONSHIPS

Match the terms dealing with interpersonal relationships with their definitions. Record the number of the definition next to the appropriate term.

_____ breadth of a relationship

_____ depth of a relationship

_____ depenetration

_____ proximity

_____ agape

_____ matching hypothesis

_____ social exchange theory

_____ contact

_____ equity

_____ complementarity

1. A theory claiming that we date and mate with those who are approximately equal to us in attractiveness.

2. The theory holding that we seek relationships from which we can derive the greatest profit, where reward exceeds the costs.

3. Physical closeness; a quality that contributes greatly to interpersonal attraction.

4. The degree to which the inner personality—the inner core of an individual—is penetrated in interpersonal interaction.

5. The first stage of an interpersonal relationship.

6. A condition in which the rewards in a relationship are distributed in proportion to the costs paid.

7. A condition where the breadth and depth of a relationship decreases.

8. A quality of interpersonal attraction more popularly referred to as "opposites attract."

9. A selfless, compassionate love.

10. The number of topics about which individuals in a relationship communicate.

11

Interpersonal
Communication
and Conflict

CHAPTER TOPICS	LEARNING GOALS	SKILLS GOALS
	After completing this chapter, you should be able to	*After completing this chapter, you should be able to*
The Nature of Interpersonal Conflict	1. Explain the nature of interpersonal conflict	Recognize the differences between content and relationship conflicts and respond appropriately to each
A Model of Conflict Resolution	2. Explain the model of conflict resolution	Deal with interpersonal conflicts in a systematic way
Conflict Management Strategies	3. Explain the unproductive and productive conflict strategies	Use more productive conflict strategies and avoid their unproductive counterparts

In ancient times the beautiful woman Mi Tzu-hsia was the favorite of the lord of Wei. Now, according to the law of Wei, anyone who rode in the king's carriage without permission would be punished by amputation of the foot. When Mi Tzu-hsia's mother fell ill, someone brought the news to her in the middle of the night. So she took the king's carriage and went out, and the king only praised her for it. "Such filial devotion!" he said. "For her mother's sake she risked the punishment of amputation!"

Another day she was dallying with the lord of Wei in the fruit garden. She took a peach, which she found so sweet that instead of finishing it she handed it to the lord to taste. "How she loves me," said the lord of Wei, "forgetting the pleasure of her own taste to share with me!"

But when Mi Tzu-hsia's beauty began to fade, the king's affection cooled. And when she offended the king, he said, "Didn't she once take my carriage without permission? And didn't she once give me a peach that she had already chewed on?"

> In a quarrel, each side is right.
> —*Yiddish proverb*

T his folktale—taken from *Chinese Fairy Tales and Fantasies* (Roberts, 1979)—tells of the common tendency to evaluate the same behavior in very different ways, depending on how you feel about the person. This tendency is especially clear in interpersonal conflict, the subject of this chapter. More specifically, in this chapter we consider what interpersonal conflict is, how it can go wrong, and how it can be used to improve your interpersonal relationships.

THE NATURE OF INTERPERSONAL CONFLICT

Tom wants to go to the movies and Sara wants to stay home. Tom's insistence on going to the movies interferes with Sara's staying home and Sara's determination to stay home interferes with Tom's going to the movies. Randy and Grace have been dating. Randy wants to get married; Grace wants to continue dating. Each has opposing goals and each interferes with each other's attaining these goals.

As experience teaches us, interpersonal conflicts can be of various types:

- Goals to be pursued ("We want you to go to college and become a teacher or a doctor, not a disco dancer")
- Allocation of resources such as money or time ("I want to spend the tax refund on a car, not on new furniture")

> It is seldom the fault of one when two argue.
> —*Swedish proverb*

Examine your assumptions about conflict. A useful critical thinking skill in studying interpersonal conflict (or any complex communication situation) is to identify the assumptions you're operating with and ask if these are true or false. For example, do you think the following are true or false?

• If two people in a relationship fight, it means their relationship is a bad one.
• Fighting hurts an interpersonal relationship.
• Fighting is bad because it reveals your negative selves, for example, pettiness, need to be in control, or unreasonable expectations.

As with most things, simple answers are usually wrong. The three assumptions may all be true or may all be false. It depends. In and of itself, conflict is neither good nor bad and is a part of every interpersonal relationship. How do your assumptions influence your approach to conflict? Your conflict strategies?

If we understand others' languages, but not their culture, we can make fluent fools of ourselves.

—*William B. Gudykunst*

• Decisions to be made ("I refuse to have the Jeffersons over for dinner")
• Behaviors that are considered appropriate or desirable by one person and inappropriate or undesirable by the other. "I hate it when you get drunk, pinch me, ridicule me in front of others, flirt with others, dress provocatively,. . . .")

Interpersonal conflict refers to a disagreement between or among connective individuals: close friends, lovers, or family members. By including the word "connected," we emphasize the transactional nature of interpersonal conflict, the fact that each person's position affects the other person. The positions in conflicts are to some degree interrelated and incompatible.

Culture and Conflict

As with other topics of interpersonal communication, it helps to view conflict in light of culture. Culture influences the issues that people fight about as well as what is considered appropriate and inappropriate in terms of dealing with conflict. For example, cohabitating 18-year-olds are more likely to experience conflict with their parents about their living style if they lived in the United States than if they lived in Sweden, where cohabitation is much more accepted. Similarly, male infidelity is more likely to cause conflict among American couples than among Southern European couples. Students from the United States are more likely to engage in conflict with another United States student than with someone from another culture. Chinese students, on the other hand, are more likely to engage in a conflict with a non-Chinese student than with another Chinese student (Leung, 1988).

The types of conflicts that arise depend on the cultural orientation of the individuals involved. For example, it is likely that in collectivist cultures, such as Ecuador, Indonesia, and Korea, conflicts are more likely to center on violating collective or group norms and values. Conversely, it is likely that in individualist cultures, such as the United States, Canada, and Western Europe, conflicts are more likely to occur when individual norms are violated (Ting-Toomey, 1985).

The ways in which members of different cultures express conflict also differ. In Japan, for example, it's especially important that you not embarrass the person with whom you are in conflict, especially if that conflict occurs in public. This face-saving principle prohibits the use of such strategies as personal rejection or verbal aggressiveness. In the United States, men and women, ideally at least, are both expected to express their desires and complaints openly and directly. Many Middle Eastern and Pacific Rim cultures would discourage women from such expressions. Rather, a more agreeable and permissive posture would be expected.

Even within a given general culture, more specific cultures differ from each other in their methods of conflict management. African American men and women and European American men and women, for example, engage in conflict in very different ways (Kochman, 1981). The issues that cause conflict and aggravate conflict, the conflict strategies that are expected and accepted, and the entire attitude toward conflict vary from one group to the other.

For example, African American men prefer to manage conflict with clear arguments and a focus on problem-solving. African American women, however, deal with conflict through expressing assertiveness and respect (Collier, 1991). In another study, African American females were found to use more direct controlling strategies (for example, assuming control over the conflict and arguing persistently for their point of view) than did European American females. European American females, on the other hand, used more problem-solution-oriented conflict management styles than did African American women. Interestingly, African American and European American men were very similar in their conflict management strategies: both tended to avoid or withdraw from relationship conflict. They preferred to keep quiet about their differences or downplay their significance (Ting-Toomey, 1986).

Among Mexican Americans, men prefer to achieve mutual understanding through discussing the reasons for the conflict while women focused on being supportive of the relationship. Among Anglo-Americans, men preferred direct and rational argument while women preferred flexibility. These, of course, are merely examples, but the underlying principle is that techniques for dealing with interpersonal conflict will be viewed differently by different cultures.

Gender and Conflict

Do men and women engage in conflict differently? Are there significant gender differences in the way people engage in interpersonal conflict? One of the few stereotypes that is supported by research is that of the withdrawing and sometime aggressive male. Men are more apt to withdraw from a conflict situation than are women. It's been argued that this may be due to the fact that men become more psychologically and physiologically aroused during conflict (and retain this heightened level of arousal much longer than do women) and so may try to distance themselves and withdraw from the conflict to prevent further arousal (Gottman & Carrere, 1994; Canary, Cupach, & Messman, 1995; Goleman, 1995a). Women, on the other hand, want to get closer to the conflict; they want to talk about it and resolve it. Even adolescents reveal these differences; in a study of boys and girls aged 11–17, boys withdrew more than girls but were more aggressive when they didn't withdraw (Lindeman, Harakka, & Keltikangas-Jarvinen, 1997). Similarly, in a study of offensive language, women were found to be more easily offended by language than were boys; but boys were more apt to fight when they were offended by the words used (Heasley, Babbitt, & Burbach, 1995).

Other research has found that women are more emotional and men are more logical when they argue (Schaap, Buunk, & Kerkstra, 1988; Canary, Cupach, & Messman, 1995). Women have been defined as conflict "feelers" and men as conflict "thinkers" (Sorenson, Hawkins, & Sorenson, 1995). Another difference found is that women are more apt to reveal their negative feelings than are men (Schaap, Buunk, & Kerkstra, 1988; Canary, Cupach, & Messman, 1995).

From a close examination of the research, it would have to be concluded that the differences between men and women in interpersonal conflict are a lot clearer in the popular stereotypes than they are in reality. Much research fails to find the differences that cartoons, situation comedies, novels, and films portray so readily and so clearly. For example, in a number of studies, dealing with both college students and men and women in business, no significant differences were found in the way men and women engage in conflict (Wilkins & Andersen, 1991; Canary & Hause, 1993; Canary, Cupach, & Messman, 1995).

Content and Relationship Conflicts

Using concepts developed earlier (Chapter 1), we may distinguish between content conflict and relationship conflict. *Content conflict* centers on objects, events, and persons in the world that are usually, but not always, external to

Do men and women use the same conflict resolution strategies? *(Interesting papers could review an article on gender differences and conflict, review the literature on the topic, or provide the stimulus for an original research paper.)*

CAUTION

How might **failing to appreciate gender and cultural variations in approaches to conflict** lead you to misread the verbal and nonverbal cues of the other person? Can you imagine an experience where this could happen?

the parties involved in the conflict. These include the millions of issues that we argue and fight about every day—the value of a particular movie, what to watch on television, the fairness of the last examination or job promotion, and the way to spend our savings.

Relationship conflicts are equally numerous and include such situations as a younger brother refusing to obey his older brother, two partners who each want an equal say in making vacation plans, and the mother and daughter who each want to have the final word concerning the daughter's life-style. Here the conflicts are concerned not so much with some external object as with the relationships between the individuals, with such issues as who is in charge, the equality of a primary relationship, and who has the right to set down rules of behavior.

Content and relationship conflicts are always easier to separate in a textbook than they are in real life, where many conflicts contain elements of both. Consider, for example, some of the issues that people argue about. Take a look at Table 11.1 and at the bulleted list that follows, which present the results of two research studies. In the first study, gay, lesbian, and heterosexual couples were surveyed on the issues they argued about most; the findings are presented in Table 11.1 (Kurdek, 1994). As you can see, real conflicts are not easy to classify into content or relationship issues, yet recognizing that there are different types of conflict will give you greater insight into the reasons for the conflicts and perhaps suggest strategies for resolving them.

In another study, four conditions led up to a couple's "first big fight" (Siegert & Stamp, 1994):

- uncertainty over commitment
- jealousy
- violation of expectations
- personality differences

CAUTION

How might **failing to distinguish relational from content conflicts** lead you to misperceive the causes of a problem or argument? Have you ever been accused of failing to see what the "real" conflict is about? Were you accused of misunderstanding the content conflict or the relationship conflict?

Where there is no difference, there is only indifference.
—Louis Nizer

Table 11.1 Interpersonal Conflict Issues

This table presents the rank order of the six most frequently argued about issues (1 = the most argued about). Note the striking similarity among all couples. It seems that affectional orientation has little to do with the topics people argue about. Are these topics similar to those you argue about? Are these topics similar to those your friends and colleagues argue about?

Issue	Gay (N = 75)	Lesbian (N = 51)	Heterosexual (N = 108)
Intimacy issues such as affection and sex	1	1	1
Power issues such as excessive demands or possessiveness, lack of equality in the relationship, friends, and leisure time	2	2	2
Personal flaws issues such as drinking or smoking, personal grooming, and driving style	3	3	4
Personal distance issues such as frequently being absent and school or job commitments	4	4	5
Social issues such as politics and social issues, parents, and personal values	5	5	3
Distrust issues such as previous lovers and lying	6	6	6

Do you find that men and women are equally likely to argue about relationship issues? Are men and women equally likely to address relationship issues in their attempts at conflict resolution?

Online Conflicts

Just as you experience conflict in face-to-face communication, you can experience the same conflicts online. A few conflict situations that are unique to online communication may be noted here.

Sending commercial messages to those who didn't request them often creates conflict. Junk mail is junk mail; but on the Internet, the receiver has to pay for the time it takes to read and delete these unwanted messages.

Spamming often causes conflict. Spamming is sending someone unsolicited mail, repeatedly sending the same mail, or posting the same message on lots of bulletin boards, even when the message is irrelevant to the focus of the group. One of the very practical reasons spamming is frowned upon is that it generally costs people money. And even if the e-mail is free, it takes up valuable time and energy to read something you didn't want in the first place. Another reason, of course, is that it clogs the system, slowing it down for everyone.

Flaming, especially common in newsgroups, refers to sending messages that personally attack another user. Frequently, flaming leads to flame wars where everyone in the group gets into the act and attacks each other. Generally, flaming and flame wars prevent us from achieving our goals and so are counterproductive.

Access ERIC, *Medline,* Psychlit, or Sociofile and locate an article dealing with interpersonal conflict. What can you learn about conflict and interpersonal communication from this article? *(Reviewing this article or a series of articles on interpersonal conflict would make an excellent review paper.)*

In what other ways is face-to-face conflict different from conflict on the net?

The Negatives and Positives of Conflict

The kind of conflict we focus on here is interpersonal, conflict among or between "connected" individuals. Interpersonal conflict occurs frequently between lovers, best friends, siblings, and parent and child. Interpersonal conflict is made all the more difficult because, unlike many other conflict situations, we care for, like, even love the individual with whom we are in disagreement. There are both negative and positive aspects or dimensions to interpersonal conflict, and each of these should be noted.

Negative Aspects

Conflict often leads to increased negative regard for the opponent. One reason for this is that many conflicts involve unfair fighting methods and are focused largely on hurting the other person. When one person hurts the other, increased negative feelings are inevitable; even the strongest relationship has limits.

At times conflict may lead you to close yourself off from the other person. When you hide your true self from an intimate, you prevent meaningful communication from taking place. Because the need for intimacy is so strong, one or both parties may seek this intimacy elsewhere. This often leads to further conflict, mutual hurt, and resentment—qualities that add heavily to the costs carried by the relationship. As these costs increase, the rewards may become difficult to exchange. In this situation, the costs increase and the rewards decrease, which often results in relationship deterioration and eventual dissolution.

Positive Aspects

The major value of interpersonal conflict is that it forces you to examine a problem and work toward a potential solution. If productive conflict strategies are used, the relationship may well emerge from the encounter stronger, healthier, and more satisfying than before. And you may emerge stronger, more confident to stand up for yourself (Bedford, 1996).

Conflict enables you to state what you each want and—if the conflict is resolved effectively—perhaps to get it. For example, let's say that I want to

Every difficulty slurred over will be a ghost to disturb your repose later on.

—*Chopin*

spend our money on a new car (my old one is unreliable) and you want to spend it on a vacation (you feel the need for a change of pace). Through our conflict and its resolution, we hopefully learn what each really wants. In this case, a reliable car and a break from routine. We may then be able to figure out a way for us each to get what we want. I might accept a good used car or a less expensive new car and you might accept a shorter or less expensive vacation. Or we might buy a used car and take an inexpensive motor trip. Each of these solutions will satisfy both of us—they are win–win solutions—each of us wins, each of us gets what we wanted.

Through our conflict and its resolution we stop resentment from increasing and let our needs be known: I need lots of attention when I come home from work; you need to review and get closure on the day's work. If we both can appreciate the legitimacy of these needs, then solutions may be easily identified. Perhaps the phone call can be made after my attention needs are met or perhaps I can delay my need for attention until you get closure about work. Or, perhaps I can learn to provide for your closure needs and in doing so get my attention needs met. Again, we have win-win solutions; each of us gets our needs met.

Consider, too, that when you try to resolve conflict within an interpersonal relationship, you're saying in effect that the relationship is worth the effort; otherwise you would walk away from such a conflict. Usually, confronting a conflict indicates commitment and a desire to preserve the relationship.

> What, if any, positive outcomes emerged from your previous interpersonal conflicts? What negative outcomes?

Before and After the Conflict

If you're to make conflict truly productive, consider these suggestions for preparing for the conflict and for using the conflict as a method for relational growth.

Before the Conflict

Try to fight in private. When you air your conflicts in front of others you create a wide variety of other problems. You may not be willing to be totally honest when third parties are present; you may feel you have to save face and therefore must win the fight at all costs. This may lead you to use strategies to win the argument rather than to resolve the conflict. Also, you run the risk of embarrassing your partner in front of others, which will incur resentment and hostility.

Make sure you're both relatively free of other problems and ready to deal with the conflict at hand. Confronting your partner when she or he comes home after a hard day of work may not be the right time for resolving a conflict.

Know what you're fighting about. Sometimes people in a relationship become so hurt and angry that they lash out at the other person just to vent their own frustration. The problem at the center of the conflict (for example, the uncapped toothpaste tube) is merely an excuse to express anger. Instead, it's the underlying hostility, anger, and frustration that needs to be addressed.

Fight about problems that can be solved. Fighting about past behaviors or about family members or situations over which you have no control solves nothing; instead, it creates additional difficulties. Any attempt at resolution is doomed to failure since the problems are incapable of being solved. Often such conflicts are concealed attempts at expressing one's frustration or dissatisfaction.

> One learns to itch where one can scratch.
>
> —Ernest Bramah

After the Conflict

Learn from the conflict and from the process you went through in trying to resolve it. For example, can you identify the fight strategies that aggravated the situation? Do you or your partner need a cooling off period? Can you tell when minor issues are going to escalate into major arguments? What issues are particularly disturbing and likely to cause difficulties? How can these be avoided?

Keep the conflict in perspective. Be careful not to blow it out of proportion. In most relationships, conflicts actually occupy a very small percentage of the couple's time and yet in their recollection, they often loom extremely large. Don't view yourself, your partner, or your relationship as failures just because you have conflicts.

Attack your negative feelings. Often such feelings arise because unfair fight strategies were used to undermine the other person—for example, blame or verbal aggressiveness. Resolve to avoid such unfair tactics in the future, but at the same time let go of guilt or blame for yourself and your partner.

Increase the exchange of rewards and cherishing behaviors. These will show your positive feelings and that you're over the conflict and want the relationship to survive.

> Beware of allowing a tactless word, a rebuttal, a rejection to obliterate the whole sky.
>
> —Anais Nin

HOW TO . . .
Deal with Complaints

Complaints—whether in an interpersonal situation (or an organizational or small group one)—are essential sources of feedback; they tell you that at least one person (perhaps many) is dissatisfied with the way things are going and that something should be changed. If you wish to keep this channel of vital information open then try these suggestions for dealing with complaints.

1. Let the person know that you're open to complaints and that you do view them as essential sources of information. Welcome complaints, stress that they are essential for improving a relationship (or an organization). And be careful that you don't fall into the trap of seeing someone who voices a complaint as a complainer and as someone to avoid.

2. Listen to complaints. Follow the suggestions for effective listening already discussed: listen supportively and with empathy. Give the person voicing the complaint your complete attention and avoid interrupting. And avoid looking at your watch; complaints are extremely hard to voice and looking at your watch only puts added pressure on the person and says, in effect, "I have more important things to do; could you hurry up."

3. Make sure you understand both the thoughts and the feelings that go with the complaint. Listen to both the complaint about working too hard and to the frustration that your partner feels when he or she has to work overtime and then come home and do additional chores. And respond to both the thoughts and feelings. Express your concern about the workload and the frustration that these excessive demands create.

4. Ask your partner what he or she would like you to do about the complaint. Sometimes, all a person wants is for someone to hear the complaint and to appreciate its legitimacy. Other times, the complaint is presented for you to do something specific. But, before you assume that you know what the person really wants, ask. The very act of asking is a further affirmation that you do welcome complaints and that you do value the person's bringing this to your attention.

[The next How To box appears on page 327.]

SKILL BUILDING EXERCISE 11.1.
Dealing with Conflict Starters

The purpose of this exercise is to preview some of the issues that will be considered in the rest of this chapter and to give you some practice in responding to potential interpersonal conflicts. Although we will provide a lot of examples of unproductive and productive conflict strategies, use your own conflict experiences as a guide in this exercise. For each situation: (1) write an unproductive response, that is, a response that will aggravate the potential conflict (why do you assume this response will intensify the conflict?), and (2) write a productive response, that is, a response that will lessen the potential conflict (why do you assume this response will help resolve the conflict?).

CONFLICT "STARTERS"

1. You're late again. You're always late. Your lateness is so inconsiderate of my time and my interests.
2. I just can't bear another weekend of sitting home watching cartoon shows with the kids. I'm just not going to do that again.
3. Who forgot to phone for reservations?
4. Well, there goes another anniversary and another anniversary that you forgot.
5. You think I'm fat, don't you?
6. Just leave me alone.
7. Did I hear you say your mother knows how to dress?
8. We should have been more available when he needed us. I was always at work.
9. Where's the pepper? Is there no pepper in this house?
10. The Romeros think we should spend our money and start enjoying life.

Thinking Critically About Conflict Starters.
After you've finished reading this chapter, you may wish to return to this exercise and do it again. At that point, ask yourself if your attitudes toward conflict have changed. Will you approach interpersonal conflict differently? Will you use different conflict strategies?

A MODEL OF CONFLICT RESOLUTION

We can explain conflict more fully and at the same time provide guidance in dealing with conflicts effectively by referring to the model in Figure 11.1. This model is based on the problem-solving technique introduced by John Dewey (1910) and used by contemporary theorists (for example, Beebe & Masterson, 1997). The assumption made here is that interpersonal conflict is essentially a problem that needs to be solved.

Define the Conflict

Your first step is to define the conflict. This is the most essential step in the entire process of managing conflict. **Define both the content and the relationship issues.** Define the obvious content issues (who should do the dishes, who should take the kids to school, who should take out the dog) as well as the underlying relational issues (who's been avoiding household responsibilities, who has been neglecting their responsibility toward the kids, who's time is more valuable).

Define the problem in specific terms. Conflict defined in the abstract is difficult to deal with and resolve. It's one thing for the husband to say that his wife is "cold and unfeeling" and quite another to say she does not call him at

Evaluating Information

Critically evaluate your decision making processes. Here are three general suggestions:

Avoid thinking through filters of unstated assumptions. Identify your assumptions and the ways in which they influence the messages you send and the messages you receive.

Massage your problem. Focus on the problem itself, rephrase it, write it, say it in different ways or even in different languages.

Introduce change. If you find yourself at an impasse sitting at your desk, get up and take a walk. Or change the popular music to rap or opera. Or get involved in a soap opera for a few minutes. You may then find yourself looking at your problem from a different perspective.

Figure 11.1

The Stages of Conflict Resolution

This model derives from John Dewey's stages of reflective thinking and is a general pattern for understanding and resolving any type of problem. This model should not be taken as suggesting that there is only one path to conflict resolution. This is just one general way. Recall a specific conflict that you had recently and try to trace it through these stages as you read about them.

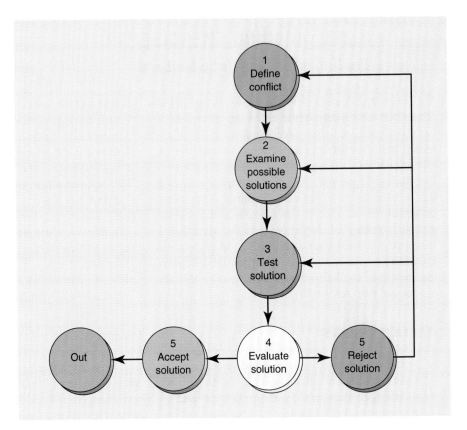

Acquiring Information

Look at a problem with three critical thinking hats. Critical thinking pioneer Edward deBono (1987) suggests that in analyzing problems, you use six "thinking hats" as a way of seeking different perspectives. With each hat you look at the problem from a different angle. Here are three hats:

- **The fact hat** focuses attention on the facts and figures that bear on the problem. For example, *How can Raul learn more about the rewards that Julia gets from her friends? How can Julia learn why Raul doesn't like her friends?*
- **The feeling hat** focuses attention on the emotional responses to the problem. *How does Raul feel when Julia goes out with friends? How does Julia feel when Raul refuses to meet them?*
- **The negative argument hat** asks you to become the devil's advocate. *How might this relationship deteriorate if Julia continues seeing her friends without Raul or if Raul resists interacting with Julia's friends?*

the office or kiss him when he comes home or hold his hand when they are at a party. These behaviors can be agreed upon and dealt with, but the abstract "cold and unfeeling" remains elusive.

Let us select an example and work it through the remaining steps. This conflict concerns Raul and Julia. Their conflict revolves around Raul not wanting to socialize with Julia's friends. While Julia is devoted to them, Raul actively dislikes them. Julia thinks they are wonderful and exciting; Raul thinks they are unpleasant and boring. Julia says that these friends make her feel important and intelligent. For example, her friends frequently look to her for advice.

Examine Possible Solutions

Look for possible ways of resolving the conflict. Most conflicts can probably be resolved through a variety of solutions. At this stage try to identify as many solutions as possible.

Look for **win–win** solutions. Look for solutions that will enable both parties to win—to get something each wants. Avoid **win–lose** solutions. These are solutions in which one of you wins and one of you loses, and will frequently cause frustration and resentment. In trying to achieve win-win solutions, consider the value of compromise where you each willingly give up a part of what you want so that you both can achieve some positive result. In our example, Raul might agree to meet with Julia and her friends *occasionally*. Julia, on the other hand, might agree to *occasionally* give up some meetings with her friends and devote this time only to Raul (Folger, Poole, & Stutman, 1997).

In examining these various potential solutions, carefully weigh the costs and the rewards that each solution will entail. Most solutions will involve costs to one or both parties (after all, someone has to take the dog out). Seek solutions in which the costs will be evenly shared. Similarly, seek solutions in which both parties share equally (or about equally) in the rewards. Once you have examined all possible solutions, select one and test it out.

Among the solutions that Raul and Julia identify are these:

1. Julia should not interact with her friends anymore.
2. Raul should interact with Julia's friends.
3. Julia should see her friends without Raul.

Clearly solutions 1 and 2 are win-lose solutions. In Solution 1, Raul wins and Julia loses. In Solution 2, Julia wins and Raul loses. Solution 3 has some possibilities. Both might win and neither must necessarily lose. Let's examine this solution more closely by testing it.

Test the Solution

Test the solution mentally. How does it feel now? How will it feel tomorrow? Are you comfortable with the solution? Would Raul be comfortable with Julia socializing with her friends without him? Some of Julia's friends are attractive unmarried men. Is this going to make a difference? Would Julia be comfortable with socializing with her friends without Raul? Will she give people too much to gossip about? Will she feel guilty? Will she enjoy herself without Raul?

Test the solution in actual practice. Put the solution into actual operation. How does it work in practice? Give each solution a fair chance. Perhaps Julia might go out without Raul once to try it out. How was it? Did her friends think there was something wrong with her relationship with Raul? Did she feel guilty? Did she enjoy herself? How did Raul feel? Did he feel jealous? Did he feel lonely or abandoned?

Evaluate the Solution

Did the solution help resolve the conflict? Is the situation better now than it was before the solution was put into operation? Share your feelings and evaluations of the solution. Use the skills for expressing emotions that we covered in Chapter 7.

Raul and Julia now need to share their perceptions of this possible solution. Would they be comfortable with this solution on a monthly basis? Is the solution worth the costs that each will pay? Are the costs and the rewards about evenly distributed? Might other solutions be more effective?

Accept or Reject the Solution

If you accept the solution, you're ready to put this solution into more permanent operation. If you decide, on the basis of your evaluation, that this is not the right solution for the conflict, then there are two major alternatives. First, you might test another solution. Perhaps the solution you thought second best might now be examined more closely. Second, you might go back

CAUTION

Can you recall a specific instance where you found yourself **dealing with ill-defined conflicts?** Did this diffuse your thinking or prevent you from centering your attention on those problems causing the conflict? What happened?

Acquiring Information

Look at a problem with three more critical thinking hats.

- **The positive benefits hat** asks you to look at the upside. *What are the opportunities that Julia's seeing friends without Raul might yield? What benefits might Raul and Julia get from this new arrangement?*
- **The creative new idea hat** focuses on new ways of looking at the problem. *In what other ways can you look at this problem? What other possible solutions might you consider?*
- **The control of thinking hat** helps you analyze what you're doing; it asks you to reflect on your own thinking. *Have you adequately defined the problem? Are you focusing too much on insignificant issues? Have you given enough attention to possible negative effects?*

SKILL BUILDING EXERCISE 11.2.

Generating Win–Win Solutions

In any interpersonal conflict, you have a choice. You can look for solutions in which one person wins, usually you, and one person loses, usually the other person (win–lose solutions). Or you can look for solutions in which you and the other person both win (win–win solutions). Obviously, win–win solutions are the more desirable, at least when the conflict is interpersonal. Often, however, people fail to even consider if there are possible win–win solutions and what they might be. To get into the habit of looking for win–win solutions, consider the following conflict situations, either alone or in groups of five or six. For each of the situations, try generating as many possible win–win solutions that you feel the individuals involved in the conflict could reasonably accept. Give yourself two minutes for each case. Write down all win–win solutions that you (or the group) think of; don't censor yourself or any members of the group.

1. Pat and Chris plan to take a two week vacation in August. Pat wants to go to the shore and relax by the water. Chris wants to go hiking and camping in the mountains.
2. Pat recently got a $3000 totally unexpected bonus. Pat wants to buy a new computer and printer to augment the office; Chris wants to take a much needed vacation.
3. Pat hangs around the house in underwear. Chris really hates this and they argue about it almost daily.
4. Philip has recently come out as gay to his parents. He wants them to accept him and his lifestyle (which includes a committed relationship with another man). His parents refuse to accept him and want him to seek religious counseling to change.
5. Workers at the local bottling plant want a 20 percent raise to bring them into line with the salaries of similar workers at other plants. Management has repeatedly turned down their requests.

Thinking Critically About Win–Win Solutions. If possible, share your win–win solutions with other individuals or groups. From this experience it should be clear that win–win solutions exist for most conflict situations but not necessarily all. And, of course, some situations will allow for the easy generation of a lot more win–win solutions than others. Not all conflicts are equal. How might you incorporate win–win strategies into your own conflict management behavior?

Recall a recent conflict. Did you follow (at least generally) the five stages identified in this model? If not, can you identify the steps you did follow? How effective was the pattern you did use? *(Your interpersonal conflict experiences and the ways you tried to resolve them would make an interesting personal experience paper.)*

to the definition of the conflict. As the diagram illustrates, you can reenter the conflict-resolution process at any of the first three stages.

Let us say that Raul is actually quite happy with the solution. He had the opportunity to use that time to visit his brother. Next time Julia goes out with her friends, he intends to go to wrestling. Julia feels pretty good about seeing her friends without Raul. She explained that she and Raul have decided that she would see her friends alone and both were comfortable with this.

CONFLICT MANAGEMENT STRATEGIES

Throughout the process of resolving conflict, try to avoid the common but damaging strategies that can destroy a relationship. At the same time, apply those strategies that will help to resolve the conflict and even improve the relationship.

LISTENING.
Messages in Conflict

Perhaps the most difficult type of listening occurs in the conflict situation, where tempers may run high and where you may find yourself attacked or at least disagreed with. Here are some suggestions for listening more effectively in the conflict situation.

1. Act in the role of the listener. And think as a listener. Turn off the television, stereo, or computer; face the other person. Devote your total attention to what the other person is saying.
2. Make sure you understand what the person is saying and feeling. One way to make sure is obviously to ask questions. Another way is to paraphrase what the other person is saying and ask for confirmation: "You feel that if we pooled our money and did not have separate savings accounts that you'd feel the relationship would be a more equitable one. Is that the way you feel?"
3. Express your support or empathy for what the other person is saying and feeling: "I can understand how you feel. I know I control the finances and that can create a feeling of inequality."
4. If appropriate, indicate your agreement: "You're right to be disturbed."
5. State your thoughts and feelings on the issue as objectively as you can; if you disagree with what the other person said, then say so: "My problem is that when we did have equal access to the finances, you ran up so many bills that we still haven't recovered from. And, to be honest with you, I'm worried the same thing will happen again."
6. Get ready to listen to the other person's responses to your statement.

[The next Listening box appears on page 335.]

This article offers a brief self-test on your style of criticism and some useful suggestions for dealing with this difficult but inevitable part of interpersonal communication.

How to Take the Bite out of Criticism

Roberta Roesch

. . . Kay has been married less than a month. But she's ready to give up on Don for his habit of dumping his clothes and belongings wherever he happens to be. "When he left his muddy running shoes on top of my new microwave I screamed at him like a fish-wife," she says, "and asked him why his mother had brought up such a slob. He immediately defended his mother and started to criticize mine. Then we both got on the defensive and had a knock-down fight."

Dr. Harriet Lefkowith, a Tenafly, N.J. human resource development specialist who leads workshops on communications throughout the country says, "Because criticism has such a negative connotation, we get into situations where the people we criticize invariably react defensively.

"Before you know it, the act of criticism turns into an armed camp with two sides. Nobody's thinking. There's no problem solving. Everyone's defending himself or herself."

Since each of us has our own systems and standards, it's human to criticize. But in order to do it in a manner that keeps personal and working relationships from landing on the rocks, it's important to understand . . . how we can give it in a way that won't make temperatures rise . . . .

HOW TO CRITICIZE

Depending on how you criticize, you can anticipate a variety of responses. Jean, for instance, got a good response when she appeared to be taking responsibility for the situation. In another case, Susan got the hoped-for results by getting to the point instead of beating around the bush. Initially, she was critical of Steve, in a general way. But Steve never got the message—especially about visiting her mother.

"In a situation such as this, it's not useful to say 'You hate my relatives and you never visit my mother,'" states Swensen. "A concrete suggestion such as 'I think my mom would really like it if you could come along with me when I go down to visit her this Saturday' will always get a better reaction than 'You never want to come with me.'"

Although responses vary with persons and circumstances, Swensen advises that usually you can expect one of these four reactions:

- People may become hostile and defend themselves and attack you as they resent and reject the criticism.
- They may point out how the criticism is based on misunderstanding or error and say, "That isn't the way it happened. That isn't what I did. That isn't what I intended."
- They may say, "I didn't know about that" or "That never occurred to me and I really don't think that's the way I react. But I'll give it some thought and see whether there's truth to it."
- Miraculously, they may agree with you.

While there's no guarantee you can always get the miracle response, there are ways to sweeten criticism and give it in a manner that won't sour relationships.

To find out how well you give criticism, take the following quiz. Circle the responses that apply to you and score yourself at the end.

1. Do you proceed cautiously by trying to understand why the behavior bothers you before you criticize it?
   (a) yes. (b) sometimes. (c) no.
2. Do you think through what you're going to say before speaking your mind?
   (a) yes. (b) sometimes. (c) no.
3. Do you criticize as soon as possible after the incident that bothers you occurs?
   (a) yes. (b) sometimes. (c) no.
4. Do you focus on what is done well and approach negatives in constructive ways?
   (a) yes. (b) sometimes. (c) no.
5. Do you suggest positive and beneficial solutions to the behavior you criticize?
   (a) yes. (b) sometimes. (c) no.
6. Do you avoid criticizing others when you're angry, overtired, or frustrated?
   (a) yes. (b) sometimes. (c) no.
7. Do you hold back from being critical when you see traits in others you don't like in yourself—or behavior patterns your parents had that always bothered you?
   (a) yes. (b) sometimes. (c) no.
8. Do you choose a place for criticism where you can be alone?
   (a) yes. (b) sometimes. (c) no.
9. Do you steer clear of putting people down when they feel worthless, hopeless, or useless?
   (a) yes. (b) sometimes. (c) no.
10. Do you avoid unmeasured honesty and frankness when criticizing?
    (a) yes. (b) sometimes. (c) no.
11. Do you speak in a concrete, tactful way and avoid vague generalities?
    (a) yes. (b) sometimes. (c) no.
12. Do you limit the length of your criticism and avoid going on and on?
    (a) yes. (b) sometimes. (c) no.

Scoring

Add up your A, B and C answers. If the majority are A, you're already at the top of the class in criticizing effectively. But if B's and C's (or overwhelmingly C's) overshadow your A's, you'll do well to smarten up the way you criticize other people.

Conclusion

In the final analysis, there's no pat formula for leveling criticism in the smartest and sweetest way. However, if your words are sincere and caring, you can provide the most benefit to your co-workers, friends, family and yourself.

Thinking Critically About "Criticism."   What additional suggestions for expressing criticism would you include if you were writing this article? If you were writing this article for the intercultural communication chapter, what additional ideas would you include? Do men and women express and receive criticism in the same way? Does criticism differ when it occurs between members of different sexes versus members of the same sex? What types of criticism are you most open to hearing? Least open to?

Source: "How to Take a Bite out of Criticism" by Roberta Roesch as appeared in *Relationships Today,* August 1988. Copyright © 1988 by Roberta Roesch. Reprinted by permission of the author.

Avoidance and Fighting Actively

Avoidance may involve actual physical flight. You may leave the scene of the conflict (walk out of the apartment or go to another part of the office or shop), fall asleep, or blast the stereo to drown out all conversation. It may also take the form of emotional or intellectual avoidance. Here you may leave the conflict psychologically by not dealing with any of the arguments or problems raised.

Nonnegotiation is a special type of avoidance. Here you refuse to discuss the conflict or to listen to the other person's argument. At times this nonnegotiation takes the form of hammering away at one's own point of view until the other person gives in. We call this technique "steamrolling."

Instead of avoiding the issues, take an active role in your interpersonal conflicts. Involve yourself on both sides of the communication exchange. Be an active participant as a speaker and as a listener; voice your own feelings and

Never go to bed mad. Stay up and fight.

—*Phyllis Diller*

listen carefully to the voicing of your opponent's feelings. This is not to say that periodic moratoriums are not helpful; sometimes they are. Be willing to communicate as both sender and receiver—to say what is on your mind and to listen to what the other person is saying.

Another part of active fighting involves taking responsibility for your thoughts and feelings. For example, when you disagree with your partner or find fault with her or his behavior, take responsibility for these feelings. Say, for example, "I disagree with . . ." or "I don't like it when you . . . ." Avoid statements that deny your responsibility, for example, "Everybody thinks you're wrong about . . ." or "Chris thinks you shouldn't . . . ."

Force and Talk

When confronted with conflict, many people prefer not to deal with the issues but rather to physically force their position on the other person. The force may be emotional or physical. In either case, however, the issues are avoided and the person who "wins" is the one who exerts the most force. This is the technique of warring nations, children, and even some normally sensible and mature adults.

Over 50% of both single and married couples reported that they had experienced physical violence in their relationship. If we add symbolic violence (for example, threatening to hit the other person or throwing something), the percentages are above 60% for singles and above 70% for marrieds (Marshall & Rose, 1987). In another study, 47% of a sample of 410 college students reported some experience with violence in a dating relationship. In most cases, the violence was reciprocal—each person in the relationship used violence. In cases where only one person was violent, the research results are conflicting. For example, Deal and Wampler (1986) found that in cases where one partner was violent, the aggressor was significantly more often the female partner. Earlier research found similar sex differences (for example, Cate et al., 1982). Other research, however, has found that the popular conception of men being more likely to use force than women is indeed true (DeTurck, 1987): Men are more apt than women to use violent methods to achieve compliance.

The only real alternative to force is talk. Instead of force, talk and listen. The qualities of openness, empathy, and positiveness, for example, are suitable starting points (see Chapter 8).

Visit some game Websites (for example, http://www.gamesdomain.co.uk or http://www.gamepen.com/yellowpages/) and examine the rules of the games. What kinds of conflict strategies do these game rules embody? Do you think these influence people's interpersonal conflict strategies?

You cannot shake hands with a clenched fist.

—*Indira Gandhi*

© 1994. Reprinted courtesy of Bunny Hoest and Parade Magazine.

"We only learned to talk yesterday, and now we're not speaking."

Defensiveness and Supportiveness

Although talk is preferred to force, not all talk is equally productive in conflict resolution. One of the best ways to look at "destructive" and "productive"
talk is to look at how the style of your communications can create the unproductive defensiveness or the productive supportiveness (Gibb, 1961). The
types of talk that generally prove destructive and set up defensive reactions
in the listener are evaluative, controlling, strategic, indifferent or neutral, superior, and certain.

Evaluation

When you evaluate or judge another person or what that person has done,
that person is likely to become resentful and defensive and is likely to respond with attempts to defend himself or herself and perhaps at the same
time to become equally evaluative and judgmental. On the other hand, when
you describe what happened or what you want, it creates no such defensiveness and is generally seen as supportive. The distinction between evaluation and description can be seen in the difference between you- and
I-messages.

Evaluative You-Messages	*Descriptive I-Messages*
You never reveal your feelings.	I sure would like hearing how you feel about this.
You just don't plan ahead.	I need to know what our schedule for the next few days will be.
You never call me.	I'd enjoy hearing from you more often.

   If you put yourself in the role of the listener hearing these statements, you
probably can feel the resentment or defensiveness that the evaluative messages (you-messages) would create and the supportiveness from the descriptive messages (I-messages).

Control

When you try to control the behavior of the other person, when you order the
other person to do this or that, or when you make decisions without mutual
discussion and agreement, defensiveness is a likely response. Control messages deny the legitimacy of your own contributions and in fact your own importance. They say, in effect, you don't count; your contributions are
meaningless. When, on the other hand, you focus on the problem at hand—
and not on controlling the situation or getting your own way—defensiveness
is much less likely. This problem orientation invites mutual participation and
recognizes the significance of your contributions.

Strategy

When you try to manipulate the other person or the situation—especially
when you conceal your true purposes, that person is likely to resent it and to
respond defensively. But, when you act spontaneously and openly, you're
more likely to create an atmosphere that is equal and honest.

Neutrality

When you act in a neutral fashion, when you demonstrate indifference or a lack of caring for the other person, it's likely to create defensiveness. It demonstrates a lack of interest in the thoughts and feelings of the other person and is especially damaging when intimates are in conflict. This kind of talk says in effect that you're not important or deserving of attention and caring. When, on the other hand, you demonstrate empathy, defensiveness is unlikely to occur. Although especially difficult in conflict situations, try to show that you can feel what the other person is feeling and that you accept these feelings.

Superiority

When you present yourself as superior to the other person, you're in effect putting the other person in an inferior position and this is likely to be resented. Such superiority messages say in effect that the other person is inadequate or somehow second-class. It's a violation of the implicit contract that people in a close relationship have, namely that each person is equal. The other person may then begin to attack your superiority and the conflict can easily degenerate into a conflict over who's the boss with personal attack being the mode of interaction.

Certainty

The person who appears to know it all is likely to be resented and likely to set up a defensive climate. After all, there is little room for negotiation or mutual problem-solving when one person already has the answer. A more provisional attitude, one that says, let's explore this issue together and try to find a solution, is likely to be much more productive.

Face-Detracting and Face-Enhancing Strategies

Another dimension of conflict strategies is that of face orientation. Face-detracting or face-attacking strategies involve treating the other person as incompetent or untrustworthy, as unable or bad (Donahue & Kolt, 1992). Such attacks can vary from mildly embarrassing the other person to severely damaging his or her ego or reputation. When such attacks become extreme, they may be similar to verbal aggressiveness—a tactic explained in the next section.

Face-enhancing techniques involve helping the other person maintain a positive image, one that is competent and trustworthy, able and good. There is some evidence to show that even when you get what you want, say, at bargaining, it's wise to help the other person retain positive face. This makes it less likely that future conflicts will arise (Donahue & Kolt, 1992). Not surprisingly, people are more likely to make a greater effort to support the listener's "face" if they like the listener than if they don't (Meyer, 1994).

Generally, collectivist cultures like Korea and Japan place greater emphasis on face, especially on maintaining a positive image in public. Face is generally less crucial in individualist cultures such as the United States. And yet there are significant exceptions that require us to qualify any such broad generalization. For example, in parts of China, a highly collectivist culture where face saving is extremely important, criminals are paraded publicly at rallies and humiliated before being put to death (Tyler, 1996). You could of course argue that the importance of face-saving in China gives this particular punishment a meaning that it could not have in more individualistic cultures.

Make the most of the best and the least of the worst.
—*Robert Louis Stevenson*

Confirming the other person's definition of self (Chapter 5), avoiding attack and blame, and using excuses and apologies as appropriate are some generally useful face-enhancing strategies.

Blame and Empathy

Sometimes conflict is caused by the actions of one of the individuals. Sometimes it's caused by clearly identifiable outside forces. Most of the time, however, it's caused by a wide variety of factors. Any attempt to single out one or two factors for *blame* is sure to fail. Yet, a frequently used fight strategy is to blame someone for it. Consider, for example, the couple who fight over their child's getting into trouble with the police. The parents may—instead of dealing with the conflict itself—blame each other for the child's troubles. Such blaming, of course, does nothing to resolve the problem or to help the child.

Perhaps the best alternative to blame is empathy. Once you have empathically understood your opponent's feelings, validate those feelings where appropriate. If your partner is hurt or angry, and you feel that such feelings are legitimate and justified (from the other person's point of view), say so; for example, "You have a right to be angry; I shouldn't have called your mother a slob. I'm sorry. But I still don't want to go on vacation with her." In expressing validation you are not necessarily expressing agreement on the issue in conflict; you are merely stating that your partner has feelings that are legitimate and that you recognize them as such.

I never take my own side in a quarrel.

—*Robert Frost*

Silencers and Facilitating Open Expression

Silencers cover a wide variety of fighting techniques that literally silence the other individual. One frequently used silencer is crying. When a person is unable to deal with a conflict or when winning seems unlikely, he or she may cry and thus silence the other person.

Another silencer is to feign extreme emotionalism—to yell and scream and pretend to be losing control of oneself. Still another is to develop some "physical" reaction—headaches and shortness of breath are probably the most

How important is face-saving to you? What did your culture teach you about the importance of face-saving?

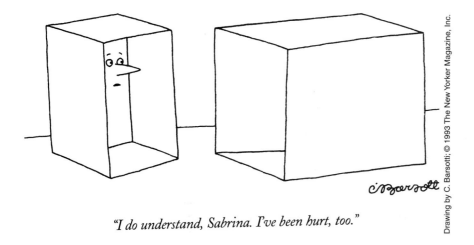

"I do understand, Sabrina. I've been hurt, too."

popular. One of the major problems with silencers is that we can never be certain that they are strategies to win the argument. They *may* be real physical reactions that we should pay attention to. Regardless of what we do, the conflict remains unexamined and unresolved.

Also, grant the other person permission to express himself or herself freely and openly, to be oneself. Avoid power tactics (raising your voice or threatening physical force) that suppress or inhibit freedom of expression. Such tactics are designed to put the other person down and to subvert real interpersonal equality.

Gunnysacking and Present Focus

A gunnysack is a large bag usually made of burlap. As a conflict strategy, *gunnysacking* refers to the practice of storing up grievances so we may unload them at another time (Bach & Wyden, 1968). The immediate occasion may be relatively simple (or so it might seem at first), such as someone's coming home late without calling. Instead of arguing about this, the gunnysacker unloads all past grievances. The birthday you forgot, the time you arrived late for dinner, the hotel reservations you forgot to make are all noted. As you probably know from experience, gunnysacking often begets gunnysacking. When one person gunnysacks, the other person gunnysacks. The result is that we have two people dumping their stored-up grievances on one another. Frequently the original problem never gets addressed. Instead, resentment and hostility escalate.

Focus on the present, on the here-and-now rather than on issues that occurred two months ago (as in gunnysacking). Similarly, focus your conflict on the person with whom you're fighting, and not on the person's mother, child, or friends.

Fighting Below and Above the Belt

Much like fighters in a ring, each of us has a "beltline." When you hit someone below it, a tactic called *beltlining,* you can inflict serious injury (Bach & Wyden, 1968). When you hit above the belt, however, the person is able to absorb the blow. With most interpersonal relationships, especially those of long standing, we know where the beltline is. You know, for example, that to hit Pat with the inability to have children is to hit below the belt. You know that to hit Chris with the failure to get a permanent job is to hit below the belt. Hitting below the beltline causes all persons involved added problems. Keep blows to areas your opponent can absorb and handle.

Which unproductive conflict strategy do you resent the most? Which unproductive conflict strategy—if any—are you most ashamed of using? Why? Which of the unproductive conflict strategies, if any, have you used in the last two or three months? What effects—both immediate and long-term—did your use of these strategies have?

Remember that the aim of a relationship conflict is not to win and have your opponent lose. Rather, it is to resolve a problem and strengthen the relationship. Keep this ultimate goal always in clear focus, especially when you're angry or hurt.

Verbal Aggressiveness and Argumentativeness

An especially interesting perspective on conflict is emerging from the work on verbal aggressiveness and argumentativeness (Infante & Rancer, 1982; Infante & Wigley, 1986; Infante, 1988). Understanding these two concepts will help in understanding some of the reasons why things go wrong and some of the ways in which we can use conflict to actually improve our relationships.

Verbal aggressiveness is a method of winning an argument by inflicting psychological pain, by attacking the other person's self-concept. It is a type of disconfirmation (and the opposite of confirmation) in that it seeks to discredit the individual's view of self (see Chapter 5). To explore this tendency further, take the accompanying test of verbal aggressiveness.

What character in a television sitcom or drama resembles the verbally aggressive personality? What character would you consider argumentative? What are some of the other distinctions that the writers have drawn between these characters?

SELF-TEST
How Verbally Aggressive Are You?

This scale is designed to measure how people try to obtain compliance from others. For each statement, indicate the extent to which you feel it is true for you in your attempts to influence others. Use the following scale:

1 = almost never true
2 = rarely true
3 = occasionally true
4 = often true
5 = almost always true

_____ 1. I am extremely careful to avoid attacking individuals' intelligence when I attack their ideas.

_____ 2. When individuals are very stubborn, I use insults to soften the stubbornness.

_____ 3. I try very hard to avoid having other people feel bad about themselves when I try to influence them.

_____ 4. When people refuse to do a task I know is important, without good reason, I tell them they are unreasonable.

_____ 5. When others do things I regard as stupid, I try to be extremely gentle with them.

_____ 6. If individuals I am trying to influence really deserve it, I attack their character.

_____ 7. When people behave in ways that are really in very poor taste, I insult them in order to shock them into proper behavior.

_____ 8. I try to make people feel good about themselves even when their ideas are stupid.

_____ 9. When people simply will not budge on a matter of importance, I lose my temper and say rather strong things to them.

_____ 10. When people criticize my shortcomings, I take it in good humor and do not try to get back at them.

_____ 11. When individuals insult me, I get a lot of pleasure out of really telling them off.

_____ 12. When I dislike individuals greatly, I try not to show it in what I say or how I say it.

_____ 13. I like poking fun at people who do things that are very stupid in order to stimulate their intelligence.

_____ 14. When I attack a person's ideas, I try not to damage their self-concepts.

_____ 15. When I try to influence people, I make a great effort not to offend them.

_____ 16. When people do things which are mean or cruel, I attack their character in order to help correct their behavior.

_____ 17. I refuse to participate in arguments when they involve personal attacks.

_____ 18. When nothing seems to work in trying to influence others, I yell and scream in order to get some movement from them.

_____ 19. When I am not able to refute others' positions, I try to make them feel defensive in order to weaken their positions.

_____ 20. When an argument shifts to personal attacks, I try very hard to change the subject.

Thinking Critically About Verbal Aggressiveness

In order to compute your verbal aggressiveness score, follow these steps:

1. Add your scores on items 2, 4, 6, 7, 9, 11, 13, 16, 18, 19.
2. Add your scores on items 1, 3, 5, 8, 10, 12, 14, 15, 17, 20.
3. Subtract the sum obtained in Step 2 from 60.

4. To compute your verbal aggressiveness score, add the total obtained in Step 1 to the result obtained in Step 3.

If you scored between 59 and 100, you're high in verbal aggressiveness; if you scored between 39 and 58, you're moderate in verbal aggressiveness; and if you scored between 20 and 38, you're low in verbal aggressiveness. In looking over your responses, make special note of the characteristics identified in the 20 statements that refer to the tendency to act verbally aggressive. Note those inappropriate behaviors that you're especially prone to commit. High agreement (4's or 5's) with statements 2, 4, 6, 7, 9, 11, 13, 16, 18, and 19 and low agreement (1's and 2's) with statements 1, 3, 5, 8, 10, 12, 14, 15, 17, and 20 will help you highlight any significant verbal aggressiveness you might have. Review your previous encounters when you acted verbally aggressive. What effect did such actions have on your subsequent interaction? What effect did they have on your relationship with the other person? What alternative ways of getting your point across might you have used? Might these have proved more effective?

Source: From "Verbal Aggressiveness," by Dominic Infante and C. J. Wigley, _Communication Monographs_ 53, 1986, pp 61–69. Used by permission of the National Communication Association and the authors.

There is some evidence to show that verbal aggressiveness can lead to physical violence (Infante, Sabourin, Rudd, & Shannon, 1990). Do you find this true in the relationships with which you're familiar?

People generally quarrel because they cannot argue.
—Gilbert Keith Chesterton

Contrary to popular usage, **argumentativeness** is a quality to be cultivated rather than avoided. Argumentativeness refers to your willingness to argue for a point of view, your tendency to speak your mind on significant issues. It's the mode of dealing with disagreements that is the preferred alternative to verbal aggressiveness. Before reading about ways to increase your argumentativeness, take the following test of argumentativeness.

SELF-TEST

How Argumentative Are You?

This questionnaire contains statements about controversial issues. Indicate how often each statement is true for you personally according to the following scale:

1 = almost never true
2 = rarely true
3 = occasionally true
4 = often true
5 = almost always true

_____ 1. While in an argument, I worry that the person I am arguing with will form a negative impression of me.

_____ 2. Arguing over controversial issues improves my intelligence.

_____ 3. I enjoy avoiding arguments.

_____ 4. I am energetic and enthusiastic when I argue.

_____ 5. Once I finish an argument, I promise myself that I will not get into another.

_____ 6. Arguing with a person creates more problems for me than it solves.

_____ 7. I have a pleasant, good feeling when I win a point in an argument.

_____ 8. When I finish arguing with someone, I feel nervous and upset.

_____ 9. I enjoy a good argument over a controversial issue.

_____ 10. I get an unpleasant feeling when I realize I am about to get into an argument.

_____ 11. I enjoy defending my point of view on an issue.

_____ 12. I am happy when I keep an argument from happening.

_____ 13. I do not like to miss the opportunity to argue a controversial issue.

_____ 14. I prefer being with people who rarely disagree with me.

_____ 15. I consider an argument an exciting intellectual challenge.

_____ 16. I find myself unable to think of effective points during an argument.

_____ 17. I feel refreshed and satisfied after an argument on a controversial issue.

_____ 18. I have the ability to do well in an argument.

_____ 19. I try to avoid getting into arguments.

_____ 20. I feel excitement when I expect that a conversation I am in is leading to an argument.

Thinking Critically About Argumentativeness

To compute your score, follow these steps:

1. Add your scores on items 2, 4, 7, 9, 11, 13, 15, 17, 18, and 20.
2. Add 60 to the sum obtained in Step 1.
3. Add your scores on items 1, 3, 5, 6, 8, 10, 12, 14, 16, and 19.
4. To compute your argumentativeness score, subtract the total obtained in Step 3 from the total obtained in Step 2.

Scores between 73 and 100 indicate high argumentativeness. Scores between 56 and 72 indicate moderate argumentativeness. Scores between 20 and 55 indicate low argumentativeness. How accurately does your score reflect your self-image concerning your tendency to speak up? Scores between 73 and 100 indicate high argumentativeness; scores between 56 and 72 indicate moderate argumentativeness; scores between 20 and 55 indicate low argumentativeness.

Can you identify relationships in which argumentativeness is the customary way of dealing with conflict? What is the primary advantage of argumentativeness? Can you identify any disadvantages?

Source: From "A Conceptualization and Measure of Argumentativeness," by Dominic Infante and Andrew Rancer, *Journal of Personality Assessment,* 1982, Vol. 46, pp. 72–80. Reprinted by permission of Lawrence Erlbaum Associates, Inc. and the authors.

The researchers who developed this test note that those who score high in argumentativeness have a strong tendency to state their position on controversial issues and argue against the positions of others. A high scorer sees arguing as exciting, intellectually challenging, and as an opportunity to win a kind of contest. The low argumentative sees arguing as unpleasant and unsatisfying. Not surprisingly, this person has little confidence in his or her ability to argue effectively. The person who scores low in argumentativeness tries to prevent arguments. This person experiences satisfaction not from arguing, but from avoiding arguments. The moderately argumentative possesses some of the qualities of the high argumentative and some of the qualities of the low argumentative.

Both high and low argumentatives may experience communication difficulties. The high argumentative, for example, may argue needlessly, too often, and too forcefully. The low argumentative, on the other hand, may avoid taking a stand even when it's necessary. Persons scoring somewhere in the middle are probably the more interpersonally skilled and adaptable, arguing when it's necessary but avoiding the many arguments that are needless and repetitive.

Here are some suggestions for cultivating argumentativeness and for preventing it from degenerating into aggressiveness (Infante, 1988):

- Treat disagreements as objectively as possible; avoid assuming that because someone takes issue with your position or your interpretation, that they are attacking you as a person.
- Avoid attacking the other person (rather than the person's arguments) even if this would give you a tactical advantage; it will probably backfire at some later time and make your relationship more difficult.
- Avoid interrupting; allow the other person to state her or his position fully before you respond.
- Express interest in the other person's position, attitude, and point of view; reaffirm the other person's sense of competence; compliment the other person as appropriate.
- Avoid presenting your arguments too emotionally; using an overly loud voice or interjecting vulgar expressions will prove offensive and ineffective.
- Allow the other person to save face; never humiliate the other person.

What changes would you like to see your relational partners (friends, family members, romantic partners) make in their own verbal aggressiveness and argumentativeness? What might you do to more effectively regulate your own verbal aggressiveness and argumentativeness? (Verbal aggressiveness and argumentativeness would make excellent subjects for a concept paper.)

SKILL BUILDING EXERCISE 11.3.

Increasing Productive Conflict Management

The following brief dialogue was written to illustrate unproductive conflict and to provide a stimulus for the consideration of alternative and more productive methods of conflict management. Identify examples of each unproductive strategy and propose more productive alternatives.

Pat: It's me. Just came in to get my papers for the meeting tonight.

Chris: You're not going to another meeting tonight, are you?

Pat: I told you last month that I had to give this lecture to the new managers on how to use some new research methods. What do you think I've been working on for the past two weeks? If you cared about what I do, you'd know that I was working on this lec-

(continued)

(continued)

	ture and that it was especially important that it go well.
Chris:	What about shopping? We always do the shopping on Friday night.
Pat:	The shopping will have to wait; this lecture is important.
Chris:	Shopping is important, too, and so are the children and so is my job and so is the leak in the basement that's been driving me crazy for the past week and that I've asked you to look at every day since then.
Pat:	Get off it. We can do the shopping any time. Your job is fine and the children are fine and we'll get a plumber just as soon as I get his name from the Johnsons.
Chris:	You always do that. You always think only you count, only you matter. Even when we were in school, your classes were the important ones, your papers, your tests were the important ones. Remember when I had that chemistry final and you had to have your history paper typed? We stayed up all night typing *your* paper. I failed chemistry, remember? That's not so good when you're premed! I suppose I should thank you for my not being a doctor? But you got your A in history. It's always been that way. You never give a damn what's important in my life.
Pat:	I really don't want to talk about it. I'll only get upset and bomb out with the lecture. Forget it. I don't want to hear any more about it. So just shut up before I do something I should do more often.
Chris:	You hit me and I'll call the cops. I'm not putting up with another black eye or another fat lip—never, never again.

Pat:	Well, then, just shut up. I just don't want to talk about it anymore. Forget it. I have to give the lecture and that's that.
Chris:	The children were looking forward to going shopping. Johnny wanted to get a new CD, and Jennifer needed to get a book for school. You promised them.
Pat:	I didn't promise anyone anything. You promised them and now you want me to take the blame. You know, you promise too much. You should only promise what you can deliver, like fidelity. Remember you promised to be faithful? Or did you forget that promise? Why don't you tell the kids that? Or do they already know? Were they here when you had your sordid affair? Did they see their loving parent loving some stranger?
Chris:	I thought we agreed not to talk about that. You know how bad I feel about what happened. And anyway, that was six months ago. What has that to do with tonight?
Pat:	You're the one who brought up promises, not me. You're always bringing up the past. You live in the past.
Chris:	Well, at least the kids would have seen me enjoying myself—one enjoyable experience in eight years isn't too much, is it?
Pat:	I'm leaving. Don't wait up.

Thinking Critically About Productive Conflict Management. Can you identify one possible effect that might result from using each of the unproductive conflict strategies? How do these effects differ from those that might result from using the more productive strategies? As you read this dialogue, did you assume the sex of the characters? On what basis did you draw your conclusions?

SUMMARY OF CONCEPTS AND SKILLS

In this chapter we examined interpersonal conflict and some of the myths that surround conflict. We looked at the distinction between content and relationship conflict and its positive and negative effects. We considered a model of conflict resolution and a variety of unproductive conflict strategies and their more productive counterparts.

1. "Interpersonal conflict" refers to a disagreement between or among connective individuals. The positions in conflicts are to some degree interrelated and incompatible.

2. *Content conflict* centers on objects, events, and persons in the world that are usually, but not always, external to the parties involved in the conflict. *Relationship conflicts* are concerned not so much with some external object as with the relationships between the individuals, with such issues as who is in charge, the equality of a primary relationship, and who has the right to set down rules of behavior.

3. Before the conflict: try to fight in private, be sure you're each ready to fight, know what you're fighting about, avoid fighting about problems that cannot be solved. After the conflict: keep the conflict in perspective, challenge your negative feelings, increase the exchange of rewards.

4. A five-step model is often helpful in resolving conflict: define the conflict, examine possible solutions, test the solution, evaluate the solution, and accept or reject the solution.

5. Unproductive and productive conflict strategies include: avoidance and fighting actively, force and talk, face-detracting and face-enhancing strategies, blame and empathy, silencers and facilitating open expression, gunnysacking and present focus, fighting below and above the belt, and verbal aggressiveness and argumentativeness.

6. To cultivate argumentativeness, treat disagreements objectively and avoid attacking the other person; reaffirm the other's sense of competence; avoid interrupting; stress equality and similarities; express interest in the other's position; avoid presenting your arguments too emotionally; and allow the other to save face.

Check your ability to apply these skills. Use a rating scale such as the following: 1 = almost always, 2 = often, 3 = sometimes, 4 = rarely, and 5 = almost never.

_____ 1. Recognize the differences between content and relationship conflicts and respond to each accordingly.

_____ 2. Prepare for conflict and follow it up so that it remains in perspective.

_____ 3. Deal with interpersonal conflicts in a systematic way, such as definition, examination of possible solutions, testing of the solution, evaluation of the solution, and acceptance or rejection of the solution.

_____ 4. View problems and solutions from the perspective of facts, feelings, negative argument, positive benefits, creative new ideas, and control of thinking.

_____ 5. Use productive conflict strategies such as active engagement in the conflict, empathy, facilitating open expression, present focus, fighting above the belt, and argumentativeness in interpersonal conflicts.

_____ 6. Avoid the unproductive conflict strategies such as avoidance, blame, silencers, gunnysacking, beltlining, and verbal aggressiveness.

VOCABULARY QUIZ. THE LANGUAGE OF CONFLICT

Match the terms dealing with interpersonal conflict with their definitions. Record the number of the definition next to the appropriate term.

_8_	six hats technique	_6_	verbal aggressiveness
_10_	silencers	_9_	spamming
_4_	argumentativeness	_5_	complaint
_2_	gunnysacking	_1_	interpersonal conflict
_3_	beltline	_7_	conflict resolution model

1. A disagreement between connected individuals.
2. An unproductive conflict strategy of storing up grievances and holding these in readiness to dump on the person with whom one is in conflict.
3. A person's level of tolerance for absorbing a personal attack.
4. A tendency or willingness to argue for a point of view, to speak your mind on significant issues.
5. An expressed dissatisfaction that's a valuable source of feedback.
6. A tendency to defend your position even at the expense of another person's feelings.
7. A relatively standard set of procedures for dealing with conflict consisting of five steps: Define the conflict, examine possible solutions, test the solution, evaluate the solution, and accept or reject the solution.
8. Varied ways of looking at a particular issue to give you different perspectives.
9. Sending unsolicited e-mail or repeatedly posting the same message.
10. A group of unproductive conflict strategies including crying and pretending to be extremely emotional.

12

Interpersonal Communication and Power

CHAPTER TOPICS	LEARNING GOALS	SKILLS GOALS
	After completing this chapter, you should be able to	*After completing this chapter, you should be able to*
Self-Esteem	1. Define *self-esteem* and identify the ways to increase it	Increase your own self-esteem
Speaking with Power	2. Define *power*, its major principles and types, and the popular power plays and appropriate responses	Manage power through verbal and nonverbal messages and respond to power plays appropriately
Assertive Communication	3. Define *assertive, nonassertive,* and *aggressive communication* and explain the principles for increasing assertive communication	Increase your own assertiveness (as appropriate)

Jackie has been having difficulties in all sorts of interpersonal situations. For example, although a competent worker, she has little confidence in her ability to do the work. She especially shies away from new tasks that may prove challenging and as a result has been overlooked repeatedly when promotions come around. Interpersonally, she has few friends and is seldom asked out. Although attractive and bright, she acts as if she is grossly unattractive and has little to offer another person.

Pedro is a counselor at a local boys club where his major problem is discipline. None of the younger boys respect him and consequently none of them will listen to his admonitions. The administration is considering letting him go. He just doesn't seem able to exert the necessary control over the boys.

Clara is employed at the local automobile showroom where she sells new Pontiacs. Although a competent salesperson, Clara often finds herself used by her coworkers. For example, when the salespeople want coffee they often ask Clara to go for it. Clara doesn't really want to be the showroom "gofer" but she doesn't know how to say no. Clara runs into similar problems at home where her brothers and sisters and even her parents take advantage of her good nature.

All of these interpersonal difficulties revolve around interpersonal power. Jackie lacks self-esteem and communicates this to those she works with as well as her friends. Jackie has to raise her self-esteem and develop a kind of self-power. Pedro's problem centers on his lack of ability to communicate his authority, his power. He needs to learn the principles for communicating power to others. Clara is a classic example of the nonassertive person. She wants to stand up for her rights but doesn't know how. Clara needs training in assertiveness.

In this final chapter, we focus on self-esteem, interpersonal power, and assertiveness. All three topics are held together by their common focus on self empowerment, on increasing your ability to exert control, whether over yourself or over others.

Communication is power. Those who have mastered its effective use can change their own experience of the world, and the world's experience of them.
—*Anthony Robbins*

What symbols of power can you identify in this photo?

SELF-ESTEEM

How much do you like yourself? How valuable a person do you think you are? How competent do you think you are? The answers to these questions will reflect your self-esteem, the value that you place on yourself.

Success breeds success. When you feel good about yourself—about who you are and what you're capable of doing—you will perform better. When you think like a success, you're more likely to act like a success. When you think you're a failure, you're more likely to act like a failure. Increasing self-esteem will, therefore, help you to function more effectively in school, in interpersonal relationships, and in careers. Here are a few suggestions for increasing self-esteem.

Substitute Self-Destructive Beliefs with Self-Affirming Beliefs

Actively challenge those beliefs you have about yourself that you find are unproductive or that make it more difficult for you to achieve your goals. Representative of such unproductive beliefs are the beliefs that you have to succeed in everything you do and the belief that you have to be loved by everyone. Replace these self-destructive beliefs with more productive ones, more self-affirming beliefs, for example: "I succeed in many things; I don't have to succeed in everything." "It would be nice to be loved by everyone but it isn't necessary to my well being or my happiness and anyway some pretty important people do love me." Further suggestions for achieving this were already covered in the Thinking About Listening box in Chapter 2.

Seek Out Nourishing People

Psychologist Carl Rogers drew a distinction between noxious and nourishing people. Noxious people criticize and find fault with just about everything. Nourishing people, on the other hand, are positive. They are optimists. Most

CAUTION

Do you know people whose thinking is distorted because of their **maintaining unrealistic beliefs about the self?** Do these beliefs influence their behavior?

CAUTION

How might **maintaining unrealistic self-destructive beliefs** prevent you from increasing your competence? Might it prevent you from achieving your professional or relationship goals?

Drawing by M. Twohy; © 1993 The New Yorker Magazine, Inc.

"So, when he says, 'What a good boy am I,' Jack is really reinforcing his self-esteem."

important, they reward us, they stroke us, they make us feel good about ourselves. Seek out these people.

Work on Projects That Will Result in Success

Some people want to fail, or so it seems. Often, they select projects that will result in failure simply because they are impossible to complete. Instead of this defeating attitude, select projects that will result in success. Each success will help build self-esteem. Each success will make the next success a little easier.

When a project does fail, recognize that this does not mean that you're a failure. Everyone fails somewhere along the line. Failure is something that happens. It's not necessarily something you have created. It's not something inside you. Further, your failing once does not mean that you will fail the next time. So, put failure in perspective. Do not make it an excuse for not trying again.

What suggestions for increasing self-esteem do you think are particularly useful? What additional suggestions might you offer?

SPEAKING WITH POWER

Power permeates all interpersonal communication. It influences what you do, when, and with whom. It influences the employment you seek and the employment you get. It influences the friends you choose and do not choose and those who choose you and those who do not. It influences your romantic and family relationships—their success, failure, and level of satisfaction or dissatisfaction. Interpersonal power is what enables the one with power to control the behaviors of others.

Power only means the ability to have control over your life. Power implies choice.
—*Nikki Giovanni*

SKILL BUILDING EXERCISE 12.1.
Rewriting Unrealistic Beliefs

Here are five "drivers," unrealistic beliefs that can get you into trouble and can lower your self-esteem: be perfect, hurry up, be strong, please others, and try hard (Butler, 1981). These beliefs are unproductive only when they are extreme and allow no room for being less than perfect. Trying hard or being strong are not themselves unhealthy beliefs; it's only when they become absolute—when you try to be everything to everyone—that they become impossible to attain and create problems. For each belief: (1) explain why these are unrealistic and counter productive and (2) identify a more realistic and productive belief to substitute for it.

• The drive to **be perfect** impels you to try to perform at unrealistically high levels in just about everything you do. Whether it's work, school, athletics, or appearance, this drive tells you that anything short of perfection is unacceptable and that you're to blame for any imperfections—imperfections that by any other standard would be considered quite normal.
• The drive to **hurry up** compels you to do things quickly, to do more than can be reasonably expected in any given amount of time.

• The drive to **be strong** tells you that weakness and any of the more vulnerable emotions like sadness, compassion, or loneliness are wrong. This driver is seen in the stereotypical American man, but also becoming more prevalent among women as well, who are not permitted to cry or ask for help or have unfulfilled needs.
• The drive to **please others** leads you to seek approval from others. Pleasing yourself is secondary; in fact self-pleasure comes from pleasing others.
• The drive to **try hard** makes you take on more responsibilities than anyone can be expected to handle. This driver leads you to take on tasks that would be impossible for any normal person to handle; yet you take them on without any concern for your own limits (physical or emotional).

Thinking Critically About Unrealistic Beliefs.   Have you internalized any of these beliefs? How do these beliefs influence your thinking and communicating? Might more realistic beliefs prove more productive?

Power in interpersonal relationships is governed by a few important principles. These principles spell out the basic characteristics of power. They help explain how power works interpersonally and how you may more effectively deal with power.

> All animals are equal. But some animals are more equal than others.
> —*George Orwell*

> Equality is what does not exist among equals.
> —*e. e. cummings*

How would you describe your own interpersonal power? In what situations are you especially powerful? In what situations do you feel you have significantly less power? *(Your own experiences with interpersonal power would make an interesting personal experience paper.)*

Some People Are More Powerful than Others

As a whole, the world is moving in the direction of greater equality, where people are equal under the law and in their entitlement to education, legal protection, and freedom of speech. But, even in the most egalitarian societies, all people are not equal when it comes to just about everything else. Some are born into wealth, others into poverty. Some are born physically strong, good-looking, and healthy. Others are born weak, unattractive, and with a variety of inherited illnesses.

Some people are born into power. And some of those who were not have managed to achieve control over it. Everyone can increase his or her interpersonal power. You can, for example, learn the principles of communication and increase your power to persuade. Power can also be decreased. Perhaps the most frequent way in which power is decreased is through ineffective attempts to control another's behavior. For example, if you threaten someone with punishment and then fail to carry out the threat, you will lose power.

Confidence communicates power. One of the clearest ways in which you can communicate power is by demonstrating confidence in your verbal and nonverbal behaviors. Recognizing these messages in the communications of others will help you recognize them in your own interactions and put you in a better position to manage and control them.

Most people have some communication apprehension or shyness (see Chapter 2). The confident communicator, however, does not let it interfere with communication. This quality also enables the speaker to make those who are anxious or shy more comfortable.

The confident communicator is relaxed (rather than rigid), flexible in voice and body (rather than locked into one or two ranges of voice or body movement), and controlled (rather than shaky or awkward). A relaxed posture, researchers find, communicates a sense of control, status, and power. Tenseness, rigidity, and discomfort, on the other hand, signal a lack of self-control (Spitzberg & Hecht, 1984). This, in turn, signals a general inability to control one's environment or fellow workers.

Here are a few additional suggestions for communicating confidence:

- Take the initiative in introducing yourself to others and in introducing topics of conversation; try not to wait for others. When you react, rather than act, you're more likely to communicate a lack of confidence and control over the situation.
- Use open-ended questions to involve the other person in the interaction (as opposed to questions that merely ask for a yes or no answer). Follow up these questions with appropriate comments or additional questions.
- Use "you-statements," which refer directly to the other person (not the accusatory kind, but those that signal a direct and personalized focus on the other person)—such as "Do you agree?" or "How do you feel about that?" This one feature, incidentally, has been shown to increase men's attractiveness to women.
- Avoid the various forms of powerless language that are identified below (see Table 12.2), for example, statements that express a lack of conviction or that are self-critical.

Another way to communicate power is with compliance-gaining and compliance-resisting strategies. *Compliance-gaining strategies* are the tactics that influence others to do what you want them to do (Table 12.1). *Compliance-resisting strategies* are the tactics that enable you to say "no" and resist another person's attempts to influence you.

Compliance-resisting strategies also demonstrate power. Let's say that someone you know asks you to do something that you do not want to do, for example, lend your term paper so that this person might copy it and turn it in to another teacher. Research with college students shows that there are four major ways of responding (McLaughlin, Cody, & Robey, 1980; O'Hair, Cody, & O'Hair, 1991):

In **identity management** you resist by trying to manipulate the image of the person making the request. You might do this negatively or positively. In negative identity management, you might portray the requesting agent as unreasonable or unfair and say, for example, "That's really unfair of you to ask

Confidence is that feeling by which the mind embarks on great and honorable courses with a sure hope and trust in itself.
—*Cicero*

Calm self-confidence is as far from conceit as the desire to earn a decent living is remote from greed.
—*Channing Pollock*

Do men and women use the same compliance-gaining strategies? *(An interesting research paper could try to answer this question by reviewing the research or conducting a survey.)*

Note that the compliance-gaining strategies are regarded as generally effective though not necessarily moral or ethical. Which strategies would you consider ethical? Which would you consider unethical?

Table 12.1 Compliance-Gaining Strategies

These compliance gaining strategies come from the research of Marwell and Schmitt (1967) and the further developments by Miller and Parks (1982). What other compliance-gaining strategies can you identify?

Strategy		Examples
Pregiving. Pat rewards Chris and then requests compliance.	Pat:	*I'm glad you enjoyed that dinner. This really is the best restaurant in the city. How about going back to my place for a nightcap and whatever?*
Liking. Pat is helpful and friendly in order to get Chris in a good mood so that Chris will be more likely to comply with Pat's request.	Pat:	*[After cleaning up the living room and bedroom] I'd really like to relax and bowl a few games with Terry. OK?*
Promise. Pat promises to reward Chris if Chris complies with Pat's request.	Pat:	*I'll give you anything you want if you will just give me a divorce. You can have the house; just give me my freedom.*
Positive or negative expertise. Pat promises that Chris will be rewarded for compliance (or punished for not complying) because of "the nature of things."	Pat:	*If you don't listen to the doctor, you're going to wind up back in the hospital.*
Positive or negative self-feelings. Pat promises that Chris will feel better if Chris complies (or feel worse if Chris does not comply) with Pat's request.	Pat:	*You'll see. You'll be a lot better off without me; you'll feel a lot better after the divorce.*
Positive or negative altercasting. Pat casts Chris in the role of the "good" or "bad" person and argues that Chris should comply because a person with "good" qualities would comply (and a person with "bad" qualities would not).	Pat:	*Any intelligent person would grant their partner a divorce when the relationship has died.*

Evaluating Information

Critically evaluate your communication strategies before applying them. When confronted with a power play, your first task is to assess your options. You have a choice as to how you can respond and only you can make that choice. In some instances, for some people, and for some relationships, it may be wiser to ignore the power play or perhaps to simply neutralize it, treating it as an isolated instance. Steiner, for example, advocates using the cooperative response because it has the potential to put an end to the power play and to restructure the interaction so that it becomes a more equal one. Under what circumstances would it be best to ignore such power plays? To neutralize them? To use a cooperative response?

me to compromise my ethics." Or you might tell the person that it hurts that he or she would even think you would do such a thing.

You might also use positive identity management. Here you resist complying by making the requesting agent feel good about himself or herself. For example, you might say, "You know this material much better than I do; you can easily do a much better paper yourself."

Another way to resist compliance is to use **nonnegotiation,** a direct refusal to do as requested. You might simply say, "No, I don't lend my papers out."

In **negotiation,** you resist compliance by perhaps offering a compromise ("I'll let you read my paper but not copy it") or by offering to help the person in some other way ("If you write a first draft, I'll go over it and try to make some comments"). If the request was a more romantic one—for example, a request to go away for a ski weekend—you might resist by discussing your feelings and proposing an alternative—for example, let's double date first.

Another way to resist compliance is through **justification.** Here you justify your refusal by citing possible consequences of compliance or noncompliance. For example, you might cite a negative consequence if you complied ("I'm afraid that I'd get caught and then I'd fail the course") or you might cite of positive consequence of your not complying ("You'll really enjoy writing this paper; it's a lot of fun").

All Interpersonal Messages Have a Power Dimension

Earlier the principle that you cannot *not* communicate was introduced (Chapter 1). We might expand that principle and note that you cannot communicate without making some comment on your power or lack of it. When in an interactional situation, therefore, recognize that on the basis of your verbal and nonverbal messages people will assess your power along with your competence, trustworthiness, honesty, openness, and so on.

No interpersonal relationship exists without a power dimension. Look at your own relationships and those of your friends and relatives. Can you tell who has the greater power? In interpersonal relationships among most Americans the more powerful person is often the one who is more attractive or the one who has more money. In other cultures, the factors that contribute to power may be different and might include one's family background or one's knowledge or wisdom.

People who are powerful communicate their power in a variety of ways. A summary of some of the major characteristics of powerful and powerless speech is presented in Table 12.2 on page 324.

Just as you communicate your power verbally, you also communicate it nonverbally. Trendiness is powerless; cheap is powerless. Conservative is powerful; expensive is powerful. It's actually all very logical. Truly powerful people have no time for new trends that come and go every six months. Further, they don't wear or have anything cheap because they have money to buy the real thing.

Similarly, nonverbal behavior often betrays a lack of power, as when someone fidgets and engages in lots of self-touching movements (adaptors) at a meeting, indicating discomfort. A powerful person may be bored but will not appear uncomfortable or ill at ease.

Territory also reflects a person's power. It's difficult for the junior analyst who operates out a cubbyhole in the basement of some huge office complex

Acquiring Information

Beware the ties that bind. Although the standard dress for the male executive is a suit and tie, some research shows that wearing a tie may not be a very good idea (Lanagan & Watkins, 1987; Stine & Bewares, 1994). There is some evidence to indicate that the tie can actually restrict the flow of blood to the brain, resulting in impaired thinking. For example, it's been shown that the response time of those wearing ties was longer (that is, slower) than the response time of those not wearing ties.

"It's all about power—getting it and keeping it."

Drawing by Brian Savage; © 1996 The New Yorker Magazine, Inc.

How would you describe your speech in terms of power? What "powerless" expressions do you use regularly?

Table 12.2 Toward More Powerful Speech

Can you identify other examples of powerless and powerful speech?

Suggestions	Examples	Reasons
Avoid hesitations.	"I *er* want to say that *ah* this one is *er* the best, *you know*."	Hesitations cause you to sound unprepared and uncertain.
Avoid too many intensifiers.	"*Really*, this was *the greatest*; it was *truly awesome*."`	Too many intensifiers make speech sound the same and do not allow for intensifying what should be emphasized.
Avoid disqualifiers.	"*I didn't read the entire article*, but . . . ." "*I didn't actually see the accident*, but . . . ."	Disqualifiers signal a lack of competence and a feeling of uncertainty.
Avoid tag questions.	"That was a great movie, *wasn't it?*" "She's brilliant, *don't you think?*"	Tag questions ask for another's agreement and therefore signal both your need for agreement and your uncertainty.
Avoid simple one-word answers.	*"Yes," "No," "O.K." "Sure."*	One-word answers may signal a lack of communication skills and a lack of interest and commitment.
Avoid self-critical statements.	*"I'm not very good at this." "This is my first public speech."*	Self-critical statements signal a lack of confidence and make public one's inadequacies.
Avoid overpoliteness.	*"Excuse me, please, sir."*	Overpolite forms signal subordinate status.
Avoid slang and vulgar expressions.	"##!!!///****!" "*No problem!*"	Slang and vulgarity signal low social class and hence little power.

to appear powerful with an old metal desk and beat-up filing cabinet. Often, however, you're more in control of your territory than you may realize. Clutter, metal ashtrays, and "cute" statues with signs like "Place your butt here" signify a lack of power and can easily be eliminated to communicate a more powerful image.

But perhaps the most important aspect of communicating power is to evidence your knowledge, your preparation, and your organization over whatever you're dealing with. If you can exhibit control over your own responsibilities, it's generally concluded that you can and do also exhibit control over others.

Some People Are More Machiavellian than Others

Before reading about this fascinating concept, take the accompanying self-test, "How Machiavellian Are You?" It focuses on your beliefs about how easily you think people can be manipulated.

Examine one of your relationships—a friendship, a romantic relationship, or a family relationship—for power. What kinds of power exist in this relationship? Who maintains greater power? How is it exercised?

SELF-TEST
How Machiavellian Are You?

For each statement record the number on the following scale which most closely represents your attitude:

  1 = disagree a lot
  2 = disagree a little
  3 = neutral
  4 = agree a bit
  5 = agree a lot

_____ 1. The best way to handle people is to tell them what they want to hear.

_____ 2. When you ask someone to do something for you, it's best to give the real reasons rather than giving reasons that might carry more weight.

_____ 3. Anyone who completely trusts anyone else is asking for trouble.

_____ 4. It's hard to get ahead without cutting corners here and there.

_____ 5. It's safest to assume that all people have a vicious streak and it will come out when they are given a chance.

_____ 6. One should take action only when sure it's morally right.

_____ 7. Most people are basically good and kind.

_____ 8. There is no excuse for lying to someone.

_____ 9. Most people forget more easily the death of their parents than the loss of their property.

_____ 10. Generally speaking, people won't work hard unless they're forced to.

(continued)

(continued)

Thinking Critically About Machiavellianism

To compute your Mach score follow these steps:

1. Reverse the scores on items 2, 6, 7, and 8 according to the following scale:

If you responded with	Change it to
5	1
4	2
3	3
2	4
1	5

2. Add all 10 scores, being sure to use the reversed numbers for 2, 6, 7, and 8.

Your Mach score is a measure of the degree to which you believe that people in general are manipulable and not necessarily that you would or do manipulate others. If you scored somewhere between 35 and 50 you would be considered a high Mach; if you scored between 10 and 15 you would be considered a low Mach. Most of us would score in between these extremes.

The concept of Machiavellianism is explained in the text. As you read the discussion, try to visualize what you would do in the various situations described. See if your score on this test is a generally accurate description of your own Machiavellianism. You will also note a similarity between this concept and self-monitoring (discussed in Unit 9). Both high self-monitors and high Machs try to manipulate others and get his or her own way. The difference is that self-monitors change their own behaviors as a way of pleasing and manipulating others; Machiavellians try to change the behaviors of others to get what they want.

Niccolo Machiavelli (1469–1527) was a political philosopher and advisor and wrote his theory of political control in *The Prince.* The book took the position (in greatly simplified form) that the prince must do whatever is necessary to rule the people; the ends justified the means. The ruler was in fact obligated to use power to gain more power and thus better achieve the desired goals (Steinfatt, 1987). The term *Machiavellian* has thus come to refer to the techniques or tactics one person uses to control another. Research finds significant differences between those who score high and those who score low on the Mach scale. Low Machs are more easily susceptible to social influence; they are more easily persuaded. High Machs are more resistant to persuasion. Low Machs are more empathic while high Machs are more logical. Low Machs are more interpersonally oriented and involved with other people; high Machs are more assertive and more controlling. Business students (especially marketing students) score higher in Machiavellianism than do nonbusiness majors (McLean & Jones, 1992).

High Machs are most effective at persuading others when the situation allows them to improvise (Christie, 1970). High Machs are also rated higher on job performance when they functioned within a loosely structured work environment that allowed them to improvise (Gable, Hollon, & Dangello, 1992).

Machiavellianism seems in part at least to be culturally conditioned. Individualistic orientation, which favors competition and being Number One, seems more conducive to the development of Machiavellianism. Collectivist orientation, which favors cooperation and being one of a group, seems a less friendly environment for the development of Machiavellianism in its members. Some evidence of this comes from research showing that Chinese students attending a traditional Chinese (Confucian) school rated lower in Machiavellianism than similar Chinese students attending a Western-style school (Christie, 1970).

HOW TO ...
Be a Power Holder

Relationships differ in the types of power that the people use and to which they respond. It's useful to distinguish among six types of power (French & Raven, 1968; Raven, Centers, & Rodrigues, 1975): referent, legitimate, reward, coercive, expert, and information or persuasion power. Differences in the amount and type of power influence who makes important decisions, who will prevail in an argument, and who will control the finances. You may find it interesting to take the self-test entitled, "How Powerful Are You?"

SELF-TEST: HOW POWERFUL ARE YOU?

For each statement, indicate which of the following descriptions is most appropriate.

1 = true of 20% or less of the people I know
2 = true of about 21–40% of the people I know
3 = true of about 41–60% of the people I know
4 = true of about 61–80% of the people I know
5 = true of 81% or more of the people I know

_____ 1. My position is such that I often have to tell others what to do. For example, a mother's position demands that she tell her children what to do, a manager's position demands that he or she tells employees what to do, and so on.

_____ 2. People wish to be like me or identified with me. For example, high school football players may admire the former professional football player who is now their coach and want to be like him.

_____ 3. People see me as having the ability to give them what they want. For example, employers have the ability to give their employees pay increases, longer vacations, and improved working conditions.

_____ 4. People see me as having the ability to administer punishment or to withhold things they want. For example, employers have the ability to reduce voluntary overtime, shorten vacation time, and fail to improve working conditions.

_____ 5. Other people realize that I have expertise in certain areas of knowledge. For example, a doctor has expertise in medicine and so others turn to the doctor to tell them what to do. Someone knowledgeable about computers similarly possesses expertise.

_____ 6. Other people realize that I possess the communication ability to present an argument logically and persuasively.

These statements refer to the six major types of power. Low scores (1's and 2's) indicate your belief that you possess little of this particular type of power and high scores (4's and 5's) indicate your belief that you possess a great deal of this particular type of power.

The Legitimate Power Holder (Statement 1) wields power because Other believes that the power holder has a right—by virtue of his or her position—to influence or control Other's behavior. Usually legitimate power derives from the roles that people occupy and from the belief that because they occupy these roles, they have a right to influence others. For example, employers, judges, managers, and police officers are usually seen to hold legitimate power. *Relate your persuasive arguments and appeals to your own role and credibility.*

The Referent Power Holder (Statement 2) wields power over "Other" because Other wishes to be like the power holder. Often the referent power holder is attractive, has considerable prestige, is well-liked, and well-respected; as these increase, so does identification and power. For example, an older brother may have power over a younger brother because the younger brother wants to be like his older brother. *Demonstrate those qualities admired by those you wish to influence.*

The Reward Power Holder (Statement 3) wields power because he or she controls the rewards that Other wishes to receive. Rewards may be material (for example, money, promotion, jewelry) or social (for example, love, friendship, respect). The degree of power wielded is directly related to the desirability of the reward as seen by Other. For example, teachers have reward power over students because they control grades, letters of recommendation, and social approval. *Make rewards contingent on compliance and follow through and reward those who comply with your requests.*

(continued)

(continued)

The Coercive Power Holder (Statement 4) wields power because he or she has the ability to administer punishments to or remove rewards from Other if Other does not do as the power holder wishes. Usually, people who have reward power also have coercive power. For example, parents may deny extended privileges concerning time or recreation or withhold money. *Make clear the negative consequences that are likely to follow noncompliance. But, be careful—this one can backfire. Coercive power may reduce your other power bases and have a negative impact when used, for example, by supervisors on subordinates in business* (Richmond et al., 1984).

The Expert Power Holder (Statement 5) wields power over Other because Other believes the power holder has expertise or knowledge. Expert power increases when the expert is seen as unbiased with noth-

ing personally to gain from exerting this power. Expert power decreases if the expert is seen as biased and as having something to gain from securing Other's compliance. For example, lawyers have expert power in legal matters and doctors have expert power in medical matters. *Cultivate your own expertise and connect your persuasive appeals to this expertise.*

The Information or Persuasion Power Holder (Statement 6) wields power over Other because Other attributes to the power holder the ability to communicate logically and persuasively. For example, researchers and scientists may be given information power because of their being perceived as informed and critical thinkers. *Increase your communication competence; this book's major function, of course, is to explain ways for you to accomplish this.*

Interpersonally, your own level of Machiavellianism will influence the communication choices you make. For example, high Machs are more strategic and manipulative in their self-disclosures than are low Machs; that is, high Machs will self-disclose to influence the attitudes and behaviors of listeners (Steinfatt, 1987). Machiavellianism influences the way you seek to gain the compliance of others (a topic discussed later in this unit). High Machs are more likely to be manipulative in their conflict-resolving behavior than are low Machs. High Machs are generally more effective in just about all aspects studied (they even earn higher grades in communication courses that involve face-to-face interaction; Burgoon, 1971). Low Mach women, however, are preferred as dating partners by both high and low Mach men (Steinfatt, 1987).

Power Follows the Principle of Less Interest

In any interpersonal relationship, the person who holds the power is the one less interested in and less dependent on the rewards and punishments controlled by the other person. If, for example, you can walk away from the rewards that your partner controls or can suffer the punishments that your partner can mete out, then you control the relationship. If, on the other hand, you need the rewards that your partner controls or are unable or unwilling to suffer the punishments that your partner can administer, then your partner has the power and controls the relationship.

> Power is the great aphrodisiac.
> —*Henry Kissinger*

Does the statement that power follows the principle of less interest explain the balance of power as you see it at work in interpersonal relationships?

The more you need the relationship, the less power you have in it. The less you need the relationship, the greater your power. In a love relationship, for example, the person who maintains greater power is the one who would find it easier to break up the relationship. The person who is unwilling (or unable) to break up has little power, precisely because he or she is dependent on the relationship and on the rewards provided by the other person.

Power Has a Cultural Dimension

In some cultures, power is concentrated in the hands of a few and there is a great difference in the power held by these people and by the ordinary citizen. These are called *high power distance cultures;* examples are Mexico, Brazil, India, and the Philippines (Hofstede, 1997). In *low power distance cultures,* power is more evenly distributed throughout the citizenry; examples include Denmark, New Zealand, Sweden, and, to a lesser extent, the United States.

These differences impact on interpersonal communication and relationships in a variety of ways. Before reading these descriptions, think about your own culture and how power is distributed. Would you consider it a high or a low power distance culture? Then, consider the interpersonal differences discussed below and see if these descriptions are consistent with your own experiences.

Also, as you go through these several differences, recognize that the differences between high and low power distance cultures are matters of degree. Characteristics are not in one culture and absent in the other but are in both, present to different degrees. For example, friendship and dating relationships will be influenced by the power distance between groups (Andersen, 1991). In India (high power distance), for example, friendships and romantic relationships are expected to take place within your cultural class; in Sweden (low power distance), a person is expected to select friends and romantic partners on the basis—not of class or culture—but of individual factors such as personality, appearance, and the like.

In low power distance cultures you're expected to confront a friend, partner, or supervisor assertively; there is in these cultures a general feeling of equality, which is consistent with acting assertively (Borden, 1991). In high power distance cultures, direct confrontation and assertiveness may be viewed negatively, especially if directed at a superior.

In high power distance cultures you're taught to have great respect for authority and generally people in these cultures see authority as desirable and beneficial; challenges to authority are generally not welcomed (Westwood, Tang, & Kirkbride, 1992; also see Bochner & Hesketh, 1994). In low power distance cultures, there is a certain distrust for authority; it's seen as a kind of necessary evil that should be limited as much as possible. This difference in attitudes toward authority can be seen right in the classroom. In high power distance cultures, there is a great power distance between students and teachers; students are expected to be modest, polite, and totally respectful. In low power distance cultures, students are expected to demonstrate their knowledge and command of the subject matter, participate in discussions with the teacher, and even challenge the teacher, something many high power distance culture members wouldn't even think of doing. The same differences can be seen in patient-doctor communication. Patients from high power distance cultures are less likely to challenge their doctor or admit that they don't understand the medical terminology than would patients in low power distance cultures.

High power distance cultures rely more on symbols of power. For example, titles (Doctor, Professor, Chef, Inspector) are more important in high power distance cultures. Failure to include these in forms of address is a serious breach of etiquette. Low power distance cultures rely less on symbols of power and less of a problem is created if you fail to use a respectful title (Victor, 1992). But, even in low power distance cultures, you may create problems if, for example, you call a medical doctor, police captain, military officer, or professor Ms. or Mr.

> We cannot live by power, and a culture that seeks to live by it becomes brutal and sterile.
> —*Max Lerner*

> All human beings are born free and equal in dignity and rights.
> —*UN Declaration of Human Rights, Article I*

Also, in the United States, two people quickly move from Title plus Last Name (Mr. Smith) to First Name (Joe). Similarly, in low power distance cultures less of a problem is created if you're too informal or if you presume to exchange first names before sufficient interaction has taken place. In high power distance cultures too great an informality—especially between those differing in power—would be a serious breach of etiquette. Again, in even the lowest power distance culture, you may still create problems if you call your English professor Pat.

In many Asian, African, and Arab cultures (as well as in many European cultures such as Italian and Greek), for example, there is a great power distance between men and women. Men have the greater power and women are expected to recognize this and abide by its implications. Men, for example, make the important decisions and have the final word in any difference of opinion (Hatfield & Rapson, 1996).

In the United States the power structure is undergoing considerable changes. In many families men still have the greater power. Partly because they earn more money, they also make the more important decisions. As economic equality becomes more a reality than an ideal, this power difference may also change. In Arab cultures, the man makes the more important decisions not because he earns more money, but because he is the man and men are simply given greater power.

In some of these cultures, the power difference is perpetuated by granting men greater educational opportunities. For example, although college education for women is taken for granted in most of the United States, it's the exception in many other cultures throughout the world.

In some Asian cultures particularly, persons in positions of authority—for example, teachers—have unquestioned power. Students do not contradict, criticize, or challenge teachers. This can easily create problems in the typical college classroom. Those students from cultures which taught that the teacher was an unquestioned authority may have great difficulty meeting the United States teacher expectation that students interact critically with the material and with its interpretation.

Take a tour of the White House (http://www.whitehouse.gov/WH/Welcome.html). What symbols of power can you identify?

What has your culture taught you about power? Have these teachings helped you get where you want to get, achieve what you want to achieve?

Power Is Frequently Used Unfairly

Although it would be nice to believe that power is wielded for the good of all, it's often used selfishly and unfairly. You see it all the time. Here are two rather extensive examples: sexual harassment and the use of power plays.

Sexual Harassment

One type of unfair use of power is sexual harassment. Sexual harassment may be defined as "bothering someone in a sexual way" (Bravo & Cassedy, 1992). "Sexual harassment," notes another team of researchers, "refers to conduct, typically experienced as offensive in nature, in which unwanted sexual advances are made in the context of a relationship of unequal power or authority. The victims are subjected to verbal comments of a sexual nature, unconsented touching and requests for sexual favors" (Friedman, Boumil, & Taylor, 1992).

Attorneys note that under the law "sexual harassment is any unwelcome sexual advance or conduct on the job that creates an intimidating, hostile, or offensive working environment" (Petrocelli & Repa, 1992).

The Equal Employment Opportunity Commission (EEOC) has defined sexual harassment as follows:

> Unwelcome sexual advances, requests for sexual favors and other verbal or physical conduct of a sexual nature constitute sexual harassment when (1) submission to such conduct is made either explicitly or implicitly a term or condition of an individual's employment, (2) submission to or rejection of such conduct by an individual is used as the basis for employment decisions affecting such individual, or (3) such conduct has the purpose or effect of unreasonably interfering with an individual's work performance or creating an intimidating, hostile, or offensive working environment. (Friedman, Boumil, & Taylor, 1992)

Behavior constitutes sexual harassment, according to attorneys Petrocelli and Repa (1992), when it's:

1. sexual in nature—for example, sexual advances, showing pornographic pictures, telling jokes that revolve around sex, comments on anatomy
2. unreasonable—for example, behavior that a reasonable person would object to
3. severe or pervasive—for example, physical molestation or creating an intimidating environment
4. unwelcome and offensive—for example, behavior that you let others know offends you and that you want stopped

In a Harris poll (*New York Times*, 2 June 1993) on sexual harassment in junior and senior high school, 56% of the boys and 75% of the girls said they were the target of some form of sexual harassment consisting of sexually explicit comments, jokes, or gestures. Forty-two percent of the boys and 66% of the girls said they were the victims of sexual touching, grabbing, or pinching. Table 12.3 presents the major behaviors and the percentage of students reporting that they were victims of such behaviors. All the behaviors are sexual in nature.

The students noted that among the effects of sexual harassment were not wanting to go to school, reluctance to talk in class, finding it difficult to pay attention or to study, getting lower grades, and even considering changing schools. This is especially true for gay and lesbian youth. In fact, in New York City, a special high school has been established—the Harvey Milk School—to accommodate gay and lesbian teens who have been sexually harassed to the point where they cannot function effectively in the school environment. Lesbian

All possibility of understanding is rooted in the ability to say no.
—*Susan Sontag*

Table 12.3 Sexual Harassment in High School

Before looking at this table which identifies the types of sexual harassment experienced by high school boys and girls, think back to your own high school days. Did you experience sexual harassment? Did you sexually harass others? What forms did the sexual harassment take?

Behavior	Boys	Girls
Sexual comments or looks	56%	76%
Touched, grabbed, or pinched	42	65
Intentionally pushed up against	36	57
Sexual rumors spread about them	34	42
Clothing pulled at	28	38
Shown, given, or left sexual materials	34	31
Had sexual messages written about them in public places	16	20

Source: From *The New York Times,* June 2, 1993. Courtesy of NYT Permissions.

and gay youth, in fact, experience such harassment in all social environments: family, school, work, and in the general community (Pilkington & D'Augelli, 1995). In one study, 77% of undergraduate lesbians and gay men reported that they experienced such harassment (D'Augelli, 1992).

To determine whether behavior constitutes sexual harassment, Memory VanHyning (1993) suggests that you ask the following four questions to help you assess your own situation objectively rather than emotionally:

1. Is it real? Does this behavior have the meaning it seems to have?
2. Is it job related? Does this behavior have something to do with or will it influence the way you do your job?
3. Did you reject this behavior? Did you make your rejection of unwanted messages clear to the other person?
4. Have these types of messages persisted? Is there a pattern, a consistency to these messages?

"Yes" answers to all four questions define the behavior as sexual harassment (VanHyning, 1993).

Three suggestions for avoiding behaviors that might be considered sexual harassment will help to clarify the concept further and to prevent the occurrence of harassment (Bravo & Cassedy, 1992):

1. Begin with the assumption that others at work are not interested in your sexual advances, sexual stories and jokes, or sexual gestures.
2. Listen and watch for negative reactions to any sex-related discussion. Use the suggestions and techniques discussed throughout this book (for example, perception checking, critical listening) to become aware of such reactions. When in doubt, find out; ask questions, for example.

Can you think of additional suggestions?

3. Avoid saying or doing what you think your parent, partner, or child would find offensive in the behavior of someone with whom she or he worked.

What should you do if you believe you're being sexually harassed and feel a need to do something about it? Here are a few suggestions recommended by workers in the field (Petrocelli & Repa, 1992; Bravo & Cassedy, 1992; Rubenstein, 1993):

1. Talk to the harasser. Tell this person, assertively, that you do not welcome the behavior and that you find it offensive. Simply informing Fred that his sexual jokes are not appreciated and are seen as offensive may be sufficient to make him stop this joke telling. In some instances, unfortunately, such criticism goes unheeded, and the offensive behavior continues.
2. Collect evidence—perhaps corroboration from others who have experienced similar harassment at the hands of the same individual, perhaps a log of the offensive behaviors.
3. Use appropriate channels within the organization. Most organizations have established channels to deal with such grievances. This step will in most cases eliminate any further harassment. In the event that it doesn't, you may consider going further.
4. File a complaint with an organization or governmental agency or perhaps take legal action.
5. Don't blame yourself. Like many who are abused, you may tend to blame yourself, feeling that you're responsible for being harassed. You aren't; however, you may need to secure emotional support from friends or perhaps from trained professionals.

What would you add to the discussion of sexual harassment presented here?

Power Plays

Power plays are patterns (not isolated instances) of communication that take unfair advantage of another person (Steiner, 1981). Put in terms of the notion of choice (Unit 1) power plays aim to rob us of our right to make our own choices, free of harassment or intimidation.

For example, in the power play *Nobody Upstairs,* the individual refuses to acknowledge your request, regardless of how or how many times you make it. One common form is the refusal to take no for an answer. Sometimes Nobody Upstairs takes the form of pleading ignorance of common socially accepted (but unspoken) rules, such as knocking when you enter someone's room or refraining from opening another person's mail or wallet: "I didn't know you didn't want me to look in your wallet" or "Do you want me to knock the next time I come into your room?"

Another power play is *You Owe Me.* Here others do something for you and then demand something in return. They remind you of what they did for you and use this to get you to do what they want.

In *Yougottobekidding,* one person attacks the other by saying "yougottobekidding" or some similar phrase: "You can't be serious." "You can't mean that." "You didn't say what I thought you said, did you?" The intention here is to express utter disbelief in the other's statement so as to make the statement and the person seem inadequate or stupid.

These power plays are just examples. There are, of course, many others that you have no doubt met on occasion. What do you do when you recognize such a power play? One commonly employed response is to ignore the power play and allow the other person to take control. Another response is to treat the power play as an isolated instance (rather than as a pattern of behavior) and object to it. For example, you might say quite simply, "Please don't come into my room without knocking first" or "Please don't look in my wallet without permission."

Have you witnessed recently any of the power plays discussed here? What is your instinctive response to such power plays? How might you respond more effectively? (Your experiences with power plays would make an interesting personal experience paper.)

The purpose of getting power is to be able to give it away.
—*Aneurin Bevan*

The object of power is power.
—*George Orwell*

CAUTION

How might **failing to recognize that power is a part of all communication** prevent you from logically evaluating, say, upward or downward messages in an organization?

A third response is a cooperative one (Steiner, 1981). In this response, you do the following:

- *Express your feelings.* Tell the person that you're angry, annoyed, or disturbed by his or her behavior.
- *Describe the behavior to which you object.* Tell the person—in language that describes rather than evaluates—the specific behavior you object to: for example, reading your mail, coming into your room without knocking, persisting in trying to hug you.
- *State a cooperative response you both can live with comfortably.* Tell the person—in a cooperative tone—what you want; for example: "I want you to knock before coming into my room." "I want you to stop reading my mail." "I want you to stop trying to hug me when I tell you to stop."

A cooperative response to Nobody Upstairs might go something like this: "I'm angry (*statement of feelings*) that you persist in opening my mail. You have opened my mail four times this past week alone (*description of the behavior to which you object*). I want you to allow me to open my own mail. If there is anything in it that concerns you, I will let you know immediately" (*statement of cooperative response*).

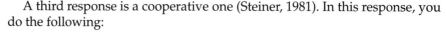

SKILL BUILDING EXERCISE 12.2.

Managing Power Plays

Here are some examples of the five power plays just considered. For each one, identify the power play and provide an appropriate three-part management strategy as identified in the text:

- State your feelings (remember to use I-messages).
- Describe the other person's behavior that you object to.
- State a cooperative response.

1. Fred continually interrupts you. Whenever you want to say something, Fred breaks in, finishes what he thinks you were saying, and then says what he wants to say.
2. One of your coworkers responds to your ideas, your plans, and your suggestions with statements like "yougottobekidding," "you can't mean that," "you can't possibly be serious." So, when you say that you're going to date Harry, she says "You can't be serious! Harry!" When you say that you're going to apply for a promotion, she says "Promotion! You got to be kidding! You've only been with the company six months."
3. Your close friend has helped you get a job in his company. Now, whenever he wants you to do something, he reminds you that he got you the

job. Whenever you object that you have your own work to do, he reminds you that you wouldn't have any work to do if it wasn't for his getting you the job in the first place.
4. Your supervisor is compulsive about neatness and frequently goes around to the various workers telling them to clean up their work areas. Frequently, this supervisor uses the power play of metaphor: "Clean up this crap before you leave tonight" or "Make sure this junk is put away."
5. Your friend, Amida, sits next to you in class but rarely listens to the instructor. Instead she waits until you copy something down in your notes and then she copies what you have written. In doing this she frequently distracts you and you miss a great deal of what the instructor has said. You have told her repeatedly that you object to this but she acts like she doesn't hear you.

Thinking Critically About Power Plays. Did the cooperative strategies you developed get to feel more comfortable as you worked from the first to the fifth example? If any of these situations or similar ones occurred in your life, would you ignore the power play? Treat it as a one-time event? Use a cooperative strategy?

LISTENING.

Listening to Empower

Much as you can empower others by complimenting or constructively criticizing or in the way you ask questions, you can also empower others through your style of listening. Thus, for example, if you manage several workers your style of listening can empower or disempower; it contributes to the sense of importance and influence that these workers will feel in dealing with you and with the organization in general. So, when you wish to empower through listening, consider these suggestions:

1. Act like you're listening willingly and eagerly. This makes the other person feel that what he or she is saying is valuable and important. As an added bonus, this person is more likely to contribute suggestions and insights on future occasions because you demonstrated a willingness to listen. In acting like you're listening, acknowledge your understanding by appropriately nodding or using such minimal responses as "I see" or "I understand," ask questions if something isn't clear or if you need more information, maintain eye contact, and lean forward as appropriate. In addition, focus on the person as exclusively as possible and try to block out your focus on anything else. Nothing is worse than speaking with someone who seems focused on what time it is or what others in the room are saying.

2. Avoid interrupting to change the topic or to shift the focus to something or someone else. When you interrupt, you say in effect, that what the other person is saying is of less importance that what you're saying—a clear way to disempower and to say, in effect, you don't really count, at least not as much as I do.

3. React supportively. Let the other person know that you're listening and that you have heard what he or she said and that you appreciate it. Let the other person know what you think of what he or she has said. If you agree, then it's easy; just say so. If you disagree, say so, also. But keep your disagreement or disapproval focused on what was said rather than on the person. And couple any disagreement with positive comments such as, "I really appreciate your bringing this to my attention, though I tried out your suggestion and it didn't work. Is there a way of doing it that might be less costly?"

ASSERTIVE COMMUNICATION

If you disagree with other people in a group, do you speak your mind? Do you allow others to take advantage of you because you're reluctant to say what you want? Do you feel uncomfortable when you have to state your opinion in a group? Questions such as these revolve around your degree of assertiveness. Before reading further about this type of communication, take the accompanying self-test, "How Assertive Is Your Communication?"

Use one of the popular search engines such as Yahoo!, Infoseek, or AltaVista to search for material on one of the topics covered in this chapter. Visit some of the websites. What can you learn from such sites?

SELF-TEST

How Assertive Is Your Communication?

Indicate how true each of the following statements is about your own communication. Respond instinctively rather than in the way you feel you should respond. Use the following scale:

5 = always or almost always true
4 = usually true

3 = sometimes true, sometimes false
2 = usually false
1 = always or almost always false

_____   1. I would express my opinion in a group even if it contradicts the opinions of others.

(continued)

(continued)

_____ 2. When asked to do something that I really don't want to do, I can say "no" without feeling guilty.

_____ 3. I can express my opinion to my superiors on the job.

_____ 4. I can start up a conversation with a stranger on a bus or at a business gathering without fear.

_____ 5. I voice objection to people's behavior if I feel it infringes on my rights.

_____ 6. I express my feelings directly, using I-messages (I need you to be more accurate in recording appointments), rather than you-messages (Your work is sloppy and inaccurate) or third-person messages (Everyone says your work is not up to par).

_____ 7. I use factual and descriptive terms when stating what I object to (The last three letters you typed contained too many errors; You complained about the service in the last seven restaurants we ate at) rather than allness or extreme terms (You *never* do the right thing; You *always* complain).

_____ 8. I try to understand and accept the behaviors of others rather than criticize them and label them with such expressions as "that's silly" or "that's insane."

_____ 9. I believe that in most interactions, both people should gain something—rather than one win and one lose.

_____ 10. I believe that my desires are as important as those of others—not more important, but not less important either.

Thinking Critically About Assertive Communication All 10 items in this test identified characteristics of assertive communication. So, high scores (say, about 40 and above) would indicate a high level of assertiveness. Low scores (say, about 20 and below) would indicate a low level of assertiveness. The remaining discussion in this chapter clarifies the nature of assertive communication and offers guidelines for increasing your own assertiveness.

Nonassertive, Aggressive, and Assertive Communication

In addition to identifying some specific assertive behaviors (as in the self-test), the nature of assertive communication can be further explained by distinguishing it from nonassertiveness and aggressiveness (Alberti, 1977).

Nonassertive Communication

Nonassertiveness refers to a lack of assertiveness in certain types of or in all communication situations. People who are nonassertive fail to assert their rights. In many instances, these people do what others tell them to do—parents, employers, and the like—without questioning and without concern for what is best for them. They operate with a "You win, I lose" philosophy; they give others what they want without concern for themselves (Lloyd, 1995). Nonassertive people often ask permission from others to do what is their perfect right. Social situations create anxiety for these individuals, and their self-esteem is generally low.

Aggressive Communication

Aggressiveness is the other extreme. Aggressive people operate with an "I win, you lose" philosophy; they care little for what the other person wants and focus only on their own needs. Some people communicate aggressively only under certain conditions or in certain situations (for example, after being taken advantage of over a long period of time) while others communicate aggressively in all or at least most situations. Aggressive communicators think little of the opinions, values, or beliefs of others and yet are extremely sensitive to others' criticisms of their own behavior. Consequently, they frequently get into arguments with others.

Assertive Communication

Assertive behavior—behavior that enables you to act in your own best interests *without* denying or infringing upon the rights of others—is the generally desired alternative to nonassertiveness or aggressiveness. Assertive communication enables you to act in your own best interests without denying or infringing upon the rights of others. Assertive people operate with an "I win, you win" philosophy; they assume that both people can gain something from an interpersonal interaction, even from a confrontation. Assertive people are willing to assert their own rights. Unlike their aggressive counterparts, however, they do not hurt others in the process. Assertive people speak their minds and welcome others' doing likewise. Not surprisingly assertiveness is found to be positively related to flexibility, discussed in Chapter 8 (Martin & Anderson, 1998).

People who are assertive in interpersonal communication display four major characteristics (Norton & Warnick, 1976). Assertive individuals are:

- *Open:* They engage in frank and open expressions of their feelings to people in general as well as to those for whom there may be some romantic interest.
- *Not Anxious:* They readily volunteer opinions and beliefs, deal directly with interpersonal communication situations that may be stressful, and question others without fear. Their communications are dominant, frequent, and of high intensity. They have a positive view of their own communication performance, and others with whom they communicate share this positive view.
- *Contentious:* They stand up and argue for their rights, even if this might entail a certain degree of disagreement or conflict with relatives or close friends.
- *Not intimidated* and not easily persuaded: They make up their own minds on the basis of evidence and argument.

Acquiring Information

Use the simple checklist to assemble your information. Checklists are common in all walks of life and are a commonly recommended critical (and creative) thinking tool (Higgins, 1994). Checklists are used by the automotive engineer and repair mechanic to discover vehicle problems, by a doctor examining a patient, by a quality control engineer examining the production of aspirin, by the social worker who investigates family conditions, and by the communication consultant who audits the communications of an organization.

Checklists are also standard thinking tools. Checklists can help you organize and prioritize your agenda items. They can also help you review a list of steps systematically to ensure that important steps will not be overlooked or neglected. Try developing a checklist for preparing for a final examination, going to a job interview, or asking for a date.

What character in a current television comedy or drama exemplifies the assertive personality? The aggressive personality? The nonassertive personality? How would you describe yourself in terms of nonassertiveness, aggressiveness, and assertiveness?

Principles for Increasing Assertive Communication

Most people are nonassertive in certain situations. If you're one of these people and if you wish to modify your behavior, there are steps you can take to increase your assertiveness. (If you're always and everywhere nonassertive, and are unhappy about this; then you may need training with a therapist to change your behavior.)

This brief article identifies the kind of language that will help you develop more assertive messages.

Direct Clear Language

Dena Michelli

Language can be a very inadequate and clumsy tool for communication. It can also be beautifully simple and, combined with reinforcing body language, can be extremely effective and evocative.

Here are some simple rules to help you practice assertive, winning, language:

- *Set the scene* by describing—very briefly—what you are referring to: "When you called a meeting last Friday, I . . . ."
- *Simplicity, clarity, and brevity* are key to assertive communication. Do not ramble; you will lose the attention of your audience. Make your point quickly.
- *Take responsibility* for what you are saying. This is done by using "I" statements. Here are two examples of "I" statements; one negative and one positive: "I am unhappy about the way this project is proceeding." "I'm delighted with the outcome of this meeting."

- *Use repetition* if you feel that your message isn't getting across, but restructure your statement the second time.
- *Use silence appropriately*—it can say more than words. Don't be afraid of it; try it out.

Thinking Critically About "Direct Clear Language."
What other suggestions would you offer for making your language more assertive? Would your suggestions be the same for men and women or would you offer different suggestions based on the gender of the speaker? The gender of the receiver?

Source: From *Successful Asssertiveness* by Dena Michelli. Reprinted by permission of Hodder and Stoughton Educational.

Analyze Assertive Communications

The first step in increasing your assertiveness skills is to understand the nature of these communications. Observe and analyze the messages of others. Learn to distinguish the differences among assertive, aggressive, and nonassertive messages. Focus on what makes one behavior assertive and another behavior nonassertive or aggressive. Table 12.4 reviews some of the verbal and nonverbal messages that distinguish assertive from nonassertive or aggressive communication.

After you've gained some skills in observing the behaviors of others, turn your analysis to yourself. Analyze situations in which you're normally assertive and situations in which you're more likely to act nonassertively or aggressively. What characterizes these situations? What do the situations in which you're normally assertive have in common? How do you speak? How do you communicate nonverbally?

> Every power is subject to another power.
> —*Shona proverb*

Rehearse Assertive Communications

Select a situation in which you're normally nonassertive. Build a hierarchy that begins with a relatively nonthreatening message and ends with the desired communication. For example, let us say that you have difficulty voicing your opinion to your supervisor at work. The desired behavior, then, is to tell your supervisor your opinions. You would then construct a hierarchy of situations leading up to this desired behavior. Such a hierarchy might begin with

Table 12.4 A Sampling of Assertive and Nonassertive or Aggressive Messages

As you read this table, consider your customary ways of interacting. How often do you use assertive messages? How often do you use nonassertive or aggressive messages?

Assertive Messages	Nonassertive or Aggressive Messages
I-messages, accept responsibility for your own feelings (I feel angry when you . . .)	You-messages, attribute your feelings to others (You make me angry)
Descriptive and realistic expressions	Allness and extreme expressions
Equality messages (recognize the essential equality of oneself and others)	Inequality (overly submissive, polite, subservient or overly aggressive, insulting, condescending)
Relaxed and erect body posture	Tense, overly rigid, overly relaxed
Focused but not threatening eye contact	Intense eye contact or excessive eye contact avoidance
Expressive and genuine facial expressions	Unexpressive or overly expressive (and often insincere) facial expressions
Normal vocal volume and rhythm pattern	Overly soft or overly loud and accusatory

visualizing yourself talking with your boss. Visualize this scenario until you can do it without any anxiety or discomfort. Once you have mastered this visualization, visualize a step closer to your goal, say, walking into your boss's office. Again, do this until your visualization creates no discomfort. Continue with these successive visualizations until you can visualize yourself telling your boss your opinion. As with the other visualizations, do this until you can do it while totally relaxed. This is the mental rehearsal.

You might add a vocal dimension to this by actually acting out (with voice and gesture) your telling your boss your opinion. Again, do this until you experience no difficulty or discomfort. Next, try doing this in front of a trusted and supportive friend or group of friends. Ideally this interaction will provide you with useful feedback. After this rehearsal, you're probably ready for the next step.

The popular view among business professionals is that assertive communication is a valuable tool for advancement. What did your culture teach you about assertive communication? How will these teachings impact on your professional advancement?

Evaluating Information

Be mindful and flexible about assertive communication. As with the general skills of interpersonal communication such as openness and empathy, use your assertiveness mindfully and with flexibility. Being assertive means that you have the control of the assertiveness skills; it does not mean that you're therefore assertive in every interpersonal encounter. It means that you can be assertive when it's appropriate. So, think critically about the situation and the people you're interacting with before acting assertively. Ask yourself, in what situations would assertiveness be inappropriate? Are there certain people in your life who would respond negatively to your assertiveness?

Whom do you consider the three most interpersonally powerful people who ever lived? Why were these people so powerful?

Do It

This step is naturally the most difficult but obviously the most important. Here's a generally effective pattern to follow in communicating assertively:

- Describe the problem; don't evaluate or judge it. *We're all working on this advertising project together. You're missing half our meetings and you still haven't produced your first report.* Be sure to use I-messages and to avoid messages that accuse or blame the other person.
- State how this problem affects you. *My job depends on the success of this project and I don't think it's fair that I have to do extra work to make up for what you're not doing.*
- Propose solutions that are workable and that allow the person to save face. *If you can get the report to the group by Tuesday, we'll still be able to meet our deadline. And I could give you a call an hour before the meetings to remind you.*
- Confirm understanding. *It's clear that we just can't produce this project if you're not going to pull your own weight. Will you have the report to us by Tuesday?*
- Reflect on your own assertiveness. Think about what you did. How did you express yourself verbally and nonverbally? What would you do differently next time?

A note of caution should be added to this discussion. It's easy to visualize a situation in which, for example, people are talking behind you in a movie and, with your newfound enthusiasm for assertiveness, you tell them to be quiet. It's also easy to see yourself getting smashed in the teeth as a result. In applying the principles of assertive communication, be careful that you do not go beyond what you can handle effectively.

SKILL BUILDING EXERCISE 12.3.

Analyzing and Practicing Assertiveness

Read each of the following five situations. Indicate how an aggressive, a nonassertive, and an assertive person would deal with each of these situations.

Cheating on an examination. You and another student turn in examination papers that are too similar to be the result of mere coincidence. The instructor accuses you of cheating by allowing the student behind you to copy your answers. You were not aware that anyone saw your paper.

Decorating your apartment. You have just redecorated your apartment, expending considerable time and money in making it exactly as you want it. A good friend of yours brings you a house gift—the ugliest poster you have ever seen. Your friend insists that you hang it over your fireplace, the focal point of your living room.

Borrowing money. A friend borrows $30 and promises to pay you back tomorrow. But tomorrow passes, as do 20 other tomorrows, and there is no sign of the money. You know that the person has not forgotten about it, and you also know that the person has more than enough money to pay you back.

Neighbor intrusions. A neighbor has been playing a stereo at an extremely high volume late into the night. This makes it difficult for you to sleep.

Sexual harassment. Your supervisor at work has been coming on to you and has asked repeatedly to go out with you. You have refused each time. Brushing up against you, touching you in passing, and staring at you in a sexual way are common occurrences. You have no romantic interest in your supervisor and simply want to do your job, free from this type of harassment.

Thinking Critically About Assertiveness. What obstacles might you anticipate in each of these situations if you chose to respond assertively? What suggestions might you offer the person who wants to respond assertively but is having difficulty putting the principles into practice?

SUMMARY OF CONCEPTS AND SKILLS

In this chapter we explored interpersonal power from three different points of view. First, we looked at self-esteem and how it might be raised. Second, we looked at how to communicate with power, how to manage power plays, and the strategies for compliance-gaining and compliance-resisting. Third, we looked at assertiveness, what it is and how it can be developed more fully.

1. Self-esteem refers to the way in which we see ourselves, the value we place on ourselves. Self-esteem is central to interpersonal power because we are more likely to be effective if we see ourselves as effective people.
2. Self-esteem may be increased by substituting self-destructive beliefs with self-affirming ones, seeking out nourishing people, and working on projects that will result in success.
3. Interpersonal power refers to the ability of one person to control the behaviors of another person. A has power over B if A can control B's behaviors.
4. The six types of power are referent, legitimate, reward, coercive, expert, and information or persuasion power.
5. Six principles govern power in interpersonal relationships: Some people are more powerful than others, all interpersonal messages have a power dimension, some people are more Machiavellian than others, power follows the principle of least interest, power has a cultural dimension, and power is often used unfairly.
6. Sexual harassment consists of sexual advances that are unwelcomed; acceptance of these advances is made a condition of one's employment or advancement. Such advances interfere with an individual's work performance or create an offensive environment.
7. Among the power plays that are used frequently in interpersonal encounters are *Nobody Upstairs* (in which the power player refuses to hear what we are saying), *You Owe Me* (in which the power player gains compliance by reminding us that we owe him or her for past favors), *Metaphor* (in which the power player uses derogatory terms to refer to people or things we care for), *Yougottobekidding* (in which the power player expresses disbelief with your statement and makes both the statement and you seem inadequate) and *Thought Stopper* (in which the power player literally stops your thinking and especially stops you from expressing your thoughts by, for example, interrupting you, raising his or her voice, or using profanity).
8. An effective management strategy for dealing with power plays cooperatively consists of three parts: stating our feelings, describing the behavior we have difficulty with, and stating a cooperative response.
9. Compliance-gaining strategies are the tactics by which we try to get other people to do as we wish. Compliance-resisting strategies are the tactics we use to avoid complying with the requests of others.
10. Assertive people stand up for their rights without denying or infringing upon the rights of others. They are open, not anxious, contentious (argumentative), and not easily intimidated.

Check your ability to apply these skills. Use a rating scale such as the following: 1 = almost always, 2 = often, 3 = sometimes, 4 = rarely, and 5 = almost never.

_____ 1. I challenge self-destructive beliefs.
_____ 2. I seek out nourishing people.
_____ 3. I work on projects that will result in success instead of projects that are doomed to failure.
_____ 4. I engage in self-affirmation.

_____ 5. I manage power through verbal and nonverbal messages.

_____ 6. I avoid behaviors that could be interpreted as sexually harassing.

_____ 7. I respond to power plays with appropriate cooperative strategies.

_____ 8. I communicate social confidence in a wide variety of interpersonal situations.

_____ 9. I use compliance-gaining and compliance-resisting strategies as appropriate.

_____ 10. I communicate assertively when it's appropriate to the situation.

VOCABULARY QUIZ. THE LANGUAGE OF POWER

Match the terms listed here with their definitions. Record the number of the definition next to the name of the concept.

__5__ self-esteem

__6__ power

__1__ assertive communication

__9__ aggressive communication

__8__ nonassertive communication

__4__ metaphor power play

__3__ compliance-gaining strategies

__2__ legitimate power

__7__ negative altercasting

__10__ management strategy for power plays

1. A willingness to speak out for one's rights but with respect for the rights of others.

2. Power held by virtue of one's position or role.

3. Stating your feelings, describing the behavior you object to, and stating a cooperative response.

4. Substituting a derogatory name for something that another person values.

5. The value we place on ourselves.

6. Tactics that influence people to do what you want them to do.

7. A compliance-gaining strategy in which we put another person into the role of the "bad" person.

8. An unwillingess to speak out for one's rights in certain situations or in all or almost all situations.

9. Expressing yourself without any concern for the rights of others.

10. The ability to control the behavior of another person.

Appendix

Writing About Interpersonal Communication

In this course you may be asked to write one or more papers. This brief appendix offers suggestions for writing several different papers that are popular in a first course in interpersonal communication. We begin with some general comments on writing the interpersonal communication paper and then explain four types of papers you may be asked to write. Specific suggestions for topics for each of these types of papers are offered in the Critical Thinking Questions in the margins as well as throughout this appendix. Note that the word "papers" is shorthand for a variety of options—e-mail (to the instructor or to the entire class), newsgroup postings, or traditional written works.

WRITING THE INTERPERSONAL COMMUNICATION PAPER: TEN GENERAL SUGGESTIONS

Here are 10 general suggestions for writing the communication paper. Although most instructors are likely to follow these, listen carefully to specific instructions for your particular paper. Following instructions can often mean the difference between a B and an A.

1. Limit your topic to manageable proportions; covering a limited topic in depth will yield greater insight than would covering a broad topic superficially.
2. Be sure to focus on communication. Your paper should advance your understanding of some aspect of interpersonal communication. If you have special competence in related fields, you can work that material into your paper, but center your paper on interpersonal communication.
3. Work from the general to the specific; read a general article or textbook chapter and then begin to explore more detailed and more specific sources.
4. Review the relevant print and online indexes (academic or scientific journals, popular magazines, newspapers) and abstracts available to

True ease in writing comes
from art, not chance,
As those move easiest who
have learned to dance.
—Alexander Pope

Write great ideas down as soon
—*Martin Woods*

compile a bibliography of potentially useful sources. Make use of the available CD-ROM databases and the Internet search engines and directories. Once you have your preliminary bibliography, you may wish to show it to your instructor to see if you're on the right track and if she or he might offer additional suggestions.

5. When appropriate and possible, try to consult the original research studies. These may be difficult to understand since they're written for professors and researchers, but you'll be able to understand the most significant aspects of the research, for example, its conclusions or limitations.

6. As you're investigating the topic, you probably have or are developing an outline of your paper. Put this outline in writing and begin to organize your thoughts around this outline. Treat this outline as a work-in-progress; revise it, enlarge upon it, reduce it, and so on as you collect additional information.

7. As you begin to write, work on the body of your paper first; once this is reasonably complete, write your conclusion and then your introduction. In your conclusion, summarize the major issues you discussed in your paper. In your introduction, identify your topic and thesis and perhaps the major issues you'll discuss.

8. Write a draft copy and revise carefully for logical development of your thesis, paragraphing, spelling, grammar, and punctuation.

9. Be sure to credit your sources. Generally, brief references are integrated into the paper and complete bibliographic references or footnotes are included at the end of the paper.

   - If you're using someone's exact words, place these in quotation marks and cite the person (according to the style manual you're using); for example: According to Judy Pearson, in *Communication in the Family*, communication refers to the process of "understanding and sharing meaning with others."
   - If you're using someone's ideas but are putting them in your own words, credit the person for the ideas (again, following your specific style manual); for example: Judy Pearson, in *Communication in the Family*, argues that communication may help but it doesn't guarantee family satisfaction.
   - If you're using easily verified facts and figures, no citations are necessary; for example: Among the 50 states, California has the largest and Wyoming has the smallest population.

10. Type up the finished paper, double spacing on $8\frac{1}{2} \times 11$ inch white paper. Be sure to follow as faithfully as possible the guidelines for the assignment (for example, adhere to requirements concerning length, footnoting format, and number and type of sources to consult). Always keep a copy of the paper just in case the one you turn in is lost.

THE PERSONAL EXPERIENCE PAPER

The personal experience paper is a lot more difficult than it seems; it's not just a retelling of something that happened to you or something you did. Rather, it involves relating that experience to some significant concept (noise, feedback, empathy) or principle of interpersonal communication (irreversibility, inevitability, adjustment) **and,** in the writing, clarifying either the experience or the concept or principle in the process. That is, the personal experience paper should help you better understand your experience or better understand the interpersonal communication principle or concept. Here are some guidelines to keep in mind while writing the personal experience paper.

1. State the communication concept or principle to which your personal experience is to be connected early in the paper—in the introduction when you explain what you'll cover and again in the body when you begin your discussion in depth.
2. Discuss the concept or principle in as much detail as is necessary for your reader to understand it; it's safest to assume that your reader knows nothing about interpersonal communication.
3. Describe the experience in as much detail as necessary, but omit those portions that are not essential to understanding the connections you'll draw.
4. Describe the connection between the concept and the experience; tell the reader very explicitly how this concept or principle helps explain your experience or how your experience clarifies the concept or principle.

THE CONCEPT OR PRINCIPLE EXPLANATION PAPER

This paper explains a concept or principle or compares/contrasts two or more concepts in interpersonal communication, for example, The Nature of Noise, Similarities and Differences between Feedback and Feedforward, Types of Relationship Repair, and Power in the Business World. In addition to the suggestions offered in the Critical Thinking Questions, look for suitable concepts or principles for papers in the boldface entries throughout the book, the items in the glossary, and the terms covered in the vocabulary quizzes. When writing this type of paper, keep the following in mind:

1. Explain the concept(s) or principle(s) so that someone who knows nothing about interpersonal communication would understand it. If you want to compare and contrast two concepts, do so after you have explained each one individually. A good way to start off this explanation is to offer simple definitions in which you first identify the category or class to which the concept belongs and then identify its unique or distinguishing characteristics (McMahan & Day, 1984), for example:

Concept to be Defined	Category or Class to which the Concept Belongs	Unique or Distinguishing Characteristics that Separate this Concept from Similar Ones
Noise [is a]	type of message	which interferes with the speaker's intended meaning getting to the listener.
Intimacy [is a]	type of relationship	characterized by psychological and often physical closeness.
Repair [is a]	relationship process	in which one or both partners try to correct relationship problems.

Writing is thinking. It is more than living, for it is being conscious of living.
—*Anne Morrow Lindbergh*

2. Follow this explanation with a concrete example. But, be careful that you only use the example as a way of illustration; an example alone does not define a concept or principle.
3. Explain the value of this concept or principle. Value can be interpreted in several ways: value in understanding communication, in improving relationships, in more effective management, in improved conflict management, and so on.

THE REVIEW PAPER

This paper is usually concerned with reviewing a specific article or book (in popular or scholarly literature), a film or television show that has special relevance to interpersonal communication, a Website, or area of interpersonal communication (such as, "self-disclosure," "excuses," "the role of power in the classroom," or "sex differences in conflict strategies"). Useful leads for review paper topics can be found in the headings throughout this textbook or in any book on communication, questions that occur to you as you read the text and that you'd like answered in more detail than you find here, as well as in many of the Critical Thinking Questions in the margins.

1. If you're reviewing an article, book, film, television show, or Website, clearly state the author's purpose, methods, and conclusions. Tell the reader what the author (writer or director, for example) set out to accomplish, what methods the author used to accomplish the task, and what the author discovered and concluded.
2. Explain why this article or area of study is of interest. Try to answer your reader's inevitable question: "Why should I continue reading this review?"
3. State some positive evaluation. Say why you think this article or book is a good one or why the research in this area is worthwhile.
4. State any negative evaluation you may have. What could the author have done to improve this article or book? What could the researchers have done, or what should they do in the future to explore this area more fully?

THE RESEARCH PAPER

The research paper is the most difficult but in many ways the most creative and the most exciting to write. In the process of writing this paper you seek to learn something new about interpersonal communication, for example: What kinds of excuses do men and women use? What type of clothing inspires confidence? What interpersonal communication skills are especially important in business? What do we know about doctor–patient communication? Suggestions for this paper can be found throughout the text, in the questions raised in the text, in the photo captions, and in the Critical Thinking Questions in the margins of each chapter. Your basic steps in writing this paper would go something like this:

1. Ask a question. Research starts with a question. Your question can be a purely theoretical one (How can a person's fear of interpersonal communication be measured?) or one of great practical importance (What

Writing is harder than anything else; at least *starting* to write is.
—Kristin Hunter

can be done to improve health care provider-to-patient communication?) A question can also be articulated in the form of a hypothesis, a statement that predicts a certain relationship will exist between different variables. For example, one such hypothesis might be: People who have high self-esteem will self-disclose more than those with low self-esteem. A hypothesis can also predict that there is no relationship between variables (this type of hypothesis is called a null hypothesis), for example: Men and women do not differ in their level of romanticism.

2. Define significant concepts. All the key terms in your research should be defined as specifically and as clearly as possible. The objective here is to define the terms so clearly that anyone looking at the same communication behavior would classify it in the same way. For example, how would you define *fear of communication? managerial effectiveness? self-esteem? effective student–teacher interaction?*

3. Review related research. Here you examine the previous theories and research studies that cover your question. You try to answer the question, "what is already known that bears on my research topic?"

4. Design the research study. How will you go about collecting your information? Will you ask people to fill out a questionnaire? Will you have them take a self-assessment test? Will you observe their interactions? How many participants will you need? What are the major characteristics of the participants you'll study (age, sex, educational level, political affiliation, religion, race, etc.)?

5. Conduct the study. At this stage you would, for example, survey your participants, have your participants fill out a self-test, or describe and record their communication behaviors.

6. Analyze the data. Using appropriate methods (which vary from the most sophisticated statistical tests to, say, simply counting the number of times teachers used humor), you would analyze the data and identify the major results.

7. Formulate the conclusions. What do the results mean? Do they help you answer your question? Do they confirm or disconfirm your hypothesis? What insights do these results provide about interpersonal communication?

Never use a metaphor, simile, or other figure of speech which you're used to seeing in print.
Never use a long word when a short one will do.
If it is possible to cut a word out, always cut it out.
Never use the passive when you can use the active.
Never use a foreign phrase, a scientific word, or a jargon word if you can think of an everyday English equivalent.
Break any of those rules sooner than say anything outright barbarous.

—George Orwell

Glossary of Interpersonal Communication Concepts and Skills

Listed here are definitions of the technical terms of interpersonal communication—the words that are peculiar or unique to this discipline—and, where appropriate, the corresponding skills. These definitions and statements of skills should make new or difficult terms a bit easier to understand and should help to place the skill in context. The statements of skills appear in italics. All boldface terms within the definitions appear as separate entries in the glossary.

Acculturation. The process by which a person's culture is modified or changed through contact with or exposure to another culture.

Active listening. A process of putting together into some meaningful whole the listener's understanding of the speaker's total message—the verbal and the nonverbal, the content and the feelings. *Listen actively by paraphrasing the speaker's meanings, expressing an understanding of the speaker's feelings, and asking questions to enable you to check the accuracy of your understanding of the speaker. Express acceptance of the speaker's feelings, and encourage the speaker to explore further his or her feelings and thoughts and thereby increase meaningful sharing.*

Adaptors. Nonverbal behaviors that, when engaged in either in private or in public without being seen, serve some kind of need and occur in their entirety—for example, scratching one's head until the itch is relieved. *Avoid adaptors that interfere with effective communication and reveal your discomfort or anxiety.*

Adjustment (principle of). The principle of verbal interaction that claims that communication may take place only to the extent that the parties communicating share the same system of signals. *Expand the common areas between you and significant others; learn each other's system of communication signals and meanings in order to increase understanding and interpersonal communication effectiveness.*

Affect displays. Nonverbal movements, mostly of the facial area, that convey emotional meaning—for example, anger, fear, and surprise.

Affinity-seeking strategies. Behaviors designed to increase our interpersonal attractiveness. *Use the various affinity-seeking strategies (for example, listening, openness, and dynamism), as appropriate to the interpersonal relationship and the situation, to increase your own interpersonal attractiveness.*

Affirmation. The communication of support and approval. *Use affirmation to express your supportiveness and to raise esteem.*

Allness. The assumption that all can be known or is known about a given person, issue, object, or event. *End statements with an implicit "etc." ("et cetera") to indicate that more could be known and said; avoid allness terms and statements.*

Alter-adaptors. Body movements you make in response to your current interactions, for example, crossing your arms over your chest when someone unpleasant approaches or moving closer to someone you like.

Altercasting. Placing the listener in a specific role for a specific purpose and asking that the listener approach the question or problem from the perspective of this specific role.

Ambiguity. The condition in which a message may be interpreted as having more than one meaning.

Apprehension. See **communication apprehension.**

Argumentativeness. A willingness to argue for a point of view, to speak one's mind. *Cultivate your argumenta-*

tiveness, your willingness to argue for what you believe, by, for example, treating disagreements as objectively as possible, reaffirming the other, stressing equality, expressing interest in the other's position, and allowing the other person to save face. Distinguished from **verbal aggressiveness.**

Assertiveness. A willingness to stand up for one's rights but with respect for the rights of others. *Increase assertiveness (if desired) by analyzing the assertive and nonassertive behaviors of others, analyzing your own behaviors in terms of assertiveness, recording your behaviors, rehearsing assertive behaviors, and acting assertively in appropriate situations. Secure feedback from others for further guidance in increasing assertiveness.*

Assimilation. A process of message distortion in which messages are reworked to conform to our own attitudes, prejudices, needs, and values.

Attention. The process of responding to a stimulus or stimuli; usually some consciousness of responding is implied.

Attitude. A predisposition to respond for or against an object, person, or position.

Attraction. The state or process by which one individual is drawn to another, by having a highly positive evaluation of that other person.

Attractiveness. The degree to which one is perceived to be physically attractive and to possess a pleasing personality.

Attribution theory. A theory concerned with the processes involved in attributing causation or motivation to a person's behavior. *In attempting to identify the motivation for behaviors, examine consensus, consistency, distinctiveness, and controllability. Generally, low consensus, high consistency, low distinctiveness, and high controllability identify internally motivated behavior; high consensus, low consistency, high distinctiveness, and low controllability identify externally motivated behavior.*

Avoidance. An unproductive **conflict** strategy in which a person takes mental or physical flight from the actual conflict.

Back-channeling cues. Listener responses to a speaker which do not ask for the speaking role. *Respond to back-channeling cues as appropriate to the conversation. Use back-channeling cues to let the speaker know you are listening.*

Barriers to intercultural communication. Those factors (physical or psychological) that prevent or hinder effective communication. *Avoid the major barriers to intercultural communication: ignoring differences between yourself and the culturally different, ignoring differences among the culturally different, ignoring differences in meaning, violating cultural rules and customs, and evaluating differences negatively.*

Behavioral synchrony. The similarity in the behavior, usually nonverbal, of two persons. Generally, it is taken as an index of mutual liking.

Belief. Confidence in the existence or truth of something; conviction. *Weigh both verbal and nonverbal messages before making believability judgments; increase your own sensitivity to nonverbal (and verbal) deception cues—for example, too little movement, long pauses, slow speech, increased speech errors, mouth guard, nose touching, eye rubbing, or the use of few words, especially monosyllabic answers. Use such cues to formulate hypotheses rather than conclusions concerning deception.*

Beltlining. An unproductive **conflict** strategy in which one hits at the level at which the other person cannot withstand the blow. *Avoid beltlining.*

Blame. An unproductive **conflict** strategy in which we attribute the cause of the conflict to the other person or devote our energies to discovering who is the cause and avoid talking about the issues causing the conflict. *Avoid using blame to win an argument, especially with those with whom you are in close relationships.*

Boundary marker. A marker that sets boundaries that divide one person's territory from another's—for example, a fence.

Breadth. The number of topics about which individuals in a relationship communicate.

Central marker. A marker or item that is placed in a territory to reserve it for a specific person—for example, the sweater thrown over a library chair to signal that the chair is taken.

Certainty. An attitude of closed-mindedness that creates a defensiveness among communication participants; opposed to **provisionalism.**

Channel. The vehicle or medium through which signals are sent.

Cherishing behaviors. Small behaviors we enjoy receiving from others, especially from our relational partner—for example, a kiss before leaving for work.

Chronemics. The study of the communicative nature of time—the way you treat time and use it to communicate. Two general areas of chronemics are cultural and psychological time.

Civil inattention. Polite ignoring of others so as not to invade their privacy.

Cliché. An expression whose overuse calls attention to itself; "tall, dark, and handsome" as a description of a man would be considered a cliché.

Closed-mindedness. An unwillingness to receive certain communication messages.

Code. A set of symbols used to translate a message from one form to another.

Collectivist culture. A culture in which the group's goals rather than the individual's are given greater importance and where, for example, benevolence, tradition, and conformity are given special emphasis; opposed to **individualistic culture.**

Color communication. Use of colors (in clothing and in room decor, for example) to convey desired meanings.

Communication. (1) The process or act of communicating; (2) the actual message or messages sent and received; (3) the study of the processes involved in the sending and receiving of messages. (The term **communicology** is suggested for the third definition.)

Communication adjustment. Adjusting our communications as appropriate to the stage of an interpersonal relationship.

Communication apprehension. Fear or anxiety over communicating; "trait apprehension" refers to fear of communication generally, regardless of the specific situation; "state apprehension" refers to fear that is specific to a given communication situation. *Manage your own communication apprehension by acquiring the necessary communication skills and experiences, focusing on success, reducing unpredictability by, for example, familiarizing yourself with the communication situations important to you, and putting communication apprehension in perspective. In cases of extreme communication apprehension, seek professional help.*

Competence. "Language competence" is a speaker's ability to use the language; it is a knowledge of the elements and rules of the language. "Communication competence" refers to a knowledge of the elements, principles, and skills of communication and the ability to use these resources for greater communication effectiveness.

Complementarity. A principle of **attraction** holding that one is attracted by qualities one does not possess or one wishes to possess and to people who are opposite or different from oneself; opposed to **similarity.** *Identify the characteristics that you do not find in yourself but admire in others and that therefore might be important in influencing your perception of complementarity.*

Complementary relationship. A relationship in which the behavior of one person serves as the stimulus for the complementary behavior of the other; in complementary relationships, behavioral differences are maximized.

Compliance-gaining strategies. Behaviors that are directed toward gaining the agreement of others; behaviors designed to persuade others to do as we wish. *Use the various compliance-gaining strategies to increase your own persuasive power.*

Compliance-resisting strategies. Behaviors directed at resisting the persuasive attempts of others. *Use such strategies as identity management, nonnegotiation, negotiation, and justification as appropriate in resisting compliance.*

Confidence. A quality of interpersonal effectiveness; a comfortable, at-ease feeling in interpersonal communication situations. *Communicate a feeling of being comfortable and at ease with the interaction through appropriate verbal and nonverbal signals.*

Confirmation. A communication pattern that acknowledges another person's presence and also indicates an acceptance of this person, this person's definition of self, and the relationship as defined or viewed by this other person; opposed to **disconfirmation.** *Avoid those verbal and nonverbal behaviors that disconfirm another person. Substitute confirming behaviors, behaviors that acknowledge the presence and the contributions of the other person.*

Conflict. An extreme form of competition in which a person attempts to bring a rival to surrender; a situation in which one person's behaviors are directed at preventing something or at interfering with or harming another individual. *See also* **interpersonal conflict.**

Congruence. A condition in which both verbal and nonverbal behaviors reinforce each other.

Connotation. The feeling or emotional aspect of meaning, generally viewed as consisting of the evaluative (for example, good-bad), potency (strong-weak), and activity (fast-slow) dimensions; the associations of a term. *See also* **denotation.**

Consistency. A perceptual process that influences us to maintain balance among our perceptions; a process that makes us tend to see what we expect to see and to be uncomfortable when our perceptions run contrary to our expectations. *Recognize the human tendency to seek and to see consistency even where it doesn't exist—to see our friends as all positive and our enemies as all negative, for example.*

Content and relationship dimensions. A principle of communication that messages refer both to content (the world external to both speaker and listener) and to the relationship existing between the individuals who are interacting.

Context of communication. The physical, psychological, social, and temporal environment in which communication takes place. *Assess the context in which messages are communicated and interpret that communication behavior accordingly; avoid seeing messages as independent of context.*

Conversation. Two-person communication usually possessing an opening, feedforward, a business stage, feedback, and a closing.

Conversational management. Responding to conversational turn cues from the other person, and using conversational cues to signal one's own desire to exchange (or maintain) speaker or listener roles.

Conversational maxims. Principles that are followed in conversation to ensure that the goal of the conversation is achieved. *Discover, try not to violate, and, if appropriate, follow the conversational maxims of the culture in which you are communicating.*

Conversational processes. Use the general five-step process in conversation, and avoiding the several barriers that can be created when the normal process is distorted.

Conversational turns. The process of passing the speaker and listener roles during conversation. *Become sensitive to and respond appropriately to conversational turn cues, such as turn-maintaining, turn-yielding, turn-requesting, and turn-denying cues.*

Cooperation. An interpersonal process by which individuals work together for a common end; the pooling of efforts to produce a mutually desired outcome.

Cooperation principle. An implicit agreement between speaker and listener to cooperate in trying to understand what each is communicating.

Credibility. The degree to which a receiver perceives the speaker to be believable; competence, character, and charisma (dynamism) are its major dimensions.

Critical thinking. The process of logically evaluating reasons and evidence and reaching a judgment on the basis of this analysis.

Cultural display. Signs that communicate one's cultural identification, for example, clothing or religious jewelry.

Cultural rules. Rules that are specific to a given culture. *Respond to messages according to the cultural rules of the sender; avoid interpreting the messages of others exclusively through the perspective of your own culture in order to prevent misinterpretation of the intended meanings.*

Cultural time. The meanings given to time communication by a particular culture.

Culture. The relatively specialized lifestyle of a group of people—consisting of their values, beliefs, artifacts, ways of behaving, and ways of communicating. Included in "culture" would be all that members of a social group have produced and developed—their language, modes of thinking, art, laws, and religion—and that are passed from one generation to the next through communication rather than through genes.

Date. An **extensional device** used to emphasize the notion of constant change and symbolized by a subscript: for example, John Smith$_{1986}$ is not John Smith$_{1999}$.

Decoder. Something that takes a message in one form (for example, sound waves) and translates it into another form (for example, nerve impulses) from which meaning can be formulated (for example, in vocal-auditory communication). In human communication, the decoder is the auditory mechanism; in electronic communication, the decoder is, for example, the telephone ear piece. Decoding is the process of extracting a message from a code—for example, translating speech sounds into nerve impulses. *See also* **encoder.**

Defensiveness. An attitude of an individual or an atmosphere in a group characterized by threats, fear, and domination; messages evidencing evaluation, control, strategy, neutrality, superiority, and certainty are assumed to lead to defensiveness; opposed to **supportiveness.**

Delayed reactions. Reactions that are consciously delayed while a situation is analyzed.

Denial. One of the obstacles to the expression of emotion; the process by which we deny our emotions to ourselves or to others.

Denotation. Referential meaning; the objective or descriptive meaning of a word. *See also* **connotation.**

Depenetration. A reversal of penetration; a condition in which the **breadth** and **depth** of a relationship decrease.

Depth. The degree to which the inner personality—the inner core of an individual—is penetrated in interpersonal interaction.

Dialogic conversation. Treating conversation as a dialogue rather than a monologue; showing concern for the other person, and for the relationship between ourselves and another, with other-orientation.

Dialogue. A form of **communication** in which each person is both speaker and listener; communication characterized by involvement, concern, and respect for the other person; opposed to **monologue.**

Direct speech. Speech in which the speaker's intentions are stated clearly and directly. *Use direct requests and responses (1) to encourage compromise, (2) to acknowledge responsibility for your own feelings and desires, and (3) to state your own desires honestly so as to encourage honesty, openness, and supportiveness in others.*

Disclaimer. Statement that asks the listener to receive what the speaker says as intended without its reflecting negatively on the image of the speaker. *Avoid using disclaimers that may not be accepted by your listeners (they may raise the very doubts you wish to put to rest), but do use disclaimers when you think your future messages might offend your listeners.*

Disclosure responses. Feedback given by the listener in response to the disclosure of another. *In responding to the disclosures of others, demonstrate the skills of effective listening, express support for the discloser (but resist evaluation), reinforce the disclosing behavior, keep the disclosures confidential, and avoid using the disclosures against the person.*

Disconfirmation. The process by which one ignores or denies the right of the individual even to define himself or herself; opposed to **confirmation.**

Discriminating. Being sensitive to differences *among* individuals prevents discrimination against individuals.

Dyadic coalition. A two-person group formed from some larger group to achieve a particular goal.

Dyadic communication. Two-person communication.

Dyadic consciousness. An awareness of an interpersonal relationship or pairing of two individuals; distinguished from situations in which two individuals are together but do not perceive themselves as being a unit or twosome.

Dyadic effect. The tendency for the behaviors of one person to stimulate behaviors in the other interactant; usually used to refer to the tendency of one person's self-disclosures to prompt the other to self-disclose, also.

Dyadic primacy. The significance or centrality of the two-person group, even when there are many more people interacting.

Ear marker. A marker that identifies an item as belonging to a specific person—for example, a nameplate on a desk or initials on an attaché case.

Effect. The outcome or consequence of an action or behavior; communication is assumed always to have some effect.

Emblems. Nonverbal behaviors that directly translate words or phrases—for example, the signs for "OK" and "peace."

Emotion. The feelings we have—for example, our feelings of guilt, anger, or sorrow.

Empathy. The feeling of another person's feeling; feeling or perceiving something as does another person. *Increase empathic understanding for your primary partner by sharing experiences, role-playing, and seeing the world from his or her perspective. Empathize with others, and express this empathic understanding verbally and nonverbally.*

Encoder. Something that takes a message in one form (for example, nerve impulses) and translates it into another form (for example, sound waves). In human communication, the encoder is the speaking mechanism; in electronic communication, the encoder is, for example, the telephone mouthpiece. Encoding is the process of putting a message into a code—for example, translating nerve impulses into speech sounds. *See also* **decoder.**

Enculturation. The process by which culture is transmitted from one generation to another.

E-prime. A form of the language that omits the verb "to be" except when used as an auxiliary or in statements of existence. Designed to eliminate the tendency toward **projection.**

Equality. An attitude that recognizes that each individual in a communication interaction is equal, that no one is superior to any other; encourages supportiveness; opposed to **superiority.** *Talk neither down nor up to others but communicate as an equal to increase interpersonal satisfaction and efficiency; share the speaking and the listening; recognize that all parties in communication have something to contribute.*

Equilibrium theory. A theory of proxemics holding that intimacy and physical closeness are positively related; as a relationship becomes more intimate, the individuals will use shorter distances between them.

Equity theory. A theory claiming that we experience relational satisfaction when there is an equal distribution of rewards and costs between the two persons in the relationship.

Etc. (et cetera). An **extensional device** used to emphasize the notion of infinite complexity; because one can never know all about anything, any statement about the world or an event must end with an explicit or implicit "etc." *Use the implicit or explicit etc. to remind yourself and others that there is more to be known, more to be said.*

Ethics. The branch of philosophy that deals with the rightness or wrongness of actions; the study of moral values.

Ethnocentrism. The tendency to see others and their behaviors through our own cultural filters, often as distortions of our own behaviors; the tendency to evaluate the values and beliefs of one's own culture more positively than those of another culture.

Euphemism. A polite word or phrase used to substitute for some taboo or otherwise offensive term.

Evaluation. A process whereby a value is placed on some person, object, or event. *Avoid premature evaluation; amass evidence before making evaluations especially of other people.*

Excuse. An explanation designed to lessen the negative consequences of something done or said. *Avoid excessive excuse making. Too many excuses may backfire and create image problems for the excuse maker.*

Expectancy violations theory. A theory of proxemics holding that people have a certain expectancy for space relationships. When that is violated (say, a person stands too close to you or a romantic partner maintains abnormally large distances from you), the relationship comes into clearer focus and you wonder why this "normal distance" is being violated.

Experiential limitation. The limit of an individual's ability to communicate, as set by the nature and extent of that individual's experiences.

Expressiveness. A quality of interpersonal effectiveness; genuine involvement in speaking and listening, conveyed verbally and nonverbally. *Communicate involvement and interest in the interaction by providing appropriate feedback, by assuming responsibility for your thoughts and feelings and your role as speaker and listener, and by appropriate expressiveness, variety, and flexibility in voice and bodily action.*

Extensional devices. Linguistic devices proposed by Alfred Korzybski to keep language a more accurate means for talking about the world. The extensional devices include **etc., date,** and **index** (the working devices) and the **hyphen** and **quotes** (the safety devices).

Extensional orientation. A point of view in which the primary consideration is given to the world of experience and only secondary consideration is given to labels. *See also* **intensional orientation.**

Facial feedback hypothesis. The hypothesis or theory that your facial expressions can produce physiological and emotional effects.

Facial management techniques. Techniques used to mask certain emotions and to emphasize others, for example, intensifying your expression of happiness to make a friend feel good about a promotion.

Fact-inference confusion. A misevaluation in which one makes an inference, regards it as a fact, and acts upon it as if it were a fact. *Distinguish facts from inferences; respond to inferences as inferences and not as facts.*

Factual statement. A statement made by the observer after observation and limited to what is observed. *See also* **inferential statement.**

Family. A group of people who consider themselves related and connected to one another and where the actions of one have consequences for others.

Fear appeal. The appeal to fear to persuade an individual or group of individuals to believe or to act in a certain way.

Feedback. Information that is given back to the source. Feedback may come from the source's own messages (as when we hear what we are saying) or from the receiver(s) in the form of applause, yawning, puzzled looks, questions, letters to the editor of a newspaper, increased or decreased subscriptions to a magazine, and so forth. *Give clear feedback to others, and respond to others' feedback, either through corrective measures or by continuing current performance, to increase communication efficiency and satisfaction. See also* **feedforward.**

Feedforward. Information that is sent prior to the regular messages telling the listener something about what is to follow. *When appropriate, preface your messages in order to open the channels of communication, to preview the messages to be sent, to disclaim, and to altercast. In your use of feedforward, be brief, use feedforward sparingly, and follow through on your feedforward promises. Also, be sure to respond to the feedforward as well as the content messages of others. See also* **feedback.**

Flexibility. The ability to adjust communication strategies on the basis of the unique situation. *Apply the principles of interpersonal communication with flexibility, realizing that each situation calls for somewhat different skills.*

Force. An unproductive **conflict** strategy in which you try to win an argument by physically overpowering the other person either by threat or by actual behavior. *Avoid it.*

Free information. Information that is revealed implicitly and that may be used as a basis for opening or pursuing conversations.

Friendship. An interpersonal relationship between two persons that is mutually productive, established and maintained through perceived mutual free choice, and characterized by mutual positive regard. *Adjust your verbal and nonverbal communication as appropriate to the stages of your various friendships. Learn the rules that govern your friendships; follow them or risk damaging the relationship.*

Game. A simulation of some situation with rules governing the behaviors of the participants and with some payoff for winning; in transactional analysis, "game" refers to a series of ulterior transactions that lead to a payoff; the term also refers to a basically dishonest kind of transaction in which participants hide their true feelings.

General Semantics. The study of the relationships among language, thought, and behavior.

Gossip. Communication about someone not present, some third party, usually about matters that are private to this third party. *Avoid gossip that breaches confidentiality, is known to be false, and is unnecessarily invasive.*

Gunnysacking. An unproductive **conflict** strategy of storing up grievances—as if in a gunnysack—and holding them in readiness to dump on the person with whom one is in conflict. *Avoid it.*

Halo effect. The tendency to generalize an individual's virtue or expertise from one area to another.

Haptics. Technical term for the study of touch communication.

Heterosexist language. Language that assumes all people are heterosexual and thereby denigrates lesbians and gay men.

High-context culture. A culture in which much of the information in communication is in the context or in the person rather than explicitly coded in the verbal messages; opposed to **low-context culture. Collectivist cultures** are generally high context.

Home field advantage. The increased power that comes from being in your own territory.

Home territories. Territories for which individuals have a sense of intimacy and over which they exercise control—for example, a teacher's office.

Hyphen. An **extensional device** used to illustrate that what may be separated verbally may not be separable on the event level or on the nonverbal level; although one may talk about body and mind as if they were separable, in reality they are better referred to as body-mind.

I-messages. Messages in which the speaker accepts responsibility for personal thoughts and behaviors; messages in which the speaker's point of view is stated explicitly; opposed to **you-messages**. *Generally, I-messages are more effective than you-messages.*

Illustrators. Nonverbal behaviors that accompany and literally illustrate verbal messages—for example, upward movements that accompany the verbalization "It's up there."

Immediacy. A quality of interpersonal effectiveness; a sense of contact and togetherness; a feeling of interest and liking for the other person. *Communicate immediacy through appropriate word choice, feedback, eye contact, body posture, and physical closeness.*

Implicit personality theory. A theory of personality that each individual maintains, complete with rules or systems, through which others are perceived. *Be conscious of your implicit personality theories; avoid drawing firm conclusions about other people on the basis of these theories.*

In-group talk. Talk about a subject or in a vocabulary that only certain people understand; such talk often occurs in the presence of someone who does not belong to the group and therefore does not understand.

Inclusion principle. In verbal interaction, the principle that all members should be a part of (included in) the interaction. *Include everyone present in the interaction (both verbally and nonverbally) so you do not exclude or offend others or fail to profit from their contributions.*

Index. An **extensional device** used to emphasize the notion of nonidentity (no two things are the same) and symbolized by a subscript—for example, $politician_1$ is not $politician_2$.

Indirect speech. Speech that hides the speaker's true intentions; speech in which requests and observations are made indirectly. *Use indirect speech (1) to express a desire without insulting or offending anyone, (2) to ask for compliments in a socially acceptable manner, and (3) to disagree without being disagreeable.*

Indiscrimination. A misevaluation caused by categorizing people, events, or objects into a particular class and responding to them only as members of the class; a failure to recognize that each individual is unique; a failure to apply the **index**. *Index your terms and statements to emphasize that each person and event is unique; avoid treating all individuals the same way because they are covered by the same label or term.*

Individualistic culture. A culture in which the individual's rather than the group's goals and preferences are given greater importance; opposed to **collectivist cultures**.

Inevitability. A principle of communication holding that communication cannot be avoided; all behavior in an interactional setting is communication. *Remember that all behavior in an interactional situation communicates; seek out nonobvious messages and meanings.*

Inferential statement. A statement that can be made by anyone, is not limited to what is observed, and can be made at any time. See also **factual statement.**

Informal-time terms. Terms that are approximate rather than exact, for example, "soon," "early," and "in a while." *Recognize that informal-time terms are often the cause of interpersonal difficulties. When misunderstanding is likely, use more precise terms.*

Information overload. A condition in which the amount of information is too great to be dealt with effectively or the number or complexity of messages is so great that the individual or organization is not able to deal with them.

Insulation. A reaction to **territorial encroachment** in which you erect some sort of barrier between yourself and the invaders.

Intensional orientation. A point of view in which primary consideration is given to the way things are labeled and only secondary consideration (if any) to the world of experience. *See also* **extensional orientation.** *Respond first to things; avoid responding to labels as if they were things; do not let labels distort your perception of the world.*

Interaction management. A quality of interpersonal effectiveness; the control of interaction to the satisfaction of both parties; managing conversational turns, fluency, and message consistency. *Manage the interaction to the satisfaction of both parties by sharing the roles of speaker and listener, avoiding long and awkward silences, and being consistent in your verbal and nonverbal messages.*

Intercultural communication. Communication that takes place between persons of different cultures or persons who have different cultural beliefs, values, or ways of behaving.

Interpersonal communication. Communication between two persons or among a small group of persons and distinguished from public or mass communication; communication of a personal nature and distinguished from impersonal communication; communication between or among connected persons or those involved in a close relationship.

Interpersonal conflict. A disagreement between two connected persons. *To engage in more productive interpersonal conflict: (1) state your position directly and honestly; (2) react openly to the messages of your combatant; (3) own your thoughts and feelings; (4) address the real issues causing the conflict; (5) listen with and demonstrate empathic understanding; (6) validate the feelings of your interactant; (7) describe the behaviors causing the conflict; (8) express your feelings spontaneously rather than strategically; (9) state your position tentatively; (10) capitalize on agreements; (11) view conflict in positive terms to the extent* *possible; (12) express positive feelings for the other person; (13) be positive about the prospects of conflict resolution; (14) treat your combatant as an equal, avoiding ridicule or sarcasm, for example; (15) involve yourself in the conflict; play an active role as both sender and receiver; (16) grant the other person permission to express himself or herself freely; and (17) avoid power tactics that may inhibit freedom of expression.*

Interpersonal perception. The perception of people; the processes through which we interpret and evaluate people and their behavior.

Intimacy. The closest interpersonal relationship; usually used to denote a close primary relationship.

Intimacy claims. Obligations incurred by virtue of being in a close and intimate relationship. *Reduce the intensity of intimacy claims when things get rough; give each other space as appropriate.*

Intimate distance. The closest proxemic distance, ranging from touching to 18 inches. *See also* **proxemics.**

Intrapersonal communication. Communication with oneself.

Irreversibility. A principle of communication holding that communication cannot be reversed; once something has been communicated, it cannot be uncommunicated. *Avoid saying things (for example, in anger) or making commitments that you may wish to retract (but will not be able to) in order to prevent resentment and ill feeling.*

Johari window. A diagram of the four selves: **open, blind, hidden,** and **unknown.**

Kinesics. The study of the communicative dimensions of facial and bodily movements.

Language fairness. Use language fairly; avoid language that offends or demeans, for example, language that excludes others from full participation.

Language relativity hypothesis. The theory that the language we speak influences our behaviors and our perceptions of the world and that therefore persons speaking widely differing languages will perceive and behave differently as a result of the language differences. Also referred to as the Sapir-Whorf hypothesis and the Whorfian hypothesis. *Because most research does not support such influence or such wide differences, the belief in this hypothesis is likely to cause undue concentration on differences when similarities really exist.*

Leave-taking cues. Verbal and nonverbal cues that indicate a desire to terminate a conversation. *Increase your sensitivity to leave-taking cues; pick up on the leave-taking cues of others, and communicate such cues tactfully so as not to insult or offend others.*

Leveling. A process of message distortion in which a message is repeated but the number of details is reduced, some details are omitted entirely, and some details lose their complexity.

Listening. An active process of receiving aural stimuli; this process consists of five stages: receiving, understanding, remembering, evaluating, and responding. *Adjust your listening perspective, as the situation warrants, between active and passive, judgmental and nonjudgmental, surface and depth, and empathic and objective listening.*

Loving. An interpersonal process in which one feels a closeness, a caring, a warmth, and an excitement for another person.

Low-context culture. A culture in which most of the information in communication is explicitly stated in the verbal messages; opposed to **high-context culture. Individualistic cultures** are usually low-context cultures.

Machiavellianism. The belief that people can be manipulated easily; often used to refer to the techniques or tactics one person uses to control another.

Maintenance. A stage of relationship stability at which the relationship does not progress or deteriorate significantly; a continuation as opposed to a dissolution of a relationship. *To accomplish relationship maintenance use such strategies as, for example, openness, sharing joint activities, and acting positively.*

Manipulation. An unproductive **conflict** strategy that avoids open conflict; instead, attempts are made to divert the conflict by being especially charming and getting the other person into a noncombative frame of mind. *Avoid it.*

Manner, maxim of. A principle of conversation that holds that speakers cooperate by being clear and by organizing their thoughts into some meaningful and coherent pattern. *Use it.*

Markers. Devices that signify that a certain territory belongs to a particular person. *See also* **boundary marker, central marker,** and **ear marker.** *Become sensitive to the markers (central, boundary, and ear) of others, and learn to use these markers to define your own territories and to communicate the desired impression.*

Matching hypothesis. An assumption that we date and mate with people who are similar to ourselves—who match us—in physical attractiveness.

Meaningfulness. A principle of perception holding that we assume that the behavior of people is sensible, stems from some logical antecedent, and is consequently meaningful rather than meaningless.

Mere exposure hypothesis. The theory that repeated or prolonged exposure to a stimulus may result in a change in attitude toward the stimulus object, generally in the direction of increased positiveness.

Message. Any signal or combination of signals that serves as a **stimulus** for a receiver.

Metacommunication. Communication about communication. *Metacommunicate to ensure understanding of the other person's thoughts and feelings: give clear feedforward,* *explain feelings as well as thoughts, paraphrase your own complex thoughts, and ask questions.*

Metalanguage. Language used to talk about language.

Metamessage. A message that makes reference to another message, for example, the statements "Did I make myself clear?" or "That's a lie" refer to other messages and are therefore considered metamessages. *Use metamessages to clarify your understanding of what another thinks and feels.*

Micromomentary expressions. Extremely brief movements that are not consciously controlled or recognized and that are thought to be indicative of an individual's true emotional state.

Mindfulness and mindlessness. States of relative awareness. In a mindful state, we are aware of the logic and rationality of our behaviors and the logical connections existing among elements. In a mindless state, we are unaware of this logic and rationality. *Apply the principles of interpersonal communication mindfully rather than mindlessly. Increase mindfulness by creating and recreating categories, being open to new information and points of view, and being careful of relying too heavily on first impressions.*

Mixed message. A message that contradicts itself; a message that asks for two different (often incompatible) responses. Avoid emitting mixed messages by focusing clearly on your purposes when communicating and by increasing conscious control over your verbal and nonverbal behaviors. *Detect mixed messages in other people's communications and avoid being placed in double-bind situations by seeking clarification from the sender.*

Model. A representation of an object or process.

Monochronic time orientation. A view of time in which things are done sequentially; one thing is scheduled at a time. Opposed to **polychronic time orientation**.

Monologue. A form of **communication** in which one person speaks and the other listens; there is no real interaction among participants. *Avoid it, at least generally.* Opposed to **dialogue.**

Negative feedback. Feedback that serves a corrective function by informing the source that his or her message is not being received in the way intended. Negative feedback serves to redirect the source's behavior. Looks of boredom, shouts of disagreement, letters critical of newspaper policy, and teachers' instructions on how better to approach a problem would be examples of negative feedback.

Neutrality. A response pattern lacking in personal involvement; encourages defensiveness; opposed to **empathy.**

Noise. Anything that interferes with a person's receiving a message as the source intended the message to be received. Noise is present in a communication system to the extent that the message received is not the message sent. *Combat the effects of physical, semantic, and psychological noise by eliminating or lessening the sources of physical noise, securing agreement on meanings, and interacting with an open mind in order to increase communication accuracy.*

Nonallness. An attitude or point of view in which it is recognized that one can never know all about anything and that what we know, say, or hear is only a part of what there is to know, say, or hear.

Nondirective language. Language that does not direct or focus our attention on certain aspects; neutral language.

Nonnegotiation. An unproductive **conflict** strategy in which the individual refuses to discuss the conflict or to listen to the other person.

Nonverbal communication. Communication without words; communication by means of space, gestures, facial expressions, touching, vocal variation, and silence, for example.

Nonverbal dominance. Nonverbal behavior that allows one person to achieve psychological dominance over another. *Resist (as sender and receiver) nonverbal expressions of dominance when they are inappropriate—for example, when they are sexist.*

Object-adaptors. Movements that involve your manipulation of some object, for example, punching holes in or drawing on the styrofoam coffee cup, clicking a ball point pen, or chewing on a pencil. *Avoid them; they generally communicate discomfort and a lack of control over the communication situation.*

Olfactory communication. Communication by smell.

Openness. A quality of interpersonal effectiveness encompassing (1) a willingness to interact openly with others, to self-disclose as appropriate; (2) a willingness to react honestly to incoming stimuli; and (3) a willingness to own one's feelings and thoughts.

Opinion. A tentative conclusion concerning some object, person, or event.

Other talk. Talk about the listener or some third party.

Other-orientation. A quality of interpersonal effectiveness involving attentiveness, interest, and concern for the other person. *Convey concern for and interest in the other person by means of empathic responses, appropriate feedback, and attentive listening responses.*

Outing. The process whereby a person's affectional orientation is made public by another person and without the gay man or lesbian's consent.

Owning feelings. The process by which we take responsibility for our own feelings instead of attributing them to others. *To indicate ownership of your feelings: use I-messages; acknowledge responsibility for your own thoughts and feelings.*

Paralanguage. The vocal (but nonverbal) aspect of speech. Paralanguage consists of voice qualities (for example, pitch range, resonance, tempo), vocal characterizers (laughing or crying, yelling or whispering), vocal qualifiers (intensity, pitch height), and vocal segregates ("uh-uh," meaning "no," or "sh" meaning "silence"). *Vary paralinguistic elements, such as rate, volume, and stress, to add variety and emphasis to your communications, and be responsive to the meanings communicated by others' variation of paralanguage features.*

Passive listening. Listening that is attentive and supportive but occurs without talking and without directing the speaker in any nonverbal way; also used negatively to refer to inattentive and uninvolved listening.

Pauses. Silent periods in the normally fluent stream of speech. Pauses are of two major types: filled pauses (interruptions in speech that are filled with such vocalizations as "er" or "um") and unfilled pauses (silences of unusually long duration).

Perception. The process of becoming aware of objects and events through the senses. *Increase your accuracy in interpersonal perception by looking for a variety of cues that point in the same direction, formulating hypotheses (not conclusions), being especially alert to contradictory cues that may refute your initial hypotheses, avoiding the assumption that others will respond as you would, and being careful not to perceive only the positive in those you like and the negative in those you dislike.*

Perception checking. The process of verifying your understanding of some message or situation or feeling. *Use perception checking to get more information about your impressions: (1) describe what you think is happening, and (2) ask whether this is correct or in error.*

Perceptual accentuation. A process that leads you to see what you expect to see and what you want to see—for example, seeing people you like as better looking and smarter than people you do not like. *Be aware of the influence your own needs, wants, and expectations have on your perceptions. Recognize that what you perceive is a function both of what exists in reality and what is going on inside your own head.*

Personal distance. The second-closest proxemic distance, ranging from 18 inches to 4 feet. *See also* **proxemics.**

Personal rejection. An unproductive **conflict** strategy in which the individual withholds love and affection and seeks to win the argument by getting the other person to break down under this withdrawal.

Persuasion. The process of influencing attitudes and behavior.

Phatic communication. Communication that is primarily social; communication designed to open the channels of communication rather than to communicate something about the external world; "Hello" and "How are you?" in everyday interaction are examples.

Pitch. The highness or lowness of the vocal tone.

Polarization. A form of fallacious reasoning by which only two extremes are considered; also referred to as "black-or-white" and "either-or" thinking or two-valued orientation. *Use middle terms and qualifiers when describing the world; avoid talking in terms of polar opposites (black and white, good and bad) in order to describe reality more accurately.*

Pollyanna effect. The condition in which one makes a prediction and then proceeds to fulfill it; a type of self-fulfilling prophecy but one that refers to others and to your evaluation of others rather than to yourself. *Be aware of your own tendency to fulfill such prophecies and of others' tendencies to fulfill their prophecies of you.*

Polychronic time orientation. A view of time in which several things may be scheduled or engaged in at the same time. Opposed to **monochronic time orientation.**

Positive feedback. Feedback that supports or reinforces the continuation of behavior along the same lines in which it is already proceeding—for example, applause during a speech.

Positiveness. A characteristic of effective communication involving positive attitudes toward oneself and toward the interpersonal interaction. Also used to refer to complimenting another and expressing acceptance and approval. *Verbally and nonverbally communicate a positive attitude toward yourself, others, and the situation with smiles, positive facial expressions, attentive gestures, positive verbal expressions, and the elimination or reduction of negative appraisals.*

Power. The ability to influence the behaviors of others.

Power bases. The sources of power, often classified into six types: referent, legitimate, reward, coercive, expert, and information.

Power communication. Communicate power through forceful speech, avoidance of weak modifiers and excessive body movement, and demonstration of your knowledge, preparation, and organization in the matters at hand.

Power play. A consistent pattern of behavior in which one person tries to control the behavior of another. *Identify the power plays people use on you and respond to these power plays so as to stop them. Use an effective management strategy, for example, express your feelings, describe the behavior you object to, and state a cooperative response.*

Pragmatic implication. An assumption that seems logical but is not necessarily true. *Identify your own pragmatic implications, and distinguish these from logical implications (those that are necessarily true) and recognize that memory often confuses the two. In recalling situations and events, ask yourself whether your conclusions are based on pragmatic or logical implications.*

Pragmatics. In communication, an approach that focuses on behaviors, especially on the effects or consequences of communication.

Premature self-disclosures. Disclosures that are made before the relationship has developed sufficiently. *Resist too intimate or too negative self-disclosures early in the development of a relationship.*

Primacy and recency. Primacy refers to giving more credence to that which occurs first; recency refers to giving more credence to that which occurs last (that is, most recently). *Be aware that first impressions can serve as filters that prevent you from perceiving others, perhaps contradictory behaviors as well as changes in situations and, especially, changes in people. Recognize the normal tendency for first impressions to leave lasting impressions and to color both what we see later and the conclusions we draw. Be at your very best in first encounters. Also, take the time and effort to revise your impressions of others on the basis of new information.*

Primacy effect. The condition by which what comes first exerts greater influence than what comes later. *See also* **recency effect.**

Primary affect displays. The communication of the six primary emotions: happiness, surprise, fear, anger, sadness, and disgust/contempt.

Primary relationship. The relationship between two people that they consider their most (or one of their most) important, for example, the relationship between husband and wife or domestic partners.

Primary territory. Areas that one can consider one's exclusive preserve—for example, one's room or office.

Process. Ongoing activity; communication is referred to as a process to emphasize that it is always changing, always in motion.

Progressive differentiation. A relational problem caused by the exaggeration or intensification of differences or similarities between individuals.

Projection. A psychological process whereby we attribute characteristics or feelings of our own to others; often used to refer to the process whereby we attribute our own faults to others.

Pronouncements. Authoritative statements that imply that the speaker is in a position of authority and that the listener is in a childlike or learner role.

Protection theory. A theory of proxemics holding that people establish a body-buffer zone to protect themselves from unwanted closeness, touching, or attack.

Provisionalism. An attitude of open-mindedness that leads to the creation of supportiveness; opposed to **certainty.**

Proxemic distances. The spatial distances that are maintained in communication and social interaction. *Adjust spatial (proxemic) distances as appropriate to the specific interaction; avoid distances that are too far, too close, or otherwise inappropriate, as they might falsely convey, for example, aloofness or aggression.*

Proxemics. The study of the communicative function of space; the study of how people unconsciously structure their space—the distance between people in their interactions, the organization of space in homes and offices, and even the design of cities.

Proximity. As a principle of perception, the tendency to perceive people or events that are physically close as belonging together or representing some unit; physical closeness; one of the qualities influencing interpersonal **attraction.** *Use physical proximity to increase interpersonal attractiveness.*

Psychological time. The importance you place on past, present, or future time. *Recognize the significance of your own time orientation to your ultimate success, and make whatever adjustments you think desirable.*

Public distance. The farthest proxemic distance, ranging from 12 feet to more than 25 feet.

Public territory. Areas that are open to all people—for example, restaurants or parks.

Punctuation of communication. The breaking up of continuous communication sequences into short sequences with identifiable beginnings and endings or stimuli and responses. *See the sequence of events punctuated from perspectives other than your own in order to increase empathy and mutual understanding.*

Pupil dilation. Detecting pupil dilation and constriction, and formulating hypotheses concerning their possible meanings.

Pupillometrics. The study of communication through changes in the size of the pupils of the eyes.

Pygmalion effect. The condition in which one makes a prediction and then proceeds to fulfill it; a type of self-fulfilling prophecy but one that refers to others and to our evaluation of others rather than to ourselves.

Quality maxim. A principle of **conversation** that holds that speakers cooperate by saying what they know or think is true and by not saying what they know or think is false. *Use it.*

Quantity maxim. A principle of **conversation** that holds that speakers cooperate by being only as informative as necessary to communicate their intended meanings. *Use it.*

Quotes. An **extensional device** to emphasize that a word or phrase is being used in a special sense and should therefore be given special attention.

Racist language. Language that denigrates a particular race. *Avoid racist language—any language that demeans or is derogatory toward members of a particular race—so as not to offend or alienate others or reinforce stereotypes.*

Rate. The speed with which we speak, generally measured in words per minute.

Receiver. Any person or thing that takes in messages. Receivers may be individuals listening to or reading a message, a group of persons hearing a speech, a scattered television audience, or machines that store information.

Recency effect. The condition in which what comes last (that is, most recently) exerts greater influence than what comes first. *See also* **primacy effect.**

Reconciliation strategies. Behaviors designed to re-create a broken relationship. *Consider using such reconciliation strategies as third-party intervention, tacit persistence, and mutual interaction to patch up a broken relationship.*

Redundancy. The quality of a message that makes it totally predictable and therefore lacking in information. A message of zero redundancy would be completely unpredictable; a message of 100% redundancy would be completely predictable. All human languages contain some degree of built-in redundancy, generally estimated to be about 50%.

Reflexiveness. The feature of human language that makes it possible for that language to be used to refer to itself; that is, we can talk about our talk and create a **metalanguage,** a language for talking about language.

Regulators. Nonverbal behaviors that regulate, monitor, or control the communications of another person.

Reinforcement or packaging (principle of). The principle of verbal interaction that holds that in most interactions, messages are transmitted simultaneously through a number of different channels that normally reinforce each other; messages come in packages.

Reinforcement theory. A theory of behavior that when applied to relationships would hold (essentially) that relationships develop because they are rewarding and end because they are punishing. *Reinforce others as a way to increase interpersonal attractiveness and general interpersonal satisfaction.*

Rejection. A response to an individual that rejects or denies the validity of that individual's self-view.

Relation, maxim of. A principle of **conversation** that holds that speakers cooperate by talking about what is relevant to the conversation and by not talking about what is not relevant.

Relational communication. Communication between or among intimates or those in close relationships; used by some theorists as synonymous with interpersonal communication.

Relationship deterioration. The stage of a relationship during which the connecting bonds between the partners weaken and the partners begin drifting apart.

Relationship dialectics theory. A theory that describes relationships along a series of opposites representing competing desires or motivations, such as the desire for autonomy and the desire to belong to someone, for novelty and predictability, and for closedness and openness.

Relationship dissolution. That relationship stage during which the bonds between the individuals are broken. *If the relationship ends: (1) break the loneliness-depression cycle, (2) take time out to get to know yourself as an individual, (3) bolster your self-esteem, (4) remove or avoid uncomfortable symbols that may remind you of your past relationship and may make you uncomfortable, (5) seek the support of friends and relatives, and (6) avoid repeating negative patterns.*

Relationship messages. Messages that comment on the relationship between the speakers rather than on matters external to them. *Recognize and respond to relationship as well as content messages in order to ensure a more complete understanding of the messages intended.*

Repair. A relationship stage in which one or both parties seek to improve the relationship. *Relationship repair may be accomplished by recognizing the problem, engaging in productive conflict resolution, posing possible solutions, affirming each other, integrating solutions into everyday behavior, and taking relational risks.* See *also* **maintenance.**

Resemblance. As a principle of perception, the tendency to perceive people or events that are similar in appearance as belonging together.

Response. Any bit of overt or covert behavior.

Rigid complementarity. The inability to break away from the complementary type of relationship that was once appropriate and now is no longer.

Role. The part an individual plays in a group; an individual's function or expected behavior.

Romantic rules. The rules that govern intimate relationships; *follow them or risk damaging the relationship.*

Rules theory. A theory that describes relationships as interactions governed by a series of rules that a couple agrees to follow. When the rules are followed, the relationship is maintained and when they are broken, the relationship experiences difficulty.

Secondary territory. Areas that do not belong to a particular person but have been occupied by that person and are therefore associated with her or him—for example, the seat you normally take in class.

Selective exposure (principle of). A principle of persuasion that states that listeners actively seek out information that supports their opinions and actively avoid information that contradicts their existing opinions, beliefs, attitudes, and values.

Self-acceptance. Being satisfied with ourselves, our virtues and vices, and our abilities and limitations.

Self-adaptors. Movements that usually satisfy a physical need, especially to make you more comfortable, for example, scratching your head to relieve an itch, moistening your lips because they feel dry, or pushing your hair out of your eyes. *Because these often communicate your nervousness or discomfort, they are best avoided.*

Self-appreciation. Appreciating ourselves; identifying our positive qualities; thinking positively about ourselves.

Self-attribution. A process through which we seek to account for and understand the reasons and motivations for our own behaviors.

Self-awareness. The degree to which a person knows himself or herself. *Increase self-awareness by asking yourself about yourself and listening to others; actively seek information about yourself from others by carefully observing their interactions with you and by asking relevant questions. See yourself from different perspectives (see your different selves), and increase your open self.*

Self-concept. An individual's self-evaluation; an individual's self-appraisal.

Self-disclosure. The process of revealing something about ourselves to another, usually used to refer to information that would normally be kept hidden. *Self-disclose when the motivation is to improve the relationship, when the context and the relationship are appropriate for the self-disclosure, when there is an opportunity for open and honest responses, when the self-disclosures will be clear and direct, when there are appropriate reciprocal disclosures, and when you have examined and are willing to risk the possible burdens that self-disclosure might entail. Self-disclose selectively; regulate your self-disclosures as appropriate to the context, topic, audience, and potential rewards and risks to secure the maximum advantage and reduce the possibility of negative effects.*

Self-esteem. The value we place on ourselves; our self-evaluations; usually used to refer to the positive value placed on oneself. *Increase your self-esteem by attacking destructive beliefs, engaging in self-affirmation, seeking out nourishing people, and working on projects that will result in success.*

Self-fulfilling prophecy. The situation in which we make a prediction or prophecy and fulfill it ourselves—for example, expecting a class to be boring and then fulfilling this expectation by perceiving it as boring. *Avoid fulfilling your own negative prophecies and seeing only what you want to see. Be especially careful to examine your perceptions when they conform too closely to your expectations; check to make sure that you are seeing what exists in real life, not just in your expectations or predictions.*

Self-monitoring. The manipulation of the image one presents to others in interpersonal interactions so as to give the most favorable impression of oneself. *Monitor your verbal and nonverbal behavior as appropriate to communicate the desired impression.*

Self-serving bias. A bias that operates in the self-attribution process and leads us to take credit for the positive consequences and to deny responsibility for the negative consequences of our behaviors. *In examining the causes of your own behavior, beware of the tendency to attribute negative behaviors to external factors and positive behaviors to internal factors. In self-examinations, ask whether and how the self-serving bias might be operating.*

Self-talk. Talk about oneself. *Balance talk about yourself with talk about the other; avoid excessive self-talk or extreme avoidance of self-talk to encourage equal sharing and interpersonal satisfaction.*

Semantics. The area of language study concerned with meaning.

Sexist language. Language derogatory to one sex, generally women. *Whether man or woman, avoid sexist language—for example, terms that presume maleness as the norm ("policeman" or "mailman").*

Sexual harassment. Unsolicited and unwanted sexual messages. *If confronted with sexual harassment, consider talking to the harasser, collecting evidence, using appropriate channels within the organization, or filing a complaint. Avoid any indication of sexual harassment by beginning with the assumption that others at work are not interested in sexual advances and stories; listen for negative reactions to any sexually explicit discussions, and avoid behaviors you think might prove offensive.*

Sharpening. A process of message distortion in which the details of messages, when repeated, are crystallized and heightened.

Shyness. The condition of discomfort and uneasiness in interpersonal situations.

Signal and noise (relativity of). The principle of verbal interaction that holds that what is signal (meaningful) and what is noise (interference) is relative to the communication analyst, the participants, and the context.

Signal reaction. A conditioned response to a signal; a response to some signal that is immediate rather than delayed.

Silence. The absence of vocal communication; often misunderstood to refer to the absence of any and all communication. *Use silence to communicate feelings or to prevent communication about certain topics. Interpret silences of others through their culturally determined rules rather than your own.*

Silencers. A tactic (such as crying) that literally silences one's opponent—an unproductive **conflict** strategy.

Similarity. A principle of **attraction** holding that one is attracted to qualities similar to those possessed by oneself and to people who are similar to oneself; opposed to **complementarity.**

Social comparison processes. The processes by which you compare yourself (for example, your abilities, opinions, and values) with others and then assess and evaluate yourself; one of the sources of self-concept.

Social distance. The third proxemic distance, ranging from 4 feet to 12 feet; the distance at which business is usually conducted. *See also* **proxemics.**

Social exchange theory. A theory hypothesizing that we develop relationships in which our rewards or profits will be greater than our costs and that we avoid or terminate relationships in which the costs exceed the rewards.

Social penetration theory. A theory concerned with relationship development from the superficial to the intimate levels and from few to many areas of interpersonal interaction.

Source. Any person or thing that creates messages. A source may be an individual speaking, writing, or gesturing or a computer solving a problem.

Spatial distance. Spatial distance signals the type of relationship we are in: intimate, personal, social, or public. *Let your spatial relationships reflect your interpersonal relationships.*

Speaker apprehension. See **communication apprehension**.

Speech. Messages conveyed via a vocal-auditory channel.

Speech rate. Use variations in rate to increase communication efficiency and persuasiveness as appropriate.

Spontaneity. The communication pattern in which one verbalizes what one is thinking without attempting to develop strategies for control; encourages **supportiveness;** opposed to **strategy.**

Stability. The principle of perception that refers to the fact that our perceptions of things and of people are relatively consistent with our previous conceptions.

State apprehension. Speaker apprehension for specific types of communication situations—for example, public speaking or interview situations. See **trait apprehension.**

Static evaluation. An orientation that fails to recognize that the world is characterized by constant change; an attitude that sees people and events as fixed rather than as constantly changing. *Date your statements to emphasize constant change; avoid the tendency to think of and describe things as static and unchanging.*

Status. The relative level one occupies in a hierarchy; status always involves a comparison, and thus one's status is only relative to the status of another. In our culture, occupation, financial position, age, and educational level are significant determinants of status.

Stereotype. In communication, a fixed impression of a group of people through which we then perceive specific individuals; stereotypes are most often negative ("Those people" are stupid, uneducated, and dirty) but may also be positive ("Those people" are scientific, industrious, and helpful). *Avoid stereotyping others; instead, see and respond to each individual as a unique individual.*

Stimulus. Any external or internal change that impinges on or arouses an organism.

Stimulus-response models of communication. Models of communication that assume that the process of communication is linear, beginning with a stimulus that then leads to a response.

Strategy. The use of some plan for control of other members of a communication interaction that guides one's own communications; encourages **defensiveness;** opposed to **spontaneity.**

Subjectivity. The principle of perception that refers to the fact that one's perceptions are not objective but are influenced by one's wants and needs and one's expectations and predictions.

Superiority. A point of view or attitude that assumes that others are not equal to oneself; encourages **defensiveness;** opposed to **equality.**

Supportiveness. An attitude of an individual or an atmosphere in a group that is characterized by openness, absence of fear, and a genuine feeling of equality. *Exhibit supportiveness to others by being descriptive rather than evaluative, spontaneous rather than strategic, and provisional rather than certain.*

Symmetrical relationship. A relation between two or more persons in which one person's behavior serves as a stimulus for the same type of behavior in the other person(s). Examples of such relationships include those in which anger in one person encourages or serves as a stimulus for anger in another person or in which a critical comment by the person leads the other person to respond in like manner.

Taboo. Forbidden; culturally censored. Taboo language is language that is frowned upon by "polite society." Topics and specific words may be considered taboo—for example, death, sex, certain forms of illness, and various words denoting sexual activities and excretory functions. *Avoid taboo expressions so that others do not make negative evaluations; substitute more socially acceptable expressions or euphemisms where and when appropriate.*

Tactile communication. Communication by touch; communication received by the skin.

Temporal communication. The messages that one's time orientation and treatment of time communicates. *Interpret time cues from the point of view of the other's culture rather than your own.*

Territorial encroachment. The trespassing on, use of, or appropriation of one's territory by another. *Generally, avoid territorial encroachment; give others the space they need; remember, for example, that people who are angry or disturbed need more space than usual.*

Territoriality. A possessive or ownership reaction to an area of space or to particular objects. *Establish and maintain territory nonverbally by marking or otherwise indicating temporary or permanent ownership. Become sensitive to the territorial behavior of others.*

Theory. A general statement or principle applicable to a number of related phenomena.

Touch. Use touch when appropriate to express positive effect, playfulness, control, and ritualistic meanings and to serve task-related functions.

Touch avoidance. The tendency to avoid touching and being touched by others. *Recognize that some people may prefer to avoid touching and being touched. Avoid drawing too many conclusions about people from the way they treat interpersonal touching.*

Touch rules. Respond to the touch patterns of others in light of their gender and culture and not exclusively on the basis of your own.

Trait apprehension. Speaker apprehension for communication generally; a fear of communication situations regardless of their context. See **state apprehension.**

Transactional. Characterizing the relationship among elements whereby each influences and is influenced by each other element; communication is a transactional process because no element is independent of any other element.

Uncertainty reduction strategies. Increase your accuracy in interpersonal perception by using all three uncertainty reduction strategies: passive, active, and interactive strategies.

Uncertainty reduction theory. The theory holding that as relationships develop, uncertainty is reduced; relationship development is seen as a process of reducing uncertainty about one another.

Universal of interpersonal communication. A feature of communication common to all interpersonal communication acts.

Unproductive conflict strategies. Avoid unproductive conflict strategies such as avoidance, force, blame, silencers, gunnysacking, manipulation, personal rejection, and fighting below the belt.

Value. Relative worth of an object; a quality that makes something desirable or undesirable; ideals or customs about which we have emotional responses, whether positive or negative.

Verbal abuse. In dealing with verbal abuse, first recognize it for what it is; second, recognize the significant consequences, and try to change the behavior.

Verbal aggressiveness. A method of winning an argument by attacking the other person's **self-concept.** Avoid inflicting psychological pain on the other person to win an argument.

Visual dominance. The use of your eyes to maintain a superior or dominant position, for example, when making an especially important point, you might look intently at the other person. *Use visual dominance behavior when you wish to emphasize certain messages.*

Voice qualities. Aspects of **paralanguage**—specifically, pitch range, vocal lip control, glottis control, pitch control, articulation control, rhythm control, resonance, and tempo.

Volume. The relative loudness of the voice.

You-messages. Messages in which the speaker denies responsibility for his or her own thoughts and behaviors; messages that attribute the speaker's perception to another person; messages of blame; opposed to **I-messages.**

Bibliography

Albas, Daniel C., Ken W. McCluskey, & Cheryl A. Albas. (1976). Perception of the Emotional Content of Speech: A Comparison of Two Canadian Groups. *Journal of Cross Cultural Psychology* 7 (December):481–490.

Albert, Rosita, & Gayle L. Nelson. (1993). Hispanic/Anglo American Differences in Attributions to Paralinguistic Behavior. *International Journal of Intercultural Relations* 17 (Winter):19–40.

Alberti, Robert. (Ed.). (1977). *Assertiveness: Innovations, Applications, Issues.* San Luis Obispo, CA: Impact.

Alessandra, Tony. (1986). How to Listen Effectively. *Speaking of Success* [Videotape Series]. San Diego, CA: Levitz Sommer Productions.

Altman, Irwin, & Dalmas Taylor. (1973). *Social Penetration: The Development of Interpersonal Relationships.* New York: Holt, Rinehart and Winston.

Andersen, Peter. (1991). Explaining Intercultural Differences in Nonverbal Communication. In Larry A. Samovar & Richard E. Porter (Eds.), *Intercultural Communication: A Reader* (6th ed., pp. 286–296). Belmont, CA: Wadsworth.

Andersen, Peter A., & Ken Leibowitz. (1978). The Development and Nature of the Construct Touch Avoidance. *Environmental Psychology and Nonverbal Behavior* 3:89–106. (Reprinted in DeVito & Hecht, 1990.)

Angier, Natalie. (1995). New View of Family: Unstable but Wealth Helps. *New York Times* (August 29): C1, C5.

Angier, Natalie. (1995). Powerhouse of Senses, Smell, at Last, Gets Its Due. *New York Times* (February 14): C1, C6.

Argyle, M., & R. Ingham. (1972). Gaze, Mutual Gaze and Distance. *Semiotica* 1:32–49.

Argyle, Michael, & Monika Henderson. (1984). The Rules of Friendship. *Journal of Social and Personal Relationships* 1 (June):211–237.

Argyle, Michael, & Monika Henderson. (1985). *The Anatomy of Relationships: And the Rules and Skills Needed to Manage Them Successfully.* London: Heinemann.

Argyle, Michael (1988). *Bodily Communication* (2nd ed.). New York: Methuen & Co.

Arliss, Laurie P. (1991). *Gender Communication.* Englewood Cliffs, NJ: Prentice-Hall.

Aronson, Elliot. (1980). *The Social Animal* (3rd ed.). San Francisco, CA: W. H. Freeman.

Aronson, Elliot, Timothy D. Wilson, & Robin M. Akert. (1994). *Social Psychology: The Heart and the Mind.* New York: HarperCollins.

Asimov, Isaac. (1983). Write, Write, Write. *Communicator's Journal* (May/June).

Aune, Krystyna-Strzyzewski, David B. Buller, & R. Kelly Aune. (1996). Display Rule Development in Romantic Relationships: Emotion Management and Perceived Appropriateness of Emotions across Relationship Stages. *Human Communication Research* 23 (September):115–145.

Aune, R. Kelly, & Toshiyuki Kikuchi. (1993). Effects of Language Intensity Similarity on Perceptions of Credibility, Relational Attributions, and Persuasion. *Journal of Language and Social Psychology* 12 (September):224–238.

Axtell, Roger. (1993). *Do's and Taboos Around the World* (3rd ed.). New York: Wiley.

Axtell, Roger E. (1990). *Do's and Taboos of Hosting International Visitors.* New York: Wiley.

Ayres, Joe, & Tim Hopf. (1993). *Coping with Speech Anxiety.* Norwood, NJ: Ablex Publishing Company.

Ayres, Joe, & Tim Hopf. (1995). An Assessment of the Role of Communication Apprehension in Communicating with the Terminally Ill. *Communication Research Reports* 12 (Fall):227–234.

Bach, George R., & Peter Wyden. (1968). *The Intimacy Enemy.* New York: Avon.

Balswick, J. O., & C. Peck. (1971). The Inexpressive Male: A Tragedy of American Society? *The Family Coordinator* 20:363–368.

Barbato, Carole A., & Elizabeth M. Perse. (1992). Interpersonal Communication Motives and the Life Position of Elders. *Communication Research* 19 (August):516–531.

Barker, Larry L. (1990). *Communication* (5th ed.). Englewood Cliffs, NJ: Prentice-Hall.

Barker, Larry, Renee Edwards, C. Gaines, K. Gladney, & F. Holley. (1980). An Investigation of Proportional Time Spent in Various Communication Activities by College Students. *Journal of Applied Communication Research* 8:101–109.

Barna, LaRay M. (1985). Stumbling Blocks in Intercultural Communication. In Larry A. Samovar & Richard E. Porter (Eds.), *Intercultural Communication: A Reader* (4th ed., pp. 330–338). Belmont, CA: Wadsworth.

Barnlund, Dean C. (1970). A Transactional Model of Communication. *Language Behavior: A Book of Readings in Communication* (Comp. J. Akin, A. Goldberg, G. Myers, & J. Stewart). The Hague: Mouton.

Barnlund, Dean C. (1988). *Communicative Styles of Japanese and Americans: Images and Realities.* Belmont, CA: Wadsworth.

Barnlund, Dean C. (1989). *Communicative Styles of Japanese and Americans.* Belmont, CA: Wadsworth.

Baron, Robert A., & Donn Byrne. (1984). *Social Psychology: Understanding Human Interaction* (4th ed.). Boston: Allyn and Bacon.

Barron, James. (1995). It's Time to Mind Your E-Manners. *New York Times* (January 11): C1.

Basso, K. H. (1972). To Give Up on Words: Silence in Apache Culture. In Pier Paolo Giglioli (Ed.), *Language and Social Context.* New York: Penguin.

Baxter, Leslie A., & C. Bullis. (1986). Turning Points in Developing Romantic Relationships. *Human Communication Research* 12 (Summer):469–493.

Baxter, Leslie A., & Eric P. Simon. (1993). Relationship Maintenance Strategies and Dialectical Contradictions in Personal Relationships. *Journal of Social and Personal Relationships* 10(May):225–242.

Baxter, Leslie A. (1983). Relationship Disengagement: An Examination of the Reversal Hypothesis. *Western Journal of Speech Communication* 47:85–98.

Baxter, Leslie A. (1988). A Dialectical Perspective on Communication Strategies in Relationship Development. In Steve W. Duck (Ed.), *Handbook of Personal Relationships.* New York: Wiley.

Baxter, Leslie A. (1990). Dialectical Contradictions in Relationship Development. *Journal of Social and Personal Relationships* 7 (February):69–88.

Baxter, Leslie A., & W. W. Wilmot. (1984). "Secret Tests": Social Strategies for Acquiring Information About the State of the Relationship. *Human Communication Research* 11:171–201.

Beach, Wayne A. (1990–1991). Avoiding Ownership for Alleged Wrongdoings. *Research on Language and Social Interaction* 24:1–36.

Beatty, Michael J. (1988). Situational and Predispositional Correlates of Public Speaking Anxiety. *Communication Education* 37:28–39.

Beck, A. T. (1988). *Love is Never Enough.* New York: Harper & Row.

Bedford, Victoria Hilkevitch. (1996). Relationships Between Adult Siblings. In Ann Elisabeth Auhagen & Maria von Salisch. (Eds.), *The Diversity of Human Relationships* (pp. 120–140). New York: Cambridge University Press.

Beebe, Steven A., & John T. Masterson. (1997). *Communicating in Small Groups: Principles and Practices* (5th ed.). New York: Longman.

Behzadi, Kavous G. (1994). Interpersonal Conflict and Emotions in an Iranian Cultural Practice: QAHR and ASHTI. *Culture, Medicine, and Psychiatry* 18 (September):321–359.

Bell, Robert A., & John Daly. (1984). The Affinity-Seeking Function of Communication. *Communication Monographs* 51:91–115.

Bell, Robert. A., & N. L. Buerkel-Rothfuss. (1990). S(he) Loves Me, S(he) Loves Me Not: Predictors of Relational Information-Seeking in Courtship and Beyond. *Communication Quarterly* 38:64–82.

Berg, John H., & Richard L. Archer. (1983). The Disclosure-Liking Relationship. *Human Communication Research* 10:269–281.

Berger, Charles R., & James J. Bradac. (1982). *Language and Social Knowledge: Uncertainty in Interpersonal Relations.* London: Edward Arnold.

Bernstein, W. M., W. G. Stephan, & M. H. Davis. (1979). Explaining Attributions for Achievement: A Path Analytic Approach. *Journal of Personality and Social Psychology* 37:1810–1821.

Blieszner, Rosemary, & Rebecca G. Adams. (1992). *Adult Friendship.* Thousand Oaks, CA: Sage.

Blumstein, Philip, & Pepper Schwartz. (1983). *American Couples: Money, Work, Sex.* New York: Morrow.

Bochner, Arthur, & Clifford Kelly. (1974). Interpersonal Competence: Rationale, Philosophy, and Implementation of a Conceptual Framework. *Communication Education* 23:279–301.

Bochner, Stephen, & Beryl Hesketh. (1994). Power Distance, Individualism/Collectivism, and Job-related

Attitudes in a Culturally Diverse Work Group. *Journal of Cross Cultural Psychology* 25 (June):233–257.

Bok, Sissela. (1978). *Lying: Moral Choice in Public and Private Life.* New York: Pantheon.

Bok, Sissela. (1983). *Secrets.* New York: Vintage Books.

Borden, George A. (1991). *Cultural Orientation: An Approach to Understanding Intercultural Communication.* Englewood Cliffs, NJ: Prentice-Hall.

Bosmajian, Haig. (1974). *The Language of Oppression.* Washington, DC: Public Affairs Press.

Bourland, D. David, Jr. (1965–66). A linguistic note: Writing in E-prime. *General Semantics Bulletin* 32 & 33.

Bravo, Ellen, & Ellen Cassedy. (1992). *The 9 to 5 Guide to Combatting Sexual Harassment.* New York: Wiley.

Bremner, John B. (1980). *Words on Words: A Dictionary for Writers and Others Who Care About Words.* New York: Columbia University Press.

Briton, Nancy J., & Judith A. Hall. (1995). Beliefs about Female and Male Nonverbal Communication. *Sex Roles: A Journal of Research* 32 (January):79–90.

Brody, Leslie R. (1985). Gender Differences in Emotional Development: A Review of Theories and Research. *Journal of Personality* 53 (June):102–149.

Brody, Jane E. (1994). Notions of Beauty Transcend Culture, New Study Suggests. *New York Times* (March 21), A14.

Brody, Jane F. (1991, April 28). How to Foster Self-Esteem. *New York Times Magazine,* 26–27.

Brown, Penelope. (1980). How and Why Are Women More Polite: Some Evidence from a Mayan Community. In Sally McConnell-Ginet, Ruth Borker, & Mellie Furman (Eds.), *Women and Language in Literature and Society* (pp. 111–136). New York: Praeger.

Brown, Penelope, & S. C. Levinson. (1987). *Politeness: Some Universals of Language Usage.* Cambridge: Cambridge University Press.

Brownell, Judi. (1987). Listening: The Toughest Management Skill. *Cornell Hotel and Restaurant Administration Quarterly* 27:64–71.

Bruneau, Tom. (1985). The Time Dimension in Intercultural Communication. In Larry A. Samovar & Richard E. Porter (Eds.), *Intercultural Communication: A Reader* (4th ed., pp. 280–289). Belmont, CA: Wadsworth.

Bruneau, Tom. (1990). Chronemics: The Study of Time in Human Interaction. In Joseph A. DeVito & Michael L. Hecht (Eds.), *The Nonverbal Communication Reader* (pp. 301–311). Prospect Heights, IL: Waveland Press.

Bull, R., & N. Rumsey. (1988). *The Social Psychology of Facial Appearance.* New York: Springer-Verlag.

Buller, David B., & R. Kelly Aune. (1992). The Effects of Speech Rate Similarity on Compliance: Application of Communication Accommodation Theory. *Western Journal of Communication* 56 (Winter):37–53.

Buller, David B., Beth A. LePoire, Kelly Aune, & Sylvie Eloy. (1992). Social Perceptions as Mediators of the Effect of Speech Rate Similarity on Compliance. *Human Communication Research* 19 (December):286–311.

Burgoon, Judee K., David B. Buller, & W. Gill Woodall. (1995). *Nonverbal Communication: The Unspoken Dialogue* (2nd ed.). New York: McGraw-Hill.

Burgoon, Michael. (1971). The Relationship between Willingness to Manipulate Others and Success in Two Different Types of Basic Speech Communication Courses. *Communication Education* 20:178–183.

Butler, Pamela E. (1981). *Talking to Yourself: Learning the Language of Self-Support.* New York: Harper & Row.

Cabello, B., & R. Terrell. (1994). Making Students Feel Like Family: How Teachers Create Warm and Caring Classroom Climates. *Journal of Classroom Interaction* 29:17–23.

Canary, D. J., & K. Hause. (1993). Is There Any Reason to Research Sex Differences in Communication? *Communication Quarterly* 41:129–144.

Canary, Daniel J., Laura Stafford, Kimberly S. Hause, & Lise A. Wallace. (1993). An Inductive Analysis of Relational Maintenance Strategies: Comparisons Among Lovers, Relatives, Friends, and Others. *Communication Research Reports* 10 (June):5–14.

Canary, Daniel, Willima R. Cupach, & Susan J. Messman. (1995). *Relationship Conflict.* Thousand Oaks, CA: Sage.

Cappella, Joseph N. (1993). The Facial Feedback Hypothesis in Human Interaction: Review and Speculation. *Journal of Language and Social Psychology* 12 (March–June):13–29.

Cate, R., J. Henton, J. Koval, R. Christopher, & S. Lloyd. (1982). Premarital Abuse: A Social Psychological Perspective. *Journal of Family Issues* 3:79–90.

Chadwick-Jones, J. K. (1976). *Social Exchange Theory: Its Structure and Influence in Social Psychology.* New York: Academic.

Chang, Hui-Ching, & G. Richard Holt. (1996). The Changing Chinese Interpersonal World: Popular Themes in Interpersonal Communication Books in Modern Taiwan. *Communication Quarterly* 44 (Winter):85–106.

Chen, Guo Ming. (1992). *Differences in Self-Disclosure Patterns Among Americans versus Chinese: A Comparative Study.* Paper presented at the annual meeting of the Eastern Communication Association, Portland, ME.

Cherulnik, Paul D. (1979). Sex Differences in the Expression of Emotion in a Structured Social Encounter. *Sex Roles* 5 (August):413–424.

Christie, Richard. (1970). Scale Construction. In R. Christie & F. L. Geis (Eds.), *Studies in Machiavellianism* (pp. 35–52). New York: Academic Press.

Clement, Donald A., & Frandsen, Kenneth D. (1976). On Conceptual and Empirical Treatments of Feedback in Human Communication. *Communication Monographs* 43:11–28.

Coates, J., & D. Cameron. (1989). *Women, Men, and Language: Studies in Language and Linguistics.* London: Longman.

Coats, Erik J., & Robert S. Feldman. (1996). Gender Differences in Nonverbal Correlates of Social Status. *Personality and Social Psychology Bulletin* 22 (October):1014–1022.

Cody, Michael J. (1982). A Typology of Disengagement Strategies and an Examination of the Role Intimacy, Reactions to Inequity, and Relational Problems Play in Strategy Selection. *Communication Monographs* 49:148–170.

Collier, Mary Jane. (1991). Conflict Competence Within African, Mexican, and Anglo American Friendships. In Stella Ting-Toomey & Felipe Korzenny (Eds.), *Cross-Cultural Interpersonal Communication* (pp. 132–154). Newbury Park, CA: Sage.

Collins, Nancy L., & Lynn Miller. (1994). Self-Disclosure and Liking: A Meta-Analytic Review. *Psychological Bulletin* 116 (November):457–475.

Cook, Mark. (Ed.). (1984). *Issues in Person Perception*. New York: Methuen.

Cooley, Charles Horton. (1922). *Human Nature and the Social Order* (rev. ed.). New York: Scribner's.

D'Augelli, Anthony R. (1992). Lesbian and Gay Male Undergraduates' Experiences of Harassment and Fear on Campus. *Journal of Interpersonal Violence* 7 (September):383–395.

Dainton, M., & L. Stafford. (1993). Routine Maintenance Behaviors: A Comparison of Relationship Type, Partner Similarity, and Sex Differences. *Journal of Social and Personal Relationships* 10:255–272.

Davis, Flora. (1973). *Inside Intuition*. New York: New American Library.

Davis, Keith E. (1985). Near and Dear: Friendship and Love Compared. *Psychology Today* 19:22–30.

Davis, Murray S. (1973). *Intimate Relations*. New York: Free Press.

Davis, Ossie (1973). The English Language Is My Enemy. In Joseph A. DeVito (Ed.), *Language: Concepts and Processes* (pp. 164–170). Englewood Cliffs, NJ: Prentice-Hall.

Davitz, Joel R. (Ed.). (1964). *The Communication of Emotional Meaning*. New York: McGraw-Hill.

Deal, James E., & Karen Smith Wampler. (1986). Dating Violence: The Primacy of Previous Experience. *Journal of Social and Personal Relationships* 3:457–471.

DeBono, Edward. (1987). *The Six Thinking Hats*. New York: Penguin.

DeCecco, John. (1988). Obligation versus Aspiration. In John DeCecco (Ed.), *Gay Relationships*. New York: Harrington Park Press.

DePaulo, Bella M. (1992). Nonverbal Behavior and Self-Presentation. *Psychological Bulletin* 111, 203–212.

Derlega, Valerian J., Barbara A. Winstead, Paul T. P. Wong, & Michael Greenspan. (1987). Self-Disclosure and Relationship Development: An Attributional Analysis. In Michael E. Roloff & Gerald R. Miller (Eds.), *Interpersonal Processes: New Directions in Communication Research* (pp. 172–187). Newbury Park, CA: Sage.

DeTurck, Mark A. (1987). When Communication Fails: Physical Aggression as a Compliance-Gaining Strategy. *Communication Monographs* 54:106–112.

DeVito, Joseph A. (1996). *Brainstorms: How to Think More Creatively about Communication (or About Anything Else)*. New York: Longman.

DeVito, Joseph A., & Michael L. Hecht. (Eds.). (1990). *The Nonverbal Communication Reader*. Prospect Heights, IL.: Waveland Press.

Dewey, John. (1910). *How We Think*. Boston: Heath.

Dindia, Kathryn, & Leslie A. Baxter. (1987). Strategies for Maintaining and Repairing Marital Relationships. *Journal of Social and Personal Relationships* 4:143–158.

Dindia, Kathryn, & Mary Anne Fitzpatrick (1985). Marital Communication: Three Approaches Compared. In Steve Duck & Daniel Perlman (Eds.), *Understanding Personal Relationships: An Interdisciplinary Approach* (pp. 137–158). Thousand Oaks, CA: Sage.

Dolgin, Kim G., Leslie Meyer, & Janet Schwartz. (1991). Effects of Gender, Target's Gender, Topic, and Self-Esteem on Disclosure to Best and Midling Friends. *Sex Roles* 25 (September):311–329.

Donohue, William A., with Robert Kolt. (1992). *Managing Interpersonal Conflict*. Thousand Oaks, CA: Sage.

Drass, Kriss A. (1986). The Effect of Gender Identity on Conversation. *Social Psychology Quarterly* 49 (December):294–301.

Dresser, Norine. (1996). *Multicultural Manners: New Rules of Etiquette for a Changing Society*. New York: Wiley.

Dreyfuss, Henry. (1971). *Symbol Sourcebook*. New York: McGraw-Hill.

Duncan, S. D., Jr. (1972). Some Signals and Rules for Taking Speaking Turns in Conversation. *Journal of Personality and Social Psychology* 23:283–292.

Duran, R. L., & Kelly, L. (1988). The Influence of Communicative Competence on Perceived Task, Social, and Physical Attraction. *Communication Quarterly* 36: 41–49.

Dusek, J. B., V. C. Hall, & W. J. Neger (1984). *Teacher Expectancies*. Hillsdale, NJ: Erlbaum.

Eakins, Barbara, & R. Gene Eakins. (1978). *Sex Differences in Communication*. Boston: Houghton Mifflin.

Ehrenhaus, Peter. (1988). Silence and Symbolic Expression. *Communication Monographs* 55 (March):41–57.

Ekman, Paul. (1985a). Communication Through Nonverbal Behavior: A Source of Information about an Interpersonal Relationship. In S. S. Tomkins & C. E. Izard (Eds.), *Affect, Cognitiion and Personality*. New York: Springer.

Ekman, Paul. (1985b). *Telling Lies: Clues to Deceit in the Marketplace, Politics, and Marriage*. New York: W. W. Norton.

Ekman, Paul, & Wallace V. Friesen. (1969). The Repertoire of Nonverbal Behavior: Categories, Origins, Usage, and Coding. *Semiotica* 1:49–98.

Ekman, Paul, Wallace V. Friesen, & Phoebe Ellsworth. (1972). *Emotion in the Human Face: Guidelines for Research and an Integration of Findings.* New York: Pergamon Press.

Ellis, Albert. (1988). *How to Stubbornly Refuse to Make Yourself Miserable about Anything, Yes Anything.* Secaucus, NJ: Lyle Stuart.

Ellis, Albert, & Robert A. Harper. (1975). *A New Guide to Rational Living.* Hollywood, CA: Wilshire Books.

Elmes, Michael B., & Gary Gemmill. (1990). The Psychodynamics of Mindlessness and Dissent in Small Groups. *Small Group Research* 21 (February):28–44.

Ennis, Robert H. (1987). A taxonomy of Critical Thinking Dispositions and Abilities. In Joan Boykoff Baron & Robert J. Sternberg (Eds.), *Teaching Thinking Skills: Theory and Practice* (pp. 9–26). New York: W. H. Freeman.

Estabrook, Noel. (1997). *Teach Yourself the Internet in 24 Hours.* Indianapolis, IN: SamsNet.

Exline, R. V., S. L. Ellyson, & B. Long. (1975). Visual Behavior as an Aspect of Power Role Relationships. In P. Pliner, L. Krames, & T. Alloway (Eds.), *Nonverbal Communication of Aggression.* New York: Plenum.

Fengler, A. P. (1974). Romantic Love in Courtship: Divergent Paths of Male and Female Students. *Journal of Comparative Family Studies* 5:134–139.

Festinger, Leon. (1954). A Theory of Social Comparison Processes. *Human Relations* 7, 117–140.

Fischer, Agneta H. (1993). Sex Differences in Emotionality: Fact or Stereotype? *Feminism & Psychology* 3:303–318.

Fischer, C. S., & S. J. Oliker. (1983). A Research Note on Friendship, Gender, and the Life Cycle. *Social Forces* 62:124–133.

Fiske, Susan T., & Shelley E. Taylor. (1984). *Social Cognition.* Reading, MA: Addison-Wesley.

Folger, Joseph P., Marshall Scott Poole, and R. Stutman (1997). *Working Through Conflict: A Communication Perspective,* 3rd ed. NY: Longman.

Fraser, Bruce. (1990). Perspectives on Politeness. *Journal of Pragmatics* 14 (April):219–236.

French, J. R. P., Jr., & B. Raven (1968). The Bases of Social Power. In Dorwin Cartwright & Alvin Zander (Eds.), *Group Dynamics: Research and Theory* (3rd ed., pp. 259–269). New York: Harper & Row.

Friedman, Joel, Marcia Mobilia Boumil, & Barbara Ewert Taylor. (1992). *Sexual Harassment.* Deerfield Beach, FL: Health Communications, Inc.

Fuller, Linda K. (1995). *Media-Mediated Relationships: Straight and Gay, Mainstream and Alternative Perspectives.* New York: Harrington Park Press.

Furlow, F. Bryant. (1996). The Smell of Love. *Psychology Today* (March/April):38–45.

Furnham, Adrian, & Stephen Bochner. (1986). *Culture Shock: Psychological Reactions to Unfamiliar Environments.* New York: Methuen.

Gable, Myron, Charles Hollon, & Frank Dangello. (1992). Managerial Structuring of Work as a Moderator of the Machiavellianism and Job Performance Relationship. *Journal of Psychology* 126 (May):317–325.

Gelles, R, & C. Cornell. (1985). *Intimate Violence in Families.* Newbury Park, CA: Sage.

Gergen, K. J., M. S. Greenberg, & R. H. Willis (1980). *Social Exchange: Advances in Theory and Research.* New York: Plenum Press.

Gibb, Jack. (1961). Defensive Communication. *Journal of Communication* 11:141–148.

Giles, Howard, Anthony Mulac, James J. Bradac, & Patricia Johnson. (1987). Speech Accommodation Theory: The First Decade and Beyond. In Margaret L. McLaughlin (Ed.), *Communication Yearbook 10* (pp. 13–48). Thousand Oaks, CA: Sage.

Glaser, Robert. (Ed.). (1987). *Advances in Instructional Psychology,* vol. 3. Mahwah, NJ: Erlbaum.

Glucksberg, Sam, & Danks, Joseph H. (1975). *Experimental Psycholinguistics: An Introduction.* Hillsdale, NJ: Lawrence Erlbaum.

Goleman, Daniel. (1992). Studies Find No Disadvantage in Growing Up in a Gay Home. *New York Times* (December 2):C14.

Goleman, Daniel. (1995a). *Emotional Intelligence.* New York: Bantam.

Goleman, Daniel. (1995b). For Man and Beast, Language of Love Shares Many Traits. *New York Times* (February 14):C1, C9.

Gonzalez, Alexander & Philip G. Zimbardo. (1985). Time in Perspective. *Psychology Today* 19:20–26. (Reprinted in DeVito & Hecht, 1990.)

Goodwin, Robin, & Iona Lee. (1994). Taboo Topics among Chinese and English Friends: A Cross-Cultural Comparison. *Journal of Cross Cultural Psychology* 25 (September):325–338.

Gordon, Thomas. (1975). *P.E.T.: Parent Effectiveness Training.* New York: New American Library.

Gottman, John M., & S. Carrere. (1994). Whey Can't Men and Women Get Along? Developmental Roots and Marital Inequities. In D. J. Canary & Laura Stafford (Eds.), *Communication and Relational Maintenance* (pp. 203–229). San Diego, CA: Academic Press.

Gould, Stephen Jay. (1995). No More "Wretched Refuse." *The New York Times* (June 7):A27.

Graham, E. E. (1994). Interpersonal Communication Motives Scale. In R. B. Rubin, P. Palmgreen, & H. E. Sypher (Eds.), *Communication Research Measures: A Sourcebook* (pp. 211–216). New York: Guilford.

Graham, E. E., C. A. Barbato, & E. M. Perse. (1993). The Interpersonal Communication Motives Model. *Communication Quarterly* 41:172–186.

Graham, Jean Ann, & Michael Argyle. (1975). The Effects of Different Patterns of Gaze, Combined with Different Facial Expressions, on Impression Formation. *Journal of Movement Studies* 1 (December):178–182.

Graham, Jean Ann, Pio Ricci Bitti, & Michael Argyle. (1975). A Cross-Cultural Study of the Communication of

Emotion by Facial and Gestural Cues. *Journal of Human Movement Studies* 1 (June):68–77.

Greif, Esther Blank. (1980). Sex Differences in Parent–Child Conversations. *Women's Studies International Quarterly* 3:253–258.

Grice, H. P. (1975). Logic and Conversation. In P. Cole & J.L. Morgan (Eds.), *Syntax and Semantics: vol. 3. Speech Acts* (pp. 41–58). New York: Seminar Press.

Griffin, Em, & Glenn G. Sparks. (1990). Friends Forever: A Longitudinal Exploration of Intimacy in Same-Sex Friends and Platonic Pairs. *Journal of Social and Personal Relationships* 7:29–46.

Gross, T., E. Turner, & L. Cederholm (1987). Building Teams for Global Operation. *Management Review* (June):32–36.

Gudykunst, W., & T. Nishida (1984). Individual and Cultural Influence on Uncertainty Reduction. *Communication Monographs* 51:23–36.

Gudykunst, W., S. Yang, & T. Nishida. (1985). A Cross-Cultural Test of Uncertainty Reduction Theory: Comparisons of Acquaintance, Friend, and Dating Relationships in Japan, Korea, and the United States. *Human Communication Research* 11:407–454.

Gudykunst, W. B. (1991). *Bridging Differences: Effective Intergroup Communication.* Newbury Park, CA: Sage.

Gudykunst, W. B. (Ed.). (1983). *Intercultural communication theory: Current perspectives.* Newbury Park, CA: Sage.

Gudykunst, W. B., & Y. Y. Kim. (1984). *Communicating with strangers: An approach to intercultural communication.* New York: Random House.

Gudykunst, William B., Stella Ting-Toomey, Sandra Sudweeks, & Lea P. Stewart. (1995). *Building Bridges: Interpersonal Skills for a Changing World.* Boston, MA: Houghton Mifflin.

Gudykunst, William B., & Young Yun Kim. (Eds.). (1992). *Readings on Communicating with Strangers: An Approach to Intercultural Communication.* New York: McGraw-Hill.

Hall, Edward T. (1959). *The Silent Language.* Garden City, NY: Doubleday.

Hall, Edward T. (1966). *The Hidden Dimension.* Garden City, NY: Doubleday.

Hall, Edward T. (1976). *Beyond culture.* Garden City, NY: Anchor Press.

Hall, Edward T. (1983). *The Dance of Life: The Other Dimension of Time.* New York: Anchor Books/Doubleday.

Hall, Edward T., & Mildred Reed Hall. (1971). The Sounds of Silence. *Playboy* (June):139–140, 204, 206.

Hall, Edward T., & Mildred Reed Hall. (1987). *Hidden Differences: Doing Business with the Japanese.* New York: Doubleday (Anchor Books).

Hall, J. A. (1984). *Nonverbal Sex Differences.* Baltimore: Johns Hopkins University Press.

Hall, Joan Kelly. (1993). Tengo una Bomba: The Paralinguistic and Linguistic Conventions of the Oral Practice Chismeando. *Research on Language and Social Interaction* 26:55–83.

Hall, Judith A. (1996). Touch, Status, and Gender at Professional Meetings. *Journal of Nonverbal Behavior* 20 (Spring):23–44.

Haney, William. (1973). *Communication and Organizational Behavior: Text and Cases* (3rd ed.). Homewood IL: Irwin, 1973.

Harris, Judy. (1995). Educational Telecomputing Projects: Interpersonal Exchanges. *Computing Teacher* 22 (March):60–64.

Harrison, Allen F., & Robert M. Bramson. (1984). *The Art of Thinking.* New York: Berkeley.

Hart, Fiona. (1990). The Construction of Masculinity in Men's Friendships: Misogyny, Heterosexism and Homophobia. *Resources for Feminist Research* 19 (September–December):60–67.

Hatfield, Elaine, & Richard L. Rapson. (1996). *Love and Sex: Cross Cultural Perspectives.* Boston: Allyn and Bacon.

Havlena, William J., Morris B. Holbrook, & Donald R. Lehmann. (1989). Assessing the Validity of Emotional Typologies. *Psychology and Marketing* 6 (Summer):97–112.

Hayakawa, S. I., & Alan R. Hayakawa. (1990). *Language in Thought and Action* (5th ed.). New York: Harcourt Brace Jovanovich.

Hays, Robert B. (1989). The Day-to-Day Functioning of Close Versus Casual Friendships. *Journal of Social and Personal Relationships* 6:21–37.

Heasley, John B., Charles E. Babbitt, & Harold J. Burbach. (1995). Gender Differences in College Students' Perceptions of "Fighting Words." *Sociological Viewpoints* 11 (Fall):30–40.

Hecht, Michael L., Mary Jane Collier, & Sidney Ribeau. (1993). *African American Communication: Ethnic Identity and Cultural Interpretation.* Thousand Oaks, CA: Sage.

Hendrick, Clyde, & Susan Hendrick. (1990). A Relationship-Specific Version of the Love Attitudes Scale. In J. W. Heulip (Ed.), *Journal of Social Behavior and Personality: Handbook of Replication Research in the Behavioral and Social Sciences* [Special Issue], 5:239–254.

Hendrick, Clyde, Susan Hendrick, Franklin H. Foote, & Michelle J. Slapion-Foote. (1984). Do Men and Women Love Differently? *Journal of Social and Personal Relationships* 1:177–195.

Hess, Eckhard H. (1975). *The Tell-Tale Eye.* New York: Van Nostrand Reinhold.

Hess, Ursula, Arvid Kappas, Gregory J. McHugo, John T. Lanzetta, et al. (1992). The Facilitative Effect of Facial Expression on the Self-Generation of Emotion. *International Journal of Psychophysiology* 12 (May):251–265.

Hewitt, John, & Randall Stokes. (1975). Disclaimers. *American Sociological Review* 40:1–11.

Higgins, James M. (1994). *101 Creative Problem Solving Techniques.* New York: New Management Publishing Co.

Hofstede, Geert. (1997). *Cultures and Organizations: Software of the Mind.* New York: McGraw-Hill.

Hoft, Nancy L. (1995). *International Technical Communication: How to Export Information about High Technology.* New York: Wiley.

Holmes, Janet. (1986). Compliments and Compliment Responses in New Zealand English. *Anthropological Linguistics* 28:485–508.

Holmes, Janet. (1995). *Women, Men and Politeness.* New York: Longman.

Hupka, Ralph. (1981). Cultural determinants of jealousy. *Alternative Lifestyles* 4:310–356.

Infante, Dominic A. (1988). *Arguing Constructively.* Prospect Heights, IL: Waveland Press.

Infante, Dominic A., & Andrew S. Rancer. (1982). A Conceptualization and Measure of Argumentativeness. *Journal of Personality Assessment* 46:72–80.

Infante, Dominic A., & C. J. Wigley. (1986). Verbal Aggressiveness: An Interpersonal Model and Measure. *Communication Monographs* 53:61–69.

Insel, Paul M., & Lenore F. Jacobson. (Eds.). (1975). *What Do You Expect? An Inquiry into Self-Fulfilling Prophecies.* Menlo Park, CA: Cummings.

Jackson, Linda A., & Kelly S. Ervin. (1992). Height Stereotypes of Women and Men: The Liabilities of Shortness for Both Sexes. *Journal of Social Psychology* 132 (August):433–445.

Jaksa, James A., & Michael S. Pritchard. (1994). *Communication Ethics: Methods of Analysis* (2nd ed.). Belmont, CA: Wadsworth.

James, Phil, & Jan Weingarten. (1995). *Internet Guide for Windows 95.* Research Triangle Park, NC: Ventana.

Jandt, Fred E. (1995). *Intercultural Communication.* Thousand Oaks, CA: Sage.

Janus, Samuel S., & Cynthia L. Janus. (1993). *The Janus Report on Sexual Behavior.* New York: Wiley.

Jaworski, Adam. (1993). *The Power of Silence: Social and Pragmatic Perspectives.* Thousand Oaks, CA: Sage.

Jecker, Jon, & David Landy. (1969). Liking a Person as a Function of Doing Him a Favor. *Human Relations* 22:371–378.

Johannesen, Richard L. (1974). The Functions of Silence: A Plea for Communication Research. *Western Speech* 38 (Winter):25–35.

Joiner, Thomas E., Jr. (1994). Contagious Depression: Existence, Specificity to Depressed Symptoms, and the Role of Reassurance Seeking. *Journal of Personality and Social Psychology* 67 (August): 287–296.

Joiner, Thomas E., Jr. (1996). Depression and Rejection: On Strangers and Friends, Symptom Specificity, Length of Relationship, and Gender. *Communication Research* 23 (August):451–471.

Jones, Stanley, and A. Elaine Yarbrough. (1985). A Naturalistic Study of the Meanings of Touch. *Communication Monographs* 52:19–56. (A version of this paper appears in DeVito and Hecht, 1990.)

Jourard, Sidney M. (1968). *Disclosing Man to Himself.* New York: Van Nostrand Reinhold.

Jourard, Sidney M. (1971a). *Self-Disclosure.* New York: Wiley.

Jourard, Sidney M. (1971b). *The Transparent Self* (rev. ed.). New York: Van Nostrand Reinhold.

Kanner, Bernice. (1989). Color Schemes. *New York Magazine* (April 3):22–23.

Keenan, Elinor Ochs. (1976). The Universality of Conversational Postulates. *Language in Society* 5 (April):67–80.

Kennedy, C. W., & C. T. Camden. (1988). A New Look at Interruptions. *Western Journal of Speech Communication* 47: 45–58.

Keyes, Ralph. (1980). *The Height of Your Life.* New York: Warner Books.

Kiesler, Sara, & Lee Sproull. (1992). Group Decision Making and Communication Technology [Special Issue: Group Decision Making]. *Organizational Behavior and Human Decision Processes* 52 (June):96–123.

Kim, Hyun J. (1991). Influence of Language and Similarity on Initial Intercultural Attraction. In Stella Ting-Toomey & Felipe Korzenny (Eds.), *Cross-Cultural Interpersonal Communication* (pp. 213–229). Newbury Park, CA: Sage.

Kim, Young Yun. (1988). Communication and Acculturation. In Larry A. Samovar & Richard E. Porter (Eds.). (1988). *Intercultural Communication: A Reader* (5th ed., pp. 344–354). Belmont, CA: Wadsworth.

King, Robert, & Eleanor DiMichael. (1992). *Voice and Diction.* Prospect Heights, IL: Waveland Press.

Kirkpatrick, C., and T. Caplow. (1945). Courtship in a Group of Minnesota Students. *American Journal of Sociology* 51:114–125.

Kleinfield, N. R. (1992). The Smell of Money. *The New York Times* (October 25):1, 8.

Kleinke, Chris L. (1986). *Meeting and Understanding People.* New York: W. H. Freeman.

Klineberg, O., & W. F. Hull. (1979). *At a Foreign University: An International Study of Adaptation and Coping.* New York: Praeger.

Knapp, Mark L., & Anita Vangelisti (1992). *Interpersonal Communication and Human Relationships.* 2nd ed. Boston: Allyn & Bacon.

Knapp, Mark L., & Judith Hall. (1996). *Nonverbal Behavior in Human Interaction* (4th ed.). New York: Harcourt, Brace, Jovanovich.

Knapp, Mark, Roderick P. Hart, W. Gustav, & Gary M. Shulman. (1973). The Rhetoric of Goodbye: Verbal and Nonverbal Correlates of Human Leave-Taking. *Speech Monographs* 40:182–198.

Koberg, Don, & Jim Bagnall. (1976a). *The Universal Traveler.* Los Altos, CA: William Kaufmann, Inc.

Koberg, Don, & Jim Bagnall. (1976b). *Values Tech: A Portable School for Discovering and Developing Decision-Making*

Skills for Self-Enhancing Potentials. Los Altos, CA: William Kaufmann, Inc.

Kochman, Thomas. (1981). *Black and White: Styles in Conflict.* Chicago: University of Chicago Press.

Komarovsky, M. (1964). *Blue Collar Marriage.* New York: Random House.

Korzybski, A. (1933). *Science and Sanity.* Lakeville, CT: The International Non-Aristotelian Library.

Kramarae, Cheris. (1974a). Folklinguistics. *Psychology Today* 8:82–85.

Kramarae, Cheris. (1974b) Stereotypes of Women's Speech: The World from Cartoons. *Journal of Popular Culture* 8:624–630.

Kramarae, Cheris. (1977). Perceptions of Female and Male Speech. *Language and Speech* 20:151–161.

Kramarae, Cheris. (1981). *Women and Men Speaking.* Rowley, MA: Newbury House.

Krivonos, Paul D., & Mark L. Knapp. (1975). Initiating Communication: What Do You Say When You Say Hello? *Central States Speech Journal* 26:115–125.

Kurdek, Lawrence A. (1994). Areas of Conflict for Gay, Lesbian, and Heterosexual Couples: What Couples Argue About Influences Relationship Satisfaction. *Journal of Marriage and the Family* 56 (November):923–934.

Labott, Susan M., Randall B. Martin, Patricia S. Eason, & Elayne Y. Berkey. (1991). Social Reactions to the Expression of Emotion. *Cognition and Emotion* 5 (September–November):397–417.

Lahey, B. B. (1989). *Psychology.* Dubuque, Iowa: William, C. Brown.

Laing, Milli. (1993). Gossip: Does It Play a Role in the Socialization of Nurses. *Journal of Nursing Scholarship* 25 (Spring):37–43.

Laing, Ronald D., H. Phillipson, & A. Russell Lee. (1966). *Interpersonal Perception.* New York: Springer.

Lanagan, Leonara M., & Susan M. Watkins. (1987). Human Factors. *Psychology Today* (October).

Langer, Ellen J. (1989). *Mindfulness.* Reading, MA: Addison-Wesley.

Lanzetta, J. T., J. Cartwright-Smith, & R. E. Kleck. (1976). Effects of Nonverbal Dissimulations on Emotional Experience and Autonomic Arousal. *Journal of Personality and Social Psychology* 33:354–370.

Larsen, Randy J., Margaret Kasimatis, & Kurt Frey. (1992). Facilitating the Furrowed Brow: An Unobtrusive Test of the Facial Feedback Hypothesis Applied to Unpleasant Affect. *Cognition and Emotion* 6 (September):321–338.

Lea, Martin, & Russell Spears. (1995). Love at First Byte? Building Personal Relationships over Computer Networks. In Julia T. Wood & Steve Duck (Eds.), *Under-Studied Relationships: Off the Beaten Track* (pp. 197–233). Thousand Oaks, CA: Sage.

Leaper, Campbell, Mary Carson, Carilyn Baker, Heithre Holliday, et al. (1995). Self-Disclosure and Listener Verbal Support in Same-Gender and Cross-Gender Friends' Conversations. *Sex Roles* 33:387–404.

Leathers, Dale G. (1986). *Successful Nonverbal Communication: Principles and Applications* (2nd ed.). New York: Macmillan.

Lee, Fiona. (1993). Being Polite and Keeping MUM: How Bad News Is Communicated in Organizational Hierarchies. *Journal of Applied Social Psychology* 23 (July):1124–1149.

Lee, John Alan. (1976). *The Colors of Love.* New York: Bantam.

Leung, Kwok. (1988). Some Determinants of Conflict Avoidance. *Journal of Cross Cultural Psychology* 19 (March):125–136.

Lever, Janet. (1995). The 1995 Advocate Survey of Sexuality and Relationships: The Women, Lesbian Sex Survey. *The Advocate* 687/688 (August 22):22–30.

LeVine, R., & K. Bartlett (1984). Pace of Life, Punctuality, and Coronary Heart Disease in Six Countries. *Journal of Cross-Cultural Psychology* 15:233–255.

Levine, R., S. Sato, T. Hashimoto, & J. Verma. (1994). *Love and Marriage in Eleven Cultures.* Unpublished Manuscript, California State University at Fresno. (Cited in Hatfield & Rapson, 1996.)

Lewin, Tamar. (1998). 1 in 8 Boys of High-School Age Has Been Abused, Survey Shows. *New York Times* (June 26), A11.

Lewis, David. (1989). *The Secret Language of Success.* New York: Carroll and Graf.

Lindeman, Marjaana, Tuija Harakka, & Liisa Keltikangas-Jarvinen. (1997). Age and Gender Differences in Adolescents' Reactions to Conflict Situations: Aggression, Prosociality, and Withdrawal. *Journal of Youth and Adolescence* 26 (June):339–351.

Lister, Larry. (1991). Men and Grief: A Review of Research, *Smith College Studies in Social Work* 61 (June):220–235.

Littlejohn, Stephen W. (1996). *Theories of Human Communication.* (5th ed.). Belmont, CA: Wadsworth.

Luft, Joseph. (1970). *Group Processes: An Introduction to Group Dynamics* (2nd ed.). Palo Alto, CA: Mayfield Publishing Co.

Lujansky, H., & G. Mikula. (1983). Can Equity Theory Explain the Quality and Stability of Romantic Relationships? *British Journal of Social Psychology* 22:101–112.

Lukens, J. (1978). Ethnocentric Speech. *Ethnic Groups* 2:35–53.

Lustig, Myron W., & Koester, Jolene. (1996). *Intercultural Competence: Interpersonal Communication Across Cultures* (2nd ed.). NY: HarperCollins.

Lutz, William. (1996). *The New Douplespeak: Why No One Knows What Anyone's Saying Anymore.* New York: HarperCollins [Harper Perennial].

Ma, Karen. (1996). *The Modern Madame Butterfly: Fantasy and Reality in Japanese Cross-Cultural Relationships.* Rutland, VT: Charles E. Tuttle.

Ma, Ringo. (1992). The Role of Unofficial Intermediaries in Interpersonal Conflicts in the Chinese Culture. *Communication Quarterly* 40 (Summer):269–278.

MacLachlan, James. (1979). What People Really Think of Fast Talkers. *Psychology Today* 13:113–117.

Maggio, Rosalie. (1997). *Talking about People: A Guide to Fair and Accurate Language.* Phoenix, AZ: Oryx Press.

Malandro, Loretta A., Larry Barker, & Deborah Ann Barker. (1989). *Nonverbal Communication* (2nd ed.). New York: Random House.

Manes, Joan, & Nessa Wolfson. (1981). The Compliment Formula. In Florian Coulmas (Ed.), *Conversational Routine.* (pp. 115–132). The Hague: Mouton.

Mao, LuMing Robert. (1994). Beyond Politeness Theory: "Face" Revisited and Renewed. *Journal of Pragmatics* 21 (May):451–486.

Marshall, Evan. (1983). *Eye Language: Understanding the Eloquent Eye.* New York: New Trend.

Marshall, Linda L., & Rose, Patricia. (1987). Gender, Stress and Violence in the Adult Relationships of a Sample of College Students. *Journal of Social and Personal Relationships* 4: 299–316.

Martin, Matthew M., & Carolyn M. Anderson. (1995). Roommate Similarity: Are Roommates Who Are Similar in Their Communication Traits More Satisfied? *Communication Research Reports* 12 (Spring):46–52.

Martin, Matthew M., & Rebecca B. Rubin. (1994). Development of a Communication Flexibility Measure. *The Southern Communication Journal* 59 (Winter 1994):171–178.

Martin, Matthew M., & Carolyn M. Anderson. (1998). The Cognitive Flexibility Scale: Three Validity Studies. *Communication Reports* 11 (Winter):1–9.

Martin, Matthew M., & Rebecca B. Rubin. (1995). A New Measure of Cognitive Flexibility. *Psychological Reports* 76:623–626.

Martin, Scott L., & Richard J. Klimoski. (1990). Use of Verbal Protocols to Trace Cognitions Associated with Self- and Supervisor Evaluations of Performance. *Organizational Behavior and Human Decision Processes* 46:135–154.

Marwell, G., & D. R. Schmitt. (1967). Dimensions of Compliance-Gaining Behavior: An Empirical Analysis. *Sociometry* 39: 350–364.

Matsumoto, David. (1991). Cultural Influences on Facial Expressions of Emotion. *Southern Communication Journal* 56 (Winter):128–137.

Matsumoto, David. (1994). *People: Psychology from a Cultural Perspective.* Pacific Grove, CA: Brooks/Cole.

Matsumoto, David, & V. Hearn. (1991). *Culture and Emotion: Display Rule Differences between the United States, Poland, and Hungary.* [Manuscript cited in David Matsumoto (1996). *Culture and Personality.* Pacific Grove, CA: Brooks/Cole.]

Matsumoto, David, & T. Kudoh. (1993). American-Japanese Cultural Differences in Attributions of Personality Based on Smiles. *Journal of Nonverbal Behavior* 17:231–243.

Maynard, Harry E. (1963). How to Become a Better Premise Detective. *Public Relations Journal* 19:20–22.

McCarthy, Michael J. (1991). *Mastering the Information Age.* Los Angeles: Jeremy P. Tarcher.

McConatha, Jasmin-Tahmaseb, Eileen Lightner, & Stephanie L. Deaner. (1994). Culture, Age, and Gender as Variables in the Expression of Emotions, *Journal of Social Behavior and Personality* 9 (September):481–488.

McCroskey, J. C., S. Booth-Butterfield, & S. K. Payne. (1989). The Impact of Communication Apprehension on College Student Retention and Success. *Communication Quarterly* 37: 100–107.

McCroskey, James, & Lawrence Wheeless. (1976). *Introduction to Human Communication.* Boston: Allyn and Bacon.

McCroskey, James C. (1997). *Introduction to Rhetorical Communication* (7th ed.). Englewood Cliffs, NJ: Prentice-Hall.

McGill, Micahel E. (1985). *The McGill Report on Male Intimacy.* New York: Harper & Row.

McLaughlin, Margaret L. (1984). *Conversation: How Talk Is Organized.* Newbury Park, CA: Sage.

McLaughlin, Margaret L., Michael J. Cody, & Carl S. Robey. (1980). Situational Influences on the Selection of Strategies to Resist Compliance-Gaining Attempts. *Human Communication Research* 7:14–36.

McLean, Paula A., & Brian D. Jones. (1992). Machiavellianism and Business Education. *Psychological Reports* 71 (August):57–58.

McLoyd, Vonnie, & Leon Wilson. (1992). Telling Them Like It Is: The Role of Economic and Environmental Factors in Single Mothers' Discussions with Their Children. *American Journal of Community Psychology* 20 (August):419–444.

McMahan, Elizabeth, & Susan Day. (1984). *The Writer's Rhetoric and Handbook* (2nd ed.). New York: McGraw-Hill.

Mendoza, Louis. (1995, March 23–25). *Ethos, Ethnicity, and the Electronic Classroom: A Study in Contrasting Educational Environments.* Paper presented at the 46th Annual Meeting of the Conferences on College Composition and Communication, Washington, D. C.

Mesick, R. M., & K. S. Cook. (Eds.). (1983). *Equity Theory: Psychological and Sociological Perspectives.* New York: Praeger.

Metts, Sandra. (1989). An Exploratory Investigation of Deception in Close Relationships. *Journal of Social and Personal Relationships* 6 (May):159–179.

Meyer, Janet R. (1994). Effect of Situational Features on the Likelihood of Addressing Face Needs in Requests. *Southern Communication Journal* 59 (Spring):240–254.

Michalko, Michael. (1991). *Thinkertoys: A Handbook of Business Creativity for the 90s.* Berkeley, CA: Ten Speed Press.

Midooka, Kiyoski. (1990). Characteristics of Japanese Style Communication. *Media Culture and Society* 12 (October):47–489.

Miller, Gerald R., & Judee Burgoon. (1990). In Joseph A. DeVito & Michael L. Hecht (Eds.), *The Nonverbal Communication Reader* (pp. 340–357). Prospect Heights, IL: Wareland Press.

Miller, Gerald R., & Malcolm R. Parks. (1982). Communication in Dissolving Relationships. In Steve Duck (Ed.), *Personal Relationships. 4: Dissolving Personal Relationships* (pp. 127–154). New York: Academic Press.

Miller, J. G. (1984). Culture and the Development of Everyday Social Explanation. *Journal of Personality and Social Psychology* 46:961–978.

Miller, Roger F. (1987). *What Can I Say? How to Talk to People in Grief.* St. Louis, MO: CBP Press.

Miner, Horace (1956). Body Ritual Among the Nacirema. *American Anthropologist* 58:503–507.

Moghaddam, Fathali M., Donald M. Taylor, & Stephen C. Wright. (1993). *Social Psychology in Cross-Cultural Perspective.* New York: W. H. Freeman.

Molloy, John. (1977). *The Woman's Dress for Success Book.* Chicago: Follet.

Montague, Ashley. (1971). *Touching: The Human Significance of the Skin.* New York: Harper & Row.

Moon, Dreama G. (1966). Concepts of "Culture": Implications for Intercultural Communication Research. *Communication Quarterly* 44 (Winter):70–84.

Morris, Desmond. (1977). *Manwatching: A Field Guide to Human Behavior.* New York: Abrams.

Murphy, Lisa. (1997). Efficacy of Reality Therapy in the Schools: A Review of the Research from 1980–1995. *Journal of Reality Therapy* 16 (Spring):12–20.

Myers, Scott A. (1995). Student Perceptions of Teacher Affinity-Seeking and Classroom Climate. *Communication Research Reports* 12 (Fall):192-199.

Naifeh, Steven, & Gregory White Smith. (1984). *Why Can't Men Open Up? Overcoming Men's Fear of Intimacy.* New York: Clarkson N. Potter.

Neugarten, Bernice. (1979). Time, Age, and the Life Cycle. *American Journal of Psychiatry* 136:887–894.

Nichols, Michael P. (1995). *The Lost Art of Listening.* New York: Guilford Press.

Nichols, Ralph. (1961). Do We Know How to Listen? Practical Helps in a Modern Age. *Communication Education* 10:118–124.

Nichols, Ralph, & Leonard Stevens. (1957). *Are You Listening?* New York: McGraw-Hill.

Nickerson, Raymond S. (1987). Why Teach Thinking? In Joan Boykoff Baron & Robert J. Sternberg (Eds.), *Teaching Thinking Skills: Theory and Practice* (pp. 27–37). New York: W. H. Freeman.

Noble, Barbara Presley. (1994). The Gender Wars: Talking Peace. *The New York Times* (August 14):21.

Noller, Patricia, & Mary Anne Fitzpatrick. (1993). *Communication in Family Relationships.* Englewood Cliffs, NJ: Prentice Hall.

Norton, Robert, & Barbara Warnick. (1976). Assertiveness as a Communication Construct. *Human Communication Research* 3:62–66.

O'Hair, Dan, Michael J. Cody, Blaine Goss, & Karl J. Krayer. (1988). The Effect of Gender, Deceit Orientation and Communicator Style on Macro-Assessments of Honesty. *Communication Quarterly* 36:77–93.

O'Hair, Mary John, Michael J. Cody, & Dan O'Hair. (1991). The Impact of Situational Dimensions on Compliance-Resisting Strategies: A Comparison of Methods. *Communication Quarterly* 39 (Summer): 226–240.

Oatley, Keith, & Elaine Duncan. (1994). The Experience of Emotions in Everyday Life. *Cognition and Emotion* 8:369–381.

Oberg, K. (1960). Cultural Shock: Adjustment to New Cultural Environments. *Practical Anthropology* 7:177–182.

Olaniran, Bolanle A. (1994). Group Performance in Computer-mediated and Face-to-Face Communication Media. *Management Communication Quarterly* 7 (February):256–281.

Olson, Robert T. (1980). *The Art of Creative Thinking.* New York: Harper & Row.

Otaki, Midori, Mary Ellen Durrett, Phyllis Richards, Lina Nyquist, & James W. Pennebaker. (1986). Maternal and Infant Behavior in Japan and America. *Journal of Cross-Cultural Psychology* 17:251–268.

Parker, Rhonda G., & Roxanne Parrott. (1995). Patterns of Self-Disclosure Across Social Support Networks: Elderly, Middle-Aged, and Young Adults. *International Journal of Aging and Human Development* 41:281–297.

Pearson, Judy C. (1993). *Communication in the Family* (2nd ed.). New York: HarperCollins.

Pearson, Judy, & Paul Nelson. (1997). *An Introduction to Human Communication* (7th ed.). Dubuque, IA: Wm. C. Brown.

Pearson, Judy C., & Spitzberg, Brian H. (1990). *Interpersonal Communication: Concepts, Components, and Contexts* (2nd ed.). Dubuque, IA: William C. Brown.

Pearson, Judy C., Richard West, & Lynn H. Turner. (1995). *Gender and Communication* (3rd ed.). Dubuque, IA: William C. Brown.

Penfield, Joyce. (Ed.). (1987). *Women and Language in Transition.* Albany: State University of New York Press.

Pennebaker, James W. (1991). *Opening Up: The Healing Power of Confiding in Others.* New York: Avon.

Peterson, Candida C. (1996). The Ticking of the Social Clock: Adults' Beliefs about the Timing of Transition Events. *International Journal of Aging and Human Development* 42:189–203.

Petrocelli, William, & Barbara Kate Repa. (1992). *Sexual Harassment on the Job.* Berkeley, CA: Nolo Press.

Phlegar, Phyllis. (1995). *Love Online: A Practical Guide to Digital Dating.* Reading, MA: Addison-Wesley.

Pierre-Pierre, Garry. (1996). Filling in Cabby's Verbal Pothole: 50 Courteous Responses Added to Driver Repertory. *New York Times* (May 6):B1, B6.

Pilkington, Neil W., & Anthony R. D'Augelli. (1995). Victimization of Lesbian, Gay, and Bisexual Youth in Community Settings. *Journal of Community Psychology* 23 (January):34–56.

Piot, Charles D. (1993). Secrecy, Ambiguity, and the Everyday in Kabre Culture, *American Anthropologist* 95 (June):353–370.

Plutchik, Robert. (1980). *Emotion: A Psycho-Evolutionary Synthesis.* New York: Harper & Row.

Porter, R. H., & J. D. Moore. (1981). Human Kin Recognition by Olfactory Cues. *Physiology and Behavior* 27:493–495.

Potts, Bonnie. (1994). Strategies for Teaching Critical Thinking. *ERIC/AE Digest.* Washington, DC: ERIC Clearinghouse on Assessment and Evaluation.

Proctor, Russell F. (1991). *An Exploratory Analysis of Responses to Owned Messages in Interpersonal Communication.* Ph.D. Dissertation, Bowling Green University.

Purnine, Daniel M., Michael P. Carey, & Randall S. Jorgensen. (1994). Gender Differences Regarding Preferences for Specific Heterosexual Practices. *Journal of Sex and Marital Therapy* 20 (Winter):271–287.

Raven, R., C. Centers, & A. Rodrigues. (1975). The Bases of Conjugal Power. In R. E. Cromwell & D. H. Olson (Eds.), *Power in Families* (pp. 217–234). New York: Halsted Press.

Reed, Mark D. (1993). Sudden Death and Bereavement Outcomes: The Impact of Resources on Grief, Symptomatology and Detachment. *Suicide and Life Threatening Behavior* 23 (Fall):204–220.

Rich, Andrea L. (1974). *Interracial Communication.* New York: Harper & Row.

Richmond, Virginia P., & James C. McCroskey. (1996). *Communication: Apprehension, Avoidance, and Effectiveness* (4th ed.). Scottsdale, AZ: Gorsuch Scarisbrick.

Roach, K. David. (1991). The Influence and Effects of Gender and Status on University Instructor Affinity-Seeking Behavior. *Southern Communication Journal* 57 (Fall):73–80.

Roberts, Moss. (Ed. and trans., with the assistance of C. N. Tay). (1979). *Chinese Fairy Tales and Fantasies.* New York: Pantheon Books.

Roger, Derek, & Willfried Nesshoever. (1987). Individual Differences in Dyadic Conversational Strategies: A Further Study. *British Journal of Social Psychology* 26 (September):247–255.

Rogers, Carl, & Richard Farson. (1981). Active Listening. In Joseph A. DeVito (Ed.), *Communication: Concepts and Processes* (3rd ed, pp. 137–147). Englewood Cliffs, NJ: Prentice-Hall.

Rosenbaum, M. E. (1986). The Repulsion Hypothesis: On the Nondevelopment of Relationships. *Journal of Personality and Social Psychology* 51:1156–1166.

Rosenfeld, Lawrence. (1979). Self-disclosure Avoidance: Why I Am Afraid to Tell You Who I Am. *Communication Monographs* 46 (1979):63–74.

Rosenthal, Robert, & L. Jacobson. (1968). *Pygmalion in the Classroom.* New York: Holt, Rinehart and Winston.

Rosenthal, Robert, & D. B. Rubin. (1978). Interpersonal Expectancy Effects: The First 345 Studies. *Behavioral and Brain Sciences* 3:377–415.

Ruben, Brent D. (1985). Human Communication and Cross-Cultural Effectiveness. In Larry A. Samovar & Richard E. Porter (Eds.), *Intercultural Communication: A Reader* (4th ed., pp. 338–346). Belmont, Calif.: Wadsworth.

Rubenstein, Carin. (1993). Fighting Sexual Harassment in Schools. *New York Times* (June 10):C8.

Rubenstein, Carin, & Philip Shaver. (1982). *In Search of Intimacy.* New York: Delacorte.

Rubin, Rebecca B. (1985). The Validity of the Communication Competency Assessment Instrument. *Communication Monographs* 52:173–185.

Rubin, Rebecca B. (1986). A Response to "Ethnicity, Communication Competency and Classroom Success." *Western Journal of Speech Communication* 50:279–282.

Rubin, Rebecca B., C. Fernandez-Collado, & R. Hernandez-Sampieri. (1992). A Cross-Cultural Examination of Interpersonal Communication Motives in Mexico and the United States. *International Journal of Intercultural Relations* 16:145–157.

Rubin, Rebecca B., & Elizabeth E. Graham. (1988). Communication Correlates of College Success: An Exploratory Investigation. *Communication Education* 37 (January): 14–27.

Rubin, Rebecca B., & M. M. Martin. (1994). Development of a Measure of Interpersonal Communication Competence. *Communication Research Reports* 11:33–44.

Rubin, Rebecca B., Elizabeth M. Perse, & Carole A. Barbato. (1988). Conceptualization and Measurement of Interpersonal Communication Motives. *Human Communication Research* 14:602–628.

Rubin, Rebecca B., & Alan M. Rubin. (1992). Antecedents of Interpersonal Communication Motivation. *Communication Quarterly* 40:3-5–317.

Rubin, Zick. (1973). *Liking and Loving: An Invitation to Social Psychology.* New York: Holt, Rinehart and Winston.

Rundquist, Suellen. (1992). Indirectness: A Gender Study of Fluting Grice's Maxims. *Journal of Pragmatics* 18 (November):431–449.

Sabatelli, Ronald M., & John Pearce. (1986). Exploring Marital Expectations. *Journal of Social and Personal Relationships* 3 (1986):307–321.

Sadker, Myra, & David Sadker. (1985). Sexism in the Schoolroom of the 80s. *Psychology Today* 19 (March):54–57.

Sadker, Myra, & David Sadker. (1994). *Failing at Fairness: How America's Schools Cheat Girls.* New York: Basic Books.

Salekin, Randall T., James R. P. Ogloff, Cathy McGarland, & Richard Rogers. (1995). Influencing Jurors' Perceptions of Guilt: Expression of Emotionality during Testimony. *Behavioral Sciences and the Law* 13 (Spring):293–305.

Samovar, Larry A., & Richard E. Porter. (Eds.). (1991). *Communication between Cultures.* Belmont, CA: Wadsworth.

Sanders, Judith A., Richard L. Wiseman, & S. Irene Matz. (1991). Uncertainty Reduction in Acquaintance Relationships in Ghana and the United States. In Stella Ting-Toomey & Felipe Korzenny (Eds.), *Cross-Cultural Interpersonal* (pp. 79–98). Thousand Oaks, CA: Sage.

Sapadin, Linda A. (1988). Friendship and Gender: Perspectives of Professional Men and Women. *Journal of Social and Personal Relationships* 5:387–403.

Saunders, Carol S., Daniel Robey, & Kelly A. Vaverek. (1994). The Persistence of Status Differentials in Computer Conferencing. *Human Communication Research* 20 (June):443–472.

Sawin, Gregory. (Ed.). (1995). *Thinking and Living Skills: General Semantics for Critical Thinking.* Concord, CA: International Society for General Semantics.

Schaap, C., B. Buunk, & A. Kerkstra. (1988). Marital Conflict Resolution. In Patricia Noller & Mary Anne Fitzpatrick (Eds.), *Perspectives on Marital Interaction* (pp. 203–244). Philadelphia, PA: Multilingual Matters.

Schachter, Stanley (1964). The Interaction of Cognitive and Physiological Determinants of Emotional State. In Leonard Berkowitz, ed., *Advances in Experimental Social Psychology,* vol. 1. New York: Academic Press.

Schafer, R. B., & P. M. Keith. (1980). Equity and Depression Among Married Couples. *Social Psychology Quarterly* 43:430–435.

Scheetz, L. Patrick. (1995). *Recruiting Trends 1995–1996: A Study of 527 Businesses, Industries, and Governmental Agencies Employing New College Graduates.* East Lansing, MI: Collegiate Employment Research Institute, Michigan State University.

Scherer, K. R. (1986). Vocal Affect Expression. *Psychological Bulletin* 99:143–165.

Schmidt, Tracy O., & Randolph R. Cornelius. (1987). Self-disclosure in Everday Life. *Journal of Social and Personal Relationships* 4:365–373.

Schwartz, Marilyn, & the Task Force on Bias-Free Language of the Association of American University Presses. (1995). *Guidelines for Bias-Free Writing.* Bloomington: Indiana University Press.

Shaffer, David R., Linda J. Pegalis, & David P. Cornell. (1992). Gender and Self-Disclosure Revisited: Personal and Contextual Variations in Self-Disclosure to Same-Sex Acquaintances. *Journal of Social Psychology* 132 (June):307–315.

Shea, Virginia. (1994). *Netiquette.* Albion Books.

Shuter, Robert. (1990). The Centrality of Culture. *Southern Communication Journal* 55 (Spring): 237–249.

Slade, Margot. (1995). We Forgot to Write a Headline. But It's Not Our Fault. *The New York Times* (February 19):5.

Snyder, C. R. (1984). Excuses, Excuses. *Psychology Today* 18:50–55.

Snyder, C. R., Raymond L. Higgins, & Rita J. Stucky. (1983). *Excuses: Masquerades in Search of Grace.* New York: Wiley.

Sorenson, Paula S., Katherine Hawkins, & Ritch L. Sorenson. (1995). Gender, Psychological Type and Conflict Style Preferences. *Management Communication Quarterly* 9 (August):115–126.

Spitzberg, Brian H., & Michael L. Hecht. (1984). A Component Model of Relational Competence. *Human Communication Research* 10:575–599.

Spitzberg, Brian H., & William R. Cupach. (1984). *Interpersonal Communication Competence.* Beverly Hills, CA: Sage.

Spitzberg, Brian H., & William R. Cupach. (1989). *Handbook of Interpersonal Competence Research.* New York: Springer-Verlag.

Sprecher, Susan. (1987). The Effects of Self-Disclosure Given and Received on Affection for an Intimate Partner and Stability of the Relationship. *Journal of Social and Personal Relationships* 4:115–127.

Sprecher, Susan, & Sandra Metts. (1989). Development of the "Romantic Beliefs Scale" and Examination of the Effects of Gender and Gender-Role Orientation. *Journal of Social and Personal Relationships* 6:387–411.

Steil, Lyman K., Larry L. Barker, & Kittie W. Watson. (1983). *Effective Listening: Key to Your Success.* Reading, MA: Addison-Wesley.

Steiner, Claude. (1981). *The Other Side of Power.* New York: Grove.

Steinfatt, Thomas M. (1987). Personality and Communication: Classic Approaches. In James C. McCroskey & John A. Daly (Eds.), *Personality and Interpersonal Communication* (pp. 42–126). Thousand Oaks, CA: Sage.

Stephan, Walter G., & Cookie White Stephan. (1985). Intergroup Anxiety. *Journal of Social Issues* 41:157–175.

Stine, Jean, & Camden Benares. (1994). *It's All in Your Head: Remarkable Facts about the Human Mind.* New York: Prentice Hall General Reference.

Sternberg, Robert J. (1987). Questions and Answers about the Nature and Teaching of Thinking Skills. In Joan Boykoff Baron & Robert J. Sternberg (Eds.), *Teaching Thinking Skills: Theory and Practice* (pp. 251–259). New York: W. H. Freeman.

Strecker, Ivo. (1993). Cultural Variations in the Concept of "Face." *Multilingua* 12:119–141.

Szapocznik, Jose. (1995). Research on Disclosure of HIV Status: Cultural Evolution Finds an Ally in Science. *Health Psychology* 14 (January):4–5.

Tannen, Deborah. (1990). *You Just Don't Understand: Women and Men in Conversation.* New York: Morrow.

Tannen, Deborah. (1994a). *Gender and Discourse.* New York: Oxford University Press.

Tannen, Deborah. (1994b). *Talking from 9 to 5.* New York: Morrow.

Tarnove, Elizabeth J. (1988). *Effects of Sexist Language on the Status and Self-concept of Women.* Paper presented at the Annual Meeting of the Association for Education in Journalism and Mass Communication, Portland, OR.

Thibaut, J. W., & Kelley, H. H. (1959). *The Social Psychology of Groups.* New York: Wiley. New Brunswick, NJ: Transaction Books. (Revised 1986.)

Thorne, Barrie, Cheris Kramarae, & Nancy Henley (Eds.). (1983). *Language, Gender and Society.* Rowley, MA: Newbury House Publishers.

Ting-Toomey, Stella. (1985). Toward a Theory of Conflict and Culture. *International and Intercultural Communication Annual* 9:71–86.

Ting-Toomey, Stella. (1986). Conflict Communication Styles in Black and White Subjective Cultures. In Young Yun Kim (Ed.), *Interethnic Communication: Current Research* (pp. 75–88). Thousand Oaks, CA: Sage.

Tolhuizen, James H. (1989). Communication Strategies for Intensifying Dating Relationships: Identification, Use and Structure. *Journal of Social and Personal Relationships* 6:413–434.

Torbiorn, I. (1982). *Living Abroad.* New York: Wiley.

Trager, George L. (1958). Paralanguage: A First Approximation. *Studies in Linguistics* 13:1–12.

Trager, George L. (1961). The Typology of Paralanguage. *Anthropological Linguistics* 3:17–21.

Trower, P. (1981). Social Skill Disorder. In S. Duck & R. Gilmour (Eds.), *Personal Relationships* (3rd ed., pp. 97–110). New York: Academic Press.

Tyler, Patrick E. (1996). Crime (and Punishment) Rages Anew in China. *The New York Times* (July 11):A1, A8.

Ubel, P., M. Zell, D. Miller, G. Fischer, S. Peters, & R. Arnold. (1995). Elevator Talk: Observational Study of Inappropriate Comments in a Public Space. *American Journal of Medicine* 99 (August):190–194.

Ueleke, William, et al. (1983). Inequity Resolving Behavior as a Response to Inequity in a Hypothetical Marital Relationship. *A Quarterly Journal of Human Behavior* 20:4–8.

VanHyning, Memory. (1993). *Crossed Signals: How to Say No to Sexual Harassment.* Los Angeles: Infotrends Press.

Veenendall, Thomas L., & Marjorie C. Feinstein. (1996). *Let's Talk About Relationships: Cases in Study* (2nd ed.). Prospect Heights, IL: Waveland Press.

Victor, David. (1992). *International Business Communication.* New York: HarperCollins.

Wade, Carole, & Carol Tavris, (1998). *Psychology* (5th ed.). New York: Longman.

Walster, E., & G. W. Walster. (1978). *A New Look at Love.* Reading, MA: Addison-Wesley.

Walster, E., G. W. Walster, & E. Berscheid. (1978). *Equity: Theory and Research.* Boston: Allyn and Bacon.

Watzlawick, Paul. (1977). *How Real Is Real? Confusion, Disinformation, Communication: An Anecdotal Introduction to Communications Theory.* New York: Vintage Books.

Watzlawick, Paul. (1978). *The Language of Change: Elements of Therapeutic Communication.* New York: Basic Books.

Watzlawick, Paul, Janet Helmick Beavin, & Don D. Jackson. (1967). *Pragmatics of Human Communication: A Study of Interactional Patterns, Pathologies, and Paradoxes.* New York: Norton.

Weinberg, Harry L. (1959). *Levels of Knowing and Existence.* New York: Harper & Row.

Weiner, Bernard, Dan Russell, & David Lerman. (1979). Affective Consequences of Causal Ascriptions. In J. H. Harvey, W. J. Ickes, & R. F. Kidd (Eds.), *New Directions in Attribution Research* (Vol. 2). Hillsdale, NJ: Erlbaum.

Weinstein, Eugene A., & Paul Deutschberger. (1963). Some Dimensions of Altercasting. *Sociometry* 26:454–466.

Werrbach, Gail B., Harold D. Grotevant, & Catherine R. Cooper. (1990). Gender Differences in Adolescents' Identity Development in the Domain of Sex Role Concepts. *Sex Roles* 23 (October):349–362.

Westwood, R. I, F. F. Tang, & P. S. Kirkbride. (1992). Chinese Conflict Behavior: Cultural Antecedents and Behavioral Consequences. *Organizational Development Journal* 10 (Summer):13–19.

Wetzel, Patricia J. (1988). Are "Powerless" Communication Strategies the Japanese norm? *Language in Society* 17:555–564.

Wheeler, D. S., A. Farina, & J. Stern. (1984). *Dimensions of Peril in the Stigmatization of the Mentally Ill.* [Manuscript cited in Edward E. Jones et al. (Eds.). (1984). *Social Stigma: The Psychology of Marked Relationships.* New York: W. H. Freeman.]

Wheeless, Lawrence R., & Janis Grotz. (1977). The Measurement of Trust and Its Relationship to Self-Disclosure. *Human Communication Research* 3:250–257.

White, Kristin. (1993). How the Mind Ages. *Psychology Today* 26 (November/December):38–42, 79–80, 91–95.

Wiemann, John M. (1977). Explication and Test of a Model of Communicative Competence. *Human Communication Research* 3:195–213.

Wilkins, B. M., & P. A. Andersen. (1991). Gender Differences and Similarities in Management Communication: A Meta-Analysis. *Management Communication Quarterly* 5:6–35.

Wilmot, William W. (1987). *Dyadic Communication,* 3rd ed. New York: Random House.

Wilson, A. P., & Thomas G. Bishard. (1994). Here's the Dirt on Gossip. *American School Board Journal* 181 (December):27–29.

Wilson, R. A. (1989). Toward Understanding E-prime. *Etc.: A Review of General Semantics* 46:316–319.

Wolfson, Nessa. (1988). The Bulge: A Theory of Speech Behaviour and Social Distance. In J. Fine (Ed.), *Second Language Discourse: A Textbook of Current Research*. Norwood, NJ: Ablex.

Won-Doornink, Myong Jin. (1991). Self-Disclosure and Reciprocity in South Korean and U.S. Male Dyads. In Stella Ting-Toomey & Felipe Korzenny (Eds.), *Cross-Cultural Interpersonal Communication* (pp. 116–131). Newbury Park, CA: Sage.

Wood, Julia T. (1994). *Gendered Lives: Communication, Gender, and Culture*. Belmont, CA: Wadsworth.

Wright, Paul H. (1988). Interpreting Research on Gender Differences in Friendship: A Case for Moderation and a Plea for Caution. *Journal of Social and Personal Relationships* 5:367–373.

Zimmerman, Don H., & Candace West. (1975). Sex Roles, Interruptions, and Silences in Conversations. In B. Thorne & N. Henley (eds.), *Language and Sex: Differences and Dominance*. Rowley, MA: Newbury House.

Zuckerman, M., R. Klorman, D. T. Larrance, & N. H. Spiegel. (1981). Facial, Autonomic, and Subjective Components of Emotion: The Facial Feedback Hypothesis Versus the Externalizer-Internalizer Distinction. *Journal of Personality and Social Psychology* 41:929–944.

Zunin, Leonard M., & Zunin, Natalie B. (1972). *Contact: The First Four Minutes*. Los Angeles, CA: Nash.

Photo Credits

Index

Note: Italicized letters *f* and *t* following page numbers indicate figures and tables, respectively.

Absolute generalization, avoiding, 128
Abstraction ladder, 118, 119*f*
Abstraction, variations in, 116–117
Accenting, nonverbal communication and, 140
Accommodation, 24–25
Acculturation, 231–233
Acquaintances, social penetration with, 277*f*
Active listening, 100
Adaptors, 142–143
      avoiding, 158
Adjustment, interpersonal communication as
      process of, 24–25
Advisor, conversational role of, 205
Aesop, 38
Affect displays, 142
Affection, self-disclosure and, 51
Affinity-seeking strategies, 271
African Americans
      and conflict styles, 292–293
      and touching behavior, 162–163
Agapic love, 266
Age, and spatial distance in communication, 149
Aggressiveness, verbal, 310
      versus assertiveness, 336–337
      messages characteristic of, 339*t*
      self-test of, 310–311
Allness, 130–131
Alter-adaptors, 142
Altercasting, 198–199
      as compliance-gaining strategy, 322*t*
Apache, silence among, 163
Appearances, deceptiveness of, 23
Apprehension, 58–63
      behaviors characteristic of, 58–59

culture and, 59–60
definition of, 58
empowering others to manage, 62–63
managing, 60–61
self-test of, 59
Arab culture, values in, 234–235
Arguer, conversational role of, 204
Argumentativeness, 312–313
      cultivating, 313
      self-test of, 312
Aromatherapy, 159
Artifactual communication, 149–152
      cultural differences in, 165–166
Ashburn, Carol, 101
Assertive communication, 335–340
      analyzing and practicing, 340–341
      increasing, principles for, 338–340
      self-test of, 335–336
Assertive language, 338, 339*t*
Assimilation, biases and, 105
Association of American University Presses, Task Force on
      Bias-Free Language, 125
Assumptions, avoiding, 23
"Attack by Question" (Lalanne), 205–206
Attitudinal positiveness, 222
Attraction theory, 272–275, 280*t*
Attractiveness, 143
      elements of, 273
      smell and, 159
Attribution, 76–77
      errors of, avoiding, 77–78
Avoidance, in conflict management, 304
Axtell, Roger, 200

Backchanneling cues, 93, 211–212
      and other-orientation, 225
Beck, Aaron, 263

Beliefs
 about interpersonal communication, self-test of, 4
 about relationships, self-test of, 262–263
 cultural
  self-test of, 232–233
  sources of, discovering, 46
 self-affirming, 318
 self-destructive, 318
 unrealistic, rewriting, 320
Beltlining, in conflict management, 309
Best friend test, 185
Biases, recognizing, 105
Blame, in conflict, 308
Blind person, interacting with, 79–80, 251*t*
Blind self, 42–43, 43*f*
 reducing, 45
Bodily reactions, emotions and, 172
Body adornment, messages perceived in, 151–152
Body appearance, communicating with, 143
Body language, 141–143. *See also* Nonverbal communication
 and assertiveness, 339*t*
 and communication of power, 158
 and confidence, 321
 in effective listening, 101, 102
Body movements, communicating with, 141–143, 143*t*
Bourland, D. David, Jr., 135
Boyd, Malcolm, 22–23
Brainstorming, 62
Business context
 directions of communication in, 28
 emotional expression in, 184–185
 listening in, 101
 problems of communication in, 2–3
Business, in conversation, 199

Certainty, in conflict management, 307
Change, openness to, 282
Channel, communication, 15
Chat groups, 195–197
Chinese culture, conversational maxims in, 209
Chronemics, 156
Civil inattention, 146
Closeness messages, 272
Closing, conversational, 201–202
 suggestions for, 214
Closure, in organization of perceptions, 68
Clothing
 communicating with, 151, 158
 and power, 323
Coercive power holder, 328
Cognitive disclaimers, 199
Cognitive labeling theory of emotions, 174–175, 175*f*
Cole, Diane, 101
Collective cultures, 239–241, 243*t*
Color
 communicating with, 150
 cultural meanings of, 163*t*
Commitment, interpersonal, 264
Communication accommodation theory, 24–25
Comparison level, in relationship, 278
Competence, interpersonal, 8–13

 critical thinking and, 9–11
 culture and, 12–13
 interpersonal skills and, 11–12
 listening and, 13
 and self-disclosure, 48
Complainer, conversational role of, 204
Complaints, dealing with, 298
Complementing, nonverbal communication and, 140
Compliance-gaining strategies, 321, 322*t*
Compliance-resisting strategies, 321–322
Complimenting, 222
Computer-mediated communication. *See* Online communication
Confidence, communicating, suggestions for, 321
Confidentiality, self-disclosure and, 55
Confirmation
 behaviors characteristic of, 121*t*
 definition of, 121
 example of, 120–121
 self-test of, 120
 skill building exercise, 129
Conflict, interpersonal
 content, 293–294
 culture and, 292–293
 definition of, 292
 fair strategies in, 282
 gender differences in, 292–293
 issues in, 294*t*
 learning from, 298
 messages in, 303
 nature of, 291–298
 negative aspects of, 296
 online, 295
 positive aspects of, 296–297
 preparing for, 297
 relationship, 294
 types of, 291–292
Conflict management, 302–313
 assertiveness and, 337
 avoidance versus active fighting in, 304–305
 beltlining in, 309
 blame versus empathy in, 308
 face-detracting versus face-enhancing strategies, 307–308
 gunnysacking in, 309
 productive versus destructive, 306–307
 silencers in, 308–309
 talk versus force in, 305
 unproductive strategy for, 313–314
 verbal aggressiveness versus argumentativeness in, 310–313
Conflict resolution, model of, 299–302, 300*f*
Conflict starters, dealing with, 299
Connotation, 112
Contact, as relationship stage, 260–261
 suggestions for, 262*t*
Contact messages, 272
Content conflict, 293–294
Context, 16–17
Context references, in conversational opening, 206
Contradicting, nonverbal communication and, 140
Contrast, in organization of perceptions, 68

Control
  in conflict management, 306
  posture as indicator of, 321
  and self-disclosure, 49
  touch and communication of, 153
Conversation(s)
  business in, 199
  closing of, 201–202
    suggestions for, 214
  definition of, 193
  effectiveness of, 216–227
  feedback in, 199–201
  feedforward in, 198–199
  gender and topics of, skill building exercise, 203
  maintaining, 207–212
  management of, 205–214
  maxims in, 207–210
  opening of, 197–198
    suggestions for, 206–207
  problems in, avoiding, 204–205
  process of, 195–203, 197f
  questions in, 204, 205–206
  repairing, 213–214
  satisfaction with, self-test of, 194
  skills of
    general, 216–220
    specific, 220–225
  taboos in, international comparison, 200t
  turns in, signaling of, 210–212, 212f
  violations of rules of, 202–203
Cooperation principle, in conversation, 207–209
Cowboy syndrome, 180–181
Creative thinking, and critical thinking, 10
Credentialing, 199
Credibility, culture and differences in, 97
Critical feedback, 201
Critical listening, 104–105
Critical thinking
  and creative thinking, 10
  and interpersonal competence, 9–11
  preserving with age, 60
  and problem-solving, 300, 301
  steps of, 9f
  suspending, 62
Criticism, styles of, 303–304
Crying, as silencer, 308
Cultural beliefs
  self-test of, 232–233
  sources of, discovering, 46
Cultural differences, recognizing, 248–249
Cultural dimension, 16
Cultural display rules, 177–178
Cultural identifiers, 125–127
Cultural maxims, 35
Cultural sensitivity, 219
  and perception accuracy, 84
  self-test of, 32
Culture
  and conflict, 292–293
  and gender differences, 287
Culture(s). *See also* Intercultural communication

  and apprehension, 59–60
  and complimenting, 222
  and conversational maxims, 209
  differences among, 239–243
  and directness, 97, 115
  and emoticons, 171
  and emotions, 172–173, 177–178
  high- versus low-context, 241–242, 243t
  individual versus collective, 239–241, 243t
  and interpersonal communication, 27–34
  and interpersonal competence, 12–13
  and listening, 96–97
  masculine versus feminine, 242–243
  and nonverbal communication, 97, 161–165, 162t, 250
  and power dimension, 329–330
  and relationship patterns, 283–284
  and self-concept, 40
  and self-disclosure, 48–49
  and spatial distance, 148
  and time orientation, 158
  transmission of, 231–233
  and uncertainty avoidance, 82t, 82–83
  values across, 234–235
Culture shock, 251–253
  reverse, 253
  stages in, 252–253
Cute-flippant openers, 207

Date, as antidote to static evaluation, 133
Deaf person, communicating with, 226t, 251t
DeCecco, John, 283
"Deconstructing Your Cubicle" (Kawachi), 150–151
Defeatist thinking, 41, 42
Defensive phrasing, avoiding, 81–82
Delayed feedback, 201
Denotation, 112
Depenetration, 277
Depth listening, 106–107
D.E.S.C. script, 185
Deterioration, relationship, 266–267
Detour taker, in conversation, 204
Dewey, John, 299
Direct openers, 207
Directness
  advantages of, 114
  culture and, 97, 115
  gender differences in, 114–115
  misunderstanding in interpreting, 116
Disabilities, people with, communicating with, 79–80, 226t, 251t
Disclaimers, 199
Disconfirmation, 120–127
  behaviors characteristic of, 121t
  definition of, 121
  example of, 120–121
  self-test of, 120
  skill building exercise, 129
  types of, 122–125
Disengagement strategies, 271
Display rules, 144
  cultural, 177–178
  gender, 178–179

Disqualifiers, in powerless speech, 324*t*
Dissolution messages, 272
Dissolution of relationship, 268–269, 277
    reasons for, 288
Distance(s)
    interpersonal, changing, 271
    spatial, in communication, 147–148
Distancing messages, 272
Distinctions, obscured by language, 133–135
Dominance. *See* Power
Doomsayer, in conversation, 204
Doublespeak, 130
Downward communication, 28
Dresser, Norine, 163
Dreyfuss, Henry, 163
Drivers (unrealistic beliefs), 320
Dyadic effect, 50
Dyads, and self-disclosure, 50

Egotist, in conversation, 204
Either-or, fallacy of, 135
Electronic communication. *See* Online communication
Ellis, Albert, 172
E-mail, 195
Emblems, 141–142
    cultural differences in, 162*t*
Emoticons, 14, 171*t*
Emotion(s)
    analyzing, 186–187
    basic, 174, 174*f*
    and bodily reactions, 172
    in business context, 184–185
    cognitive labeling theory of, 174–175, 175*f*
    communicating, 171–180
        guidelines for, 184–189
        obstacles in, 180–183
        principles of, 179–180
        self-test of, 175–176
        skill building exercises, 181, 188
    culture and, 172–173, 177–178
    deciding whether to express, 184
    echoing speaker's, 100
    expression of, variations in, 176–177
    facial expressions and, 144–145
    gender differences in expression of, 178–179, 180–181
    interpretations and, 172
    James-Lange theory of, 174, 175*f*
    listening to, guidelines for, 182
    negative, expressing, 183
    owning, 187–189, 220
    paralanguage and communication of, 154–155
    silence and communication of, 156
    as silencers, 308
    touch and communication of, 153
    understanding one's own, 184
    venting, 185
Emotional arousal, 174–175
Empathy, 221–222
    in conflict, 308
    in intercultural communication, 245
    in relationship communication, 282

Emphatic listening, 103–104
Encoding-decoding, 7
Enculturation, 231
E-prime, thinking with, 135
Equity theory of relationships, 278–279, 280*t*
Eros love, 265
Ethics
    gossiping and, 215–216
    in interpersonal communication, 17–18
        skill building exercise, 19
    in listening, 93–94
Ethnocentrism, 231
    continuum of, 247*f*
    recognizing and reducing, 246
Euphemisms, 130
Evaluating
    in conflict management, 306
    listening and, 90*f*, 92–93
Excuses
    formulating, skill building exercise, 215
    good versus bad, 214*t*
    motives for making, 213
Exercise, and clear thinking, 80
Expert power holder, 328
Expertise
    as compliance-gaining strategy, 322*t*
    gender differences in emphasizing, 98
Expressiveness, 224–225
    in intercultural communication, 245
Extensional orientation, 130
Extroversion, and self-disclosure, 47
Eye avoider, 106
Eye contact
    breaking, 158
    cultural differences in, 161
    and empathy, 222
    and immediacy, 223
Eye movements, communicating with, 145–146

Face-enhancing strategies, in conflict management, 307–308
Face-saving, culture and, 242
Facial communication, 144–145
    and assertiveness, 339*t*
Facial feedback hypothesis, 144–145
Facial management techniques, 144, 145*t*
Fact-inference confusion, 131–132
Fair fighting, 282
Family, problems of interpersonal communication in, 2–3
    resolving, 193, 281
Farson, Richard, 88
Fear(s)
    emotional expression and, 182–183
    and intercultural communication, 248
Feedback, 14
    in conversation, 199–201
    culture and differences in, 97
    dimensions of, 200–201, 201*f*
    eye communication and, 146
    monotonous, 106
Feedforward, 14, 198–199
Feelings. *See* Emotion(s)

Feminine culture, 242–243
Figurative analogies, resisting, 268
Filtering out messages, avoiding, 105
Financial difficulties, and relationship deterioration, 266
First impressions, 72–73
Flaming, 295
Flexibility, 68, 217–219
 assertiveness and, 337
 and interpersonal relationships, 282
 self-test of, 217–218
 suggestions for cultivating, 219
Formal time, 164
Friend-or-foe factors, 104
Friendship
 cultural differences in, 284
 gender differences in, 285–286
 right to know in, 47
 rules of, 275–276, 276t
 social penetration in, 277f
Fuller, Linda K., 257
Fundamental attribution error, 78
Future orientation, 156
 and income, 158
 versus present orientation, 159
"Galileo and the Ghosts," 71

Gender differences
 in conflict styles, 292–293
 in content versus relationship messages, 21
 in conversational topics, skill building exercise, 203
 culture and, 287
 in directness, 114–115
 in emotional expression, 178–179, 180–181
 in interrupting, 212
 in listening, 98–99
 in nonverbal communication, 149, 150
 in politeness, expression of, 210
 in power, 330
 in relationships, 285–288
 in responding, 238
 in self-disclosure, 49–50
 in spatial communication, 149
 in verbal messages, self-test of, 117
Gender display rules, 178–179
General Semantics, 66
Ghost-thinking team, 71
Gift giving, cultural differences in, 165–166
Gobbledygook, 130
Goffman, Erving, 146
Gordon, Thomas, 100
Gossip, 215–216
Gould, Stephen Jay, 237
Grapevine communication, 28
Greeting, 197–198
Grief-stricken, communicating with, 189
Group size, and self-disclosure, 50
Gunnysacking, 309

Halberstam, Joshua, 41–42
Hall, Edward, 139, 147
Hall, Mildred, 139

Halo effect, 74
Handshake, communicating dominance with, 158
Haptics, 152
Hatfield, Elaine, 284
Hedging, 199
Height, 143
Helping
 interpersonal communication and, 26, 27f
 listening and, 89t
Hesitations, in powerless speech, 324t
Heterosexism
 in language, 123–124
 in listening, 239
Hidden self, 43, 43f
 revealing. See Self-disclosure
High power distance cultures, 329–330
High-context culture, 241–242, 243t
High-monitored feedback, 201
Hispanic culture, self-disclosure in, 48–49
Hoft, Nancy, 163
Homophobia
 in language, 123–124
 in listening, 239
"How to Really Talk to Another Person" (Boyd), 22–23
"How to Take the Bite out of Criticism" (Roesch), 303–304

Identification messages, smell and, 161
Identity management, as compliance-resisting strategy, 321–322
Illustrators, 142
I-messages, 187–189, 220, 225
 and assertiveness, 339t
 in conflict management, 306
Immediacy, 223
 of feedback, 201
 in intercultural communication, 245
Implicit personality theories, 73–74
Inactive responder, in conversation, 204
Income, time orientation and, 158
Index, as antidote to indiscrimination, 134
Indirect messages
 advantages of, 113
 disadvantages of, 114
 gender differences in use of, 114–115
 misunderstanding in interpreting, 116
Indirect style of communication, 97
Indiscrimination, 133–134
Individual cultures, 239–241, 243t
Inevitability of communication, 25
Inferences, versus facts, 131–132
Inflated language, 130
Influencing
 interpersonal communication and, 26, 27f
 listening and, 89t
Informal communication, 28
Informal time, 164
Information power holder, 328
Ingham, Harry, 43
Innocuous openers, 207
Intensifiers, in powerless speech, 324t
Intensional orientation, 129–130
Interaction management, 223–224

in intercultural communication, 245
Interactional contact, 260
Interactional view of communication, 4–5, 5f
Intercultural communication, 233–236. *See also* Culture
definition of, 233
effectiveness in, characteristics of, 245
improving, 246–253
obstacles to, dealing with, 253
openness to, self-test of, 237–238
process of, 233f
skill building exercise, 244
Intercultural setting, problems of interpersonal communication in, 2–3
Internet. *See* Online communication; Online relationships
Internet relay chat (IRC) groups, 195–197
Interpersonal commitment, 264
Interpersonal communication
areas of, 18t
beliefs about, self-test, 4
characteristics of, 25–26
culture and, 27–34
elements in, 6–18
ethical dimensions of, 17–18
interactional view of, 4–5, 5f
linear view of, 4, 4f
principles of, 20–27
problems in, 2–3
process of, 6f
purposes of, 26, 27f
transactional view of, 5, 5f
Interpersonal deterioration, 266
Interpersonal difficulties, explaining, 29
Interpersonal distance, changing, strategies for, 271
Interpersonal perception, 66–69
barriers to accuracy in, 85
definition of, 66
increasing accuracy in, 80–84
principles of, 71–77
self-test of, 71–72
Interpersonal Perception (Laing, Phillipson, & Lee), 111
Interpersonal repair, 267
Interpersonal separation, 268–269
Interpersonal skills
and interpersonal competence, 11–12
lack of, in emotional communication, 183
Interpretation-evaluation, of perceptions, 68–69
Interpretations, and emotions, 172
Interrogator, conversational role of, 204
Interrupting
breaking habit of, 101
gender differences in, 212
Intimacy, 264
gender differences in, 285, 286
social penetration in, 277f
Intimate distance, 147
Intrapersonal dissatisfaction, 266
Intrapersonal repair, 267
Involvement, as relationship stage, 261–263
Iranian culture, silence in, 163–164
IRC groups. *See* Internet relay chat groups
Irreversibility of communication, 25

James, William, 121, 174
Japanese culture
conflict in, 292
conversational maxims in, 209
emotional expression in, 177
masculinity in, 243
nonverbal communication in, 161–162
self-disclosure in, 48
values in, 234–235
Jargon, 130
Jenkins, Jerry B., 127–128
Jewelry, communicating through, 151
Johari window, 42–43, 43f
Justification, as compliance-resisting strategy, 322

Kawachi, Yutaka, 150–151
"Keeping Your Cool at Work" (Monson), 184–185
Kim, Young Yun, 231
Kleinke, Chris, 207
Korzybski, Alfred, 66, 132

Labeling, and intensional orientation, 129–130
Laing, Ronald D., 111
Lalanne, Jacques, 205–206
Landers, Ann, 193
Lange, Carl, 174
Language
abstraction in, variations of, 116–117
assertive, 338, 339t
nature of, 111–117
and reality, 129–131
and speech, differences in, 96–97
Lateral communication, 28
Lazarus, Emma, 237
Learning
interpersonal communication and, 26, 27f
listening and, 89t
Lee, Russell, 111
Lefkowith, Harriet, 303
Legitimate power holder, 327
Levant, Ronald, 181
Liking, as compliance-gaining strategy, 322t
Linear view of communication, 4, 4f
Listener cues, 211–212
Listening
active, 100
in business context, 101
in conflict situation, 303
critical, 104–105
culture and, 96–97
depth, 106–107
to emotions, guidelines for, 182
emphatic, 103–104
to empower, 335
ethical, 93–94
gender and, 98–99
increasing effectiveness of, 102–107
ineffective versus effective, 88–89
with inner ear, 23
and interpersonal competence, 13
nonjudgmental, 104–105

Listening (cont.)
    nonparticipatory, 102–103
    objective, 104
    offensive, avoiding, 104
    to other perspectives, 71
    paraphrasing and, 107–108
    participatory, 102–103
    problematic styles of, 106
    purposes and benefits of, 89*t*
    reducing barriers to, 95–96
    rules of, 23
    and self-awareness, 44–45
    to self-disclosure, 54
    self-test of, 95
    stages of, 89–93, 90*f*
    to stage-talk messages, 272
    stereotypes and, 239
    suggestions for improving, 101
    surface, 106–107
    time spent on, 19
    to yourself, 44
Loneliness, 258
    after relationship breakup, dealing with, 269
Looking-glass self, 39
Love, 264. *See also* Romantic relationship(s)
    gender differences in, 286, 287–288
    types of, self-test, 265–266
Low power distance cultures, 329–330
Low-context culture, 241–242, 243*t*
Low-monitored feedback, 201
Ludus love, 265
Luft, Joseph, 43
Lurking, in electronic communication, 118, 197

Machiavelli, Niccolo, 326
Machiavellianism, 326–328
    self-test of, 325–326
Mailing list group, 195
Maintenance messages, 272
Manic love, 266
Manner, conversational maxim of, 209
Masculine culture, 242–243
Masculine pronouns, use of, 122
Matching hypothesis, 274
Maxims, conversational, 207–210
McLaughlin, Margaret, 193
Meaning
    connotative, 112
    context and, 112
    denotative, 112
    levels of, 106–107
    people and, 111–112
Memory, smell and, 159
Message-focused feedback, 201
Messages
    assertive versus nonassertive, 339*t*
    content versus relationship, 20–22
    cultural differences in, 249–250
    direct versus indirect, 113–116
    in initial encounter, 262*t*
    and interpersonal communication, 14

    stage-talk, 272
Metacommunicational ability, 219–220
Mexican Americans, conflict management strategies, 293
Michelli, Dena, 338
Miller, Tom, 185
Mind reading, avoiding, 81
Mindfulness, 216–217
    in intercultural communication, 246–248
Miner, Horace, 230–231
Monitoring, in feedback, 201
Monochronic time orientation, 164, 164*t*
Monotonous feedback, 106
Monson, Nancy, 184–185
Moralist, conversational role of, 204

Nacirema culture, 230–231
National Council of Teachers of English, guidelines for nonsexist language, 122–123
Negative feedback, 200
Negative feelings, expressing, 183
Negotiation, as compliance-resisting strategy, 322
Nelson, Paul, 4
Netiquette, 118–119
Neutrality, in conflict management, 307
Nobody Upstairs (power play), 333
Noise, 15–16
    major types of, 16*t*
Nonassertive communication, 336
Nonassertive messages, 339*t*
Nonjudgmental listening, 104–105
Nonnegotiation, 304
    as compliance-resisting strategy, 322
Nonparticipatory listening, 102–103
Nonverbal communication, 139–141
    artifactual, 149–152
    body, 141–143
    channels of, 141–161
    culture and, 97, 161–165, 162*t*, 250
    in effective listening, 101, 102
    emotional meaning in, 14
    of emotions, 172, 180
    expressiveness in, 225
    eye, 145–146
    facial, 144–145
    functions of, 140–141
    in initial encounter, 262*t*
    paralanguage, 153–155
    of power, 158, 323–324
    silence, 155–156
    skill building exercise, 160–161
    smell, 159–161
    space, 146–149
    temporal, 156–159
    touch, 152–153
    and verbal communication, integrating, 141
Note-taking, listening and, 101
Nourishing people, 318–319
Noxious people, 318

Oberg, Kalervo, 251
Object-adaptors, 142–143

Objective listening, 104
Oculesis, 145
Offensive listening, avoiding, 104
Office decoration, messages perceived in, 150–151, 323–324
Olfactics, 159
One-clue conclusion, avoiding, 80
One-word answers, in powerless speech, 324*t*
Online communication, 6
    conflict in, 295
    emoticons in, 14, 171*t*
    etiquette in, 118–119
    and face-to-face communication
        differences, 7, 197
        similarities, 6
    lurking in, 118, 197
    noise in, 15
    politeness maxim in, 210
    skills of, 226–227
    temporal aspect of, 20
    types of, 195–197
Online relationships, 257, 258, 259
    advantages of, 258
    disadvantages of, 259
Open self, 42, 43*f*
    increasing, 45
Opening, conversational, 197–198
    suggestions for, 206–207
Opening line(s), 207, 226*t*
Openness, 220
    assertiveness and, 337
    to change, 282
    in conflict management, 309
    intercultural
        guidelines for, 245
        self-test of, 237–238
    and relationship maintenance, 270*t*
Organization(s). *See* Business context
Organizing, perception and, 67–68
Other-orientation, 225
    in intercultural communication, 245
Overattribution, 77–78, 124
    avoiding, 249
Overly expressive listener, 106

Paralanguage, 153–155
Paraphrasing, to ensure understanding, 107–108
Parents, visits with, increasing satisfaction in, 193, 281
Participatory listening, 102–103
Past orientation, 156
Pearson, Judy, 4
People perception. *See* Interpersonal perception
Perception(s)
    definition of, 66
    interpersonal (people). *See* Interpersonal perception
    interpretation-evaluation of, 68–69
    organization of, 67–68
    process of, 66–69, 67*f*
    selective, 67
    of self, 69–70
    sensing and, 67

Perceptual contact, 260
Personal distance, 147
Personal risks, of self-disclosure, 52
Personality, paralanguage and judgments of, 155
Person-focused feedback, 201
Perspective taking, 78–79, 185
Persuasion power holder, 328
Phatic communion, 198
Phillipson, H., 111
Phlegar, Phyllis, 257
Physical dimension, 16
Physical noise, 15, 16*t*
Physiological noise, 15, 16*t*
Play function
    of interpersonal communication, 26, 27*f*
    of listening, 89*t*
Playfulness, touch and communication of, 153
Plutchik, Robert, 174
Polarization, 134–135
Politeness
    cultural differences in, 209
    gender differences in, 210
    in online communication, 210
    in powerless speech, 324*t*
    Wolfson's bulge model of, 210*f*
Polychronic time orientation, 164, 164*t*
Positive feedback, 200
Positiveness
    and apprehension reduction, 61
    in communication, 222
    in intercultural communication, 245
    and relationship maintenance, 270*t*
    and self-confidence, 42
Posture, body. *See* Body language
Power, interpersonal
    confidence and, 321
    cultural dimension of, 329–330
    difficulties with, 317
    gender dimension of, 330
    in interpersonal relationship, 323, 328
    nonverbal communication of, 158, 323–324
    speaking with, 319–334
    types of, 327–328
    unfair use of, 331–334
Power plays, 333–334
Power tactics, in conflict, 309
Powerless speech, 324*t*
Pragma love, 265–266
Pregiving, as compliance-gaining strategy, 322*t*
Preoccupied listener, 106
Present orientation, 158, 159
Primacy effect, 72
The Prince (Machiavelli), 326
Problem-solving, model of, 299–302, 300*f*
Professional risks, of self-disclosure, 52–53
Promise, as compliance-gaining strategy, 322*t*
Proxemic distance, relationship and, 147–148, 148*t*
Proxemics, 146
Proximity
    and interpersonal relationships, 274
    in organization of perceptions, 67

Psychiatrist, conversational role of, 205
Psychological health, self-disclosure and, 51
Psychological noise, 15, 16*t*
Public distance, 148
Pygmalion effect, 75

Quality, conversational maxim of, 208
Quantity, conversational maxim of, 208
Questions
    in active listening, 100
    in conversation, 204, 205–206

Racism
    in language, 124–125
    in listening, 239
Rapson, Richard, 284
Raye-Johnson, Venda, 184, 185
Reading, while listening, 106
Reasonableness, in relationship communication, 283
Receiving, listening and, 90, 90*f*
Recency effect, 72
Reciprocity, in self-disclosure, 54
Reconstruction, remembering and, 91–92
Referent power holder, 327
Regulating, nonverbal communication and, 140
Regulators, 142
Reinforcement, and interpersonal relationships, 274–275
Reinforcing comments, 221
Rejection
    versus disconfirmation, 121
    example of, 120–121
    skill building exercise, 129
Relating
    interpersonal communication and, 26, 27*f*
    listening and, 89*t*
Relation, conversational maxim of, 208
Relational dialectics theory, 270
Relational references, in conversational opening, 206
Relationship(s). *See also* Friendship; Romantic relationship(s)
    advantages of, 258
    attraction theory of, 272–275
    beliefs about, self-test of, 262–263
    breadth of, 277
    cultural differences in, 283–284
    depth of, 277
    deterioration of, 266–267
    disadvantages of, 258–259
    dissolution of, 268–269, 277
    equity theory of, 278–279
    exceptional, 257
    gender differences in, 285–288
    improving communication in, 281–288
    initial contact in, 260–261, 262*t*
    initial encounter, suggestions for, 262*t*
    intimacy in, 264
    involvement in, 261–263
    maintaining, strategies for, 270*t*
    online, 257, 258, 259
    power dimension in, 323, 328
    and proxemic distances, 147–148, 148*t*
    repair of, 267*f*, 267–268
    rules of, 275–276
    social exchange theory of, 278
    social penetration theory of, 276–277
    stages of, 259–272, 261*f*
    testing in, 261, 263
    theories of, 272–279, 280*t*
        application to problems, 280–281
    violence in, 305
Relationship conflict, 294
Relationship messages, 20–22
Relationship risks, of self-disclosure, 52
Relationship rules approach, 275–276
Remembering, listening and, 90*f*, 91–92
Repair messages, 272
Repair, relationship, 267*f*, 267–268
Repeating, nonverbal communication and, 140
Repulsion hypothesis, 274
Responding, 93
    effectively, skill building exercise, 227
    gender differences in, 238
Reward power holder, 327
Rich, Andrea, 124
Risks, self-disclosure and, 52–53
Ritual, touch and, 153
Roesch, Roberta, 303–304
Rogers, Carl, 88, 318
Romantic relationship(s). *See also* Love
    conflict in, issues leading to, 294*t*
    cultural differences in, 284
    gender differences in, 286–288
    problems of interpersonal communication in, 2–3
    right to know in, 47
    rules of, 276
    turning points in, 273*t*
Rosenfeld, Lawrence, 49
Rules
    of conversation, violations of, 202–203
    cultural display, 177–178
    display, 144
    of emotional expression, 180–181
    gender display, 178–179
    of listening, 23
    relationship, 275–276, 280*t*
    of speaking, 23

Same-sex relationships, cultural differences in attitudes toward, 284
Selective perception, 67
Self, Johari model of, 42–43, 43*f*
Self-acceptance, self-disclosure and, 51
Self-adaptors, 142
Self-affirming beliefs, 318
Self-affirming statements, 44
Self-awareness, 42–45
    increasing, 43–45
Self-concept, 38–41
    sources of, 39*f*
"Self-Confidence: The Art of Being You" (Halberstam), 41–42
Self-critical statements, in powerless speech, 324*t*
Self-destructive beliefs, 318
Self-destructive statements, 44

Self-discloser, in conversation, 204–205
Self-disclosure, 45–58
 dangers of, 52–53
 deciding for or against, 55
 definition of, 45
 and empathy, 221
 facilitating, 56–58
 factors influencing, 47–50
 guidelines for, 53–54
 Machiavellianism and, 328
 and openness, 220
 in relationship communication, 282
 responding to, guidelines for, 54–55
 rewards of, 51–52
 self-test of, 51
Self-esteem, 318–319
 and emotional reactions, 185
 lack of, problems associated with, 317
 raising, suggestions for, 269
 relationship and, 258
 and self-confidence, 41
 unrealistic beliefs and, 320
Self-feelings, as compliance-gaining strategy, 322t
Self-fulfilling prophecies, 41, 74–75
Self-knowledge
 and self-confidence, 42
 self-disclosure and, 51
Self-monitoring, 224
 self-test of, 223–224
Self-perception, 69–70
Self-references, in conversational opening, 206
Self-serving bias, 77
Self-talk, 44
Semantic noise, 15, 16t
Sensing, and perception, 67
Sex role stereotyping, in language, 122–123
Sexism
 in language, 122–123
 in listening, 239
Sexual dissatisfaction, and relationship deterioration, 266
Sexual harassment, 331–333
 in high school, 332t
Sexual relationships, cultural differences in attitudes toward, 284
Sharpening, biases and, 105
shi gu, 74
Signals, other person's, learning, 24
Signal-to-noise ratio, 15
Significant others, and self-concept, 39
Silence
 cultural differences in, 163–164
 functions of, 155–156
Silencers, 308–309
Similarity
 and interpersonal relationships, 273–274
 in organization of perceptions, 68
Sin licenses, 199
Slang, in powerless speech, 324t
Smell communication, 159–161
Social bonding, 264
Social clock, 165
Social comparison, 38, 39–40

Social distance, 147
Social exchange theory, 278, 280t
Social penetration theory, 276–277, 277f, 280t
Social rules, and emotional expression, 180–181
Social separation, 269
Social-psychological dimension, 17
Socioeconomic class, and time orientation, 158
Soder, Dee, 101
Source-receiver, 6–8
Space communication, 146–149
Space decoration, communication through, 150–151, 152
Spamming, 295
Spatial distances, in communication, 147–148
Speaker cues, 210–211
Speaking
 with power, 319–334
 rate of, 155
 rules of, 23
Speech
 and language, differences in, 96–97
 powerless, 324t
Spencer, Duffy, 184, 185
Stage-talk messages, 272
Stanley, Julia, 122
Static evaluation, 132–133
Static listener, 106
Statue of Liberty, poem on, 237
Status
 and spatial distance, 148
 territoriality and, 149
Steamrolling, 304
Steil, Lyman K., 101
Stereotypes, 76
 antidote to, 134
 indiscrimination and, 133
 and listening, 239
Storge love, 265
Story teller, conversational role of, 204
Subject matter, and spatial distance, 149
Substituting, nonverbal communication and, 141
Success
 focusing on, and apprehension reduction, 61
 and self-esteem, 319
Successful Listening (Wyatt & Ashburn), 101
Superiority, in conflict management, 307
Support, self-disclosure and, 55
Supportive feedback, 201
Surface listening, 106–107
Suspension of judgment, appeals for, 199
Sympathy, expression of, 189

Taboos, conversational, international comparison of, 200t
Tag questions, in powerless speech, 324t
Tannen, Deborah, 98, 114
Task-related touching, 153
Taste, smell and, 159
Tavris, Carol, 170
Temporal communication, 156–159
 cultural differences in, 164
Temporal dimension, 17
Temporal principle, in organization of perceptions, 67

Temporary relationships, and self-disclosure, 50
"10 Things You Should Never Say to Anyone" (Thompson & Jenkins), 127–128
Territoriality, 146, 149
    and power, 323–324
Testing, in relationship, 261, 263
Thompson, George J., 127–128
Thought-completing listener, 106, 204
Time. *See also under* Temporal
    attitudes toward
        cultural differences in, 164–165
        self-test of, 156–157
    and feedback effectiveness, 201
    formal, 164
    informal, 164
    monochronic versus polychronic, 164, 164*t*
"to be," omitting in speech, 135
Touch communication, 152–153
    cultural differences in, 162–163
Turn(s), conversational, 210–212
Turn-denying cues, 211, 212*f*
Turn-maintaining cues, 210–211, 212*f*
Turn-requesting cues, 211, 212*f*
Turn-yielding cues, 211, 212*f*

Uncertainty
    culture and avoidance of, 82*t*, 82–83
    reducing, strategies for, 83–84
Understanding, listening and, 90*f*, 91
United States
    ancestry of residents, 30*f*
    cultural diversity in, 30–31
    self-disclosure in, 48
    values in, 234–235
U.S. Department of Labor, "What Work Requires of Schools," 3
Unknown self, 43, 43*f*

Unpredictability, reducing, and apprehension management, 61
Unrepeatability of communication, 25
Upward communication, 28

Values, across cultures, 234–235
VanHyning, Memory, 332
Verbal aggressiveness, 310
    versus assertiveness, 336–337
    messages characteristic of, 339*t*
    self-test of, 310–311
Violence, in relationship, 305
Visual dominance behavior, 146
Visual noise, 16
Vulgarity, in powerless speech, 324*t*

Wade, Carole, 170
Waiting listener, 106
"Want to do better on the job?—Listen up!" (Cole), 101
Weasel words, 133
"What Work Requires of Schools" (U.S. Department of Labor), 3
Win-lose solutions, 300–301
Win-win solutions, 297, 300–301
    generating, skill building exercise, 302
Work. *See* Business context
Work dissatisfaction, and relationship deterioration, 266
Writing, while listening, 106
Wyatt, Nancy, 101

You Just Don't Understand: Women and Men in Conversation (Tannen), 98
You Owe Me (power play), 333
Yougottobekidding (power play), 333
You-messages, 187, 220
    and assertiveness, 339*t*
    and confidence communication, 321